The Stations of the Sun

A HISTORY OF THE RITUAL YEAR IN BRITAIN

Ronald Hutton

OXFORD
UNIVERSITY PRESS

OXFORD
UNIVERSITY PRESS

Great Clarendon Street, Oxford OX2 6DP

Oxford University Press is a department of the University of Oxford.
It furthers the University's objective of excellence in research, scholarship,
and education by publishing worldwide in

Oxford New York

Auckland Bangkok Buenos Aires Cape Town Chennai
Dar es Salaam Delhi Hong Kong Istanbul Karachi Kolkata
Kuala Lumpur Madrid Melbourne Mexico City Mumbai Nairobi
São Paulo Shanghai Taipei Tokyo Toronto

Oxford is a registered trade mark of Oxford University Press
in the UK and in certain other countries

Published in the United States
by Oxford University Press Inc., New York

© Ronald Hutton 1996

First published 1996 by Oxford University Press
First issued as an Oxford University Press paperback 1997
Reissued 2001

British Library Cataloguing in Publication Data
Data available

Library of Congress Cataloging in Publication Data
Data available

ISBN-13: 978-0-19-285448-3

6

Printed in Great Britain by
Clays Ltd, St Ives plc

TO LISA

as promised
twelve years ago

✎ PREFACE ✎

'THERE is a peculiar charm to be found in the reading of a book such as this. It is redolent of the English countryside, its inarticulate love of ancient things, its immemorial speech, its stubborn resistance to the encroachments of changing Time.' So wrote the reigning president of the Folk-Lore Society, Professor S. H. Hooke, in 1936. The work which he was commending consisted of a large collection of information about English calendar customs made by a former president, A. R. Wright, edited after his death by a colleague and published by the society in three volumes. A comparable edition for Scotland was brought out during the following few years. The result was a huge, though very far from complete, amount of raw material for a history of the ritual year in Britain, presented in individual entries according to source and almost devoid of comment or analysis. Today, over half a century later, they still represent the staple work on the subject. No attempt to employ and to assess the data comprehensively, and to write such a history, has ever been made.

There have, on the other hand, been a great many studies of individual calendar customs or groups of them, and until recently almost all embodied the attitudes expressed by Professor Hooke. First, such activities were 'of the countryside', part of an agricultural society much older than, and being destroyed by the expansion of, urban and industrial culture. Secondly, they were 'immemorial', preserved unchanging over the centuries. Thirdly, they were 'inarticulate', the people who performed them often being incapable of explaining their true significance, so that this task had to be undertaken by scholars. Fourthly, they were 'ancient', a term which was most often taken by folklorists to mean that they were survivals of pre-Christian religious practices, which could in large part be reconstructed by a study of them. All of these notions enjoyed some academic respectability at the beginning of the twentieth century, having been propounded in England most prominently by Sir Edward Tylor, Sir Laurence Gomme, and Sir James Frazer. By the 1930s the consensus among historians and anthropologists had turned decisively against them, but those disciplines did not evolve new conceptual approaches to the study of folklore. Instead, they abandoned the whole subject to enthusiasts from other disciplines (or none), who continued to interpret calendar customs in the old terms, and who dominated the discussion of folk rites and practices, and the public perception of them, until the 1970s. In that decade the very popular series of books on county folklore edited by Venetia Newall, for Batsford, treated seasonal customs as survivals from an almost wholly amorphous past, with virtually no sense of chronological perspective. So did coffee-table volumes upon the subject like those by Homer Sykes, Brian Shuel, and the *Reader's Digest* team. Other works from these years, such as Ralph Whitlock's *In Search of Lost Gods*, played up the theme of pagan origins without any further attempt to investigate it; the 'search' consisted of no more than a portrayal of surviving customs.

It was during the 1970s that my own interest in folklore caused me to project a study of the British ritual year which challenged the attitudes encapsulated by Professor Hooke on every count. It seemed clear that, far from being definitively rural, many seasonal pastimes had flourished in or around industrial towns. It was equally plain that some had altered their form and content during the time over which they had been recorded, in response to changing social needs. Their purpose at particular moments was therefore all-important, and their practitioners had often been extremely articulate in explaining this. Finally, the claim that they were relics of ancient pagan religions needed to be examined from historical evidence, not just asserted from supposition or analogy. By 1981 I had mapped out a plan of research and discussed it with colleagues and publishers, but did not wish to commit myself wholly to it at that stage. For one thing I had also undertaken major research projects into the history of the Restoration period. For another, the sheer scale of study involved, and the number of fields with which it over-lapped, meant that too rapid a pace was likely to produce a shamefully inadequate result. I decided therefore to work upon both big ventures, Restoration Britain and the ritual year, for a decade, testing my ideas as they developed by giving papers and publishing essays. This scheme was pursued until 1985, during which time my research for the book on rituals yielded an article upon early modern popular culture for *History Today* and an essay in the volume edited by Christopher Haigh under the title *The English Reformation Revised*. At that point I threw most of my energy into my books upon seventeenth-century history, partly because the general pace of research in that area was increasing, but also because it was now obvious that my work on folk customs was yielding three substantial publications instead of one. In 1989 I became free to concentrate upon these, and the first, *The Pagan Religions of the Ancient British Isles*, was published in 1991. It tackled the question of the pagan origins of folk rites from the opposite end, by assessing what can be known of the pre-Christian religions of these islands. In 1994 it was followed by *The Rise and Fall of Merry England*, a study of the ritual year in England and Wales between 1400 and 1700, which represented the research carried out in the central, and least studied, part of the chronological range of the subject.

The Stations of the Sun is a larger work than those two put together, and is erected upon the foundation provided by both, being a complete survey of what is known of the history of the communal rituals and customs which have marked the year in Britain from the earliest recorded time until the present. It incorporates and reworks the relevant portions of *Pagan Religions*, and in-cludes much of the data from *Merry England*, augmented by some new material from early modern England and Wales and a large amount from the published sources for Scotland. The relationship between *Merry England* and the present work is umbilical, and it is assumed that scholars will use the two together. Although large parts of the earlier book dealt with other issues, it also served the function of presenting arguments and providing evidence which would be employed in the later one without the need to repeat them in detail. In several of the chapters of *Stations of the Sun*, material from *Merry England* is reproduced wholesale in the text. I had considered the option of leaving it out to avoid this repetition, but to do so would have been to leave chunks of the larger book looking curiously threadbare while, as said, it augments the data in detail. Only one of the six sections of the conclusion deals with the preoccupations of the earlier work.

The Stations of the Sun also makes full use of the recent monographs upon the nature and context of British seasonal customs; but by far the largest addition of evidence to that provided by my preceding books consists of the collections made by folklorists since the late eighteenth century. These are represented by hundreds of published works and some major archives, and the present book incorporates the former and also items from the latter which have not yet appeared in print. No original research has been undertaken into the eighteenth, nineteenth, and twentieth centuries because the body of material already assembled by the collectors is so enormous. It was assembled, however, with a very limited number of objectives in mind, and consequently leaves questions of major importance to current historians still wanting an answer. One function of this book is to draw attention to these.

If it has limitations of evidence, then it also has some of scope. It is concerned with communal customs, and especially those involving the public life of societies. Thus private seasonal rites, such as divination and magic, will be almost wholly excluded for the sake of space. So will customs unique to one or two communities, however colourful, unless they have been used in the past to exemplify more general theories. This book only considers activities specifically linked to the passage of the year, and ignores sports and entertainments which are no more than superficially related to particular festivals. Although it gives detailed treatment to the whole island of Britain, and also to the Isles of Scilly and Man, the Hebrides, the Orkneys, and the Shetlands, it deals with Irish customs only when they shed light upon those in Britain. The enormous collections of the Irish Folklore Commission and related bodies require a labour, and resources, beyond the span of what is already an ambitious undertaking. The same consideration applies with even more force to customs on the continent of Europe. Likewise, this book does not attempt to make reflections upon perceptions of the nature of time or of the seasons in earlier British societies for, despite an apparent near relation to its concerns, such themes do need separate and detailed treatment. Furthermore, the reasons supplied in the introduction to *Merry England* for my reluctance to participate in debates over the true meaning of expressions such as 'ritual', 'ceremony', 'community', or 'religion' apply equally to this work.

The structure is that of a classic old-fashioned 'Book of Days', working its way around the circle of the year. Festivals are sometimes given chapters to themselves, while at other times themes within them are accorded separate treatment. The simplicity, flexibility, and familiarity of this framework made it the most attractive one, but it also has the obvious disadvantage of dividing as much as relating the material gathered for it. For example, the ploughboys of the east Midlands were responsible for Plough Monday gatherings, Molly dancing, and May singing, just as the youth of the Lancashire textile region were the driving force behind Pace-Egging, rush carts, and north-western morris. It would therefore be profitable to study these activities together as aspects of the culture of the groups concerned and their interaction with the wider community; and yet they appear in different parts of the book. Likewise, to group harvest and Maying customs together would probably make some interesting points about the relationship of humans to the world of vegetation, and begging customs and ritual dances are very clear categories of activity even if they are scattered across the seasons. The suppression of Shrove Tuesday football and Guy Fawkes celebrations in nineteenth-century towns were clearly two parts of an identical process; yet again they are dealt with in completely different sections of the book. In general the preoccupation of the work is with the genealogies of seasonal customs. Although an important part of this process is to illustrate the way in which they developed or disappeared in changing social and cultural contexts, constraints of space and resources often precluded the complete reconstruction of those contexts. In some cases my own expertise simply did not stretch to the work in periods with which I was less familiar, while in others denser description would have caused a loss of pace and focus, and clogged an already very large book with detail.

To overcome these problems would have required another sort of work altogether, and some readers may well feel that a more thematic and analytical approach would have produced a better one. As I wrote the conclusion, I was acutely aware that had I divided its six parts into as many chapters, supporting their arguments with the data distributed through the bulk of the existing book, then I would probably have produced a result more attractive to specialists in each of the respective areas under consideration. The trouble was that it would not have been more attractive to anybody else, and here I am not thinking of any theoretical general readership but simply of colleagues and students in departments of history, religious studies, and literature, who wished to have an overview of the history of the British ritual year as a whole. My format had the virtue of positively compelling readers to take that broader view. It suited the specific tasks in which I was most immediately interested, and if its relatively conservative and pedestrian structure inspires my readers as well as myself to adopt different approaches in the future, then I shall be the more delighted.

During the many years in which I was working on this project, several other scholars arrived quite independently at all of my attitudes towards the subject-matter. Even before my research commenced, social historians of different periods were coming to treat folk customs as an important part of their subject; the pioneering efforts of E. P. Thompson, Sir Keith Thomas, and Robert Malcolmson were followed up by Robert Storch, Bob Bushaway, David Underdown, David Cressy, and others. I have gratefully incorporated their insights into my own survey, to which they did not represent a pre-emption as our interests merely overlap. More directly relevant was a development during the 1980s, whereby folklorists turned decisively against the attitude towards popular customs which had prevailed in their field and criticized it for precisely the faults stated earlier. Roy Judge, E. C. Cawte, Venetia Newall, Georgina Boyes, Craig Fees, and Theresa Buckland were among the most prominent of those who did so, and they and others provided some superb studies of the recent history of popular customs. Their work made me feel that mine was the more, and not the less, necessary. For one thing, it has failed so far to make much impact upon academic, let alone popular, perceptions of the subject, partly because it is so marginalized and underfunded. A folklorists' conference upon calendar rites was held in London in 1984 at which papers were presented which were so important and innovative that they effectively opened a new epoch of work in the field; but nine years elapsed before the proceedings could be published. Most university libraries do not purchase, or in a time of financial pressure have ceased to purchase, the specialist journals in which folklorists publish. If the present book serves the purpose of making the achievements of these admirable scholars apparent to a wider audience, then I shall be pleased for us all.

There are, however, special difficulties for a historian even in the new scholarly folklore studies. Many of them could be accused of being quite as ahistorical as those which they have replaced, though in a quite different way. By suggesting that a quest for the origins of folk customs is fruitless, and that it is more important to relate them to the society in which they are best recorded, the new studies have effectively confined consideration of them to the last two hundred years. Furthermore, at times what may appear to an outsider to be the folklorist establishment can seem to speak with two voices. In the Folklore Society's own review of my *Rise and Fall of Merry England*, written by Gillian Bennett and published in *Folklore* in 1995, I was accused of belittling her and her colleagues by failing to make clear that the theory of pagan origins for British folk customs had recently been forcefully challenged by eminent folkorists—an omission which the present book should, as said, fully correct. In the same year, however, the only work devoted to those customs which was cited in the Society's own list of new books in folklore was Michael Howard's *The Sacred Ring* (Capell Ban, 1995). This represented a confident restatement of that very theory, not delivered as a refutation of the recent attacks upon it, but as though those attacks had never been made.

The moment therefore may be ripe for a comprehensive review of what is known of the history of seasonal customs in Britain, synthesizing the recent research and introducing it to a wider public (in and out of academe), and incorporating a large body of original work. Such a task is arguably undertaken with some advantage by a historian whose centre of gravity lies in the early modern period, permitting perspectives both forward and backward. If it achieves no more than to encourage others to improve on the result, then it will still have made a significant contribution to the subject.

R.H.

Lammas 1995

➢ ACKNOWLEDGEMENTS AND NOTE ❧

THE greatest single piece of assistance towards this book was given by my own university, of Bristol, in appointing me to a Research Fellowship for the year 1994–5, which enabled me to complete the writing a year ahead of schedule. The secretarial support of my departmental office also allowed me to set a rapid pace in writing by typing up final versions of chapters while I was working on drafts of others. The text and references will disclose a number of debts owed to individuals and groups in the course of field work, but I would wish to single out the novelist Lizzie Gibson for the particular attention which she has paid to my research over the past ten years, and for her determination to infect me with her own enthusiasm for the folklore of her beloved Kent.

Throughout the text, whenever dates are given they are rendered according to old style; that is, those before 1752 are left as they were before the calendar change of that year. According to the same long-established convention, I have none the less treated the year throughout as beginning on 1 January. In another matter I have been more innovative, by abandoning the conventional division of time into BC and AD, based upon a Christian world-picture, for the symbols BCE and CE, still anchored on the presumed date of Christ's birth, but referring to the subsequent epoch, in less partisan terms, as the Common Era. It is a system adopted for a few years now by scholars of literature and of religious studies, but is still almost unknown among archaeologists and historians. The Folk-Lore Society altered its name, and that of its journal, *Folk-Lore*, to the spelling 'Folklore' in 1960, and both versions are used here, according to whether I am referring to its activities, or to publications in the journal, before or after that date. Throughout the text I have modernized the language of quotations from early modern or medieval documents written in prose, to make them more accessible to a general readership. I have, however, left quotations in verse as they were originally recorded, as modernization there would sometimes destroy the rhythm of the work; in practice early poetry is seldom quoted, and so the discrepancy is not very obvious.

❧ CONTENTS ❧

· CONTENTS ·

ఌ LIST OF MAPS ఌ

ఌ FIGURE ఌ

THE ORIGINS OF CHRISTMAS

❧

No modern Biblical scholars would rate the Nativity stories very highly among sources for the life of the historical Jesus. It now seems to be generally accepted that they are an extreme case in the Christian gospels of inventions by the authors to place Christ in traditional Jewish salvation history.[1] In one major respect the accounts contradict each other (that of how he comes to be born in the expected birthplace of the Redeemer at Bethlehem), while two other aspects of them, the Roman census and the Massacre of the Innocents, are historically implausible. The tales make sense, however, on a mythological level, not merely as confirmations of specifically Hebrew prophecy, but as archetypal representations of the birth of a hero, at the junction of many worlds: engendered partly human and partly divine, coming into life at a place neither a house nor the open air, belonging partly to humans and partly to animals, and in a strange land, and adored by people living upon the margins of society.

Furthermore it is patently clear that the New Testament provides not the slightest indication of the date at which Christ was born.[2] Early Christian tradition preserved no knowledge of one, and different writers made different guesses, most preferring dates in the spring.[3] The first absolutely certain record which places it upon 25 December is the calendar of Philocalus, produced in 354 and apparently at Rome. From there it seems to have spread to Constantinople, Antioch, and Bethlehem by the end of the century, although it is not recorded at Jerusalem for almost two hundred more years and was never recognized by the Armenian Church.[4] The reason for the choice of this date, and the success of it, was stated with admirable candour by a Christian writer, the Scriptor Syrus, in the late fourth century:

It was a custom of the pagans to celebrate on the same 25 December the birthday of the Sun, at which they kindled lights in token of festivity. In these solemnities and revelries the Christians also took part. Accordingly when the doctors of the Church perceived that the Christians had a leaning to this festival, they took counsel and resolved that the true Nativity should be solemnized on that day.[5]

The pagan feast which Christmas replaced was not, however, itself much older. It had apparently been decreed only in 274, by the emperor Aurelian, as a major holy day of a new and syncretic state cult with the sun as its official chief deity. The imperial reform built upon a much older Syrian cult of the

Unconquered Sun which had spread across the western Roman empire in the second and third centuries. Aurelian's official religion was, none the less, something far more ambitious, being an attempt to provide a universal focus of worship to help bond the Roman world together. It lasted only until 323, when Constantine transferred imperial sponsorship to Christianity.[6]

Curiously, the 'doctors of the Church' (whoever they were) did not impose the feast of the Nativity upon the principal one of Aurelian's state cult. The Syrian progenitor of that had celebrated its annual festival in late summer, while Aurelian's Sol Invictus (Unconquered Sun) was honoured every four years with games held in mid-October. Perhaps it was also given a small annual festival at the winter solstice, or perhaps the Scriptor Syrus was describing a private and informal pagan celebration at that time. It is even possible that, being (by definition) a Syrian, he was guessing at what had happened in Rome and that there had in fact been no pre-Christian celebration upon that date. Whatever the truth of the matter, to locate the Nativity in the turning-point of winter at once gave it a considerable symbolic potency and presented conscientious Christians with worries about the confusions of the festival's identity which were to keep resurfacing; Augustine of Hippo and Pope Leo the Great, the most famous Fathers of the fifth-century western Church, both felt compelled to remind people that Christ, and not the sun, was being worshipped then. By contrast Maximus of Turin, in the same century, exulted over the appropriation of a pagan festival of sun-worship for Christian use.[7]

The Romans were not, indeed, absolutely sure of which was the shortest day and longest night: Pliny, in the first century, put them at 26 December, while Columella, writing around the same time, guessed at the 23rd.[8] The official calendar of Julius Caesar marked them at the 25th. The uncertainty was perfectly natural, for at midwinter and midsummer the solar orb does appear to rise and set in the same places for a few days; the very term, solstice, is taken from the Latin for 'the sun stands still.' The traditional pagan Roman calendar had left this period as a quiet and mysterious one, and flanked it instead with a festival of preparation and one of completion: the former was the feast of Saturn, the Saturnalia, in the days after 17 December, the latter the New Year feast, the Kalendae, from 1 to 3 January. In very early Roman times it seems that the year had opened with March, which is why the months from September to December were all numbered from then and not from January. During the period of the empire the sacred fire kindled by the Vestal Virgins was still rekindled then, and new foliage put in temples of all kinds. If the month which opened the farming and fighting season was one obvious time for new beginnings, however, the moment at which the strength of the sun was perceived to be returning was an even more powerful, and universal one, and from 153 BCE the Roman year had officially commenced upon 1 January.[9]

In Rome itself, and among wealthy Romans living elsewhere, the Saturnalia was by far the more popular and lavishly celebrated feast. The religious rites were confined to 17 December, but the revelry continued for a minimum of two and a maximum of seven days afterwards. Shops, schools, and lawcourts were closed, gambling in public was allowed, and there was general noisy rejoicing. Presents—especially candles, symbols of light—were exchanged between friends, and masters or mistresses waited at mealtimes upon their servants.[10] Sociable men who shared a common age-group would throw lots to choose one of them as a 'king', who would organize party pranks. Lucian wrote of the fun of becoming 'sole king of all with a win at the knuckle-bones, so that you not only escape silly orders but can give them yourself, telling one man to shout out something disgraceful about himself, another to dance naked, pick up the flute-girl, and carry her three times around the room'.[11] The Kalendae, sacred to Janus, were marked by more feasting and merry-making, but distinctively by the exchange of gifts to bring luck during the coming year, traditionally of figs, honey, and pastry, but more often (by the time of the empire) of coins.[12]

The new Christian feast of the Nativity extinguished or absorbed both of them, and a string of other holy days sprang up in its wake. From the second century the eastern churches had celebrated the baptism of Christ, by John the Baptist, on 6 January. This feast, under the Greek name of the Epiphany, was known in Gaul by the fourth century. During the next few hundred years it was generally adopted in the western Christian world and associated with various other incidents in the career of Jesus, such as the miracle of Cana and the feeding of the five thousand. One of these, however, came to eclipse all others, including the baptism, in the popular imagination, and drew its appeal from the proximity of the festival to Christmas; the adoration of the infant Christ by the Magi. In the original gospel story (of St Matthew), they are described only as an unspecified number of wise men from the east, bringing gold, frankincense, and myrrh. By the sixth century, however, they had been combined with the figures of the three kings whom the Book of Psalms had predicted would come to honour the Messiah.[13] Around the year 400, also, feasts were being established on the days immediately following the Nativity: on the 26th for the first Christian martyr, Stephen, on the 27th for John the Evangelist, reputedly Christ's favourite disciple, and on the 28th for the Holy Innocents slaughtered by Herod's soldiers at Bethlehem (another link with the Nativity stories). In 567 the council of Tours declared that the whole period of twelve days between the Nativity and the Epiphany formed one festal cycle. It also confirmed that three of those days, representing the old Kalendae, would be kept as fasts between the two blocs of rejoicing. The old festive tradition of the New Year, however, gradually reasserted itself, and by the eighth century the western Church had honourably surrendered by declaring 1 January to be the feast of Christ's Circumcision.[14] The medieval system of twelve days of celebration following the winter solstice, with peaks at 25 December, 1 January and 6 January, was now in place. In the eastern Christian lands, and across much of the Mediterranean, Easter remained the principal annual festival. In most of northern and central Europe, where the cold and darkness of mid-winter were much greater, it was the cycle of merry-making anchored by the Nativity which was emerging as the more considerable. As it developed there it would have run into local patterns of pre-Christian seasonal celebration, and it is now necessary to see what is known of those in the British Isles.

It has long been appreciated that some of the most spectacular prehistoric monuments of these islands were aligned upon cardinal points of the sun, and recent excavation has only served to reinforce this. In particular, it is true of three separate groups, erected in each of what were then the major focuses of activity in the archipelago in the period 3200–3000 BCE; a transitional time of intense creativity when the concentration of religious activity upon mega-lithic or earthen tomb-shrines was starting to give way to use of circular ceremonial enclosures. In the Boyne valley of Ireland the enormous passage grave of Newgrange was given a special aperture above the entrance, through which the rising sun at midwinter could shine down the passage to the chamber even when the entrance was blocked up.[15] Nearby at Knowth a similar, and contemporary, monument apparently had its two entrances, and passages, aligned upon the sunrise and sunset at the equinoxes.[16] One of the cemetery of passage graves at Loughcrew, on a hill to the north-west of the valley, may well have had its opening in line with the equinoctial sunrise, so that the beams would, as at Newgrange and Knowth, light up decorated stones within the tomb; this certainly happens now, but the tomb was heavily 'restored' in the 1940s, so that its original structure will never now be known.[17] North of Scotland, in the mainland of Orkney, the huge passage grave of Maes Howe is Britain's equivalent to Newgrange, sharing many features of its design and roughly contemporary with it. One of the common features is that the midwinter sun shone into the chamber through a gap left above the blocking stone at the passage's entrance; the difference being that the moment was that of sunset and not of sunrise. A short walk away to the west, in full view and at about the same time, a large building was constructed with a doorway facing in just the same direction.[18] Finally in southern England a number of the enigmatic 'cursus' monuments made around this time, long narrow rectan-gular enclosures defined by banks, seem to have had significant solar align-ments. The seven-mile one in Dorset points at the midwinter sunset, that near Stonehenge at the equinoctial sunrise, and that near Dorchester on Thames at the midsummer sunset.[19]

All this is impressive, and must be significant, but needs to be put in a wider perspective. These are almost all unusually sophisticated and elaborate structures of their kind, and as such highly atypical. None of the other fifty-odd cursuses known in Britain has obvious solar alignments, nor do any of the other passage graves, which number over a hundred. An occasional one is found among other classes of megalithic tomb, but these cases may be coincidental; thus, of twenty 'Clyde'-style tombs upon the Isle of Arran, one faces the midsummer sunrise fairly exactly but all the rest have very dispersed orientations.[20] Much the same is true of the 'henge' monuments and stone circles of the third and early second millennium; thus, the large circle in Cumberland called Long Meg and Her Daughter has one entrance in line with the midwinter sunset, but none of the other stone rings of the Cumbrian region has apparent solar connections.[21] The resounding exception to this rule is a monument even more utterly atypical of stone circles than New-grange and Maes Howe are of megalithic tombs: Stonehenge itself. Around 2100 BCE this was reconstructed to provide the famous alignment upon the midsummer sunrise, through its only entrance and between two sighting stones. This possibly also furnished a corresponding orientation upon the midwinter sunset, through the uprights of the 'great trilithon' behind the centre of the monument.[22] Stonehenge is, however, utterly unique in its structure. To sum up, it is clear that at particular times and places in British and Irish prehistory the cardinal points of the sun, and particularly the winter solstice, had considerable ritual importance. None the less, the vast majority of prehistoric monuments in these islands do not relate to any of them, so that no overall or enduring pattern of cult can be detected. Furthermore, a considerable gulf separates all these monuments from the pre-Roman British Iron Age, not one of the temples of which has yet been found to have possessed a significant solar alignment.[23]

Literary sources do not tell us anything conclusive about the midwinter practices of the ancient British Isles. The Irish tales which most commonly reflect a pagan past, the Ulster cycle, do not mention any midwinter feast at all, but emphasize those at the beginning of the seasons. Indeed, that cycle, and the mythological stories such as the Book of Invasions, contain no apparent trace of a cult of the sun or of a solar deity. They were all, however, composed at least two hundred years after the end of Irish paganism, and are directly contradicted by St Patrick himself, writing in the fifth century when that paganism was very much alive; he denounced those in Ireland who adored the sun. *Sanas Chormaic*, a glossary produced around the year 900, states that the solar symbol was carved upon certain altars.[24] Certainly the Christian cycle of a twelve-day midwinter feast was well established in Ireland by the eleventh century, when *The War of the Gaedhil with the Gaill* could portray the high king Brian Boru as holding court near Dublin *ó nodlaic mór co nodlaic becc*, 'from great Christmas to little Christmas', that is from Christmas to Epiphany.[25] The early Welsh literature is, notoriously, much less helpful as a source for pagan belief and practice than the Irish, and the ancient Greek and Roman writers, useful in other aspects of the field, say nothing about seasonal festivals among the tribes of north-west Europe. Instead, one of them, Pliny, has been the source of an enduring popular confusion over a connection between Druids, mistletoe, and midwinter. He recorded that the plant was regarded by the tribes of Gaul (modern France) as an antidote to poison and a giver of fertility to animals. He added that it was treated by their Druids, or magical specialists, as especially sacred when it was found growing on an oak (which it rarely does). Then it was ritually gathered on the sixth day of the moon, a day upon which, Pliny added, these Gallic tribes traditionally began their months and their years.[26] A brief glance at this passage is sufficient to demonstrate that it does not describe a seasonal custom, but an *ad hoc* one prompted by a rare botanical event, and linked to the phases of the moon and not a solar calendar. Furthermore, Pliny specifically locates it in Gaul and not in Britain.

At first sight the Anglo-Saxon evidence seems to be much better. The key witness here is Bede, writing a history of the calendar around the year 730. He stated, confidently, that the most important annual festival of the English had formerly been what they called the *Modranicht*, or 'Mother Night', on 24 December of the Roman calendar. This was the night which opened their new year, and they kept watch during it with (unspecified) religious rites.[27] The information seems perfectly straightforward, but conceals difficulties which were thoroughly exposed in 1889 by Alexander Tille. He pointed out that Bede's knowledge of these earlier practices had been very sketchy and that Bede himself had admitted that he understood imperfectly the significance of the little that he knew. Tille suggested that it was possible that the festival described by Bede had simply been the Christian feast of the Nativity, and that the 'Mother' concerned was the Virgin Mary. He supported his scepticism by pointing out that the term *Modranicht* is not found in any other early English or Continental sources. Instead, until 1038 the feast of the Nativity was described in Anglo-Saxon literature simply as 'midwinter' (*midne winter* or *middum wintra*), a name stark enough to have an archaic ring about it. Much more rarely it was given its correct ecclesiastical name of *Nativited*. In 1038 there occurs the first recorded appearance of its enduring English name of *Cristes Maessan*, Christmas.[28] The tradition of twelve days of celebration following 'midwinter' was firmly established by 877, when the law code of Alfred the Great granted freedom from work to all servants during that span.[29]

In the eleventh century Danish rule over England resulted in the introduction of the colloquial Scandinavian term for Christmas, 'Yule', which provided an alternative name for it among the English. It became popular with them in the next century, and in the thirteenth is first recorded in Scotland, where it had become standard in vernacular speech by the end of the Middle Ages.[30] In Old Norse it is *jol*, in Swedish *jul*, and in Danish *juul*. The derivation of the name has baffled linguists; it is possibly related to the Gothic *heul* or Anglo-Saxon *hweal*, signifying a wheel, or to the root-word which yielded the English expression 'jolly'. Nothing certain, however, is known,[31] and there is equal doubt over whether it was originally attached to a midwinter festival which preceded the Christian one. The earliest Scandinavian literature does not refer to it but to an undoubted pagan feast in October, the 'Winter Nights', which opened that season. Some medieval writers did believe that Yule was just as old, notably the learned Snorri Sturluson in the thirteenth century. He asserted that the pattern had been to sacrifice for an easy winter during the 'Winter Nights', for a good crop at Yule, and for a successful fighting season on 'Summer's Day' (in April).[32] He added that Yule had lasted for three nights, the first being midwinter night and that of the New Year, and that a Christian ruler of Norway, Hakon the Good, had made this synchronize with the feast of the Nativity.[33] Another Icelandic author, probably in the same century, portrayed a warrior operating in pagan times as postponing a single combat until three days after Yule, so that he would not break the sacred peace of that festival.[34] This writer may, however, have been projecting Christian sentiments back into a dimly known past, while we do not know how reliable Snorri's sources were and whether he was correct in his interpretation of them.

When this is said, the consensus between Bede and Snorri, that the winter solstice was a major feast of the ancient Scandinavian and Norse peoples, and opened their year, is still an impressive one. It would fit in with a famous series of complaints made by churchmen and church councils about the revelry attending the New Year, between the fourth and the eleventh centuries. In 1903 Sir Edmund Chambers could list forty such denunciations.[35] The Saturnalia seems to have perished remarkably easily, perhaps indicating that it had, after all, a narrow geographical base. By contrast, the Kalendae, or rather ancient European festivals of midwinter and New Year which churchmen compared to the Roman Kalendae, proved to be very resilient indeed. Among those who attacked them were some of the most renowned Fathers of the early medieval Church, including Jerome, Ambrose, Augustine, and John Chrysostom. Especially concerned, and voluble, were Maximus of Turin, Chrysologus of Ravenna, Caesarius of Arles, and Pacian of Barcelona. In the eleventh century the denunciations had ended in these southern regions, but they were repeated by Burchard of Worms, writing in more recently evangelized Germany.[36] More interesting for our purposes, they were still being issued in England. At some point between the years 1005 and 1008 Archbishop Wulfstan of York, facing a province recently given a fresh infusion of paganism by heavy Viking settlement, condemned (among many other observations) 'the nonsense which is performed on New Year's Day in various kinds of sorcery'.[37] At the other end of the realm, in the late twelfth century, Bartholomew Iscanus, bishop of Exeter, prescribed a penance for 'those who keep the New Year with heathen rites'.[38] If these rites were of divination, to see what the year would bring, then the condemnations were ineffectual. The fourteenth-century *Mirk's Festival* warned readers against being tempted into 'magic' on New Year's Day.[39] In the early years of the next century, the tract *Dives and Pauper* complained of 'their folly that divining be Christmas Day or be the first day of January, or be pondering what shall fallen all be the year following'.[40] These writers were no more successful than the earlier prelates, to judge by the very large number of divinatory customs for New Year's Eve and Day recorded by nineteenth- and twentieth-century folklorists.

There is also good evidence in early medieval Welsh literature that the most important annual festival in Wales at that period was a midwinter one, never identified with the Christian holy day of the Nativity but always known by the secular title of 'the New Year feast'. In the celebrated epic poem *Y Gododdin*, composed at any time between the seventh and tenth centuries, the warrior Gorthyn ap Urfai was admired for the fact that he 'provided song at the New Year feast'. The verses *Etmich Dinbych* (The Praise of Tenby), dating from the ninth or tenth centuries, contain the lines

> My custom it was on New Year's Eve
> To sleep beside my prince, the glorious in battle,
> And wear a purple mantle, and enjoy luxury.[41]

One of the most famous of all early Welsh prose tales, *Culhwch ac Olwen*, which seems to be tenth-century, sets the beginning of its action at a New Year feast of the war band of King Arthur, where there were 'hot peppered chops and an abundance of wine and entertaining songs.' There is a widespread if unproven modern notion that the pagan 'Celtic New Year' was not in midwinter, which will be discussed much later in this present book. The Welsh sources at least strongly suggest that by the tenth century at the very latest, a midwinter New Year's festival was being celebrated with a vigour which suggests a long-established tradition.

It must be obvious now that, in seeking for pagan feasts which underlie the British Christmas, the issues are complex and the evidence difficult to assess. This is true even in the case of the Roman material, which is the fullest, and infinitely more so in that of the north European data. Nevertheless, there is sufficient to argue strongly for the existence of a major pre-Christian festival marking the opening of the new year, at the moment at which the sun had reached the winter solstice and its strength was being renewed. There is testimony to this in the Anglo-Saxon, the Viking, and the Welsh components of the medieval British heritage. If so, this tradition would explain the pattern which set in after 1155, when the English Crown determined to revert to the presumed early Roman system of commencing the official year in March, which made more sense of the names of the months which the English had taken over from Rome. The precise date selected was the 25th, the Christian feast of the Annunciation, and first English and then British years were reckoned from that until the calendar reform of 1752, when it was returned to 1 January. At the same time, however, everybody from the monarch downwards continued to observe rituals and superstitions upon 31 December and 1 January; this abundantly demonstrated that these remained the New Year's Eve and Day which were recognized in practice and to which all emotional significance was attached. It is clear that the alteration of 1752 was simply a long-overdue recognition of the realities of the situation, and likely that the highly charged atmosphere which still prevails upon the British New Year's Eve is a faithful reflection of one of the oldest festivals of the island.

2

THE TWELVE DAYS

⟡

I T is time now to see how the cycle of midwinter celebration established in the early part of the Middle Ages had developed in Britain by the end of that period. The opening of it, Christmas itself, began very early indeed for the devout. The book of ceremonies most widely used in England and (until the early sixteenth century) in Scotland was the Use of Sarum, compiled at Salisbury cathedral. This directed that the day should have three masses, the first of which, Matins, commenced before dawn. At the end of this the genealogy of Christ, from St Matthew's Gospel, was sung by a man standing in the rood loft, the carved wooden platform over the top of the nave which supported the rood, an image of the crucified Christ, flanked by Mary and John. Another person held a candle to light him as he performed, while others in the body of the church carried burning tapers.[1] Fifteenth- and sixteenth-century churchwardens' accounts, therefore, often contain payments for candles and tapers, made or bought in bulk for Christmas morn. Some specified that the largest of these should be for the rood loft, and, by process of association, a collection often accompanied the service to pay for the candle or lamp which lit up the rood during masses throughout the year.[2]

When the people left church they could enjoy, if they chose, their first unrestricted meal for over four weeks. From Advent Sunday, the fourth before the Nativity, they had been enjoined to limit their diet. For the wealthy, this apparently meant having soups, stews, and fish instead of roasts or pies. The poorer, however, could find the reduction a misery. In the fifteenth century James Ryman complained of eating 'no puddings nor sauce, but stinking fish not worth a louse'. Christmas Eve was kept as a strict fast, meat, cheese and eggs all being forbidden. The feasting upon the Day was thus something of an emotional release, and also an occasion for generosity. All household accounts surviving from the Middle Ages and Tudor period record the purchase of abnormal quantities of foodstuffs for it and the following days. The ideal of hospitality was expressed by Thomas Tusser in the mid-sixteenth century:

> At Christmas we banquet, the rich with the poor,
> Who then (but the miser) but openeth his door?

The wealthy were naturally expected to open theirs with particular munificence, although it seems that in reality they mostly entertained their social equals and immediate inferiors. In the 1510s the earl of Northumberland and duke of Buckingham received a string of clerical dignitaries and local gentle-folk. The earl's dinner always included four swans, the duke's several barrels of Malmsey wine. In the 1520s Sir Henry Willoughby, a midland landowner, entertained all his tenants. Nevertheless, his namesake, contemporary, and relatively near neighbour, Henry Rogers, mayor of Coventry in 1517, seems genuinely to have kept 'open house' for all.[3]

This meal ushered in the twelve days of merriment which were to last until the Epiphany, and which had been developing steadily all through the medieval period. During the central portion of that period literary sources for merriment are supplemented by two new categories of material: manorial records and household accounts. Most manorial custumals specified that villeins were to do no work on the lord's land during the Twelve Days and that the lord would provide a feast for them; but they were also expected to bring him gifts, which being normally in farm produce would provide most of the meal. Sometimes the one was explicitly conditional on the other.[4] Monarchs and magnates would hold feasts on Christmas Day itself and on some others of the twelve, much as the Welsh princes had done for their war bands at New Year. In this high medieval period, foodstuffs and entertainments are rarely itemized in the accounts, only the most remarkable being picked out; thus we know that in 1289 the bishop of Hereford ensured a boar's head as a stylish centrepiece for his table,[5] while in 1328 the Scottish king Robert the Bruce had minstrels perform for his court.[6] The descriptions of Christmastide amusements in the famous fourteenth-century poem *Sir Gawaine and the Green Knight* [7] bear out what the accounts up to and including that period suggest:[8] that even wealthy households tended to find entertainments within themselves.

Towards the end of that century, the itemization of purchases of food and the detail in which the feasting is recorded tend to grow more elaborate, which may reflect a better record-keeping or a genuine increase in sophistication. Most grandiose of all were of course the royal banquets: one held by Richard II had 10,000 guests and consumed 200 oxen and 200 tubs of wine. Another provided by Henry V consisted of brawn (in this case boar's flesh from the belly, strapped in rolls), dates with mottled cream, carp, prawns, turbot, tench, perch, fresh sturgeon with whelks, roasted porpoise, crayfish, roasted eels and lampreys, leached meats garnished with hawthorn leaves, and marzipan.[9] It is also notable that wealthy households began to avail themselves much more of the services of visiting entertainers, whether professional artists or groups of village players, in a way not apparent in the accounts before. This is obvious at the highest level, as in the case of the Jack Travaill and his company, who were paid £4 for making plays and interludes before the young King Henry VI at Christmas 1428.[10] It is equally plain at a regional one. In 1406 Richard Mitford, bishop of Salisbury, kept the Twelve Days at his manor of Potterne in a crevice of Salisbury Plain. He enjoyed the usual 'interludes', 'games', and 'disguisings' within his own little court, but also watched players who came from Potterne itself, Devizes, Urchfont, Seend, and Sherborne.[11] Near the lower end of the landowning élite was the widow Alice de Bryene, who kept the 1412 season at her seat of Acton Hall in central Suffolk. On Christmas Day she held a feast for her household and estate officials, and on New Year's Day one for her 300 tenants, entertaining various guests between. For the whole week she hired a single harper.[12]

A hundred years later the same pattern still held. In the Twelve Days of 1520–1, the duke of Buckingham watched a troupe of French players, as well as three jesters, the corporation musicians of Bristol, and an acrobat. In 1540–1 the earl of Rutland paid for players from Lincoln and Wighen, minstrels from Derbyshire, and a performance by 'the children of Newark'. Most aristocrats, however, watched only one or two plays and concerts in each Christmas season, and Henry VIII himself marked his first one as monarch with just three dramatic productions and one sequence of music. Religious houses and urban councils frequently, but not invariably, invited in the same sorts of entertainers as the nobles, and parishioners sometimes pooled their resources to hire players or to present their own productions in the village church. The latter were occasionally turned into fund-raising events, with food and drink sold by the churchwardens. We can only guess at the nature of the great majority of the plays which were performed. From the evidence of the late sixteenth and early seventeenth centuries, when theatrical records become more detailed, we can surmise that they would often have been just the current repertoire of the groups which staged them. Some, however, must have been upon the theme of the Nativity, like the one acted annually before the fifth earl of Northumberland in the 1510s. In addition to these performances, there were always many private parties at all levels of society and a great deal of card-playing and board-gaming.[13]

The mention of 'disguisings' at the manor house of Bishop Mitford is one reference to a fashion of considerable importance during the late Middle Ages. It was also commonly known in Britain as 'mumming', a term which, in the form of 'momerie', is first recorded there in the thirteenth century. This latter form was also used across western Europe from the same period, its earliest appearance apparently being at Troyes in 1263, where the corporation banned 'momment' among the populace. It signified the wearing of festive masks or other disguises and may have derived from 'mommo', the Greek word for a mask. References to it become much more frequent in the fourteenth century, which may indeed reflect a growing popularity at all levels of society; it certainly became a favourite courtly entertainment then in a way not known before. Edward III introduced it into English royal recreation during the Christmas season of 1347. The disguised people entered the King's presence in six groups of fourteen; the first three sets were merely masked, as women, men, and angels respectively, and the remainder wore whole heads, of dragons, peacocks, and swans. The following year all the groups wore heads, including some of animals and some of 'wild men'. The tradition persisted; in

1377 the Common Council sent 130 men to salute the young Richard II, 'to go on mumming to the said prince'. They rode in pairs with music and torches, 'clothed in coats and cloaks of red saye or sendall and their faces covered with vizards well and handsomely made'. First came those clad as squires, then knights, then an emperor, then a pope, next cardinals, and finally devils. They paraded through the City, moved on to Kennington Palace, presented gifts, and then drank and danced before returning. In 1414 Lollard heretics plotted a coup at Eltham Palace 'under colour of the mumming'. During the fifteenth century the performances appeared at the Scottish court, and at the English one they became more allegorical and symbolic, with speeches, plots, songs, and scenery. They grew during the sixteenth into the distinctive theatrical genre of the masque.[14]

'Mummers', 'maskers', and 'guisers' were also recorded among the inhabitants of British towns, and posed a problem to law and order because the combination of dark evenings and revellers in disguises afforded marvellous opportunities for crime. This is almost certainly why the custom was banned at Troyes, and at other European urban centres during the fourteenth century. It was explicitly the reason for a municipal order forbidding 'mumming' on the streets of London in 1405. Similar measures were subsequently taken at Bristol and Chester.[15] An Act of Parliament in the third year of Henry VIII's reign prohibited the 'wearing of visors' across England, as 'a company together naming themselves Mummers have come in to the dwelling place of divers men of honour and other substantial persons; and so departed unknown'.[16] The same problem affected Scotland, where a man was hanged in 1508 for stealing 'under guise of mumming.'[17]

In the English countryside a much more benign, and mysterious, sort of people were abroad at this season, known variously as Hognells, Hogglers, Hogans, or Hogners, or Hoggells, or by other versions of those names. In the fifteenth and sixteenth centuries, they are recorded in parishes in Gloucestershire, Somerset and Devon, Surrey, Sussex and Kent, and the Lincolnshire Fens. In the south-western counties and in Sussex and Surrey, they appear in the majority of (but not all) country parishes for which Tudor accounts survive. In some, especially in Devon and Somerset, they provided the largest annual contribution to parochial finances. In the two neighbouring Lincolnshire villages where they are known to have existed, Sutterton and Wigtoft, they maintained their own light burning in the churches. At Pilton and Tintinhull in central Somerset and Ashburton and Chagford on the fringe of Dartmoor in Devon, they were formally organized into a guild, Tintinhull's having a steward and Chagford's possessing wardens. At times they included some of the wealthiest people in their villages. At Ashburton they handed in their contribution at Easter, but most of the accounts imply what those of Surrey and some in Sussex make explicit, that their period of activity was during the Christmas holidays. At Bolney in the Sussex forest lands, 'the hognel time' lasted longer, until 2 February.

What we are never told is what happened in that time. The derivation of the name or names is unknown. The Old English *hagenhune* meant a protected guest, while the Norman *hoguinane* signified a New Year present; and these are the dictionary's only clues. We do not know whether the hogglers or hognells performed any service or gave any performance in return for their collections. We cannot account for their curious geographical distribution. We cannot say how or why they first appeared, for they feature in the first year of every book of expenses in which they occur, and none of these is older than the 1450s. We can only say that, according to a late Elizabethan Somerset court book, their fundamental activity was to go about the parish gathering money for it, and that every piece of evidence testifies to their efficiency in doing so.[18]

A different sort of Christmastide activity concerned the wassail bowl, or cup. The custom connected with it was first described by Peter de Langtoft, writing in the 1320s; the leader of a gathering took it, and cried 'wassail', Old English for 'your health'. That person was answered 'Drinkhail', drank from it, and passed it to the next of the company with a kiss. Each then repeated these actions. The custom may not, in fact, have been much older than Langtoft's time. From the famous eighth-century poem *Beowulf* to the fourteenth-century conduct-book of Robert of Brunne, the word 'wassail' appears as a toast: it is simply Anglo-Saxon for 'be of good health'. The bowl is first mentioned by Matthew Paris in the thirteenth century, as one in which cakes and fine white bread were communally dipped. Near the end of the same century Robert of Gloucester retold the legend of the marriage of the British king Vortigern with the English princess Rowena, making the latter drink to the former with the words *Waes hael*. The exchange reported by Langtoft, therefore, may have become traditional in the intervening few decades, around 1300, but this is impossible to prove. By the end of the fourteenth century, great families preserved wassail cups of considerable value— Edmund, earl of March, left a silver one upon his death in 1382—and it remained a diversion in high society for the rest of the Middle Ages and beyond. At the court of Henry VII it was accompanied into the royal presence by the chief officers of the household, bearing staves.[19]

An especially flamboyant version of the custom was experienced by the Londoner Henry Machyn, when a guest at a party at Henley on Thames on Twelfth Eve 1555. Into the room came 'twelve wessells with maidens singing, with their wessells; and after came the chief wives singing with their wessells; and the gentlewoman had ordained a great table of banquet, desserts of spices and fruit, as marmalade, gingerbread, jelly, comfit, sugar plate and divers others'.[20] What is not clear is whether the whole entertainment was arranged by the household, or whether the wassail-bearers were going from house to house and were lucky enough to receive a very generous welcome at this one. If the latter, it is the earliest known reference to a custom which was to become commonly recorded a generation or two later. From about the same time dates the following song, which may have accompanied the cup or bowl around the household or (if that custom did yet obtain) around the streets:

> Wassail, wassail, out of the milk pail
> Wassail, wassail, as white as my nail,
> Wassail, wassail, in snow, frost and hail,
> Wassail, wassail, that much doth avail,
> Wassail, wassail, that never will fail.[21]

This was one of a very large number of songs which were by that date associated with the season. 'At Christmas of Christ many carols we sing,' wrote Thomas Tusser in the 1570s, and scores have survived from fifteenth- and early sixteenth-century England. By 1500 they were also well established in Scotland, William Dunbar writing some for the court of James IV. Most were of the Nativity, but they were also devotional, or about saints, or about the mass, or were satiric, amorous, or humorous. In the late Middle Ages they represented a distinctive type of lyric, made to accompany a ring dance of women and men holding hands. As such, they first appear in extant English records in the *Cursor Mundi*, written around 1300. During the following century and a half, Robert of Brunne, Chaucer, and Gower all referred to the song and dance as inseparable, and only in the fifteenth century did the two come apart, and the former acquire its association with Christmas. Even then, however, the specific term 'Christmas carol' was needed, and the word 'carol' signified a form of verse not a subject. Its origins are uncertain, but the Franciscan friars were so closely associated with popular religious songs by 1300, and their compositions are so similar in style and subject-matter to the early carols, that they probably either directly inspired or assisted the adoption of the entertainment in England. No record survives of the setting for their performance there. Some were by their nature suited to the home, but many could have been sung door to door as they have been in modern times. There is no evidence, however, that it was usual to perform them in church.[22]

Most of the customs and diversions mentioned above were common to all or most of the Christmas season; but certain days among the Twelve were especially important. The first such, after Christmas itself, was 1 January, known as New Year's Day throughout the medieval and early modern period despite the formal change of date for beginning the year to March. The Roman custom of giving presents then was retained across much of Europe all through the Middle Ages. In England the thirteenth-century monarch Henry III was criticized for extorting them from his subjects.[23] Two centuries later, those sent by young Henry VI to members of his family included tablets of gold studded with jewels, a ruby set in a gold ring, and a gold crucifix decorated with sapphires and pearls.[24] The court ordinances of Henry VII directed that he would receive his gifts in the morning after he had put on his shoes. Trumpets then sounded, and the presents arrived carried by servants, first from the queen and then from his leading subjects. In her own chamber the queen received hers. The royal couple had arranged for gifts from each of them, usually in cash, to be sent out to the officers of the household and to the chief lay and clerical dignitaries of the realm. If the latter were at their own seats, the presents were carried thither by Yeomen of the Guard. Upon the same morning the fifth earl of Northumberland was awoken by minstrels playing before his door, followed by his own fanfare of trumpets. He then received his gifts, making them in turn to his sovereigns and his household. Similar scenes were probably enacted at the residences of other Tudor magnates, while gentry exchanged presents with their servants and often despatched them to local aristocrats. Some great nobles, like the earl of Rutland, sent gifts to servants of the king and of other peers, from whom they expected or had received favours. Religious houses gave to their own staff and to each other.[25] Schoolboys at Eton played games in order to win gifts, and made presents of verses to their masters and to each other.[26] New Year's gifts appear in every full set of household accounts surviving from the period 1400–1550, underpinning the social and political order. What is not clear is whether they were exchanged between commoners. Polydor Vergil, at the opening of the sixteenth century, stated that they were sent by those who served lords; but Tusser, in the middle of the same century, commented that Christmas was a time when people in general 'gave many gifts'.[27] In 1419 the corporation of London ordered the servants of City officers to stop the custom of asking for Christmas offerings from victualling trades, sometimes with menaces when refused.[28] It is clear therefore that a wider tradition of exchanging gifts at this time existed, but the extent of it seems impossible to quantify.

The date was marked by festivity as well as reciprocal generosity. The Scottish king James IV was greeted with a 'New Year ballad' sung by the clerks of his chapel.[29] His English contemporary Henry VII held a banquet at noon, processing to it with the sword of state carried before him. The nobles and gentry keeping the season at their seats almost certainly all held feasts then as well (or so the household accounts suggest); the fifth earl of Northumberland, in the 1510s, had his honours proclaimed by his herald as the meal commenced. The evening was a notable one for entertainments, from royal to parish level.[30]

The same was even more true of Twelfth Night, which ended the Christmas holidays. Twelfth Day (in Scotland 'Uphaliday' or end-of-holiday) began as Christmas itself had done, with a dramatic religious service. This time it was the commemoration of the Three Kings, in places with the appearance of a Star of Bethlehem, sometimes gilded and sometimes made of brass, suspended from the rood loft or in 'the body of the church'. It seems to have been used almost wholly in urban parishes, Holbeach in the Lincolnshire Fens being the only rural one where it is recorded. It was, indeed, apparently favoured only by some churches even within towns, and it is striking that none of the surviving sets of London parish accounts seems to mention it. It may have played a part in a theatrical performance featuring the Three Kings, but of this

15

there is evidence only in the grandiose setting of Lincoln cathedral. In the Chapels Royal of Scotland and England it was the tradition by 1500 for the monarchs to make offerings symbolizing their spiritual kinship with the Wise Men; Henry VII gave packets of gold, frankincense, and myrrh, and James IV gave three gold crowns.[31]

After the service Henry VII donned his own crown and royal robes, to preside over another banquet. For him, his successor Henry VIII, and many others of all social ranks, the festivities of that night were the most sumptuous of the whole year. The fifth earl of Northumberland regularly watched a play followed by a masked dance interspersed with pageants. In 1486 Henry VII held a banquet and then went in procession to Westminster Hall to watch a play, and then a pageant of St George and the dragon, and then a 'disguising' by various courtiers. For Henry VII in 1512 the Master of the Revels prepared the pageant of 'The Dangerous Fortress', a castle complete with towers, bulwarks, iron chains, cannon, and a banner, inhabited by six ladies and seven gentlemen in yellow and russet, six lords in gold and russet, and twelve great nobles in yellow and blue.[32]

There were a few other customs associated with the Twelve Days during this period which, because of their special character, will be considered later. It is time now to trace the subsequent history of those which have been delineated above. The religious ceremonies of Christmas morn and the Epiphany were, of course, swept away when the medieval liturgy was replaced by Protestant Prayer Books, first under Edward VI and then under Elizabeth. Between these two Reformations, they were restored by Mary Tudor, and the hanging of a Star of Bethlehem is recorded during her reign at two Chester churches.[33] With their final disappearance, they left a remarkable and enduring regional (or national) legacy, in the Welsh *plygain*, or *plygien*, a candlelit assembly before dawn on Christmas Day. Although the reading from the rood loft had gone (along with the liturgy and most of the lofts), the service was apparently retained. At Swansea the purchase of candles for Christmas morn is already recorded by the 1610s, a decade from which no other parish accounts survive in Wales.[34] As more begin, in the course of the seventeenth century, the same purchase features in a minority, always now in the north of the principality. There is a clear trend, nevertheless, for the custom to become more popular in the 1680s.[35] The enduring term *plygain* seems to be recorded first at Wrexham, in the far north-east, in 1663,[36] it apparently derives from the Latin *pulli cantus*, or 'cock-crow song'.[37] The reference to song indicates that the provision of carols was already an integral part of the custom, and indeed many Welsh Christmas carols were written in just this period by Edward Morris (d. 1689), and Huw Morris (1622–1709). Both men worked in Denbighshire, bearing out the suggestion of the parish accounts that this was an especial centre of the growing tradition.[38]

Most descriptions of it, however, derive from the nineteenth century, by which time it was found all over Wales except in the 'Englishry' of Pembrokeshire, as well as in Shropshire parishes just over the border.[39] Most colourful of all seems to be the Carmarthenshire version, by which people carried torches around the streets on the *nos y polgen* (Christmas Eve), before processing to church with green candles in the early morning.[40] At the opening of the century the usual time for the service was three o'clock, but as it wore on the hour was either pushed later into the morning or further into the following evening, or else the custom was abolished altogether. The reason for this was not religious; indeed, as dissenting denominations spread among the Welsh during this period, those in the south often adopted the *plygain*, while those in the north cheerfully allowed their congregations to attend it in the local parish church. The problem was, rather, that the service was becoming increasingly disrupted by drunkenness; and whether this was a result of growing population, spreading industry, or a weakening of communal ties is a question which Welsh social historians have yet to solve. At any rate, by the early twentieth century the custom had contracted into the parishes of the central Tanat valley in the Berwyn mountains of what was then Montgomeryshire, and there it remains. It does so as a straightforward carol service, without any other religious observance, held on an evening between mid-December and early January. From twenty to thirty carols are sung, mostly in Welsh, almost always by adults, and usually without any accompaniment, although a harp is sometimes used. It is an art form of powerful simple beauty; it is also, apparently, the last surviving echo, in a British parochial setting, of the seasonal liturgy of the medieval Church.

By the nineteenth century, at latest, the Isle of Man had a similar custom, the *Oie'l Verrey* ('Eve of Feast of Mary') service. This was held on Christmas Eve, the parishioners crowding into churches at midnight carrying lighted candles decorated with ribbons. After it was concluded, the priest would usually go home and leave groups of people to sing carols in the church. It is not known how long this had obtained, how it evolved, and (therefore) how it was related to the *plygain*.[41] In addition to these local traditions of the established Church, the Methodists developed the habit of a 'watch-night' service, extending from Christmas Eve to Christmas morn. It arose during the eighteenth century,[42] it was sustained through the nineteenth, although sometimes diverted to New Year's Eve, and in the twentieth it helped to inspire the increasingly popular Anglican tradition of a 'midnight mass' on Christmas Eve.

The royal presentation of gold, frankincense, and myrrh at the Epiphany survived the English Reformation without difficulty, reflecting as it did a direct relationship between deity and monarch which the rejection of papal authority only served to enhance. Elizabeth duly presented her papers containing the gifts,[43] and so did every English sovereign until George III lost his reason and so was unable to perform the ritual in person. In his place, two gentlemen from the Lord Chamberlain's Office laid the offerings upon a dish held by the officiating priest in the Chapel Royal, taking them from a box with a star on its top. Under Victoria the procedure was simplified to the delivery of them in a single red bag, the monarchs never having resumed attendance in person, and this system still obtains.[44] In its almost perfunctory fashion, it stands as witness to the medieval popularity of the cult of the Three Kings.

The royal entertainments of the Christmas season also continued, of course, unaffected by the political and religious changes of the Tudor period. Under Elizabeth the mummery at court completed its transformation into the more stately and formal diversion of the masque. Each Twelfth Day she drew up lists of nobles who were to attend her at the feast, when the Children of the Chapel Royal opened the musical accompaniment with a carol.[45] James I established a pattern of having plays at court on almost every evening of the Twelve Days, with a masque upon Twelfth Night. When he wanted a performance upon Christmas Night 1608, and was told by his 'lords' that it was not the fashion, he snapped that he would make it one. Under Charles I the tradition of the Twelfth Night masque was continued, to lapse only with the fall of the monarchy itself in the 1640s.[46] Masques were out of fashion after the Restoration, and the tone of elegance combined with vulgarity which Charles II set for his court was neatly symbolized by the new Twelfth Night custom there of heavy gambling. The other evenings of the holidays were filled with royal balls and parties as before.[47] The passion for gaming on Twelfth Night persisted under more sober monarchs, until abolished at the accession of the exceptionally prim George III.[48] With this a more domestic pattern set into royal Christmases, which will be discussed later.

Likewise the round of aristocratic and genteel entertainment remained fairly constant. The feasting was still ample; even an unusually pious and serious-minded gentlewoman like Lady Mildmay, seated in 1594 at Apethorpe in Northamptonshire, could stock up with bread, butter, eight hogsheads of beer, beef, mutton, pork, blackbirds, larks, rabbits, hens, and wild game.[49] Household entertainments also showed little development, so that another Mildmay, Sir Humphrey, based at Danbury near the Essex coast for the Christmases of 1639 and 1640, could play dice, cards, and board games on most evenings and hire a 'fool' for New Year's Day.[50] An author in the 1640s also listed bowling, hawking, and hunting among the usual Christmas diversions of the landed élite.[51] The great houses rewarded visiting players and musicians as they had during the later Middle Ages, and this habit was maintained through the seventeenth century, as will be seen. The early Stuart period also furnishes novel insights into the pastimes of commoners, the most detailed being provided by John Taylor, himself a Thames waterman. In his account, ordinary rural people enjoyed feasting (especially upon normally scarce and expensive commodities such as meat), dancing, card-playing, carol-singing, story-telling, and party games. The latter included 'hot cockles' (which involved a whack on the hand), 'shoeing the wild mare' (which involved a whack on the foot), and attempting to bite apples which were tied at one end of a stick which had a lighted candle stuck at the other.[52]

The decades between 1610 and 1650 also provide the first detailed evidence of the popular association of special foods and drinks with the season. One was the 'minced pie', a mixture of meat, fruit, and spice baked in a pastry case. Another was 'plum porridge', thick beef broth with prunes, raisins, and currants stirred into it. Among meat dishes, beef and brawn, both stuck with rosemary, were especially favoured. The seasonal drink identified at this time was hot spiced ale with apples floating in it, which would be commonly known by the nineteenth century as 'lambswool'.[53] All these were to remain standard for the next two hundred years.

One of the principal problems in the history of Christmas during this period is how much of this food, drink, and entertainment was diffused in the form of hospitality. It was the opinion of James I that the quantity was decreasing to an alarming extent, as landowners increasingly chose to remain in London during the Christmas season instead of spending it at their country residences and dispensing hospitality and charity in the traditional manner. In 1616 he made a formal speech in Star Chamber calling upon them to reverse the trend, which helped to inspire a masque by Ben Jonson, a poem by George Wither, at least one popular ballad, and (eventually) the tract by John Taylor quoted above, all supporting the king's view.[54] It has been cautiously supported also by the historian of early modern hospitality Felicity Heal, partly because it seems logical that the complaints must have been inspired by some genuine development, and partly because she uncovered examples to illustrate them. From the Tudor age she recovered several cases of heroic quantities of Christmas largesse, while from the Jacobean one came the story of the Thynnes, who took to living in the capital during at least some Christmases during the 1600s, leaving their enormous new country mansion at Longleat closed up.[55]

What is less clear is how far these examples were in fact typical. As mentioned above, the household accounts of late medieval and early Tudor England do not suggest that many gentry kept open house in the Twelve Days; the rule was to entertain neighbours and often tenants. On the other hand, Dr Heal herself has detected several cases of a far more liberal hospitality in the early Stuart period. They include gentry such as the Petres, Stanleys, and Mildmays, parsons of country livings, and (above all) prelates. Toby Matthews, archbishop of York, held six huge feasts between 26 December 1624 and 3 January 1625, which between them fed hundreds of commoners. A poor woman could spend the season of 1616–17 moving between five gentry households in the Stilton area.[56] It seems clear that if there was a decline it was only relative, and it is even possible that there was little or none absolutely. The Elizabethan and Jacobean periods were a time of growing economic strain and a burgeoning poverty problem, and calls for a return to an ideal standard of old-fashioned seasonal hospitality may have been propelled by a growing need for the latter rather than an actual decrease in it.

At any rate, the complaint became a historical constant. In 1702 Poor Robin's Almanac could declare that

> But now landlords and tenants too
> In making feasts are very slow;
> One in an age, or near so far,
> Or one perhaps each blazing star;
> The cook now and the butler too
> Have little or nothing for to do.
> And fiddlers who used to get scraps
> Now cannot fill their hungry chaps;
> Yet some true English blood still lives,
> Who gifts to the poor at Christmas gives,
> And to their neighbours makes a feast,
> I wish their numbers were increased.[57]

In the last third of the seventeenth century the same theme had been treated, with about the same degree of literary talent, in at least three other popular publications.[58] On the other hand, a fourth one had claimed that hospitality had been revived with such liberality that

> All travellers as they do pass on the way
> At gentlemen's halls are invited to stay.[59]

The truth is once more difficult to determine. Felicity Heal, again, has suggested that the pattern of long-term decline was sustained,[60] and the known evidence from the late Stuart years can fit either argument. At one extreme was Sir George Downing, who gloated over the money which he saved by giving only broth to the neighbours whom he entertained. At the other was Sir Justinian Isham, who fed the paupers, labourers, and 'better class inhabitants' of two Northamptonshire villages on successive evenings. In Lancashire Nicholas Blundell sometimes kept open house. Generally, however, landowners seem to have provided for their neighbours and tenants just as before.[61] Almost the same remarks could be made for the following 150 years. In Devon in 1816 labourers still claimed food and drink at Christmas from any farmer whose crop they had reaped in the autumn. Four years later the issue was alive enough one for Washington Irving to produce a literary portrait of an Essex squire who attempted to keep open house in the Twelve Days, only to be 'overrun by all the vagrants of the county'. He subsequently retrenched to a Christmas Day feast for 'the decent part of the neighbouring peasantry'. At the opening of the nineteenth century a Dr Falconer lamented the manner in which the nobility and gentry had recently adopted the 'pernicious custom' of deserting their 'native mansions' at Christmastide, as if the same condemnation had not now been made almost continuously for two centuries.[62] Perhaps, indeed, upper-class generosity had been ebbing over that whole span, but it is equally likely that perception and idealization were more important here than reality.

What the ages of Elizabeth and James did destroy, beyond doubt, was the mysterious world of the 'hogglers' or 'hognels'. It is clear that the Reformation was inimical to them, although so little is known of their activities that the reason for this is lost. Three villages in which they collected have left accounts for the reign of Edward VI, and in each they ceased to operate as soon as the religious changes got under way; by contrast, they re-emerged at the opening of the reign of the Catholic Mary Tudor, although now recorded only in the West Country and at one village in the Sussex Weald. With the enforcement of the more moderate Elizabethan Reformation, the decline was resumed at a slow but steady pace. By 1600 they were confined to Somerset and Gloucestershire, and becoming rare there, and by 1630 they are only mentioned at the little market town of Cheddar, where the Mendip Hills meet the Somerset marshes. Even there they now only visited those who did not pay the usual parish rate, and they ceased operations in 1636. They resumed them seven years later, when the Civil War had disrupted the area enough to make the formal levy of a rate difficult, and continued to collect money door to door, and provide most of the church income, until the end of the fighting. Then, in 1646, they vanished again, and are heard of no more in any place.[63] The imposition of new and more regular means of fund-raising, by rates, clearly made them redundant, but the Tudor evidence obviously indicates that they also offended Protestant sensibilities.

Other popular seasonal customs persisted without difficulty. One was mumming. In 1616 Ben Jonson could portray a typical mummer's costume as being a pied suit and a mask.[64] The tradition was 'put down' in the Fylde district of Lancashire in 1648 as part of the local dimension of the 'Puritan Revolution',[65] but is repeatedly recorded in southern England during the Interregnum. A set of Christmas 'mummers' got into a dispute with an alehouse-keeper at the Wiltshire clothing town of Calne in 1655,[66] another solicited rewards at the manor house of North Aston, Oxfordshire, in 1657, and two more did the same at that of Weston Underwood, Buckinghamshire, in 1659.[67] At the end of December 1657 another inhabitant of a western cloth-making town, Frome, complained to the county bench that he had been beaten up on the 26th by a group who had been 'drinking, playing cards and fiddling all day in disguised habits'.[68] A definition of mumming as carried on around Newcastle in the 1720s was provided by Henry Bourne, who characterized it as an exchange of clothing between young people of opposite sexes, who thus costumed went from house to house asking for hospitality.[69] As such it persisted in Yorkshire into the mid-nineteenth century, where groups were usually composed of 'one man in sailor's dress, the rest being women, or rather men in women's dress'. If a house which they entered needed cleaning, then they would sweep hearth and kitchen, 'humming all the time "mum-m-m"'.[70] In the south, mummers continued to call at great houses, and to be given money and food there, all through the eighteenth century,[71] though there are no descriptions of what they actually did until the end, when references multiply to the famous play which will be discussed later.

Christmas carols likewise remained in constant use. James I's favourite preacher, Lancelot Andrewes, recommended the singing of them at home,[72] and many more were written during the seventeenth century, often specifically for family use.[73] The wassail bowl is apparently not heard of at the royal court after the time of Henry VIII, but is reported at all other levels of society in the years 1600–30. Jonson portrayed it as a brown bowl decorated with ribbons and rosemary. To the author of *Pasquils Palinodia* it was a symbol of peace and communality. It is in this period, too, that the bowl first features, unequivocally, as an object carried from door to door by poor people seeking hospitality. This may, as mentioned, have been what is implied in Machyn's mid-Tudor account. It is also probably what was described by Nicholas Breton in 1602 when he wrote of how 'hearty welcome fills the wassail bowl', or by George Wither in 1618 when he wrote of wealthy people who aid the poor once a year and 'entertain their Christmas wassail bowls'. John Taylor, however, was quite clear when in 1631 he described how a 'company of maids' would call at a rural household at Christmas crying 'Wassell, Wassell, jolly Wassell' and bringing cakes and a bowl of drink. In return they would be given white bread, cheese, and minced pies.[74] If this development of the custom indeed dated from the mid-Tudor period or earlier, it seems reasonable to suggest that it would have been increased (if it was not, indeed, actually provoked), by the much greater polarization of local society under the economic strains of the late sixteenth and early seventeenth centuries. Payments to 'wassailers' feature in gentry household accounts throughout the late Stuart and Hanoverian ages.[75] During the same years the domestic wassail continued as well: around Leeds, in Yorkshire, during the 1780s, a cup of ale with roasted apples in it was passed round after supper on every Twelfth Eve. Each person spooned out an apple and wished the company a merry Christmas and happy New Year. The date was known locally as 'Wassail Eve'.[76]

Much the same story attaches to the New Year's gifts. Throughout the Tudor and Stuart periods they remained a vital symbol of relationships at the heart of the body politic. Elizabeth gave gold or silver plate in fixed quantity, from the 136 ounces due to a reigning favourite such as Robert Dudley to the 2 ounces received by the court dwarf. In return she accepted rich clothing, money, jewels, and individual presents in kind down to the marzipan sent by her cook.[77] By the time of Charles II the sovereign was still presenting plate, but generally got purses of money from his courtiers in reciprocation. The annual income to the Crown from this source was about £3,000, and a classic piece of gossip reported about Charles was that in 1663 he had handed over the lot to his mistress Barbara Villiers. It was only under the Hanoverians that the exchange seems to have withered quietly away, following a general fashion.[78]

In the seventeenth century, also, it is possible both to prove that the custom was found throughout society, and to document it in some detail. In 1616

Jonson provided examples of the sort of present commonly made: an orange, rosemary, brooches, gingerbread, marzipan, and wine.[79] At Cambridge in the 1660s the aldermen sent fowl or rabbits to the mayor, who provided a feast in return.[80] In the same decade Samuel Pepys, fairly well representative of the prospering 'middling sort' of London, exchanged various gifts with friends, and on New Year's Day 1669 gave his wife a valuable walnut cabinet.[81] At Newcastle in the 1720s Henry Bourne noted that the presents were very common among the populace, who regarded it as lucky to make them.[82] It is not surprising therefore that, with the greater commercialization of leisure and the growth of provincial newspapers in the early half of that century, advertisements began to appear for them. In 1728 *The Country Journal* offered necklaces for children, adding that the queen always gave them to her own. Samuel Richardson's edition of Aesop's *Fables*, in 1739, was perhaps the earliest of a run of didactic works specially produced as 'proper New Year's gifts to the youth' in the middle of the century. This emphasis upon children was not, however, a sign of health in the tradition, for as the Georgian period wore on adults came increasingly to send written greetings rather than gifts, and these tended to become more formal and then more intermittent as well.[83] By the early nineteenth century, writers upon popular customs could agree that the New Year's gift had become almost obsolete, for reasons which neither they nor anybody since has managed to discern.[84]

Nevertheless, both a specific and a generalized tradition of gift-making at Christmastide survived the decay of the ancient New Year one. The former is first recorded in the early Stuart period, when several writers referred to the kind habit of dropping money at Christmas into an earthenware box kept by an apprentice, which he would break when it was full and so furnish himself with a treat. The first citation of this is in 1621, and by the 1640s the custom had been extended to servants in general.[85] During the 1660s it is clear that it had been widened again to make cash gifts, now euphemistically known as 'boxes', to tradespeople whose services a customer had enjoyed during the year, to enable them to enjoy the holidays more. Pepys 'dropped money at five or six places' on Christmas Day 1667 to accomplish this.[86] By the eighteenth century the upper middling sort, at least, were starting to find the tradition oppressive. In 1710 Jonathan Swift declared. 'By the Lord Harry, I shall be undone here with Christmas boxes. The rogues of the coffee-house have raised their tax, every one giving a crown, and I gave mine for shame, besides a great many half-crowns to great men's porters, etc.' In 1756 Sir John Fielding was snarling that everybody who did anybody else the slightest service in the year now demanded a 'box' at Christmas, so that the total cost to some families was up to £30. He thought it 'a very scandalous imposition upon the fair trader'.[87] It is not, however, one that the beneficiaries would allow to lapse without a struggle, and flourished so steadily through the nineteenth and twentieth centuries that during the later reign of Victoria the feast of St Stephen became, for ever, 'Boxing Day'. As well as sending the old-fashioned

New Year's gifts to the mayor, the city officials of Cambridge in the 1660s made him others upon Christmas Eve (the treasurers, for example, presenting a sturgeon).[88] Even a Quaker like Sarah Fell, who did not believe in holy days, still exchanged gifts of venison and game birds with neighbouring gentry families in the Furness district of Lancashire during the same period.[89] A century later a vague feeling still existed that the season was an appropriate one for the exchange of good wishes, even if there was no longer any formalized and universal mechanism for doing so.[90]

The fortunes of some of the customs described above will be followed further in later chapters, and a few which were important in the early modern Twelve Days have yet to be discussed. It is time now, however, to destroy the impression of continuity which this chapter has conveyed. In the course of the sixteenth and seventeenth centuries the festival of Christmas became the centre of political and religious tensions which were for a long time to remove the former essential similarity of observation across the island of Britain and for a short one to make possible the complete abolition of the feast itself. It is this process which must now be addressed.

3

THE TRIALS OF CHRISTMAS

~⟨✛⟩~

EUROPE'S Reformations made a particular point of attacking the cult of saints as divine intercessors, and each therefore involved a pruning of holy days associated with them. The feasts of the apostles and evangelists, however, were in an entirely different category, while those of Christ himself remained sacrosanct in the main reformed churches. Thus it is not surprising that during the most radical of the Tudor Reformations, that under Edward VI, the English Parliament retained the holy days of Christmas, Circumcision (New Year), and Epiphany, in Christ's honour, that of St John the Evangelist, and also those of St Stephen and the Holy Innocents, both of which could be held to have scriptural warrant.[1] The traditional structure of the Twelve Days was thus preserved, and this was confirmed by the Reformation of Elizabeth in 1559–60.[2] Until this point the English and Scottish observation of Christmastide had been almost identical. English examples initially had a marked influence upon the Scottish Reformation, neatly symbolized by the expeditionary force which Elizabeth sent in 1560 to put the Protestants of Scotland into power. In view of this, and of the Continental pattern, it is not surprising that during the 1550s the reformed churches gathering in Scotland observed the feasts of Christ.[3] Thereafter the practices of the two nations dramatically diverged, because the Scots chose to make a clean break with tradition and also with foreign example, to produce a national Kirk which was in this respect the most 'perfectly reformed' in Europe. Both the inception and the enforcement of the policy have been virtually ignored by historians of the Scottish Reformation, preoccupied as they have been by Kirk government, finance, and organization, by national politics, by theology, and by the social foundations of the changes. The sole exception seems to be Ian B. Cowan, but only to the extent that he accords the matter rather less than two pages of a large and beautifully researched book upon the social history of the reforms.[4] Nevertheless, these paragraphs do provide a framework to which a visitor to the field can add a large quantity of evidence from published primary sources.

The break came in 1561, when the First Book of Discipline issued by the newly established reformed Kirk claimed that 'the Papists have invented' the feasts of Christmas, the Circumcision, and Epiphany, along with those of the Virgin Mary, the apostles and all other saints. It therefore abolished the lot, as unscriptural. When, in 1566, the General Assembly of the Kirk adopted the Helvetic Confession of the Church of Zurich as the model for a national profession of faith, it explicitly deleted the clause which recognized the feasts of Christ. In 1575 it petitioned the current regent of Scotland, the earl of Morton, to enforce the prohibition with all the power of the central government.[5] The reality of the situation was that the Kirk simply needed Morton to provide his blessing to a drive which had already commenced, at least in the all-important Lowlands, at the local level. It seems to have opened at St Andrews, in 1573, when the kirk session, the local unit of church government, punished a number of people for 'observing of superstitious days and specially of Yuil-day.' The following year it made a particular example of a baker, for filling his house with lights and guests on New Year's Day and shouting 'Yuil! Yuil! Yuil!' In that year, too, the kirk session at Aberdeen tried fourteen women for 'playing, dancing and singing of filthy carols on Yule Day at even'. In 1575 the leaders of the craft guilds in the town were 'ordained to take trial of their crafts for sitting idle on Yule Day'. The appeal to Morton was provoked by the first check received by the campaign; at Dumfries, where the corporation defiantly paid a musician with a pipe and tabor to accompany the preacher to the town kirk 'all the holy days' of Christmastide.[6]

The efforts of the reformers were now strengthened and extended. From 1583 the Glasgow kirk sessions ordered that those who kept Yule were to be excommunicated and also punished by the secular magistrates. A few years later bakers at Perth were questioned for making 'Yule Bread', and in 1588 the Haddington presbytery forbade the singing of carols at this time. In 1593 the minister of Errol equated this pastime with fornication and in 1599 the local élite of Elgin prepared for the season by forbidding 'profane pastime . . . viz. footballing through the town, snowballing, singing of carols or other profane songs, guising, piping, violing and dancing.' In that decade also a piper from Dunblane was forced to promise not to play upon Christmas Day or any other old festival, having been hired to do so by Yuletide revellers in villages along the Allan Water.[7] The same sorts of record (which are all that we have) also make clear the large amount of opposition which these measures encountered. The ruling at Glasgow had to be repeated four times up to 1604, a sure sign of resistance to it. At Aberdeen in 1606, thirty years after the campaign of repression began, the kirk session had to condemn anew 'the superstitious time of Yule or New Year's Day' and direct that henceforth the citizens should not 'presume to mask or disguise themselves in any sort, the men in women's clothes, nor the women in men's clothes, nor otherways, be dancing with bells, other on the streets of this burgh or in private house'. The Elgin session ruling of 1599 had been the third, and most detailed, of its kind within five years. Every one of those before had been defied by revellers disguised by blackened faces, masks, handkerchiefs, or fancy dress; traditional festival costume now assuming a practical advantage. So was this order, by at least two young women going abroad attired as men. At Yule in 1603 a man rode through the town with a cloth over his head, while another was accused of 'singing and hagmonayis' at New Year. Two years later a set of Aberdonians got into trouble by going through the streets 'masked and dancing with bells'.[8]

The reformers might have taken consolation from the fact that by the new century such conflict seems to have been concentrated in these north-eastern towns and to have receded from the south; although the continuing total lack of evidence from the Highlands probably suggests that the old ways continued there largely unmolested. It may have been more worrying to the stricter kirkmen that some of the ruling élite showed equally little disposition to accept the reforms. The promise obtained from the piper of Dunblane had to be waived, explicitly, in the case of seasonal celebrations held by noblemen. Most striking of all, the King himself, James VI, had shown an increasing disposition towards the old feasts. In 1598 and again in 1599 the presbytery of Edinburgh campaigned in vain to stop the celebration of Yule at the royal court.[9] To some extent this problem was relieved in 1603 by the migration of James and his household to England, where his enthusiasm for Christmas revelry has been noted. In 1617, however, he was (briefly) back in his ancestral realm and intent upon reforming the Kirk further with the package of measures known to history as the Five Articles of Perth. One of these reimposed the religious celebration of seasonal holy days. It was a royal campaign parallel to, and in some ways connected with, James's more celebrated defence of English summer games embodied in the royal Book of Sports. To the local lairds and burgh merchants or tradesmen who made up the bulk of the lay membership of kirk sessions and presbyteries, just as to English gentry confronted with the Books of Sports, the Crown's measures carried a real threat that their control of local society, never apparently more necessary than in a time of population growth and price rises, would be weakened.

In the event, a workable compromise seems to have been achieved. One aspect of this was that the Five Articles do not seem to have been rigorously enforced.[10] Another was that while Yuletide services were resumed in at least some large kirks, this did not mean that revelry among the populace was necessarily accorded any greater toleration. Nevertheless, at least in its stronghold of the conservative north-east, such revelry does seem to have been encouraged by the revival of the main holy days. The much-tried kirk sessions at Elgin fulminated regularly against it for the next twenty-five years. At Yule 1618 cross-dressing and 'hurling with stools in the streets' were the main problems. In 1623 five 'guisers' performed a sword dance in the kirkyard, and being masked they evaded all punishment.[11] Such incidents make it all the less surprising that as the more radical kirkmen seized control and threw off royal authority in the Scottish Revolution of 1637–41, the royal ruling on festivals should be repealed. The General Assembly of 1638 called for the total abolition of Yule, and the recension of the Five Articles was eventually ratified by Charles I in 1641, after his defeat by the Covenanting Scots in two wars. In

1640 the religious observation of Yule Day at the episcopal stronghold of St Andrews was brought to an end, and kirk services upon it are not recorded after that, at least in the Lowlands where records survive. Secular celebration was once again going to be another matter, a fact demonstrated resoundingly at Aberdeen on Yule Day 1642. To compound the offence, the date was also a sabbath day, but despite the preaching of the ministers and the warnings of the bellman, many Aberdonians 'made good cheer and banqueting', while university students stole the bellman's bell.[12]

Repression was made possible by the wars and *coups d'état* of the 1640s, which delivered Kirk and State increasingly into the hands of precisely those zealous ministers and godly lairds and traders who had staffed the more active sessions and presbyteries. After 1643 there is no more sign of trouble at Elgin or Aberdeen. Instead, across the Lowlands in the later 1640s, there is abundant evidence of a campaign to prevent any private celebration, let alone public revelling, at Yule. People were expected to be seen at work, and questioned if they were not.[13] For the first time, also, there are signs that the campaign was getting into the Highlands; at least in the region around the top of the Great Glen. There one kirkman, Murdoch Mackenzie, became notorious 'for searching people's kitchens on Yule Day for the superstitious goose, telling them that feathers of them would rise up against them one day'. At Urquhart on Loch Ness the minister reported that he had inspected all the houses in his parish on that date, and found the people at work, 'but was suspicious that some of them wrought no longer than he was present'.[14] This drive came to an end in the years 1650-2, in which English armies conquered Scotland and the Kirk was stripped of political power. The English concerned were, however, of a kind who agreed completely with the kirkmen upon the question of holy days.

This was a new, remarkable, and very rapid development, which owed its success not merely to Scottish example but to Scottish intervention. Until 1640 only a tiny number of extraordinarily radical English Protestants had shared the hostility of the Kirk towards seasonal festivals. Even prominent advocates of a further reform of the Church of England, such as William Harrison in the 1570s or William Prynne and Henry Burton under Charles I, had only urged that the old feasts be reduced in status to enhance that of Sunday, not abolished altogether. Harrison, indeed, would have increased the importance of Christmas and Easter, by turning the whole of the week following each into a succession of holidays, created by concentrating the festivals of all the apostles and evangelists in them.[15] In 1616 the presence in the land of people who reviled Christmas as a mere survival of Catholicism was sufficiently well known for Ben Jonson to write a masque for the royal court ostensibly intended to answer them.[16] He seems, however, to have been setting up the flimsiest of straw men, for all the evidence suggests that such individuals were very few indeed. An example of one was the widow of a separatist lay preacher at Bristol in the 1630s, who kept her grocer's shop open on Christmas Day to signify her disapproval of the feast as a Papist survival.

The significant thing about her is that she was considered to be so eccentric that she escaped prosecution.[17] In the same decade a number of country folk in Buckinghamshire were accused by the rector of Beaconsfield of honouring only Sunday, but the accuracy of his complaint cannot be verified.[18] Such sentiments were strikingly lacking among those who wielded even local political power. The Barringtons, an Essex gentry family which favoured ecclesiastical reform and patronized godly preachers, still gave money to wassailers and spent lavishly on their own celebration of Christmas.[19] The last statement was equally true of Lord Brooke, the most radical member of the English nobility in his attitude to religion.[20] The only distinction of these 'puritans' was that they termed the day 'Christ-tide' in preference to the old name with its memory of the mass. When Scottish representatives arrived in London in 1640 to conclude a treaty after their decisive defeat of Charles I, they were surprised and angry to find that their English counterparts (many of whom had considerable sympathy for the Scots) suspended the negotiations for what the Scotsmen termed 'their Christmas'.[21]

This situation was to be ended by the fortunes of what is traditionally called the English Civil War. Historians have of late tended to prefer the term 'the War of the Three Kingdoms', correctly seeing the English conflict as one part of an interlinked series of crises which destroyed royal power in Scotland and Ireland as well. It may be suggested that the names are appropriate to different phases of the fighting in England. In 1642–3 it was indeed an English Civil War, waged over English issues and between soldiers who were almost wholly English or Welsh (or Cornish). In 1643, however, the Long Parliament signed the Solemn League and Covenant with the reigning Scottish government, purchasing military support from it in exchange for a number of undertakings. One was a further reform of the Church of England, and there was no doubt that this would involve its holy days. Until now, the status of Christmas had not been an issue in the war with the royalists, but an attack upon it followed immediately upon the signature of the Solemn League. That December, Parliament continued to sit upon the 25th, while some London ministers kept their churches closed. What ensued has, in contrast to the campaign in Scotland, been relatively well studied, first in the pioneering work of Christopher Durston,[22] which has now been followed up by further research.[23] It opened with a literary debate which broke out in December 1643 and was to continue intermittently (though latterly without much novelty) until 1656. Despite a few desperate efforts upon both sides to find some scriptural indication of the true date of Christ's birth, a common ground was established almost at once; that as there was indeed no objective evidence of when Christ was born, the feast of the Nativity was wholly a creation of later authorities and supported by tradition and not the Bible. Royalists and orthodox Anglicans argued that only the King possessed the legal right to abrogate it, and that tradition deserved respect. Parliamentarians and ecclesiastical reformers insisted (of course) that the Long Parliament was a sovereign institution and that the tradition thus invoked was a compound of Catholic superstition and godless self-indulgence.[24]

Parliament, though increasingly inclined to abolition, would not act until it had received a clerical mandate, and this was provided by the Westminster Assembly of Divines, to whom was entrusted the task of reforming the Church of England in accordance with the Solemn League. On 19 November 1644 this resolved that Sunday was the 'only standing holy day under the New Testament' and within a week had decided to recognize no other.[25] The new national liturgy which it delivered to Parliament, and which was issued on 4 January 1645, accordingly made no provision for Christmas, and its abolition was thus legally achieved, although more than two years passed before a parliamentary ordinance was produced to declare its celebration an offence.[26] By that time the royalists had been completely defeated and so the abrogation could be imposed upon the whole of England and Wales, and reinforced by repeated orders from parliaments and Councils of State right up until the end of the Interregnum. It was one of the few respects, indeed, in which English practice was brought into conformity with Scottish.[27]

Enforcement of the change was, of course, another matter. One of the most obvious features of the literary debate over Christmas was that its defenders assumed that they would have a popular audience and its opponents did not. This was borne out by behaviour. The loss of a well-beloved festival compounded hostility felt by the majority of the population towards a regime which was associated with high taxation and the quartering of a huge army among civilians. Expression of this was muted in Parliament's territory during the war years, when it could be taken as treachery, but by December 1647 the old feast could be made a rallying-point for condemnation of the government. On what should have been Christmas Day there were riotous celebrations at Bury St Edmunds, Norwich, Ipswich (where one reveller was killed), and Canterbury, where they developed into a full-scale royalist uprising. At London they were prevented by patrolling militiamen, but Parliament was still affronted on its very doorstep, when the wardens of St Margaret, Westminster, decked the church with holly and ivy in preparation for a service. Parliament's response was to arrest them, and the preacher, and all the other demonstrations were met by force.[28] In the following summer its armies crushed a set of provincial uprisings in what is generally known as the Second Civil War, and after that the populace was too cowed to mount any more direct challenges to the ordinance. The evidence of the 1650s strongly suggests that the 'Puritan Revolution' was indeed largely successful in ending Christmas as a holy day. Literary comment agrees that most churches remained closed then, and this is borne out by a sample of accounts from 367 parishes, of which thirty-four (9 per cent) paid for communion then. All, save one brave London example, St Mary Woolchurch Haw, were in small villages. John Evelyn's diary illustrates the difficulties of a devout Anglican searching for a Christmas service in the London area; he could find none until 1656, when he began to attend worship held by royalist clergy in private settings. On one occasion the congregation was detected and arrested by soldiers.[29]

The secular celebration of Christmas was, however, a different matter. A newspaper which had called for the abolition of the festival paid unconscious tribute to the psychological need to retain it in December 1647, when the editor referred lugubriously to the 'depth of the winter' and 'the sloth of these winter nights'.[30] England during the Interregnum possessed none of those institutions, like kirk sessions and presbyteries, which had led enforcement of the Scottish reform; the republican regimes deliberately avoided setting them up in order to produce a feebler national Church. As a result, successive commentators noticed how small a number of shops were open or people at work upon what had been Christmas Day, while in 1656, as is well known, an MP complained to a House of Commons (itself suspiciously low in numbers) that he had been kept awake on the previous night by revellers.[31] Examples of mumming and other traditional seasonal pastimes from these years have been noted in the previous chapter. Also noticed there was the famous Welsh writer of Christmas carols, Huw Morris; the bulk of his work was actually composed in the 1650s, as a response to the official proscription of the feast.[32] The accounts of gentry households generally show a pre-war level of expenditure upon food and rewards for passing entertainers.[33] The impact of the Puritan Revolution had been only to strip the festival of its public aspect and (ironically) of much of its Christian content.

Both were replaced at the Restoration, as is well known. As the government of England was declared in May 1660, to be comprised of monarch, Lords and Commons, all the legislation since early 1642 was automatically invalidated, including that which had endorsed the new liturgy and abolished the old feasts. Christmas in 1660 was therefore celebrated with royal entertainments and religious services, just as before the wars.[34] In Scotland the monarchy had never been formally abolished and so no measure was needed to restore it. On the other hand, the reforms produced by the revolution of 1637–41 had all been endorsed, however reluctantly, by Charles I. A mood of reaction and revulsion set in among the Scottish ruling élite, provoked by the various humiliations of the previous twenty years. To have an episcopalian Kirk which stressed hierarchy and order now seemed to be a guarantee of stability, and so in 1661 a Parliament repealed all legislation since 1637. This effectively reactivated the Five Articles of Perth, and with them the legal status of holy days. It is not clear, once again, how far these were accepted, or imposed, across the country, especially as Scotland was now far more bitterly divided over religion than it had been in the 1620s and 1630s. At Elgin cathedral, for example, an episcopal seat in a conservative district, a Christmas service was not revived until 1665, although it was regular after that.[35] Formally, however, the two British kingdoms were once again in harmony upon the issue.

This was to end for a very long time with the next set of revolutionary changes, in 1688–90, which uncoupled the practice of the two national churches completely, as the new rulers William and Mary allowed their Scottish allies to remove both bishops and festivals, once again, from the Kirk. This time the abolition was permanent. Its results seem to have varied considerably, once again, according to region. Some communities in the Outer Hebrides effectively never experienced a Reformation at all, and in these during the early nineteenth century Christmas was still celebrated in the traditional fashion. Christmas Eve was known as *Oidhche Choinnle*, Candle Night, because of the custom of lighting up windows upon it.[36] In eighteenth-century Shetland, Yule was maintained as a prolonged celebration lasting a full twenty-four days, 'and on each of the nights, Sundays excepted, a dance was held in some house in the community'. The most intense celebration was on the evening of Yule Day itself.[37] The 'Yule bread' for which bakers had been prosecuted in the sixteenth century was still made in the nineteenth, as 'Yule Cake' in the Shetlands or 'Yule Brehd' or 'Yule Bannock' in the shires all around the Moray Firth; in all cases it was a large round cake.[38] In Caithness during the early part of the nineteenth century, 'continued festivity' was the rule from Christmas to the end of January, with dances and reciprocal entertainment of friends.[39] Throughout most of the Highlands at that period Yule Day was a time for sports followed by feasting, on haggis, 'sour scones', and bannocks.[40] In the north-eastern districts of Buchan and Mar, the week between Christmas and New Year was known collectively as 'Yeel'. Balls were held in barns, and an especially large breakfast and dinner were provided on Christmas Day itself, with meat eaten even by those who could never otherwise afford it.[41] Wealthy townsmen in Angus and Aberdeenshire entertained friends all through the same period. The simple truth was that the further north one went in Britain, the colder and longer the midwinter nights were and the less there was for farmers and fisher folk to do at that season; northern Scotland and the Isles provided both the need and the opportunity to spend it in making merry. All that the Kirk had achieved was to remove the religious services, much as the Long Parliament had done.

In the Central Lowlands and Southern Uplands things were different, for not only was the need slightly less but the grip of the Kirk considerably stronger. Once again after 1690 we come across cases of punishment of those who kept the festival, and members of the social élite were no longer immune; in 1703 the laird of Clackmannan was summoned by the local kirk session for holding a feast in his house upon it.[42] Nevertheless, it is notable that in the nineteenth century certain specific customs associated with the season, which will be discussed later, had either survived or been reintroduced in Galloway and the Border areas. Much more to the point, the emotional requirement for a midwinter feast was met by transferring the revelry traditionally associated with Christmas to New Year's Eve and Day (long themselves, of course, festive occasions) which were less tainted by religious associations. All through the eighteenth century the Eve was kept with an ever greater ebullience at Edinburgh until by the 1800s there were more people abroad on the streets in the hour after midnight than at noon.[43] At first the kirk sessions tried to keep their hold upon this festival as well; thus, that at Falkirk rebuked a group of youths for going out disguised on New Year's Eve 1702 and 'acting things unseemly'.[44] Later in the same century, however, this was relaxed, and during the next one metropolitan, lowland, and expatriate Scots developed another winter festival which was both wholly secular and specifically patriotic in its associations. It was Burns Night, the anniversary of Robert Burns's birthday upon 25 January, which came to be celebrated first with suppers alone and then with dances as well. The celebration was conceived in Burns clubs, the first of which was founded at Greenock on the Clyde in 1802. As these spread so did the feast, until by the mid-century it was achieving the status of a national festival, built around the reputation of Scotland's most famous literary figure. It represented one part of a process by which the Scots of the period strove to assemble a distinctive set of costumes, customs, and symbols to prevent the submergence of their national identity in that of the English.[45] It also embodied the irony that the Scottish Enlightenment had produced a holy day to replace those removed by the Kirk.

The feast of the New Year was (and is) called in Scotland by the distinctive name of Hogmanay, also known in earlier centuries as 'hagmena' or several variants between the two. The older applications of the word were both to the date and to the gifts which were made then. *The Oxford English Dictionary* gives the first appearance of it as 'Hogmynae-night', condemned in the declaration of a radical Protestant group, the Gibbites, in 1680;[46] the reference to 'hagmonayis' at Elgin in 1603, cited above, takes its history, effectively, back to the sixteenth century. Its derivation is certain enough, for it descends from the medieval French *aguillanneuf*, commonly used likewise to describe either the New Year or a New Year's gift. We do not know, however, where the French word came from, or how the Scots took it over.[47] What is patent enough is that the long and desperate efforts of the reformed Kirk had simply caused the Lowlanders, at least, to abandon the Christian festival of the Nativity for a semi-secular one to honour the New Year, much closer to the pattern of the pagan Vikings and Saxons, and perhaps of the ancient British as well.

4

RITES OF CELEBRATION AND
REASSURANCE

~·¾¾·~

THE point has now been adequately made that the habit of a midwinter
festivity had come by the dawn of history (and probably very long before)
to seem a natural one to the British, and not one to be eradicated by changes
of political or religious fashion. What may now be investigated are specific
components of that festivity and the manner in which they have developed up
to the present. In many respects, feasting and entertainment were in themselves fundamental responses to the tedium and melancholy which a northern
winter could engender. Here, however, it is proposed to consider direct
ripostes to the three most obvious privations of the season: the lack of green
leaves, light, and warmth.

It was a general custom in pagan Europe to decorate spaces with greenery
and flowers for festivals, attested wherever records have survived. One of the
problems addressed by early Christian churchmen was that of how far this
custom could be adopted by the new religion and, as usual, they disagreed.
Those who condemned the practice included St Gregory Nazianzen, Bishop
Martin of Braga, and the clerics who gathered at the latter's Council of Braga.[1]
Most, however, did not, and among those who positively recommended it was
Pope Gregory the Great, at the opening of the seventh century, with England
specifically in mind. How much he actually knew of English conditions, and
how far all his directions were followed may never be known,[2] but in this
respect at least his suggestion was adopted sooner or later. By the time that
parish accounts became available, from the late Middle Ages, virtually all those
of urban churches show payments for the purchase of holly and ivy as
decorations at Christmastide. Their absence from rural accounts is almost
certainly due to the fact that they were to be found in the parish. Occasionally
there are glimpses in these sources of the kind of decorating which resulted,
such as the frame which was made at St Mary on the Hill, Chester, in the 1540s,
covered in holly, stuck with candles, and suspended from a line. At the
important Sussex port of Rye during the same decade, holly twigs were wound
up with broom and also had candles placed among them. The same sorts of
adornment were found in private homes, for John Stow, remembering in old
age the London of Henry VIII, asserted that 'every man's house' was decked
with holly and ivy at this season. A fifteenth-century poem directed

> Nay, ivy, nay, it shall not be, I wys,
> Let holly have the master as the manner is,
> Holly stood in the hall, fair to behold,
> Ivy stood without the door, she is full sore a-cold.

This may reflect a tradition whereby the holly was fastened in the interior and the ivy in the porch.[3] Another late medieval writer produced a Christmas carol, 'Holvyr and Heyvy', which embodied a belief that holly represented the male and ivy the female. In the song a contest breaks out between them:

> Holly and ivy made a great party,
> Who should have the master
> In lands where they go.
>
> Then spake Holly: 'I am fierce and jolly.
> I will have the master
> In lands where we go.'
>
> Then spake Ivy: 'I am loud and proud,
> And I will have the master
> In lands where we go.'
>
> Then spake Holly, and set him down on his knee:
> 'I pray thee, gentle Ivy, say me no villainy,
> In lands where we go.'[4]

Certainly there appears to have been no sense in this period that either plant was chosen for arcane properties. It was the custom to fill buildings with greenery for any celebrations, and ivy and holly were simply, in Stow's words, 'whatsoever the season of the year afforded to be green'. He also mentioned bay, and broom (as said) had a supporting role at Rye; but there seems to be no reference to the use of mistletoe in medieval or Tudor English Christmases.[5]

As a custom of demonstrable pagan origin, irrelevant to any of the requirements of the Christian religion, decking with greens would not recommend itself to Protestant reformers. The latter seem to have regarded it as too trivial to be worth denunciation in print, but it is noticeable that, as a Protestant national Church was constructed under Edward VI, payments for the Christmas foliage vanish from the surviving churchwardens' accounts, with the exception of those for the London parish of All Hallows Staining. Equally significant is the fact that they reappear in the reign of the Catholic Mary, as generally as before, and persist widely in the first decade after the more moderate Reformation of Elizabeth. From that decade, however, the custom atrophied again as Protestantism spread at the local level, until by 1590 it had almost vanished.[6] The sole known exceptions were the two parish churches flanking the royal winter palace of Whitehall,[7] which must be linked to the fact that Elizabeth herself paid for holly and ivy to deck the palace each Christmas.[8] In this as in other respects, the queen's tastes were remarkably conservative for a Protestant, and when Stow made his comment upon the former observation of the tradition, at the very end of her reign, there was a distinct air of nostalgia about them which may suggest that it had waned in private homes as well as in churches.

From the 1590s, however, it began to wax again as part of a much wider drift back towards ornamentation and ceremony now that the population had been decisivly converted from Catholicism and these phenomena were no longer regarded as so dangerous by many Protestants. Around 1600 western towns such as Chester and Bristol began to deck their churches with Christmas greenery again, and over the following forty years the revival spread across the nation, so that by 1639 it obtained (for example) in twenty-three out of the fifty-one London parishes which have left good records for that year. Only at Norwich does it seem to have been very muted, the proportion there being one church out of four. The practice does not seem to have been a test of general attitudes to religion, for at Chester it was certainly readopted in parishes which had prominent 'puritan' ministers. It also seems to have acquired a new sophistication, especially in London, where rosemary and bay leaves were used to add their astringent fragrance to the holly and ivy or to replace them. Laurel was purchased at the single Norwich church recorded as reviving the custom.[9]

The same tendency seems to be reflected in literary accounts of secular practice. In the 1610s George Wither could declaim that

> Each room with ivy leaves is dress'd,
> And every post with holly.[10]

The botanist Parkinson could identify yew and box as other Christmas greenery in 1629,[11] while Robert Herrick, writing in the 1620s or 1630s, listed holly, ivy, rosemary, bay, and (at last) mistletoe as the favourites.[12] Another botanist could comment in 1656 that mistletoe 'is carried many miles to set up in houses around Christmas-time, when it is adorned with a white glistening berry'.[13] In the later seventeenth century a ballad could still extol holly and ivy as the best-known decorations,[14] while John Aubrey wrote that 'We dress our house at Christmas, with bays, and hang up in the hall, or etc., a mistletoe-bough'.[15] The proliferation of choice obviously continued, for the author of a tract upon Christmas merriment in the early eighteenth century could list all the plants named above, and add cypress.[16]

The adorning of churches naturally underwent a dramatic hiatus during the period between 1645 and 1660 in which the festival itself was officially illegal in England. It is an illustration of its popularity that, despite this, St Michael at Gloucester, St John Baptist at Bristol, and three London churches all continued to be given their seasonal holly and ivy in the 1650s although none can be shown to have held Christmas services.[17] At the Restoration it was widely readopted along with the festival, and by 1712 The Spectator was starting to feel that, in some parishes at least, a surfeit was being provided: 'The middle aisle is a very pretty shady walk, and the pews look like so many arbours on either side of it. The pulpit has such clusters of ivy, holly and rosemary about it that a light fellow in our pew took occasion to say that the congregation heard the Word out of a bush, like Moses.'[18]

Little altered in this pattern over the following 150 years, except for a single major development: the appearance of the 'kissing bush'. The custom of kissing under a bunch of foliage seems to have commenced in the late eighteenth century, and by the mid-nineteenth it was found across most of England, from Yorkshire southward, with especial popularity in the southwest, the Welsh Border, and the north-east Midlands.[19] It was also widely adopted in Wales.[20] The custom had begun, and long remained, one of common people, found in farm kitchens, cottages, and servants' quarters. The 'bush' could be made of mistletoe alone, and this plant was often a valued component in it, either because of some significance (never explained) or simply because it was relatively hard to find and so acquired the value of scarcity. In many places, the bush was an elaborate structure which gave tremendous pride to the makers. Some were five or six feet around, the most common forms being a basin shape or two to four crossed hoops. Any evergreens could be used to decorate it, with mistletoe followed by holly at the top of the scale of value and gorse at the bottom; very often a mixture of species was used. Apples, oranges, oat ears, dolls, candles, coloured paper, and ribbons could all be employed in the decoration. In most places it was made for Christmas, but in some for New Year's Day. As should be clear from the sources cited above, the hanging of mistletoe is well recorded from the seventeenth century; but the kissing custom seems to have been a device of the next one. Washington Irving, in his short story 'Christmas Day' (1819), gave his readers a romantic *frisson* by suggesting that it was a pagan plant, beloved of Druids and never trusted by the Church. In reality, churchwardens' accounts prove that it was employed in church decoration from the time that it became fashionable in the seventeenth century.[21]

The rich folklore collections of the Victorians and Edwardians reveal some local variation in the length of time for which the greenery was to be kept in place, and what was to be done with it when it was removed. Herrick had asserted that it remained in the home until Candlemas, the traditional end of winter, and that the superstitious believed that the house would be haunted by a goblin for every twig left behind. Two hundred years later this was still the rule in Wiltshire.[22] Generally in England and Wales, however, and also in Ireland, the decorations were now removed on the day after Twelfth Night,[23] although in Devon and the Welsh Marches the 'kissing bush' was left up for the year in the belief that it gave magical protection to the house.[24] Once the plants had served their purpose, they were usually burned, in Lancashire being used first as fuel in the making of the Shrove Tuesday pancakes.[25] Worcestershire farmers, however, gave the kissing bough as fodder to the first cow to calve in the new year.[26]

The pattern of festive greenery thus described for England holds good for Ireland, although the custom of kissing under the mistletoe (or any other bush) was till recently very rare there and apparently an English introduction.[27] It is Scotland which presents the largest contrast, for references to decking with midwinter greenery are rare; the exception is that holly was often hung in the house by Highlanders, especially upon New Year's Eve, 'to keep out the fairies.'[28] There are several apparent reasons for the disparity: early parish and household accounts are not available for Scotland; the Christmastide festivities were banned across much of the country during the time from which most evidence survives; and the favourite winter plants would be hard to find in some parts of the north. Nevertheless, as said before, midwinter merry-making was kept up by many Scots, with sufficiently detailed accounts of it to make the comparative silence about holly and ivy surprising.

What the Scots did emphasize, in common with many of the English, was light. In 1725 Henry Bourne, a Newcastle clergyman, commented that many people in the north of England lit huge 'Christmas candles' on Christmas Eve.[29] He also believed that the custom was declining, but during the nineteenth century it was still found all over the North Country, from the Scottish Border down to Derbyshire. The candles were also common in the northern half of Scotland, up to the Shetlands, and had an isolated occurrence in Cornwall. The Irish were likewise fond of them.[30] There was no agreed time for lighting them by then, some families preferring to do so on Christmas Eve like those mentioned by Bourne, while others burned them on the following morning or night. Likewise, it was a matter for individual or local taste whether there was a single large candle or many of standard size, and whether or not they were painted. In both the English and Scottish parts of their range, under Victoria, grocers commonly presented them to regular customers. The aim was to fill a family's common living space with light, just as churches had been on Christmas morning before the Reformation. Yule candles were also common in Scandinavia, a region which had strong contacts with those parts of Britain which maintained them.

For most families until the latter part of the nineteenth century, however, the main illumination on a winter evening, as well as the principal source of heat and means of cooking, was the fire in the kitchen or (in poorer homes) the main room. At Christmas in the nineteenth century, this was commonly given the additional fuel of an enormous log of wood, sufficient (ideally) to burn through the whole of the Day itself, or through the preceding or succeeding nights. In the Welsh Border counties, a little of it was burned in the embers overnight between each of the Twelve Days, and everywhere it was common to keep the last portion and use it for kindling the log the following year. Folklorists have usually called it the Yule Log, a name indeed found across its English range although it was known by many others. Yule Clog was a favourite in the north-east and the north-east Midlands, although also heard in Devon. Yule Block was often used in the west Midlands and West Country, with the variants Gule Block in Lincolnshire and the Stock or the Mock in Cornwall. The different appellation Christmas Brand (or Braund, or Brawn) was often used in Cornwall, Devon, Dorset, and the Welsh Marches. In Wales it was *Y Bloccyn Gwylian* (the Festival Block), in the Scottish Highlands the 'Yeel Carline' or 'Yeel Cyarlin' (the Christmas Old Wife), and in Ireland *Bloc na Nollaig* (the Christmas Block).[31] It was only missing from the Northern and Western Isles, where wood was scarce, from southern and central Scotland, where Christmas was hardly celebrated in the nineteenth century, and from East Anglia and most of south-eastern England, where it seems to have been considered unsophisticated by then. It was above all a tradition of rural districts, where logs were readily obtainable.

That tradition was apparently first recorded in Britain by Robert Herrick, writing in the 1620s or 1630s, He called it 'the Christmas log', and portrayed it as being brought to the farmhouse by cheering lads, whom the farmer's wife rewarded with all the drink that they could take. He also commented that the presence of the log was thought to bring prosperity, and that it was lighted to music, with the remnant of the last year's one. The latter, he added, was believed to protect the house from evil if laid up there safely during the intervening months.[32] All this suggests a body of belief and ritual already well established by the early Stuart period; probably in Devon, where Herrick spent the 1630s as a country clergyman. Certainly a description of the custom in that county almost two centuries later is remarkably similar, the young men fetching in the log 'with every sign of exultation.[33] An account of Christmas pastimes in the West Riding of Yorkshire, received by John Aubrey between 1650 and 1687, included 'a large Yule log or Christmas block',[34] and Henry Bourne noted that the 'Yule-Clog or Christmas block' was common around the Tyne valley in the 1720s.[35] It had therefore appeared across most, if not all, of its subsequent range by the late seventeenth century, if not before.

Bourne opined that it might have descended from an Anglo-Saxon fire ceremony of the winter solstice, and Sir James Frazer added it to his collection of putative pagan fire rituals from ancient Europe.[36] Objections may be raised against both. Alexander Tille pointed out in 1889 that, whereas there is no record of the custom in Britain before 1600, the earliest one in Germany comes from 1184, and subsequent medieval references to it are found there. He suggested, plausibly, that it might have been introduced to Britain from Germany after the end of the Middle Ages.[37] One route for such an introduction could have been Flanders, where it also enjoyed an early and enduring popularity; and indeed by the nineteenth century it ringed Germany, being especially common in France, the Italian Alps, and Serbia, but also found in most parts of northern Europe.[38] The Swedish scholar C. W. von Sydow made a direct attack upon the suggestion of Frazer, and of some German writers, that the log represented part of a religion essentially concerned with agricultural fertility and the veneration of vegetation spirits. He suggested that the most obvious function of the custom was simply festive; that a big piece of wood was needed to keep the fire burning through the unusually protracted feasting and merry-making of Christmastide, and that households competed against each other to get the biggest—a form of jovial contention certainly well documented in peasant societies.[39]

Even von Sydow, however, conceded that at times the log was regarded as conferring some kind of magical protection upon the home; and this function is abundantly clear in the earliest account of it in Britain, that of Herrick. To be fair to von Sydow, however, it is largely missing from the nineteenth-century folklore collections with which he was mostly concerned. In the British examples, at least, the aspects of competition and frivolity are much more to the fore. They tend to emphasize the sheer size of the log, usually sufficient to fill a hearth and often enough to be dragged in by a team of men or by one or more horses. It was not traditionally taken from any special species of tree, but from those most readily available which provided the best logs for burning.[40] Local elaborations of the custom could increase both the mirth and the competitive element in fetching it; thus, while being dragged home in eastern Somerset, it was ridden by a young man who earned a reward of mulled ale and hot cakes if he could avoid being thrown off.[41] Here and there, however, are traces of the sort of magical association in which Frazer was primarily interested. In parts of Montgomeryshire, the ashes of the log were put on the cereal fields to fertilize them.[42] The people of Penistone in Derbyshire preferred to pile them in the cellar, 'to keep the witch away.'[43] In the Highlands the log was sometimes said to be 'against scaith', meaning misfortune, and was occasionally carved to represent a woman.[44] This would fit well with the local name 'Carline', or hag, often applied in the region to a fearsome tutelary nature spirit, though the equivalent Cornish custom of chalking on the figure of a man seems to have had no arcane associations and been merely for fun.[45] It is hard to argue conclusively that any of these local variants were originally integral to the custom, rather than grafted onto it, and the other early British sources, Aubrey and Bourne, say nothing about superstitions equivalent to those in Herrick. The matter therefore remains open.

A very distinctive local alternative to the Yule log, in Devon, western Dorset, and western Somerset, was the ashen faggot, a bundle of ash stakes tied round with bands of bark. Unlike the log, it was burned on one evening only, which could be any from Christmas Eve to Twelfth Night. The largest recorded were twelve feet long, the bands could be of willow, ash, or hazel bark, and the number of them could vary from one to fifteen.[46] Herrick, perhaps significantly, did not write about the custom despite his long residence in Devon, and indeed there is apparently no mention of it until the end of the eighteenth century. Both of the first extant accounts, in 1795 and 1806,[47] stress an enduring aspect of it which much contributed to its popularity; that a fresh round of drinks was served and a toast proposed, every time that a band broke in the fire. This was, of course, why the total number of bands could be highly significant, and as the faggot was usually made by farm-workers, for farmers (or, more rarely, innkeepers) who would provide the drink, it formed the centrepiece of a classic reciprocal social relationship. The fetching of the Yule log could, of course, play the same part.

The Yule log vanished steadily from the late nineteenth century onwards, removed by the reduction in farm labour and the disappearance of the old-fashioned open hearths. The same factors caused an atrophy in the use of the ashen faggot, but that was to some extent protected by its special status as a distinctive local piece of folklore, and its association with the conviviality of the bursting bands. It was still burned at many homes in Devon's Teign valley in the 1950s, and in a few pubs and houses in the south-east of the county at the end of the 1960s,[48] and may survive there yet, unadvertised. It certainly still exists at pubs in the other parts of its old range, having been revived at the Luttrell Arms in Dunster, on Somerset's Exmoor coast, in 1935, and at the Squirrel Inn at Thorncombe in the hills of west Dorset, in 1972. The William IV, in Curry Rivel, a village upon a ridge among the mid-Somerset marshes, has apparently maintained it without cessation. The burnings are on Christmas Eve, Twelfth Night, and Twelfth Eve, respectively. The Luttrell Arms occasion is the grandest, with a local carol sung as the flames rise, and couples laying wagers upon which will be the first band to burst (a successful bet being said to bring luck in marriage). Those at the Squirrel and the William IV are intimate communal gatherings, although the joviality can be the less restrained for that. As the proprietors, or a particular villager, provide the faggot, there are, however, no longer any free drinks at any of these places.

All these customs have been characterized principally as a means of compensation for the various deprivations of the season. It must be plain, however, that at points they overlapped with another class of ritual: that concerned with protecting a home from evil. It is with this other kind of ceremony that the next chapter must be concerned.

5

RITES OF PURIFICATION
AND BLESSING

⋙⋘

ONE of the most important aspects of the Yule season in eighteenth-century Shetland was 'saining', signifying rituals intended to safeguard people and property against the powers loose in that time of darkness and also during the coming year. It began on 'Tul-yas-e'en', seven nights before Yule Day, when farmers would put a straw cross at the entrance to the cornyard, hang a plait of hairs from all the beasts on the croft over that of the byre, and carry a burning peat through the outbuildings. On the 20th, Tammasmas or Tundersmas E'en (St Thomas's Eve), all had to keep quiet, avoiding either work or games. On Yule E'en itself the house was cleaned and all locks polished, after which an iron blade was left inside the main door to scare off trows (trolls), and a light burned all night. The following morning the trows were defied again, as each person in a home drank a dram of whisky with the words

> Yule gude an' Yule gear
> Follow da trow aa da year.[1]

Further south, in the Highlands, that bitter and astringent shrub, juniper, featured prominently in the saining customs. In the 1770s Thomas Pennant recorded that people burned it in front of their cattle upon New Year's Day.[2] During the following century it was still observed as being set alight in houses and byres upon that date or on Yule morn, all openings being stuffed to hold in the acrid smoke, as a literal and spiritual fumigation.[3] The purifying element of fire was also sometimes employed in itself, especially around the Moray region. In 1655 ministers of the Duffus district censured fishermen who 'superstitiously carried fir torches about their boats' on New Year's Eve. In 1714 the kirk session at Inveravon in Banffshire passed 'an act against clavies', a local word apparently derived from the Gaelic *cliabh*, a basket, and referring to pots or torches of fire carried round cornfields and byres of livestock at this season to bless them.[4] One 'clavie' survives, at Burghead on the Moray Firth, being the lower part of a tarbarrel, filled with kindling and carried blazing through the streets on 11 January, which would be New Year's Eve were it not for the calendar change of 1752. There are some self-consciously archaic aspects to the custom. In the nineteenth century the people making it would use only a stone hammer, following the very old Highland belief that metal should not be employed in the lighting of a sacred fire (to be considered again below, under Beltane).[5] Even now, it is considered very lucky to a building to have the clavie carried into its entrance, and charred fragments are kept as charms.

Burghead is not, however, itself an old town, but one designed in the early nineteenth century, and it looks as if a genuine local tradition was transplanted there, and endured, precisely because it provided a focus for an artificial (and isolated) community. Other New Year's Eve fire customs in Scotland and neighbouring parts of England are themselves relatively recent innovations. The swinging of fireballs (ropes and rags soaked in paraffin and tied in wire cages) at Stonehaven, near Aberdeen, was commenced under Victoria.[6] So, apparently, was the carrying of blazing tar barrels on the heads of men in fancy dress at Allendale in Northumberland's Pennine hills. It developed out of a Methodist watch night service in about 1858, although the local people now believe that it is pagan and prehistoric.[7] Much the same antiquity attends the even more spectacular Up-Helly Aa procession at Lerwick, capital of Shetland, now held at the end of January. Hundreds of men costumed as Vikings tow a replica of a longship through the town, carrying torches with which they set the boat on fire at the end. It was sponsored by the local Total Abstinence Society after 1870, to divert the island's young men from their accustomed drunken rowdiness on Christmas Eve and New Year's Eve. The name is derived from Upholiday, the Lowland Scots' one for Twelfth Day, brought to Shetland by immigrants at that period; now, however, the festival is used as a means to assert the islanders' separate cultural identity from the rest of Scotland.[8]

When these are removed from the record of older practices, there remain a number of local Scottish New Year's Eve fire ceremonies of indeterminate origin. There is the Flambeaux Procession of torch-bearers which continues at Comrie in Strathearn, and the large bonfires lit at Biggar and Westrow in the upper Clyde district, of which the latter is now defunct. Also now gone are the pair of processions and fires at Newton Stewart and Minnigaff in Galloway, but Wick, far up in Caithness, preserves a municipal blaze. So does Dingwall on the coast of Easter Ross and Campbelltown in the Kintyre Peninsula, while nineteenth-century accounts survive of fires kindled by lads before dawn on New Year's Day upon the hills around Inverness and at Auchterarder in Strathearn.[9] Put together, this makes quite an impressive list, but it represents a number of communities very widely separated on the map. Only in the cases of Dingwall and Inverness can the customs be connected to an old regional tradition, that of the clavies of Moray, and it is possible that some were of relatively recent creation such as those of Stonehaven, Allendale, and Lerwick. The lack of a well-recorded regional custom behind most is the more striking in comparison with the other Scottish ritual fires, at Beltane, Midsummer, and Hallowe'en. Nor does a comparison with other 'Celtic' lands help much. The only midwinter fires recorded there (other than on the hearth) were lit on cliff-tops in the Isle of Man, upon 21 December, called 'Fingan Eve'. 'Fingan' to the Manx merely signified cliffs, and there were no rituals or superstitions connected with the blazes.[10] Once again, it is possible that it was another isolated custom which was never involved with the process of saining. Most of these practices may be more useful in teaching us about the way in which certain small Scottish towns defined and regulated the sense of community in the nineteenth century.

In an altogether different category was the mode of saining once widespread in the Western Isles and adjacent areas of the Highland coast. It may well have been pre-Christian, and can certainly be said to have come down from prehistory in the limited sense that it was long firmly established by the eighteenth century, when accounts of the culture of the region begin. The first to record it was Dr Johnson, on Coll in the 1770s, who was told how a man dressed in a cow's hide would run round the hall of a laird's house or castle at New Year, while others beat him with sticks. Their gambols would drive the rest of the people outside, and they could only be readmitted after speaking a verse.[11] This seems to have been a debasement, into a glorified party game, of a ritual next mentioned by John Ramsay, recalling the last third of the eighteenth century. He wrote that it was then very important on the West Highland coast and on St Kilda, and consisted of a visit by the local youths, led by a cowherd, to each house of a settlement on New Year's Eve. One, wearing the cow's hide, would run three times sunwise (*deosil* or *deiseal*, the lucky direction) around the outside of the building, while others hammered at the hide. This would gain the attention of the family inside, who would admit the party. One of the latter then spoke a blessing on the home, beginning *Gum beannaichrad th' Dia an ligh's nath ann* (May God bless the house . . .). Each then lit a small piece of the hide on the end of a staff and held it, smouldering, to the nose of every person and pet animal in the home, believing that the pungent smoke (like the burning juniper further east) would drive away ill luck.[12]

The same practices lingered in the Outer Hebrides into the early nineteenth century, sometimes identical to that described by Ramsay,[13] and sometimes as variations or parallels. On Lewis, as upon Coll, it had become more of a game. The lad in the hide ran round the fire inside the home while the family struck at him with broomsticks, and he used a shield to ward them off. If he made it round, then his party were given food.[14] A distinctive variant on South Uist was for the boys to take a piece of hide from the breast of a freshly killed sheep, tie it to the end of a stick, and set it alight. On reaching a house they would walk round it sunwise chanting a New Year rhyme (a *Duan Callaig* or *Rann Calluinn*) such as this one (in translation):

> I am coming to you tonight
> To renew for you the gift of the year.
> I have no need to tell you of it,
> It existed in the time of my grandfather;

> My New Year skin-strip is in my pocket
> And good is the smoke that comes from it.
> It will go sunwise round the children
> And especially around the housewife.
> 'Tis the housewife who deserves it,
> Hers is the hand for the New Year blessing.
> A small thing of the good things of summer
> To keep a promise got with the bread.
> Open the door and let me in!

The housewife was then expected to open it. The lads trooped in, and the skin-bearer swung the smouldering hide three times round her head; very bad luck was expected if it went out. The group were rewarded with food and went away calling *Beannachdan Dhia's na Callaig libh* (the Blessing of God and the New Year to you).[15] At times in the Hebrides the two rites were combined, the youths banging the cow hide and then carrying in the strip of sheep (or deer, or goat) skin. A rhyme used with this variant went:

> The New Year blessing of the yellow bag of hide.
> Strike the skin (upon the wall)
> An old wife in the graveyard,
> An old wife in the corner,
> Another old wife beside the fire,
> A pointed stick in her two eyes,
> A pointed stick in her stomach,
> Let me in, open this.[16]

The reference to the three old women is a riddle, as the third is plainly a quern, but it also has a striking echo of the pagan European veneration of triple goddesses (especially strongly marked among the Irish) and of the common Irish and Welsh fear and reverence of the hag. All told, specific accounts of the animal-hide blessing come from the whole of the Hebrides except for Skye and Jura, and from parts of Argyll on the mainland. It had died out everywhere by the mid-nineteenth century.[17] The local names for it, *a calluinn, a challuinn*, or *na callaig*, all signify a New Year gift or a New Year blessing; a fairly exact equivalent of the Lowland Scots 'hogmanay'. Sir James Frazer proposed that it was a relic of the worship of a sacred animal, portions of whose sacrificed carcase were distributed for luck.[18] It may be suggested instead, once more, that the fumigation was the essential part of the rite, juniper being employed in the east and animal skin in the west. The custom was also, like that of the ashen faggot, one of hospitality and social reciprocity, as the boys usually expected a reward. Indeed, other names for it were *a calluinn a bhuilg*, 'the New Year blessing with the sack' (after the receptacle in which food was taken away) or simply *Oidhche nam Bonnag*, 'Bannock Night' (as the usual reward was in cakes).

In southern England a parallel set of customs to the saining at the other end of Britain was grouped under the name of wassailing. They consisted, in essence, of wishing health to crops and animals much as people passing the wassail bowl wished it to each other. Most are well recorded by the early modern period, and they may quite easily have descended directly from pagan practices, although it is also possible that they developed outward from the domestic wassail. The most widespread, famous, and enduring concerned fruit trees. It is first mentioned at Fordwich, Kent, in 1585, by which time it was already in part the preserve of groups of young men who went between orchards performing the rite for a reward.[19] Robert Herrick, almost certainly writing about Devon and in the 1630s, spoke of 'wassailing' the fruit-bearing trees in order to ensure good yields,[20] and in the 1660s and 1670s a Sussex clergyman gave money to boys who came to 'howl' his orchard (being the enduring local term).[21] John Aubrey, describing West Country customs in the same period, said that on Twelfth Eve men 'go with their wassel-bowl into the orchard and go about the trees to bless them, and put a piece of toast upon the roots, in order to it'.[22]

From the 1790s onward, detailed accounts of the practice proliferate. The *Gentleman's Magazine* reported from the South Hams of Devon, in 1791, how farmers and workmen would circle the best tree in an orchard, and drink to it three times in cider, saying:

> Here's to thee, old apple tree,
> Whence thou mayst bud
> And whence thou mayst blow!
> And whence thou mayst bear apples enow!
> Hats full! Caps full!
> Bushel—bushel—sacks full,
> And my pockets full too! Huzza![23]

Around Cornworthy in the same district in 1805, the action was performed by one man of the group, advancing to the finest tree with a cider jug in one hand, taking a branch in the other, and singing:

> Huzza, Huzza, in our good town
> The Bread shall be white, and the liquor be brown
> So here my old fellow I drink to thee
> And the very health of each other tree.
> Well may ye blow, well may ye bear
> Blossom and fruit both apple and pear.
> So that every bough and every twig
> May bend with a burden both fair and big
> May ye bear us and yield us fruit such a stors
> That the bags and chambers and house run o'er.

All then shouted, 'so that the country rings for miles'.[24]

We have here, then, two rather different versions of the rite, with different words, observed a few miles from each other in the same generation. It was the former rhyme which was, or was to become, the most popular, versions of it being recorded in the nineteenth and twentieth centuries from Devon, Dorset, Cornwall, Sussex, and Surrey.[25] In the last two counties a preface was often added:

> Stand fast root, bear well top
> Pray the God send us a howling good crop.
> Every twig, apples big,
> Every bough, apples now.

This embodies the traditional local name for the custom, of 'howling'. Peter Robson, observing the remarkable similarity of the rhymes over this large range, has suggested that they spread through printed versions,[26] and this may well be correct; indeed, it is possible that some at least of this print may not have been in the form of song-sheets but of popular works on folklore such as John Brand's *Observations*, published in 1813. For all this the variants could still be broad, and completely independent chants or songs survived. Another from the South Hams embodied a threat to the tree:

> Apple-tree, apple-tree,
> Bear good fruit,
> Or down with your top
> And up with your root.[27]

The single example from Worcestershire runs:

> Bud well, bear well
> God send you fare well;
> Every sprig and every spray
> A bushel of apples next New Year Day.

It then turns into a common New Year rhyme.[28]

During this period the custom was recorded, as it had apparently always been, in three distinct areas. One consisted of eastern Cornwall, Devon, west and south Somerset, and the western fringe of Dorset. The others were southern Surrey and northern Sussex, and western Worcestershire.[29] Orchards in Kent were blessed as part of the Rogation ceremonies of May, and the Worcestershire version of the ceremony was incorporated with the local fire wassail, to be described below. The activity was also carried on in a rather different way in each of its two principal locations. In the West Country it was the responsibility of workers on the farms concerned or (occasionally) of the whole parish, going on a round. In the Surrey and Sussex Weald it was the preserve of groups of labourers going from property to property and soliciting reward. They would often blow horns to announce their approach, and sometimes wore special costumes. For fifty-four years the team at Duncton, Sussex, was led by Richard Knight, who in the 1900s sported 'a grotesque costume, principally composed of patches rivalling the rainbow in multitudinous tints, the whole surmounted by an indescribable hat, bearing, displayed in front, a huge rosy-cheeked apple'.[30] Farmers in the Weald who were not visited by such groups would do the job themselves; those who were visited would usually provide beer, food, and money, or just the latter in gratitude. The date of the operation could be any of the Twelve Days, Christmas Eve, New Year's Eve, and Twelfth Eve all being favourites; as the calendar was shifted twelve days in 1752, some of the observations were left behind in what was now mid-January. The singing or chanting of the conjuration, and shouting, was integral to the custom. In Sussex and Surrey the performers commonly rapped the trees with sticks and sometimes splashed ale on them. In the West they often fired guns over them, splashed cider on them, and put cider-soaked cakes or bread in the branches. The shots were later explained to (or by) folklorists as attempts to drive away evil spirits; Bob Pegg has recently suggested that they could, as plausibly, have been merely an expression of high spirits.[31] The cakes and bread may originally have been gifts to the tree, though latterly it was said in some places that they were for robins, regarded as lucky birds. Sometimes one particular tree in an orchard was wassailed, and sometimes all.

From the early nineteenth century the custom was in fairly steady decline. It was gone from Worcestershire by the middle part of that century and vanished in the Weald and from most of the West in the early decades of the next one. In Devon various attempts were made to revive it from the 1920s onward, but none seems to have lasted.[32] In Somerset, however, two revivals have persisted, and become institutions. The longer-running is at the Butcher's Arms, Carhampton, in the strip of Somerset between the Brendon Hills and the sea. It takes place on 17 January, old Twelfth Eve. Having lapsed twice since 1900, it is now famous enough to be secure and includes the full accompaniment of guns and soaked bread and the standard rhyme out of Brand. The tree is splashed with cider which is also shared, hot and spiced, very generously among those present. The folk-singing afterwards is well performed and the friendliness of the atmosphere notable. More formal, and usually more crowded, is that carried on a dozen miles southward by the Taunton Cider Company at its base in Norton Fitzwarren. This includes the innovation of a Wassail Queen who performs the blessing, but otherwise the ritual is similar, as is the amplitude of the hospitality.

Those who know their cider will have observed that one considerable orchard land, Herefordshire, is missing from this distribution pattern, while it was stated above that in adjacent areas of Worcestershire tree-blessing was a secondary part of a different custom. The latter was a distinctive form of wassailing confined to the region around the Wye and lower Severn. It was apparently first described in the *Gentleman's Magazine* in 1753, from a farm at Huntingdon, west of Hereford,[33] and again by the traveller Thomas Pennant in 1776, speaking of the Newent district in the north-western corner of Gloucestershire.[34] The latter portrayed it in detail:

All the servants of every particular farmer assemble together in one of the fields that has been sown with wheat; on the border of which, in the most conspicuous or most elevated place, they make twelve fires of straw, in a row; around one of which, made larger than the rest, they drink a cheerful glass of cider to their master's health, success to the future harvest, and then returning home they feast on cakes made of carraways etc., soaked in cider, which they claim as a reward for their past labours in sowing the grain.

In 1791 another Herefordshire correspondent of the *Gentleman's Magazine* noted that the activity was called 'wassailing', that it was accompanied by a lot of shouting, and that at one time on Twelfth Eve fifty or sixty such fires could be seen at once.[35]

The custom was recorded in the eighteenth and nineteenth centuries across most of Herefordshire, in parts of Worcestershire west of the Severn, in the area of Gloucestershire bordering upon those two counties, and in the southern fringe of Shropshire. It took place upon Twelfth Eve, Twelfth Night, or Christmas Eve, and was commonly held to prevent blight from striking the next year's crop. Sometimes there were twelve small fires and a large one. There was no generally accepted theory of what the fires represented: some held that they symbolized the apostles, and some that they were witches, while the single large fire was to some Judas, to others the Virgin Mary, and to yet others, Old Meg, a traditional Herefordshire heroine.[36] In the Ross on Wye district twelve fires were made in a horseshoe pattern, with a tall pole in the centre crowned with a human effigy of straw, called 'the Maiden' or 'the Mary'. This was set alight as well.[37] In Worcestershire, as said, the people proceeded from the field to the orchard to wassail the trees. A curious outlier of the tradition was also recorded in the 1820s at Stanton, on the edge of the Staffordshire Moorlands, where men ran around wheat fields with torches of straw on Twelfth Night 'to scare witches and other enemies'.[38] The fire-wassail declined over the same period as the apple-wassail, but more completely, so that there is no more trace of it after the first years of the twentieth century. In 1994, however, it was revived near Leominster as part of a folklore package of local customs including the apple-wassailing, Border morris dancing, and a Mummers' Play. As a reflection of the popular assumption (which in this case may well be correct) that such traditions are survivals of ancient pagan ceremonies, it was confidently stated that the large fire represented the sun, and the twelve smaller fires the months of the year. This is, however, an interpretation never credited to the country people who used to light them.

Aubrey described another form of wassail among West Country ploughmen: on Twelfth Eve 'they go into the ox-house to the oxen, with the Wassellbowl and drink to the ox with the crumpled horn that treads out the corn; they have an old conceived rhyme'.[39] After this no more is heard of the custom in the west, but it still obtained in the nineteenth century in South Wales and its March. In the former it was 'common' in unspecified districts to go into the stall of the finest ox on Christmas Eve, men on one side and women on the other. The bowl, decorated with evergreens and filled with hot spiced ale, was passed round while a toast was sung. Then a basket, similarly decorated and containing a cake, was put on the animal's horns. If he

remained quiet, it was taken as a good omen.[40] In Herefordshire the ceremony took place on Twelfth Eve, often after the fire-wassail. There a plum
cake was stuck on the horns of a cow and the oldest person present took a pail
of cider and chanted

> Here's to thy pretty face, and to thy white horn,
> God send thy master a good crop of corn,
> Both wheat, rye and barley, of grains of all sort,
> And next year, if we live, we'll drink to thee again.

The others then repeated this in chorus and the first speaker threw the cider in
the cow's face. If she tossed the cake forward, then the omen for the harvest
was good. These practices, too, had ceased by the end of the century.[41] So,
also, had the last and worst-recorded of this group of blessing rituals, the
'wassailing' of beehives in Sussex and Hertfordshire, of which only a bare
mention survives.[42]

The large area between the northern Scottish saining and the southern
English wassailing was occupied by the tradition of the First Foot; the belief
that the nature of the first person to enter a home at the New Year (usually
members of the household) determined its luck during the coming twelve
months. It also prevailed in the West Country 'wassailing' zone, and all over
Wales; indeed, the only parts of Britain in which it was not found by the
nineteenth century were the Northern and Western Isles, and most of the
Highlands of Scotland, and the quarter of England south of Leicestershire and
Suffolk and east of Wiltshire and Warwickshire. In Ireland it was confined to
communities of Scottish immigrants,[43] but it was well established in the Isle of
Man, where Scottish influence was strong.[44] Across this huge range, the
favoured First Foot was almost always male, preferably adult and darkhaired.[45]
This preference served, of course, to reinforce prevailing stereotypes of gender
dominance and biological normality. Women were not excluded from the
rite; at the north Yorkshire fishing village of Staithes, for example, their task
was to sweep the hearth clean and wash any dirty crockery in preparation for
the First Foot's coming, and to welcome him.[46] Such a role was, however, very
obviously a supportive and subservient one. In places the implicit misogyny of
the tradition took stronger forms, notably in central Shropshire. There, the
visit of a woman on New Year's morn was regarded as unlucky even if many
men had preceded her, while an actual female First Foot could be blamed for
deaths or monstrous births in the household. In the north-west of the county
it was considered almost as unfortunate to meet a woman on one's first
journey out of the house at New Year.[47] In neighbouring Montgomeryshire
a home cursed by a female first visitor would engage a troupe of small boys to
parade through it to 'break the witch'. Carmarthenshire and Cardiganshire
people provided a more equitable balance of fortune by holding that it was
lucky for each person to come across a member of the opposite sex on a first
journey at New Year.[48] What needs to be stressed is that scattered across the

range of the custom were places which, by local caprice, had different priorities (without suffering any worse luck). At Minchinhampton in the Cotswold hills of Gloucestershire, it did not matter what the gender of the first visitor was; dark hair was, however, crucial.[49] Along the Anglo-Scottish Border, male gender was required, but it was fair hair that was prized,[50] and the same was true in the Lincolnshire Marshland.[51] The people of Hunmanby, near the coast of northern Yorkshire, prized a dark-haired girl,[52] and women were also welcomed at various places in the Fife and Angus regions of Scotland. In Banff, near the Moray coast, it helped if the women were barefoot, and at Thurso, near the very tip of Caithness, children were preferred.[53] Around Bradford and Huddersfield in Yorkshire's West Riding, the single taboo still enforced everywhere else was joyfully broken, and a red-haired man was considered lucky, along with all shades of blonde.[54]

Despite its very wide distribution, there is no doubt that the custom was most elaborate and highly developed in northern England and the Lowlands of Scotland, and may indeed have sprung from there. There was a vague idea in western and midland England that the First Foot should bring a token gift or perform a brief ceremony; thus pieces of wood were presented on the Lincolnshire Wolds and a handful of sand in Cornwall, while in the Staffordshire Black Country the vital visitor would run through the house from the front to the back door shouting 'Please to let the New Year in'.[55] At neighbouring Birmingham he was expected to go three times round the table, poke the fire, and speak a rhyme as well.[56] Further north this more formal pattern was general. In County Durham the First Foot had to bring bread and a bottle of spirits, and recite: 'Happy New Year t'ye! God send ye plenty! Where ye have one pound note I wish ye may have twenty'.[57] At Staithes he gave a silver coin to a woman, put a coal in the hearth, said 'May your hearth never grow cold', cut a cake, and made a speech of goodwill.[58] Near Sheffield in 1907 the well-qualified First Foot brought a mince-pie, coal, and whisky, and generally in the north he was expected to put some food on the table and fuel in the hearth. The same was true in Scotland, where whisky was the most valued component among the gifts.[59] There seems to have been a tendency for First-Footing further south in England, and in Wales, to grow more ornate in the twentieth century, until it reached northern standards. In Nottinghamshire by the 1950s the caller was expected to bring silver, bread, and coal, while Staffordshire First Footers had a glass of wine in one hand and a lump of coal in the other. In southern Lincolnshire and western Monmouthshire, by transference, the gifts of silver, bread, and coal were left out on the doorstep as presents for the spirit of the New Year.[60]

As this account would indicate, the custom did not, like those described above, atrophy as the modern period wore on. Indeed, in the mid-twentieth century it actually extended its range as immigration and improved communications carried it into south-eastern England.[61] As it could essentially be a ritual based upon family and friends, it easily survived changes within the wider society. What is far more difficult to determine is how long it has been operating, for there is apparently no record of it anywhere before the eighteenth century. The point must certainly be made that its strongholds lay in regions for which evidence is generally lacking before that time. The absence of data, however, is only relative, and it is surprising that, had the First Foot enjoyed its later importance from the Middle Ages, it is apparently not mentioned in a single poem, ballad, household account, or kirk sessions minute. The significance of the accounts is that homes were often, naturally enough, glad to receive prompt visits from people who matched the most fortunate characteristics of a first caller, and to provide rewards. In nineteenth-century Lancashire a dark-haired man could earn up to 10s. in gold each time by going door to door in a wealthy district after midnight on New Year's morn.[62] Youths at Berwick were entertained with cakes, cheese, and spirits for the service,[63] while in Edinburgh they fought each other in the streets to obtain the rights to lucrative neighbourhoods once midnight had struck.[64] It is possible (but no more) that the custom gained importance with the increasing intensity with which the Scots celebrated the New Year, and then travelled south into England.

Finally, some communities observed blessings by water at New Year, and a ritual prohibition concerning fire. The former were commonly used in the Highlands of Scotland during the early nineteenth century, households sharing some of a pitcher of spring water on New Year morning and sprinkling some of the rest in each room.[65] The same tradition was found at the same period in Pembrokeshire and Carmarthenshire, although here appropriated as a means of profit for children. They would go about at any time from 3 a.m. on New Year's Day, carrying jugs of water and tufts of evergreen or sea spurge. With these they would sprinkle passing people and call at houses offering to shake drops in each room. In either case a reward was expected. Doors which stayed closed would still, however, very often get their liquid benediction. While processing, they often sang:

> Here we bring new water
> From the well so clear,
> For to worship God with,
> This happy New Year.
> Sing levy-dew, sing levy-dew,
> The water and the wine;
> The seven bright gold wires
> And the bugles they do shine ...

No observer of this chant could ever make sense of the last four lines. The custom went into decline from the latter part of the century, when it was increasingly stigmatized as begging, but lingered at Tenby into the 1940s or 1950s.[66]

The fire superstition was a version of a common one in Europe, associated with days which began years or seasons. In much of lowland Scotland, northern England, and the West Midlands it was considered very bad luck to give anybody a light from one's own home upon New Year's Day, for the luck of the house would be stolen with it. Those unhappy enough to have their fire go out on 1 January would be left without one until the following day, and this situation was only altered with the invention of safety matches.[67] The symbolism and context of the tradition is plain enough; what remains baffling is why it should have occupied this particular geographical range.

It must be obvious that some of the practices discussed in this broad category overlapped in turn, considerably, with another, that of customs focused upon groups of people travelling about a district soliciting food, drink, or money, often in return for a service or entertainment. It is to the bulk of these that this book must now turn.

6

RITES OF HOSPITALITY
AND CHARITY

⟶⟨❦⟩⟵

THE long tradition of generosity at Christmastide (whether or not realized in practice) has been described in a previous chapter. The expectation that resident landowners would entertain tenants and guests from the neighbourhood continued right up until the later nineteenth century, when the decline of British agriculture and increasing rural depopulation put paid to the old social and economic relationships of the countryside. For some time before then, however, the scale of entertainment had probably been decreasing with the diminishing size of gentry households, and the increasing commercialization of labour services: a story much better illustrated in the case of harvest suppers, to be considered below. Echoes of the traditional festive obligations are occasionally found in the mid-nineteenth century, such as the case of the farmer in 1847 who made sure to entertain all his labourers 'as usual' to a dinner of goose and plum pudding on Christmas Day with plenty of cider.[1] This is an aspect of Victorian social history which has been very little studied, and not much is at present known about it.

The folklore collections are much more useful for certain related practices. One was the development, and public endorsement, of early winter celebrations related to particular trades and crafts. Just as agricultural workers had their sheep-shearing feasts and harvest homes, so artisans held equivalent festivities associated with medieval patron saints, at a time of year when food was abundant but the season of privation on its way. They began near the end of autumn, with the day of the cobbler saints Crispin and Crispinian on 25 October. At Cuckfield in the Sussex Weald, master cobblers in the nineteenth century always gave a dinner to their employees on that date. At nearby Horsham all shoemakers 'could be depended upon to get thoroughly drunk'.[2] In Herefordshire at the same time boys sang:

> The 25th of October:
> Cursed be the cobbler
> That goes to bed sober.[3]

On 23 November fell the old feast of Clement, patron of ironworkers, carpenters, blacksmiths, and anchor-makers. In Staffordshire country almanacs of the late seventeenth century, this was marked with a pot, 'from the

54

ancient custom of going about that night, to beg drink to make merry with'.[4] It cannot be a coincidence that this county had a thriving early iron industry; until 1860 the corporation of one centre of it, Walsall, threw apples and nuts to the crowd on this date from the windows of the town hall.[5] Carpenters were rewarded in eighteenth-century Pembrokeshire, where local people paraded an effigy of the saint as a member of this trade and distributed its clothing to local practitioners at the end before kicking it to pieces.[6] Blacksmiths celebrated with especial exuberance in nineteenth-century Hampshire and Sussex, commonly exploding gunpowder on their anvils and holding suppers at inns in some small towns. At Steyning and Bramber they went door to door for contributions towards the meal, and sometimes advertised the latter with an effigy of 'Old Clem', tricked out in wig, beard, and pipe, hoisted above the door. Occasionally one would dress up as 'Clem' and be carried in procession by his fellows.[7] Farriers also regarded the saint as their own, by extension from smiths, and had communal meals at London inns on his day in the same century.[8] At the private dockyards of Bristol, Liverpool, and Brighton, master craftsmen provided suppers for their juniors, and at the naval one at Woolwich, on the Thames, the apprentices carried one of their number round the town dressed as 'Old Clem', with wig, beard, and greatcoat. Like the Sussex smiths, they collected towards a feast; this procession, which developed in the late eighteenth century, became controversial in the nineteenth when it became attended by a mob carrying torches and throwing fireworks. In 1837 it frightened a horse pulling an omnibus into bolting through a shop window, and was stopped soon after.[9]

Two days later came the feast of Catherine, patron saint of wheelwrights, carters, spinners, rope-makers, and all celebrated it at places in the nineteenth century. The first of these groups were particularly enthusiastic about it in the Isle of Ely, and the second in the Isle of Thanet, while the third poured out of Chatham naval dockyard late at night, with a band, torches, and a crowned 'Catherine' in white muslin borne in a chair.[10] Most widespread were the festivities in the spinning and lace-making communities of the Chiltern hills and Hertfordshire plain, from Wendover to Ware. The people gathered for parties of hot buttered cakes with tea, hot spiced ale, metheglin, or hot elderberry wine. Those of Ware held a procession of a girl riding in a cart with a spinning-wheel, and sang:

> Here comes Queen Catherine, as fine as any queen,
> With a coach and horses, a-coming to be seen;
> And a spinning we will go, will go, will go,
> And a spinning we will go.

The parade and song were imitated at Peterborough by the girls of the workhouse.[11] The queen in these places, and at Chatham, was supposed not to be the saint but the historic Catherine of Aragon, remembered as a special friend of the poor and alleged foundress of lace schools and the ropery. None the less, she was honoured on the saint's feast day, which provided a special prominence for the women of the community, who were the principal practitioners of the skills concerned.

Finally, 30 November was St Andrew's Day, 'Tandrew' in Northampton-shire and Bedfordshire, where the lace-making villages chose to celebrate now instead of upon the feast of Catherine; perhaps because unlike the latter it was still a holy day under the post-Reformation Church of England. In many, during the first decades of the nineteenth century, 'drinking and feasting prevailed to a riotous extent'. The sexes changed clothes with each other, and visited friends to drink hot elderberry wine.[12] This closed the sequence of craft feasts. Most, not surprisingly, declined and vanished along with cottage industry in the course of the nineteenth century, or atrophied along with the establishments and labour practices to which they were connected. What is likely, but less easy to document, is that most had developed along with the proliferation of such domestic industry in the course of the seventeenth and eighteenth centuries, a process which peaked along with most of the observa-tions towards the end of that period. What is striking about them all is their intense regionalism; there were smiths all over England, but only those of two southern counties made much of 'Clem'. They embodied, nevertheless, some very old traditions. Most were held upon feasts which had not been included in the Church's official calendar since 1559, and depended upon medieval associations of the saints concerned. Where St Catherine was conflated with an actual queen, the result was no more Protestant, for the Catholic Catherine of Aragon would hardly be a heroine to a reformed Church and was honoured in this case for reputed actions which were not prominent in official histories. The story of these festivities is a neat illustration of how popular culture managed with an equal intensity to be localized, constantly creative, conser-vative, and independent.

The same seems to be true of the chain of regional begging customs which occupied the same chronology in the same period and were calculated to appeal to the generosity of donors while supplies were still ample but winter had arrived. They commenced with 'souling' or 'soul-caking' in Cheshire at the opening of November, which will be dealt with as part of a consideration of Hallowtide customs. The tradition by which Staffordshire people (presum-ably ironworkers) went around soliciting gifts upon St Clement's Day was imitated by children in what became known as 'Clementing'. Their custom is recorded wholly in the nineteenth century, and consisted of going from house to house with a rhyme. A standard Staffordshire version ran:

> Clemany! Clemany! Clemany mine!
> A good red apple and a pint of wine,
> Some of your mutton and some of your veal,
> If it is good, pray give me a deal;
> If it is not, pray give me some salt.
> Butler, butler, fill your bowl;

> If thou fillst it of the best
> The Lord'll send your soul to rest;
> If thou fillst it of the small,
> Down goes butler, bowl and all ...

Four other versions are known from the same county, with such alternative opening lines as 'Clemancing, clemancing, year by year', and 'Clemency, Clemency, God be wi' you'.[13] Others were found in Warwickshire.[14] The words are not very appropriate to youngsters, and may well have been taken over from the earlier begging tradition of adult men. In most cases they were succeeded by others, very similar to 'souling' verses and more suited to juveniles:

> Pray, good mistress, send to me,
> One for Peter, one for Paul,
> One for him who made us all
> Apple, pear, plum or cherry
> Any good thing to make us merry;
> A browning buck, or a velvet chair.
> Clement comes but once a year;
> Off with the pot, and on with the pan,
> A good red apple and I'll begin.

The centre of the practice remained Staffordshire, spilling over into neighbouring parts of all the adjacent counties.[15] This range overlapped considerably with the identical custom of 'catterning' at the same time or on St Catherine's Day; this was found in northern Herefordshire and Worcestershire and in southern Staffordshire. Despite the close geographical proximity of the two, there was a sharp distinction between them, no villages containing them both, so that their distribution pattern in the overlap resembled that of a chess-board or quilt. Charlotte Burne, who plotted this pattern on the map while they were still active, was at a loss to account for the choice made by communities between one or the other. They were found in agricultural, industrial, or mixed-economy settlements, with a slightly greater emphasis on manufacturing centres.[16] Really all that distinguished them was the date (not a constant difference) and the rhyme used. Catterning chants ran like this one from Alvechurch in north-eastern Worcestershire:

> Catteny, Clemeny, year by year,
> Some of your apples and some of your beer;
> Some for Peter, some for Paul,
> Some for God who made us all.
> Clemeny was a good old man;
> For his sake give us some,
> Some of the best and none of the worst,
> And pray God give you a good night's rest.
> Plum, plum, cherry, cherry.
> All good things to make us merry.
> Up the ladder and down the pan.

> Give us a red apple and we'll be gone.
> Missis and Master sit by the fire
> While we poor children trudge in the mire,
> All for apples that grow on the tree.
> So Missis and Master, come listen to me.[17]

The basic similarity to clementing (and souling) rhymes is obvious, structure and many lines being identical; the basic message is a demand for food, usually coupled with an appeal to the pious associations of charity and often with one to sympathy.[18] An oddity about catterning was that, by some caprice which no records explain, it was also found among the children of some villages in eastern Sussex. The chant used there was virtually the same as those of the West Midlands for the first four lines, and then concluded simply:

> Clemen was a good man,
> Cattern was his mother.
> Give us your best
> And not your worst
> And God give your soul good rest.[19]

The stated relationship between the saints was, of course, a local invention.

These regional begging customs were dwarfed in importance by that which occurred on St Thomas's Day, 21 December. It provided an opportunity for the poorer members of a community to appeal to the better nature of the wealthier at a time associated with generosity and goodwill, by asking for money or provisions for a Christmas feast of their own. It was occasionally associated with children but much more often with adult women, and especially the elderly and indigent female population. The finest (if a patronizing) evocation of it was left by a writer in the Midlands in 1894:

In the days of the Georges, when red cloaks were commonly worn by elderly women, it was a common sight to see, in the grey light of a December morning, groups of bent and withered figures going from door to door and hear them piping in a childish treble the following lines:

> Well a day, well a day,
> St Thomas goes too soon away,
> Then your gooding we do pray
> For a good time will not stay.
> St Thomas gray, St Thomas gray,
> The longest night and shortest day
> Please to remember St Thomas's day.[20]

In general, the rhymes which were essential to 'legitimize' the children's begging customs were rare in this one, as its claim was held to be so self-evidently just. One of the few others to be recorded came from Warwickshire:

> Little Cock Robin sat on a wall,
> We wish a merry Christmas
> And a great snowfall:

> Apples to eat and nuts to crack.
> We wish you a merry Christmas
> With a rat, tap, tap.[21]

The activity was known commonly as 'Thomasing', 'gooding', 'mumping', and 'corning', and occasionally as 'doleing', or 'gathering', or (frankly) as 'Begging Day'. There was no striking regional correlation for the terms; the first three were all found in Somerset,[22] while Shropshire had Thomasing and gooding with two most unusual local variations, 'courantin' in the south and 'clogging' in the north-west.[23] 'Mumping' seems to have derived from 'mumper', a common expression for a beggar, in turn based upon a dialect word signifying 'to mutter', as so many beggars were old and toothless.[24] 'Gooding' may have come from 'goody', a traditional term for an old woman or just from the expectation of good being done. 'Corning' signified the grain which farmers often gave in response. 'Courantin' seems to be related to a set of old English and French words to indicate 'running about', and 'clogging' likewise means trudging, being derived from footwear. In the course of the nineteenth century the custom was recorded all over England south of, and including, Cheshire, Derbyshire, and the West and East Ridings of Yorkshire.[25] It apparently never took root in most of the North Country, in Wales, or in Scotland, and within its range was found mostly in villages and small towns with (again) a variety of economies. In places scattered over this vast geographical extent all members of poor families were involved in it, and many local doles provided by legacy were directed to be made upon that date.[26] Generally, however, it was associated with females, and in Sussex and Hampshire widows amongst them received double amounts.[27]

The custom seems to have been at its peak in the first half of the nineteenth century, and to have declined thereafter until it vanished in the first few decades of the twentieth. In some places it remained vigorous for a long time; at Lewes in east Sussex clothes shops always put their surplus stock out on the pavement upon St Thomas's Day in the 1870s, while at Mayfield in the same county an old gentleman in 1903 was still saving up his 4d. coins all year to give to the poor women on their rounds.[28] Even now the congregation of Hinton Martell parish church, on the Dorset edge of the New Forest, get 5p each after communion on the feast of Thomas. The reasons for decline are obvious enough. The practice was never a very just or rational way of relieving the poor, for it was the sickest, feeblest, and most heavily burdened who were least able to profit from it. From the mid-nineteenth century, Shropshire farmers preferred to make presents to a common town or parish fund which was distributed on 21 December according to need.[29] A more fundamental blow was struck by rising standards of living and more stable food prices, and the institution of old age pensions was decisive in terminating the tradition. The same changes, producing a general hardening in attitudes to begging, put paid to clementing and catterning, aided by the 1870 Education Act which kept the older children at school upon those dates in most years. Few of those who abetted their demise were as gleefully forthright as a Mr Ray of Brewood in the Staffordshire ironworking belt: 'Clementing was a great pest. I used to take my stick to them.'[30]

The question of when these begging traditions arose is much harder, and more interesting. Charlotte Burne's suggestion, that they were descended from a dole once made at the 'Pagan Celtic' New Year (allegedly Hallowe'en) and later moved to medieval saints' days, was based upon no historical research at all.[31] Against it may be set the total absence of them from Wales and Scotland, and also from either literary sources or household accounts dating from before 1700. All we have from this earlier period are the rounds made by men in the Staffordshire ironworking communities. On the other hand, Thomasing was well established by the late eighteenth century, when (for example) the parson of Weston Longville on the Norfolk clay plateau made gifts to fifty-six poor people upon St Thomas's Day 1788.[32] It is possible to suggest that the practice grew up during this period as traditional genteel charity and hospitality waned. One thinks again of the poor woman who had spent Christmas 1616 living off successive gentry houses in the Stilton area; two centuries later, she would have been a-gooding. The trouble is that, as stated above, there is no solid evidence that upper-class provision for the poor at this season ever was extensive enough to make make begging unnecessary. The rise of customary beggary on such a large scale is, therefore, a puzzle.

Ever since the later Middle Ages, a different sort of caller bent on reward had often been welcome at wealthy houses; those with an entertainment to offer in exchange. The pattern of fifteenth-century household accounts is reproduced throughout the next three hundred years: to choose one example among many, at Christmastide 1662 Sir Miles Stapleton of Carlton in Yorkshire paid out 2s. 'to two fiddlers of Selby', 3s. 'for fiddling two days' when neighbours and tenants came to dinner, 10s. when the villagers of Carlton acted 'The Gentle Craft', and a mere 6d. 'to Mummers'.[33] The season provided a triple reason for such services to be offered: they were much in demand, poorer people had an exceptional need for extra earnings, and the absence of opportunity for agricultural work, fishing, or trading left their practitioners seeking alternative employment. No wonder that all over Europe it was associated with songs, dances, rhymes, music, or plays performed by adults or children going around houses which had food or money to spare. Some in England offered varieties which had become more normally associated with other seasons, such as morris dancing, which in the West Midlands was principally a Christmastide activity. Others were practitioners of forms most closely associated with midwinter, and it is these which must be considered now, mostly as they were recorded in the last three hundred years.

One of the simplest was carol-singing, with or without an instrumental accompaniment. Across much of England, and including London and Westminster, this was carried on by the town 'waits', the body of musicians retained by the corporation. They were usually allowed, or in the metropolis formally licensed, to go about the streets in the week or weeks before Christmas, performing or collecting money. During the nineteenth century their repertoire consisted increasingly of the carols printed in national collections; they were as familiar a sight in the towns and neighbouring villages of Lancashire, Cambridgeshire, or Dorset as in the capital.[34] In addition, the West Country, the South Welsh Marches, the Midlands, and Sussex possessed a vigorous tradition of singing by informal groups of poor villagers. They tended to be less often equipped with musical instruments and their carols were inclined to be older although still usually drawn from a common stock found in national printed works. Different parishes or small towns did, however, make different selections and combine them in distinctive cycles. A common size for a group was about a dozen, and the favourite time to operate was upon Christmas Eve and Christmas morning, but both were subject to wide local variation. Once again, the heyday of this tradition seems to have been in the eighteenth and early nineteenth centuries, and atrophy to have set in during the latter because of a withdrawal of public support.[35]

Two accounts from the West illustrate the different forms which the circuits of singers could take. One is from Exmoor, where the carollers were called Holly Riders. They made tours of the remote farms carrying lanterns and wearing a sprig of holly on jacket or coat and a holly wreath around each hat. After each performance they were rewarded with pennies or with cakes and cider.[36] In Wiltshire the visits occurred in ascending order of importance. The children would be out singing from house to house for up to a month before Christmas, and the adults only appeared after dark upon the Eve itself. They usually numbered about a dozen, with lanterns, fiddles, and viols, performing through the middle of the night and ending each serenade with the cry, 'Good Morning, we wish you a Merry Kersmass and an Happy New Year.' Two of them would reappear at breakfast time with a collecting box.[37]

Ireland had similar traditions.[38] Scotland, where Christmas no longer existed as part of a national culture, generally did not, but with one exception— the Catholic settlements of the Outer Hebrides which had never accepted the Reformation. There young men variously called *gillean nollaig* (Christmas lads), *fir duan* (song men), *gaisearan* (guisers), or *nuallairean* (rejoicers) went about providing Gaelic carols and wearing long shirts and tall white hats to imitate surplices and mitres. They combined the choruses with a typically Hebridean blessing rite by putting the youngest child of a household on a white lambskin and carrying it three times around the fire; the baby was held to represent the Christ Child or Lamb of God.[39]

Carol-singing was also closely bound up with the custom of taking a wassail bowl from house to house to solicit gifts, described earlier. In the mid-seventeenth century this remained especially associated with young women, and could already be a matter for grumbling: the famous lawyer John Selden became momentarily a forerunner of Scrooge when he complained to friends of 'wenches with wassells at New-Year's-Tide' who 'present you with a cup and you must drink of the slabby stuff, but the meaning is, you must give them monies, ten times more than it is worth'.[40] The connection with females persisted long in some areas. On Christmas Eve 1759 a young girl at Wootton Wawen, in Warwickshire's Forest of Arden, saw 'two tall women' call at her grandmother's house, carrying between them a large wassail bowl 'finely dressed on the outside with holly, mistletoe, ribbons, Laurustinus, and what other flowers could be had at that season'. The brew inside was offered in a 'pretty silver cup', and the women sang a 'long carol'.[41] Female wassail-bearers remained the rule in that county, Staffordshire, and Nottinghamshire; in the latter shire their bowl was decorated with evergreens and ribbons and contained spiced ale, roasted apples, and toast, seasoned with nutmeg and sugar, and it is likely that this was so elsewhere. The song which they used in this region had twelve verses, of which the first three ran

> A jolly Wassail-Bowl,
> A Wassail of good ale,
> Well fare the butler's soul,
> That setteth this to sale;
>   Our jolly Wassail.
>
> Good Dame, here at your door
> Our Wassail we begin
> We are all maidens poor,
> We pray now let us in,
>   With our Wassail.
>
> Our Wassail we do fill
> With apples and with spice,
> Then grant us your good will
> To taste here once or twice
>   Of our good Wassail ...

Often only the second verse was employed, ending in a succession of whoops. The story of the song is almost a classic case of how folklore could be disseminated; it was printed and published by a Mr Rann of Dudley in 1819, specifically for the use of local wassailers, and soon became their favourite all across the north Midlands.[42]

Much more famous was the Gloucestershire wassail carol noted down by Samuel Lysons in the late eighteenth century and published prominently in the hugely influential edition of John Brand's collection of folklore brought out in 1813, upon which Mr Rann (among many others) drew for material:

> Wassail! Wassail! All over the town,
> Our bread it is white, our ale it is brown:
> Our bowl it is made of the Maplin tree,
> We be all good fellows who drink to thee.
>
> Here's to our horse and to his right ear,
> God send our master a happy New Year.
> A happy New Year as e'er he did see—
> With my wassailing bowl I drink to thee.

Here's to our mare, and to her right eye,
God send our mistress a good Christmas pie;
A good Christmas pie as e'er I did see—
With my wassailing bowl I drink to thee.

Here's to Fillpail and to her long tail,
God send our master us never may fail
Of a cup of good beer; I pray you draw near,
And our jolly wassail it's then you shall hear.

Be there any maids? I suppose there be some;
Sure they will not let young men stand on the cold stone;
Sing hey O maids, come trole back the pin,
And the fairest in the house let us all in.[43]

'Fillpail' was, of course, the cow. This song, or very similar versions of it, was subsequently found throughout the whole southern English zone in which the wassail bowl was taken round villages and towns; comprising southern Cornwall, northern Dorset, most of Somerset, Gloucestershire, Wiltshire, and Herefordshire. In this region the custom was by the nineteenth century distinctively that of adult men, usually gathered into one group in each community where it obtained.[44] The standard verses were given still further prominence by being collected again in Gloucestershire by Ralph Vaughan Williams at the end of the century and published by him in turn;[45] although they never quite eclipsed some completely different local wassailers' songs.[46] In addition versions of them were sung by carollers in Lancashire, Yorkshire, Worcestershire, Warwickshire, and the western end of the Isle of Wight. In the last three of those areas it was children who had appropriated them, and the variants used were often corrupt; the West Midland renderings usually began 'whistle, wastle, through the town', or even 'wisselton, wasselton, who lives here?'[47] In none of these 'fringe' cases, moreover, do the singers seem to have taken round a bowl. The latter remained very much a feature of the nineteenth-century western heartland of the tradition, usually of wood but sometimes of china, and usually decorated with greenery, ribbons, or coloured paper.[48] It seems to have been in the eighteenth century that the carrying of it from house to house became, for reasons which the sources do not provide, purely a western custom. In the early 1790s, for example, only one elderly couple still perambulated Guthlaxton Hundred in Leicestershire every Christmas, 'with a fine geegaw which they call a Wassail', and it was expected that the practice would die with them; as apparently it did.[49]

The use of a wassail bowl in a domestic setting, on the other hand, continued to flourish under Victoria in exactly those areas where the perambulating bowl had died out or never been adopted: in much of northern England, the northwest Midlands, and Sussex. Its traditional contents remained hot spiced ale, with apples, toast, or Christmas cake floating in it. In at least some places in Sussex, those gathered to drink from it first walked round it sunwise, stirring it with silver spoons.[50] It was also customary in North Wales, where a writer in 1831 could portray a household on Twelfth Night seated round a huge oaken table, with the yuletide log blazing on the fire, and the wassail bowl with its contents (generally sugared ale, toast, etc., and sometimes enriched with eau de vie) sparkling, the large sirloin of beef...smoking on the board, the old harper increasing the mirth with the melodious strains of his harp and 'the joke and jest going round'[51]

In South Wales the bowl was taken house to house in search of profit, as a direct geographical extension of the practice of the English West Country. The activity is attested there back to the seventeenth century by a song intended to accompany it.

> Arfer y nydalig yw
> Rhodiolr nos lle bytho gwiw
> I edrych ple bo diad dda

(The custom of Christmas is to wander the night where it is proper to find where there is good drink...)[52]

Other native Welsh wassailing songs are recorded, while a version of the familiar Gloucestershire one was used by the late nineteenth century in English-speaking districts of the Gower peninsula and vale of Glamorgan. Some of the bowls could be very elaborate, one variety having twelve handles, while those used in the vale were commonly made of local (Ewenny) decorated pottery.[53]

The custom underwent a unique regional development in Yorkshire and adjoining areas of Derbyshire and Nottinghamshire. There, by the 1810s, women or children were observed going from house to house with a box instead of a bowl, likewise decorated with greenery and ribbons. Instead of containing drink, it held fruit and sugar, or (very often) a decorated doll to represent the infant Jesus. Sometimes a second doll (for the Virgin Mary) was added. The assemblage was covered with a cloth or glass front, which was raised to allow those who gave food or money to view it: a procedure very similar to that of southern and midland English May-dolls, although it is not clear how the two traditions were related. The people carrying it sang versions of a wassailing song or Christmas carols, and the object was itself known as a 'wassail box', 'vessel box', 'vessel cup', 'bezzle cup', 'milly' (My Lady) box, or (even) 'Wesley-box'.[54]

The perambulating wassails declined at the same time and rate as other nineteenth-century Christmastide begging customs, both supply and demand being subject to atrophy. In 1932 some of the former Cornish wassailers were still alive and healthy even though the practice was by then obsolete; an observer commented bluntly of them that they gave it up when they no longer needed to beg.[55] By the 1970s, however, groups had revived it at Bodmin and Truro, the main towns of the east and west divisions of the county. They sing traditional local wassailing carols and offer beer or cider from the bowl, getting money in return which they now donate to charity. The wassail survived in a different from at Drayton, in the southern Somerset Levels, where the repertoire was carefully developed into an all-round village entertainment each Twelfth Eve, including songs, jokes, and repartee. On that date, also, it has been revived at nearby Curry Rivel, where the round of the wassailers, to the homes of friends and hospitable local notables, ends at the William IV inn for the burning of the ashen faggot; the custom functions there neither principally as a fund-raising exercise, nor as an entertainment, but as a bonding exercise in communal solidarity. In such ways can a practice now firmly consigned to 'folklore' still contribute to the life of the modern West Country.

Wassail bowls and 'vessel' boxes could be out at any point in the Twelve Days; Christmas Eve, New Year's Eve, Twelfth Eve, and Twelfth Night being particular favourites. There remains to be considered, however, a clutch of begging customs concentrated upon the New Year and drawing upon traditions associated with it. The ancient tradition of New Year's gifts, and the helpful ambivalence of the word 'hogmanay', signifying either a present or a blessing, encouraged many poorer people, and especially the young, to solicit charity at that time. By the end of the eighteenth century it was a well-established custom for children in small towns all over the Scottish Lowlands and in the far north of England, down to and including Richmond, to do so. They went from door to door on New Year's Eve or New Year's Day, asking for 'hogmanay' or (in England) 'hagmena', meaning food or money. In most cases they did so with a song or chant, which came in two main local varieties. The Richmond version began with an appeal to tradition:

> Tonight it is the New Year's Night, tomorrow is the day,
> And we are come for our right and for our ray,
> As we used to do in old King Harry's day.
>   Sing, fellows, sing Hagman heigh!

Along the east coast of Scotland, from Sutherland to Fife, there was also an assumption of right:

> Rise up, aul wife, an shack yer feathers;
> Dinna think it we are beggars;
> We'er only bairnies come to play—
> Rise up and gee's wir hogmanay.

Variants of these, and independent local compositions, were found across the range of the custom, and a form of the second was still used in eastern Scottish ports in the 1950s.[56] Some of these rhymes also reached Skye, though the fact that they were recited in English indicates that they were recent importations from the Lowlands when recorded there in the nineteenth century.[57] Alongside them, and all over the northern Hebrides, were collected examples of the home-grown Gaelic *rann*, or *duan*, or *beannachadh blhadhna uir*, recited by groups of young men from poorer crofts going begging at the richer. From Skye comes (in translation):

> I have come out on the night of the New Year
> From a homestead of the moorland.
> Here I stay till I get a bannock
> From each village that I know ...

> Let each give me the bannock,
> That the New Year may go well with you.
> May he who gives no bannock
> Have his reward from Black Bad Donald.

The later character was the Devil. An equivalent from Lewis, *A nochd oidhche nam bonnag*, can be rendered:

> This is the night of the cakes.
> We will take bread without butter
> We will take butter without bread,
> We will take cheese all by itself,
> So how can we possibly lack food?
> One thing alone we do refuse—
> Small wart-covered potatoes:
> They'd keep nine times later abed
> The strongest man in the village.

On South Uist a favourite song was *Oidhche Challaig*:

> We are come to the door,
> To see if we be the better of our visit,
> To tell the generous women of the townland
> That tomorrow is New Year's Day.

If given food they would continue by going sunwise about the fire singing:

> May God bless the dwelling,
> Each stone and beam and stave,
> All food and drink and clothing
> May health of men always be here.

If spurned, they would pile a cairn of stones near the door as a warning to others, and tramp off shouting:

> The curse of God and the New Year be on you
> And the scath of the plaintive buzzard,
> Of the hen-harrier, of the raven, of the eagle,
> And the scath of the sneaking fox.
> The scath of the dog and cat be on you,
> Of the boar, of the badger and of the ghoul,
> Of the hipped bear and of the wild wolf,
> And the scath of the foul polecat.[58]

In the Northern Isles the custom was the same, differing only (of course) in the song, which in both Orkney and Shetland began with a variant of:

> Güde New Year and Güde New Year Nicht.
> St Mary's men are we.
> We're come here to crave our right
> Before Our Leddie

Sometimes it was secularized to 'Queen Mary', although as the only Scottish queen of that name was a Catholic, it achieved no more to Protestantize the verse than turning St Catherine to Catherine of Aragon.[59] The Isle of Man had its equivalent, the 'Quaaltagh', with a standard song which translates from Manx as:

> Again we assemble, a Merry New Year
> To wish to each one of the family here,
> Whether man, woman, or girl, or boy,
> That long life and happiness all may enjoy.
> May they of potatoes and herrings have plenty,
> With butter and cheese and each other dainty,
> And may their sleep never, by night or by day,
> Disturbed be by even the tooth of a flea,
> Until at the Quaaltagh again we appear
> To wish you, as now, all a happy New Year![60]

The Welsh form of the tradition was to go door to door on New Year's morning asking for the *calennig* or *calenia*, signifying a New Year's gift. It was not youths who carried out this work but local poor people in general, although it increasingly became a children's custom in the course of the nineteenth century. Over the same period, also, bread and cheese tended to be replaced by money as the form of gift made.[61] Sometimes those asking used local rhymes, such as this, still recited near Aberystwyth in the 1950s:

> Dydd calan yw hi heddiw,
> Rwy'n dyfod ar eich traws
> I mofyn am y geiniog
> Nev grwst a fara caws.
> O dewch i'r drws yn sirios
> Heb neusid dim o'ch gwedd;
> Cyn daw dydd calan eto
> Bydd lawer yn y bedd.

(It's New Year's Day and I'm coming to ask you for a penny or bread and cheese. Come to the door smiling. Before next New Year's Day many will be in their graves.)[62]

In south-east Wales and the neighbouring English areas of Herefordshire and the Forest of Dean, the perambulating children carried a symbol of blessing, itself often called the *calennig*. In its most elaborate form, it consisted of an apple or orange, resting on three sticks like a tripod, smeared with flour, stuck with nuts, oats or wheat, topped with thyme or another fragrant herb and held by a skewer. These three components, of fruit, cereal or nuts, and herb, were supposed to represent the gifts of the Three Wise Men, of sweetness, wealth, and immortality. Again, it is possible that what had been an adult practice had descended to children, for in Herefordshire, at least, back in 1821 it had been the 'peasantry' in general who sent the token round, but only their youngsters by the 1880s.[63] Either by some transference or by independent development, by the late nineteenth century children in Nottinghamshire were also carrying fruit about on New Year's morning, often gilded or stuck with cloves.[64]

The whole arc of England between the *calennig* and the 'hagmena', comprising the west and north Midlands and Yorkshire, was occupied by an almost identical parallel to both, distinguished only by its rhymes and its often explicit linkage to the custom of the First Foot. The latter was fulfilled by a youngster, often also called 'the lucky bird', who accorded well with the requirement and who was usually part of a group requesting gifts on New Year's morning. The most common verse, found across the full extent of the practice and overlapping with 'hogmanay' gathering far into Scotland, was a variant of:

> I wish you a merry Christmas
> And a happy New Year
> A pocket full of money
> And a cellar full of beer,
> And a good fat pig
> To serve you all the year.
> Ladies and gentlemen
> Sat by the fire,
> Pity we poor boys
> Out in the mire.[65]

It was also found in Hertfordshire,[66] though apparently not elsewhere in south-eastern England and even in that country not definitely attached to actual solicitation of gifts. Across much of its range, like most such commonly used rhymes, it coexisted with local equivalents used for the same purpose.[67]

There is, then, excellent evidence for early and mid-winter begging customs, sanctioned within particular traditional forms, across more or less the whole of Britain and its satellite islands during the eighteenth and nineteenth centuries. Some areas, such as the west Midlands, had successive opportunities for them. Throughout, there was an opportunism and a flexibility in their application, as illustrated nicely at the Shropshire village of the folklorist Charlotte Burne, where in the 1880s 'souling' was checked by the disapproval of a new vicar but 'Thomasing' burgeoned with the arrival of a rich and openhanded family.[68] What is important, and also frustratingly difficult to ascertain, is the antiquity of these traditions. It has already been suggested that in England the wassailing customs go back at least to the beginning of the seventeenth century, while 'Thomasing', for all its later importance, does not. At first sight the Scottish islands promise still more antiquity for their equivalents; after all, the standard rhyme in the Northern Isles refers to a religion proscribed in the sixteenth century, while the Gaelic curse from South Uist called upon the wild boar, extinct in Scotland by the seventeenth, and the wolf, reduced to a tiny number by 1700 and last recorded in 1753. Both animals, moreover, would have vanished from the Hebrides much earlier. The problem with the former argument is that an appeal to antiquity could be a way of legitimating an action; the reference to 'King Harry's day' at Richmond is probably in this category, as is the appeal of children begging at New Year in eighteenth-century Cumberland to 'the bounty we were wont to have in old King Edward's days'.[69] The Hebridean curse also refers to the bear, an animal which had been wiped out all over the British Isles by the Middle Ages; so that either it is amazingly old or else it assembled a catalogue of well-known European menaces, starting with those actually found in the Hebrides by the eighteenth century and moving on to bears and ghouls. Bereft of either records or inferential evidence, a historian can only leave the matter open. What is beyond doubt is the major importance of these traditions in the years around 1800.

Most of those considered in this chapter were relatively easy procedures, offering only a rhyme, a song, or a bowl in exchange for reward. In a class of their own were the midwinter ritual plays and dances which have always excited much more interest among folklorists; and they now deserve a proportionately extended treatment.

7

MUMMERS' PLAY AND
SWORD DANCE

❧

The typical Mummers' Play opens with a naive introduction in which one of the performers craves the spectators' indulgence, asks for room and promises a fine performance. When this is concluded the two protagonists appear, and after each has boasted of his valour they fall to fighting. In this duel one or the other is wounded or killed. A doctor is then summoned who vaunts his proficiency in medicine and proceeds to revive the fallen hero. Here the main business of the play ends. It is now the turn of minor characters to enter and provide irrelevant amusement of a simple sort. One of them collects money and the performance finishes with a song.

So wrote Reginald Tiddy, in the first full-length study of the play, published (posthumously) in 1923.[1] By then it was already clear that in this 'classic' form it was found all over southern England and the south Midlands, and performed in the Christmas season. Several elements of it were also present in plays presented in the east Midlands on Plough Monday, in Cheshire in November, and in the north-west at Eastertide, to be described later; and also in the north-eastern Christmastide Sword Dance. Over much of the West Country, Father Christmas made the introduction, while everywhere St George or King George was the most common champion, fighting either a Saracen knight or a swaggering soldier called, most frequently, Slasher. The doctor was ubiquitous, and often had an assistant, and the combats could be single or multiple. The lesser characters were most often a fool, who also danced and played music, a man with a club and frying-pan or dripping-pan (usually called Beelzebub), a poor man who speaks of his wife and family, and a sweeper and money-collector (most often named Devil Doubt). The tone was consistently comic and the structure loose, with no integrated plot, love interest, or sense of historic setting. Scores of local names were substituted for those commonly given to the cast and, although they were roughly divided into two regional traditions by the Thames valley, there was both a consistent framework of action across the whole range and tremendous differences of detail everywhere. Costumes consisted usually of shirts or smocks hung with ribbons, bits of cloth, or strips of paper, but again there were many variations. The actors, always male and usually young, could be called Mummies, Guisers, Guizards, Seven Champions, Johnny Jacks, or Tipteerers, as well as Mummers. By 1900 they were rapidly disappearing in all their old haunts.

Ten years after the appearance of Tiddy's book, a renowned scholar of medieval and Elizabethan drama, Sir Edmund Chambers, published a more detailed appraisal of this play, and added a lengthy discussion of the northern Sword Dance, to which it had already been linked.[2] In the 1920s this was still fairly common in Yorkshire, County Durham, and Northumberland, and had occasionally been recorded in Cheshire, Derbyshire, Nottinghamshire, Devon, Hampshire, and (by some trick of dispersal) on the Shetland Island of Papa Stour. Whereas the play was usually performed in houses or pubs, the dance was generally an outdoor activity, howbeit also in the Christmas period. It was provided by five to eight men, accompanied by one or more fools or clowns, and a man in woman's dress; the latter was often called Betty or Bessy. Sometimes the team had a captain or a king and queen. There were always musicians and could be flag-bearers. The dancers dressed in a uniform costume, consisting most often of a white or coloured shirt and trousers or breeches. Their swords were long and straight in Yorkshire and short and flexible, with two handles, in Northumberland and Durham (where they were commonly called 'rappers'). A few Yorkshire teams used wooden specimens, but in general the swords were of steel. The costume of the extra characters was more fantastic, the fool being in shreds or in particoloured circus garb. Occasionally fools or dancers blackened their faces, which was also rarely found in the Mummers' Play.

The dance usually began with calling-on verses, naming the dancers, with little sign of any consistent tradition behind them. The key point of the performance came when the men meshed swords to form an interlocking pattern called the lock or the nut, which was laid on the ground, held breast-high, or raised overhead. Usually the group turned clockwise above it. Often the fool or transvestite stepped into the ring and the lock was placed around his neck; sometimes a spectator was put in this position. Several dances ended in a combat and a cure like that of the Mummers' Play.

Both forms of entertainment first entered the orbit of scholarship at the beginning of the nineteenth century, in the works of folklore collectors such as John Brand and county historians such as George Ormerod. For most of that century they were viewed primarily as colourful pieces of drollery or as a means for working men to make extra money to provide for their Christmas celebrations; this was certainly a very important aspect of them, a hat or other receptacle being passed round the spectators at the end of each performance, while food or drink was often given instead in a private house. Some commentators were impressed by the size of the crowds drawn, and indeed up to a hundred people attended sword dances at Eskdaleside and Sleights on the North York Moors.[3] Others were more struck by the nuisance value of the traditions, such as a writer upon the Mummers' Play in Northamptonshire in 1864: 'in this age of refinement few only will allow their dwellings to be the scene of this antic pastime, as the performers enter uninvited, suddenly throwing open the door, and one after the other act their different parts'.[4]

Ten years later the mummers of the Wiltshire cloth town of Melksham attacked those of Wraxall for performing in their community. The fight was waged along the streets, 'and the bridge was quickly strewn, not with corpses, but with the remnants of Wraxall paperhangings'.[5] Such notices began to be replaced, from the last decade of the century onward, by others, marked with a new tone of acute interest and profound respect. No new evidence had been produced; what had happened was that scholars were looking at the entertainments with different eyes.

The process was initiated by a civil servant, Thomas Fairman Ordish, who had been inspired to take an interest in folklore by reading German and Scandinavian mythology, especially in the works of the Brothers Grimm. The sword dance struck him as a probable ancient Germanic ritual, and his consideration of it led to one of the Mummers' Play in its different local forms. He suggested the first classification of these, and employed (or invented) the term 'folk play' to include the whole genre.[6] Ordish, however, died before he could publish much of his material, and the work of fostering interest was left to his fellow civil servant, Sir Edmund Chambers, whose thoughts upon the matter were first published in 1903.[7] By that time a new and powerful spell had fallen over the subject, that of Sir James Frazer, whose immensely influential book *The Golden Bough* had gone into its first edition in 1890. The context of Frazer's work will be considered later; for now it is sufficient to repeat that he popularized a theory that the nature of ancient pagan religion could be reconstructed partly by a consideration of modern folk rituals, which were presumed to be descended from it. This argument, and Frazer's own application of, it were fiercely criticized from the beginning by historians and experts in comparative religion, and had the most favourable impact upon writers who fell outside those categories (and were thereby less able to evaluate the evidence).[8] Chambers was exactly a person of this sort: a government employee who earned his knighthood through devoted service, but also a superb amateur research scholar, patient and assiduous in his collection of historical data and passionately interested in medieval and Tudor drama. His main weakness was that he relied heavily upon others, and upon Frazer above all, for the ideas which he applied to his material.[9] In 1903 he proceeded to impose the theory of pagan survival upon a range of English popular customs, notably the morris dance. With the midwinter plays and dances, however, he could do no more than make passing suggestions, as he was not a field collector himself and the printed works of the time simply did not have enough information.

The latter was now provided, by Cecil Sharp and his pupils of the English Folk Dance Society, of which he was the principal founder. Sharp went up to the north-east of England to collect sword dances in 1910, and published two long-sword and two 'rapper' examples during the following year. After this he sent a postcard to every parish minister in the three north-eastern counties, and this prodigious effort yielded details of ten more dances, published in 1912 and 1913. The collecting was often done in the nick of time, from a single survivor of a team; the old man who gave him the Escrick dance died two days later.[10] Some of the dances were demonstrated, along with much of the morris also collected by Sharp, by a team of six young men who included an Oxford don, Reginald Tiddy. It was he who set to work during the same period finding examples of the folk-drama, especially the combat and resurrection to which he applied the name 'the Mummers' Play'. Tiddy died in the battle of the Somme, but his work was published, as described above, in 1923. In their interpretations of the dances and plays, the two writers accepted and extended the work of Chambers, and through him of Frazer. They asserted with perfect confidence that both traditions descended from ancient pagan rites concerned with fertility, death, and resurrection.

This conclusion was reinforced by the parallel impact of Frazer's work upon studies into ancient Greek drama carried out by the 'Cambridge School' of classical anthropology. From 1912 onwards its members tried to find the origins of Greek drama, mythology, and religion in a basic seasonal ritual drama representing the life-history of a dying and reviving fertility god. They were assisted in their arguments by the discovery by British scholars in the 1900s of modern Greek popular plays which appeared to embody aspects of this theme and had some resemblance to the English folk-drama. From Cambridge the theory swiftly crossed the Atlantic and was taken up with equal enthusiasm in American universities. In England it flourished until 1927, when Arthur Pickard-Cambridge made a thorough analysis of it against the ancient dramatic texts and showed that there was actually no real evidence to support it. Despite this, it continued to enjoy popularity among literary scholars in the USA into the 1960s, the English Mummers' Play being used as a *proven* instance of the persistence of the primitive ritual pattern in modern folk usages to bolster the same argument for the Greeks.[11]

At the same time, by a process of perfect circularity, the Greek evidence was being used to foster confidence in the view of the English traditions propounded by Chambers and Sharp. The latter was enthusiastically taken up by leading members of the Folk-Lore Society,[12] and in 1933, as described earlier, Chambers revisited his own theory. Being now equipped with a lot more English data, and the presumed Greek parallels, he was able to restate it triumphantly with respect to both the play and the dance. He suggested that both stemmed from a prehistoric European fertility rite in which 'skin-clad worshippers, accompanied by a traditional Woman, capered about the slain figure of a man who had been King of the feast'.[13] After this the theory of an origin in pagan ritual remained dominant for almost fifty years, specialists differing only over the classification of the different plays and dances and the nature and chronology of the original rites. To the prominent English folk-lorist Violet Alford, in 1962, the sword dance was 'firmly rooted in and beneath Mother Earth', meaning that it incorporated a Neolithic rite to waken the earth from its winter sleep, led originally by matriarchal priestesses serving a Mother Goddess, with a Bronze Age rite of manhood. Her evidence for the former was pure supposition, her evidence for the latter that many of the dances had been recorded in modern mining communities.[14] To the American academic Alan Brody, in 1969, the dance had been the ancestor of the Mummers' Play, because it involved the community as an anonymous group, unified in ritual; whereas the play, including characters and symbols, represented an intermediate stage between ritual and true drama. Both, however, were still prehistoric in origin.[15] Another American, E. T. Kirby, got carried away in 1971 by the fashionable new interest in tribal shamanism in the universities of the USA, and declared that the doctor in the play had once been a shaman.[16] The notion of the ancestral pagan ritual remained powerful among folklorists in the 1970s,[17] was still confidently repeated in academic studies rather distant from the subject in the 1980s,[18] and was widely believed among the general public even in the mid-1990s.

Over this long period, more and more evidence was amassed. By 1962 references to sword dances in seventy-eight English communities had been collected.[19] In 1903 Chambers could draw upon twenty-nine examples of the Mummers' Play; by 1933 he had over a hundred at his disposal. By 1967 the total of complete texts was 156, with thirty-eight fragments, while references to the play had been found in over eight hundred communities. The Christmas-tide combat-and-revival drama had been performed all over England except in East Anglia, eastern Kent, and the east Midlands—and in the last area its place was taken by the Plough Play. It had been especially popular in the south Midlands and Cotswolds, Wiltshire and Hampshire, and the north Midlands, being found in both industrial towns and large, stable, agricultural communities. It was also found across southern Scotland, although it had never apparently reached the Highlands and its only known Welsh locations were in the Glamorgan coalfield, where it had fairly obviously been introduced from England.[20] The same pattern was traced in Ireland, where the play was found only in areas of English immigration even though it overlapped easily with some native popular entertainments.[21] In England, however, even the present assemblage of evidence may be just the tip of an iceberg; the survey of 1967 found the play in eleven communities in Dorset, while a more recent study of that county traced it in forty-five.[22]

Alongside the labour of collection (in which the work of the Cheshire schoolmaster Alex Helm was especially remarkable) went on the work of revival. The play at Marshfield, in the Cotswolds north-east of Bath, was recreated in 1932 by Violet Alford. She happened to be the sister of the vicar, and employed her enthusiasm and her social status to reproduce the action after a lapse of about fifty years. Expediency forced her to compromises, so that a work formerly performed on several nights, by boys, and indoors, now became the preserve of men, operating out of doors upon St Stephen's Day. Against her will the performers insisted upon adding a town crier and a closing song, but she in turn impressed upon them the idea that they were enacting an ancient ritual and that they formed a magic circle as they worked. Once patched together, this new version of the play became 'traditional', to be reproduced without innovation or deviance thereafter.[23] The play at Chipping Campden, further north in the same hills, was restored two years later by another newcomer. He was F. L. Griggs, an artist who had settled there in 1903 and devoted himself subsequently to opposing any redevelopment in order to preserve what he regarded as the true spirit of rural England. In 1934 he organized a broadcast of the play of the former Campden Mummers, on a BBC radio programme, and provoked so much interest that the local head-master had it performed in the town henceforth.[24] By such means was the play 'restored' in scores of places as part of the successive phases of the 'folk revival'; schoolteachers and local morris teams were especially important in the process. Frequently the texts used were those published by folklorists, so that the majority of those employed in recent Dorset revivals, for example, actually came from outside the county.[25] Likewise, Cecil Sharp's pupils made the sword dances a standard part of folk-dance repertoire, most popular (of course) in their native region; but the texts used were rewritten by Sharp to make them both more 'decent' and more complex, and to enhance the importance of the dance itself.[26] What all these recreations had in common was that they were invariably undertaken in the belief that an ancient ritual was being saved from oblivion; without this it is unlikely that the perfor-mances of nineteenth-century working men would have excited anything like the same degree of interest.

As Chambers had seen at the beginning, the belief possessed one serious weakness: the extant records of sixteenth- and seventeenth-century England were filled with references to popular customs, but included not a single one to this supposedly ancient folk-drama. Mummers indeed there were in plenty but none was described as performing the combat- and-resurrection play. The contrast with the luxuriant evidence from the nineteenth century could hardly, in fact, have been more complete. The earliest full text was found in a printed, chapbook, version, dating from anywhere between 1746 and 1769 and intended specifically to be used by groups requiring a piece of theatre to be acted around Christmastide. Before then came only four lines, extracted from a play of this sort acted around Exeter in about 1738, and it was only after 1750 that references to the custom began to multiply across the country, and in the American colonies.[27] There is indeed an account of a mumming at Cork city in 1685, which included most of the characters of the later plays, such as St George, the Turk, the doctor, Beelzebub, and the little devil, under the name of 'an ancient pastime.' It does not, however, describe the action, and is not an original document. It is, rather, one of a collection of jottings made by the antiquary Thomas Crofton Croker, probably in the 1820s. In this case his source is lost, and its worth, or his accuracy of transcription, cannot be verified; for example, a slip when copying the date, of '1685' for '1785' would make a crucial difference.[28] As Chambers spotted, some of the personalities and material in the later plays derived from Richard Johnson's prose romance, *The Famous Historie of the Seaven Champions of Christendom* (1596), probably filtered through John Kirke's dramatization of it in 1638.[29] Neither Johnson nor Kirke, however, included the essential actions of combat and resurrection.

Sword dances, on the other hand, were certainly found in early modern Britain. One at Elgin has already been mentioned, and the Glovers Company of Perth performed another in 1617 which was so successful that it was repeated for the coronation of Charles I as King of Scots in 1633.[30] In England too they could occur as *ad hoc* occasions; the Lancashire gentleman Nicholas Blundell taught one to eight men to celebrate the making of a new marl-pit in June 1712.[31] Another is mentioned in John Marston and John Webster's play *The Malcontent*, written in 1604. The genre of such dances was very well established in Germany and the Netherlands from the fourteenth century onward, sometimes including formations of dancers, and the locking of blades in a pattern, later found in England. The problem with all this is that the 'lock', and the additional characters, are not recorded in England until 1777, when the antiquary John Brand watched such a dance on Tyneside. In 1769 another observer had described a sword dance team in Northumberland, led by a man with a fox's skin on his head, but before then there are no records for the custom in what was to be its characteristic homeland; the earliest from Yorkshire date to 1810 and 1811, while the isolated Papa Stour dance was established by 1788, with a highly polished literary text clearly composed by some classical scholar. E. C. Cawte has pointed out that the 'rapper' variety would have been technologically impossible before the appearance of steel in the region in 1701, and that the 'rapper' knots were developments from a few well-known figures of the Yorkshire long-sword type. He therefore proposed that long-sword dances got into Northumberland and Durham from Yorkshire in the mid-eighteenth century, and mutated there into the 'rapper' tradition around 1800.[32] How the Germanic, Dutch, or Flemish sword dance got into Yorkshire or the Shetlands, and when, is anybody's guess.

It was this sort of difficulty which inspired Lord Raglan, a folklorist who was normally one of the most devoted followers of Frazer, to remind the Folk-Lore Society in 1947 that there was no trace of the Mummers' Play in medieval England. His lack of tact earned him a rude letter from Violet Alford, who accused him of ignorance,[33] and intensified a search for parallels which might extenuate the lack of direct evidence. Alford's own favourite tactic was to list the large number of sword dances, men–women, Fools, and death and resurrection dramas to be found in peasant societies in modern Europe, and suggest that they all derived from the same prehistoric ceremony; her essential sense of the rural past as a timeless continuum prevented her from making an attempt to reconstruct the actual history of a single one of these.[34] Others preferred to point to the apparent echoes of the Mummers' Play in early literature. Tiddy had already drawn attention to the fifteenth-century *Play of the Sacrament*, which includes a similar quack doctor.[35] Chambers had found that medieval and Tudor English literary works were sprinkled with heroic combats, comic braggarts, deaths followed by revival, and (of course) devils.[36] After Raglan's intervention, a succession of articles in the periodical of the Folk-Lore Society emphasized that characters, actions, and structures in the same works bore a resemblance to those in the later Mummers' drama. In every case the argument rested upon the assumption that the latter must be older and the literary parallels drawn from it; in none did the author confront the possibility that the Mummers' texts might themselves have drawn in part upon these earlier models.[37] Violet Alford had stated the basic principle of this exercise with admirable candour: 'it does seem to me that imagination is needed. On the vision evoked facts can be built, and pulled down again if they do not fit'.[38] It never seems to have troubled her or those who followed her in the work that the vision had not been composed of facts in the first place and that those 'built on' to it were being wrenched from other contexts.

All this labour did, however, have the effect of keeping scholars of literature, especially in the USA, aware of the existence of folk-drama and inclined to treat it with respect. It inspired a new generation of students in the 1970s and 1980s to carry out research in the field with a new concentration and academic rigour. A crop of postgraduate theses duly sprouted, an occasional newsletter, *Roomer*, was launched in 1980 to co-ordinate work, and in 1985 a periodical, *Traditional Drama Studies*, was founded to encourage it further. From 1978 the Centre for English Cultural Tradition at Sheffield sponsored annual conferences upon it. Inevitably, however, this systematic application of academic interest was bound to produce new emphases and to challenge old assumptions. A harbinger of these developments was Roger D. Abrahams, who studied the Mummers' Plays transplanted to the British West Indies. At the end of the 1960s he pointed out that they functioned perfectly well there even though cut off from the whole context which folklorists had presumed for them in Europe.[39] His work had the effect of concentrating attention upon the plays as performances, and upon the people known to have performed them, for the first time since Ordish wrote. He also pointed out that there was still absolutely no sign of any 'original' drama from which the known versions derived, and that the dominant theme of the latter was comedy, not a celebration of a particular season. P. S. Smith complained at the same time that folklorists had been so fond of theorizing about the origins of the plays that they had paid little attention to collecting full and precise information about their actual identity.[40] In 1972 A. E. Green used a review to launch a direct attack upon the view of the custom as an enduring relic of ancient ritual, pointing out that there was still absolutely no evidence for this; and now there was nobody in the Folklore Society willing to reply.[41]

The actual origins of the play and the dance thus remain a mystery. In 1989 and 1990 Gareth Morgan refloated the idea that Greek parallels could be useful, by pointing again to similarities between the modern Greek and the modern English folk-drama, including plays which had come with Greek refugees from Asia Minor. He suggested that the drama had been brought back by Crusaders from the Byzantine world to England, via Flanders, in the thirteenth century. The linchpin of the argument was that the Greek performers were called *momoeri*, a word so close to 'mummer' that it is unlikely to be unconnected. The whole piece of research drew on fascinating material, and neatly side-stepped the whole morass of speculation about northern European pagan rites. It also, however, was susceptible to several criticisms, which were presented by Craig Fees. One was that the Greek term *momoeri* was not recorded until the twentieth century, and may even have been adopted from the first English scholars to watch the drama concerned, who applied their own word 'Mummers' to it. The action of the Greek and English plays is not so similar as to be beyond the possibility of coincidence, and the Morgan thesis also fails to explain the total absence of records of this drama in England before the 1730s.[42] It should perhaps be stressed again how remarkable this silence is to a specialist in early modern studies. The Early Morris Project, to be discussed later, has recovered several hundred references to morris dancing before 1700, indicating quite how much material there is for the study of popular pastimes in Tudor and Stuart England. By contrast, the folk-drama is not represented by a single one.

It therefore looks at present as if the Mummers' Play and the sword dance with the locked blades evolved between 1700 and 1750, spreading rapidly thereafter and reaching a peak of popularity in the early nineteenth century. This seems to have been the consensus among those directly concerned with the issue since 1980, with an emphasis upon the importance of printed sources such as chapbooks in spreading the play.[43] As the performances seem invariably to have been given by labouring men, artisans, or youths, to earn extra money, their wide and speedy dissemination can only be explained by the facts that the presenters were in need of food, drink, or cash, and the audiences found the drama acceptable entertainment; Flora Thompson, in her semi-fictionalized account of childhood in a south Midland hamlet in the 1880s, made the telling comment that mummers never visited her settlement because it was too small to be financially worth while.[44] Unhappily, the observation of both performers and audiences in the crucial period 1750–1850 was so slight and careless as to furnish very little information about either. As Barry Ward has pointed out, the surviving texts were generally so heavily reworked in the course of the nineteenth and twentieth centuries as to provide only a slight sense of their nature in the earlier period; and indeed to render the terms 'traditional' virtually meaningless if applied to them.[45] The actual evolution of the play remains a complete mystery, and a very intriguing one as the assemblage of characters and sequence of action is apparently unlikely. For the present writer, the most remarkable of the former remains 'Beelzebub', with his club and pan. As Chambers noted, medieval stage devils carried pitchforks, not these accoutrements. In 1929 the archaeologist Stuart Piggott suggested that he was so like the celebrated prehistoric hill-carving of the Cerne Abbas Giant that he was surely a personification of an ancient deity, a remark which inevitably found an enthusiastic reception in the Folk-Lore Society of the time.[46] The particular comparison no longer works, because there is now considerable doubt as to whether the Giant itself is older than the late seventeenth century.[47] Piggott's instinct was, however, a sound one, because Beelzebub does look amazingly like the ancient Celtic god-form venerated in Gaul under the name of Sucellus and in Ireland as the Daghda, a male figure carrying a club and a pot or cauldron.[48] This sort of deity does not, however, seem to have been popular in ancient Britain, and how this image manages to leap-frog over a thousand years to turn up in eighteenth-century England is a real puzzle; unless, of course, the date of the 1685 Cork play is correct and he really is the Daghda, given a devil's name and trans-planted from Irish folklore to English folk-drama via Munster. All told, the collapse of the theory of pagan origins has created more problems that it has solved in the quest for the origins of the Mummers' Play.

At present scholars of the play and dance seem to have lost interest in that quest, being concerned wholly with performance in a modern context where it can be properly studied. All the recent works of this sort concur that the action is intended to be at once comic and disturbing.[49] The dance is both stylish and menacing. The play's characters are essentially outcasts; devils, tramps, half-wits, quacks, and bragging, fighting adventurers. Through their essential lack of realism, they make acceptable the representation of social misconduct, mock violence, irony, and disrespect; in many ways they are a popular counterpart of the professional theatre of (say) Brecht. The same studies also emphasized that the mummers and dancers functioning in the 1970s and 1980s had a considerable range of values and goals, which may always have been the case. In general the plays entertained and amused, and served as a platform for people who were articulate and yet normally denied a means to express themselves or win esteem within a local society. Some honoured the past, some parodied it, and some afforded a romantic journey into it. Like a club or a sports team, all provided cohesion for small groups within a wider community.

A few case studies of such groups may serve to illustrate and conclude this discussion. For the Ripon Blue Stots (at least in the 1970s) the personal financial motive was still uppermost; the performers toured working-class streets, pubs, and clubs, trying to make as much money or earn as many free pints as possible, getting very drunk, and occasionally brawling. The Bampton Mummers also enjoyed the process of inebriation, but collected for local charities and tended to be much more distant and formal when acting in private homes than in the knockabout atmosphere of pubs.[50] The Marshfield Mummers are the centrepiece of a genuine communal celebration upon Boxing Day, producing their play at successive points in the village street. There is a collection for charity, but this is almost incidental to the occasion, which functions more as a symbol with which the whole settlement identifies and of which it is proud; as befits Violet Alford's pet play, it is the most heavily ritualized of all.[51] At Chipping Campden the atmosphere is more convivial and informal, the play functioning at once as a symbol of conservatism and continuity in a self-consciously pretty Cotswold town, and a shared world with the wealthy newcomers and tourists who are its principal patrons.[52] The players at Headington, Oxford, operate in pub car-parks during the daytime and act as a reminder of the separate identity of a historic community now physically swallowed up by an expanding city. Last, the Waterley Bottom Mummers function as a link between two old towns upon the Cotswold Edge, taking their name from a valley half-way between Dursley and Wotton under Edge. The members are drawn equally from the two, and although their performances are based in pubs and not open spaces, their relationship with their communities is intense; not only do they give all proceeds to local charities but their costumes are made of rags which have each been donated by a different household. I asked one of them if he thought that his play was pagan. He replied that, whether it was ancient or not, it was certainly pagan in spirit, for nothing could be less Christian than the resurrection from death of a braggart, performed by a quack armed with a medicine bottle. I asked him if he regarded it as a ritual. He answered that anything becomes a ritual if you have to do it ten times in a single night. It seemed to me then that the romantic Edwardian picture of the natural wisdom of the countryman, so often rightly derided as a cultural artefact, might not at times be so far from the truth.

8

HOBBY-HORSE AND HORN DANCE

E very May Day two hobby-horses dance their way through the Cornish coastal town of Padstow, representing different halves of the community. Each consists of an oval frame covered in black oilskins, with a small horse's head in front but also a fearsome mask in the centre, red and white with glaring eyes and snapping jaws. For twelve hours they move around separate circuits, each led on by a 'Teaser', a person in white prancing in front with a painted club. Each also has a retinue of people, also in white clothes, some playing accordions and drums. They sing the local version of a Mayers' song, with the unique addition that at times the tune becomes a dirge, and the 'Oss sinks to the ground and lies flat; till the chorus swells triumphantly again and the beast rises and progresses on the next stage of its course. The tradition represents a tremendous reaffirmation of communal pride and solidarity in this small and normally quiet settlement; nobody is allowed to take part in either procession unless their family has lived there for at least two generations. It is also a major attraction for visitors, and one of the most famous and most dramatic folk customs of modern Britain.

In 1931 it attracted Mary Macleod Banks, soon to be the President of the Folk-Lore Society, who took it upon herself to upbraid the 'Teaser' (a name only later adopted) for dressing as a clown and so 'spoiling the rite'. Her point was that on her previous visit in 1929 he had been attired as a woman. For once the bonds of social deference snapped, and he told her angrily that there was no one traditional costume for his part. What she was hearing was valuable folklore but it made no favourable impression upon her because she had already decided that the custom was a relic of a pagan sacred marriage between earth and sky, and the presence of a man–woman was as essential to her theory as that of a clown was inconvenient.[1] Other luminaries of the Folk-Lore Society obviously made a more favourable impression later on, because on my own visit in 1985 the tradition was confidently explained to me by townspeople as a particular stage of devolution from a prehistoric ritual in which a man representing a fertility god was sacrificed for the good of his people. The details of this theory made it instantly recognizable as one propagated by one of Mrs Banks's colleagues, Lord Raglan, ultimately based (like hers) upon those of Sir James Frazer, and systematically refuted within academe in the late 1960s.[2] The official pamphlet printed by the town avoided any specific schemes of origin, simply stating that it is a Celtic custom about four thousand years old.

Systematic research into its history has now been carried out by E. C. Cawte and Roy Judge, two of the same society's new breed of rigorous archival scholars.[3] The former revealed that the oldest known record dates from 1803, when the horse consisted of a stallion's skin and the man inside splashed water over the crowds from the town's pools. The author of the account thought that such an entertainment was 'not British', that is, Cornish; and indeed all previous descriptions of the county are barren of references to it, including some, like that of Richard Carew, which pay particular attention to its customs. In the course of the nineteenth century some details of the Padstow celebration were dropped, such as the tall maypole which had been erected annually,[4] and others were added, such as the second horse and the masks. Roy Judge discovered that the tradition had been little regarded until Francis Etherington, a close friend of Cecil Sharp, drew attention to it in 1907 as a colourful piece of folklore. In 1913 Thurstan Peter, following Frazer's ideas, suggested that it might be a remnant of pagan ritual, and this launched it on its way to becoming a tourist attraction. There is no doubt that the *frisson* of ancient and arcane ceremony which has been attached to it is in large part responsible for its popularity, and indeed the ferocity of local pride manifested in Padstow on May Day, the pounding of the drums, and the clumsy lunges of the great beasts do combine to produce an archaic atmosphere of disturbing or exhilarating intensity; even though there is now no reason to assign the tradition a greater age than the late eighteenth century.

The same is true of another surviving May Day hobby-horse, that which perambulates the West Somerset port of Minehead, eighty miles from Padstow. Its tour lasts for three evenings, and it consists of a heavy frame eight feet long and three feet broad, covered in a cloth painted with roundels and with coloured ribbons coating the top. The head of the man carrying it sticks out of the middle wearing a painted mask and a crested, ribbon-dangling hood. It has a seven-foot tail of ribboned rope, and until about 1880 had a snapping wooden head at the other end. Melodeon-players and a drummer accompany it. Its traditional role is to raise money from the spectators, and the inscription 'Sailors' Horse' traditionally painted on its side may suggest that it was a particular venture of the town's seamen. This is borne out by the earliest description, in 1830, when it was said that they, and the fishermen, used to bring out several hobby-horses each May Day and punish anybody who refused donations with a ceremonial beating. Similar mock-beasts are recorded along the same stretch of coastline in the nineteenth and early twentieth centuries, and since the 1960s a second 'horse' has appeared at Minehead.[5]

Model horses of this sort featured as common entertainments in early modern May-games, and it is no accident that those preserved to the present day should be found at that season. None the less the authors of the most comprehensive studies of them, Violet Alford and E. C. Cawte,[6] both considered them, rather hesitantly, to have originated as, or to have been more essentially, a midwinter custom. This was partly because it had no special seasonal association in early modern England, being provided at peak times of festivity. Thus, the royal court of Edward VI ordered thirteen hobby-horses for the Twelve Days in 1551–2, that of Elizabeth regularly provided sets of them for the same period, and the Crown officials in charge of Wisbech castle brought one out at Christmas 1594.[7] Gentry households obtained the same diversion by rewarding performers who toured them during 'the Christmas time'; for example two in Essex did so in different generations, the Catholic Petres in 1576 and the Puritan Barringtons in 1635.[8] Another reason for the tentative conclusion of Alford and Cawte, however, was their concurrence that the model horses should be grouped together with a set of customs recorded in the nineteenth century which consisted of the carrying of animal figures from house to house to earn money.

To take them in the order employed by E. C. Cawte, the first was the 'Hooden Horse', a carved wooden horse's head on a pole about four feet long, decorated with brasses and ribbons, clacking a jaw worked by a string and carried by a man covered in a dark cloth. It was accompanied by three to seven other men, one with a whip to lead it, one who tried to mount it, some musicians, and a man called 'Mollie', dressed as a woman and carrying a broom. The name has no proven derivation, but the simplest one is that it refers to the 'hooded' man carrying it. The custom was carried on at Christmas by farm labourers in eastern Kent, and especially the north-eastern corner from Swalecliffe to Ramsgate. It was recorded from 1807 to 1908 but revived at Canterbury in 1952 and now flourishes again in the Whitstable area under the mantle of the 'Ancient Order of Hoodeners' (the word is traditionally pronounced without the 'H'); its success has been due largely to the desire of many people in Kent to preserve a separate identity from London.[9] The same forces of local patriotism have helped a revival of the South Welsh 'Mari Lwyd', or Grey Mare, a horse's skull on a pole, decorated with ribbons and carried by a man covered with a white sheet which also partially concealed the skull. The latter often had glass eyes and a clashing jaw. An essential part of the custom was that the group with the 'mari' would sing outside a house to be admitted and the inhabitants sang back providing a reason for refusal. A common opening was:

> Wel dyma ni'n dwad,
> Gy-feillion di-niwad,
> I ofyn am gennad
> I ofyn am gennad
> I ofyn am gennad i ganu.
>
> (Well here we come,
> Innocent friends,
> To ask leave
> To ask leave
> To ask leave to sing.)

After a few verses both parties began to extemporize, and continued until one or the other gave up; if those on the outside cracked first, they would appeal for generosity. The 'mari' party would then be admitted and given food and drink, and the 'mare' would usually chase people. On departing, the team would sing a blessing, often:

> Dy-mun wn i'ch lawenydd,
> I gynnal blwyddyu newydd,
> Tra paro'r gwr i dincian cloch,
> Well, well, y bo'ch chwi beunydd'

> (We wish you joy,
> To sustain a new year,
> While the man continues to ring a bell,
> May you prosper more every day.)

The teams usually consisted of four to seven men, often wearing best clothes decorated with ribbons and coloured paper and operating around Christmas or (more rarely) New Year. Sometimes two dressed as Punch and Judy, and the latter carried a broom to sweep the house; there was also sometimes a fiddler. During its recorded history the custom was principally one of Glamorgan, both in the Vale and the mining valleys, with extensions into the Monmouthshire coal-producing area and the farmlands of Carmarthenshire and Cardiganshire. It is a distribution which overlaps not only some very different economic regions but also crosses the boundary between English and Welsh-speaking districts, although more a feature of the latter. The tradition was first recorded in 1800, and seems to have become defunct in the early twentieth century; but it was revived at Llangynwyd, on the edge of the vale of Glamorgan, in the middle of that century. During the 1980s it also reappeared around Caerphilly, Llantrisant, and St Fagans in the same borderland between Vale and mountains, partly because of the need of Glamorgan people to reaffirm a sense of cultural identity during the collapse of traditional industries, and partly because of the presence of the Welsh Folk Museum in this area.[10]

The Mari Lwyd also operated under a set of differing local names, such as 'The Horse's Head' in the English-speaking Gower peninsula, *Y Pen Ceffyl* (meaning the same) or *Y Wassel* (the Wassail), in Carmarthenshire, or *Aderyn bec y llwyd* (the Grey-Beaked Bird) in parts of West Glamorgan.[11] In addition she had an apparent sister in the nineteenth-century Isle of Man; the *Laare Vane* or 'White Mare', a horse's head carved of wood and painted white, also held by a man covered in a white sheet, which was brought into the communal room of a household after supper on New Year's Eve. It chased the girls, until it caught one, who had to assume the disguise and sit as an intricate stick dance was performed. In the end the fiddler was blindfolded and put through a mock beheading, after which his head was laid in the lap of the *Laare Vane* and he had to answer questions about the nature of the coming year.[12] There seems to be a genuinely old Celtic literary and folkloric motif here, of the magical properties of a severed head, and the *Laare* itself looked west to Ireland, where she had an exact equivalent during the same period. This was the *Lair Bhān* (pronounced in the same way and meaning just the same thing), a complete wooden framework of a horse with snapping mouth, covered in a white sheet and carried by a man. It was found in many districts of the south and east of the island at different festivals of the year, including Christmas;[13] just as the Manx *Laare* was also paraded in harvest celebrations.[14]

A similar Christmastide beast was the 'Old Horse', which was a feature of the coal-mining and iron-working area in which Derbyshire, Yorkshire, and Nottinghamshire meet. This was essentially the same as the Mari Lwyd, except that the head was more commonly wooden and the sheet could be of any colour. It was taken round by groups who sang versions of the fairly common popular song 'Poor Old Horse' as in this version from Derbyshire:

> It is a poor old horse,
> And he's knocking at your door,
> And if you please to let him in,
> He'll please you all I'm sure,
> Poor old horse, poor old horse.
>
> He was once a young horse,
> And in his youthful prime
> My master used to ride on him
> And thought him very fine.
> Poor old horse, poor old horse.
>
> And now that he's grown old,
> And nature doth decay,
> My master frowns upon him,
> And these words I've heard him say—
> Poor old horse, poor old horse
>
> His feeding it was once
> Of the best of corn and hay,
> That grew in yon fields,
> Or in the meadows gay.
> Poor old horse, poor old horse.
>
> But now that he's grown old,
> And scarcely can he crawl,
> He's forced to eat the coarsest grass
> That grows against the wall.
> Poor old horse, poor old horse.

There were five more verses. While the song was in progress, comedy was provided by attempts made by a blacksmith to shoe the 'horse', which the latter strenuously resisted. The struggle often spilled over into the audience. This northern 'horse' was first noticed in the 1840s, and seems to have become obsolete, again, in the early twentieth century.[15] A variant of the song reached the Gower peninsula of South Wales, where it was tacked onto the Mari Lwyd

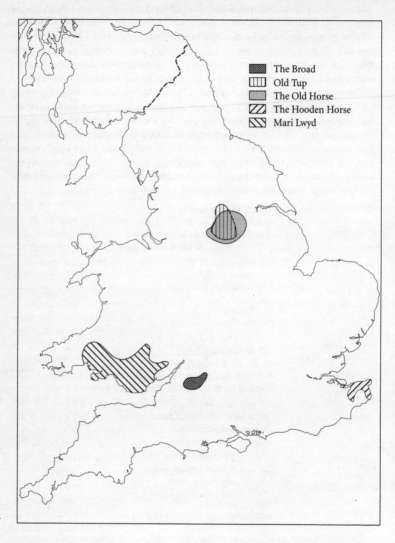

The Broad
Old Tup
The Old Horse
The Hooden Horse
Mari Lwyd

MAP 1. Range of nineteenth-century midwinter animal heads (after E. C. Cawte, *Ritual Animal Disguise*)

custom with the unique development that the death of the animal was acted out.[16]

In just the same area as the 'Old Horse', but much more closely concentrated where the three counties met, was the equivalent custom of the 'Old Tup'. Again it was a Christmas pursuit, with some performances at New Year, and again it involved an animal head on a staff worked by a man under a covering. This time, however, the beast was a sheep, usually made of wood, and the covering was a sack; sometimes children would dispense with the carving by putting one of their number in the sack and tying the top to represent horns or ears. It featured in a piece of drama staged by a team of four to six men or boys. First the group entered a dwelling and sang another famous traditional song, 'The Derby Tup' or 'Derby Ram', about an enormous ram. Sometimes this was enough, but more often the 'tup' was then slaughtered by a 'butcher', wearing an apron and carrying a knife. After a few moments the animal revived itself, and the presentation ended. In some places, characters out of the Mummers' Play introduced themselves at the finish, such as the doctor, Beelzebub, and Little Devil Doubt.[17] Again, the first certain reference to the custom is in 1845, but unlike all its equivalents it has continued to flourish, as a seasonal means by which adolescents earn extra money. In the 1970s there were forty-one groups recorded as performing it in north-east Derbyshire. It was still a working-class tradition, based strongly upon families and finding its audience in pubs and clubs. It also retained a considerable variety of styles of performance and some of characters, the main difference being that girls were now included. As such it represents the most noteworthy example of continuously performed regional 'folk-drama' in Britain.[18]

Neither survival nor revival has been the fate of the 'Broad', a bull's head carried about by Christmastide wassailers in a triangular area of the southern Cotswolds bounded by Stroud, Cricklade, and Chipping Sodbury. It was usually a stuffed skin or cardboard mask, and was mounted on a staff which was either beaten on the floor or used to poke the head at, or chase, spectators while a version of the famous Gloucestershire wassail song was rendered. The difference in this one was that the bull, and not a range of different farm animals, was saluted at the opening of each verse wishing success to the family. It often accompanied the more usual wassail bowl, and its records occupy the same trajectory as most of the similar customs, appearing in the 1830s and ending a hundred years later.[19] This concludes the catalogue of distinctive nineteenth-century regional traditions involving carrying of animal heads around at Christmastide; but there were several related practices in other contexts and at other times, such as the model horses which featured in some Dorset Mummers' Plays, some Lincolnshire Plough Plays, and Cheshire Soulers' Plays, and the Lancashire Easter version of the Old Horse.[20] Animal hides could be prominent in other midwinter customs, such as the Hebridean blessing rite examined earlier and the use of bulls' horns by some of the

Cornish 'goose-dancers', to be described below.[21] There is also the occasional magnificent enigma, notably the Dorset Ooser, a terrifying horned mask with human face, staring eyes, beard, and gnashing teeth, which was kept by farmers near Melbury Osmond in the chalk downs. It was brought out at village events until lost in 1897.[22] Before then antiquarians had already suggested that it was a relic of pagan worship,[23] and in the Reader's Digest encyclopedia of folklore it is described confidently as 'the idol of a former god of fertility'.[24] E. C. Cawte was far more cautious, pointing out that the mask was unique and that there was no reliable information about its use or origins.[25] Recently Peter Robson has reopened the matter, emphasizing that the object was too big and heavy to be carried, let alone worn, and speculating that it had originally been mounted in an urban carnival procession.[26] The name, which remains a mystery in itself, may be related to the Wiltshire dialect word 'Wooset', used for a horse's skull with deer's horns fixed upon it, set on the end of a pole. This was carried by youths in the Marlborough district until the 1830s, in noisy processions to mock neighbours whose partners were suspected of marital infidelity; horns were the traditional sign of a cuckold.[27] They were used in just the same fashion in Wiltshire and Somerset back in the early Stuart period,[28] and may well indicate the original association, if not the actual use, of the Ooser.

So then, what did all the local Christmastide animal-head customs signify? Their function was obviously to provide the poorer members of a community with another means of raising money or obtaining food and drink at midwinter. What is less obvious is why the means should have taken this particular form. Violet Alford, of course, was in no doubt; to her all the local forms descended form a widespread pagan ritual to honour wild beasts as symbols of the fertility of the sleeping earth.[29] Other folklore-collectors, from Sidney Addy in 1907 to Brian Rose and Theo Brown in the 1950s, agreed that they must be remnants of prehistoric animal cults.[30] After 1970 a new note of caution began to be sounded. E. C. Cawte thought that pagan origins for the customs were still possible, but could not be demonstrated, while Luke Lyon subsequently stated flatly that there was such a total lack of evidence for the theory that it was of no practical value.[31] The same drift of feeling is present in studies of individual practices. In 1943 Iorwerth Peate could insist that 'no one doubts that Mari Lwyd is a pre-Christian horse ceremony', while adding that it has become united with a standard South Welsh wassailing custom.[32] To Trefor Owen thirty years later, the priorities were reversed, so that the wassail appeared to be the basic activity onto which the horse had been grafted, perhaps from the hobby-horse of the early modern morris dance. Pagan origins were dismissed with the simple comment that none of the surviving accounts of the 'mari' implied any ritual or religious significance.[33]

The earlier writers who spoke confidently about such origins were greatly encouraged by the existence of a series of denunciations, issued by churchmen between the fourth and eleventh centuries, of popular practices at the tradi-tional midwinter festivals. These consisted pre-eminently of dressing up in the skins of animals, especially stags but also bulls, and also sometimes of 'making the old woman'. In the former case, where details are given (which is rare), the animal hide and head is usually being donned by somebody, but there is occasionally a hint that the beast is a model being taken about like the modern British and Irish animal figures. The latter reference was sometimes clearly to ritual transvestism, of the sort often noted in British Christmastide customs, but at others it might have been to a hideous effigy representing winter and death, called 'the Old Woman' and ritually destroyed in parts of Italy, Sicily, Spain, and the Balkans until the eighteenth and nineteenth centuries.[34] The various clerical invectives were scrupulously searched out and listed by Sir Edmund Chambers in an appendix to his influential volumes on medieval drama, published in 1903.[35] They originate from Italy, Spain, Greece, Africa, France, and Germany, although mainly from the first of those; there is a possibility that some of the directives concerned were merely repeating for-mulas found in others. For those who wish to use them as evidence for the origins of the modern British and Irish animal heads, there are two problems. The first is that none occurs after the very early eleventh century, although the publications of churchmen become still more abundant (and their anxiety about popular superstition remains constant). The second is that none of these texts refers to Britain.

The former objection hardly mattered to folklorists such as Violet Alford to whom (following Frazer) popular culture was something essentially unchang-ing and essentially illiterate, so that a reference from the tenth century (and indeed from a different country) could be quite feasibly used to interpret one from the nineteenth despite the lack of any to fill the gulf. The latter one was, however, long apparently contradicted by a pair of scholarly errors. The first concerns the Penitential issued by Theodore of Tarsus, archbishop of Canter-bury in the late seventh century. About two centuries later it was copied by an unknown cleric working somewhere in what is now France or Germany, who made his own additions. One was a particularly vivid condemnation of the wearing of animal skins at midwinter celebrations. The editors of the standard text of the 'real', English, Penitential of Theodore, working in 1871, did not confuse it with the other,[36] but within twenty years two respected scholars writing popular works had done so.[37] Chambers was too good a researcher to make the mistake, but his identification of it was buried in an appendix and noted by only the most scrupulous readers such as Cawte.[38] As a result the work of the 'Pseudo-Theodore' has been taken as evidence for Anglo-Saxon or prehistoric British religion right up to the 1980s.[39] Chambers himself, how-ever, did accept a second apparent reference from an English source, a letter from St Aldhelm in the mid-seventh century which speaks of the former worship of the *ermulus* (a word which seems unique to this source) and the stag in pagan shrines.[40] While good evidence for a stag cult among the pre-

Christian Anglo-Saxons, the passage has absolutely no connection with seasonal rites, at midwinter or any other time.

There is, however, one surviving folk custom which can be said to link the epochs of the early medieval denunciations, the Tudor and Stuart hobby-horse, and the nineteenth-century animal heads: the famous Horn Dance at Abbots Bromley in Staffordshire's Forest of Needwood. Although now performed on the first Monday after 4 September, it was in the early seventeenth century an entertainment of the Christmas season, and the date was probably changed when it was revived in the early eighteenth century, after a lapse of up to a hundred years. In the nineteenth, the dancers acquired their present costumes and the addition of a man–woman who was subsequently called Maid Marian. Revival and preservation was made much easier by the existence of a famous description of the event as it would have been in about 1630, published in 1686 by the antiquary Robert Plot: It was then

called the Hobby-horse dance, from a person that carried the image of a horse between his legs, made of thin boards, and in his hand a bow and arrow, which passing through a hole in the bow, and stopping upon a shoulder it had in it, made a snapping noise as he drew it to and fro, keeping time with the music; with this man danced 6 others, carrying on their shoulders as many reindeer's heads, three of them painted white and three red, with the arms of the chief families (viz. of Paget, Bagot and Wells) to whom the revenues of the town chiefly belonged, depicted on the palms of them, with which they danced the Hays, and other country dances. To this Hobby-horse dance there also belonged a pot, which was kept by turns, by 4 or 5 of the chief of the town, whom they called reeves, who provided cakes and ale to put in this pot; all people who had any kindness for the good intent of the institution of the sport; giving a pence for themselves and their families; and so foreigners too, that came to see it; with which money (the charge of the cakes and ale being defrayed) they not only repaired their church but kept their poor too.[41]

Apart from the later developments noted above, the antlers are now painted white and brown, and no longer bear coats of arms, and the dance is a special set one. The antlers are genuine, but are (and may always have been) fitted into carved wooden heads held on short staves. The connection of the dance with parish finance seems to have been broken at the Civil War, when the lapse in the custom began.[42] The date of the earliest record of the latter has now been pushed back to 1532, when it was already a well-established tradition; the hobby-horse alone is mentioned, but the antlers may have been present already and passed over in silence.[43] The latter have at last been submitted to a proper examination by naturalists and to chemical dating procedures, and were found to be, indeed, very old, for they were worn by reindeer which had been castrated, that is, domesticated, and lived at some time in the eleventh century.[44] This does, however, make them even more of a puzzle, as wild reindeer were certainly extinct in England and Wales, and probably in Scotland too, by that period; and there are no records of or archaeological traces of domesticated herds. The antlers must therefore have been imported from Scandinavia, or even further afield, at any time between the eleventh and the seventeenth centuries. The priority which the Tudor and Stuart references give to the hobby-horse in the custom strongly suggests that this was the original component onto which the antlers were grafted as an exotic extra; thereby, indeed, making it unusual enough to ensure its notice in Plot's work, and its revival and survival. It has long been regarded as an archetypal relic of a pagan custom, and this plays a large part in the importance attached to it in the present. Perhaps unsurprisingly, it was Violet Alford (again) who made this view an orthodoxy of folklore studies for many years, following a note published by her in 1933.[45] As E. C. Cawte has pointed out, however,[46] it is not an archetype but an anomaly, because it is so completely unique, not only in Britain but in Europe, that it does not even remotely resemble any other known custom, past or present, and cannot be taken as representative of anything. It is, in effect, an Abbots Bromley original, and all the more worthy of respect for that.

On the other hand, once the dance is stripped of its antlers it has a perfectly recognizable context, that of a north Midland tradition of hobby-horse dances employed to raise money for parish funds, which is well-attested in the early Tudor period. Virtually all the information comes from churchwardens' accounts, of which only relatively few survive for this time in the region concerned. Enough do, however, to suggest that the custom was especially well established in Staffordshire and carried on in Nottinghamshire and Northamptonshire as well.[47] In the parishes concerned, it took the part of the church ales, May games, Plough Monday collections, and Hocktide bindings which were equivalent fund-raising events during the same age elsewhere in England. At Abbots Bromley, as said, the dance was at Christmastide (specifically New Year and Twelfth Day). At Stafford it was apparently upon St Nicholas's Night (6 December) in the 1520s and on New Year's Day a century later, as the feast of Nicholas was abolished at the Reformation.[48] The performance there included a fool, in a special coat. At Culworth in Northamptonshire 'hobby horse night' was almost certainly 1 January, and the 'horse' had a painted covering.[49] The performance at Holme Pierrepont in the Trent valley of Nottinghamshire was 'with lights', which also suggests a winter season,[50] and for the other places there is no reliable information on the matter.[51] We have here, therefore, good evidence of an important regional midwinter custom. How long it had been established before the first record of it in the 1520s is impossible to say, but it seems generally to have been suppressed, along with most festive fund-raising for churches, in the Protestant Reformation of the duke of Somerset's Government in 1547–9.[52] At Stafford and Abbots Bromley it was apparently revived later and came to grief there again in the general abandonment of parish festivity following the condemnations made of it by the Long Parliament.[53] The Horn Dance, however, rose again, probably because of the glamour of those remarkable antlers, and survives, from this perspective, as a single living reminder of north Midland winter revelry half a millennium ago.

This consideration brings the present enquiry, at last, to the history of the hobby-horse itself; and here again the main evidence has been assembled by E. C. Cawte. The name itself is of no help, being a tautology as a 'hobby' was just a word used from the fourteenth century in England to denote a small horse. It is Anglo-Saxon, or at any rate Germanic, in origin, but the first known record of the expression, and object, of hobby-horse is in a Welsh poem by Gruffudd Gryg, writing in Anglesey in the latter half of the same century. He called it by its English name and mocked it for having been a much-admired recent novelty, though it was actually 'a miserable pair of lath legs, kicking stiffly'. In 1460 the London parish of St Andrew Hubbard paid a child of one of its members 'for dancing with the "hobye" horse', as an unusual entertainment. The third certain reference is in the Cornish play *Beunans Meriasek*, completed in 1504, which speaks of a 'hebyhors' accompanied by *cowetha*, 'comrades'.[54] From this year on, municipal, parochial, household, and literary records of the object multiply rapidly. Of these three early records, all that can be said with confidence is that a model horse with human 'rider' or operator was a popular entertainment in Britain by the late fourteenth century, having originated in England and reached North Wales by that period. It was then a novelty to the Welsh, but there is no evidence of whether it was also one to the English, for the time concerned was the first in which records of seasonal customs begin to exist in anything more than an occasional and accidental form. All that can be said is that the invectives of early medieval churchmen on the Continent, cited above, do not seem to mention horses. It is possible that the popularity of the tournament, from the twelfth century onward, may have inspired the entertainment of a model steed controlled by a human rider, but this is pure conjecture.

As said above, the hobby-horse remained popular at both the main festive times of year, Christmastide revels and summer games, all through the sixteenth century and into the early Stuart age. It soon became an almost integral part of the morris dance, and remained so until the 1630s, when horse and dance came apart again until the Victorian revival of May games in a Tudor image. The various references make clear that it was primarily a comic entertainment, but one demanding considerable skill, to imitate the movements and noises of a real horse, and also stamina, as the framework must often have been quite heavy. All the extant illustrations and detailed descriptions of the latter reveal a structure sitting about the rider's hips so that his body stuck up out of the centre as if he were riding a genuine horse. The model was usually caparisoned with a cloth just like a steed in a tournament, increasing (but far from clinching) the suggestion of origins made above. That suggestion gains a little further substance from the general loss of interest in the entertainment from the 1630s onward, as tournaments finally ceased to be a part of national culture.[55] The horses at Padstow, Minehead, and Abbots Bromley are based upon this 'tourney' variety of construction. By contrast, none of the surviving early modern pictures shows a pole-and-head animal, with the operator concealed under a sheet, of the sort commonly used in the nineteenth-century local customs. It is still possible, nevertheless, that some (or many) of the less elaborate hobby-horses of the period were of this design. Plot's description of the seventeenth-century Abbots Bromley horse sounds somewhat like it, even if the later version was different. There is also a reference by the Scottish poet Sir David Lindsay, in his *Satyre of the Thrie Estaits*, to a mock-animal in an interlude performed at the royal court at Linlithgow palace in 1540, which seems to portray a pole-and-head construction.[56] All this, however, is conjecture, and the eccentricity of the Linlithgow case is highlighted by the fact that neither hobby-horses nor the carrying of animal heads from door to door seem to be recorded in Scotland at any period.

So, we are left with three separate groups of customs: the midwinter animal disguises condemned by early medieval churchmen on the Continent, the fashion for the hobby-horse as an entertainment in late medieval and early modern southern Britain, and the local traditions of taking animal heads about in nineteenth-century Britain and Ireland. There seem to be no demonstrable links between them, and after the most diligent possible search for some, E. C. Cawte was reduced to crying out that 'there must have been *something* going on'.[57] In the end he fell back upon Violet Alford's favourite device (and one that does deserve serious consideration) of comparative folklore drawn from across Europe. He drew attention to the common presence of a man–woman in the modern British customs, to the condemnation of transvestism as well as animal disguise by the medieval clerics, and to the way in which mock-beasts in modern European folk customs often chased young women, to suggest that 'it seems beyond reasonable doubt that the animals were once intended to distribute fertility'.[58] This explanation is not susceptible of disproof, and there is nothing inherently unattractive about it; there are, however, grounds for 'reasonable doubt'. All the features noted may owe their widespread and long-lived popularity to functional value, because two of the simplest ways of expressing festive licence and signalling the existence of legitimate misrule have always been for the sexes to cross-dress or for people to put on animal skins or masks. Both indicate the suspension of the normal. Likewise, in societies in which most of this formalized misbehaviour is carried on by young men, young women are always going to be the favourite objects of attention.

Looking again at the available evidence, some new, though still tentative, suggestions can be made. There seems to be no way of making any direct connection between the animal disguises cited in the early medieval clerical complaints and the early modern hobby-horse. Evidence from the intervening period is certainly so meagre that the problem may be one of surviving data, but there is also a mismatch between the two phenomena. On the other hand, it is possible to suggest (though with some difficulty) a relationship between the Tudor and Stuart fashion for the hobby-horse and the later animal heads.

The comparable case is the morris, which having been a nation-wide craze in the Tudor and early Stuart periods gradually evolved thereafter into a set of sharply delineated regional traditions, associated very often with areas peripheral to its original, metropolitan heartland such as Wales and its Marches, and Lancashire and Cheshire. If the hobby-horse did do the same, often turning into simpler, head-and-pole, forms, then it is possible to see patterns in the distribution; the survival of the 'tournament' horse in the south-west, the development of the isolated 'hooden horse' in East Kent and of the linked dramas of Old Tup and the Old Horse in the Sheffield region, and the evolution of the 'white' or 'grey' horses of southern Ireland, South Wales, and Man. The Cotswold 'Broad', by contrast, may have developed out of the wassailing song itself. All, like the other midwinter customs of wassailing, carolling, blessing, dancing, and acting of plays from household to household, not only provided money and cheer for the poorer members of a community, but helped to bond that community together at a time of year when the weather hardly permitted large festive assemblies.

Furthermore, the nature of the entertainment seems also to have remained consistent between the hobby-horse and the later animal disguises. All depended for effect upon the same mixture of clowning and dexterity; all likewise provided opportunities for rather *risqué* and exciting licensed misconduct, as the model beast kicked, gambolled, and pretended to attack. E. C. Cawte shrewdly commented that the experience of being inside a hooden horse has an odd character of its own, involving a sense of slackening personal responsibility for what occurs as the role of playing the creature takes over.[59] The present author, who has had that experience, must agree, and testify to the nervousness in the laughter of most spectators at the approach of something that is, and yet is not, a human being. As was said earlier of the celebrations at Padstow, these customs do have a way of communicating something genuinely archaic, whatever their actual age.

9

MISRULE

༄༅

THE theme of festive disguise and of similar suspensions or reversals of normality at Christmastide has been sounded with increasing strength in the last few chapters. It is time now to deal with it directly in its remaining manifestations. From one end of nineteenth-century Britain to another there were districts in which young people, and sometimes adults, used fancy dress as a means both to personal enjoyment and to profit. In the Shetland Isles the 'skeklers' or 'gulicks' were abroad during the evenings of the Twelve Days; youths dressed in straw costumes with conical hats, handkerchiefs covering their faces. They would fire a gun on approaching a farm, and if the proprietor wished to make them welcome an answering shot would be fired. Once admitted to a home, the skeklers would dance and be rewarded with refreshments and a little money.[1] 'Guisers' were out at New Year across most of eastern Scotland from the Sutherland coast to the Lothians and the Tweed valley, including Edinburgh. Their disguises included straw heads, ribbons, and blackened faces. Doors were often left unlocked for them, and if they entered a household of their own social rank they sometimes claimed the right to kiss every woman in the room.[2] At Golspie in Sutherland the youngsters 'guised' at Christmas, the girls in the clothes of adult women and black muslin masks, and the boys daubed with charcoal or flour and wearing long overcoats, large hats, and false whiskers. They went from house to house singing comic songs and dancing for pennies. New Year's Eve was reserved for misbehaviour, such as playing practical jokes and beating noisily on pails.[3] In the Border district of Roxburghshire, the Christmas dancers were adult, and their performances real displays of agility; comedy was provided by 'a person called Bessie the besom, dressed in petticoats and disguised as an old woman; and another called the Fool, in a grotesque costume. These two collected donations from the bystanders.[4]

Similar pastimes were recorded in nineteenth-century England. 'Guising' of some sort went on in Hertfordshire.[5] The same term was used in the Uttoxeter area of Staffordshire, where the information is more detailed; working men went round pubs with blackened or reddened faces, performing a rhyme and passing round a hat for pennies. The patter was loosely based on a Mummers' Play, ending in the offer of a nip of drink to a man lying on the floor with the words, 'Take a little of my nick-nack, get up Jack and walk'. Other lines included 'In come Mary Ann with a frying pan', apparently an echo of the part of Beelzebub; but the whole seems to have made little sense to actors or audience, and was really a piece of nonsense aided by the fact that the performers immediately spent their takings on drink at each place.[6] At the west Yorkshire industrial town of Bradford, working-class men and boys in costumes and with blackened faces invaded middle-class neighbourhoods on New Year's morning. They entered houses without warning and expected to receive food and drink as of right; in 1868 a youth knocked down a couple at their door for refusing it. What had presumably begun as a tradition by which communal solidarity was reaffirmed had become one of social confrontation and aggression.[7]

During the Christmas season the pubs and wealthier households of the Cambridgeshire and Huntingdonshire Fens were visited by the 'Molly Dancers'. These were young labourers in fancy dress ('Molly' like 'Bessie' being a common term for a transvestite), who performed a morris and other dances to a fiddle and a dulcimer or concertina. Those who had no money to spare for them gave them hot beer or elderberry wine with sugar and spices.[8] The equivalent in west Cornish towns were the 'guise-dancers', sometimes corrupted to 'goose-dancers'. All were masked, and some wore bulls' horns or carried hobby-horses. The tradition seems to have undergone the same metamorphosis, as local society grew apart, as at Bradford. Around 1800 they were welcomed as entertainers and poor neighbours, but by the latter part of the century 'they often behaved in such an unruly manner that women and children were afraid to venture out. If the doors of the houses were not locked, they would enter uninvited, and stay, playing all kinds of antics, until money was given to them to go away'. As a result they were banned at Penzance by the corporation around 1880,[9] but lingered for more than ten years more at St Ives, where one observer described them as 'a lawless mob, who go about yelling and hooting in an unearthly manner'. The masks provided an opportunity for anonymous attacks to settle grudges.[10] Accounts of the Isles of Scilly in the late eighteenth century reveal either an earlier and less polarized version of the custom or else a more relaxed parallel to it in a smaller and more cohesive society. There the young men and women exchanged clothes or dressed in parti-coloured garments divided down the middle. They danced in the streets during the Twelve Days and held parties in the evenings. Thus, said a commentator in 1796, 'by this sort of sport according to yearly custom and toleration, there is a spirit of wit and drollery kept up among the people'.[11]

What must be clear from the above is that festival disguise may in places have been an expression of merry-making, but was generally, by the nineteenth century, another part of the considerable number of ritualized means of making money or earning hospitality at midwinter. That this was always so is suggested by the number of payments to 'mummers' in early modern household accounts. Into the same pattern fits one of the most curious, and celebrated, of Christmastide 'ritual reversals', the hunting, killing, and display of wrens. The wren is the smallest bird native to Europe, and to kill it has generally been regarded as an especially craven and unlucky act, a belief equally well recorded among the ancient Greeks and Romans as among modern Italians, Spaniards, French, Germans, Dutch, Danes, Swedes, English, Welsh, and Scots.[12] To the early medieval Irish writer Cormac of Cashel, one derivation of the Old Irish name for the wren, *dreean*, was from '*drui-én*, druid-bird, i.e. a bird that makes prophecy'. In another early Irish text, the Life of St Moling, it is called 'the magus bird, as some take auguries from it'.[13] During the nineteenth century it was observed that at certain places in the south of France and in the British Isles the wren was killed at the Christmas season by groups of youths who would take it about, displayed, and ask for money. Sir James Frazer regarded this as a classic case of the sacrifice at an annual festival of an animal normally considered to be sacred, of which there are various ancient and ethnographic cases.[14] His theory may well be correct, but is not susceptible of proof or disproof because of the total lack of any record of the hunt in any ancient or medieval literature. It may have been instead a striking demonstration of a festive suspension of norms, developed at a time when the old superstition about killing the bird had decayed to the point at which it could be mocked.

In the nineteenth century the centre of the custom was Ireland, from which it may indeed have spread along the trade routes to France as well as Britain. It was found across the whole land with the exception of most of Ulster, an anomaly which may reflect the denser British settlement there.[15] It was first recorded in Ireland by Thomas Crofton Croker in 1824, as being well established in the form in which it was to endure; on St Stephen's Day groups of 'wren-boys' went from house to house seeking money, carrying 'a holly bush adorned with ribbons, and having many wrens depending from it'. They sang a song with many local variations but almost always beginning:

> The Wren, the Wren, the King of the birds
> St Stephen's Day was caught in the furze...[16]

Occasionally in the later decades of the century the bird was carried in a box, and increasingly it became incidental to the entertainment offered by the lads, of dancing, songs, clowning, or mock combats. By the twentieth century it had all but vanished, and the 'wren-boys' themselves were following it. They survive, however, in districts such as the Dingle peninsula as a self-conscious part of 'folk' heritage, and the song or rhyme is still very familiar to Irish children. It seems to have originated in English, as the few Irish versions are translations, but this need not indicate that the tradition itself began in areas of English settlement.[17]

That tradition is recorded in Britain most densely in areas exposed to direct contact with eastern and southern Ireland: the Isle of Man and West Wales. The Welsh records are, in fact, the earliest of all, beginning with an account of it in late seventeenth-century Pembrokeshire by Edward Lluyd. It took place there upon Twelfth Night, two or three young men carrying the tiny corpse 'in a bier with ribbons' and singing carols. They paid special attention to the houses of sweethearts, but visited most where there was a chance of money.[18] Thereafter versions of wren-hunting songs were noted all over Wales, but the custom itself remained confined to Pembrokeshire and adjacent parts of Cardiganshire and Carmarthenshire, where it occupied the niche filled elsewhere among the South Welsh by wassailing and Mari Lwyd. As such it flourished all through the eighteenth and early nineteenth centuries. Over most of its range, the use of a bier was retained, but in the Englishry of Pembrokeshire the hunters had by the nineteenth century taken to putting the bird or birds alive into a special box with a glass window at either end, two candles stuck at the sides, and coloured ribbons or paper hung from the top. It was carried along slung on two long poles. The custom also now obtained on St Stephen's Day as well as Twelfth Night. The beauty of taking the wrens alive was not merely that it displayed superior skill but that they could be released afterwards and so the hunters could counter growing moral objections to the custom. In the last stages of the later, as in Ireland, the actual bird was dispensed with altogether and replaced by a decorated bush; but even in this form it had totally vanished by the 1920s.[19]

Among the Manx the practice was recorded on Christmas Day in the late eighteenth century. Servants would attend a midnight service at the end of the Eve, and then hunt the birds while they roosted in the early hours of the morning. After daybreak they would hoist the body of a successful catch, wings spread, on top of a pole, and carry it from house to house chanting a rhyme and gathering money. At the end they buried it in a churchyard, reverently, and danced. By the early nineteenth century the date had been shifted to St Stephen's feast, so that Irish, Welsh, and Manx hunts were all in harmony. The corpse was hung by its legs at the centre of two crossed hoops decorated with evergreens and ribbons. Donors of money were given a feather each, as a charm against shipwreck, and the bird was now buried in wasteland instead of consecrated ground. The song used was a version of the usual Irish one:

> We hunted the wren for Robin the Bobbin,
> We hunted the wren for Jack of the Can,
> We hunted the wren for Robin the Bobbin
> We hunted the wren for everyone.
>
> The wren, the wren, the King of all birds
> St Stephen's Day was caught in the furze;
> Although he is little, his family's great,
> I pray you, good landlady, give us a treat.

As elsewhere, the use of an actual wren vanished before the custom did. On St Stephen's Day 1911 parties of boys were still out all over the island singing of the death of the bird but bearing poles decked with ivy and streamers. Despite this metamorphosis, the custom died out in Man also during the next couple of decades, a victim of the general British drift away from ritualized begging.[20]

In addition, the vagaries of fortune carried it to a number of isolated districts of Britain. It is no surprise to find it in nineteenth-century Galloway, the area of Scotland closest to eastern Ireland; as Christmas had been suppressed in that region, the hunt was held on New Year's morn instead.[21] Nor is it remarkable that a version of the Irish practice, on St Stephen's Day, was carried on at the royal naval base of Devonport, which a large number of Irish sailors must have visited. A wonderful Chinese Whispers effect during its transmission resulted in the rhyme beginning 'The Ram, the Ram, the King of the Jews', and a pair of ram's horns being carried round in a bush instead of the bird.[22] It is a mystery, however, that copies of the Irish wren hunt should have seeded themselves in small areas of Suffolk (on St Valentine's Day),[23] Essex (a perfect facsimile, including the song),[24] and Oxfordshire.[25] It is possible to speculate that Irish migrant labour may have carried them; but there is no evidence for this, and the matter serves to illustrate how much of a puzzle the nature of Victorian popular culture can still be.

All these were traditions of reversal and legitimate misbehaviour centred upon working people and best recorded at a relatively recent date. It is time now to turn to equivalents recorded among social, political, and religious elites at a much more remote period. The institution in medieval Europe which consistently left the largest number of records was the Church, and they testify abundantly to how by the twelfth century some of its clergy had developed a custom which (to certain of their superiors all too obviously) evoked the anarchic spirit of the ancient Saturnalia and Kalendae. This was the Feast of Fools, or of Asses, or of Sub-Deacons, essentially a celebration of the lower clergy of cathedral chapters who held only minor orders. By the year 1200 it was familiar in France, which remained its stronghold for the rest of the Middle Ages, until its gradual repression in the fifteenth century and its complete abolition in the sixteenth. From France it rapidly spread into Flanders and into Britain. At its inception it was an exercise in Christian humility on the part of the higher clergy, whereby they handed over to the lowest the leadership in religious ceremonies at the time of the New Year feast. Soon, however, it spread backwards into the holy days between Christmas and New Year and began to involve burlesques of the same rites.[26]

Its history in England can, therefore, be traced through the complaints of pious prelates. In 1236 and 1238 Robert Grosseteste, bishop of Lincoln, forbade in his diocese the practice of inverting the proper order of worship and pretending to praise demons at the New Year. During the fourteenth century his example was followed by four other churchmen. In 1331 the dean of Wells prohibited displays held by his chapter between Christmas and Holy Innocents, in which costumed figures 'exercised silly pranks and gesticulations'. Two years later John de Grandisson, bishop of Exeter, began a thirty-year campaign to stop similar japes in his own cathedral. It appears that on the feast of Holy Innocents some of its clergy, assisted by the choirboys, were putting on masks and staging irreverent mimes. Later they took to throwing mud at each other during services on the three holy days after Christmas, causing the congregation to become 'dissolved into disorderly laughter and illicit mirth'. In 1390 the reigning archbishop of Canterbury, William Courtenay, visited the Lincoln diocese and was angered to find that some clerics were putting on lay clothes at New Year and interrupting services with rude songs and games. His example may have inspired his colleague at York, Archbishop Thomas, to forbid similar high jinks at Beverley Minister in the following year. These were, however, a set of unusually high-minded and energetic churchmen, and the silence on the issue which obtains otherwise may conceal a widespread toleration of it by most. The occasional cathedral inventory lends support to this presumption; one for Salisbury in 1222 includes costumes for the 'Feast of Fools', as does one for St Paul's in 1425. Nevertheless, the custom is not recorded in any source after the latter date, and it does seem that by the early fifteenth century opinion had at last decisively swung against it in England.[27]

This result may have been assisted by complete acceptance of a much more decorous, and endearing, development from the same tradition; the institution of the boy bishop.[28] It grew directly out of a custom settled in the Church in Germany by the early tenth century, whereby the junior clergy and assistants of cathedrals were honoured by being allowed to hold processions on the successive holy days after Christmas; deacons on St Stephen's, priests on St John's, and choirboys on Holy Innocents, the commemoration of the slaughtered children of Bethlehem. This quickly spread west through France to Britain, where it remained standard throughout the high and later Middle Ages. In the twelfth century the choristers' feast became linked with the burgeoning cult of St Nicholas of Myra, patron of children. Before the end of that century it had become a practice to choose a cathedral choirboy, either on the feast of the saint (6 December) or upon Holy Innocents, to impersonate the bishop and to lead the boys' procession as well as presiding over other parts of the religious service. This was known throughout most of western Christendom for the rest of the medieval period, but seems to have been especially popular in Britain, where it rapidly took root at all stages of religious organization. Its existence at Salisbury cathedral by 1222 is implied by the note, in an inventory, of a gold ring for use at the 'feast of boys'. Three years later a prebendary presented a little mitre to St Paul's for use in the ceremony, while the earliest record of all in England may be a statute of York Minister, probably written by 1221, giving the boy bishop the duty of finding rushes for the Christmas and Epiphany feasts. Within a century, the tradition had reached parish level, for Edward I, on his way to Scotland, was met by the 'bishop' from Hedon chapel, in the Tyne valley, who said vespers before the King while his fellow boys sang. Once among the Scots, the same monarch was entertained by another belonging to the royal chapel at Dunfermline palace; whether or not he introduced it to Scotland, this is the first reference to the institution there.[29] As rites of reversal went, it was much more easy to regulate and control than those of adult men; but in any case it was only in one sense a ceremony of festive inversion. In another, it was a reaffirmation of Christ's own teaching about the special relationship of children to the kingdom of heaven, and of the Church's especial respect for innocence and purity—a celebration of norms.

It is therefore attested at every cathedral in Britain at which a medieval archive has survived,[30] though with some local variety in practice. At Salisbury the choirboys retained the right to elect the 'bishop' from among their number. He appeared after vespers on St John's Day, leading the choristers to the high altar dressed in his full episcopal robes while his companions wore silk copes (mantles) like higher clergy, carried candles, and sang. He censed the altar and images while the genuine bishop (if present) and the chapter followed the procession bearing books and candles as the boys normally did. The lads then took the stalls normally reserved for the chapter, and their 'bishop' presided over all services for the next twenty-four hours, except mass itself. At St Paul's the higher clergy reformed procedures in 1263 to reserve the choice of the boy bishop to themselves and to excuse themselves from menial functions while he reigned. The boy was expected to lead a cavalcade through London to bless the populace and to preach a sermon; in 1329 an almoner took care to collect into a single volume all those delivered in his time. He may indeed have written them, as did other adult clerics at other cathedrals in later times, utilizing the occasion to display a sardonic wit at the expense of the world of maturity. The boy bishop of Salisbury also went on tour of the district, at least to the homes of prominent clergy, although after 1443 he was forbidden to have an adult escort or for the boys with him to carry staves (one vicar in his retinue that year having brained a townsman in a quarrel). *En route*, he collected money from hosts and spectators, raising in 1459 the large sum of 89s. 11d. By that time too the staff of the St Paul's boy had been fixed for perambulations, at two chaplains, two taper-bearers, five clerks, two vergers, and four canons. At Winchester and York he was allowed the supreme privilege of saying mass, and at the latter cathedral the 'Bairn Bishop' was apparently the most hard-worked of his kind. The statutes, uniquely, prescribed that he had to be good-looking and have a fine voice. After 1481 his mitre was of cloth of gold. His staff consisted of a tenor singer, leading his horse, a steward, a preacher, a 'middle voice singer', and two others, with whom he perambulated Yorkshire for a fortnight on a sixty-mile circuit. *En route* they visited and sang at religious houses and noble and gentry seats and collected money. The boy was allowed to pocket whatever was left after the deduction of expenses and the cost of a large supper on the nights of St John or Holy Innocents; a typical menu for the latter around 1500 consisted of pears, woodcock, plover, fieldfares, and smaller birds.

The custom was also observed at major abbeys which included schools, such as Westminster, Bury St Edmunds, Winchester, and Holyrood (Edinburgh). The Westminster boy was clad in a jewelled mitre and velvet robes embroidered with gold, and the one from Winchester traditionally visited St

Mary's convent, with a retinue of companions dressed as girls, to sing and dance before the good sisters. In the thirteenth century, indeed, it had been a practice for nunneries themselves to let the sacred offices and prayers be performed by girls on Holy Innocents' Day, but this met with the disapproval of Archbishop Peckham in 1279. In 1526 Bishop Richard Nicke of Norwich suppressed the 'Christmas Abbess' at Carrow Nunnery.[31] The little 'bishops' also featured at wealthy collegiate churches like St Peter's, Canterbury, Beverley Minister in Yorkshire's East Riding, and Ottery St Mary in East Devon, and educational establishments such as Eton, and the local grammar schools at Rotherham in Yorkshire and at Canterbury. The master of Aberdeen Grammar went from house to house in the city on St Nicholas's Day with its own 'bishop', collecting money which in 1542 the corporation fixed at a minimum contribution of 4s. Scots per household; all proceeds went to the school.[32] Boys performed the same office at the university colleges of Magdalen and All Souls Oxford, and King's, Cambridge. At King's it was associated with the feast of St Nicholas, and an inventory of 1506 describes the whole costume: a white wool coat, a scarlet gown with its hood furred with white ermine, fine knitted gloves, gold rings, a crozier, and a mitre of white damask with a rose, a star, and a cross embroidered upon it in pearls and green and red gems. The wearer presided at services and at theatrical performances. On that feast, at least from the time of Henry VII, English monarchs presented money to their own 'St Nicholas Bishop', apparently chosen from the choristers of the Chapel Royal. At least one great aristocrat, the fifth earl of Northumberland, kept a 'bishop' of his own on Holy Innocents' Day, with his outfit preserved in store for the rest of the year.[33] Scottish royalty preferred to be generous to those sent forth by others, so that James IV gave money to a total of six from different institutions, annual sums going to the boys of Holyrood Abbey and the High Kirk of Edinburgh.[34]

The popularity of the custom is illustrated particularly well by its transplanting to parish churches, which (as said) had taken place by the end of the thirteenth century. At least seven London parishes (none dedicated to St Nicholas) had adopted them by the 1520s.[35] In 1485–6, for example, that of St Mary at Hill paid out 'for a mitre for a bishop at St. Nicholastide, garnished with silver and enamel, and pearls and counterfeit stones', plus 'six copes for children' to process with him.[36] At Bristol in the same period it was indeed the church of St Nicholas which sent one out into the city on his feast, accompanied by eight banners, while a white cloth was hung before the statue of the saint. The mayor and corporation attended morning and evening services at the church and listened to a choral concert by the boy and his companions at the mayor's counter between.[37] The 'bishop' attached to the major Norwich parish of St Peter Mancroft had four attendant children,[38] the one in the Suffolk arable farming village of Boxford had a crozier and a 'coat of red',[39] and the one at Ludlow, capital of the Welsh Marches, wore a 'short scarlet gown'.[40] They are also recorded at parishes in Cambridge, Nottingham,

Coventry, Leicester, Lincolnshire, Yorkshire, Derbyshire, Staffordshire, Worcestershire, Somerset, Dorset, Sussex, Kent, and Surrey;[41] and in the Scottish
towns of Edinburgh, Leith, Linlithgow, Stirling, and Cupar.[42] References to
many more have doubtless perished. It is clear that while going on procession
the little prelates blessed spectators and collected money from them for parish
funds; sometimes, as in Aberdeen, they were taken determinedly from door to
door. Nor did all stay within their parish boundaries. The one from New
Romney near the coast of Kent visited nearby Lydd, while the Lambeth
'bishop' toured the surrounding countryside. The six rewarded by James IV
of Scotland had all turned up at the royal court. Their good reputation among
the people is suggested not just by their wide distribution and by the sums
collected, but by the fact that several of the vestments mentioned above were
bequests from parishioners. In 1520 a dying man at Whitchurch in Buckinghamshire's vale of Aylesbury got the local 'Nicholas presbyter' to witness his
will after the parish priest.[43] Nevertheless, they are recorded in a small
minority of the parishes in each locality for which records survive, while that
minority which did adopt them spanned a considerable range of size and
economic function. Nor were the parishes which set forth the 'bishops'
obviously spaced out to provide each with a suitable 'catchment area'. Their
institution seems in most cases to have been the result of local caprice.

What is clear is that their popularity, and range, continued to grow until
Henry VIII suddenly turned against them in 1541, and banned them by royal
proclamation as a late part of his reformation of the Church; he had been
persuaded that they affronted an ecclesiastical dignity of which he was now
the guardian. With them he forbade the costuming of children to represent
Sts Catherine and Clement upon their feast days, a custom which must by
contrast have been so rare, and localized, that nothing else is heard of it. In
the Chapel Royal henceforth the choirboys were given money on St Nicholas's
Day, but no little bishop appeared there again, and the royal order seems
likewise to have been obeyed immediately everywhere else.[44] As soon as the
Catholic queen Mary succeeded, however, they were restored at London. In
1554, the first year of the reign, a royal order did indeed reimpose the ban
upon them, solely because it was feared that they would distract attention
from the grand ceremony of reconciliation with the papacy. At least three City
parishes ignored it, however, and the next year Mary herself entertained the
boy bishop from St Paul's on St Nicholas's and Holy Innocents' Days at St
James's Palace. In 1556 they were 'abroad the most part in London singing
after the old fashion, and received with many good people into their houses,
and had such good cheer as ever they had'. A woman parishioner of St
Katherine by the Tower refused to admit the one who called at her door, and
rapidly had to excuse her behaviour to an angry priest backed by a crowd.[45] In
the provinces, however, the tradition is only recorded in cathedrals under
Mary, and it vanished altogether as soon as she died and the Elizabethan
Reformation followed. Almost simultaneously, in 1560, the Scottish Reforma-

tion swept it away in the northern kingdom. A hundred years later, however, John Aubrey could still note that West Country schoolboys observed the feast of St Nicholas informally, as their patron, and that at Curry Rivel in Somerset a barrel of ale was brought into the church for them.[46] The institution of a parish boy bishop was revived in 1899 at Berden in the north-western corner of Essex, as a piece of sentimental antiquarianism devised by an Anglo-Catholic country vicar.[47] It lapsed there when he retired in 1937, but has reappeared and persisted since at other centres of Anglican worship, the grandest of which is Hereford cathedral, upon the old feast of Nicholas.

Some early modern schoolboys, at least, were left with a more thorough-going, and immediately satisfying, ritual of festive liberty and legitimate mis-behaviour; the custom of 'barring out'. It seems to have arisen as part of the large expansion in school education under the Tudors, and as a response to the initial absolute authority of masters. The regular pattern was for boys to gather weapons and provisions as Christmas drew near, and then seize the school one morning; which normally in practice meant barricading the single room in which lessons were provided. If they could hold out for a set period (usually three days), then they were allowed an addition to the usual Christmas holiday period or a relaxation of the normal rate of flogging. If the master broke in, however, they were generally beaten severely. The first record of the custom is in the foundation statutes of Witton School, Cheshire, in 1558, which estab-lished it immediately on the grounds that it was already 'old' in 'other great schools'. Charles Hode, author of the manual *A New Discovery of the Old Art of Teaching Schools* (1660) suggested a regulation of it, whereby masters were given due warning and formal treaties were drawn up, incorporating demands agreed by form captains and head boys. The master would sign one of these on the school door and enter to receive a congratulatory oration from the pupils.

What is by no means evident is whether it was ever more than a tradition of northern grammar schools. It seems to be no accident that the earliest reference is in Cheshire, and the most southerly known example seems to have been at Lichfield in the 1680s, where a 'barring' was organized by the future writer Joseph Addison. The tradition was known in Scotland from 1580 until the late seventeenth century, and there are a few Irish cases from 1678. By the Georgian period, however, it was very much a regional curiosity, confined to Cumber-land, Westmorland, County Durham, and Lancashire. The growing tendency to spell out the rights of pupils in school charters was rendering it increasingly obsolete in practical terms, but it had a long afterlife as a source of seasonal fun and as an embodiment of institutional tradition in particular schools, such as Bromfield and Scotby in Cumberland. By 1828 the *Gentleman's Magazine* could describe it as 'ancient but almost obsolete', and indeed the qualification seems to have been redundant as there are no certain examples of it after 1800.[48]

In an ancient or medieval European society, midwinter was an especially appropriate time for role-reversal and relaxation of norms. Farming, trade, and warfare were all equally difficult and could be set aside for a time, permitting the ruling élites in particular to take life, and themselves, a little less seriously than usual, even if the forms of recreation adopted were inevitably designed to confirm the usual hierarchy either explicitly or by parody. The Roman mock-kings at the Saturnalia are an early example of this tendency, and they were either continued directly or imitated at medieval courts. Late medieval French royalty were especially fond of such figures, and sponsored several different kinds including a 'bean king' who seems to have been chosen (like the Saturnalian monarchs) by lot; in this case by baking a bean into a cake and crowning the man who selected the slice containing it. This was apparently imitated at the courts of Edward II and Edward III, where a 'bean king' was rewarded at the Christmases of 1315, 1316, and 1335. After this, however, royal interest in the custom seems to have lapsed, and the mock-monarchs most generally recorded in thirteenth- and fourteenth-century Britain were the village youths crowned for summer games.[49]

Midwinter sovereigns reappear in some of the lesser houses at Oxford University in the early fifteenth century; a 'Prester John' operated at Canterbury College between 1414 and 1430, while 'King Balthasar' held court at Hinksey Hall in December 1432. In 1485 Merton College regarded it as customary to elect a 'bean king' of the old French style.[50] In a famous episode at Norwich in 1443 a local politician rode through the streets as 'King of Christmas', with a crown, a sceptre, and a horse 'trapped with tinfoil and nice disguising things'. Three men carried swords before him and twelve others followed him in costumes representing the months of the year.[51] This conceit may have drawn upon an existing tradition, or may have been an original device. Likewise, the seasonal sovereigns at Oxford may have been inspired directly by Roman literature, and it may have been as a conscious piece of Renaissance classicism that they suddenly became fashionable at the apex of British society near the end of the century. Henry VII of England paid for the services of both a 'Lord of Misrule' and an 'Abbot of Unreason' (presumably to parody leaders of State and Church respectively) in all Christmases from 1489 onward, while James IV of Scotland retained both an 'Abbot of Unreason' and a 'King of the Bean' from the 1490s. In 1496 the 'Abbot' was so boisterous that a householder at Stirling had to be paid compensation by the royal treasurer for the 'spilling' of his home by the mock-cleric and his mates.[52] Henry VII's mother, Lady Margaret Beaufort, had a Lord of Misrule in her own household for 'divers disguisings and plays' during the Christmas seasons,[53] and Henry VIII continued the custom with tremendous enthusiasm at his own court.[54] In 1525 he was considering the appointment of a separate 'Lord' for the household of his little daughter Mary.[55] His devotion to the institution remained constant in a way remarkable for a king who abandoned so many other enthusiasms. In 1545 he wrote into the statutes of St John's College, Cambridge, which had been founded by Lady Margaret, a clause directing that its Christmas festivities be supervised by a Lord of Misrule. The office was to be undertaken by each Fellow in turn, and he had to stage a fresh spectacle upon every one of the twelve nights. At his own foundation of Trinity, established in the following year, the same office was instituted at once.[56]

In the reign of his son and successor, little Edward VI, the position of royal Lord of Misrule reached its apogee, and climax, in England. Its most celebrated occupant was the last, George Ferrers, who combined the traditional fun of inversion and parody with a dash of Renaissance metaphysics, both lavishly funded by the King's protector, the duke of Northumberland, who was anxious to divert his child master. At one Christmas Ferrers appeared out of a moon, and at the next from 'a vast airy space'. He had his own coat of arms (a hydra) and his own crest (a holly bush). His retinue consisted of three pages, eight councillors, a clergyman, a philosopher, an astronomer, a poet, a physician, an apothecary, a Master of Requests, a civil lawyer, a fool, a Master of Horse, an ambassador (who spoke nonsense and was partnered with an interpreter), two gentlemen, jugglers, acrobats, comic friars, and guardsmen. His spectacles in the 1552–3 season included a triumphal entry, a naval battle on the Thames, a hunt, and a hobby-horse joust. His own robes were blue (for his entry), white (for his Christmas Day feast), red (upon New Year's Day), and purple (when he rode forth from court). He was originally chosen by the permanent Master of the Revels, but devised all his own entertainments; and the latter were designed to delight not only Edward and his court, but the people of London. One of his annual escapades was a state visit to the City, to be welcomed by a sheriff's Lord of Misrule who had his own musicians and retainers in blue and white liveries. The spectacle thus created was one of the most elaborate (and frequently recorded) in Tudor history. Ferrers was at his grandest, dressed in purple trimmed with ermine and braided with silver, and his followers included bagpipers, morris dancers, and gaolers bearing instruments of punishment. They processed through the capital, the mock-sheriff bearing a sword of state before his royal counterpart, and observed the delivering of a comic proclamation. The 'royal cofferer' threw money to the crowd, and all then processed to a banquet provided by the Lord Mayor or Lord Treasurer.[57]

The close association of the office with Northumberland's regime proved to be its undoing, for when Edward died and Mary succeeded, the duke was beheaded and no royal Lord of Misrule ever appointed again in England. Mary's taste in Christmas entertainment was opulent enough, but the arrangements were left in the hands of the usual Master of the Revels. It was probably as a gesture of tact, rather than because of the stated reason, of economy, that the Lord Mayor and sheriffs decided not to appoint any such 'Lords' themselves after 1554.[58] At the Scottish royal court the custom took a different, and more demure, form, of appointing a 'Queen of the Bean', presumably by lot like the former 'kings'. One of these reigned at Christmas 1531, but the best-recorded was the last, chosen in 1563 when the presence of a genuine queen regnant, Mary, made a female counterpart all the more appropriate. She was the queen's namesake Mary Fleming, a notable royal favourite, and reigned upon Twelfth Day in 'a gown of cloth of silver; her head, her neck, her shoulders, the rest of her whole body, so beset with stones, that more in our whole jewel-house were not to be found'.[59] In this (literally) glittering manner the tradition ended in British royal households, for the troubles of Mary's reign intervened in successive winters and her son James did not revive it; it had flourished for a little over eighty years.

The emulation of it among subjects was to last about the same amount of time again. John Stow, looking back upon the reign of Henry VIII, asserted confidently that a 'Lord of Misrule, or Master of merry disports' had been found then 'in the house of every nobleman, of honour and good worship'.[60] This would seem, to judge from household accounts, to have been an exaggeration, and it was only a minority of nobles who troubled to retain these figures themselves; among them were the unusually festive fifth earl of Northumberland, who had both a Master of the Revels and an 'Abbot of Misrule' at Christmas 1522, and in Scotland a Lord Borthwick who installed an 'Abbot of Unreason' at his castle south of Edinburgh in 1547.[61] With the collapse of royal interest in such entertainers, aristocrats also seem to have forsaken them, and they remained as features in homes of gentry who wished to provide unusually elaborate Christmas entertainment. One such was the Lincolnshire squire who in 1560 gave a servant money 'to furnish himself Lord Christmas and his men in a livery'.[62] Another was John Evelyn's father Richard, who in the 1630s gave his own Lord of Misrule permission to break down doors to get at those who disobeyed his commands.[63] There were enough such landowners around to make writers, from Polydor Vergil, in the reign of Henry VII, to John Selden, in that of Charles I, assume that the 'Lords' would be relatively familiar figures in gentry households.[64] Stow also held that high churchmen retained them, but among these the chapter of Exeter cathedral, in 1533, is apparently the only case in which the custom can be proved.[65] It was more common among municipal officers. The example of the leaders of the city of London has been cited, and it is recorded that the Mayor of Coventry made one of his servants a 'Lord' when he entertained the public in 1517, and his counterpart at Chester did so in 1567.[66] In 1610 a mayor of Carlisle prevailed upon the corporation to pay for a 'Lord Abbot' with a special coat to delight the citizens during the Christmas holidays.[67] Other municipalities found it cheaper and more convenient to lay on a reception for a visiting Lord or Abbot of Misrule from the seat of a local gentleman, as Gloucester did in 1550 (when 'Master Kingston's Abbot' arrived with a troupe of players) or Marlborough did in 1578 (providing wine and fireworks).[68] Urban enthusiasm for them waned, however, as part of a general decrease in élite support for visiting players and traditional popular recreations, and the Carlisle case is apparently the only one of its kind after 1600.

In one area of the country the upper-class fashion for such comic heroes found a genuinely popular counterpart, in the institution of parish 'lords' to preside over local revelry, of the kind more prominent, and ancient, in the summer games. It included a single known example in the City of London, at St Bride's, where a man was 'Master de Misrule in the Christmas games' of 1523. It was hardly an inspiring one, however, because he got carried away and managed to kill somebody by accident, being pardoned for manslaughter the following May;[69] perhaps it is no coincidence that he apparently had no successors in the parishes of the capital. Instead, from the same decade until the 1560s, 'Lords of Misrule' or 'Christmas lords' featured as a well-documented local tradition in Norfolk, Suffolk, and Essex, raising money for church funds.[70] They may indeed have been characteristic of East Anglia before that, and helped to inspire the pageant at Norwich in 1443 but, despite the existence of a number of parish records from the area predating 1520, there is no trace of these mock-rulers until the succeeding decade. Only at the Essex port of Harwich (in 1535) is there any indication of how they were chosen or what they did; the 'lord' there was elected by the town's youth, gathered in the parish church, from among their number, and went about the streets with musicians, calling out the people to make merry.[71] The heyday of these local 'lords' was in the later reign of Henry VIII. They vanish from sight in the general disapproval of parish festivity under Edward, reappear in western Norfolk alone under Mary and in the early years of Elizabeth, and then disappear permanently in the renewed campaign against popular revels in the middle Elizabethan period.[72]

The Christmas mock-sovereigns were best established, and endured longest, where they had appeared in the early fifteenth century: in educational establishments filled with wealthy and energetic young men. Schools, where misrule was a phenomenon of only limited desirability, and which were in any case vacated for the holidays, naturally featured very little upon the list although Westminster had a 'Paedonomus' chosen before Christmas in the reign of Elizabeth. He dressed in black silk trimmed with gold lace and silver buttons, sported a cloak of crimson taffeta, was accompanied by a guard bearing halberds, and presided over feasting, a firework display, and a play.[73] The 'lords' were much more common in their old stronghold of the universities. At Cambridge, it is true, the enthusiasm of Henry VIII seems to have worn out the senior members, because soon after his death the heads of colleges agreed that nobody would henceforth be 'a lord of games at Christmas in whatever way he is titled'. At some time later, however, resistance collapsed once more, for in 1569 or 1570 it was ruled there that these officers could exist providing that the head of the house concerned approved the choice. In 1610 it was said that a Fellow of Christ's College had preached against them and been forced to resign as a result. At Oxford the tradition continued without need for either royal encouragement or regulation. What seems to have altered was that something that had been annual and low-level became ever more elaborate, spectacular—and rare. The best-documented of these later examples was at St John's College, Oxford, in 1607, when the students arranged to elect a 'Christmas Prince' for the first time since the 1570s. He named a council of nine ministers with their own individual insignia, and presided over and helped to devise plays, revels, and disputations on all holy days from the feast of Andrew until Shrove Tuesday.[74]

Exactly the same pattern can be discerned in the great London law schools known as the Inns of Court. At Lincoln's Inn during the 1519–20 season there was a 'King over Christmas Day' and also a 'King over New Year's Day'. They could be the same person, normally a high-ranking officer of the Inn, and were attended by a Sewer and a Cupbearer, chosen from colleagues, who were fined if they refused to serve. There was, however, also a 'King of Cockneys' on Holy Innocents' Day, who had his own Marshal, Butler, and Constable and was apparently chosen or elected from the students. The figure that the governing body of the Inn would not tolerate was 'Jack Straw' (named after the rebel leader of 1381), who was clearly an instigator of wild pranks among the young men. At the Christmas three years before, a student wearing this title had led his follows in smashing down doors and invading rooms, and his reappearance had been officially prohibited.[75] Forty years later, the Inner Temple had but a single 'lord', the 'Prince Palaphiles', and invited to the post a real Lord, Robert Dudley, the reigning favourite of Queen Elizabeth. He processed to the Inn in gilded armour and followed by eighty gentlemen 'riding gorgeously with chains of gold'. Twenty-four knights clad in white were his constant attendants. His 'rule' commenced after dark on Christmas Eve and lasted until Twelfth Night, consisting of nothing more onerous than presiding over feasting and dancing. The most celebrated fun was upon St Stephen's Night, when the 'Prince' was joined by the Lieutenant of the Tower of London, both in white armour. A fox and a cat were hunted around the hall with about a score of hounds. The two animals were cornered and torn to pieces in front of the fire, after which everybody sat down to enjoy a good supper.[76] In 1635 Charles I himself asked the Middle Temple to appoint a student to provide a Christmas diversion for his nephew, the exiled Prince Palatine, who was on a state visit to England. A young Cornishman, Richard Vyvyan, was duly elected 'Prince d'Amour', and contributed £6,000 of his own money towards the £20,000 which the Inn spent on feasts, dances, and a masque, between Christmas Day and Shrovetide. Nevertheless, the law students still managed to keep low-budget and disreputable versions of the tradition going by themselves. In 1623 the 'Lord' of Lincoln's Inn had visited the Middle Temple and got uproariously drunk. Five years later one from the Temple was arrested by the Lord Mayor for extorting money from householders in the surrounding streets.[77]

What killed the taste for those figures among the English ruling classes was an experience of genuine 'misrule' and political inversion in the form of the Civil Wars and Revolution of the 1640s. When the traditional political and social order was restored in 1660, almost nobody felt much like simulating that experience any more. By the 1680s John Aubrey could declare Lords of Misrule to be a thing of the past.[78] The single exception seems to have been at Lincoln's Inn in 1661, when a 'young spark' from a royalist family in Pembrokeshire, Mr Lort, became 'Prince de la Grange' as a deliberate evocation of the festive past. He arranged a grand masque and a formal trial before a full imitation royal court, and the genuine monarch, Charles II, arrived to see the fun. Nobody, however, seems to have felt impelled to follow Lort's example, and although Christmases at the Inns remained notoriously lavish and riotous, they did without mock lords henceforth.[79]

Instead, misrule metamorphosed into a much more harmless, inexpensive, scaled-down and domesticated from, based apparently upon the reintroduction to England from Europe of the medieval tradition of the 'bean king'. In the sixteenth-century Netherlands and in Germany there was a popular custom of choosing a household king or lord upon Twelfth Night by baking a coin in a cake and awarding the title to the man who found it in his slice. In the next century the same procedure was also common in France and Spain, save that it corresponded much more closely to the medieval one in that the token was not a coin but a bean.[80] It had reached England by the late Tudor period, when it was referred to obliquely in a speech made to Queen Elizabeth at Sudely Castle, and it was cited again in the 1610s, when Ben Jonson could count a 'great cake with a bean and pea' among the trappings of Christmastide.[81] The pea was probably the token which featured later in the custom as being that to enable the person who got it to act as (or to choose) the 'queen' for the night. Within three decades of Jonson, the lawyer John Selden could turn the Twelfth Night king and queen into an example to make a debating point.[82] On that night in 1669, Samuel Pepys held a supper-party with a 'noble cake'. He and his guests followed a 'new fashion' in drawing titles from a hat instead of seeking tokens in the cake itself, a practice which afforded a much greater range of characters to add to the royal couple. Several were taken from a recent stage comedy.[83] At a party aboard a royal warship at about the same time, the old practice still obtained, the pieces of cake being chosen from a napkin. Bean was still for king, pea for queen, a clove for a knave, 'etc'.[84]

Both methods continued to obtain for the next couple of hundred years. In 1774 it was regarded as a common custom, in the south of England at least, to choose an entire royal court by lot at parties upon Twelfth Night.[85] Londoners in the 1820s were still doing so, children especially being fond of the tradition because the characters of courtiers were so often comic (Sir Gregory Goose, Sir Tunbelly Clumsy, Miss Fanny Fanciful, and so forth) and had to be acted out.[86] For smaller gatherings, and further out in the provinces, Twelfth Night cakes with the pea and bean were still popular, now usually being obtained from confectioners. As the nineteenth century wore on, the vegetable tokens tended to be replaced by silver equivalents, to indicate not a character but a promise of the future, such as a sixpence for wealth, a ring for marriage, and a thimble for lack of it.[87] The tradition provided an excellent focus for gatherings to conclude the Christmas season, and only vanished, or rather was relocated, as that season was increasingly reshaped under Victoria. A Twelfth Night cake was still served annually to the Parish Clerks' Company of London, which held its audit feast upon that date, until the Second World War.[88] The last survivor appears in the Green Room of Drury Lane Theatre after the evening performance on Twelfth Night, according to the bequest of

Robert Baddeley, an actor who died in 1794. His legacy also provides wine in which the performers drink to his memory; and the accident of his whim ensures that a relic is also preserved of all the 'bean kings' who lorded it over royal courts and family homes since the time of the Saturnalia.

10

THE REINVENTION OF CHRISTMAS

An elegiac note has prevailed through most of the preceding chapters, chronicling as they do a series of customs which were at their apogee in earlier centuries and have declined or vanished since. It is, however, absolutely patent that the Christmas season is the most important complex of festivals in the modern British year and contains by far the largest number of customary practices. In the last twenty years, as intellectuals have become ever more conscious of the artificial and socially engineered nature of human conventions, there has been a flowering of books and essays devoted to the 'making' or the 'construction' of the modern Christmas.[1] The object of this final chapter upon the season is to pool the findings of this research, with a few additional reflections.

A tone of elegy was, indeed, predominant among the writers contemplating Christmas in the first four decades of the nineteenth century. In part this was the product of nostalgic illusion, as authors such as Sir Walter Scott, Washington Irving, William Wordsworth, Robert Southey, and Charles Dickens contemplated with alarm the apparent growth of division and instability in a society undergoing rapid industrialization.[2] They turned instinctively to traditional festivities as relics of a time of greater order, deference, and harmony, an impulse even more pronounced in the case of May games, in connection with which it will be considered more fully later in this book. On the other hand, the perception of decline was firmly anchored in reality. Between 1790 and 1840 employers, led by the government, carried out a ruthless pruning of the Christmas holidays without encountering any resistance. In 1797 the Customs and Excise Office, for example, closed between 21 December (St Thomas's Day) and 6 January (the Epiphany) on all of the seven dates specified by the Edwardian and Elizabethan Protestant calendars. In 1838 it was open on all except Christmas Day itself. The Factory Act of 1833 put the seal upon this process by declaring that Christmas and Good Friday were the only two days of the year, excepting Sundays, upon which workers had a statutory right to be absent from their duties. In 1837 the Middlesex and Westminster House of Correction, one of the capital's principal prisons for lesser offenders, no longer commemorated Christmas at all.[3] In twenty of the years between 1790 and 1835 *The Times* did not mention the festival, and it never referred to it with enthusiasm. To the fashionable world it was increasingly an anachronism, and a bore.

The rot was not confined, moreover, to the higher levels of society. It is true that the celebration of the date was more noticeable among the middle classes, and especially those with children. It is also correct that in some traditional industries—iron-working around Sheffield, lace-making in the West Country, mining in the North—workers insisted on observing all of the old holidays.[4] The customs detailed above indicate that the season was still ebulliently kept in many areas. None the less, a closer look at them reveals that a more pronounced importance was accorded to other remnants of the old twelve-day cycle, such as New Year in the northern counties (as in Scotland) and Twelfthtide in the West of England, rather than to the feast of the Nativity. Furthermore there were a number of regions—parts of Wales, the south Midlands, and the Home Counties are examples[5]—in which observers in this period found that Christmas had become a remarkably colourless and hum-drum day of rest for ordinary people.

The reversal in these attitudes was swift and dramatic, and can now be discerned to have had more than a single cause. One was the appearance of the Oxford Movement in the Church of England, embodying an enhanced feeling for ritual and decoration, and therefore for the old holy days. John Keble's book of poems, *The Christian Year* (1827), was a wholehearted cele-bration of the traditional festive calendar. More important were a complex of emotions waxing within the rapidly growing middle class: a fear of the rift between rich and poor, an enhanced consciousness of the value of family ties, a novel interest in protecting children from the world, and a yearning for a 'safer' pre-industrial England.[6] These impulses were constantly articulated by writers and addressed by parliamentary legislation, and the enhancement of the image of Christmas, a feast which combined associations of piety, charity, and family reunion, was another result of them. In 1840 and 1841 *Punch* devoted parts of its first two Christmas issues to harrowing stories about lack of charity at that season; the villain of the second was a wealthy miser. In 1841 also, Prince Albert deliberately publicized an image of himself, Victoria, and their children gathered to celebrate at Windsor Castle which promoted an atmosphere of familial domesticity to replace the flamboyant Christmastide revelry of earlier royal courts. The drift of feeling was reaching a point at which it would both inspire and be catalysed by a literary genius, and this occurred in 1843 with the publication of Charles Dickens's *A Christmas Carol*. Dickens had treated the theme of Christmas merry-making six years before, in *The Pickwick Papers*, and done so in wholly traditional, if deeply sentimental, manner. The *Carol* was different; it was a passionate avowal of how the festival ought to be kept, dashed off in six weeks by a writer in love with his subject.

Dickens succeeded in turning Christmas celebration into a moral reply to avarice, selfishness, and greed. He linked worship and feasting, within a context of social reconciliation. The story owed much of its power to the way in which it interwove nostalgia for the past and anxiety about the present, and presented Christmas as a palliative to both. From the centre of the festival Dickens displaced the wider community, and guests, and substituted the family, and children. He linked the new prosperity of the age with its social unease, and put the middle classes in the vortex of both, equipped with a feast which employed the former to allay the latter. Christmas, as portrayed by Dickens, invested materialism with a spiritual quality which enabled the newly-rich to enjoy their wealth. Within one year the book sold 15,000 copies, and at the following Christmas it was dramatized at nine London theatres. It has subsequently been adapted for stage and screen more than any other of Dickens's works.[7]

Once again, it may be necessary to stress that neither Charles Dickens nor Prince Albert 'invented' the new attitude to Christmas; as the case of the *Punch* stories shows, they were responding to a mood already coming into existence. After *A Christmas Carol*, however, that mood was immeasurably stronger. In 1847 the Poor Law Board permitted a special Christmas dinner in all workhouses. During that decade and the next the *Illustrated London News* and other magazines ran a series of drawings of English Christmases through the centuries, to inculcate a sense of their continuous identity as a time of festivity and benevolent hierarchy. The growing reputation of it as a national feast of harmony and charity began to wear down denominations which had traditionally rejected it as a holy day; in 1868 the *Baptist Advertiser* published an advertisement for Christmas presents. By then the flow of seasonal generosity was so considerable that the inmates of prisons and workhouses enjoyed more food and games on Christmas Day than many working-class families. In 1871 the Bank Holidays Act began to reverse the attrition of midwinter holidays, by declaring St Stephen's Day (now officially secularized as 'Boxing Day') to be a day of leisure again in order to allow the nation a double dose of pleasure. In that year also Lord and Lady Amberley dropped their former complete refusal to celebrate Christmas. It had been based upon their rejection of Christianity itself, impelled by rationalism; but when their eldest child was 5 years old they felt obliged to organize festivities in order to evade a suspicion of parental cruelty.[8] Their consciences may have been placated by the fact that virtually none of the new set of Christmas customs adopted in this same period had any Christian context whatsoever.

The most spectacular was the Christmas tree, a perfect combination of the two qualities of greenery and light so much in demand at midwinter. It had long been a custom in the Rhineland, although even there it was not a medieval one, as the first record of it comes from the 1520s. From 1789 to 1840 it was regularly mentioned as used in England by German settlers, guests, or governesses, and by the 1820s was starting to spread out from the German community in Manchester to the local people of that city. On Christmas Eve 1840 a medic, H. W. Acland, mentioned seeing one at Roehampton in Surrey, in terms which suggest that it was a rarity but not a complete novelty. The next year, however, that good German Prince Albert made the custom fashionable by setting one up at Windsor Castle, and by 1845 the author of a piece upon it could say that it had 'long been well known to a few in England' but was now becoming familiar. In 1850 Dickens could still call it 'the pretty German toy', but recommended it enthusiastically to the readers of *Household Words*, portraying one lit by a 'multitude of little tapers' and hung with dolls, miniature furniture for their houses, musical instruments, 'books, work-boxes, paint-boxes, sweetmeat boxes, peep-show boxes...there were tee-to-tums, humming-tops, needle-cases, pen-wipers, smelling bottles, conversation-cards, bouquet-holders; real fruit, made artificially dazzling with gold leaf; imitation apples, pears and walnuts, crammed with surprises'. Five years later, the *Lady's Newspaper* could describe the trees as 'very popular'.

The English had, in fact, taken to them relatively late, for by 1840 they had already become well established in Finland, Sweden, Norway, the Netherlands, the whole of Germany, and the United States. Their particular appeal was to the middle classes, for they represented a perfect focus for a family gathering while (as Dickens made clear) it was at first customary to hang the Christmas presents from the branches before distribution, providing a display of the household's wealth, generosity, and popularity. Children in particular found them exciting and beautiful, although until the invention of electric lights in the 1890s the habit of tying candles to their branches did make them notable fire hazards. In rural areas the trees were often lit up at first on Twelfth Night, but by the 1880s a more homogeneous national bourgeois culture had caused them to be universally a feature of Christmas itself. Among the working class they spread far more slowly, families often being content with the old holly and ivy, and (in appropriate regions) the kissing-bough. Only in the 1950s did the tree become virtually ubiquitous.[9]

The Christmas card represented a convenient and sophisticated evolution of the ancient custom of giving blessings or good wishes for the New Year. By 1840 it was often carried on among the wealthier classes by sending a short poem engraved within an ornamental framework. In 1843 the social reformer Henry Cole engaged an artist, John Calcott Horsley, to respond to the new interest in Christmas by designing a card showing a family Christmas dinner, with side panels illustrating acts of charity. This, and some imitations, proved to be commercial failures because they were too expensive. In 1862, therefore, a fresh start was made by the stationers Messrs Charles Goodall, which printed cheap plain greetings. By the end of the decade these were becoming deco-rated, and other firms were producing them. At first many referred only to the New Year, as before, and it was long into the 1870s before the enhanced importance of the family Christmas made this an essential preface to the greeting. In 1878 the volume sent was sufficient for the Post Office to com-mence a separate record of Christmas mail, and in the 1890s the cards became a popular craze, and continued to expand their market over the next century. In 1992 1,560 million were sent, and the commercial value of the Christmas card trade was £250 million.[10]

From the beginning, the proportion of religious themes in the designs was small. Examples from before 1890 (of which the Jonathan King collection has 163,000) show an overwhelming concentration upon the natural world and upon jollity; the favourite images were holly, mistletoe, Christmas pudding, Father Christmas, the Christmas tree, bells, and robins. The robin had become associated with the season as a convention among urban artists, in the late eighteenth century, for reasons that remain mysterious. There is nothing to connect it with the ancient veneration of the wren, and painters may simply have found it to be the most colourful common and well-loved bird in the winter garden. The choice of imagery has remained more or less constant ever since; an evocation of survival, rejoicing, and the resilience of nature, usually constructed around the (literally) vivacious colours red and green.[11]

If the Christmas card descends directly from the New Year blessing, the Christmas present is equally obviously a continuation of the New Year's gift. The latter custom, as described earlier, was in decline by the early nineteenth century as part of the general run-down in enthusiasm for the season. The upsurge in support for Christmas as a family festival of generosity and charity, from the 1840s, created a slow but steady transfer of the date of giving, backwards from New Year to the feast of the Nativity. The process was very protracted at both the top and the bottom of society; Queen Victoria was still sending New Year's gifts and not Christmas presents in 1900, and the balance did not shift from one to the other among English working-class families until about 1900, and among crofters in the Northern Isles until the 1960s. The movement occurred first—indeed in London from the 1820s onward—among the English middle classes. This was partly because the new Christmas was designed by and for them, and partly because of the development of nurseries, run by maids, in their homes, making the parent–child relationship more formal. The greater segregation of children from the rest of the family also created a greater need for toys and board games to divert them. From the 1880s market forces were slowly starting to respond; in 1887 Christmas shopping advertisements appeared in *The Times* from 12 December onward, but in 1898 from 30 November. George Bernard Shaw started an enduring myth in 1897 by declaring that 'Christmas is forced upon a reluctant and disgusted nation by the shopkeepers and the press'. In reality, there is no evidence that businessmen sponsored the revival of the festival either individually or collectively; and indeed under Victoria they would have lacked the publicity techniques to do so. *Punch* and Dickens both personified them as the natural enemies of the holiday, and authors, journalists, preachers, and hymn-writers were all more important in its re-creation. By 1900, however, the market was becoming geared to it at last, and in the following decade one firm, Woolworths, pioneered the production of toys cheap enough to be within the range of working-class families. The resulting industry flourished in Britain until the 1970s, when it crashed in the face of competition from US based multinational companies using cheap Far Eastern labour and targeted mainly at working-class children through television.[12]

Gift-making pulled other rituals and traditions in its train. The new emphasis on seasonal care for the pauperized and imprisoned created a major growth in charitable organizations, usually run by middle-class women.[13] This growth may in turn have helped to stigmatize the efforts of working-class people to earn extra money for themselves by presenting seasonal plays, dances, or songs, which atrophied everywhere that the proceeds were not being applied to specifically charitable purposes. Christmas presents also summoned into England the German custom of the Christmas stocking, which had already reached France and Italy by the early nineteenth century. This was a child's stocking, hung at the end of the bed and filled with a present or presents overnight on Christmas Eve (or sometimes that of another major feast) by an adult impersonating the Christ Child. It is first referred to in an English setting by Susan and Ann Warner, who made it the centre-piece of a Christmas story published in 1854, which in turn advertised it further. It subsequently became very common among working-class and lower middle-class families, who could afford only gifts sufficient to fill such a receptacle. Among the upper middle class it was always more the habit to hang gifts from the tree or pile them under it, to be exchanged or presented on Christmas morn; and growing general affluence has made this more and more the norm at all levels of society since 1960.[14] The idea that the Christ Child filled the stocking did not last long in England, for as the custom caught on there it became linked instead with a far more flamboyant and secular figure, imported from America.

Nobody seems to have thought of personifying Christmas until the early seventeenth century. It was done then partly because of the general taste of the age for allegory and partly because the criticism of observation of the feast by radical Protestants made a representation of it convenient to writers determined to defend it. Thus in 1616 Ben Jonson introduced to the world, *Christmas His Masque*, presented by a figure 'in a round hose, long stockings, a close doublet, a high-crowned hat with a brooch, a long thin beard, a truncheon, little ruffs, white shoes, his scarfs, and garters tied cross'.[15] 'Christmas' appeared again in a masque by Thomas Nabbes performed before the young Prince of Wales twenty-two years later, as 'an old reverend gentleman in furred gown and cap'.[16] Over the next 250 years this sort of character was to feature repeatedly in pictures, stage plays, and folk-drama, known variously as Sir Christmas, Lord Christmas, or (increasingly) as Father Christmas. He was essentially concerned with the adult world, personifying feasting and games, he had no connection with presents, and he was not treated with much respect, being generally a burlesque figure of fun. Then Santa Claus turned up. In origins he was, of course, the medieval patron of children, St Nicholas, who remained a favourite popular figure amongst the Dutch. They continued to put presents, ostensibly from the saint, in the shoes (later the stockings) of sleeping children on the night before his feast, and this custom became naturalized in their American colony of New Amsterdam, eventually captured by the English and renamed New York. It seems to have died out there, however, as the Dutch influence waned. In 1809 Washington Irving, whose sentimental interest in traditional Christmases has been mentioned, drew attention to the old tradition in his *Knickerbocker's History of New York*, rescheduling it from St Nicholas's Eve to Christmas Eve. Irving's portrait was repeated in an 1821 issue of the *Children's Friend*, published in the same city, and that may have been the direct inspiration to another New Yorker, Clement Clark Moore, to create the modern Santa.

He was the Professor of Hebrew and Oriental Languages at the episcopalian theological college in the city, and also a good classicist (making a much-admired translation of Juvenal) and minor poet. In 1822 he wrote a poem called 'A Visit from St Nicholas' to amuse his own children, and in doing so his powers of inspiration took a remarkable leap. His saint was not the traditional, sentimental, figure of the Dutch, but a magical spirit of the northern midwinter. He wore fur clothes, had a bushy white beard, travelled through the sky merrily in a sleigh drawn by reindeer, and came down chimneys with a sack of gifts to fill the stockings of children on Christmas Eve. To Moore's initial anger, somebody passed a copy to a local newspaper, the *Troy Sentinel*, and upon being printed (without attribution) it became wildly popular. It was not illustrated until 1863, when the artist Thomas Nast portrayed him in *Harper's Weekly* as a sort of large gnome. Soon after, however, it became more conventional to represent him in a red suit (perhaps derived from St Nicholas's red bishop's robes), trimmed with white fur and with a matching cap. He arrived in England in 1854, in that same story by Susan and Ann Warner, *The Christmas Stocking*, which introduced the latter custom. Not until the 1870s, however, did he begin to be adopted by ordinary people in England; in 1879 the newly formed Folk-Lore Society, not knowing about US practices, was excitedly trying to discover the source of the new belief. By the 1880s he was firmly established in the English popular imagination, having swapped his cap for the hood of the native Father Christmas and usually having acquired the latter's name as well. Associated with children, bounty, and charity, he was the perfect personification of the new sort of festival; in adopting him as in adapting to other customs, retailers only followed where novelists, poets, and public demand had led.[17]

In 1980 a young academic, Rogan Taylor, started a completely new run of speculation about the Santa Claus figure by suggesting that his characteristics were derived ultimately from Siberian shamanism; he flies through the air like a shaman, his reindeer resemble the reindeer spirits of Siberian tribes, his robes are red and white like the hallucinogenic fly agaric mushrooms which shamans consumed to enter trances, and he comes down chimneys like Siberians entering and leaving homes by the smoke-hole in their dwellings. He conceded that 'no definite link can ever be established between Moore's Santa Claus and Siberian shamanism', but thought it 'most appropriate that a shaman should direct our Christmas entertainment'.[18] The ingenuity of the suggestion earned it a well-deserved popularity, although almost entirely outside academe. A careful survey of the evidence for Siberian shamanism[19] reveals the following discrepancies: shamans did not travel by sleigh, did not usually deal with reindeer spirits, rarely took the mushrooms to achieve trances, did not have red and white clothes, did not bring gifts, and did not usually leave dwellings by physical entrances while in trance, because they operated in an entirely different dimension. Nor is there evidence that Americans knew anything about Siberia until the late nineteenth century; it may be that Dr Taylor has not given sufficient credit to the sheer originality of Clement Moore's creative vision. His hypothesis formed a part of the preoccupation of many Western intellectuals with tribal magical practices and altered states of consciousness during the 1970s and 1980s. As things stand, the traditional Dutch image of the red-robed, bearded St Nicholas, flying through the winter night on his grey horse with his sack of presents and magically entering houses to fill the stockings of children, makes a much better fit with the modern Santa Claus than the Siberian shaman, clad in an animal-hide kaftan hung with metal images, drumming and dancing into a trance to confront the spiritual enemies of the tribe. Behind that image of the saint *may* well lie those of ancient northern European deities; but that is a different matter.

The Christmas dinner changed only slightly under Victoria. From the late eighteenth century the turkey, brought into Europe from America, had begun to replace the traditional roast beef as the centre-piece; it was cheaper, and its size suited a middle-class family gathering. For most of the nineteenth century, working-class households had to make do with the still cheaper, and tougher, goose, but twentieth-century affluence removed that need. Plum porridge died out in the Victorian period, and the fruit pudding took over completely in its stead. The Twelfth Night cake, in its later form with silver tokens, was transferred to Christmas Day over the same span of years, and Twelfthtide collapsed almost completely as a festival, its functions and trappings being moved to swell the burgeoning importance of Christmas.[20] The ritual meal also acquired the only Christmas custom invented by a businessman, a London confectioner called Tom Smith who produced the Christmas cracker. He had introduced the French bon-bon into England in 1844, and found that the swelling enthusiasm for Christmas meant that sales were best at that season. In 1846, hearing a log pop on the fire, he hit on the idea of marketing the sweet at that time in a paper wrapping with two handles which detonated a firecracker. This proved so successful that he later altered the focus by dropping the sweet and substituting a small gift. By the 1870s manufacturers had added paper hats, perpetuating the tradition of festive misrule in a harmless and contained setting.[21] Exactly the same effect was achieved in a different setting when the eighteenth-century harlequinade, imported from Italy and linked to no season, developed into the Christmas pantomime. From the 1860s onward only nursery-tale themes were treated, and by the 1890s it was established that the principal boy would be played by a woman and the dame by a man.[22] The ancient seasonal motifs of cross-dressing, absurd comedy, and animal disguises had all been appropriated, professionalized, and placed at a much safer distance from the audience. In the same period the older, amateur, expressions of these motifs went into terminal decline.

The same was true of the old seasonal music. In the early nineteenth century antiquarians became convinced that carolling was dying out as part of the general run-down of the feast, and a number—David Gilbert, William Howitt, William Sandys, Thomas Wright, E. F. Rimbault, and William Henry Husk—made collections of traditional specimens as a self-conscious rescue operation. Their activities, however, impressed only learned colleagues, until in 1871 two Fellows of Magdalen College, Oxford, published *Christmas Carols Old and New*. The simple and attractive nature of most of its contents came as a gift to the Church of England at a time when both of its wings were determined to revive hymn-singing. In 1880 the future archbishop, Edward Benson, devised the basic modern English Christmas service, the 'Festival of Nine Lessons and Carols', for his see of Truro. The hoped-for appearance of carols as staple items in church and school worship took place, luxuriantly, in the succeeding decade and has persisted. This was, however, because virtually all the songs concerned were in fact new or newly remodelled; which is precisely why they had seemed so attractive. 'The First Nowell' was indeed entirely seventeenth or eighteenth century, but this was true of nothing else in the repertoire now adopted. 'O Come All Ye Faithfull' was French, and translated into English in 1840, and 'While Shepherds Watched' and 'Hark the Herald Angels Sing' had Georgian words but Victorian tunes. All the rest were products of the mid- and late nineteenth century. The old examples lovingly collected by the antiquarians remained fossilized in learned tomes; as people flocked to the new carol services, the remaining village singers gave up and the last urban waits had their licences revoked.[23]

The decorations provided for the settings of the redeveloped festivities altered in keeping with the other changes. From the 1880s onward, commercially produced paper hangings became available in towns and, being convenient and easily reused, they spread out into the country, and downward in society, in the twentieth century. The holly was eventually reduced to wreaths upon doors on the American model or around 'Advent' candles of the German sort; ivy, bay, laurel, box, and yew vanished altogether. Mistletoe, however, was retained as the eighteenth-century custom of kissing beneath it ascended the social ladder from the servants' quarters in the mid-Victorian period, being taken over by the middle class as another form of licensed misbehaviour. For most of the time between about 1860 and 1940 the most fashionable middle-class families decked their homes with a mixture of holly and artificial materials put together at home. Women's magazines of the period were most emphatic that this work be taken seriously and weeks devoted to it; in 1896 *The Lady* applied pressure with brutal directness by informing its readers that hostesses who provided 'meagre decoration' were disgracing their families.[24]

The main development of the twentieth century was that the now fully remodelled Christmas spread outwards from the wealthier third of society to take in the whole of it, and the nation's public life as well. As the average size of families shrank, more middle-class children were sent away to school, and family relationships were stretched by mobility of labour, the importance of the festival as a time of reunion and reaffirmation was enhanced in proportion. In 1923 Lord Reith, controller of the British Broadcasting Corporation, began trying to persuade King George V to deliver a Christmas message over the radio to his subjects. After nine years the monarch gave in, and Reith's script treated the whole British Empire as an extended kinship of the Crown, getting a friendly admonition from its father. The 1934 message declared Christmas to be 'the festival of the family', and the increasingly standardized and homogenized nature of it was becoming a bond between British people all over the world.[25] The remarkable spread of the nativity play as a junior school entertainment, also a feature of the 1920s and 1930s, testified to the same process. It was not linked to any enhanced religiosity in society; indeed the general trend was all the other way. Rather, the Christian Holy Family was being used as a symbol of the new seasonal concentration upon the human family, to give it a historical and spiritual legitimacy.[26] Physically, the new customs entered public space. In the 1930s Christmas trees appeared in churches, and after the Second World War (following American precedent), in streets, squares, and shopping centres as well.[27] From the 1950s, also, cities began to hang illuminated decorations over their streets, at public expense, and as the intensity of celebration increased with general affluence and the Christmas shopping period extended, so the lighting-up time of the displays pushed backward, into mid-November. The period of preparation for the national, secularized, Christmas is now therefore over a month in duration, corresponding to no previous festive calendar.

Being now defined as a patriotic and social obligation rather than a religious one, and with all the mass media on its side, the new Christmas was unstoppable. During the first half of the twentieth century it was adopted by all the dissenting Protestant denominations which had rejected it in the seventeenth, and became generally accepted in Scotland. In 1958 it was declared an official holiday there for the first time since 1690.[28] The Scots, however, returned the compliment, for the mass media also helped to carry their veneration of New Year's Eve and Day into England over the same period. In the 1920s Scots living in London took to imitating their long-established (eighteenth-century) custom of gathering outside the Tron Kirk in Edinburgh for the chimes of midnight on 31 December. They did so initially outside St Paul's, where thousands were gathered by New Year 1938, but also subsequently thronged Piccadilly and Shaftesbury Avenue.[29] After the Second

World War the favourite location shifted to Trafalgar Square, and by now English far outnumbered the Scots in the revelling crowds, a reflection of the adoption of the festival as an important one in England's domestic culture. It served, in fact, an invaluable purpose there as an antidote to the new style of Christmas, for adults who had spent the latter indulging children, parents, or relations, and engaging in harmless and controlled misbehaviour, could now indulge themselves, and engage in misbehaviour that was (potentially at least) neither harmless nor controlled. Into the frequently cloying atmosphere of the Victorian Christmas, Hogmanay blew like a raw northern wind, smelling of alcohol. Its 'natural' community was that of friendship, not family, and its deity was not Father Christmas but the more menacing one of Father Time.[30]

By the early 1990s a mood of criticism and anxiety concerning the festival was once again manifesting itself in the mass media. The British Safety Council had demonstrated that the weeks before it were the worst time of year for disorders related to strain, and in 1993 Christmas Stress Syndrome had been formally identified. Courses and workshops upon How to Cope with Christmas were springing up across the country, and marriage guidance counsellors proclaimed that their numbers of clients rose by 50 per cent each January.[31] The historical reasons for this were obvious enough. For most of the British direct experience of the reformed Christmas was only a generation old, for it had been in the 1950s that the majority of working-class people had become able to afford the tree, the turkey, the systematic sending of cards, and the large-scale purchase of presents, for the first time, and only then did large-scale family Christmas gatherings become common among them.[32] All this had been buoyed up upon an unprecedented economic boom, and since the 1970s the economy had generally been in recession. Until the 1970s, also, advertising of presents had been generally in written material and targeted at adults, but in that decade virtually all households came to own a television set, a medium especially well suited to children. The multinational companies which took over the international toy industry at that time efficiently and unscrupulously aimed their advertisements directly at youngsters. The mode of Christmas conceived in the 1840s had at last expanded throughout the entire national community; entropy of some sort might have been expected after this point.

A related complaint, often heard at the same time, and the subject of various radio and television debates, could be described as more illusory or artificial: that the 'true', Christian message of Christmas had recently been destroyed by commercialism. It was often accompanied by the suggestion that the festival was now reverting to its pagan origins. The fallacy in this was that, as emphasized repeatedly above, the overtly Christian content in the Victorian revival of Christmas had been minimal from the beginning—which had been a large part of its success. It was not pagan in the strict sense, of honouring ancient deities, but in the looser and more secular one, of being concerned with honouring natural forces and human responsibilities. Furthermore, grumbles about the destruction of the 'true' spirit of Christmas, the absence of religion, and the predominance of commercialism and self-indulgence were heard as soon as this new sort of Christmas became established. *The Times* could be relied upon to articulate them in leaders from the 1870s onwards.[33] It should not be forgotten, moreover, that writers like Dickens who had sponsored the Victorian Christmas had done so explicitly with an appeal to the 'true', 'original', spirit of the festival. It is, indeed, rather hard to determine what exactly that is supposed to be. As soon as the Christian churches had adopted the custom of celebrating the Nativity at about the time of ancient pagan midwinter feasts, they encountered the problem of ensuring that the veneration of Christ would remain predominant in it; some of them abolished the feast in the seventeenth century precisely because they believed that the battle had long been lost. St Gregory Nazianzen, who died in 389, urged upon his flock 'the celebration of the feast after a heavenly and not after an earthly manner', and complained that instead they were 'feasting to excess, dancing, and crowning the doors'.[34] His words were paraphrased unconsciously by many an evangelical preacher giving comment on British radio or television in the 1990s; it seems that in this context the word 'human' is more relevant than 'pagan'.

In view of these different complaints, it is worth keeping firmly in mind that in 1975 a National Opinion Poll found that 88 per cent of adults interviewed expected to have a happy Christmas,[35] and there is no reason to believe that the proportion has declined since. The most obvious reaction of people to the increasing opulence and stress of the festival has been to extend the holiday period after it in order to have time to recover. By 1993, 80 per cent of English and Welsh local businesses were closing from the day before Christmas Eve to that after the newly restored public holiday of New Year's Day (Scotland having an extra day after that),[36] a modern nine-day cycle to replace the medieval twelve-day one. What was being created was a period between the winter solstice and the traditional (Roman) time of the New Year, in which politics, education, commerce were alike suspended, of peace, privacy, domesticity, revelry, and charity: a sacred period in a much broader sense than that associated with any one religion.[37] At this point a sense of overpowering familiarity strikes a historian interested in the long-term development of the festival. It seems only right to agree with David Miller's recent emphasis upon its essential continuity (or perhaps one should say, episodic re-creation) from pre-Christian times onward,[38] and to close with a key passage from the fourth-century writer Libanius, describing the Roman New Year feast:

The feast of the Kalendae is honoured as far as the Roman Empire stretches... Everywhere is singing and feasting; the rich enjoy luxury but the poor also set better food than usual upon their tables. The desire to spend money grips everybody... People are not merely bountiful to themselves but to their fellow humans. A stream of presents pours itself out on all sides... The Kalendae bring all work to a halt, and allow humans to surrender themselves to pure pleasure.[39]

11

SPEEDING THE PLOUGH

I N medieval and early modern England the ploughing season began immediately after the end of the Christmas holidays; and indeed this remained true until the widespread adoption of winter cereal crops in the twentieth century. Since the harvest, arable fields would have been left spiked with fading stubble; now the soil, wet through by the autumn and winter rains, would be turned over by ploughs dragged first by oxen, later by horses, and latest of all by tractors. It was a process which would last far into March. Medieval records contain stray references to customs associated with the opening of it. In the late thirteenth century, for example, the villagers of Carlton in Lindrick, at the northern tip of Nottinghamshire, held a plough race in the common fields on 7 January. Each contestant was allowed to sow later the land which he succeeded in ploughing up.[1] The author of *Dives and Pauper*, written between 1405 and 1410, condemned the superstition of 'leading the plough abouten the fire as for good beginning of the year'.[2] By that time, or at the latest by the mid-fifteenth century, the rites of the opening of this work were becoming concentrated on the first Monday after Twelfth Night, known familiarly as 'Plough Monday'.

Only the richer members of a village could afford their own ploughs, so that others had to take turns to borrow a communal one. At Leverington in the Cambridgeshire fenland, money from the 'town stock' was loaned out in the early Tudor period together with the plough, to enable the poorer farmers to launch their annual operations.[3] In the main arable regions of England at the time, the east Midlands and East Anglia, there were 'plough lights' kept burning in many churches, in some cases maintained by special guilds. At Knapton near the Norfolk coast, each of the three traditional divisions of the parish paid to keep its own light in the church.[4] Each may have had a plough (probably the communal one) placed in front of it, for at Holbeach in the Lincolnshire marshland, and at the major Norfolk port of Great Yarmouth, there were certainly ploughs mounted in churches upon special stands. Lincolnshire was especially fond of the 'lights', which are recorded in the majority of its surviving pre-Reformation churchwardens' accounts. They are also mentioned in Northamptonshire, Cambridgeshire, and Norfolk. Even in Lincolnshire, however, they were not universal, for records of churches in the same districts as those which kept up the custom show no trace of them. It seems likely that the ploughs kept in churches, and perhaps some that were not, were blessed upon 'Plough Sunday', the first after Epiphany; John Bale, a Protestant writing under Edward VI, condemned 'conjuring of ploughs' among a list of traditional seasonal rites.[5]

In 1413 an official of Durham Abbey (which functioned as the cathedral) gave 4d 'on the day after Epiphany in Old Elvet to the people who were drawing a plough'.[6] Old Elvet was a street in Durham city, and this seems to be the earliest reference (and a geographically isolated one) to a custom widespread by the end of the century in Essex, Suffolk, Norfolk, Cambridge-shire, Lincolnshire, and Northamptonshire. This entailed the dragging of a plough (again, perhaps that from the church) around a community while money was collected behind it for the parish funds. It took place, unlike the Durham version which may represent an earlier form, on Plough Monday. In East Anglia this collection is mentioned in virtually all (but again not all) of the accounts for arable parishes. Boxford, in southern Suffolk, and Great Dunmow, in central Essex, held feasts upon the same day. At another Suffolk village, Brundish, and at Saxilby near Lincoln, it was specifically the young men of the village who made the gathering, and so it may have been every-where. Sometimes the proceeds went directly to the upkeep of the 'plough light'. What is never made clear is whether those who dragged the plough upon these occasions performed a song, dance, or play as they did so.[7] The parish gatherings are not recorded until the 1460s,[8] but as the documents for the communities in question only commence from that decade onward, there is no way of telling how much older they might have been.

Their subsequent fate is much more apparent, as the Reformation struck repeatedly at the parochial aspects of this complex of customs. Henry VIII's injunctions of 1538 forbade most sacred candles or lamps in churches, and so the 'plough lights' were extinguished in all those parishes where they were maintained and which have left records for the year. In the autumn of 1547 an Act of Parliament introduced by the Government of the Lord Protector, the duke of Somerset, suppressed the guilds upon which some of the 'plough shrines' had depended. In the same year the royal injunctions issued by the same regime, in the name of the young Edward VI, forbade all shrines of saints, and it is likely that this ruling would have been extended in practice to cover the mounting of ploughs in churches. At Holbeach the plough was cleared out of the church with the images of saints at some time in 1547, and the stand upon which it had been displayed was sold off.[9] It was probably in the following January that the visitors enforcing the injunctions in the Yorkshire deanery of Doncaster forbade the gatherings behind the plough on Plough Monday.[10] Their stated reason was a practical one, that they caused drunkenness and brawling, but it is also likely that their motivation was religious and political. The former concern derived from the hostility which this Government and its local agents displayed in general towards the raising of parish funds by festivity, the latter from fear that gatherings of any kind might prove to be opportunities for rebellion, at a time when the government of a royal minor was introducing controversial religious changes. The penalties were certainly stiff, including fines for both the owner of the plough used and the householders to whom it was drawn; the more substantial people of settlements were being forced to turn against the custom. It is hardly surprising, if other teams of visitors were of like mind, that the contributions to church funds from these gatherings disappeared in 1548 from all those parishes which have left accounts.[11]

As in the case of other traditional festivities, the gatherings revived under the Catholic regime of Mary, but without their full vigour. Their range was much the same as under the young Henry VIII, from Lincolnshire to Suffolk, but in a thinner scatter of communities. Furthermore, only at Leverton, in the Lincoln-shire Fens, is there mention of the rekindling of a 'plough light'.[12] That was snuffed out again after the accession of the Protestant Elizabeth, but (once more in keeping with a general pattern of seasonal customs) there was no immediate suppression of the Plough Monday collections. During the 1560s they persisted across the same region, although in Suffolk apparently with-drawn to the northernmost parts, and only occasionally are there traces of the process spilling over into behaviour which produced disapproval; in 1560 ten men at North Muskham, on the Nottinghamshire side of the Trent, were indicted before the archdeacon 'for ploughing up the churchyard and misusing themselves in church upon plough day last'.[13] As the reign progressed, how-ever, the gatherings became susceptible to the slow tendency for parish finances to be separated from communal merry-making once more, which is a feature of the Elizabethan period. The last trace of the link was at Bungay, on the Suffolk bank of the river Waveney, where it was finally broken in 1597.[14] A few relics of it were left, here and there, in parochial custom. At Leverton the churchwardens held a feast upon Plough Monday until 1611. All through the seventeenth century the bells of Rolleston, another village on the Trent, were rung then. Into the eighteenth century, the parish funds of Waddington, in the uplands just south of Lincoln, were administered by 'ploughmasters' ap-pointed them with much ringing and provision of music. Stuart ecclesiastical officials in Cambridgeshire (especially), Nottinghamshire, and Lincolnshire were occasionally annoyed to find ploughs still kept in churches; at Belton, in the Isle of Axholme, the one discovered there in 1601 was towed there as part of a 'plough game'.[15] What was probably the last of these old-style ceremonial ploughs was kept in the belfry of Castor church, near Peterborough, in the 1840s. It was described then as 'an old town plough, roughly made, decayed and worm-eaten...about three times as large as an ordinary plough'.[16]

Private 'plough games' continued unabated. Under Elizabeth, Thomas Tusser could rhyme gleefully:

> Plough Monday, next after that Twelfthtide is past,
> bids out with the plough, the worst husband is last.
> If ploughman get hatchet or whip to the screen,
> maids loseth their cock if no water be seen.

This verse was entered in a set dealing with Leicestershire, and describes a competition whereby ploughmen would try to put an object on the fireside screen or settle of a farmhouse before the maids had managed to get a kettle boiling there in the morning; the prize for either party was a cockerel.[17] The most common entertainment of Plough Monday, however, during the following three hundred years, was a 'privatization' of the medieval gatherings, whereby plough boys dragged a plough around their neighbourhood, collecting money from homes and passers-by to be spent upon a feast for themselves. During the eighteenth and nineteenth centuries, this was observed regularly in Norfolk, Cambridgeshire, Bedfordshire, Huntingdonshire, Northamptonshire, Lincolnshire, Leicestershire, Rutland, Nottinghamshire, Derbyshire, the East Riding of Yorkshire, County Durham, and Northumberland.[18] It was also occasionally known in Staffordshire and Hertfordshire, with possible isolated examples in Sussex, Somerset, and Devon.[19] To increase both the formality and the festivity of the action, and to make it more enjoyable for all concerned, the lads generally wore fancy dress. Sometimes this just involved putting on white shirts with ribbons, or blackening faces. At others the teams wore cloth patches cut to the shape of ploughs or of farm animals. In places (such as the Norwich area in the mid-eighteenth century), they all put on female clothing, but more often just one of their number did so, being called the Bessy. At times they were all simply described as being in 'antic' dress or 'bright' clothes, or straw garments. Some teams played music, and one in Northamptonshire included a pair of hunchbacked Fools with knaves of hearts, from playing cards, sewn onto their clothes. They could have a leader, called in places Tommy, Billy Buck, or Captain Calf's Tail, who often doubled as a clown where he appeared; his costume might have included a coat of tattered cloth or shredded skin, a fox-skin hood, a bullock's tail, or a whip with the traditional Fool's bladder on the end. There was little more standardization in the names for them than in their dress: they were commonly just known as Plough Boys, Lads, or Jacks, but also as the Stot Plough (in Northumberland and Durham), Plough Bullocks or Stots (meaning the same thing, in Yorkshire and the north-east Midlands), Kitwitches (in Norfolk, from their women's garb), and Plough Witches (in the southern part of their range). During the nineteenth century, as metal ploughs became usual, they emphasized their traditional nature by continuing to appear with an old-style wooden one; along Tyneside they used a small anchor instead, but still called it a plough.

There always seems to have been at least a potential element of coercion in the custom, as it was conducted by a group of young men, seeking money or some equivalent donation towards a feast, and equipped with a piece of machinery which could inflict damage to property. An observer in Derbyshire in 1762 commented dispassionately that 'if you refuse them, they plough up your dunghill'.[20] As the population grew, social divisions widened, and the new populist radicalism of the end of the century made an increasing impact, the friction generated by the tradition seems to have worsened in proportion. At Derby Assizes in 1810 a Peak District farmer sued over twenty 'plough bullocks' from Blackwell, who had arrived on his property dragging 'the common plough' and accompanied by a piper. When he refused money, they ploughed up his drive, lawn, and bench, and he claimed £20 damages; the jury, however, was against him and he got 1s.[21] Six years later, however, similar japes in Staffordshire earned a team leader a heavy fine. In 1821 the Lincoln-shire JPs issued a threat to deal with any misbehaviour by the local 'bullocks' 'with exemplary severity'.[22] Twenty years later William Howitt, surveying the whole east Midland region, declared that 'the insolence of these Plough-bullocks as they are called, which might accord with ancient custom but does not suit all modern habits, has contributed more than anything else to put them down'. His sentiments were expressed by various local newspapers.[23] The rowdiness of the practice, and the drunkenness which it often funded, made it as obnoxious to sections of the working population as to the social élite, and in particular to Primitive Methodists, who campaigned strenuously to stop it during the early nineteenth century.[24] Farming families in the East Riding could find the 'Ploo Lads' frighteningly 'rude and bold' if their houses stood in isolated places. A writer in 1890 had 'a vivid recollection of his mother keeping one of these fellows at bay with a sweeping-brush, while he bolted the door to prevent any further inroad'.[25] Even later in the century, Plough Monday in the Huntingdonshire Fens was a principal occasion for satisfying grudges.[26]

Some of the teams did try hard to provide entertainments which would encourage a greater acceptance and generosity. The simplest of these was to chant rhymes, according to strongly marked local traditions. In the St Neots area of Huntingdonshire, the usual one began:

> Remember us poor plough boys
> A-ploughing we must go.
> Whether it's rain, blow, hail or snow,
> A-ploughing we must go...

At Kimbolton, not far away in the same county, it commenced:

> A hole in my stocking
> A hole in my shoe,
> Will you spare a poor plough boy
> A copper or two...[27]

The appeal here was to charity and pity. Eastward in the Fenland, comedy was used to elicit sympathy instead. Either on Plough Monday or on the following day, the 'Plough Witches' would lead around one of their number on a chain, covered in straw and pretending to be a bear, growling and capering. Sir James Frazer thought that this costume was probably a remnant of an ancient pagan rite and represented a corn spirit. This is still possible, but the custom was confined to a small area of the Huntingdonshire Fens, from Ramsey to Whittlesey, is not recorded before the late nineteenth century, and may well represent an outgrowth of the earlier local custom of wearing straw costume when going around with the plough, inspired by the popular entertainment of the dancing bear.[28]

Further north, the youths often provided a more spectacular entertainment; indeed the most elaborate of all English seasonal folk-drama, the Plough Monday Play. It had been recorded by 1967 in seventy-seven communities, being especially important in northern Lincolnshire, common in the southern half of the county and in Nottinghamshire, and found occasionally in Leicestershire and Rutland. Fifty-six texts have been recovered. The action usually began with a leader (the 'Fool' or 'Tommy') calling in the players one by one. A recruiting sergeant then invited men to enlist in the army, and was refused by a ploughboy or farmer's man. The latter then wooed a lady (played of course by a lad), who rejected him in turn and chose the Fool. In over half the texts another, coarser, transvestite called 'Dame Jane' appeared, and accused the Fool of fathering her child. Usually there was now a combat and revival sequence like that in the Mummers' Play, sometimes a dance, and sometimes a gambol by a hobby-horse based loosely on the 'tournament' model. The performance ended with a leading-out oration or general dance. It is clear from this summary how much variety existed between the plays even in this confined range, and indeed they were really a fund of speeches around which individual teams arranged actions. Ballads, and quotations from stage plays, were often added. Costumes were, of course, equally heterogeneous, some groups dressing in character, but most in rags, old sacks, or ribbons, commonly blackening their faces as well to distance themselves further from the spectators and lend a greater theatricality to their actions. The basic unit which provided the teams was a single farm, the players being its young labourers. In cases where motivation is recorded, the need for money ranks as most important, but most of the performers clearly also enjoyed their work. Their competence varied considerably, and so did their welcome; some Lincolnshire teams carried sticks to beat off the dogs set on them by hostile farmers. The squire of Alkborough, near the Humber, stopped the play there in the 1890s because the actors were incapable of remaining sober.[29]

The distinctive nature of the wooing motif in the 'Plough Play' was recognized from the moment that T. F. Ordish began the serious study of English folk-drama in the 1880s, and it was treated by subsequent writers upon the Mummers' Play. Sir Edmund Chambers suggested that it was grafted onto the hero-combat but was itself an old theme, appearing in the *Satyre of the Thrie Estatis* written by Sir David Lindsay for the early sixteenth-century Scottish court.[30] It may be added here that the same plot, of a lady who is won by a Fool, seems to have featured prominently in the late medieval morris dance, from which Lindsay may have taken it. Chambers considered that it was a 'natural' theme in any society. Similar reflections were produced by other detailed studies of the Plough Play between 1920 and 1960.[31] They were challenged by Alan Brody in 1969, in what was probably the last major work of the old sort of folklore studies,[32] with the argument that the 'wooing ceremony' was actually older than the combat and resurrection. To him the man–woman and Fool were figures left from a very ancient fertility ritual.

The problem with this sort of speculation was the familiar one: that the first datable Plough Play text derives from Bassingham, near Lincoln, in 1823, and the second from Broughton, at the north end of that county, in the following year. Even taking literally the accompanying declaration that the Broughton version had been performed for about sixty years before it was recorded, this does not get further back than the 1760s.[33] In October 1779, however, a play was performed at the hall at Revesby on the southern edge of the Lincolnshire Wolds, the seat of Sir Joseph Banks. The text survives in the British Library, and combines the sword dance, wooing motif, and death and resurrection plot in unique fashion, and this caused a succession of scholars of folk-drama to regard it as ancestral, the original combination of rituals from which all the rest had hived off.[34] Otherwise, rather desperate efforts were made to identify particular sixteenth-century plays as antecedents. In 1953 M. W. Barley cited one performed in the 1560s by the parishoners of Donington in the Lincolnshire Fens, as a Plough Play. There is, however, no evidence of the season at which it was performed, and the cast list (which is all we have) bears no resemblance to those of the later plough drama.[35] Two years later, H. M. Shire and K. Elliott[36] identified a Scottish 'Plough Song' dating from around 1500 as a parallel to that later drama. As, however, it describes the slaughter of a dying ox and the harnessing of a new one, it has nothing in common save the theme of death and renewal (in this case by replacement not resurrection). Nor is there any proof that the actions of the song were mimed out as these authors suggested.

The question clearly needed the application of proper techniques of source analysis, investigation of local records, and the careful reconstruction of context, and all these were provided in the 1980s. The Revesby play text turned out to be a polished work composed by a scholarly hand, almost certainly that of Sir Joseph Banks's sister, Sara, a keen antiquarian interested in popular pastimes. The performers all came from the Revesby district itself, and were plainly provided with a script which put together a range of customs currently enjoyed by country people. There was, in short, nothing ancestral about it.[37] Since the 1950s, scholars had recognized that, even within Lincolnshire and Nottinghamshire, the Plough Play was almost confined to the clay and limestone regions, and almost totally absent from the Fens, coastal marshes, forests, or vale of Belvoir.[38] In other words, it was found not in the more remote and conservative communities, but in areas of large-scale arable farming, supported by large numbers of young workers living in their employers' houses. Alun Howkins and Linda Merricks now studied these areas and found that it was precisely in the later eighteenth century that this sort of farming developed, representing some of the most advanced and commercia-lized agriculture in England. It sucked in crowds of unmarried youths as labour, hired for the year and noted for their strong sense of group identity and their rowdiness. Howkins and Merricks suggested, convincingly, that the old Plough Monday gatherings were developed by this new labour force into the plays, a grand celebration of licensed misrule. The verses vaunted the performers' strength and pride in their work. The action was public and noisy, the costumes mocked normality, and the characters (notably the Fool) mocked authority. They also expressed a fear of women, with a great deal of adolescent ribaldry. At the same time, at a more profound level, the plot reinforced traditional morality, and so affirmed the values of the whole society.[39]

Much the same sort of process occurred in the study of one of the most famous and most bizarre of British calendar customs, the Haxey Hood Game on Twelfth Day in the Isle of Axholme. It centres upon a Fool, a Lord, and eleven 'boggins' in strawberry-hued coats or sweaters, who preside over a succession of struggles in a huge ploughed field between the villages of Haxey and Westwoodside. The object of each is to capture a coil of old rope inside a leather tube (called a 'hood') and to get it into a pub in one of the two settlements. Beforehand the Fool stands up on the stump of a cross outside Haxey church and announces the rules of the game, while a fire is lit behind him so that the smoke blows about his body (and into the crowd). The scrums around the 'hoods' rarely result in serious injury because the mud of the field is so soft, deep, and clinging; the same phenomenon, however, does mean that a typical contest can push round and round the same spot for hours. In 1896 Mabel Peacock drew the attention of the Folk-Lore Society to it, with the suggestion that it was a rite of ancient solar worship (the hood representing the sun) and human sacrifice (smoking the Fool) held near Haxey church, a former pagan holy place (the evidence for which was the game).[40] This notion, with or without all of the detailed suggestions, became an orthodoxy among folklorists; another luminary of the Society almost seventy years later, E. O. James, could describe it as 'a transitional rite at the end of the Midwinter festival, of ritual combat and sacrifice'.[41] It was left to Venetia Newall, one of the first of the new breed of rigorous scholars in folklore studies, to make a comprehensive investigation of the game's history in 1980.[42] She found that, with the exception of the smoking of the Fool, which seems to be a unique local invention, all the components of the game were common Lincolnshire Twelfthtide events of the eighteenth century. They seem to have been put together by the villages' 'plough bullocks', to provide sport on the Epiphany holiday before setting out on the usual Plough Day gatherings. Their alternative name, at Haxey, was 'boggins', probably derived from a dialect word for marsh fairies. The process of construction was complete by 1815, and all that happened thereafter was that the plough collections, and therefore the name of 'plough bullocks', were dropped.

As in the case of the Padstow 'Oss and the Horn Dance, the very atypicality of the custom enabled it to survive, as the expression of a unique community, while the norm from which it had derived completely disappeared. During the nineteenth century the agriculture of the east Midlands passed into long-term recession, demand for labour fell off yet further with mechanization of processes, and the culture of the plough boys collapsed. As wages rose for the relative few who remained, the need to beg extra money was reduced. The plays and gatherings accordingly atrophied, and although both were still observed in a few places in the 1930s, the former in Lincolnshire and the latter in Huntingdonshire, Cambridgeshire, and north Bedfordshire, they all seem to have ended with the outbreak of the Second World War.[43] Over precisely the same span of time, however, an equally old tradition was being revived; the blessing of a plough in the local church to mark the opening of the traditional season of tillage on Plough Sunday. Bob Bushaway has indeed suggested that the two phenomena were related, and that the church services represented a form of enhanced social control of the populace by the local élite to replace the rowdy importunities of the 'plough bullocks'.[44] No detailed research exists to substantiate or refute this point, but it does appear that the adoption of the services was a very slow business, even now affecting only a minority of rural parishes; that it commenced in the West Country, which had no general tradition of 'plough games'; and that it was more bound up with the antiquarianism of the Anglo-Catholic movement than efforts of social engineering. It acquired a much higher profile with the pressure upon English agriculture created by the Second World War, which made the farmlands seem once again, to many, to be a sacred resource. In 1943 the Council for Church and Countryside set about sponsoring the blessings, and they were instituted subsequently in the cathedrals of Chichester, Salisbury, and Exeter. At the first of those the local Young Farmers' Club drew a plough to the cathedral chancel, where the bishop himself read the new form of prayer. There was also a further adoption of the rite by parish churches, scattered thinly across eastern and southern England, and it has persisted in most of these and in the three cathedrals. Its traditional nature is emphasized by the fact that an old-fashioned wooden wheel-plough is generally used for (and made for) the occasion.[45] The service did not, however, always manage to take root in areas which had no previous history of rituals concerned with arable cultivation; an attempt to introduce it to Dorset churches in the 1970s failed completely, as did one by the morris dancer Rolf Gardiner in the 1930s, to persuade his colleagues in that county to take up a Plough Play as well as reviving the morris and the Mummers' Play.[46]

On the other hand, the second great wave of 'folk revival', which began in the 1960s, had much more success in restoring semblances of plough customs to districts where they had once been very popular. In the 1970s the 'straw bear' reappeared at Whittlesey in the Huntingdonshire Fens, and has remained there ever since on the day after Plough Monday.[47] The latter celebration was revived in 1971 at Balsham in the Cambridgeshire chalk hills, by the local folk club. Its members discovered that by-laws now forbade them to call from door to door, so they arranged calls in advance as 'guests', and dragged a plough around collecting money for the elderly.[48] That revival persisted, and was joined by another in 1984 at Fenstanton out in the fenland to the north-west. The plough here was drawn by a horse, and accompanied around the village by about forty singing and dancing people in fancy dress, gathered from three counties; the proceeds went to local charities. From 1979 onward, also, the 'Molly Dancers' reappeared in pubs and streets in a growing number of villages in the Huntingdonshire and Cambridgeshire Fens (to use the old county names).[49] The performers in all these cases represent the cultural inheritance and financial needs of a whole community rather than a group within it. None the less, some of them were children of people who had carried out the customs in their twilight years of the 1930s, so that it might be most objective to speak of these re-creations as a latest development within an ongoing local tradition now spanning more than half a millennium of re-corded history. Furthermore, the shift to a communal focus is, after all, a faithful reversion to the form in which the gatherings first appear, in the parish records of the later Middle Ages.

12

BRIGID'S NIGHT*

ONE of the 'Ulster Cycle' of early medieval Irish tales is *Tochmarc Emire*,
the story of the wooing of Emer by the hero Cú Chulainn, which (at
least in its extant form) was probably composed in the tenth or eleventh
century. One of the tests which she set her semi-divine suitor was to go
sleepless for a year, and in setting her challenge she named the main calendar
points of the yearly cycle as they feature repeatedly in Irish literature of the
time. Instead of denoting the cardinal points of the sun or the main Christian
festivals, she indicated the opening of the four seasons. One of those which
she named was 'Imbolc, when the ewes are milked at spring's beginning'.[1] The
same feast, marking the end of winter and the opening of spring, is cited
repeatedly in the early medieval literature under the names Imbolc, Imbolg, or
Óimelc; as the 'b' in the first two is silent and the first syllable in the last is a
short 'i', the different words have a very similar pronunciation, as 'imolk' or
'imelk'. It was placed in the Roman calendar, adopted by the Irish by the time
that written records begin, on 1 February. The festival must be pre-Christian
in origin, but there is absolutely no direct testimony as to its early nature, or
concerning any rites which might have been employed then. There is, in fact,
no sign that any of the medieval Irish writers who referred to it preserved a
memory of them, and some evidence that they no longer understood the
meaning of the name itself. *Sanas Chormaic*, a glossary probably produced
around the year 900, suggested that it originally meant 'sheep's milk', a
derivation which modern Celticists have pointed out to be linguistically impossible. The latter part of the word, however, certainly has something to do
with milking, so that Emer's comment must be near the mark: that this is the
time when ewes begin to lactate. Eric Hamp has recently suggested, by analogy
with other old European languages and customs, that the Old Irish words for
milk and milking derived from a lost Indo-European root-term for 'purification', and that this was the aim of the festival; but this remains a speculation.[2]

Whatever did happen at it, the feast was important enough for its date to be
dedicated subsequently to Brigid, Bridget, Bride, Brighid, Brid, or Brig, the
major figure in the early Irish Church after Patrick himself, and the Mother
Saint of Ireland. It seems reasonably certain that behind this alleged holy

---

* Seamús Cathain's important book, *The Festival of Brigid* (Dublin, 1995) appeared too late for
use in this work.

woman, of whom no contemporary or near-contemporary records survive, stands a pagan goddess of the same name. What is by no means clear is whether there was one goddess, or a triple one, or several, and whether there was in addition a real Christian woman of the same name with whom the deity became conflated. In legend the goddess-figure was associated with learning, poetry, prophesying, healing, and metal-working, and was in general the most pleasant Irish female deity. The saint was portrayed more as a provider of plenty and a friend of animals, with a very close association with the whole natural world. She could also be a battle goddess, the particular patroness of the armies of the province of Leinster, where her cult centre was situated at Kildare. She may therefore have begun as a local tutelary goddess, but some modern writers have preferred to view her as a pan-Celtic deity, and linked her to the Romano-British Brigantia. The latter was, however, essentially the tutelary goddess of one major tribe, the Brigantes, although the Roman identification of her with their own Minerva, the goddess of war, crafts, and skills, indicates a group of characteristics very similar to those of the Irish Brigid. The name of the latter means 'fiery arrow', and by the twelfth century it was traditional for an eternal flame to be kept burning in her shrine at Kildare, which many modern writers have surmised to have been a survival from an original pagan temple there. In legend, however, the goddess was not especially associated with fire, and (more significantly) the very important seventh-century life of St Brigid written by Cogitosus at Kildare makes no mention of the custom; it is possible, therefore, that it grew up between the seventh and twelfth centuries as a derivation from the meaning of the saint's name. The goddess may already have been linked to Imbolc, or it could be that the festival's association with milk drew the saint to it, because of a popular medieval Irish legend that she had (somehow) been the wet-nurse of Christ. It must be obvious from all this how rich the material is for imaginative reconstructions of the ancient cult of Brigid, and how little it supports absolutely certain conclusions.[3]

By the opening of the eighteenth century, if not long before, the belief had developed that the saint would visit virtuous households upon the eve of her feast, and bless the inhabitants as they slept. During the nineteenth, traditions regarding this visit were recorded all over Ireland. Their starting-point was usually a formal supper, shared by the family, to mark the last night of winter. Very often some of the food, such as a cake, or bread and butter, was placed outside on a window-sill as a gift for the saint. More frequently still, people would plait a *críosog Bridghe*, or a St Brigid's cross woven of rushes (or, occasionally, straw), and hang it over a door or window or in the rafters as a sign of welcome for her; others were commonly put in stables to obtain blessings for the beasts. These objects took many different forms, partly according to region. The straightforward three-armed Christian cross was rarely used; instead four-armed examples, often set in lozenges or crooked at the ends as swastikas, were normal. Such shapes are known in prehistoric

European art, so may in this case have been adopted directly from the ancient past. On the other hand, the first record of the crosses comes from 1689, when they were associated with the summer feast of Corpus Christi, and their enduring linkage with St Brigid's Eve was not noted until 1728. The dearth of information upon Irish popular customs before the eighteenth century prevents anything more than speculation as to the date and means of origin of this one. The crosses were generally left up for the next year, to protect the house from lightning, and replaced on the next St Brigid's Eve. Frequently they were made from a sheaf of rushes or straw representing the saint, wrapped in a garment and (usually) brought into the house by a young woman. There was often a ceremony of welcome for it, with set questions and responses, and at times the remainder of the bundle, or some birch twigs, were made into a bed by the fire in case the saint wanted to rest awhile on her visit.[4]

It was also a common custom to put a *bratog Bride*, *brat Bride*, or *ribín Bride* outside upon a window-sill overnight, being a cloth, garment, or ribbon which St Brigid would bless in passing and which would subsequently prevent headaches in the wearers. The following day, her feast, a straw figure dressed in baby clothes was carried round by children, women, or young men at places in all parts of Ireland except the most Anglicized (north Leinster and Ulster). It was called the *Breedhoge*, *Brídeóg*, or Biddy, and represented the saint; the bearers collected money or food as the appearance of the image was supposed to be lucky; it probably replaced the parish statue carried round upon her feast before the establishment of the Protestant Church of Ireland. In western Connacht lads took round instead a *crios Bride*, St Brigid's girdle, a huge circle of straw with a cross woven in the centre. People were invited to step through it, and so be blessed.[5]

In so many ways, therefore, did the Irish honour, and seek favour from, their national Mother Saint. By contrast, her cult was comparatively weak in Britain, being developed mostly in cities which possessed Irish visitors or immigrants, or stations for Irish pilgrims crossing the island, such as Glastonbury Abbey. Glastonbury, indeed, carefully nurtured its association with her, claiming to possess her relics in rivalry with Kildare, a process undoubtedly encouraged by the ambitions of the abbey's royal English patrons to extend their influence in the British Isles. For similar reasons Glastonbury also claimed to possess the bodies of St Patrick, St David, and several Northumbrian holy men. Elsewhere in Britain, however, Brigid was essentially a foreigner, and practices like those so plentiful in Ireland were found only in peripheral places where Irish influence was strong. One of these was the Isle of Man, where in the eighteenth century 31 January was called *Laa'l Breeshey*, Brigid's Festival, and

the custom then was to gather a bundle of green rushes, and standing with them in the hand on the threshold of the door, to invite the holy Saint Bridget to come and lodge with them that night. . . . saying 'Brede, Brede, come to my house tonight. Open the door for Brede and let Brede come in.' After these words were repeated, the rushes were strewn on the floor by way of a carpet or bed for St Bridget.[6]

In the nineteenth century old Manx women still sometimes made up a bed in the barn for 'Breeshy' on this night, with bread, cheese, a jug of ale, and a lighted candle left beside it.[7]

The other area was the Hebrides, where at the end of the seventeenth century a traveller noted that in Catholic communities

the mistress and servants of each family take a sheaf of oats and dress it up in woman's apparel, put it in a large basket, and lay a wooden club by it, and this they call Brüd's bed; and then the mistress and servants cry three times 'Brüd is come, Brud is welcome.' This they do just before going to bed, and when they rise in the morning they look among the ashes, expecting to see the impression of Brüd's club there; which if they do, they reckon it a true presage of a good crop and a prosperous year, and the contrary they take as an ill omen.[8]

In the later eighteenth century another observer recorded that in the same islands and on the neighbouring coast of Scotland (he did not specify districts or communities) it was usual on 1 February

to make a bed with corn and hay, over which some blankets are laid in a part of the house near the door. When it is ready, a person goes out and repeats three times 'a Bhrid, a Bhrid, thig a sligh as gabh do heabaidh'—'Bridget, Bridget, come in; thy bed is ready.' One or more candles are left burning near it all night.[9]

During the early part of the next century St Bride's Day (*Latha 'ill Brídhe*) was still remembered 'in some places' of this region. Feasts were held, at which women would dance holding a large cloth by the corners and call '*Bridean, Bridean, thig an nall's dean do leabaidh*' (Bride, Bride come over and make your bed). The bed itself, however, was by then rarely made, although a little straw might be thrown together in a corner.[10]

The most elaborate of all such descriptions come from the later part of the century, being derived from the Catholic settlements of the Outer Hebrides, at a time when such customs had died out elsewhere and were presumed by other observers to have done so there as well. They were published by Alexander Carmichael,[11] and it may be charitably argued (and will be assumed when dealing with his work henceforth in this book) that the discrepancy is due to his more profound knowledge of the islanders concerned; though some confusion is created by the fact that he always used the present tense for portraits of customs which in a few cases he explicitly acknowledged to have vanished a generation or two before he wrote. In this case he recorded that

On St Bride's Eve the girls of a townland fashion a sheaf of corn into the likeness of a woman. They dress and deck the figure with shining shells, sparkling crystals, primroses, snowdrops and any greenery they may obtain...A specially bright shell or crystal is placed over the heart of the figure. This is called *reul-iuil Bride*, the guiding star of Bride, and typifies the star over the stable door at Bethlehem.

He went on to speak of how the girls called the image 'Brideag' and carried it in procession singing a hymn to the saint. All wore white with their hair unbound, as symbols of purity and youth. They visited every house in the townland and received either more decorations for the figure or bannocks, butter, and cheese. At the end they feasted on the foodstuffs in a house with a barred door and the image set in a place of honour. When the meal was done, the young men humbly asked for admission, made obeisance to the Brideag, and joined the girls in dancing and making merry until dawn. Then all formed a circle and sang the hymn *Bride bhoidheach muime chorr Chriosda* (Beauteous Bride, foster mother of Christ). The fragments of food left over were given to local poor women.

Adult females spent the Eve making an oblong basket in the shape of a cradle, called *leaba Bride*, 'the bed of Bride'. They also made an oatsheaf into the form of a woman and decked it with ribbons, shells, bright stones, and flowers. This was the *dealbh Bride* (icon of Bride). When both were ready, one went to the doorstep and called softly into the darkness, 'Bride's bed is ready.' One behind her replied, 'Let Bride come in, Bride is welcome.' The woman at the door called again: 'Bride, Bride come in. Thy bed is made. Preserve the house for the Trinity.' The icon was laid in the bed and a peeled wand of birch, broom, bramble, or willow put beside it. Then they smoothed out the ashes and retired to sleep. If the mark of the wand was found there in the morning, this was a good sign. If a footprint was found, this was wonderful, but if there was nothing then the household would be dejected because Bride had not listened to it. Bad fortune was almost guaranteed unless the people buried a cock as an offering at the junction of three streams and burned incense on their fire before they next went to bed.

Nothing quite like this is recorded outside this group of islands (and there only by this single writer), but all of it represents an exceptionally ornate version of the St Brigid's Eve customs noted elsewhere in the Hebrides and in Ireland and Man. In the islands and some Irish communities, they were designed to give a particular prominence, and dignity, to the women of a community—an appropriate phenomenon at the feast of Ireland's greatest female saint. Nothing like them is known from the other areas of the British Isles which spoke Celtic languages; from the Scottish Highlands, Wales, or Cornwall. The first of those regions shared a Gaelic tongue with Ireland and the Western Isles, but (clearly) not sufficient of an Irish identity. The whole of mainland Britain celebrated the opening of spring, instead, with a pan-European Christian festival which must be the subject of the next chapter.

13

CANDLEMAS

❧⟨⟩☙

In the Gospel of Luke there occurs a story of how the infant Jesus was taken to the Temple at Jerusalem by his parents because his mother needed to make the traditional offering to purify herself, forty days after childbirth. The baby was recognized there, according to the tale, by an old man called Simeon, who hailed him as the Messiah of Israel and a 'light to lighten the Gentiles'. It was an important episode in Luke's construction of the life of Christ, furnishing the first proof of a theme especially dear to this evangelist: that Jesus had come to save all humanity and not, as some early Christians had held, the Jews alone. As the Gentile churches came rapidly to outnumber those among the Jews, it could only be enhanced in significance. A commemoration of the event would, moreover, have a double message, for it was also a major episode in the career of the Virgin Mary, marking the end of the process which had commenced with her conception of the Messiah. As the status of Christ as a semi-divine being was emphasized ever more strongly with the triumph of the Church in the Roman world, the cult of his mother as a mortal who had become more than human waxed in its train. Both came together in the feast of the Purification of the Blessed Virgin Mary, at once a festival of Christ and of his mother, which (as the event had to have occurred, according to Hebrew law, forty days after the Nativity), was installed upon 2 February.

None the less, it took a long time to develop and its origins are obscure. It is first definitely recorded in seventh-century Rome, in a context which suggests that it had arrived from Gaul but with a name which suggests that it had first appeared in the Greek world. Some sort of festival of the Purification was certainly operating among the eastern churches by the fourth century. Once the Roman Church had taken it up, its adoption throughout western Europe was assured, and rapid; it had reached England by the end of the seventh century, and by the time that Bede wrote (some three to four decades later) had acquired its characteristic ritual of a candlelit procession.[1] Its success was clearly not due merely to its exposition of an important point of scripture, but to the manner in which it fulfilled profound seasonal needs. The Roman word *februa*, which gave the month its name, signified purification, and the ceremonies of the pagan Roman February had mostly been rites of cleansing, in preparation for a fresh start to many activities in the coming spring.[2] A Christian feast of purification therefore fitted into a long tradition. There was, however, apparently nothing in the ancient Roman February rites which prefigured the Christian ceremony of kindling candles, an action which seems to have been directly suggested by the words attributed to old Simeon in the gospel. This point matters because some Protestant writers at the time of the Reformation tried to defame the medieval ritual by declaring that it had been taken directly from a pagan Roman festival of lights upon the same date,[3] an assertion occasionally repeated by later folklorists. In Ireland the feast of the Purification fell right next to the pre-Christian one of Imbolc but, as said, the latter was consecrated to St Brigid instead; this development produced a direct clash as Christians were supposed to fast upon the eve of the Purification, whereas the Irish were making merry then in honour of Brigid. The Viking sagas do not seem to preserve a memory of any traditional festival between Yule and the 'Summer Nights' in April. According to Bede, on the other hand, the pagan Anglo-Saxons called February 'Sol-monath', 'cake month', and in it they offered special cakes to their deities.[4] This looks like a convincing record of an early English feast at the opening of spring, only providing that Bede was not just guessing at the meaning of the name. He gave, however, no indication of when in the month it fell, and the Christian celebration was concerned with purification and lights, not with cakes. The Christian feast has, therefore, no demonstrable links with ancient northern European practices.

It clearly, however, had a tremendous emotional appeal in the north. If its association in the Mediterranean world was chiefly with purification, its importance further north, where winters were darker and colder, was primarily as a celebration of returning light. The words of the Use of Sarum, the form of service most commonly employed in later medieval England and Scotland, made the point strongly. They played upon images of the appearance of divine light in the darkness of human sin, of renewal and rebirth of light in the dark time of the year, and of the new light of heaven manifested to an old world. The liturgy also testifies with equal strength to the way in which, by this period, the candles carried in procession on the feast had become objects of veneration in themselves. Every parishioner was obliged to bring and carry one, and to offer it to the priest to be blessed, paying a penny for the service. The benediction was accomplished by placing each candle before the high altar, sprinkling it with holy water, perfuming it with incense, and pronouncing the blessing over it. Part of the latter stated that once the sanctified candle was lit 'the devil may flee away in prayer and trembling'. What happened to the consecrated objects next seems to have varied according to local custom or to individual wish. They were carried round the church again after mass, and then some seem to have been burned before a statue of the Virgin, and others taken home to be lit in times of storm or sickness, or in the hands of the dying.[5] From this ceremony the feast took its popular British name of Candlemas; it marked the formal opening of spring and of the month which drives the darkness from the afternoon and (in England at least) usually restores the first flowers to the earth and the first buds to the trees.

Late medieval records testify amply to its celebration in Britain. Upon 1 February, when the Irish, Hebrideans, and Manx were (presumably) feasting in honour of Brigid, the British were expected to eat only bread and drink only water. Then the next day dawned and (in the words of a fourteenth-century Shropshire monk, John Mirk) churches 'made great melody', and worshippers prepared to have their candles blessed. Some parish churches bought them in bulk for the feast, either to be presented to parishioners or to light up the building further. Some made a 'trendle', a circular frame which either operated as a conventional chandelier or rotated each candle in turn beneath the priest's hands for benediction. The candle of Henry VII was carried at his right-hand side by the Lord Chamberlain as he processed into the Chapel Royal. Under the young Henry VIII, the fifth earl of Northumberland presented them in his own chapel on behalf of himself and his family, while the Warwickshire gentleman Sir Henry Willoughby offered them for his servants as well.[6] Some towns staged processions to the churches. At Beverley in the East Riding, the Guild of the Blessed Virgin dressed up one of its members as its patroness, carrying a doll to represent Christ. She was followed by two men costumed as Joseph and Simeon, two people attired as angels bearing a frame which held twenty-four candles, and then the remaining sisters and brothers bearing their own, with musicians. At the church the 'Virgin' offered the doll to 'Simeon' at the high altar and the others presented their candles to be blessed.[7] The craft guilds of Aberdeen in the fifteenth and early sixteenth centuries provided pageants to accompany their members through the streets with their candles; in 1442 these consisted of the Three Kings, an emperor, Saints Bride, Helena, and Joseph, bishops, angels, 'woodmen', knights, and minstrels.[8] Once the service was over, people could feast to the utmost of their ability. Grimsby, Coventry, and Cambridge held municipal banquets, and in the last of those places the town musicians toured the streets. Winter regulations for urban street-lighting and watchmen, in force since All Saints' Day, came to an end.[9] Villagers began to drive their livestock from fields which they had manured in the cold season, to make way for sowing.[10] Some of the worst cold and privation of the confined season might well still be ahead, but there was now the promise of better times not far away.

The Reformation, inevitably, tore out the central ritual from the feast, as Protestants viewed the sanctification of the candles as a 'superstitious' act turning the minds of people from true religion. Henry VIII compromised by confirming the ceremony in a proclamation of 1539, but emphasizing that it was to be seen only as a means to honour Christ as the light of the world and not as a way of producing magical objects. It was left to the far more Protestant regime of the duke of Somerset to abolish it altogether, just over a year after Henry's death, in another proclamation of February 1548. Like the other religious measures of Somerset's Government, it seems to have been swiftly enforced, and there is no further trace of the hallowing of candles in the remaining reign of the young Edward VI. Candlemas itself remained a holy day, but as a feast of Christ and not of the Virgin. Then Mary succeeded, and her Catholic prelates made the blessing of the candles compulsory once more; the extant records indicate that it once again became widespread in England. It was banned again by Elizabeth in 1559, and this prohibition in turn seems to have been immediately effective. The only known exceptions were at Crediton in central Devon, where wax was bought for Candlemas 1560, and Ludlow in the Welsh Marches, where a pound of candles was obtained for the feast in 1562. In both cases it is likely that the rite of blessing was intended, but not certain, and they seem to be the last of their kind, at least until the Anglo-Catholic readoption of a form of the ceremony in the nineteenth century.[11]

In 1560, also, the Scottish Reformation swept the ritual away in that country, although enforcement must have been a much more lengthy affair because of the persistence of Catholic communities in the Highlands and Western Isles. Nevertheless, it may be significant that these communities were subsequently found to be celebrating St Brigid's Eve and Day, and not Candlemas, and the latter feast lingered longest, instead, in the Shetlands, which were just as remote but Norse and not Gaelic in culture. Until 1711 people used to bear candles to the Crosskirk at Northmavine after dark on Candlemas night. They would burn them there and feast, even though there was no longer any blessing by a cleric. Instead the people themselves offered them with prayers, and kept them to be lit, as before, when ill fortune threatened. The tradition ended when a zealous minister razed the kirk. A traveller in 1700 also found candles burning at Candlemas upon the altar of the ruined kirk on St Ninian's Isle. Later in the eighteenth century there is no further reference to such practices.[12] In Ireland, where the feast had apparently been kept as a supplement to that of Brigid, local priests continued quietly to bless candles for people as part of the general survival of Catholicism.[13]

That is not, however, the whole story, for the ritual of the feast migrated, in some places, into folk custom. In Dorset until the late eighteenth century candles were exchanged as private gifts at Candlemas, and at Lyme Regis it was the tradition for each household to burn one and to stand and drink about it.[14] In 1853 it was remembered as having been customary 'to light up a number of candles in the evening' in the villages along the Trent in Nottinghamshire.[15] Both records are retrospective, and indeed until the nineteenth century notices of domestic customs outside the south-east of England are very rare. It is difficult to tell whether these were the only cases in the country of a 'privatization' of the feast, and whether they themselves represented an empty formality or actions genuinely intended to bring good luck. In the Border districts of Scotland it was certainly deemed lucky to light fires of broom or gorse on hills at Candlemas, these blazes replacing the sacred flames of the churches.[16]

The situation in Wales was, however, of a different order altogether. From the seventeenth century there survive songs speaking with deepest reverence of the old feast, such as the one which translates as: 'It was a custom to bear drink at the Festival of the Virgin Mary at the beginning of spring...Mary went meekly to the church, with virgins from the locality, their candles all alight. The purification of Mary, with all their drink meeting her.' These 'Candlemas carols' occur in great number from the eighteenth century, and were clearly designed to be sung by groups going from house to house in North Welsh communities on the eve of the festival. A description survives from Caernarvonshire in that century, of the rite which accompanied them. When the singers performed outside a home they would be answered, through the closed door, with a series of riddles (a parallel to the South Welsh Mari Lwyd custom). Upon passing this test, they were admitted, to find a room lit with candles and (ideally) a maiden seated in a chair, with a baby boy in her arms, personifying the Virgin and Child. They then sang to her again in her praise and pledged her in the drink offered to them by way of reward. As in the Gaelic areas where Brigid was welcomed, a feast at the opening of spring had developed into a means (among other things) of paying respect to womanhood. This may reflect a pre-Christian tradition in these Celtic areas, or it may have been the natural result of the convergence of the two festivals of Brigid and Mary. The popularity of the carols suggests that the Welsh custom was widespread, at least in the north, but it had died out before 1800.[17] There is no trace of it in South Wales, but Candlemas (known in Welsh as *Gwyl Fair y Canhwyllau*, the Virgin's Feast of the Candles) remained important there as well. It is recorded that in many (though unspecified) places candles were always lit in the home or placed upon window-sills on that night until the nineteenth century. Their arcane associations were emphasized by the fact that they were employed for divination.[18] All over Wales, therefore, for about 200 years after Reformation, there are signs that aspects of the medieval rite of Candlemas had simply been taken from the churches and relocated in homes—a fact the more significant in that so little actual Catholicism survived there.

Candlemas remained a holy day in the Church of England, and was observed as such by the public until the late seventeenth century, when attention to it began gradually to ebb away, a process completed by its effective disappearance about a century later. It was, however, over this same period, when all remnants of the medieval festival were in decay, that a new early spring celebration developed among an important social group. It focused upon the following day, which until the Edwardian and Elizabethan Reformations had been the feast of St Blaise, a Cappadocian bishop who had become the medieval patron of wool-combing, wax-chandling, wild animals, and (appropriately for a saint with a holy day in February) sufferers from sore throats. It was the first of those responsibilities which became of considerable significance in the late eighteenth century, as the English woollen industry enjoyed a boom period based upon the traditional system of production whereby clothiers put out processing functions to workers operating in their own homes. These workers seem increasingly to have required a ritualized means of expressing communal pride and solidarity, and found it in the feast which had technically been abolished in the mid-Tudor period. It was the last and greatest of those craft celebrations which flowered in the earlier part of the Industrial Revolution and which had commenced with the shoemakers upon St Crispin's Day.

Already in the 1670s it was noted that on St Blaise's Day Oxfordshire wool-workers 'went about and made good cheer, and if they found any of their neighbour-women a-spinning, set their distaff on fire'.[19] From the 1760s onward processions upon this date appeared in woollen districts all over England, from Devon to Hampshire, Hertfordshire, and Essex, and so north-ward to Yorkshire.[20] They always included 'Bishop' Blaise (or Blaze, Blase, or Blasius) in his mitre and robes; these Protestant artisans would have no time for saints. Jason and the Argonauts represented another favourite subject, because of the symbolism of the Golden Fleece, as did shepherds and shep-herdesses. The following parade, observed at an unnamed town in the North of England in the 1800s, seems to have been typical. It

was led by Jason . . . who was followed by shepherds and shepherdesses; a beautiful girl elegantly dressed, carried a lamb in her lap, with a bouquet of flowers made from wool in her bosom; next followed the venerable bishop, his mitre with the keys of St Peter gilt in front were formed of wool; and he had a large wig of the same material which reached down to the saddle; his bridle was held on each side by a page, and another was at the stirrups carrying a Bible in one hand and a wool-comb in the other; his followers dressed in white, with sashes, scarfs and high caps, carrying two large flags, all made of wool, and wands; two persons elevated on a stage were at work showing the manner in which the wool is combed.[21]

The public was thus edified as well as entertained.

The most ornate of these events were, naturally enough, in the district which was becoming the main woollen-manufacturing one of the country, around Bradford in Yorkshire. There they were subsidized by employers, and grew so elaborate that by the end of the eighteenth century it was customary to hold them only once every seven years. That in 1825 began at 10 a.m. First rode a herald, bearing a flag, and then the wool-staplers, upon horses saddled with fleeces. The worsted-makers followed in white wool waistcoats and sashes, their mounts having necks covered with yarn. Now came merchants in coloured sashes; apprentices in scarlet coats, white waistcoats and blue pantaloons; two local bands; a mace-bearer; a king and queen with guards; Jason and Medea, with their own armed retinue; Bishop Blaise; a shepherd and shepherdess with their company; and then the wool-sorters, comb-ma-kers, charcoal-burners, combers, two more bands, and finally the dyers in red cockades and blue aprons.[22] The entire industry was on display; but this was the last time that it could be. Later that year the Bradford combers went on strike, and the industrial and class conflict which ensued ruptured, for ever, the communal solidarity which the processions had expressed.[23] The strike itself, moreover, was a symptom of new strains upon the industry. All over England the system of domestic piece-work was dying, to be replaced by concentrated production in mills, and in fewer areas. The seasonal combination of workers in processions was slowly giving way to permanent combinations in clubs and trade unions. The St Blaise's Day celebrations withdrew into these during the early nineteenth century,[24] and then withered away there, as an anachronism.

Their disappearance left Britain bereft of any national festivals formally to mark the traditional end of winter and the opening of spring. During the twentieth century the notional beginning of spring came itself to be moved backwards to the vernal equinox, by a slow process induced by the mass media. This was part of an adoption of the American system of reckoning seasons from the solstices and equinoxes, which works admirably in the climate of most of the USA, but is nonsensical in the rhythm of the British year. February became for most people a friendless month, too far after Christmas and too long before Easter. All that rescues it now, in the popular imagination, are two other seasonal rituals surviving from the time when it was regarded as a time of hope and renewal. It is to these that the present study must now turn.

14

VALENTINES

꘏꘎꘍

Two out of the three most celebrated fourteenth-century English writers, Geoffrey Chaucer and John Gower, mentioned the same popular belief, that the birds choose their mates upon the feast of Valentine, their patron saint. Although still more credible further south in Europe, where spring would be more advanced, the idea made sense in Britain as well. By that date, 14 February, the mating flights of ravens, crows, and rooks would usually be visible, and they would be starting to repair their nests, while in a good year the spring songs of thrushes, finches, and woodpeckers would be beginning to swell. These were further omens of the approaching end of the time of cold and deprivation. How much further back in time the tradition goes is impossible to say, for the fourteenth century is the first in which literary works became available in sufficient quantity in England to make the recording of such notions likely. The third famous author to operate in it, Langland, did not refer to this one, but the most prominent writer in the first half of the fifteenth, John Lydgate, not only did so but went on to speak of a custom which had grown out of it. As part of a poem in honour of Queen Katherine, widow of Henry V, he referred to the way in which Englishmen were habituated upon St Valentine's Day

> To look and search Cupid's calendar
> And choose their choice, by great affection.

It seems a little strange that neither of the fourteenth-century poets thought of mentioning this in works which gave prominence to the belief about birds—unless the human custom had grown up between the time of Chaucer's work in the 1380s and that of Lydgate's, around 1440. It is possible that this is indeed what happened, and that the amorous conceit was invented in the rather frivolous courtly circle among which Lydgate moved; but neither suggestion can be proved. The same conceit was known in Lorraine, yet is not recorded there with a precision which enables us to tell if it had appeared earlier than in England. Lydgate's verse suggests that he regarded it as distinctively English.[1]

During the next hundred years the practice is recorded at regular intervals, but (rather curiously) among the gentry rather than royalty or aristocracy. The letters of the Paston family, seated near the Norfolk coast, mention it three times in the 1470s, while Sir Henry Willoughby, a gentleman in northern Warwickshire, paid 2s. 3d., for his 'Valentine' in 1523. These entries prove that people of both sexes were by then expected to send tokens of affection or admiration to the person of their choice. That purchased by Sir Henry must have been more than a mere trifle, and it is a pity that we shall never know what it was, and that indeed no other medieval or Tudor Valentine was ever described. Another puzzle concerns the manner of choice. To Lydgate, clearly, it was a question of personal affection, but by the time of the Pastons it seems that sometimes, at least, the recipient of the token was chosen by lot. Nor is it possible to tell whether the custom obtained further down in society during this period.[2] The actual holy day of Valentine was abolished first in the Edwardian Reformation and then in the Elizabethan one, but the amorous practices continued unabated. Two of the best-known poets of the early Stuart period, John Donne and Robert Herrick, celebrated them,[3] and a third, Michael Drayton, confirmed that the two modes of choice were still in existence; he mocked those who drew their Valentines by lot and then proudly wore their names. Like Herrick, he preferred to avow true affection.[4] By 1641 the system of lots was also well known in Edinburgh, where a wag proposed that a Lord Chancellor be chosen in the same fashion.[5]

In the mid-seventeenth century, it is plain that the tradition had become genuinely popular, if it had not always been so. On almanacs used by Staffordshire country people the day was marked by 'a true lovers knot'.[6] At the same time it reached to the highest levels in society; in 1668 the heir to the throne, the duke of York, gave a jewel worth about £800 as a Valentine, to the current court beauty Lady Frances Stewart.[7] A Dutch visitor to London in 1663 observed it as practised among the middling sort:

it is customary, alike for married as for unmarried people, that the first person one meets in the morning, that is, if one is a man, the first woman or girl, becomes one's Valentine. He asks her name which he takes down and carries on a long strip of paper in his hat band, and in the same way the woman or girl wears his name on her bodice; but it is the practice that they meet on the evening before and choose each other for their Valentine, and, come Easter, they send each other gloves, silk stockings, or sometimes a miniature portrait, which the ladies wear to foster the friendship.[8]

The diary of Samuel Pepys shows the system at work in the same decade; although the gifts within his circle were made at once and not at Easter. During the early 1660s Pepys would compliment a colleague in the naval administration by calling at his house early in the day in order to make his daughter Pepys's Valentine, and he would arrange for a personable young man to do the same for his own wife—although he then sometimes paid for her presents! In one year in which Pepys was short of money, no man called, much to Mrs Pepys's irritation. Sometimes women friends would call upon, and so choose him, and at times the Pepyses would draw names the night before to determine who would be the object of their attentions in the morning. After a number of years they settled down to a regular system whereby Samuel's cousin called annually to honour his wife and could make presents, such as a ring, which Pepys already knew that she desired.[9] Similar manœuvres in the early 1670s are documented in the family of the earl of Lindsey.[10]

The same sort of pattern held through the eighteenth century. Henry Bourne, writing on Tyneside in the 1720s, noted that the 'vulgar' invariably drew names from a vessel on St Valentine's Eve, those of one gender being drawn by an equal number of the other. The choice, he added, was in theory a genuine matter of chance and regarded as a good omen of an actual match.[11] An identical system obtained across the Border in Scotland, where it was alluded to later in the century by the traveller Thomas Pennant, and then by Robert Burns.[12] It remained the standard form of selection in Scotland, and in England down to, and including, northern Nottinghamshire and Derbyshire and the parts of Lancashire above the river Ribble; only dying out near the end of the nineteenth century.[13] In the West of England during the same long period, from Gloucestershire to Devon, the other old tradition remained constant. There it was the first person of the other sex seen upon the morning who became the Valentine, and would (like a person whose name was drawn in the North) expect a gift. Some people would walk blindfolded to the home of their chosen person.[14] Across most of the rest of England, however, a new procedure was becoming customary by the late eighteenth century; of choosing a recipient privately, and by design, and sending them the token of affection. Written greetings and salutations were as common in this function as the old-fashioned presents, and it was increasingly usual to send them anonymously. The same practice obtained in Victorian Wales, at first upon the old feast of Dwynwen, the Welsh patron saint of love (25 January), and then upon that of Valentine, in conformity with metropolitan culture.[15]

The future was, of course, to lie with this method, but before tracing its development it is necessary to consider two customary outgrowths from the giving of tokens of love or respect. One was 'Valentining', a begging tradition equivalent to those at the winter feasts of All Souls, Catherine, Clement, Thomas, and New Year. It was essentially one for children, who went about asking wealthier neighbours for Valentine gifts for themselves, of money or food (later on, of sweets). This activity is recorded first in the mid-eighteenth century, in Leicestershire and Norfolk,[16] and in the nineteenth covered the whole of East Anglia plus Hertfordshire, and a zone of the Midlands comprising Berkshire, Oxfordshire, Northamptonshire, Leicestershire, Derbyshire, Warwickshire, Worcestershire, and Herefordshire.[17] These were for the most part areas in which children did not engage in ritualized begging in the winter; although, once again, many communities in its range never took it up. As with the winter activities, Valentining was legitimized, from its first appearance, by use of a standard rhyme; almost always beginning 'Morrow, morrow, Valentine', 'Good morrow Valentine', or 'Good morning Valentine'. The most common was also the most inconsequential, being a variant of

> Morrow, morrow, Valentine,
> Curl your hair as I do mine
> Two before and two behind,
> Good morning to your Valentine.[18]

This was found all over East Anglia, as far west as Huntingdonshire and Hertfordshire. In Oxfordshire, Warwickshire, and Northamptonshire the basic rhyme referred directly to the romantic tradition, running something like:

> Morrow, morrow, Valentine,
> I'll be yours if you'll be mine,
> Please to give me a Valentine.[19]

At places in both East Anglia and the midlands this could take a more impudent twist, as in

> Good morrow, Valentine,
> First 'tis yours and then 'tis mine,
> So please give me a Valentine.[20]

or

> Good morrow, Valentine,
> Change your luck and I'll change mine.
> We are ragged and you are fine,
> So pray give us a Valentine.[21]

As with Clementing and Catterning, the point of origin for the chants is apparently lost, and so is the means of dissemination. In addition every area in which the custom obtained had its own unique rhymes, often as idiosyncratic as this one from the Norfolk coast:

> Good morrow Valentine,
> How it do hail
> When Father's pig die
> Yow shall have its tail.[22]

Around Norwich and in south-eastern Norfolk, the other distinctive offshoot from the romantic traditions had appeared by 1840: the leaving of small anonymous gifts for children in parallel to the greetings and presents being made to adults. All through the early twentieth century the custom continued to thrive among working-class families in this area, youngsters expecting the visit of an invisible character called 'the Valentine Man' or 'Father Valentine' after nightfall on St Valentine's Day. Apparently inspired by Santa Claus, he left sweets, fruit, pencils, or a book for each child on a window-sill or inside a hallway; in reality, he could be either a parent or a family friend.[23] The custom still obtained in a few villages of the district in the 1970s,[24] and may do so yet. Likewise, in the 1950s it was still a common superstition that a person was destined to marry the first eligible individual seen upon the day, and 'Valentining' by children still went on in a suburb of Birmingham and in several Norfolk villages.[25] Both traditions may also still survive.

It is, however, the commercial aspect of the day which most obviously flourishes, and to that we must return. The habit of sending written compliments for St Valentine's Day seems to have been a development of the mid-eighteenth century; the oldest known, in Hull Museum, has been dated to 1750. During the years between 1780 and 1800 it was starting to become popular,[26] and in south Devon in the 1800s an observer noted 'Valentine Letters containing a Love Device or the sportive and frequently highly indecorous effusions of the rustic Muse' were now sent in large numbers.[27] By 1825 the London Post Office was handling 200,000 more letters on 14 February than on any other date. It was in about 1820 that stationers began to make paper with embossed headings designed specially for the romantic messages, and ten years later these were being lithographed. During the 1840s they started to appear with lace or satin decorations, matching envelopes, and set messages; the Valentine card had arrived.[28] By the 1860s it was as familiar in the countryside as the town, at least in southern England,[29] and some examples had become very elaborate, with artificial flowers, real feathers, and pieces of silk. During the 1870s cheap printed and coloured alternatives were produced to cater for the other ends of the market. In 1880 one and a half million Valentine cards passed through the Post Office.[30]

That, however, represented a peak, and a very marked decline set in from the next decade. It was partly the result of a passage of fashion, but also of the increasing production of mocking, insulting, or 'indecent' Valentines. The latter seem to have been similar to the 'naughty' seaside postcard, which also appeared at this time, and persisted.[31] The former could take forms like these, which were obtainable in the Huntingdonshire Fenland villages around 1900: 'you'd open the card and a great long paper snake would unfold itself and instead of a nice greeting there'd be a message like

YOU ARE A SNAKE IN THE GRASS

or perhaps a black man with a terribly ugly face would stick his tongue out at you when you opened the card'.[32] Cards of this sort were popular enough with purchasers and detested enough by recipients to assist the passage of the whole custom into disrepute, and then into abeyance. By 1914 the sending of Valentine cards had become a rarity or died out altogether in every part of England and Wales.[33] In the 1920s a modest revival began in London, which continued during the following decade,[34] but it was only in the 1950s that a national readoption of the custom got under way, making it completely ubiquitous. Like the parallel boom in Mother's Day cards, this was the result of commercial promotion, working through the powerful new mass media, and inspired by American fashion. Like 'Mothering' also, it drew directly upon an older native tradition, because the American cards were not generally anonymous but the British equivalent was customarily so, as it had been under Victoria. The cards were mass-produced, inexpensive, and avoided the fate of their predecessors by remaining overwhelmingly affectionate and sentimental in tone. The net result is to ensure that if Christmas is now the celebration of the family and New Year of the network of adult friends, then couples have to wait only six weeks for a festival dedicated to them. With Mothering Sunday in the next month, the modern run of feasts dedicated to different roles within the life cycle, stretching from the middle to the end of the cold and confined season, is complete.

15

SHROVETIDE

EITHER before or after St Valentine's Day fell a much bigger and more general festival, effectively the biggest and wildest of early spring. It began on 'Shrove Sunday', the seventh before Easter, continued on 'Collop Monday', and reached its climax on 'Shrove Tuesday'; the sequence of Sundays meant that it was effectively a February feast, although it might occur anywhere from a third of the way through the month until its very end. Its origins lay in the early Middle Ages, along with those of the long fast of Lent, which it directly preceded and which thus created it. The peculiar febrility of Shrovetide sprang from two causes. The first was that it was a last opportunity for fun before the dietary, recreational, and sexual restrictions of Lent set in, and indeed imposed a need to consume remaining stocks of meat, eggs, and cheese before they were interdicted. The second was that by this season stocks of food would have been low for many people in any case and privation considerable, so that an opportunity for the frenetic release of emotion would have been very welcome. The names for the component days in England indicated the dual nature of preparations for the fast. 'Shrove' was from 'shriving' or confession of sins and receipt of absolution, so that congregations went into Lent with clean consciences; this was what the Church expected from these days. 'Collop' referred to the eating of collops, or cuts, of fried or roasted meat. In English-speaking Scotland, and in northern England, the Tuesday was 'Fastens (or Fasten's or Fastern's) E'en', 'Fasting's Eve', while in Gaelic-speaking areas it was 'Inid', signifying 'the beginning'.

In medieval and early modern high society, Shrovetide marked the end of the chain of cold season celebrations which had commenced with the Twelve Days of Christmas and continued at Candlemas. From the time at which royal, aristocratic, and episcopal household accounts become abundant, in the fourteenth century,[1] payments for food, drink, and entertainment at this time rank only behind those at Christmas. Sixteenth-century accounts for the English and Scottish royal revels show regular and heavy expenditure upon plays, music, and masquerades for Shrove Tuesday. With the arrival of the Stuarts it became customary for the court to conclude its winter season then with the most elaborate and expensive diversion of the age, a formal masque. Charles I and his queen, Henrietta Maria, instituted from 1631 the tradition of presenting these extravaganzas for each other, celebrating their love and marriage, as well as monarchy, piety, and hierarchy, before their servants, the aristocracy, and foreign ambassadors.[2] Municipalities likewise often provided entertainments: in the early sixteenth century, the corporation of Hull paid for wine and cakes on Collop Monday, and Rye for a bear-baiting on Shrove Tuesday, when Chester annually sponsored a football match.[3] When the corporation records of Carlisle commence in 1602, the city fathers were hosting either a play or 'silver games' (presumably referring to the prizes) every year on the Tuesday.[4] In 1555 those of York had met the expenses of young men who had produced an 'honest and pleasant pastime' before them and the public on that day, 'one sort in defending a fort and the other in making the assaults'.[5] Celebration seems to have been universal throughout the island and throughout society. The very first detailed record of seasonal celebration in north-west Wales is in the diary of the Anglesey farmer Robert Bulkeley. On the Saturday and Monday nights of Shrovetide 1635 he and a crowd of friends went on a tour of neighbouring farmhouses carrying drink with them.[6]

Other medieval and early modern sources illustrate activities especially associated with the festival. One, naturally enough, was the consumption of the foodstuffs soon to be forbidden—and meat salted down for the winter and batter or fritter dishes would also require a proportionate amount of drinking. A Protestant preacher in 1571 characterized Shrovetide as a time of 'great gluttony, surfeiting and drunkenness'.[7] Fifteen years later, the poet William Warner made the first reference to its most enduring foodstuff, when he wrote of 'Fast-eve pan-puffs'.[8] In 1622 the satire on London, *Vox Graculi*, could term the festival 'Prime Peer of the Pullets, First Favourite of the Frying Pans, greatest Bashaw to the Batter Bowls, Protector of the Pan Cakes, First Founder of the Fritters, Baron of Bacon-flitch, Earl of Egg-baskets'.[9] The finest and most famous early description of the most popular dish was that produced by another London satirist, John Taylor, in 1621, in his account of Shrove Tuesday,

at whose entrance in the morning all the whole kingdom is in quiet, but by that time that the clock strikes eleven, which (by the help of a knavish sexton) is commonly before nine, then there is a bell rung, called the Pancake-bell, the sound whereof makes thousands of people distracted, and forgetful either of manners or of humanity; then there is a thing called wheaten flour, which the sulphury Necromantic cooks do mingle with water, eggs, spice and other tragical, magical, enchantments, and then they put it by little and little into a frying-pan of boiling suet, where it makes a confused dismal hissing (like the Lemean snakes in the reeds of Acheron, Styx or Phlegeton) until at last, by the skill of the cooks it is transformed into the form of a Flap-Jack, which in our translation is called a Pancake, which ominous incantation the ignorant people do devour very greedily.

Taylor added that in addition 'they do ballast their bellies with meat for a voyage to Constantinople'.[10]

The two other principal pastimes associated with the day were noted as early as the late twelfth century, when William Fitzstephen included in a life of

St Thomas Becket a description of how Londoners spent the morning of Shrove Tuesday in cock-fighting and the afternoon in ball games.[11] In 1314 the City corporation banned the latter, and in 1409 it prohibited the forcible levying of money by youths from pedestrians to cover the expenses of both activities.[12] They embodied, indeed, the intrinsic propensity of Shrovetide sports to express both violence and cruelty as part of the feast's cathartic role. The term concerning the cocks in the 1409 order was 'cock-threshing', rather than the traditional cock-fighting, and represents the earliest known reference to a distinctive game of the day, whereby people competed to kill a cock with missiles or blows. Pleasure in this act spanned society, for the fourth Lord Berkeley, who died in 1417, was a noted 'thresher of the cock' and in 1493 Henry VII paid for the birds to be delivered to his palace for Shrovetide.[13] It made sense to kill off poultry if eggs were forbidden in Lent, and to a brutal society it was equally logical to have some fun in the process. A first glimpse of the latter is provided by Thomas Tusser, writing (in this case) of Essex and Suffolk, under Elizabeth:

> At Shroftide go shroving, go threshe the fat hen,
> If blindfold can kill her, then give it thie men.[14]

This leaves open the matter of whether the bird was being thrown at, or struck. The Dutch tourist who provided such a fine description of Valentines in 1663, William Shellinks, is equally helpful in this case. He described two methods in use on Shrove Tuesday during that year:

In London one sees in every street, wherever one goes, many apprentice boys running with, under their arms, a cock with a string on its foot, on which is a spike, which they push firmly into the ground between the stones. They always look for an open space and, for a penny, let people throw their cudgel from a good distance at the cock and he, who kills the cock, gets it. In the country or among countryfolk they bury a cock with only its head above ground, and blindfold a person and turn him two or three times round himself, and he then tries to hit the cock with a flail, and the one who hits it or comes closest to it gets the prize.[15]

That, then, was how Tusser's 'fat hen' died. Sometimes a public body as well as apprentices could make money out of the game. At the village of Pinner, in Middlesex, the churchwardens bought cocks for Shrovetide at the parish expense in the early Stuart period and again at the Restoration, and returned the profits to the church funds.[16] At the same time fights between cocks remained a rival attraction of the feast. The Hospital of God's House at Southampton provided them to amuse the inmates upon Shrove Tuesday 1326 and the antiquarian John Stow recalled that they had been common on London streets in Shrovetides under Henry VIII. Fitzstephen, in the twelfth century, had recorded that they were found in schools on Shrove Tuesday morning, and John Aubrey, five hundred years later, described how in his schooldays the boy who owned the cock which emerged as the champion would parade 'through the streets in triumph decked with ribbons, all his school fellows following with a drum and a fiddle to a feast at their master's school house'.[17]

Football provided another release for sadistic impulses, with the added attraction that the victims were human and the drawback that they might include one's self. Governments and writers interested in the reform of manners were generally agreed that the risk to bones and property involved outweighed the advantages of recreation. The game in its traditional form had no clearly defined teams and effectively no rules; and goals, if they existed at all, were of secondary importance to the thrill of fighting for possession of the ball. Its proscription by the corporation of London has been mentioned; it was also banned by Edward III, Richard II, Henry IV, and Henry VIII. The reiteration of these prohibitions gives an ominous indication of their effectiveness, and James I was content to forbid it within the precincts of the court, remarking that it was 'meter for laming than making able the users thereof'. In 1531 Sir Thomas Elyot, writing to encourage the development of a better-educated and more polished social élite, described it as 'nothing but beastly fury and extreme violence, whereof procedeth hurt, and consequently rancour and extreme malice do remain'. Philip Stubbs, campaigning in 1583 for a more godly and better ordered society, called it

a devilish pastime ... a bloody and murdering practice ... For doth not every one lie in wait for his adversary, seeking to overthrow him and to pick him on his nose, though it be upon hard stones? So that by this means, sometime their necks broken, sometime their backs, sometime their legs; sometime their arms; sometime one part thrust out of joint, sometime another, sometime the noses gush at with blood, sometime their eyes start out ... But whosoever scapeth away the best, goeth not scotfree, but is either sore wounded, crazed, and bruised, so he dieth of it, or else scapeth very hardly and no marvel, for they have sleights to meet one betwixt two, to hit him under the short ribs with their griped fists, and with their knees to catch him upon the hip, and to pick him on his neck, with a hundred such murdering devices.[18]

The reasons for its popularity, therefore, are obvious, and during the sixteenth and seventeenth centuries several official bodies sponsored it upon Shrove Tuesday. At Chester the Shoemaker's Company provided a ball for a game through the streets in the afternoon, although admittedly the corporation intervened in 1540 and forced the substitution of a foot-race because of the 'great inconvenience' caused by 'evil disposed persons' among the players.[19] Under the early Stuarts the sport was one of the 'silver games' encouraged by the Carlisle city council, being held in a meadow beside the river Eden. In 1614 the city presented a prize to the lad who had won the ball.[20] It was the same story in Scotland. Admission to the Tailors' Craft in sixteenth-century Perth was made conditional upon the presentation of a football for use on 'Fastern's E'en'. In 1601 the 'Cordiners'' (Cordwainers') Craft ordered every married man among its members to contribute towards the purchase of one. The city of Glasgow bought six footballs for use by its people on the same day every year between 1574 and 1579.[21] Within some communities different social groups were traditionally matched against each other; a play of 1600 refers to Shrove Tuesday football games between the bachelors and the married men of a parish.[22] Cornwall had its own distinctive sport, of hurling, which was essentially the same game but using a smaller, lighter, and harder ball. The local squire Richard Carew, writing in 1602, commented that in the east of the country there were goals, marked by bushes two or three hundred yards apart, but in the west the victor was the person who got the ball to a village, or gentleman's seat, which could be miles from the starting-point. He compared the ball 'to an infernal spirit, for whosoever catcheth it fareth straightways like a madman, struggling and fighting with those that go about to hold him'. Like Elyot and Stubbes, he added that the game caused many injuries, but unlike them he insisted that these left no malice among the competitors.[23]

The Shrovetide ball games, therefore, had a decided element of licensed misrule about them, and this aspect of the festival became more overt as the early modern period advanced. In medieval and Tudor times it was not, indeed, noted for serious disorder; riot and rebellion tended to arise instead out of the summer games when the climate was better for taking to the streets or the battlefield.[24] During the reign of James I, however, it developed into a celebrated time of misbehaviour for London apprentices. Under Elizabeth the potential for trouble at Shrovetide had been recognized, as Lord Mayors had routinely doubled the watch and ordered the 'prentices to stay indoors. There are, none the less, no signs of actual violence before 1598. By contrast, riots occurred on twenty-four out of the twenty-nine Shrove Tuesdays of the early Stuart period, normally in the suburbs of the City and especially in those on the northern side, where traditional areas of recreation were situated. All apparently included apprentices, but they were regularly reinforced by craftsmen and could involve thousands of people. The targets were not random, but consisted overwhelmingly of brothels and playhouses. In 1612–14 one Shoreditch bordello was attacked every year until it was demolished. On Shrove Tuesday 1617 a new playhouse in Drury Lane was wrecked, the inmates of Finsbury prison released, and several houses at Wapping destroyed. Such actions were certainly criminal, and ringleaders sometimes received heavy fines and gaol sentences. They were, however, directed against targets disliked by the respectable—the brothels were technically illegal—and could thus be regarded as a form of community policing. Their eruption at this particular period cannot be coincidental, and may perhaps best be viewed as a popular dimension to that campaign against theatres, sports, and prostitution which had been undertaken by the City authorities under Elizabeth and was itself a part of the wider Protestant 'Reformation of Manners'.[25] At the same time it fitted into a much older tradition of cleansing a community before Lent.

Literary works of the time accordingly reflected a profound ambivalence towards the Shrovetide riots. Playwrights could regard the apprentices as natural enemies because they attacked playhouses; and yet some sympathy for the young men might be expected among audiences because of their more usual animosity towards brothels. Four works for the stage mentioned the riots between 1606 and 1638, and all did so with uneasy humour, avoiding judgement.[26] Among the satirists of the same years, the author of *Vox Graculi* skirted round the subject, Sir Thomas Overbury took the same attitude as the playwrights, and only John Taylor dared both to treat the subject in detail and to pass a judgement upon it, howbeit temperately. He portrayed how 'ragged regiments' of 'youths armed with cudgels, stones, banners, rules, trowels and hand-staves, put playhouses to the sack and bawdy-houses to the spoil, in the quarrel breaking a thousand quarrels (of glass I mean)'. He also described them as ripping away tiles, pulling down chimneys, and tearing up feather beds. Then he pointed out that the true wrong of their actions lay in the 'contempt of justice: for what avails it for a poor constable with an army of reverend rusty bill-men to command these beasts, for they with their pockets instead of pistols, well charged with stone-shot discharge against the image of authority, whole volleys as thick as hail'.[27]

The coming of the Civil Wars and English Revolution gave the apprentices more important concerns, and thereafter the presence of a ring of regular regiments quartered about the City to watch it provided a much more effective deterrent to disorder than 'rusty bill-men'. Instead, Shrove Tuesday revelry by youth became an issue at the realm's second city, of Bristol, where annually during the Interregnum the magistrates (clearly without avail) forbade the apprentices to throw at cocks, play football, or (as another opportunity for cruelty) toss dogs in the air. The lads eventually wove these sports into a political protest, for on Shrove Tuesday 1660, when demonstrations against the tottering republic were breaking out all over southern England, they used the letter of the prohibition to insult the republicans who ran the city. Outside the mayor's house they threw at geese and hens and tossed up bitches and cats, and knocked down the sheriff who tried to prevent them.[28] The Restoration occurred within three months, and ushered in a period in which, unsurprisingly, the gambols of the 'Shrovetide 'prentices' continued to provide headaches for local authorities. Those at Bristol tried to stage a fight with clubs and staves in 1670, and the ringleaders went to gaol for abusing the mayor. Fifteen years later several of them were whipped through the city at a cart's tail for using excessive violence during the day's fun.[29] At York in 1673 the Dean tried to keep that city's youth out of the Minster, where they had become accustomed to begin the sport; they not only forced their way in but smashed the windows of his house.[30] These notices, however, seem to die out before the end of the century, and it is still more striking that there is no evidence of a resumption during the Restoration period of the Shrovetide rioting at London, even though its apprentices were still unruly in general. The memory of their former activities remained proverbial into the reign of Queen Anne,[31] but the writers who referred to them did so as a phenomenon of the past. In this respect it seems as if bawds, as well as Catholics, actually lived more easily as a result of the Puritan Revolution than they had done under the early Stuart monarchy.

The status of Shrovetide declined very slowly in England and Wales from the later seventeenth century onward, along with the Lenten fast to which it was so closely linked. It had never been an official set of holy days, sanctioned by the Church or confirmed by Act of Parliament. The feasting on Collop Monday was undertaken between or after work, while the undoubted leisure and liberty on Shrove Tuesday was an informal matter for employers, school-masters, and whole communities to grant according to long custom. In many places, by the seventeenth century, it was announced as Taylor described it, by the ringing of a 'pancake bell' near noon; the London parish of St Benet Gracechurch invested in a special small bell for this purpose in 1691.[32] In the late Stuart period John Aubrey recorded how at Eton the boys waited until the school clock struck nine upon Shrove Tuesday morning, and then shouted, stamped, thumped sticks, and ran out for a day of leisure.[33] In Scotland there were no more official seasonal fasts after 1690, so that Fastern's E'en became even more of an informal celebration, but the need for a February feast caused it to linger even there. In the Shetlands a special supper, followed by dancing and games, was still customary in the nineteenth century.[34] In the Orkneys and in the Moray district it was known as Brose Day or Brose Night after the beef broth which was a favourite dish. Other traditional foods in the northern half of Scotland were Fastyn (or Festy, or Fitless) Cock, which were roasted oatmeal dumplings, and Sauty Bannocks, cakes of eggs, salt, and meal which took the role of the pancakes in the south.[35] In the Highlands and Western Isles, 'Inid' was a time for 'saining' the cattle in the stalls again, with burning juniper as at New Year, it was clearly regarded (as the name suggested) as opening another stage of the year.[36] Until the beginning of the nineteenth century the Manx also spent Shrove Tuesday in sports and feasted in the evening upon meat, with a large pudding and pancakes to follow.[37] The later history of the festival in the rest of Britain, where records are much more ample, is best traced by examining that of its component activities.

The ritualized mistreatment of poultry continued at full pace into the eighteenth century. Cock-fighting in schools remained particularly common in Scotland, where the schoolmaster was generally supposed to provide the birds but the pupils to pay him a penny each in recompense. He could also claim any cock which fled the fight. In the Buchan district pupils supplied their own cocks, and the captain of the victorious side was declared leader of the school and led a procession to feasting and games. In Ross and Cromarty a cock that would not fight had to be ransomed by its owner. It is notable that all the terms used for the cock-fighting in Highland areas were in Latin, not Gaelic, so that the custom was clearly imported into them from the south. Every pupil in a large number of grammar schools scattered across the Cumbrian region of England—Cumberland, Westmorland, northern Lancashire, and north-west Yorkshire—was also expected to pay a 'cock-penny' to the headmaster on Shrove Tuesday. It is not clear, however, that the money was still used for its traditional purpose in most of these cases.[38] Further south, 'cock-throwing' remained the preferred sport, some communities having special venues for it like Cock Throwing Close at Ashwell in the chalk hills at the top of Hertfordshire.[39] In Sussex special throwing sticks were made, weighted with lead at each end.[40] The brutality of the sport varied. Joseph Strutt noted that its promoters were so keen to make money that they would not accept a win until the bird was killed outright; a crippled one was propped up on a stick.[41] At Kingsbridge in south Devon, death was likewise the customary object of the game.[42] The birds at Heston in Middlesex, in 1791, were the targets of broomsticks, thrown from twenty-two yards at three goes for twopence. Here the idea was to catch them before they regained their feet, and a victor to keep the cock; but the observer who recorded this noted that in practice the birds were always destroyed. At Birstall in the west Yorkshire woollen area, during 1783, a throw killed an onlooker instead.[43] In Lancashire, however, the sticks were lighter, and the cocks expected to survive—so that they could be used for fighting. The same was true in parts of Wales and at Bewdley, on the Severn in Worcestershire.[44] In the alleys of the Brighton 'Lanes' quarter, and at North Walsham in Norfolk, a cock was hung in a clay pot overhead and could be won by the person who broke the pot with a throw. On one Shrove Tuesday at Walsham in the 1760s a wag put in an owl instead.[45]

In the same century hens (and sometimes cocks) were still 'threshed'. In Wales, the procedure was the same as before.[46] The south-east of England, by 1710, had produced a different one: 'The hen is hung at a fellow's back, who has also some horse-bells about him, the rest of the fellows are blinded, and have boughs in their hands, with which they chase this fellow and his hen about some large court or small enclosure ... After this the hen is boiled with bacon'.[47] In Sussex in the mid-nineteenth century the game was conducted in the same manner:

They was all blindfolded 'ceptin the Hoodman, and he had a hen in a sack, and bells tied to his coat-tails. All the others had sticks an' run after he, tryin' to beat him, an' he'd jump behind one of the others so he got hit instead ... They was supposed to beat [the hen] to death, but Granfer says she didn't never get killed that way, but when they got tired of the game she was killed and plucked, an' then they all had her for dinner, boiled with plenty of fat bacon.[48]

By the years around 1700 sensibilities were already starting to shift to the point at which commentators were finding the sadism of all this disturbing. Their nervousness is betrayed by the way in which they were repeatedly trying to find historical justifications for what was clearly just a joy in cruelty. Thus, Sir Charles Sedley in 1693 claimed that cocks were belaboured in memory of St Peter's denial of Christ (three times before cock-crow); the *British Apollo* suggested in 1708 that cocks had alerted Danish oppressors to an attempted English revolt; and Hearne subsequently asserted that they were symbols of the hated French.[49] Throwing at them now became the first blood sport in

English history to be determinedly attacked and then suppressed. The City of London led the way by banning it within its precincts in 1704, though constables were still trying to control it in the fields beyond the suburbs in 1766. The towns of Worcestershire followed suit in the late 1740s.[50] The *Gentleman's Magazine* published its first condemnation of the sport in 1737, and six more followed each other through its pages between 1750 and 1762. In the three decades after 1750 several provincial newspapers took up the call, and under the impact of this campaign opinion among the social élite moved decisively. Most remaining towns banned cock-throwing during this period, and it was last seen in an urban setting at Liverpool in 1787 and at Manchester in 1800. In the years 1750 and 1780 also, gentry first withdrew support from the practice, and then (as landlords and magistrates) began trying to stop it. By the end of the century it was very rare in public, and last observed in the open at Quainton, in Buckinghamshire's vale of Aylesbury, in 1844. During the 1790s its promoters began to find alternatives to throwing at live birds, such as making clay cocks to be used as targets, or having people throw sticks at a bobbin with a cock or hen as a prize. How long the cruel old game continued in private is much more difficult to say; at Llansanffraid ym Mechain in eastern Wales it was still carried on in farmyards in 1870. Likewise, the 'threshing' of hens was still enjoyed by servants of an (unnamed) mansion in Sussex in the mid-nineteenth century. The most that can be said is that there is no trace of either after 1900. As a public sport it made a relatively easy target for humanitarians working on upper-class sympathies. It was, after all, a pleasure of small groups among the common people, and as the animals were tethered it could be made to appear unsporting to those accustomed to chase their quarry with guns or hounds.[51] Cock-fighting began to come under pressure later, at the end of the eighteenth century, and was made illegal at a national level in the 1830s. Again, suppression was much easier in the public than the private sphere; the cock-pit at Penzance was closed in about 1800, but Shrovetide fights were still staged among miners on the coasts of West Penwith, the port's hinterland, until the 1880s.[52]

Shrove Tuesday football, of course, had always been at once more popular and more controversial. By 1800 it was a custom of small, stable, and conservative towns, at which it was thoroughly entrenched. In the far north of England these consisted of Alnwick, Workington, Chester-le-Street, and Sedgefield. At the first of those it was patronized by the duke of Northumberland, whose seat was (and is) the big castle overlooking the town. At 2 p.m. the town waits would come, playing loudly to its walls, and the ball was thrown over them to the crowd. In the Midlands the game's centres were Derby, Ashbourne, Caistor, and Nuneaton. In the last of those the glove factory girls would line the pavements in their best dresses, to cheer the young men who turned out hundreds strong to fight for the balls. Derby supplies the best English record of a match for the period, being a contest between townsmen and local villagers involving up to 2,000 players. The goals were the gate of a nursery ground and the wheel of a mill, each a mile outside the town in opposite directions. In most years the play careered into the river Derwent. Unpopular or richly dressed people foolish enough to be out among the spectators were pelted with bags of soot or powder. The sport had a solitary West Country outpost among the marble-quarrymen of Dorset's Isle of Purbeck, who held a free-for-all in a field. Otherwise its remaining stronghold lay in the neighbouring areas of southern Middlesex and northern Surrey, where *The Times* found it in 'almost every parish' in 1840: the balls were pursued 'by hundreds through the most public thoroughfares, the shops and windows of which are customarily closed, and the windows barricaded with hurdles'. Normally one half of each town played the other, reinforced by crowds of Londoners. Two or three matches were held, the main struggle being preceded by a boys' contest. The actual results were almost never noticed, the excitement and danger of play being the main object. There was little trace of lasting rivalries or resentments resulting, and almost none of the events was used to mock authority. It was essentially a young men's activity, but their elders cheered them on.[53]

In Scotland it was also most obviously a small-town sport, surviving in the Border districts at Jedburgh, Melrose, Hawick, Westruther, Coldingham, Denholm, Duns, and Foulden. In the Lothians it was found at Inverness and Musselburgh, on Tayside at Scone, and in the Moray region at Keith, and in some villages. There was usually a traditional local rivalry involved, between the two halves of a town, or the bachelors and the married men, or the town and its rural hinterland. Little Inverness, in Midlothian, was unique in pitting married and unmarried women against each other; apparently the former always won. Play was as furious as in England, so that at Hawick 'cuts, contusions and bloodshed were common occurrences; and all the evil passions that are excited by a state of war frequently pervaded the place'. Once again, however, no lasting animosity seems to have been created. A few towns introduced rules to limit the damage, such as Scone and Jedburgh, which forbade kicking; in the latter case the reform was made in 1704 after a succession of deaths. Some had a reckoning for scores—the married men of Scone had to get the ball thrice into a hole in the moor, the bachelors to dip it thrice in the river—but as usual the play was an end in itself.[54] In Wales the game was a feature of the Anglicized towns of Pembrokeshire, where six or eight balls were made for each Shrove Tuesday from bulls' bladders covered in leather. Windows were shuttered and the local youth assembled before the town hall, from where the ball was thrown. The play went on till dusk, the formal object being to get to one edge of town or another. Sometimes the balls were sent forty feet into the air, hurtling over roofs. Women sold horns of ale and pancakes to refresh the combatants, and thousands of spectators came in from the countryside.[55]

Shrovetide football, then, had become by the modern period a tenaciously held tradition of a particular set of communities; of just the same sort, in social terms, which were strongholds of Guy Fawkes celebrations, although the two customs rarely coexisted as they fulfilled much the same annual function as an enormous release of emotion and energy. Both became intensely controversial in the nineteenth century and were mostly wiped out. Wherever the process can be traced in detail it was because of a withdrawal of support from the respectable tradespeople upon whose goodwill local government depended. In the case of the football they became less and less tolerant of a guaranteed loss of trade when their shops were boarded up, and a possible risk of damage to their property. Moral considerations always ranked behind practical issues in the complaints, although a swelling working-class movement for greater temperance and responsibility (linked to a quest for more political and economic power) sometimes opposed the game as degrading. The principal fact behind the change in attitude, however, seems to have been the growth in the population in general and in that of towns in particular, meaning that the crowds at the matches were ever larger and more composed of strangers who had used improved transport facilities to travel in for the fun. In 1835 the Highways Act made the traditional form of the game technically illegal by banning sports from public throughfares. The co-operation of town councils and magistrates was required to make the law effective, but between 1840 and 1870 most of those involved, throughout Britain, not only gave it but banned the game outright within their precincts.

At times a desperate struggle resulted. That at Derby began in 1845, when the mayor was petitioned to forbid the custom and some leading players, convinced that it was becoming too dangerous, led a subscription to pay for alternative attractions. On Shrove Tuesday in that year, a band parade was held instead, and it was proposed to follow with competitions usually associated with summertime fairs and wakes, such as climbing a greased pole and pulling faces through horse collars. While the bands played, however, somebody kicked a ball in the crowd, a scrum began, and the other activities were hastily cancelled. The following year the corporation swore in several hundred special constables, and persuaded the Home Secretary to lend two troops of dragoons, to prevent the play. Instead the ball moved so fast that the police and soldiers were either knocked over or left behind, and the magistrates ended up by reading the Riot Act. Though victorious, the players had come close enough to serious criminality to be scared; although the town filled up with policemen and dragoons again on every Shrove Tuesday until 1849, they faced no more opposition. At Kingston upon Thames, Surrey's county town, the council banned the game in 1840 after several gentlemen had complained and the senior officer of the newly formed local police force offered his help to enforce the order. The mayor, however, noted that many of Kingston's wealthy citizens still supported the sport, and countermanded the ban. In 1857, after much of this support had been withdrawn, another mayor tried to move the play out of town, but was resisted by a publican who hosted the celebration after the game. The following year this man became mayor himself and persuaded the council to pay for the balls. After another decade, however, the influx of badly behaved strangers each year became so large that the decisive vote for abolition was taken. The result was a serious riot on Shrove Tuesday 1867, in which the houses of councillors were stoned. In 1868 the game was allowed in a park but, when it spilled out into the town, players were arrested and fined. After that heavy police reinforcements prevented any revivals of the sport. It remained at Dorking, a tightly-knit town much deeper in Surrey and so safer from interlopers. In 1873, however, the local paper turned against it because players snowballed spectators, including a Catholic priest. By the 1890s shopkeepers were starting to complain in large numbers. The urban district council ignored them, but in 1897 the county council took up their cause and called in the police. The players who were arrested by them appealed to law, but here the Highways Act stood in their way and they received heavy fines. Extra policemen were brought into Dorking for every Shrove Tuesday until 1909, when attempts to play were finally abandoned.[56]

The suppression of the Dorking game left only eight still active. That at Chester-le-Street, in County Durham, was stopped by police, on magistrates' orders, in 1930.[57] The one at Corfe Castle still survives, but as a token only, about a dozen men from the Ancient Order of Purbeck Marblers and Stone-cutters kicking a ball down the main street. That at Jedburgh is larger and more ebullient, having avoided repression by its local council in 1848 when Scotland's Lord Justice Clerk ruled that it had an 'immemorial right' to continue; of all the other Scottish matches only that at Kirkwall, Orkney, was as lucky.[58] The one at Ashbourne, on the edge of the Peak District in Derbyshire, was saved by shifting it to the perimeter of the town. In the early twentieth century it came to be seen as a quaint and colourful survival, patronized again by civic officials, the Church, and (in 1927) the Prince of Wales.[59] As such, it has acquired the status of the little town's emblem, its distinctive feature and a focus for traditional communal loyalties, the two 'sides' being still the two halves of the settlement. Play is furious, with the single limitation that, as at Derby, it almost always moves quickly into the local river (in this case the Henmore). There it can remain for hours, the scrum pushing slowly up or downstream, although there is something re-markable about the sight of the fog which forms as the heat of the straining bodies meets the surface of the cold water. I asked one old man why he still played, and he told me that it gave him a chance to pay off every grudge which he had acquired in the past year. At Alnwick in Northumberland the duke saved the match by moving it to a meadow and forbidding use of hands. This makes it look very much like conventional soccer, save that the teams are about a hundred strong, representing rival parishes, and the ball is brought out with the duke's piper playing. Sedgefield, in the rural south-eastern side of County Durham, also preserves a local game; about a thousand people compete to get the ball into a pond or a stream. The most convincing (or overwhelming) evocation of early modern Shrovetide football, however, is probably that at Atherstone, Warwickshire, which sprang into prominence when the famous one at nearby Nuneaton was forbidden. It is still played in the main street and, save that veterans are present as stewards to impose a modicum of good behaviour, justifies most of the remarks made about the game by Elyot and Stubbes. The ball is large and filled with water to increase the weight, and there are no goals; instead the point is to win a struggle for possession of the ball itself and so have the honour of the next kick-off. The overall victor is the person holding it when exactly two hours are over. As all falls are taken onto stone, concrete, or tarmac (unless one is lucky enough to land on a fellow player), it is difficult to emerge without severe bruising. The present author, in his sole experience of a day's play, witnessed the person to his left in one scrum sustain a spectacularly broken nose. It is an event which, in its own rather magnificent way, firmly resists any categorization of surviving folk traditions as sanitized, stilted, or precious.

The pressures which removed most of the street football killed off more localized Shrovetide combats. In the central Marches of Wales, Ludlow and Presteigne both had tugs of war between men from different sections of the community. The former was stopped in 1851 as it caused so much violence, while the latter was banned at the end of the century.[60] 'Hurling' declined in Cornwall during the same period, Methodism reinforcing the growing antipathy of local authorities to the destructive and disruptive potential of the game.[61] By the end of Victoria's reign the remaining Shrove Tuesday match was at St Columb Major, half-way down the peninsula, and this survives. About a thousand people participate annually, the little town is boarded up to protect it, and play goes on long after dark. The goals are two miles apart, and even to touch the silver-cased ball is considered lucky as well as honourable, for it flies through the air fast enough to bear out all of Carew's comments upon it four hundred years ago.

Alongside the old ritualized violence there appeared in the eighteenth century a regional juvenile begging custom of precisely the same sort as Souling, Clementing, Catterning, New Year blessing, and Valentining. It occupied the area of the provinces, southern England, in which all those did not occur. Known as 'shroving', it is not recorded before the end of the century,[62] and its origins are as obscure as those of the others. There are occasional traces of low-key localized traditions in communities from the Thames valley to Wales or County Durham, whereby poor people went to richer neighbours to collect money or foodstuffs to enable them to enjoy a Shrovetide feast.[63] The children's 'shroving' may have grown out of this, and indeed the earliest definite reference to it (from south Devon) describes it as a tradition of the poor in general.[64] Peter Robson, who has made the best study of the juvenile custom, has suggested rather tentatively that it may have been a survival of local medieval doles, because five out of the seventeen Dorset settlements in which it is recorded had been the sites of abbeys; but there is no direct evidence of such doles at Shrovetide in the Middle Ages, and nothing to indicate why the custom should have arisen in the west and south. What can be said with confidence is only that during the nineteenth century it was found in villages scattered thinly across much of Somerset, Dorset, Wiltshire, Hampshire, the Isle of Wight, Berkshire, Oxfordshire, and Hertfordshire.[65] Just as in all the comparable begging customs, there was a standard rhyme which gave the request legitimacy. These showed a rather greater variety than those used at the other feasts, although most of them commenced either with a line like 'Shroving, shroving, I be come a shroving', or 'Tippity, tippity, tin', or 'knick a knock upon the block', or 'Pitt a patt, the pan's hot'. Even within a county, however, there could be considerable variety. In Hertfordshire a rhyme heard at Baldock in 1894 went:

> I've come a shrov'in
> Vor a little pancaik
> A bit of bread of your baikin'
> Or a little truckle cheese o' your maikin':
> If you gie me a little, I'll ax no more,
> If you don't gi me nothin', I'll rattle your door.

At Breachwood Green to the north, the one heard about six years later ran:

> Pancake in a pan,
> Pray ma'am give me some,
> You've got some and I've got none,
> So pray ma'am give me some.[66]

The equivalent in the same period at Newchurch, in the centre of the Isle of Wight, was:

> A-shroven', a-shroven', we be come a-shroven',
> Nice meat in a pie, my mouth be very dry,
> I wish'e was as well a wet,
> I'd sing the louder for a nut,
> A pancake or a truffle cheese,
> Or a bit of your own making,
> I'd rather have than none at all,
> A bit of your own baking![67]

A few miles away at Brighstone it was:

> Shroving, shroving, I am come to shroving.
> White bread and apple pie,
> My mouth is very dry;
> I wish I were as well a-wet,
> As I could sing for a nut.[68]

Between the two lay Hampshire, where around Basingstoke children chanted:

> Knick a knack upon the block;
> Flour and lard is very dear,
> Please we come a shroving here.

Your pan's hot, and my pan's cold,
(Hunger makes us shrovers bold)
Please to give poor shrovers something here.[69]

About ten miles westward, at St Mary Bourne, the words were

Knick knock, the pan's hot,
And we are come a shroving,
For a piece of pancake,
Or a piece of bacon,
Or a piece of truckle cheese
Of your own making.[70]

Most often small groups of children were involved, but couples or isolated individuals are also recorded in most places across the range of the practice.

The threat implied in the Baldock verse was implemented at the western end of the 'shroving' region, and further west still, in a parallel tradition. The first full description is found along with the first of shroving itself, in a letter from Cornworthy in the South Hams of Devon written in 1805. Its author, a gentleman farmer called Robert Studley Vidal, recorded that it had originated as a game by which poor people earned the right to a Shrovetide dole by putting a potsherd on the table of a householder without being seen; he thought that originally it might have been a plate, for the expected food. During living memory, he said, it was usual for ungenerous proprietors to have their nature advertised to the world by the sign of sherds left at their door by disappointed paupers. At the time of writing, however, this had degenerated into the throwing of potsherds and filth into a front hallway or at a front door on Shrove Tuesday, by 'the most worthless and despicable of the rabble'. It was a pure act of malice, to express local animosities, and in Vidal's opinion served only for 'insulting and damaging many of the most peaceable and deserving inhabitants of the neighbourhood'. It seems to have been connected with a tradition observed in the Isles of Scilly in the 1740s, whereby boys claimed the right to throw stones at doors on Shrove Tuesday until the owners gave them money or pancakes.[71]

During the nineteenth century juvenile variants of this activity, mostly functioning as ritualized begging, are recorded in many places in Devon, and also in Cornwall, western Somerset, Dorset, and Carmarthenshire, to which it had presumably been taken across the Bristol Channel.[72] It was known variously as Lent Crocking, Pan Sharding, Lent-Sherding, Drawing of Cloam, Dappy-Door Night, or (in Cornwall) Nicky-Nan Night. In its mildest form, found across its English range, it consisted of leaving the broken crockery as a sign of parsimony if 'shroving' was refused. Equally widespread was the tradition of throwing it at doors which remained closed or at which an unfriendly reply had been given. Occasionally the children would throw once and then wait to see if they were bought off with a pancake or pennies. The Carmarthenshire variant was to try to put an eggshell or a hollow turnip containing food scraps on a kitchen window-still, without being seen. In

Devon and Cornwall, however, it was still an option simply to pelt the homes of unpopular neighbours, and in Cornwall this could be combined with general mischief, such as clubbing doors and running away, stealing gates, or blackening the faces of passers-by with soot. In places there was a traditional reprisal expected, such as in west Somerset where 'crockers' could be chased and have their faces blackened, in Carmarthenshire where a captured child would have to shine the household's boots, and in west Devon where the penalty was to turn an old shoe hung painfully close to a fire. Generally, however, the punishment was followed by a compensation, of a pancake.

Once again, the activity was customarily attached to a song or rhyme. The simplest was heard in Somerset:

> Tippety, tippety toe;
> Give me a pancake and then I'll go.[73]

A west Devon equivalent was more elaborate and menacing:

> I see by the latch
> There is something to catch;
> I see by the string
> The good dame's within;
> Give me a cake, for I've none;
> At the door goes a stone,
> Come gie, and I'm gone.[74]

The 'crockers' at Milton Abbas on the Dorset downs sang:

> Please live come a shroving
> For a piece of pancake,
> Or a little truckle cheese
> Of your own making
> If you don't give me some,
> If you don't give me none,
> I'll knock down your door
> With a great marrow bone
> And away I'll run.[75]

The cry at Polperro, a tiny fishing port on the southern coast of Cornwall, went:

> Nicka, nacka, nan
> Give me some pancake and I'll be gone;
> But if you give me none,
> I'll throw a great stone
> And down your door shall come.

Westward at St Ives it was still more peremptory:

> Give me a pancake, now, now, now,
> Or I'll souse in your door with a row, tow, tow.[76]

The coercive element in all this was very unusual in British seasonal begging customs, although perhaps suited to the cruel or abrasive quality of Shrovetide traditions in general. Both 'shroving' of a more bland variety, and 'crocking', waned in pace with all the other winter and early spring festival solicitations during the middle and later part of the nineteenth century. The confrontational aspect of 'crocking', however, meant that it did not die as peacefully as most. Perpetrators were fined for damaging doors at Crewkerne in 1858, Bridport in the 1880s, and Allweston in the 1890s, all those places being in southern Somerset or western Dorset.[77] After 1900 there is apparently no more sign of the threats actually being implemented, and 'shroving' as a whole had become very rare. It was still found in the Torridge valley of north Devon, and among the farms of Exmoor and the Brendon hills, in the 1950s, and survives now at Durweston in the eastern Dorset chalklands as a result of a bequest made in 1925.[78]

What lasted longest and most generally of the old Shrovetide customs was the feasting, gradually diminishing in scale and range as the Lenten fast decayed until it was reduced to the single distinct dish of the festival, the pancake. This was made and eaten all over England in the nineteenth century, and the records of the practice would be a roll-call of all the hundreds of local collections of popular customs. Its equivalent in Scotland was the bannock, equally ubiquitious on Fasten's E'en, and in Wales the same day is summed up by the couplet 'Dydd Mawrth Ynyd, Crempog bob munud' (Shrove Tuesday, pancakes every minute).[79] The pancake bell was retained in the eighteenth and nineteenth centuries as a common tradition in the north of England, in Kent, and in the Midlands north of and including Gloucestershire, Berkshire, and Hertfordshire. It was rung either at 11 a.m. or noon to announce the half-holiday. Around 1800 it became rare in large towns, and thereafter disappeared slowly across its whole range along with the holiday itself.[80] It is rung still, or has been revived at, the villages or small towns of Ashford in the Water in the Peak District, Audlem, Congleton, and Tarvin in Cheshire, Toddington in Bedfordshire, and Chesham in Hertfordshire. Under Victoria children in Somerset, west Dorset, and Cornwall were observed to be using up eggs on Shrove Tuesday by cracking them against each other on pieces of string or in sieves; the object was always to be the owner of the egg left at the end.[81] Known in Somerset as 'egg-shackling', it remains in schools at Stoke St Gregory and Shepton Beauchamp in the Somerset levels and has been revived in that of Powerstock in Dorset (although near Easter). The tossing of pancakes became a much wider activity, seemingly growing into a sport in itself in the eighteenth century as it is not mentioned by earlier writers such as Taylor. In the later Victorian period, races of people tossing them in pans were instituted, the earliest being apparently that at Winster in the Peak District, which is first recorded in 1870;[82] it may (like the unique local morris) have been the brainchild of the local antiquary Llewellyn Jewitt. The races subsequently spread to most parts of England, reaching a peak of popularity in the mid-twentieth century. The most famous is at Olney in the northern tip of Buckinghamshire, and is confined to adult women from that village and nearby Warrington. They run from the market square to the church, using standard-sized frying pans in which each pancake must be tossed at least three times *en route*. In their regulation aprons and headscarves they look the very image of the early twentieth century's ideal housewife; yet in their own way they represent just as much as the courage and the contusions northward along Watling Street at Atherstone, an echo of the fever of celebration and fear which heralded the opening of the medieval Lent.

16

LENT

~❧~

FROM its earliest recorded occurrence, in Anglo-Saxon texts dated to the beginning of the eleventh century, the word 'lenten' had the dual meaning of the season of spring and the major annual Christian fast. It seems to derive simply from the 'lengthening' of the daylight. The connotations of joy, and of abstinence, were intimately combined in it from the beginning, and this dual aspect was retained as it evolved into 'Lent' in the thirteenth century. Not until the seventeenth did the term become confined to the fast.[1] It was wholly appropriate to a season at which flowers, foliage, warmth, and light were all increasing and yet food and fuel would also be at their shortest. The time was admirably suited to a period of self-denial and spiritual doubt culminating in the rejoicing of the most important of all Christian festivals. It took up the season in which most of the ploughing and sowing was carried out in agrarian areas, and relaxation and celebration was hardly appropriate.[2]

The bounds of the fast were standardized for the Church in western Europe by Pope Gregory the Great at the end of the sixth century, to exclude meat, milk, cheese, butter, and eggs. These regulations were susceptible to amendment in areas where alternative foodstuffs were not available, and especially where the authority of Rome was not fully recognized: at the Scottish island monastery of Iona in the seventh century, the monks ate nothing during the day and supped upon bread, milk, and eggs.[3] In the late tenth-century English capitula of Archbishop Aelfric all food was interdicted until after evensong except for the old and the sick, and then 'delicious meat', cheese, eggs, fish, and wine were prohibited. The capitula also bade people to confess their sins every Sunday, and to avoid fighting and sexual intercourse. In the 1020s Canute put the royal law behind the ban upon violence and sex, with fines as the penalty for culprits. By Aelfric's time the restrictions were already sufficiently well enforced for people to be loosening them in ways of which he disapproved, such as ending the complete fast at noon, or believing that all or some of the regulations could be ignored by people who gave enough alms.[4]

By the late Middle Ages the scope of the fast was fixed to exclude meat, eggs, and cheese, and the principal prohibition of social activity was that nobody could marry or make love.[5] The first dent put in the code was the work of Henry VIII, as a minor flexing of his muscles as Supreme Head of his new Church of England. In 1538 he proclaimed permission to his subjects to eat dairy produce during Lent, because of the high price of fish. He still, however, forbade meat on the grounds that this was the dietary equivalent of the moral renunciation of 'corrupt works of flesh' at that season. When he died, further reformation was expected from the more unequivocally Protestant Government of Lord Protector Somerset, and many people ceased to observe Lent at all. They were met with another royal proclamation, reimposing the ban upon meat with the new, and more secular, arguments that it encouraged self-discipline and helped the fishing industry. Catholic Mary restored the whole fast, and then Elizabeth narrowed it to meat again, carefully avoiding any articulation of principle in retaining that prohibition. James VI and I followed her example, having instituted the same system in Scotland. The principal targets of these oft-repeated royal proclamations were butchers and poulterers, who could be fined, pilloried, or imprisoned if they slaughtered an animal, let alone dressed its flesh and sold it, during this period. Those of London put their leisure to use by going into the countryside to arrange their purchases for the rest of the year.

Charles I reacted to continued breach and criticism of the fast with a new secular argument, that it encouraged 'the navy and shipping of this realm' by fostering the fisheries, and so aided national defence. In this fashion he hoped to answer the perennial charge that a seasonal fast, like seasonal feasts, had no place in a Protestant Church: the poet John Taylor remarked that Lent's main enemies were 'a dog, a butcher and a Puritan'. He was quite correct, in that the architects of the Puritan Revolution, despite an even greater need of warships, proceeded to abolish it. In 1664 the restored monarchy of Charles II issued a proclamation for England, and in the next year one for Scotland, to reimpose the old regulations. Neither, however, was repeated and, whereas prosecutions for breach of the fast represent a regular, if not common, item in the published quarter session records of the early Stuart period, they do not seem to appear after the 1660s. In this respect, as in the associated disinclination to prosecute people for working on Saints' days, the Church and State which returned at the Restoration had moved a further step away from its medieval post.[6] Thereafter the observation of Lent became a private matter, and so it remains, within an ever-diminishing proportion of the population. Abstinence has ceased to be regarded as a virtue in Britain.

If the realities of the season did prescribe want in previous ages, then the Church set itself firmly against nature in inculcating fear at a time when optimism might have been a more obvious emotion. Throughout the Middle Ages, the long fast began in the morning after Shrovetide when parishioners (some badly bruised or hung over) were expected to file into their local church and kneel before a priest. He would bless ashes, sprinkle them with holy water, and either give the mixture to the people or dab some of it upon their foreheads, with the Latin formula for the words 'Remember O Man that thou art dust and to dust thou shalt return'. The more pious of the congregation made the sign of the cross in the damp ash.[7] If this ritual of 'Ash

Wednesday' brought mortality to mind, then another reminded the congregation of damnation: the hiding of the altars and lectern, as representing twin ways to redemption, beneath cloths. The cloths could be objects of considerable beauty, fashioned of white silk or linen with red crosses embroidered upon them. In cathedrals the decoration could be more elaborate, the crosses at Salisbury Cathedral in the 1460s being purple with a crown of thorns over the head of each. The London churches displayed sets of individual motifs, the cloths at St Christopher le Stocks in 1483 having suns, crosses, and scourges, while by the 1540s those at St Nicholas Cole Abbey had drops of blood. Wealthy provincial parishes went in for similar forms of display in the early Tudor period, when the cloths of St Lawrence, Reading, were worked with images of the Virgin and angels, those of Christ's College, Canterbury, had pageants of the Passion, and those of Long Melford, Suffolk, had whips and angels.[8]

Probably yet more disturbing to the pious were the similar articles used to veil the images of Christ and the saints, who were expected to intercede on behalf of sinners. These were white, blue or black, the first usually bearing a red cross at the centre. Largest, of course, was the one which hid the rood, hung from a line across the church and drawn up, when needed, by a pulley. It could be painted or embroidered with pictures and was normally white, although green or red specimens were also common. Even this, however, was small beside the Lent Veil par excellence, which concealed the chancel from the laity in the nave, and was drawn up (by a line) only during the reading of the gospel each mass. Once again, this was commonly white and stained or worked with a red, blue, or black cross. Religious houses were more adventurous, St Mary's convent at Leicester having a blue one in 1485 and Lindisfarne Priory a black specimen in 1533. Westminster Abbey possessed both a green one and a red and white one in about 1540, while the churches of early Tudor London used combinations of two colours.[9]

It is difficult to say when these beautiful and distressing items arrived in British churches. The Lent Veil itself may have been a recent institution in the ninth century, for at the end of that Alfred the Great decreed the heavy fine of £6 for tearing it down, noting that congregations deeply resented being excluded from a sight of the high altar. In 1250 Archbishop Gray made a point of requiring every parish to possess one. From the previous year dates the first surviving record of a rood cloth.[10] How much progress both customs had made after the next hundred years may be indicated by an inventory of church goods taken in the Archdeaconry of Norwich (hardly a remote corner of the realm) in about 1360. Out of 358 town and village churches, 261 owned Lenten cloths of any kind.[11] Early Tudor inventories give the impression that they became general thereafter, and the number in each church must have multiplied with the steady addition of images recorded in churchwardens' accounts. What seems plain is that the choice of colour and decoration remained very much at the whim of the individual parish or set of clergy involved. Henry VIII supported all these rituals during his Reformation, enjoining the blessing of ashes as a gesture of penance,[12] and permitting the retention of images unless they had been 'abused' by excessive adoration. It was left to the regime of Protector Somerset, acting in the name of young Edward VI, to outlaw the former in a Proclamation of 6 February 1548, and the latter in a Privy Council order two weeks later.[13] The last recorded clearances of statues of saints took place at Worfield in the Severn Valley of Shropshire and at Ashburton on the edge of Dartmoor, in Devon, during 1549–50.[14] The hallowing of ashes is not known anywhere after it was forbidden. It was, however, enjoined once more, together with the making of images and their veiling during Lent, when Mary took the throne. Most churches had disposed of their various cloths in the reign of Edward, selling them off for the profit of the parish before the government set about trying to seize such obsolete goods for its own gain in 1553.[15] The majority of the churchwardens' accounts from Mary's reign therefore record the purchase and painting or staining of fresh material. It was all in vain, for Elizabeth's accession allowed just one more Lent of such rites, in 1559, before her regime forbade the Ash Wednesday consecration, and the presence of religious statues in churches. The images were not removed from Belton in Axholme, among the north Lincolnshire marshes, until 1566. They stood in two churches in the eastern peninsula of Yorkshire, Holderness, and in still more among the mountains of Snowdonia, in 1567.[16] By the 1570s, however, there is nothing more heard of them, and with their passing it was left to sermons to inculcate the dread of Lent until the Anglo-Catholic movement of the nineteenth century restored statues and the placing of ashes upon worshippers to some parishes. In Scotland they appear to have been suppressed permanently in the Reformation of the 1560s, but no records comparable to those in England exist to chart the process. In much of Wales during the eighteenth century it was a tradition for old people to veil themselves instead during Lent, by wearing only black clothes as a sign of penance and mourning; by 1815 this too was 'wholly laid aside'.[17]

By the sixteenth century, at latest, young Londoners had acquired a means to displace some of the frustrations produced by the restrictions of the season. This was the making of a straw human effigy, a 'Jack o' Lent' or 'Jack a' Lent', which was hung up in a public place and pelted by boys: it was supposed to remain available for this treatment for the whole six weeks, if it could survive that long. The character, and presumably the custom, was already known by March 1553, when the sheriff of London rode through the city followed by pageants including a farce in which a dying 'Jake of Lent' was tended by a physician at his wife's behest.[18] The effigy is first mentioned in 1596, and during the next sixty years half a dozen writers alluded to it, usually as a simile.[19] The most famous of these, Ben Jonson, included the detail that the lads were charged to hurl at it, 'three throws a penny'. With the abolition of Lent in the Puritan Revolution and its enfeebled resurrection under the later

Stuarts, no more is heard of the custom in the capital. The records leave uncertain the matter of whether it was a mid-Tudor novelty, part of the relative decline of respect for the fast under Protestantism, or a survival from the Middle Ages. Equally insoluble is the related question of how far it obtained outside the metropolis. Certainly during the early nineteenth century it was still carried on in eastern Cornish fishing villages such as Polperro, the difference being that the effigy was just paraded at the opening of Lent and then destroyed.[20] Whether this was a transplantation of the tradition from London, or a final remnant of a widespread one, is an open question. 'Jack' is mentioned in a children's song from the villages north of Oxford in the late seventeenth century, but not any image of him.[21]

Within a few weeks of Ash Wednesday, early modern Londoners had the option of savaging another sort of effigy. The origins of this lay in the fact that the slow and episodic way in which the Christian ritual year had evolved meant that the fast of Lent had trapped within it a number of feast-days. The most important of these was that of the Annunciation on 25 March, fixed by the fact that it had to be nine months before Christmas. Known popularly as Lady Day in honour of the Virgin Mary, it was a favourite date for the payment of quarterly rents and dues. From the twelfth century to 1752 it also (as mentioned earlier) marked the formal beginning of the year, which was thus conceived as commencing in the season of opening and of new life rather than in the dead of winter. Lent also contained the holy day of the 'additional' apostle, Matthias, and of a relatively large number of saints from the Celtic realms, including the patrons of Ireland and Wales, Patrick and David. St Patrick's Day was hardly noticed in Britain until the influx of Irish immigration in the nineteenth century. By contrast that of St David, on 1 March, was a matter for remark three hundred years before, when the accession of the Tudor dynasty, and the subsequent relaxation of the discriminatory laws against the Welsh and assimilation of Wales into the English framework of government, made Welshmen a familiar sight in the capital and in government service. They, and the English about them, chose different ways of marking the feast.

To the Welsh, of course, it was a matter for pride, symbolized by the wearing of a leek as a national emblem. It had been associated with St David since the Middle Ages, being linked to him in the *Salysburye Prymer* of 1533: despite much later antiquarian speculation, the reasons for this are lost.[22] What was always clear was that the sporting of it was always much more common among the Welsh when abroad than at home.[23] The earlier reference to it is also the most famous, when it is made the occasion for some broad comedy in Shakespeare's *Henry V*, apparently written in 1599. During the Stuart period it grew into a tradition which affected metropolitan society from top to bottom. A Dutch visitor to London on 1 March 1662 noted that

His Majesty and many great lords and gentlemen, common people, and even lackeys, coachmen, porters and all kinds of riffraff and layabouts wear one in their hats. NB. The office to fix the leek to the King's hat on this day is worth 600 guilders. We saw some country folk carry such large leeks on their hats that their heads hung almost sideways because of them.

The same observer also recorded the response of the cockneys: 'not only by calling after them Taffey, Taffey, or David, David, but also by hanging out all kinds of dolls and scarecrows with leeks on their heads'.[24] Five years later, in the City, Samuel Pepys encountered '(it being St David's Day) the picture of a man dressed like a Welshman, hanging by the neck upon one of the poles that stand out at the top of one of the merchant's houses, in full proportion and very handsomely done'.[25]

Not surprisingly, all this gave rise to a great deal of fighting, so that in 1661 alone one Welsh gentleman stabbed a local commoner near Westminster, while the retinue of another got into a pitched battle with a London crowd.[26] The pattern was repeated regularly thereafter. A more exalted Dutchman, William of Orange, gamely donned his leek as part of his transformation into a British monarch,[27] while Londoners continued to abuse the Welsh in effigy on 1 March,[28] until the large-scale immigration of Irish and Jews in the nineteenth century provided other targets for xenophobia. As for the Welsh, the more delicate daffodil was substituted for the leek as the national symbol by Lloyd George, to lend a greater dignity to the investiture of the Prince of Wales in 1911.[29] The only group still to wear the vegetable on St David's Day seems to be the Royal Welch Fusiliers.

The obvious disadvantage of any holy day which fell in a medieval or early modern Lent was that it was still bound by the dietary restrictions of the season, and that no merry-making could begin until after sundown. The great compensation was that alcohol was still permitted. By the seventeenth century, however, the fast had become divided by a much gentler celebration, which has descended to the present. The earliest certain reference to it is in the journal of the royalist officer Richard Symonds, for the year 1644: 'Every Mid-Lent Sunday is a great day at Worcester, when all the children and godchildren meet at the head and chief of the family and have a feast. They call it the Mothering-day'.[30] To Symonds, an Essex man, the tradition was unfamiliar, and he did not hear of it elsewhere on his marches across southern England. Probably earlier still is the poem by Robert Herrick, published in 1648 but written at any time in the previous twenty years:

> I'le to thee a simnell bring,
> 'Gainst thou go'st a *mothering*,
> So that, when she blesseth thee,
> Half that blessing thou'lt give me.

A 'simnell' in this context was a cake made from fine flour, the term already being used by 1267.[31] Herrick entitled the poem 'A Ceremonie in Glocester' and so, between him and Symonds, we seem to have a picture of a custom peculiar to the lower Severn valley and flourishing there in the early seventeenth century. Mid-Lent would have been an excellent time for families to remeet and inform themselves upon each other's needs, when the conditions for travel were improving after winter and want would be greatest. Widowed mothers would have been especially vulnerable. In addition a cue may have been given by the epistle for that Sunday recommended in the Anglican Prayer Book: 'Jerusalem Mater Omnium'. A long-established argument, that the custom also derived from a medieval rite whereby parish congregations processed to their 'mother church' (the cathedral of their diocese) upon this day, remains unproven. The records of Lichfield apparently show such processions until the Reformation, when they were reduced to visits by clergy from collegiate and deanery churches. Elsewhere the situation is less clear, as is any connection with the Worcester and Gloucester 'mothering'.[32]

By the nineteenth century the latter had expanded to become common in all the counties of the West Midlands[33] and of the Welsh Border,[34] in Gloucestershire, Somerset, and Devon,[35] and in Lancashire.[36] It was not recorded in any in the eastern half of the country except Leicestershire,[37] and although the name of Mothering Sunday was known in Wales (in translation as Dydd Sul y Meibion), the only record of the practice comes from Radnorshire, on the Border.[38] This distribution reinforces the impression that it had spread out from an epicentre in the shires around the Severn, but in the process its character had altered. In Lancashire it still seems to have retained the nature of a general reunion at a parental home, but everywhere else it had become primarily a holiday granted to apprentices and young servants, to visit their families. Different regions had also evolved their own traditions of the proper fare to be enjoyed at the remeeting. Simnel cake was still popular for the occasion across most of the range of the tradition, although it had become spicy and filled with fruit, often made commercially by confectioners and a noted speciality of certain centres such as Bury in Lancashire. In that county it was washed down with 'bragget', hot, spiced ale. In the West Midlands frumenty, or boiled, spiced wheat, was popular in the early nineteenth century, but as standards of living rose Worcestershire and Shropshire took to veal and Warwickshire to pork stuffed with bay leaves.

With the decline of live-in apprenticeship and domestic service in the twentieth century, the practice went into rapid decline and was almost gone by the 1930s.[39] What revived it, in yet another form, was the determination of a Miss Anna Jarvis of Philadelphia, whose guiding passion in life was a devotion to her own mother. Miss Jarvis was well-connected enough to turn her personal obsessions into public laws, and her tireless lobbying caused the Senate and House of Representatives of the United States to legislate in 1913 that the second Sunday in May should be set aside as a national day of remembrance of mothers. It seems to have been the arrival of American soldiers in the Second World War which introduced the concept to England, where the memory of the old Mothering Sunday was still strong enough for the two to become merged. Whereas Congress promoted the festival in the

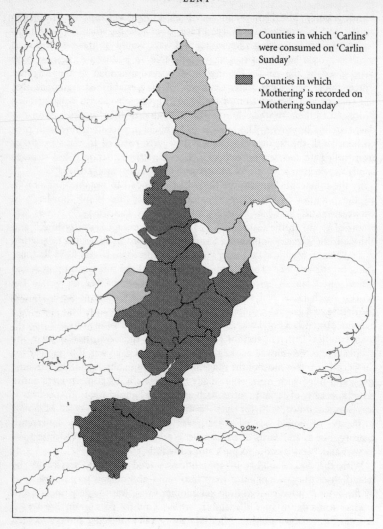

Counties in which 'Carlins'
were consumed on 'Carlin
Sunday'

Counties in which
'Mothering' is recorded on
'Mothering Sunday'

Map 2. Range of 'Carlins' and 'Mothering'

USA, in Britain it was private enterprise which did the trick, as manufacturers immediately saw the commercial potential of the idea. By the 1950s it had become nation-wide, and classless.[40] Thus a regional tradition, developed to ease unequal relationships in a hierarchical society, has (like Christmas) been reinvented to serve the new cult of the family.

Over the same extended period one, and in some years two, other customs were developed to provide entertainment in what the Church had once designated as a sombre season. The first was the practice of eating peas cooked in butter upon the fifth Sunday of Lent. Peas and beans had always been principal foods during the fast, being cheaper and more easily obtained than fish. In 1355 the will of a Lady Clare bequeathed sixty-one quarters of both for use in it.[41] The use of butter, however, was only possible after the Reformation. Peas eaten in this way, on this day, were recorded, only from the eighteenth and nineteenth centuries and almost wholly from the north-east of England (Nottinghamshire, eastern Yorkshire, County Durham, and Northumberland), Cumberland, and parts of Scotland.[42] The peas were known as 'carlins' or 'carlings' and the day as Carlin, Carling, or Care Sunday, but it is hard to tell which came first. Certainly the popular nickname of 'Care Sunday' in Welsh, Dydd Sul y Gwrychon, was much more widespread than the custom, and there is no clear origin for the term.[43] The eating of the peas was a feast of the poor,[44] and lingered into the more affluent twentieth century in a few villages and urban pubs[45] before, apparently, disappearing.

The other innovation could fall either towards the end of Lent or in the rejoicing immediately after it had concluded: the mock-festival of All Fools' Day upon 1 April. This is not recorded at all by the dramatists or comic poets of Elizabethan and early Stuart England, nor in the diary of Pepys or the other sources for Restoration social life; it can hardly have existed in England, therefore, in these periods, providing as it did such a rich potential source of comic theatre and of simile. Its first recorded appearance is in John Aubrey's notes, in the 1680s. It features again in 1698, when several persons were gulled into turning up to the moat of the Tower of London, 'to see the lions washed'. The *British Apollo* journal and a literary work, *Wars of the Elements*, both refer to it in 1708. Jonathan Swift and his friends sat up on the last evening of March 1713, devising 'a lie' for the next day, and thereafter in the eighteenth century the tradition features regularly in almanacs and personal records.[46] It seems, therefore, to have been imported into the country at the end of the seventeenth century, probably from France, where it was already proverbial in 1656, or Germany, where it was well known in the 1680s.[47] By the nineteenth century it was found in every part of Europe, all over Ireland, and in every corner of Britain and its offshore islands, including the Outer Hebrides;[48] as the old season of licensed misrule at Christmas waned, the need for another had become more acute. The new was much more closely circumscribed, being confined to a single day and to a single category of misbehaviour, the deceiving of others in order to make them objects of fun. None the less, this could still be extremely potent, especially if deployed against opponents, or individuals slightly higher in a hierarchy than the prankster(s). During the twentieth century, as both rigid social structures and recognized opportunities for misbehaviour have declined, it has inevitably become largely a festival for children, who remain restricted and governed in a way from which their elders are now in the main set free. Thus All Fools' Day (now more usually 'April Fools' Day') is still one of 'the most joyous' in the calendar of the young.[49] The principal change at this level is that metropolitan culture has substituted 'fool' for the more traditional provincial term of 'gowk', 'gawby', 'gobby', or 'gob', signifying a cuckoo.[50]

Lent itself, however, was not designed to culminate in such relative trivialities, but in a set of rituals and celebrations proportionate to the scale of the gloom and deprivation preceding them. These will be the concern of the next section of this book.

THE ORIGINS OF EASTER

⚜

As the execution and resurrection of its founder were the principal events upon which Christianity has based its claims as a messianic religion, it was inevitable that the annual commemoration of them would be the principal festival of the Christian year. Its location in that year, unlike that of the Nativity, was fixed by Scripture, for it had to be in spring, around the time of the Jewish Passover when the trial and crucifixion of Christ took place. 'Pesach', the proper Hebrew name for that festival, forms the basis for most of the terms for the Christian Feast of the Resurrection used across Europe. Indeed, the latter was celebrated at the same time as the Passover until the Council of Nicaea in 325, when a distinction from the Jewish celebration was deemed necessary. The Council also agreed upon a means of reckoning its date, compromising between the Asian churches' custom of calculating it according to the phases of the moon, and the practice of the Church in Rome, of fixing it upon a particular Sunday in the calendar: henceforth it was to fall after the first full moon following the spring equinox. This ruling still left room for considerable divergence of practice, as different Christian communities regarded the equinox as occurring at different dates, and varied also in the number of weeks which they left between the full moon and the feast. Not until the eighth century were all these in the British Isles agreed upon the rule which was becoming standard in Western Europe, of the first Sunday after the moon had achieved its fullness.[1]

Over the same period the number of days involved in the celebration slowly multiplied. By the late fourth century the churches in Palestine were keeping the preceding Sunday in memory of Christ's triumphal entry into Jerusalem, with a bearing of palm branches to imitate the actions of the crowds upon that occasion. By the ninth century this 'Palm Sunday' was also a common festival in Western Europe. Towards the end of the fourth century the Church in Jerusalem decided to separate the commemoration of the Crucifixion and the Resurrection, removing the first to the preceding Friday. The habit spread westward during the following few hundred years. At first the Anglo-Saxons dubbed the preceding feast 'Long Friday', because of the unusually protracted services: by the high Middle Ages the more pious name of 'Good Friday' had been substituted, almost certainly imported from Germany, where the expression 'Gute Freytag', probably derived from 'Gottes Freytag' (God's Friday), had been established earlier. By 385 it was also the custom at Jerusalem to keep the preceding day in memory of the Last Supper, and this had likewise reached Britain by the eighth century. During the high Middle Ages it acquired the popular nickname of 'Maundy Thursday', perhaps from the 'maunds' or baskets in which gifts were given to the poor, or perhaps from the 'mandatum' or final set of instructions given by Christ to his apostles.[2] The law code of Alfred the Great, promulgated in 877, directed all masters to free their servants from labour during the whole seven days before and after Easter, being the longest holiday in the year.[3] At its centre lay the most important religious celebration, firmly established by Alfred's time as the principal one for baptism and for the taking of communion, all over the British Isles.[4]

There remains, however, the problem of why the Germanic-speaking areas of Europe, in sharp contrast to the others, did not derive their name for this celebration from the Passover, but from a term which is rendered into modern German as Ostern and modern English as Easter. On the face of it, the issue ought to have been solved by Bede in the early eighth century, as part of his work on the calendar mentioned earlier.[5] He declared that the name had derived from that of a goddess, Eostre, after whom the month in which Easter fell had been dubbed the 'Eøstur'-month. This passage has been so often quoted without any inspection or criticism that it is necessary to stress that it is subject to all the reservations lodged by Tille against Bede's assertions concerning the 'Mother Night', cited in the section dealing with Christmas. It falls into that category of interpretations which Bede admitted to be his own, rather than generally agreed or proven fact. A number of German scholars cast doubt upon its utility during the nineteenth and early twentieth centuries, although not with sufficient evidence to disprove it in turn. Two facts do seem to emerge from the discussion. One is that versions of the name given by Bede were used widely among speakers of Germanic languages during or shortly after his time; thus the Christian festival was known as Ostarstuopha in the Main valley during the eighth and ninth centuries. The other is that the Anglo-Saxon eastre, signifying both the festival and the season of spring, is associated with a set of words in various Indo-European languages, signifying dawn and also goddesses who personifed that event, such as the Greek Eos, the Roman Aurora, and the Indian Ushas. It is therefore quite possible to argue that Bede's Eostre was a Germanic dawn-deity who was venerated, appropriately, at this season of opening and new beginnings. It is equally valid, however, to suggest that the Anglo-Saxon 'Estor-monath' simply meant 'the month of opening' or 'the month of beginnings', and that Bede mistakenly connected it with a goddess who either never existed at all, or was never associated with a particular season but merely, like Eos and Aurora, with the dawn itself.[6]

With the removal of this shadowy deity from the canon of historical certainty, there evaporates any reliable evidence for a pre-Christian festival in the British Isles during the time which became March and April.[7] It may be that there was none, the ancient inhabitants being wholly taken up with ploughing, sowing, and caring for young livestock. Alternatively, some of the later Easter rites and customs may echo practices which attended old feasts of which we have now lost sight. Of one thing alone it is possible to be confident; that, although the timing of the feast of the Resurrection was dictated by historical accident, it could not have fallen at a more appropriate point of the European calendar, when so much in nature conduced to a mood of celebration and renewal.

HOLY WEEK

F OR medieval British clergy and congregations, the first clear sign that Lent was drawing to a close came upon Palm Sunday, the fifth in the fast, with one of the longest passages of ceremony in the whole religious year. Where the Use of Sarum was fully observed, it took the following form. First the priest blessed water, and the narrative of Christ's entry into Jerusalem was read to the parishioners, taken from St John's Gospel. Then the priest blessed branches, almost certainly gathered and presented by the people, of what was supposed to be palm in memory of the palms said to have been strewn before Jesus in that entry. The churches of the Mediterranean could, of course, actually use that tree, but in England fronds of willow or sallow in fresh leaf, or of box, yew, or other evergreens, were usually employed instead. The consecrated host was put in a shrine or monstrance and carried out by the clergy into the churchyard. The laity followed in a procession of their own, bearing the branches behind a priest carrying a plain cross, and the two groups halted to hear another version of the tale of the entry, this time from St Matthew's Gospel. Next the two processions met, and one or more people read or sang the prophetic lesson, being rewarded later with bread and ale or a potation of wine. The two groups united and moved to a scaffold at the south door of the church, from which seven boys sang 'Gloria, Laus et Honor', and flowers and cakes were thrown to the congregation. The procession then entered the church through the west door and watched as the rood cloth was drawn aside to reveal the image of Christ, for the first time since Shrove Tuesday. An anthem was sung as this happened, and was followed by mass, incorporating the Passion from the Gospel of Matthew sung (where possible) by a tenor voice providing the narrative, trebles for the parts of Jews or disciples, and a bass representing Christ. During this, either the priest or the congregation made small wooden crosses, almost certainly from the branches, and the former then blessed them with incense and holy water; they were subsequently treasured by the laity for their presumed protective powers. At the end of the service the veil was drawn back across the rood, and the church emptied.[1]

This was, at any rate, the sequence of ritual prescribed by the Salisbury tradition (and with minor variations, in the others) by the end of the Middle Ages. What needs to be emphasized now is, first, that it took a long time to evolve, and secondly, that it was enacted in full in relatively few places. The basic ceremony, of the procession, was known to St Aldhelm in the seventh century and to Alcuin in the eighth. The hallowing of fronds was enjoined in a mid-eighth-century pontifical of Archbishop Egbert of York, and this is Britain's first record of the custom.[2] Not only was it long-established by the early Tudor period but very widespread and probably universal, to judge both from literary comment and the quantity of local names for the day which relates to the custom. Apart from 'Palm' Sunday itself, 'Branch', 'Sallow', 'Willow', and 'Yew' Sunday, and (in Wales) Sol y Blodau or 'Flowering' Sunday, are all recorded.[3] By contrast, the singing of the Passion by a choir appears almost wholly in urban parishes and in cathedrals, the sole village where it is mentioned being Denton in the prosperous Waveney valley of Norfolk.[4] The presence of a 'prophet' to read the lesson is recorded only from the 1490s, and seemingly remained confined to towns in the southern half of England. Even there not all parishes adopted the practice: some in London, for example, entered no payment for it in their accounts. Others, however, tried to make it as dramatic as they could; thus, St Peter Cheap, in the capital, hired a wig or false beard to make its own prophet look suitably grave. The custom certainly became more popular in the early sixteenth century, in which period the scattering of cakes and flowers seems to have been adopted, also at urban churches.[5] In the overwhelming majority of rural parishes, Palm Sunday seems to have been essentially a festival for processing with and blessing of foliage, at once a commemoration of a key event in the life of Christ and of the coming of spring. In the fourteenth century it was already so popular that the people of Romsey, on the edge of the New Forest in Hampshire, could become furious with the local abbey for failing to consecrate their 'palms'.[6] A Protestant under Elizabeth was to recall contemptuously how the common people had put the twig crosses over their doors, or in their purses, as bringers of good luck.[7]

Henry VIII allowed the continuation of the whole complex of rites, endorsing the blessing of branches in the proclamation of 26 February 1539 which also supported the consecration of ashes on the first morning of Lent and of candles at Candlemas. Its only amendment was to emphasize that the act was one of commemoration alone, not investing the crosses with any sanctity.[8] The succeeding Government, of Lord Protector Somerset, behaved equally in character, by banning both the procession and the blessing of the crosses in its first religious injunctions, of July 1547.[9] It followed this on 6 February 1548 with a proclamation to prohibit the consecration of foliage.[10] After this volley of commands there is no certain evidence in either churchwardens' accounts or contemporary comment of the enactment of any of these rites. A curate in south Yorkshire stated specifically that all were forbidden there in that spring, and a chronicler at Worcester recorded the same in the cathedral. The sole possible occurrence was at Winchester Cathedral, where Bishop Gardiner was subsequently accused by the government of allowing the blessing of 'palms'.

These reforms left only two Palm Sunday ceremonies still permitted, the appearance of the 'prophet' and the reading or singing of the Passion. These declined in turn, probably because of the removal of so much that had provided a context for them. In Yorkshire in 1548 they were replaced by a sermon. Only at two parishes which have left accounts, one in Reading and one in Bristol, did the prophet speak his lines that spring, and there he vanished after Palm Sunday 1549, as part of the general reform of the liturgy.[11]

Five years later, after the accession of Mary, the whole complex of ceremonies could return: the blessing of 'palms', indeed, was made compulsory by royal order.[12] One of the religious works published during the reign, Nicholas Doncaster's *Doctrine of the Mass Book*, provides the best picture known hitherto of the rite. The priest, wearing a red cope, or mantle, stood on the third step of the altar, upon which branches and flowers were laid. He then prayed over them, made the sign of the cross, sprinkled them with holy water, and distributed them.[13] The practice was certainly restored throughout the capital, and payment for branches is recorded at many urban churches, which had no easy access to woodland. It seems safe to assume that the revival was general. The singing of the Passion, by contrast, reappeared at just a few parishes, in towns, while the 'prophet' is only recorded at Chester Cathedral, where he was rewarded with a jug of malmsey and a pair of gloves.[14] The restored rituals were conducted for the last time on Palm Sunday 1559, and then the new Protestant liturgy of Elizabeth put paid to them permanently. None of them is recorded after the royal visitation of that year.[15]

The popularity of the bearing of foliage and the making of 'palm crosses', however, can be gauged by the way in which they got absorbed into secular custom by way of compensation. During the eighteenth century, all over England, working people were going out into the countryside in groups upon Palm Sunday morning to fetch home branches, especially those of willow and hazel, with which to decorate their houses. The special significance of those trees was that they were hung with buds, or catkins, as a symbol of the ripening spring. These expeditions were still known as 'going a-palming' or, in the northern counties, 'a-palmsoning'. Although houses had usually replaced the church as the focuses of these now informal processions, at times a natural feature was employed as a place of convergence: on the north Wiltshire chalk downs, for example, Martinsell Hill and the huge prehistoric mound of Silbury were favourite assembly-points. By the end of the eighteenth century the custom had evolved into an opportunity for young East Enders to carouse all night in the fields and woods of Essex, and in the early nineteenth a natural resentment grew among the country people whose land was being invaded in this fashion by people sallying forth from the city and other swelling towns in the south-east. From that time onward the custom was on the wane in southern England. In the north during the mid-nineteenth century it was still a common saying that 'He that hath not a palm in his hand on Palm Sunday must have his hand cut off', yet even there by the early twentieth century the plucking of foliage had been reduced to a practice for children.[16] It seems now to have disappeared at last.

The little 'palm crosses', made on the Sunday and treasured as lucky charms in houses, had almost as long a history after priests ceased to bless them. In County Durham they were fashioned until about 1840, being tied with blue or pink ribbons. They still appeared all over northern Yorkshire, from the Pennine dales to the coast, in the central decades of that century, but by its end they had apparently disappeared everywhere. They had vanished from the south a couple of generations before, being last recorded in Dorset's Frome valley in the 1820s.[17] Over the same period, Sul y Blodau in Wales developed in a quite different fashion. The initial reaction to the end of the ecclesiastical ceremonies, apparently, was to develop a full-blown popular equivalent. Parishioners wheeled a human effigy to represent Christ, seated on a stuffed donkey, up to the church door. Both the dummies and the people who processed with them were hung with flowers, branches, and herbs. The minister spoke a blessing over these and they were kept as charms against misfortune.[18] In the late nineteenth century this custom was 'long obsolete', but by then the spring blooms had been put to a different use. Throughout that century the habit burgeoned, especially in the industrial towns of the south, of visiting family graves on Sul y Blodau and decking them with blossoms and flowers. It spread eastward to the borders of England, appearing at the villages of St Briavel's in the Forest of Dean and Albrighton near Shrewsbury.[19] It still persists in South Wales, illustrating once again how the family has replaced the church as the modern focus of ceremony and of sanctity.

Palm Sunday opened Holy Week, which by the late Middle Ages culminated in a series of increasingly crowded and spectacular ceremonies. First, upon Wednesday, the passage concerning the rending of the veil in the Temple at Jerusalem was read, and at that moment the Lenten cloth which concealed the high altar was either torn or dropped away. After dark that evening the first of the Tenebrae, the Services of Shadows, could be held. In the Use of Sarum, a triangular or cruciform candle frame was placed on the south side of the now visible altar and lit with twenty-four candles representing the apostles and prophets. When the office as sung, one was sometimes extinguished at the opening of each response, so that only a single taper, representing Christ, was left burning in the darkness at the end. In some places the candles were snuffed in groups, or all at once but, whatever the method preferred, the rite is recorded wholly in cathedrals and major urban churches.[20] It vanished with the reforms of liturgy under Edward VI, and after a presumably brief revival under Mary must have been suppressed finally in 1559, with the issue of Elizabeth's Protestant Prayer Book.

The next day was Maundy Thursday, the commemoration of the Last Supper. One of the actions ascribed to Christ at that gathering had been to wash the feet of his disciples as a gesture of humility, and according to Bede the monks of Lindisfarne were already performing the action for each other upon this day before the year 700. On the Continent clerics had used the custom almost two centuries earlier than that, and by the year 1000 French kings were washing the feet of paupers to imitate Christ. The first English sovereign to follow their example was John, almost certainly as part of an attempt to demonstrate his piety in the aftermath of his excommunication by the Pope. In the year 1210 an entry occurs among his accounts for the presentation of robes and money on Maundy Thursday to thirteen poor men, representing the first appearance of the gifts which became standard procedure after the monarch had laved the feet of the recipients. The number was that of Christ and the apostles, but later sovereigns chose to benefit more, and there was no standard rule for the 'royal Maundy' until 1361, when Edward III marked his fiftieth year by washing the feet of as many individuals as he had years of age.[21] This became the tradition for royalty thereafter. As the Reformation increased the sanctity of monarchy while decreasing that of clerics, the custom survived it with ease. A particularly well-documented 'maundy' was that of Elizabeth I at Greenwich palace in 1572. The monarch being aged 39, and female, it was that number of poor women who were honoured. To rescue the monarch from any actual contact with dirt, their feet were cleaned thoroughly beforehand by the yeoman of the laundry, then the sub-almoner, and then the almoner. Elizabeth knelt before them on carpets and cushions in her great hall and washed one foot of each in a silver basin of warm, scented water. She then wiped them and kissed the toes, after which the almoner presented each one with cloth, shoes, claret, fish, bread, an apron, and two bags of money, a white one containing 39 pence, and a red one with 20s.[22] As always, there is no indication of how the lucky recipients were chosen.

The custom had, however, begun among churchmen, and archbishops, bishops, abbots, and priors observed it all through the medieval period, although there is no way of telling how many of them did so. Alcuin, in the eighth century, included it in his Book of Offices, and there are intermittent accounts of important clergy giving clothes, food, and money after it during the later Middle Ages.[23] Only at early Tudor Durham is there a full description of the rite, the prior of the cathedral (which was also an abbey) performing the action at 9 a.m. in the cloisters, for eighteen old men seated on a long bench. They were then given money, drink, and bread.[24] In addition one noble of the same period, the fifth earl of Northumberland, is known to have carried it on, self-consciously imitating the monarch down to the last detail including the one about years of age.[25] No clearer indication could have been given of the earl's self-image as one step below royalty, but none of his peers can be shown to have made the same gesture. With the coming of the Reformation it seems to have disappeared among churchmen as well, although no source demonstrates how or when.

Its decline at the royal court, by contrast, is well documented. Under the Stuarts the sovereign ceased to wash any feet, merely sprinkling them with water. James II, characteristically, was the last to perform the rite puncti-liously. William III did so irregularly and without enthusiasm, ending the reckoning by years of age to care for a mere dozen men. Anne apparently gave the whole job to the royal almoner, and under George II, in the 1730s, the washing was abandoned altogether and the occasion converted into a dole: no simpler indication can be given of the progressive desacralization of monarchy after the Revolution of 1688. The gesture of charity, however, remained, and George III increased its munificence to gratify an equal number of poor women and men according to his years of age. In 1814 his sub-almoner received seventy-five of each in the Chapel Royal and presented them with salt fish, beef, bread, and ale for a midday meal. At 3 p.m. the sub-almoner followed the yeomen of the guard back into the chapel, one of the latter bearing a gold dish each with seventy-five bags containing seventy-five silver pennies each upon it. After evening prayer the money was given out, together with linen, cloth, shoes, stockings, and a cup of wine for each pauper, in which the royal health could be drunk.[26] Today the Queen distributes her own gifts herself, to the appropriate number of elderly people of slender means and respectable character, at Westminster Abbey on the morning of Maundy Thursday. All the beneficiaries are from the diocese of Canterbury. If the royal participation has been restored, the presents, like the whole ceremony, are token, being specially minted 1*d.*, 2*d.*, 3*d.*, and 4*d.* pieces delivered in individual bags. What commenced as a clerical gesture of humility, and was subsequently used to enhance the status of the monarchy, is now primarily a means of according pleasure, and pride, to senior citizens.

To many late medieval English people, however, the day was 'Sheer', 'Char', 'Shrift', or 'Sharp' Thursday, all names which the fourteenth-century writer John Mirk believed to derive from the cutting of hair and beards in prepara-tion for Easter. This was part of a process of personal renewal, and the same spirit was accorded to the religious rites of the day. The altars were stripped of their Lenten cloths, washed with water and wine, and scrubbed with birch besoms. The devout laity made confession, to prepare their souls for the ceremonies to come. Important urban churches such as Great St Mary at Cambridge, or St Mary Pattens in London, kept a special 'shriving stool' or 'pew' for this purpose by the early sixteenth century. Bishops blessed oil, as they had done upon this day since before the year 500, to be distributed to parish priests for the unction of the sick during the next year, or retained at the cathedrals for the making of new clergy. Before the washing of the altars, mass was celebrated with unusual solemnity, two extra wafers being conse-crated for the morrow. The bells were not used to summon the congregation, but left silent while wooden clappers or rattles were employed instead. In this fashion the spiritual and physical stage was set for Good Friday.[27]

That evening the Tenebrae were sung again in those places where they were observed, and the following morning the commemoration of the crucifixion and burial of Christ began. In some churches the altars were sprinkled or rubbed with herbs. Individuals whose sense of sin had not been assuaged by confession sometimes asked a priest to beat their hands with 'disciplining rods': payment for these is recorded at a few London parishes.[28] Medieval monarchs demonstrated again the semi-divine nature of their office by blessing gold or silver 'cramp rings' in the belief that the royal healing power thus transmitted would alleviate the effects of epilepsy and palsy. The custom seems to have originated with Edward II, who tried to employ against epilepsy the ring of Edward the Confessor, kept at his shrine in Westminster Abbey. His son and successor Edward III developed this into the Good Friday custom of consecrating specially made rings by touch. The ceremony used in 1522 began with a form being set in the Chapel Royal before the crucifix. The king knelt on a cushion before it, with his almoner kneeling at his right holding the service book for the rite. The Master of the Jewel House then set the rings upon the form in a silver basin and the king read the blessing before rising and proceeding up to the high altar. The greatest lord attending would then follow him with the basin of rings and hand it to him to be dedicated. The procedure, as a manifestation of sacred majesty, was not offensive to Protestants and was carried on with equal devotion throughout the Henrician and Edwardian Reformations and by Mary Tudor, whose form of words for the blessing has survived. Elizabeth, however, took against the procedure for wholly mysterious reasons, and it was discontinued permanently at her accession.[29]

There is also some evidence that the rite existed at parish level, supplied by a fourteenth-century treatise which described how pennies offered at five different churches were gathered in one of them before the crucifix on Good Friday. After Paternosters were recited, they were beaten into a ring with Hebrew names engraved upon it, which was used to cure cramps. This is the only such reference, and if the ceremony persisted until the Reformation it would have been ended then. In the 1790s, however, observers in two different places recorded that the populace was still carrying on the custom even though it was now bereft of both royal and ecclesiastical support. In Devon people had turned to the numinous power of the dead, fashioning the rings out of the nails of old coffins dug out of the churchyard. In Berkshire they echoed the fourteenth-century procedure, by making them from the silver coins offered to the collection tray upon Easter Day. In both cases the intention was still to cure fits.[30]

The clappers were out again that morning, to call parishioners to a service which, uniquely, included no mass. Instead, according to the Use of Sarum, the whole of the Passion from St John's Gospel was read, with the tearing of two linen cloths laid upon the high altar at the words 'they parted my garments'. After the gospel and prayers, a crucifix was held up veiled behind the altar by two priests while a series of scriptural verses were sung to contrast the goodness of the Christian god and the ingratitude of humanity. The crucifix was then unveiled and laid upon the third step in front of the altar, and the ceremony of Creeping to the Cross ensued. First the clergy went barefoot, on hands and knees, to kiss its feet, and then it was carried down to the laity who would do the same. Communion followed, employing one of the hosts consecrated on the Thursday.[31] At Durham Cathedral the ceremony was very similar, the crucifix being of gold and laid upon a velvet cushion embroidered in gold thread with the arms of St Cuthbert. It was held on the lowest steps of the choir by the two oldest monks of the abbey.[32] Royalty crawled barefoot to a cross in the Chapel Royal, in the case of Henry VIII and Catherine of Aragon being equipped with a rich carpet to make the process more comfortable. They also led the laity in making offerings to the Church after the action. They, and magnates such as the earl of Northumberland, gave money. Poorer people presented in kind, eggs and apples being favourite items. Literary comment of the late medieval and early Tudor periods suggests that the rite was very widely observed, but it is impossible to lend any precision to this impression. It is specifically recorded at the cathedrals of York, Lincoln, Wells, and Hereford, as well as at Salisbury and Durham, in several Benedictine and Augustinian monasteries, and in some urban churches, but Cistercian and Carthusian monks did not use it and it is impossible to tell how far it was observed in rural parishes.[33]

Whatever its maximum range, the rite was certainly venerable by about 1500. It was recorded in parts of Continental Christendom before the late ninth century, when Aelfric, archbishop of Canterbury, admonished all to 'greet God's cross with a kiss' on Good Friday, and so provided the earliest English reference.[34] It was enjoined once more by two thirteenth-century prelates, Henry of Sisteron and Giles of Salisbury, and thereafter references to it become frequent.[35] Its repression is better documented than its inception. Although a ritual of especial abhorrence to Protestants,[36] it was supported by Henry VIII in his proclamation of February 1539, provided that it was re-membered that Christ and not the crucifix was the true object of adoration.[37] Nevertheless, in January 1546 Archbishop Cranmer almost persuaded the King to abolish it,[38] and it was hardly going to survive long under Edward VI. It was, in fact, forbidden in the same proclamation of February 1548 which proscribed Ash Wednesday ashes and Palm Sunday 'palms'.[39] No clear proof exists that the order was flouted upon the following Good Friday, although this was one of the charges made against the very conservative bishop of Winchester.[40] This is the last that is heard of it until the counter-Reformation of Mary, when it was not merely permitted by royal decree but commanded by the visitation articles of Archbishop Pole of Canterbury and Bishop Bonner of London, and probably of other prelates. The enactment of the rite is difficult to prove because it did not involve expenditure and so feature in account books. None the less it certainly took place at Cambridge and at Tarring in Western Sussex, and one of the London chroniclers stated that it was restored all over the capital.[41] It was legal for the last time in Holy Week 1559, and then banned as part of Elizabeth's Reformation. No further reference is made to it, although in the 1560s there were still reports of people going 'bare-legged to the church' on Good Friday as if ready to make the adoration.[42]

According to the Use of Sarum, the crucifix employed for the latter rite was laid upon the altar while the liturgy was concluded. It was then washed with wine and water and prepared for the second, and greater, ceremony of the day, the Easter sepulchre. The priest, stripped to a surplice and barefoot, brought the second host consecrated the previous day, enclosed in a casket. This and the cross were wrapped in cloths and taken to the north side of the chancel or choir, where a miniature tomb had been prepared for these representations of Christ. They were closed up in it together. Much the same rite existed in the cathedrals at Durham, Lincoln, and York: at Durham, crucifix and casket were combined as the host was placed in a crystal container set into the breast of an image of Christ. The nature of the sepulchre itself varied considerably by the early sixteenth century. Some were simple recesses in the wall, others richly carved stone structures with decorated arches and figures, and yet others chambers built into the tombs of wealthy and pious individuals who had provided for this in their wills. Examples of all these varieties survive today with especial frequency in the east Midlands: at Heckington, Navenby, and Irnham, in the woods and farmlands of Lincolnshire's Kesteven district, Maxey, in the nearby Welland valley, Bottesford, in the marshes by the Humber, and Hawton, Sibthorpe, and Arnold in Nottinghamshire's Trent valley. Others are scattered more thinly across the rest of the country. More often the sepulchre was a richly ornamented chest. The most elaborate of these upon record was given in 1470 by the very rich Bristol merchant Nicholas Canynge, to the church of St Mary Redcliffe. It was gilded, with an image of God rising out of it, a Heaven of timber and dyed cloth over it, a timber and iron Hell with thirteen devils beneath it, an armed knight at each corner, four angels of painted wood, and 'a Father, Crown and Visage and orb with cross on it, all gilt, the Holy Ghost coming out of Heaven'. In the majority of parishes, however, the sepulchre was a wood, canvas, and paper construction, made anew in most years and fastened together by pins, nails, or wires. Sometimes, as at Leverton in the Lincolnshire Fens, it was gilded.

Whatever the nature of the sepulchre, when the host was inside it, a cloth was draped over it or hung before it: at Durham cathedral this was of red velvet embroidered with gold, while even in village churches it could be richly painted. Sometimes the sepulchre was surrounded by candles, and in the early 1480s a duchess of Norfolk made regular payments to ensure this. At times it was illuminated by a smaller number of large tapers, three being specified at the London church of St Andrew Hubbard in 1510–12. Most commonly it had its own 'light', a big candle or lamp paid for in many places by a particular collection and tended by its own guild. At Heybridge on the Essex coast, the unmarried youth of the village maintained it. St Lawrence, Reading, built a special loft for it in 1516. In many parishes, especially in towns, volunteers watched the sepulchre from the moment that it was closed until the Easter morning, in memory of the soldiers who guarded Christ's tomb. The church-wardens paid for bread and ale for them, and sometimes for coals to keep them warm at night. At St Mary at Hill, London, the number of watchers was recorded as three, and this may have been standard. The popularity of the custom is vouched for by the fact that it is mentioned in the majority of parishes for which early Tudor accounts survive, and by the number of bequests made to support it or its light. A survey of Northamptonshire wills for the period 1490–1546 reveals an average of just over one bequest per parish, far exceeding that for sums left to any other seasonal rite. On the other hand, there remains a total of twenty-three parishes which have left good early Tudor churchwardens' accounts, where a reference to the custom is entirely lacking. This number represents about one-seventh of all those surviving from the period. They are scattered across the country and are found in most types of environment, and all they have in common is that they are rural. It seems that there were many districts of countryside in which the sepulchre had not been adopted by the time of the Reformation.[43]

The history of the ritual is essentially that of other major Holy Week rites: inception under the Anglo-Saxons, growing popularity in the later Middle Ages, and suppression by Protestant reformers. It was known in southern England by the mid-tenth century, being especially associated with Win-chester cathedral.[44] None the less, its rate of adoption was very slow, to judge from the inventory of church goods taken in the Archdeaconry of Norwich (hardly a remote corner of the realm) in 1360. Out of a total of 358 town and village churches, only five possessed the cloth which traditionally covered the sepulchre when the host was lying within it.[45] The surviving churchwardens' accounts show that it was employed in some urban parishes during the late fourteenth century and in most of them by the middle of the fifteenth. In the early sixteenth century it was present in all of them and becoming popular in the countryside but (as said above) had not yet become universal when it was forbidden.[46]

That process followed a now familiar course. Henry VIII's reforming injunctions of 1538 specifically excepted the sepulchre light from an order abolishing most ceremonial candles and lamps in churches.[47] The government of the duke of Somerset was wary of a direct attack upon so popular a custom, but before Easter 1548 Archbishop Cranmer launched one himself. The effect of this was dramatic, for the sepulchre was not watched in that year at any of the London and Westminster churches which have left accounts. The same is true of most of the rest of the country, in both town and village. In many cases the sepulchre itself was sold (if portable) or demolished (if a stone structure) during this year and the next. At the important administrative centre of Ludlow in the Welsh Marches, at St Dunstan, Canterbury, at St Michael, Worcester, and at the southern Lancashire village of Prescot, the sepulchre was prepared and watched in 1548. This pattern of survival clearly owed more to the strength of local feeling than to a remote or rural situation. It certainly survived that Good Friday in at least two cathedrals: at Worcester, and at Winchester, where Bishop Gardiner this time cheerfully admitted to encouraging it upon the grounds that it was not forbidden by royal authority. None the less, he was hauled before the Privy Council to apologize, and his treatment must have helped to ensure what followed; that after Easter 1548 there is no certain reference to the custom anywhere in England for the rest of the reign.[48] Then Mary succeeded, and issued injunctions for the restoration of all the traditional ceremonies in time for Easter 1554. The sepulchre subsequently features in eighty-four of the 168 sets of parish accounts surviving from her reign, and as more villages are represented in them than in the sample from the early sixteenth century, this reflects about as wide a distribution as before, comprising all urban and many rural communities.[49] This distribution continued until Easter 1559, and then Elizabeth's Reformation swept the old seasonal rites away once more. Sepulchres featured among the Catholic goods of which the royal visitors made bonfires all that summer, and there is no clear reference to their use in ritual after then.[50]

In place of ceremony, the reformed Church of England substituted an increased emphasis upon preaching to drive home the religious significance of Good Friday. The latter was not kept as a holy day during the period of the Puritan Revolution between 1645 and 1660, but with the Restoration it resumed its place in the Anglican calendar. By the nineteenth century it was one of only two days in the year (the other being Christmas) upon which all shops were closed in London and all work ceased.[51] People tended to remain within doors, or to attend the sombre religious services, and the atmosphere of the day, as one of gloom relieved only by the promise of the Easter holidays to come, lingered long into the twentieth century and has not wholly dispersed. In this sense only the negative aspect of the medieval festival survived, while the rites which afforded it some sort of cathartic effect were destroyed. None the less, the latter did make a considerable impact upon popular custom. Creeping to the Cross, it is true, was never imitated once it was prohibited in the churches, but the more popular ritual of the sepulchre was transplanted whole in at least one place. This was Tenby, in the 'Englishry' of Pembrokeshire, where until the early nineteenth century many young people would make 'Christ's bed' on Good Friday. The latter was a human figure woven of reeds and laid solemnly together with a wooden cross in a concealed place in a field or garden.[52] It was, as said, an apparently unique survival: far more common were the sacred qualities long attributed to Good Friday bread.

During the nineteenth century, across virtually the whole of England and in parts of Wales, folklorists discovered the superstition that bread, buns, or biscuits baked upon this day had especially beneficial powers. They were generally believed never to go mouldy and to be capable of curing diseases, especially intestinal disorders, if eaten. If hung in a house, they were thought to protect it against misfortune. Not merely the day of manufacture was important, however, for like a pre-Reformation host they had to be marked with the sign of the cross.[53] The faith in them crossed a surprising number of confessional boundaries: thus a lady in the Cambridgeshire fenland village of Brandon Creek manifested it to the full although she was a strict primitive Methodist. Her Good Friday bread was kept in a tin to bring good luck to her family during the following year. Only after a new one had replaced it was the twelve-month-old loaf moistened, rebaked, and eaten on Easter Day by the whole household. The person given the cross was considered especially blessed, and the end slice was thrown into the river Ouse to protect the neighbourhood from floods.[54] Only in Northamptonshire, to illustrate the twists which popular belief was capable of taking, was the tradition reversed, and baking upon Good Friday regarded as unlucky.[55] That the medieval veneration of the consecrated bread of the mass should have left a profound impact upon the popular imagination is not surprising. That the home-made bread stamped with the cross should be especially associated with Good Friday does, however, call out for some particular explanation, and the one most apparent is surely that the host was most obviously venerated upon this day, in the rite of the sepulchre.

By the nineteenth century, these special pieces of bread were known very widely by the name of Hot Cross Buns, and they survived as the traditional Good Friday morning or midday dish in areas where their magical qualities had been forgotten, and they had become commercialized. This happened earliest, naturally enough, in London, where the street vendors' cry:

> One a-penny, two a-penny
> Hot Cross Buns

was familiar by 1733.[56]

It was still heard repeatedly from dawn onwards on every Good Friday in the metropolis during the 1820s,[57] and the sale of the buns spread in that century to towns right across England, in the Anglicized areas of Wales, and in Scotland.[58] In the latter country they were very clearly a recent importation from across the Border, and rested upon no folk tradition of magical bread of the sort which obtained in England: on the other hand there were districts of the Western Lowlands where some transference of the belief seems to have been made, in that eggs laid and butter made on Good Friday were regarded as being exceptionally beneficial.[59] Long after their associations with divine or supernatural power have faded everywhere, the round currant buns with their white cross remain distinctive products of bakers and confectioners across Britain, a last echo of one of the most dramatic rituals of medieval Christianity.

On the evening of Good Friday the Tenebrae could be sung for the last time, and then came the Saturday, Easter Eve. That morning, according to the Salisbury rite, was held the ritual of the extinguishing of every light in the church and the striking of fire anew from flints by the priest. This had entered the Christian calendar at Jerusalem in the fourth century, and become well known in England by the twelfth,[60] but Sir James Frazer was perfectly correct to point out that it has 'abundant analogies in popular custom and super- stition'. Quite apart from a pagan parallel in the British Isles (Beltane), the custom of a ritual of renewal whereby all fires in a community were put out and relit from a single, freshly kindled, sacred flame was familiar alike to the Incas, Mexican natives, Inuit, African and Indian tribes, Russian peasants, and the civilizations of China, Japan, ancient Greece, and pagan Rome.[61] In most of these cases the drama of it was much enhanced by setting it at night, and this is still the case in the Roman Catholic and Orthodox churches. The Use of Sarum, however, for some reason had transferred it to the morning, and this may explain the relatively little impact which it seems to have made upon late medieval literature.[62] At Durham cathedral the fire was remade on Maundy Thursday, though it is not clear at which hour.[63] Urban churchwardens' accounts of the early Tudor period usually record the purchase of coals or wood to be kindled from the flint, while country people would almost certainly have used their own local supplies of fuel.[64]

The new flames were blessed and censed, and from them was lit the largest candle to burn in any medieval church, the paschal. It apparently originated in Spain in the sixth century and was well known in England by the twelfth. At that period, however, the time of its ignition varied considerably between localities, and thirteenth-century prelates were concerned that it should be more widely adopted.[65] Their hope was fulfilled, for the taper is recorded in all the surviving pre-Reformation churchwardens' accounts, from their first appearance in the fourteenth century.[66] During that later period it normally weighed about 20 pounds, but examples as small as 3 pounds in weight and as gigantic as 300 (in cathedrals) have been recorded. It could be wreathed with ribbons, or painted, or made of coloured wax. It could be given the illusion of greater size by being set upon a wooden stick, painted to resemble a con- tinuation of the candle and nicknamed a 'Judas'. With or without this, the paschal taper was sometimes put in a metal candlestick proportionately bigger than the norm. The one at Durham cathedral stood upon the steps before the high altar and was so tall that the candle had to be lighted from the roof. The metal of the stick was wrought with flowers, dragons, soldiers, and other forms. In some parish churches the candle was stuck upon a wooden post or hung in a basin. In most, a special collection was taken up to pay for it. Once it was burning, another large taper was kindled to illuminate a procession to the font, to bless the water there anew for baptisms. After that, the sepulchre light and all the others of the church could be renewed.[67]

The history of this complex of ceremonies under the Tudors is of a piece with that of the other Holy Week rites. So important was it that Henry's Reformation did not touch it, and it was not at first attacked by the Govern- ment of Somerset. The first prohibition of it was issued by the archbishop of

Canterbury, Thomas Cranmer, in the same articles of early 1548 in which he denounced the sepulchre. The paschal candle is recorded at the Easter following only at Prescot in Lancashire, Ludlow, Halesowen in north Worcestershire, the Oxford parishes of St Martin and St Michael, and the market town of Bungay in Suffolk, and Worcester Cathedral, where it was set up but set up not blessed. There is no trace of it in 1549. The case of Worcester proves that the lighting of the paschal could now be uncoupled from the consecration of new fire. The latter was made at St Michael, Oxford (this time without the paschal candle) in 1549, but it is recorded nowhere else and by 1550 it seems to have vanished.[68] Both reappeared under Mary, being made compulsory in the visitation articles of her most important churchmen. The paschal is recorded in every set of parish accounts remaining from the reign, and the purchase of coals appears in the same proportion of them as under Henry VIII; once again, almost all in towns. This situation altered drastically with the substitution of Elizabeth's liturgy, and at Easter 1560 there is no sign of either, and none thereafter.[69]

In most churches at the beginning of the sixteenth century, the first ceremony of Easter Day was the opening of the sepulchre. At Durham cathedral this took place before four o'clock, and it was probably held before dawn in other places as well. The Durham monks placed the crucifix bearing the host upon a velvet cushion and carried it to the middle of the high altar. The anthem 'Christ is Risen' was sung, and then the crucifix and host were carried about the cathedral under a canopy of purple velvet fringed with gold hung with red silk tassels.[70] Elsewhere the rite of opening seems to have been similar, if seldom so gorgeous and never so well described. In the popular Salisbury rite, it was the crucifix alone which was borne about the church by the clergy while the bells were rung for the first time since the Wednesday. It was then placed on an altar on the north side of the church, and the ritual of Creeping to kiss it was repeated. The empty sepulchre was left with candles burning before it during service time, and given a censing every evening, until it was removed or closed up on the morning of the following Friday.[71] A few urban churches placed carved wooden angels beside it, in memory of those said to have appeared beside the tomb of Christ.[72] The ceremony of the opening may have been the 'play of the Resurrection' recorded in some parishes and in the fifth earl of Northumberland's chapel, though the payments for this piece of drama suggest that something more elaborate was involved. It was probably an acting out of the events set around Christ's tomb in the gospels. At the Devon seaport of Dartmouth, the parishioners themselves painted the costumes for it.[73]

At the mass upon Easter Day, the Use of Sarum prescribed the blessing of herbs sprinkled upon the altar, which must have added fragrance to the joyous human atmosphere in those churches which followed the custom. It is disappointing that only a few, in London and Bristol, record payment for them; perhaps they were a refinement of large cities, or perhaps elsewhere they were contributed free.[74] Everywhere the figures of Christ and of the saints, veiled since Ash Wednesday, stood accessible once more, ready to receive the prayers of devotees. Parishioners were expected to express their delight by making offerings to the church funds, in cash or kind, and to confess their sins anew and then to take communion. Failure in any of this could lead to citation before an ecclesiastical court.[75] Having begun as the favourite day for reception of converts into the Christian faith, Easter remained a popular one for baptisms, so much so that in 1279 Archbishop Peckham ruled that the latter be restricted to children born in the previous week. By keeping their babies to receive the ceremony on the great feast, he warned, parents were endangering their souls if they died in the interim.[76] Only when the Easter mass was over could the Lenten fast finally be ended.[77]

The Reformations of Edward and Elizabeth substituted sermons for ceremony to bring home the significance of the Resurrection to church-goers. The offerings, naturally enough, were retained. In the early Stuart period a few churches in county towns, such as St Petrock at Exeter and St Lawrence, Reading, began to be beautified for the day with decorations of greenery: rosemary was used at the former, and box and yew at the latter.[78] Towards the end of Elizabeth's reign, also, the practice of communion on Easter Day began to revive, until by the 1630s it had become the rule almost everywhere.[79] The exceptions to this picture were Chester and Cheshire, Bristol and (by far the most significant) the City of London. It was notably absent from parishes served by more radical Protestant clergy, which was an omen for the future.[80] So was the course of events in Scotland. There has hitherto been a striking lack of data from either there or Wales in this account of medieval Holy Week ritual, the consequence of the absence of the kind of local records which make such a study possible in England; the presumption is that practice in them was similar. When the Scottish Reformation began, in 1559, its leading ministers were charged to continue communion at Easter. The First Book of Discipline, in 1561, implicitly overturned this ruling by ignoring the existence of the feast. When the General Assembly of the Kirk took the Church of Zurich as its model of practice in 1567, it explicitly rejected the Zurich practice of celebrating the feasts of Christ. In 1570, however, it relented sufficiently to allow a communion on Easter Day if no 'superstition' were involved in the proceedings.[81]

This grudging toleration, and the increasingly enthusiastic celebration south of the Border, were both terminated in 1640s, when Scottish and English reformers joined forces to purge the last remnants of 'Popery' from the island. The Westminster Assembly of Divines abolished Easter with every other seasonal festival in November 1644, and its Directory of services, issued on 4 January 1645, had no place for it.[82] On what ought to have been Easter Day 1647, the captive Charles I issued a much-publicized statement that the festival of the Resurrection was as scriptural as Sunday. The Government printed a denial of this view, asserting that the feast had been instituted by the primitive

Church and so could be abrogated by a reformed one. On 10 June the Long Parliament seconded the Westminster Assembly by passing an ordinance for its abolition.[83] The result of these measures was impressive, in that communions as Easter shrank from being the regular practice of most parishes in 1640 to that of a small minority: fifty out of a total sample of 367 kept them up all through the 1650s, and virtually all were in small villages.[84] This statistic is vitiated by two considerations. The first is that a devout Anglican determined to celebrate Easter in the later 1650s could usually do so, even in London where John Evelyn received the sacrament at St Gregory by St Paul's in 1656 and heard sermons for the feast there and in other City churches in following years.[85] The second is that conformity to the Directory was reluctant in many of those communities which obeyed it. At Easter 1660, when the authority of the republic was obviously crumbling, just under half the parishes which have left accounts recorded the taking of communion.[86]

After the Restoration the proportion of communities where the sacrament was offered at the festival continued to increase, steadily but very slowly: it comprises 58 percent of the parishes which have left accessible accounts for the period from 1660 to 1700. As before the Puritan Revolution, most were rural, and York is the only major urban centre where a majority of churches from which accounts survive carried on the custom.[87] In the eighteenth century it seems to have become the norm in England, although not in Wales, and as part of the general trend to a greater use of ceremony in Anglicanism in the nineteenth, the tradition of decking churches for the feast also became well established in specific regions. By the reign of Victoria, yew (functioning as a symbol of immortality) was commonly used in Herefordshire, Worcestershire, and West Somerset, and box was also employed in much of the Welsh Marches.[88] Above all, the position of Easter as the principal festival of the Church of England has never been challenged since the collapse of the republican experiment.

It must be plain from the account above, moreover, that some of the most popular rituals of the pre-Reformation Holy Week were transmuted into folk customs and so given a second life until relatively recent times. They joined a number of secular rites of the season, which can themselves be traced in some cases into medieval antiquity, and which formed the lay counterpart to the religious ceremonies. These must be the subject of the next two chapters.

AN EGG AT EASTER

THE bird's egg has always been one of the most ubiquitous human symbols of new life in general and of spring in particular. The classic study of this image was made in 1971 by Venetia Newall, in a book which documented the giving of eggs at Easter, often decorated, all across Europe and western Asia in historic times. In this respect, the medieval prohibition of the eating of them in Lent was neatly contrived to enhance the exchange and consumption of them at the most appropriate season, in which the fast terminated. This was the more important in that they represented one of the chief delicacies possible to that large proportion of the population which was too poor to afford meat. The rich certainly delighted in them as well: in 1290 the household of Edward I purchased 450 to be coloured or covered in gold leaf and distributed among the royal entourage at Easter. Over two centuries later young Henry VIII received one enclosed in a silver case as a seasonal present from the Vatican.[1] They also represented one of the principal commodities in which the Good Friday and Easter offerings to the Church could be made. The latter were known as 'eggsilver' at late medieval Durham,[2] while the Protestant ministers William Kethe and John Bale mocked the presentation of eggs after 'Creeping to the Cross'.[3] Easter dues to the Church were still paid in them by most people in south-west Lancashire during the early eighteenth century, while the gentry gave cash.[4] Secular levies were also made in the same kind during earlier periods: thirteenth-century English villages brought gifts of eggs to their manorial lord every Easter.[5]

Just as before Christmas, so prior to this next extended period of holidays there was provision made for the poor to obtain foodstuffs for a feast. Parish doles were very common at this time and, whereas it was women who went about before the midwinter festival, so it was children who did so before the spring one. In the villages north of Oxford during the mid-seventeenth century, they would go door to door beating the wooden clappers which had been used before the Reformation to summon people to church in the last days of Holy Week.

Their chant went:

> Herrings herrings white and red
> Ten a penny Lent's dead
> Rise dame and give an Egg

> Or else a piece of Bacon
> One for Peter two for Paul
> Three for Jack a Lent's all
> Away Lent away.

If gratified they provided a blessing:

> Here sits a good wife
> Pray God save her life
> Set her upon a hod
> And drive her to God

If not, there was a malediction:

> Here sits a bad wife
> The devil take her life
> Set her upon a swivel
> And send her to the Devil.

The disappointed children would then cut the door latch, fill the keyhole with dirt 'or leave some more nasty token of displeasure'.[6] Two hundred years later the clappers had apparently vanished from England, but survived in north-west Wales.[7] Under the name of 'Clapio wyau' they continued in Anglesey during the early twentieth century, children banging pieces of slate instead of wooden blocks and chanting:

> Clap, clap, gofyn wy,
> Bechgyn bach ar ben plwy.
>
> (Clap, clap, ask for an egg
> Small boys on the parish.)[8]

The tradition of going about begging food for Easter remained strong in the nineteenth century among children in Cheshire and Lancashire. One Cheshire rhyme associated with it echoed some from the early winter period:

> Eggs, bacon, apples or cheese,
> Bread or corn if you please,
> Or any good thing that will make us merry.

Another, from the Wirral, embodied the aggressive spirit of the seventeenth-century Oxfordshire one:

> Please, Mrs Whiteleg,
> Please to give us an Easter egg.
> If you won't give us an Easter egg,
> Your hens will lay all coddled eggs,
> An your cocks lay all stones.[9]

In outlying parts of Scotland, such as Caithness and Islay, the same simple practice also obtained in the nineteenth century. Elsewhere in that country it could be absorbed into, or collide with, quite different social norms. In parts of the Highlands, for example, boys were expected to steal the eggs as a test of daring and to make a pancake feast on Easter Day around a fire in some hidden place. In strongly Presbyterian Galloway, by contrast, any customs involving eggs at Easter were avoided as Catholic. In the early part of the century one 'strict old Cameronian' in the Isle of Whithorn 'would not even let eggs be cooked on Easter Sunday, lest he might be doing something that savoured of Popery'.[10]

It was in north-west England that the habit of collecting food or money for the feast developed into its most elaborate form, whereby an entertainment was provided as part of the solicitation. The actors were young people somewhat older than those who went singing and begging in the southern part of the region or (more rarely) adults. They seem to have been first recorded in the cotton-making district of south-eastern Lancashire, at the end of the eighteenth century, as 'young men grotesquely dressed, led by a fiddler, and with one or two in female attire'. Their performances varied according to their powers and the tastes of their patrons, but usually included dancing and the recitation of 'quaint' verses. They were known as 'peace-eggers', a term which will be discussed below.[11] During the early nineteenth century they were found commonly in the textile-making communities of the Lancashire Pennines and those just over the border in Yorkshire, but also in villages and towns of Cheshire, Westmorland, and Cumberland. After the mid-century they became rarer and also more inclined to perform on Easter Monday, as the motive for doing so became more purely one of raising money or getting beer, rather than finding food for the festival. They survived into the twentieth century around Blackburn in Lancashire, in the Upper Calder valley of Yorkshire, in the Furness peninsula, and amongst communities in the south-east fringe of the Cumbrian mountains. For most of this period they were known either as Pace-Eggers or Jolly Boys.

Their repertoire naturally became both more varied and at times more sophisticated in the nineteenth century. At Kendal lads merely blackened their faces and paraded the streets dragging old tins and buckets and chanting:

> Trot, 'errin, trot, 'orn,
> Tris Good Friday tomorn.[12]

Around Blackburn young men also blackened their faces, but put on animal skins in addition to increase their disguise. More commonly in Lancashire and Yorkshire the groups, which numbered from three to twenty, wore ribbons or coloured paper, masks, or 'fantastic garbs'. Some bore wooden swords. In the cotton district in the earlier part of the century it was common for groups to fight each other if they collided on their circuits; in 1842 one youth was killed in such a brawl. The most ubiquitous character among them was an individual with a blackened face called Tosspot, who carried a container which in the earlier decades was used to collect eggs, and in later times money, by way of reward. His comrades sang, usually patriotic ballads, and danced (or 'capered').[13]

Most colourful were the customs adopted from winter pastimes of the same period. One was the carrying of a horse's head on a pole, very similar to the Old Horse or Old Ball of the Derbyshire Christmas players. This one, likewise named Old Ball, went about the industrial towns on either side of the Forest of Rossendale, taken by about six men with blackened faces or masks. It consisted of an actual horse's skull with bottle-ends for eyes, clashing jaws, and a sackcloth body to cover the performer, and followed the practice of its winter cousins in cavorting and chasing onlookers.[14] A more widespread borrowing was of the southern English Mummers' Play, versions of which were performed by Pace-Eggers across their nineteenth-century range from Cheshire to Cumberland. The only distinctively regional touches to the surviving texts are the presence of Tosspot and the common addition of a song referring to 'Pace-Egging Time'. Unlike the Christmas presentations, these tended to occur in daylight: in the Calder valley the boys would start out early enough to earn money from engineers on their way to work. Perhaps the most distinctive tradition was that evolved by the youngsters of Far and Near Sawrey, two villages nestling among the oak woods beyond Lake Windermere in Westmorland. The chief literary fame of this community is that it became the home of the children's writer Beatrix Potter, and in view of this it is wholly appropriate that in the twentieth century the actors were all girls, who opened with a chorus of

> Now we're jolly pace-eggers all in one round,
> We've come a pace-egging, we hope you'll prove kind;
> We hope you'll prove kind with your eggs and strong beer
> For we'll come no more near you until the next year
> Fol de diddle ol, fol de dee, fol de diddle ol dum day.

Individual verses were then sung to introduce the characters: Old Betsy Brownbags, Jolly Jack Tar, Lord Nelson, Old Paddy from Cork, and (of course) Old Tosspot. A standard hero-combat play followed. The reference to 'strong beer' and the complete lack of any local identity to the characters indicate how far the play had travelled across boundaries of age-groups, groups, gender, and communities to reach this form.[15]

Pace-Egging would make an admirable subject for a monograph of the sort recently devoted to wakes, north-western morris, and rushbearing, all pastimes carried on the same communities at the same time by much the same people. The same social changes, of growing affluence and wider horizons, which sapped the vigour of these, also put paid to the Pace-Eggers. By the 1920s the custom was moribund. Only one part of it, the plays, was easily susceptible to a revival, and this occurred in the Calder Valley in 1931–2, produced by a request for readings of the texts for radio broadcasts upon folk culture. Schoolteachers duly set their pupils to work performing versions from Brighouse and Midgley, and they are still presented by schools and children's theatres in the villages on either side of Halifax upon Good Friday.[16] Although almost certainly derived from a winter custom, the plays' central actions of death and resurrection were equally well suited to the Easter season.

Pace-Egging, however, had a much broader context in the nineteenth-century north, sharing its name with a very common children's custom which derived in turn from an ancient seasonal pastime of ruling élites. This has been referred to above, and consisted of the decoration of eggs and their use as presents, adornment for homes, and items in competitions. It became practicable for commoners as soon as standards of living reached the point at which the eggs were no longer essential as foodstuffs. None the less, northern Britain was the region in which this practice became most firmly established, under the various names of peace-, pace-, paes-, paste-, or pasch-eggs. All were probably based upon the adjective 'paschal', from the Latin name for Easter. The term 'pace egg' is first mentioned in early eighteenth-century Lancashire and dyed or gilded specimens were first recorded as popular in Northumberland in the 1770s.[17] In the 1950s they were still made by or given to children in many areas of north-western England and in a few communities in south-east Wales.[18] In between those two periods they were observed as customary in all the six northern English counties and in Notting-hamshire,[19] up the east coast of Scotland and in the Shetlands,[20] and (apparently as an outlying example) in Somerset.[21] They were also found in County Down, a part of the north of Ireland which has easy communications with north-western England.[22] Rural and urban communities of all kinds enjoyed them. Often the simplest means of colouring the eggs was to boil them with onion skins, which gave a rich yellow hue to the shells; at the Durham port of Hartlepool in the 1920s, they were wrapped in gorse flowers before going into the pot, and emerged with delicate yellow and brown patterns.[23]

Decorated or not, many eggs in northern Britain and northern Ireland were put to a further use, in the children's sport of rolling them down hillsides: again, this could only have developed in a time when ordinary people had food to waste. It was first noticed in Cumberland and Westmorland in the 1790s, and this remained its principal English stronghold up to the mid-twentieth century. Around 1900 hundreds of youngsters would gather for the fun at traditional spots such as Castle Hill at Kendal, Castle Moat at Penrith, and Honey Pot Farm near Edenhall.[24] In the nineteenth and early twentieth centuries it was also thinly scattered all over the rest of northern England, with especial concentrations of enthusiasm on the North Yorks Moors and around Preston, Derby, and Manchester.[25] The rolling was found in addition on the Lincolnshire side of the Humber, in Staffordshire, and in an isolated occurrence at the south-east Welsh town of Pontypool, perhaps brought thither by northerners coming to work in the coal-mining industry.[26] Over the same period, however, the custom was just as common in Scotland as in the English north; although it was not recorded there as early, it could indeed be of Scottish origin. Reports of it derive from all over the country, including both the largest cities and rural districts from Ayrshire to the Shetlands and the Outer Hebrides.[27] The areas of Ireland in which it was carried on were those of Ulster in which Scots had settled in large numbers, and it was also popular in the Isle of Man.[28] Most enterprising, however, seem to have been the rather older children of Wednesbury, in Staffordshire's Black Country, who took to rolling themselves, instead of eggs, down slopes. This tradition flourished in the very early nineteenth century, but 'it was scarcely suitable for young women clothed in skirts and petticoats to engage in; so as times progressed and manners became less coarse, this old-time revel was gradually frowned out of existence, and we hear no more of it after 1830'.[29]

In three areas in which they were decorated or rolled, the eggs were submitted to still rougher treatment, for the children held them in pairs and cracked them together until one broke. Both the decoration and the rolling could be competitive, but this was invariably and blatantly so. In Cumberland and Westmorland the sport was known as 'dumping', and in the north-east of England, from Northumberland down to the Cleveland district, as 'jarping'.[30] It was also noted at one isolated place in the south; at Taunton during the years 1905–12.[31] Canny children soon learned that the sharp ends broke less swiftly than the round.[32]

From foodstuff and symbol of new life, to courtly art object, to household decoration, to focus for juvenile games, the Easter egg had travelled a long way. That so much of this journey was made in the northern two-thirds of Britain can only be put down to one of those caprices of regional taste which abound in the history of calendar customs. There is no theory of social or economic causation which can embrace at once Hebridean crofters, Hartlepool fisher folk, and workers in Tyneside industries, while excluding all comparable communities in the south. The lack of interest in the latter is remarkable by contrast: in Hertfordshire, for example, Easter eggs were hardly heard of in the nineteenth and early twentieth centuries,[33] and they are conspicuously missing from the seasonal traditions of early Victorian Londoners. After 1850, however, artificial specimens began to be made in the capital, and by 1874 the *Illustrated London News* could remark upon their growing popularity.[34] It was only in the mid-twentieth century, however, that the chocolate Easter egg became mass-produced and took up its now ubiquitous role as the national symbol of the feast. It fitted perfectly into the now familiar pattern of the conversion of a former religious and communal celebration into one centred upon the family and, more particularly, the pleasures of children. In the past few years it has been joined by the traditional central European Easter Hare, taken by German immigrants to the USA and given tremendous popularity there as the Easter Bunny before being re-exported to Britain. Simnel cakes, relocated from Mothering Sunday, seem also to be turning into a further association of the festival. There is every sign that, like Christmas, Easter is developing rapidly as a public holiday devoted to intense private celebration.

20

THE EASTER HOLIDAYS

As mentioned earlier, Alfred the Great decreed a cessation of any need to labour in the fortnight on either side of Easter. If the first of those weeks was intended to be given up principally to religion, then the second could be devoted mainly to feasting and making merry. Sports, which had also been banned during Lent, could now be enjoyed as well. By the thirteenth century, the period of rest from labour had been curtailed to remove the first part of Holy Week, but extended at the other (festive) end to include the second Monday and Tuesday after Easter. This latter period was known as the Hock or Hoke Days, or Hocktide, the derivation of which is now completely mysterious. Hocktide was to Easter what Twelfthtide was to Christmas, the uproarious climax to a major period of celebration, and yet it was also an important time for business meetings and transactions. Court leets frequently sat then, work-shifts were fixed for the coming season, and taxes and rents were paid.[1] This span of leisure remained until the Reformation of Edward VI, one component of which was a severe reduction in what the reformers regarded as an excessive number of holy days. An act of Parliament in 1552 restricted the period of recreation after Easter to the Monday and Tuesday immediately following,[2] and it was generally observed as such until the institution of bank holidays in the late nineteenth century cut it back to the Monday alone. By then the adoption of the weekend and of paid annual leave had removed the apparent need for seasonal periods of leisure.

The point at which the feasting and fun could commence itself seems to have altered over time. In the Middle Ages, as said above, it was upon returning from mass on Easter Day. By the early seventeenth century it had been pushed back to the previous evening.[3] The joyous character of the Sunday was, however, not a whit diminished by this. The fourteenth-century Shropshire cleric John Mirk could write of it as a time when fires were at last extinguished in homes, hearths strewn with rushes, and flowers and houses cleaned.[4] To the Jacobean poet Nicholas Breton, it was a time for 'nothing but play and mirth': 'the sun's dancing-day and the earth's holy-day.[5] This may well be the earliest reference to a belief found subsequently all over the British Isles, that the sun danced for joy as it rose at Easter.[6] Like a similarly wide-spread tradition, that it was essential to wear new clothes on the day, it embodied the sense of delight, relief, and optimism which attended the festival. Thirteenth-century manorial lords held a dinner for their servants, and perhaps for their tenants also,[7] and all surviving late medieval household accounts testify to the manner in which aristocrats and gentry stocked up for a feast upon the day.

It was upon Easter Monday that the sports and fairs began in earnest. During the seventeenth and eighteenth centuries there are several well-recorded cases of urban corporations organizing special entertainments. In the early Stuart period it was a tradition for the mayor and aldermen of Chester to watch a public archery contest before breakfast, held between local teams.[8] More energetic were those of Leicester, who by 1668 at latest were going hare-hunting on horseback in their scarlet gowns of office. The custom lasted until the early nineteenth century, by which time the hare had been replaced by a dead cat trailed in front of the hounds through the streets.[9] Almost a hundred years before, their counterparts at Nottingham had given up their own tradition of marching with their wives to St. Anne's Well, the town musicians playing before them.[10] Most of the corporation of Georgian Newcastle upon Tyne processed behind the mace to preside over handball competitions and dances, sometimes joining in.[11] All these gatherings were intended to foster a sense of civic pride and unity, and were duplicated in miniature at rural parish level at an earlier period. Village 'ales', of the sort which were to become much more common in the warmer months, were held at an unknown Warwickshire village in 1523, and were customary at North Bradley in the west Wiltshire clothing and dairying country during the early seventeenth-century.[12] At this early and chilly season, however, parochial solidarity was more commonly and enduringly displayed in the giving of customary doles to the poor.

Informal festivity was more the rule. In early modern Britain spells of uncommonly warm weather at Easter could be the signal for the first appearance of morris-dancing, may poles, and other activities normally associated with the summer.[13] On Tyneside in the 1720s there were 'public shows, gamings, horse-races,[14] while in the cotton-manufacturing district of Lancashire, at the other end of the century, people sported new clothes, held dinners, and met at alehouses. They displayed, according to one observer, much 'folly, intemperance and quarrelling, amidst the prevailing good humour'.[15] In the early decades of the nineteenth century thousands of south Londoners sallied forth to Greenwich Fair,[16] while their counterparts in the East End went on the Epping Forest Stag Hunt. This had begun its life as a municipal celebration like those mentioned above, by which members of the corporation hunted in the forest on Easter Monday to mark the medieval grant of rights in it. By this later period, however, it was left to a huge crowd of Cockneys, including 'numberless Dianas', to chase an old stag released from a cart. The growth in the size of the event, and thus of the disruption which it caused, resulted in its prohibition by 1847.[17] All across England and Ireland in the same century smaller communities engaged in dancing, athletics, racing of horses and dogs, feasting, and a variety of local games.[18] The tradition persists to the present day in the scheduling of fun-fairs and professional sports. What has perished is any sense of a celebration of communal identity.

Two aspects of the Christmas holidays surfaced again as minor themes at Eastertide. The first was a local tradition of wishing success to crops, the 'wassailing' of midwinter being paralleled in Herefordshire by 'corn-showing' and in Monmouthshire by 'walking the wheat'. Farmers or bailiffs would go round the fields under their care on the afternoon of Easter Day, carrying plum-cakes and cider and eating and drinking to the good fortune of the sprouting cereals. In Monmouthshire they buried pieces of the cake and scattered others, saying:

> A bit for God, a bit for man,
> and a bit for the fow's of the air.

The Herefordshire recitation was:

> Every step a leap, every leap a sheaf,
> And God send the master a good harvest.

Recorded only in the nineteenth century, it was last heard of in the Golden Valley in about 1880, 'when owing to the importation of the wheat from abroad the crop had no longer so much importance, and also it gave rise to a noisy assemblage on Easter Sunday'.[19]

The other theme was misrule, which played a very minor part indeed in most of the Easter holidays. At Melton Mowbray, a market town in the rolling Leicestershire arable lands, a parish 'lord' organized entertainments and collected money for the church in a manner much more familiar at summer revels.[20] Less usual was the custom observed in late Tudor Lostwithiel, a Cornish seaport, on the Sunday after Easter. A mock-king was chosen by lot from amongst the freeholders and led them in a procession to the church 'gallantly mounted' with a crown upon his head, a sceptre in his hand, and a sword borne before him'. After the service he presided over a feast.[21] Sir James Frazer was to assimilate this to his general theory of a prehistoric divine and sacrificial kingship,[22] but it is more likely to have derived from the common medieval British custom of summer kings or lords, to be dealt with later in this book. Far less decorous were two other offshoots from that tradition, the mock-mayors chosen at Middleton in the Lancashire textile-making district, and Randwick, a cloth-weaving village on the Cotswold scarp, on Easter Monday and Hock Monday respectively.[23] The first was recorded in the 1790s, the second in about 1703, and both had a heyday in the late eighteenth and early nineteenth centuries. The Middleton man was elected by the town drunks, from among their number, dressed in rags and daubed with soot, flour, and grease before being placed in a chair or on a pole and carried from door to door to collect money. Randwick's 'mayor' was by contrast elected by the parish to preside over its annual revel; though it was a notably rough and disreputable community. He was carried in state, with drums, flags, and acclamations, to the horse pond, where all present sang a song to celebrate equality, communality, and the weaver's trade, and engaged in a water-throwing battle which commenced the games and drinking. After over a hundred years of opposition from local magistrates, the tradition was suppressed in 1892; by then the village cloth industry which had helped to support it had long collapsed.

Misrule, however, appeared in a far more important and distinctive form at Hocktide, in a medieval and early modern custom whereby groups of one sex caught members of the other upon the public street and released them upon payment of a forfeit. In many cases it was the men who were the pursuers on the Monday and the women on the Tuesday, but this was not constant: indeed, in many places the custom seems wholly to have been one by which females captured males and held them to ransom. This situation was a far more perfect reversal of the social norm, which held women in a position of subservience, so that they not only seem to have taken to the role of captors with gusto but to have found more willing victims. From the earliest notices of the custom, it was claimed to have originated in the Anglo-Saxon struggle against the Danish invaders, either in celebration of the massacre of Danes in England under Ethelred or of the death of Hardicanute, the last Danish sovereign to rule the English.[24] No historical evidence has ever been discovered to substantiate this belief, nor indeed so remote an origin. Instead the first certain reference to the custom is at London in 1406, when the corporation forbade anybody to constrain anyone else in the city, either indoors or on the street, by 'hokking' them on the 'Hokkedays'. This was repeated in 1409, with the additional information that people were using the practice to raise money for sports.[25] It was forbidden again at Worcester in 1450, by the bishop, Carpenter, who thought it a 'disgraceful sport'.[26] The literary historian Sir Edmund Chambers thought that it might have had courtly antecedents, relating it to a payment by Edward I 'to seven ladies of the queen's bedchamber who took the king in bed on the morrow of Easter and made him fine himself'.[27] This seems, however, to refer instead to an aristocratic game by which ladies who caught gentlemen still abed could exact a forfeit from them; it features prominently in the famous fourteenth-century poem *Sir Gawaine and the Green Knight*.[28] The removal of this from the record reduces the earliest appearances of the Hocktide captures to a disreputable popular custom, buttressed by a patriotic myth. The latter is first mentioned by the midland commentater John Rous, who remarked upon the festive bindings in Warwickshire in the later fifteenth century.[29] By then, however, it was enjoying a notable upturn in its fortunes, for it had achieved respectability in some places by being linked to parish finances.

This development seems first to have been recorded at the Oxfordshire market town of Thame in 1457, when the churchwardens received a donation

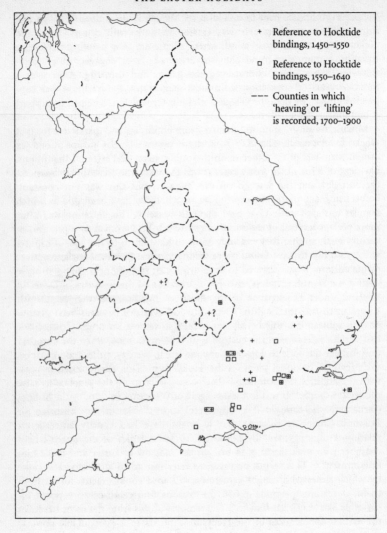

MAP 3. Range of Hocktide bindings, 'heaving', and 'lifting'

from the profits of Hocktide. Those of the Staffordshire town of Walsall apparently did the same in 1462. By 1469–70 the wives of the parish of the university church, Great St Mary, were going about the Cambridge colleges collecting money, and by 1471 the practice had appeared at Oxford. It then seems to have spread southward, with gathering momentum, until by 1500 it was established in Canterbury, Reading, and Salisbury, and in at least one London parish. In the first half of the sixteenth century it appears in more communities within this range, virtually all towns but including the villages of Bassingbourn on the Cambridgeshire clay plateau, Badsey in Worcestershire's vale of Evesham, and Lambeth, opposite Westminster on the Surrey bank of the Thames. For some reason, it never outgrew this, not apparently reaching East Anglia, most of the south-east, the West Country, the north Midlands, or the north of England. Nor was it ever much used in the capital, its classic home being a provincial town.[30] The largest urban centre at which it was popular was apparently Coventry, where the theme of the defeat of the Danes was developed into a much-loved Hock Tuesday play, culminating in the leading of the humbled foreigners in chains by the women of the city.[31] By contemporary standards the sums raised for churches by female gangs at Hocktide were very impressive: at Lambeth, for example, they became the biggest single source of parochial income. Usually it was specifically the married women who gathered, but at Badsey the maidens went out instead. In Salisbury the menfolk continued to make their own efforts, always getting less cash, but in most places the female parishioners were given a clear field, and at St Mary at Hill, London, as the male contingent abandoned the unequal struggle in 1526. In several parishes the ladies were rewarded for their efforts with a dinner at public expense: at St Mary at Hill in 1499 the menu consisted of two ribs of beef, plus bread and beer.[32] A number of other communities, mostly in the counties between Oxfordshire and Suffolk, held parish feasts at Hocktide.[33]

The government of the duke of Somerset, fatal to so many ecclesiastical ceremonies, and apparently to Plough Monday collections, 'hoggling', and hobby-horse dances, also took its toll of 'hocking'. After 1549 there is no further trace of the custom in any records of the reign of Edward VI.[34] Like many other seasonal rites and celebrations, it underwent a spectacular revival under Mary Tudor, which continued without check into the early reign of her sister Elizabeth. The sources for the 1560s permit glimpses of the details of the pastime which are lacking before, such as of the succession of 'goodwives' who organized the teams at Battersea, or of the unusual contest at Hexton in Hertfordshire, where the men of the village tried to prevent the women from dragging a pole down a steep hill—traditionally without success.[35] None the less, the Hocktide captures and contests flourished at this later period only within the same geographical range within which they had operated earlier, and even there they began to disappear steadily after the first decade of the Elizabethan era. By its end they were confined to Oxford, to towns and villages in the Thames valley west of London, and to parts of Hampshire.[36] This pattern of decline was shared by many other forms of seasonal merry-making during the same years, and I have suggested elsewhere that it was the result chiefly of hostility on the part of evangelical Protestants,[37] reinforced by a growing fear of disorder on the part of the governing élite. It is true that only one of the reformers who wrote against popular pastimes, the Ipswich curate Samuel Byrd, specifically attacked Hocktide bindings, which he called cruel and abusive.[38] None the less, they so perfectly fitted into the model of behaviour which men like Byrd deplored that it is difficult to avoid the conclusion that they fell victim to the same campaign. This impression is reinforced by the well-documented fate of the Coventry Hock Tuesday play. It was suppressed by the corporation in the early 1570s, an action driven on by the city's new ministers. In 1575, however, the supporters of the play, led by Coventry's muster-master, brilliantly outflanked its critics by presenting it as one of the entertainments offered to Queen Elizabeth during her stay at nearby Kenilworth Castle. Its prologue denied that it set any 'ill example of manners, papistry or any superstition', and its climax, of foreigners led captive by Englishwomen, was calculated to flatter a female monarch. Elizabeth was indeed pleased, and this permitted the revival of the play as an annual event in the city itself, to the 'great commendation' of the populace. In 1591, however, its enemies felt able to strike again, for the corporation moved it to the summer, and having thus cut it from its roots abolished it permanently a few years later.[39]

It is of a piece with this picture that the last traces of Hocktide gatherings in parish records, at Oxford and Brentford, vanish as soon as the Long Parliament took control of English politics in 1640, and commenced the reforms which would become known cumulatively as the Puritan Revolution.[40] At the Restoration they were restored also, but only, it seems, linked to parish finance at two churches in Oxford. At one of these, St Peter in the East, the revival was abandoned in 1677, for reasons which are not recorded; the accounts of the other, St Cross, ran out too soon for a historian to trace the end of the tradition there.[41] The link to public fund-raising seems to have survived in other parishes at this time, for in his account of Oxfordshire, written in the mid-1670s, the Oxford don Robert Plot portrayed women as still catching men with ropes or chains at Hocktide. They gave some of their profits to churches, and kept the rest for merry-making.[42] Nevertheless, by then he clearly considered it to be a local curiosity, and after this time there is no more trace of it in its old strongholds of the south and south midlands of England.[43] In at least one place in Yorkshire (not identified), schoolboys at the beginning of the twentieth century put a rope across a street on Hock Tuesday and demanded kisses of all girls who passed.[44] At the East Riding fishing port of Filey, in the early nineteenth century, young men tried to steal the shoes of young women on Easter Day, and the women stole the hats of the youths on Easter Monday.[45] Both are obvious transfers from the Hocktide games, as is the custom of the two Tutti men at the large Berkshire town of Hungerford. This community preserved its annual festivity on Hock Tuesday, last survivor of the old 'Hock ales'; as part of this two men, distinguished by the poles crowned with flowers which they carry are allowed to kiss all women whom they meet and to call at houses to demand the same tribute. This case, and the Yorkshire one, suggest that by the modern period menfolk had at last deprived women of any initiative in the Hocktide revels. It is also easy to conclude that, once the profits ceased to go to the common good, the custom of binding and exacting money upon the streets had returned to being as intolerable as it had seemed to the authorities of late medieval London and Worcester.

There was, however, one resounding regional exception to both those suggestions, and its epicentre seems to have lain in the west Midlands, where Hocktide revels had been noted at the very beginning of their recorded history. Indeed, the custom is described in the parish accounts from those counties[46] by a distinctive name, that of 'heaving'. Under that title, or 'lifting', it was very strongly established in the eighteenth century, all over the region and also in north-east Wales and Lancashire;[47] in the latter county at least it was not mentioned earlier, despite the survival of records relating to many other customs, and seems to have been an importation from the Midlands. What was distinctive about it was that those captured were also lifted bodily into the air, theoretically in symbolic celebration of Christ's resurrection, and that it took place on Easter Monday and Tuesday and not at Hocktide. It may always have done so, or it may have been transferred back a week with the shortening of the legal holiday; for the pattern was the classic one of 'hocking', with men allowed to 'lift' on the Monday and women on the Tuesday.

The most decorous form of the custom was in Wales and its borderland, where groups of young people went from house to house upon the appropriate day, carrying a chair decorated with greenery and ribbons. They would place willing members of the opposite sex in this and raise them up three times before being rewarded with money, food, drink, or kisses. Demure girls would simply not open their doors when the men knocked, and sometimes mothers paid the latter to go away. In parts of Wales the lads processed with a fiddler playing before them. In Herefordshire and around Ludlow in Shropshire, the 'lifters' carried a bowl of water and a posy of flowers as well, using them to sprinkle the feet of the person in the chair. Herefordshire parties were sometimes mixed-gender, and sang 'Jesus Christ is risen again' before they performed the lift. A chair was also used upon the streets of Shrewsbury, Chester, and Kidderminster, and employed by servants at a hotel in Crewe upon the guests. Mostly, however, people caught by gangs on the streets were swung up bodily by their limbs, and this could be extremely unpleasant. Indeed, at worst 'heaving' could be a custom of assault, extortion, and humiliation. In a few places it may have been an expression of high spirits, but mostly, in the words of an observer at Manchester in 1784, it was 'converted into a money job'.[48] Most impressions of it were naturally recorded by men of the educated classes, and refer to the experience of being ambushed by working-class women; they vary according to the youth and looks of the latter and perhaps to the gallantry of the former. To an observer at Wolverhampton the captors were 'beauteous nymphs', while to one in Warwickshire they were 'jolly matrons', to another at Wednesbury they were 'brawny pit-bank wenches', to yet another at West Bromwich they were 'sturdy viragos', and to one more Staffordshire writer they were 'amorous Amazons'.[49] Usually the 'heaving' teams operated in their own neighbourhoods, but in 1771 they barred every gate into Chester, demanding money from each man who passed.[50] The feelings of women, pursued by gangs of men, are unlikely to have been more appreciative than the male views expressed above.

For a shy person, indeed, the tradition could turn Eastertide into an ordeal. Samuel Parr, the scholarly minister of Hatton, near Warwick, was chased over hill and dale every year.[51] A squire in the Shrewsbury district was especially afraid of the custom, and Easter Tuesday 1838 was a nightmare for him: he 'escaped from a posse of his own tenants' wives and daughters in Coleham, Shrewsbury, and fought a host of resolute females assembled in the Castle Foregate; but at Acton Reynald he could neither fight nor run away'. This was because he was a guest at the hall there, and caught by its female servants. In the same decade a young doctor working in northern Shropshire was an especial quarry for female teams, who knew that he would pay large sums to avoid being touched. Forty years later the vicar of Ketley in the same county sent out his maid to post a letter on Easter Monday. The poor girl was beset so often by different parties of men determined to 'heave' her or make her pay that in the end her employer had to rescue her.[52] A modern liberal may find much that is attractive in a tradition which at times so perfectly reversed the usual balance of power between classes and genders, and at times contemporaries felt the same: a commentator in nineteenth-century Staffordshire thought that 'it was sometimes amusing to see tall and strong young men running as for their lives from a gang of aggressive and determined-looking women'.[53] None the less it is by no means clear that the majority of victims of 'heaving' or 'lifting' actually were young or wealthy, and the custom waned without need for a concerted campaign by magistrates and police of the sort conducted against Shrovetide sports.

All observers seem to have agreed that its heyday was the eighteenth century, and that all over its range it was in decline during the early nineteenth. Even the elegant Herefordshire method was thought to have 'degenerated into wickedness' and been 'discontinued' by 1869.[54] By then, indeed, it seems to have been confined to the iron-working and collier communities of Shropshire and Staffordshire, the Birmingham backstreets, an occasional village in the Cotswold Edge of Warwickshire, and some Lancashire textile-making towns. There is no trace of it in any of these after the mid-1880s.[55] A final echo of it persisted in the Peak District of Derbyshire, where village youths lifted up and kissed the girls on Easter Monday. This was still practised at Bakewell in the early 1890s, but after that no more is heard of it.[56] Almost half a millennium had passed since the corporation of London had first expressed concern about the Hocktide captures, but now they had gone at last.

ENGLAND AND ST GEORGE

꩜

THE vagaries of the Easter cycle meant that Hocktide could be followed by a fortnight of lull in celebration or might itself by preceded by the first calendar Festival to be widely celebrated in late medieval England after St Valentine's. This was the feast of the military saint George upon 23 April. As befitted that of a Christian warrior, his cult burgeoned in western Europe in the wake of the Crusades, and his festival day was officially established in England in 1222.[1] During the next two centuries he was carefully promoted by the conqueror kings Edward III and Henry V, to rival the French St Denis and to replace the less martial Edward the Confessor as England's patron saint. As such he proved a considerable success, being a glamorous figure, perfect for a society imbued with chivalric ideals and associated with one of hagiography's most dramatic legends. In particular, he was taken as dedicatee by a large number of the religious guilds which were founded in late fourteenth- and fifteenth-century England,[2] and these in turn often provided the 'ridings' on his day, which were to be some of the most colourful rites of the early Tudor period.

The earliest and best-known of these was at Norwich, first recorded in 1420 and provided by a guild which was itself founded in 1385. A hundred years later, and fully developed, it took the following form. First the corporation heard mass at the cathedral on St George's Eve, followed directly by a banquet. The next day, the guild provided a procession including a model dragon and people attired as George himself, St Margaret, and their retinue. The George wore a gilt helmet and coat armour of white damask woven with a red cross, while Margaret had a gown of tawny velvet. He rode a horse caparisoned in black velvet with copper ornaments, while her steed was harnessed in crimson velvet with gold flowers. Their followers were dressed variously in more crimson velvet, green satin, red buckram, and red or white wool or satin.[3] Upon the same date the corporation of Newcastle upon Tyne paraded its own dragon, of canvas nailed to a wooden frame.[4] The St George's guild of Leicester provided its own costumed parade, with their hero wearing real plate armour, partly funded by the town council, which joined the procession.[5] The saint went about Canterbury and another George and dragon sallied forth on behalf of the guild at Stratford-upon-Avon. All the guilds of Chester processed through its streets behind another monster, while at York

St Christopher and a 'royal family' appeared with George.[6] Monarchy mustered the Order of the Garter for its annual service and chapter, while the fifth earl of Northumberland held a banquet of his own with a generous distribution of gifts.[7] Bristol and Coventry parish churches held processions with the carrying of a cross at the head, Croscombe in central Somerset provided a parish feast, and more dragons were carried or towed around Little Walsingham near the Norfolk coast and the Cornish port of Lostwithiel.[8] The popularity of St George continued to grow up to the very beginning of the Reformation, the establishment of new shrines to him after 1490 being recorded in the accounts of parishes in Somerset, Yorkshire, Salisbury, Reading, and Westminster.[9]

By 1530, therefore, the feast had the beginnings of a truly national celebration. It was not yet universal, for no festivities are recorded in London or in other towns for which good early Tudor records survive, nor in the vast majority of the period's churchwardens' accounts. None the less, it was found across the country, was spreading rapidly, and represented an excellent fusion of patriotism, religion, and entertainment. It turned out, however, to have one tremendous weakness: that it was linked to the veneration of a saint, and the Reformation was about to attack the whole notion that saints could act as divine intercessors. Henry VIII was content to rule that they could only be honoured as fine human beings, and (in 1538) to condemn images of them which had been 'abused' by adoration. This halted the St George's Day procession at Canterbury because the statue of the saint carried in it was held to have fallen within the prohibition. It was removed from public view by the warden and curates of its church and then destroyed by the archbishop's commissary.[10] After this no more 'ridings' or shrines of the saint are known to have been instituted, although the existing parades continued. They lasted until the reforms of Lord Protector Somerset in 1547–8, as part of which the other statues of George were removed like those of any saints, and the guilds dedicated to him were dissolved with all such institutions. The special status of the national patron was indicated only by the fact that churchwardens tended to specify the removal of his images (and of the horse and dragon which often accompanied one), while failing to name almost any of the other saints whose representations were being stripped away.[11] At Norwich the corporation did its best to preserve the guild, but only by removing its religious function and using its funds to clean the river. The three men appointed to arrange the usual dinner on St George's Day 1548 refused to do so unless the ceremonies were restored, and suffered the punishment of being disenfranchised. The dinner became simply a municipal feast, and in April 1550 the council sold all the costumes of the 'riding'.[12] The corporation of York could not at first believe that the Government intended to dissolve that city's St George guild, and sent a clerk to discover the truth and ask for a reprieve if needed. None, however, could be obtained.[13] At Leicester the trappings of the shrine were sold in 1547, and the procession through the streets was stopped.[14] The government of Somerset thus made an absolute end of the day's celebrations in towns and villages. For a while the Crown retained its own portion of them, the parade and service of the Knights of the Garter which provided the prime means for display of the realm's principal chivalric order. In 1548 its rites were reformed to make them more acceptable to Protestants. Many of the latter, however, were still offended by them, and they included young Edward VI himself. At one chapter he demanded, 'What saint is St George that we do here honour him?' The Marquis of Winchester replied gamely, 'St George mounted his charger, out with his sword and ran the dragon through with his spear'. 'And pray you my lords,' answered the royal child mockingly, 'and what did he with his sword the while?'[15] In 1552 the feast was dropped from the new religious calendar approved by Parliament, as it had no scriptural warrant.

The obverse of all this was, of course, that it was restored in the Catholic reaction of Mary Tudor. Her husband Philip personally led the Knights of the Garter in their traditional procession on St George's Day 1555, together with priests wearing copes (mantles) embroidered with gold, and three cross-bearers.[16] At York in 1554 the corporation ordered that on his day St George 'be brought forth and ride as hath been accustomed'. The next year he was accompanied by a dragon, St Christopher, a mock-king and a mock-queen, and a May.[17] The 'riding' at Leicester was restored by that municipality, while at Norwich the council resolved in 1555 to re-establish the saint's guild and procession as of old. St George also rode once more through the streets of Chester.[18] His images were set up again in parish churches in Devon, Essex, and Worcestershire, and may also have been carried in procession there.[19] Once again, however, the rapid development of the feast was blasted by a Protestant Reformation, that of Elizabeth. In this as in other respects, that queen's greater moderation and taste for ceremony in matters of religion led to a less radical alteration than that of her brother. The procession and service of the Garter was continued, with a Protestant liturgy, and the feast itself was retained in the new list of holy days issued in 1560. On the other hand, neither Crown nor Church attempted to enforce any public observance of it, the statues of George were destroyed once more along with all religious imagery in churches, and his 'ridings' ended again in the face of renewed official hostility to veneration of saints.

At Norwich, however, one character was allowed to escape the prohibition; the dragon, which continued to be paraded upon St George's Day by popular demand. During the course of the reign its appearances became more intermittent but they persisted none the less and could be quite dramatic, so that in the early Stuart period the snapping model was accompanied by 'beating of drums', 'sounds of trumpets', 'fellows dressed up in fools' coats and caps', a 'standard with the George thereon', and 'hanging of tapestry cloth' in the streets.[20] All this was abolished in 1645, along with the whole concept of saints' days of any sort,[21] but restored with the former Church and the monarchy in

1660. With it reappeared a dragon which had survived the Reformation at Chester, 'made anew' with 'six naked boys to beat at it' on the next feast of St George.[22] This vanished again, however, in the 1670s, and the Norwich dragon, 'Old Snap', only survived because the day had been made into the one upon which the new mayor took office, and 'Snap' formed part of a parade intended to honour him and the city rather than the saint. It lasted, in fact, right up until the national reform of corporations in 1835, 'Old Snap' was then retired, but imitations were made by the different quarters of the city, being stored in pubs and brought out for local junketings. The last of these appeared at the Norwich Festival of 1951, and is now in the Castle Museum as a lone relic of all the lost pageantry of the medieval feast.[23]

The compromising of St George's Day by its Catholic associations combined with England's subsequent lack of any dramatic national renewal to leave it unusual among nations in its total lack of a patriotic holiday. As it never underwent an enduring change in the fundamental nature of its government, nor a war of independence, the realm never threw up a political anniversary worth commemorating as a symbol of its very existence. In the late nineteenth century a drift back to the celebration of St George's Day began, propelled by a more self-conscious nationalism, a resurgence in chivalric imagery, and a waning of the Anglican allergy to saints. It was wholly spontaneous and localized, being manifested in towns and villages scattered across southern England: in 1914, for example, the council and clergy of Kidderminster, the iron-making town on the Severn in Worcestershire, co-operated to hoist the national flag with its red cross over churches and public buildings and provide a religious service. By the 1930s the revival was at its height, many communities of different sizes attending churches, flying flags, and sporting the roses, which had become adopted as the national flower.[24] Stratford-upon-Avon worked hard to promote the solution made by the Scots to an identical problem, by turning the country's foremost literary figure into a secular saint around whose memory his compatriots could rally: a kind providence had placed Shakespeare's birthday on the feast of St George. England, however, never felt beleaguered enough to require a rallying-point, and as its cultural norms began to be questioned after the Second World War the sort of jingoism represented by the resurgence of celebration upon 23 April became increasingly unfashionable. It seems, therefore, to have gone into a quiet decline, leaving England in the curious position of having a day which honours the nation upon which everybody works, virtually no religious services are held, and the government itself does not pause for the slightest celebration. This is despite the wonderful irony that the cult of St George, so long tainted for the English by its Catholic associations, was abolished in the Church of Rome in the 1960s, leaving him with impeccably Anglican qualifications.

BELTANE

꩜

THUS far in the present book two themes must be uncomfortably obvious. One is the almost total absence of concrete evidence concerning pre-Christian seasonal rituals in the British Isles. The other is that the overwhelming majority of material for a history of British calendar customs derives from the southern half of the island. When dealing with the major Celtic feast which opened the warmer half of the year, both those considerations are firmly negated. It is best known today by a variant of the Gaelic name for its main custom: out of about a dozen different spellings, the very influential scholar Sir James Frazer selected one Scottish example which, being itself an Anglicized version, was best for English readers.[1] In popular literature in the English language it has thus, ever since, been 'Beltane'.

The earliest reference to it is probably in *Sanas Chormaic*, an early medieval Irish glossary attributed (perhaps wrongly) to the Munster churchman Cormac of Cashel, who lived around the year 900. Under the entry 'Beltane', both surviving texts have ' "lucky fire", i.e. two fires which Druids used to make with great incantations, and they used to bring the cattle against the diseases of each year to those fires'. In the margin of one is the additional jotting 'they used to drive the cattle between them'. Both manuscripts have under 'Bil' the words 'from Bial i.e. an idol god, from which beltine i.e. fire of Bel'. One has the further information that 'a fire was kindled in his name at the beginning of summer always, and cattle were driven between the two fires'. Finally, in both under 'Cetsoman' is the definition 'First May, i.e. the first motion . . . of summer'.[2] In the tale *Tochmare Emire*, the wooing of Emer, which is probably later in its present form, the festival is described as 'Beltine at the summer's beginning'.[3] Put together, this is good evidence for a fire-ritual on May Day to protect cattle before they were driven out to the summer pastures. Its name may have replaced an original Irish one, Cetsoman, for the date on which it was held. The author of the *Sanas* seems to have been uncertain of the origins of the name, suggesting in one place that it signified 'lucky fire' and in another that it derived from a god Bil, Bial, or Bel. The latter may be nothing more than the Old Testament's Baal, with whom the Irish writer would have been thoroughly familiar as the Bible's most prominent pagan god. At times modern Celticists have suggested that he might have been the northern European deity Belenus.[4] This was, however, the main god of Noricum (modern Austria), and although he was also popular in parts of Italy and France, only two, slightly doubtful, dedications to him have yet been found in Britain.[5] Perhaps even more to the point, there is absolutely no trace of him, or 'Bel', in other early Irish literature. There is hardly any need for him, for our purposes, for the common Celt preface 'bel-' did indeed apparently mean 'bright' or 'fortunate'.[6]

With that the reliable ancient evidence runs out. The seventeenth-century Irish antiquary Geoffrey Keating described, from unknown sources, an annual early medieval assembly on the feast of 'Beltane' at the hill of Uisnech in the centre of Ireland. He asserted that men came from all over the land to trade and to sacrifice to Bel, 'the principal deity' of the pagan Irish. The rites included the lighting of two sacred fires, as indeed were lit at that time (says Keating) in every district in the country. The late and unreliable nature of this account, and the total lack of any reference to such a gathering in the early medieval Annals, make it impossible for this information to be accepted at face value. None the less, the medieval Dindsenchas, the collection of Irish place-name legends, did include a tale of a holy fire lit by a hero on Uisnech which blazed for seven years, and this may just possibly preserve a tradition of Beltane ceremonies there.[7] It is also true, however, that Keating or his source may simply have conflated this legend with the information in *Sanas Chormaic* to produce a piece of pseudo-history.

Early Welsh literature furnishes nothing in the way of probably pre-Christian seasonal rituals; but then it is both much smaller in quality and much more restricted in scope than the Irish. It does, however, testify to the attribution of an especially arcane quality to May Day ('Calan Mai') and its eve. Each 1 May, according to the tale of *Culhwch ac Olwen* (probably tenth century), the undying heroes Gwythyr and Gwyn ap Nudd were fated to do battle. It was on May Eve, in the eleventh-century story of Pwyll, that a demon stole new-born children and farm animals in the land of Dyfed, while on the same night two dragons always fought each other in the contemporary fable of *Lludd ac Llevelys*.[8]

Certainly the ritual portrayed in the *Sanas*, minus its Druids, survived in Ireland to the nineteenth century. Bonfires were lit at Beltane over most of the country, especially in Leinster and Munster, in the first half of that period.[9] In the rural south in the 1820s, cows were made to leap over lighted straw or wood on 'near na Beal tine' (May Eve) in order to save the milk from being pilfered by the 'good people' or fairies, who were 'supposed then to possess the power and inclination to do all sorts of mischief without the slightest restraint'.[10] In southern Leinster in 1838 the farmer Humphrey O'Sullivan casually noted in his diary how he had driven his cattle between two fires on that night exactly as 'Cormac' had recorded almost a thousand years before.[11] The flames on the eve or the day were also used to bless and protect humans, who leaped them. The best description of this custom in country districts was furnished in 1852 by Sir William Wilde:

With some, particularly the younger portion, this was a mere diversion, to which they attached no particular meaning, yet others performed it with a deeper intention, and evidently as a religious rite. Thus, many of the old people might be seen circumambulating the fire, and repeating to themselves certain prayers. If a man was about to perform a long journey, he leaped backwards and forwards three times through the fire, to give him success in his undertaking. If about to wed he did it to purify himself for the marriage state. If going to undertake some hazardous enterprise, he passed through the fire to render himself invulnerable. As the fire sunk low, the girls tripped across it to procure good husbands; women great with child might be seen stepping through it to ensure a happy delivery, and children were also carried across the smouldering ashes. At the end the embers were thrown among the sprouting crops to protect them, while each household carried some back to kindle a new fire in its hearth.[12]

Conversely, it was considered very dangerous for others to be allowed to take fire from one's home on May Eve or May Day, because they would thereby gain power over the inhabitants. In sixteenth-century Ireland a woman who tried to borrow a light from neighbours then was reckoned to be a witch.[13]

It is time now to see how far such beliefs prevailed in Britain and its neighbouring islands. In view of the heavy cultural colonization of northern Scotland and its Isles by the Irish in the early Middle Ages, nobody should be surprised to find them there, as in the case of Bridget's Night, and so indeed we do. The earliest and most famous description was by the early travel-writer Thomas Pennant, who repeated what he was told by an acquaintance who had seen it in the Highlands during 1769:

On the first of May, the herdsmen of every village hold their Bel-tein, a rural sacrifice. They cut a square trench on the ground, leaving the turf in the middle; on that they make a fire of wood, on which they dress a large caudle of eggs, butter, oatmeal and milk; and bring, besides the ingredients of the caudle, plenty of beer and whisky, for each of the company must contribute something. The rites begin with spilling some of the caudle on the ground, by way of libation: on that every one takes a cake of oatmeal, upon which are raised nine square knobs, each one dedicated to some particular being, the supposed preserver of their flocks and herds, or to some particular animal, the real destroyer of them: each person then turns his face to the fire, breaks off a knob, and flinging it over his shoulders says 'This I give to thee, preserve thou my horses; this to thee, preserve thou my sheep'; and so on. After that, they use the same ceremony to the noxious animals: 'This I give to thee, O Fox! Spare thou my lambs; this to thee, O hooded Crow! this to thee, O Eagle!' When the ceremony is over, they dine on the caudle.[14]

Previous references are oblique, though still significant. At Peebles in the Scottish Lowlands during 1571, the corporation doubled the watch 'on Beltane even, Beltane at even, and the morn after Beltane day' to control festivities.[15] At the end of the next century a traveller in the Hebrides noted the common proverb *edir da hin Veaul* or Bel, 'he is between two Bel fires'.[16] After Pennant's portrayal, however, soon came a host of others. The fullest were written in the last twenty years of the eighteenth century by John Ramsay of Ochtertyre, friend of Sir Walter Scott and patron of Robert Burns.[17] He believed that by then it was simply a festival of the young, who would kindle fires and feast, and that even this was confined to the interior of the High-lands. Until the middle of the century, however, it had been a truly communal practice found all over the Isles as well:

The night before, all the fires in the country were carefully extinguished, and next morning the materials for exciting this sacred fire were prepared. The most primitive method seems to be that which was used in the islands of Skye, Mull and Tiree. A well-seasoned plank of oak was procured, in the midst of which a hole was bored. A wimble of the same timber was then applied, the end of which they fitted to the hole. But in some parts of the mainland the machinery was different. They used a frame of green wood, of a square form, in the centre of which was an axle-tree. In some places three times three persons, in others three times nine, were required for turning round, by turns, the axle-tree or wimble. If any of them had been guilty of murder, adultery, theft or other atrocious crime, it was imagined either that the fire would not kindle, or that it would be devoid of its usual virtue. So soon as any sparks were emitted by means of the violent friction, they applied a species of agaric which grows on old birch-trees and is very combustible. This fire had the appearance of being immediately derived from heaven, and manifold were the virtues ascribed to it. They esteemed it as a preservative against witchcraft, and a sovereign remedy against malignant diseases, both in the human species and in cattle; and by it the strongest poisons were supposed to have their nature changed. This was termed *tein-eigin*, forced fire or need-fire. A feast was then prepared, with singing and dancing, and lots drawn to select one man. He was called *cailleach bealtine*, Beltane carline, a term of great reproach. Upon his being known, parts of the company laid hold of him, and made a show of putting him into the fire, but, the majority interposing, he was rescued. And in some places they laid him flat on the ground, making as if they would quarter him. Afterwards he was pelted with eggshells, and retained the odious appellation during the whole year.

He had to leap thrice through the flames, and this concluded the ceremony. Cailleach, signifying an old woman, was a common term of abuse or fear throughout Gaelic-speaking Scotland.

In the 1790s the successive volumes of Sir John Sinclair's survey of the country revealed that the fires were indeed by then chiefly made in Perthshire and by young cowherds. They confirmed Pennant's information about the baking of the cakes with raised lumps, and near Callander the 'carline' was still chosen, by drawing pieces of bannock, the unlucky one daubed with charcoal, out of a bonnet.[18] During the century and a half after Pennant's description further scraps of memory about the earlier observances trickled into the record. It was recalled how herdsmen in north-east Scotland had struck the fire with flints and processed three times sunwise around it.[19] An aged minister described in 1893 how his father had told him that as a boy he had known the *tein' eigin* made in Rannoch and Lochaber, each family relighting its hearth from it unless a member had been guilty of some moral of criminal offence.[20] It was reported that in Caithness the making of the fire by rubbing wood had required eighty-one men, divided into nine shifts of nine; clearly (if true) to create an outsize blaze. Another account stated that on Mull in 1767 it had been made by turning a wooden wheel over nine spindles of wood. Joseph Logan, working in the 1820s, gathered the information that the special fire was made on a circular platform (at variance with Pennant), and by turning a horizontal post against a vertical one by four short spokes; relays of men were required, and all had to divest themselves of iron before working. Logan also heard how Highlanders had carried brands around their fields and how in the Isles people and cattle had passed over the embers as the Irish did. Other informants recounted how in Ross and Sutherland young men had walked round the 'Beal' fires carrying branches of rowan, a tree which gave special protection against evil. In Caithness the unlucky person chosen by lot was also remembered, and had to jump the fire seven times.[21] A woman in the Isle of Arran told in 1895 how in her father's time people still drove their livestock around a fire on a knoll upon the first of May.[22]

The most elaborate of these later descriptions came from the hinterland of Aberdeen concerning 2 May, and explained how in 'some districts' the

belief was that on that evening and night the witches were abroad in all their force, casting ill on cattle and stealing cows' milk. To counteract their evil power ... fires were kindled by every farmer and cottar. Old thatch, or straw, or furze, or broom was piled into a heap and set on fire a little after sunset. Some of those present kept constantly tossing up the blazing mass, and others seized portions of it on pitch-forks or poles and ran hither and thither, holding them as high as they were able, while the younger portion, that assisted, danced round the fire or ran through the smoke, shouting 'Fire! blaze and burn the witches; fire!, fire! burn the witches!' In some districts a large round cake of oatmeal was rolled through the ashes. When the material was burned up, the ashes were scattered far and wide, and all continued till quite dark to run through them still saying 'Fire! burn the witches'.[23]

In the course of the nineteenth century the flames slowly died in Scotland: they were last heard of in Arran and Helmsdale around 1820, in North Uist in 1829, and in Reay in about 1830.[24] In these same decades they were last recorded at Strathpeffer, Ross, and in the mid-century they vanished from the Ochil Hills of Western Fife.[25] They lasted into the later part among the children of Inverness-shire, the cowherds of Perthshire, and, most imposingly, among the Shetlands. There until the 1870s fisher folk as well as farmers had their fires to launch the season, and fathers leaped them with children in arms.[26] By then they were no longer lit in the Outer Hebrides, but the crofters there still drove their flocks and herds up to the summer pastures at 'Bealltain', feasted there, and then called on divine protection. The Protestants of Lewis, Harris, and North Uist invoked the Trinity:

> Bless, O three-fold true and bountiful
> Myself, my spouse and my children
> My tender children and their beloved mother at their head.
> On the fragrant plain, on the gay mountain sheiling,
> On the fragrant plain, on the gay mountain sheiling.

The Catholics of Benbecula, South Uist, and Barra called on St Michael, St Columba, St Bride, and

Mary, though mother of saints,
Bless our flocks and bearing kine,
Hate nor scathe let not come near us,
Drive from us the ways of the wicked.[27]

Two relics of the fire-ceremony survived into the early twentieth century. One was a Scottish parallel to the Irish belief that it was dangerous to give fire from one's home on May Day: this was found all over the Highlands, the Hebrides, and Galloway in the reign of Victoria.[28] The other was the cake, or bannock, once baked by the holy flames. By the late nineteenth century the 'Bannoch Bealltainn' had shed its knobs and was instead marked with a cross on one side like a Hot Cross Bun. It had become widely employed by children in the central and eastern Highlands after the same manner as Easter eggs, of being rolled down hillsides. The custom was still associated with the arcane, however, for if the bannock landed with the cross underneath it, this spelled bad luck to the person to whom it belonged. The tradition still continued in the 1950s, and may do so yet.[29]

Hence there is good evidence that the Irish ritual was also found throughout Gaelic Scotland. What remains now is to examine that for the holy fires in the rest of Britain, and to discuss whether they represented a general 'Celtic' custom once covering the whole archipelago. It is not surprising to find them in the Isle of Man, which was mainly Gaelic in language and culture, and indeed in 1837 a visitor described the island as presenting 'the appearance of a universal conflagration' after sunset on May Day. The inhabitants were not making bonfires, but setting the gorse bushes alight, theoretically in order to deny fairies and witches cover in them.[30] It was none the less a recognizable local version of the Scottish and Irish tradition. Further back, around 1790, the parallel is still more exact, for villagers would kindle a fire so that its smoke blew over cattle and fields, and relight their own hearths from it.[31] In complete contrast to the Manx case, the solitary May Eve bonfires lit on Stapleford Hill, Nottinghamshire, and near Horncastle in Lincolnshire, in the eighteenth century, are too isolated a pair of cases to appear part of the same pattern; they look more like aberrant local customs.[32] The rest of England is bare of May Eve or May Day fires in recorded history, with two very significant exceptions. One was Cumbria, where they were lit until the late eighteenth century, and people brought rowan branches to them, as in Scotland.[33] Scottish influence might be suspected in such a location, but it can hardly have operated in the other area, west Devon and Cornwall, where they were 'familiar' until the end of the same century. Upon Dartmoor farmers performed the rite of driving cattle over the embers to protect them.[34] These were precisely the parts of England in which native British culture lingered longest.

The test case, therefore, is Wales: if the May fires were lit there, then their status as a general 'Celtic' custom is proven. The key piece of information comes from Glamorgan, where Marie Trevelyan reported that May Day fires had been made in the vale until the 1830s. Her description ran as follows:

Nine men would turn their pockets inside out, and see that every piece of money and all metals were off their persons. Then the men went into the nearest wood and collected sticks of nine different trees. These were carried to the spot where the fire had to be built. There a circle was cut in the sod and the sticks were set crosswise. All around the circle the people stood and watched the proceedings. One of the men would then take two bits of oak, and rub them together until a flame was kindled. This was applied to the sticks, and soon a large fire was made. Sometimes two fires were set up side by side. These fires, whether one or two, were called coelcerth or bonfire. Round cakes of oatmeal and brown meal were split in four, and placed in a small flour-bag, and everybody present had to pick out a portion. The last bit in the bag fell to the lot of the bag-holder. Each person who chanced to pick up a piece of brown-meal cake was compelled to leap three times over the flames, or to run thrice between the two fires, by which means the people thought that they were sure of a plentiful harvest.[35]

This is so close to Highland accounts of the Beltane that it might almost have been copied from one, yet it is found far away and across a language barrier. The one really puzzling feature about it is that it comes from one of the most Anglicized parts of Wales, though employing a Welsh term for the custom. From the interior and north of the principality there seems to be nothing comparable, although May Eve fires were recorded at one other place, Trefedryd in Montgomeryshrine (again, not a very 'Welsh' part of Wales) all through the nineteenth century.[36] The pattern of distribution does look a little puzzling, therefore, but the presence of comparable customs in the south-west of England and Cumbria, and the absence of any apparent means of transference from Scotland, makes the opinion that they were all survivals of a widespread tradition seem to be the most plausible.

Over the whole of their range, the fires were only the most spectacular of a set of different means of protecting livestock and humans at the opening of May and of the summer pastures. In nineteenth-century Ireland, the bright yellow flowers of the primrose or marsh mallow were commonly scattered before doors to secure the interiors from bad magic: they might have suggested flames. Any hares found among the cattle on May Day were killed, upon suspicion that they were witches in disguise. Above all, rowan was hung about cows, doorways, and equipment for milking and butter-making on the Day and its Eve.[37] All over the Highlands of Scotland in the eighteenth century, rowan was used in just the same way, often fashioned into crosses to provide it with additional symbolic power.[38] It was also employed, or primroses substituted, to identical ends in eighteenth- and nineteenth-century Cumbria, Man, western Somerset, Wales, and Herefordshire.[39] Rowan, sometimes called mountain ash, may have been regarded as effective because its bright red berries also suggested fire. In places in Wales and its Marches where it, or primroses, could apparently not be obtained, people chalked crosses above doorways, or made them of birch or hawthorn.[40] In Somerset the astringent plants rue, hemlock, and rosemary were burned in houses by men who had been blessed by the local parson.[41] Across this whole vast range of the

'Celtic' parts of Britain, the adversaries of these precautions were occasionally described as fairies, but most commonly as witches.

This collection of data is very imperfect. Most of the British section is derived from regions for which there are no or virtually no records of seasonal practices until about two and a half centuries ago, by which time the Beltane customs were not merely in decline but existed only in a reduced and marginalized form. Indeed, it is striking that not one of our descriptions of the fire rituals in Britain was made by somebody who observed them at first hand. None the less, enough has been salvaged to permit certain conclusions to be drawn. First, that all over the ancient British Isles summer was reckoned as beginning around the time which was to become the opening of May. Secondly, that in a pastoral economy, this was the period when livestock, penned in folds, byres, and home fields during winter and spring, could be driven out to the new grass of the pastures. Thirdly, that rituals were conducted at that moment to protect them against the powers of evil, natural and supernatural, not merely in the season to come but because those malign powers were supposed to be particularly active at this turning-point of the year. The most obvious means of protection was by symbolic use of fire, the archaic weapon against darkness and large predators, although certain plants (perhaps because they evoked it) were also effective. To increase the potency of the holy flames, in Britain at least they were often kindled by the most primitive of all means, of friction between wood. There was also a widespread rite involving a scapegoat, which may always have been symbolic or may embody a memory of actual human sacrifice.

Nevertheless, the word 'Celtic', when applied to the Beltane tradition, remains in inverted commas because, although it perfectly fits the areas of the British Isles in which Celtic language and realms survived longest, it does not correspond to the Celtic cultural province which earlier generations of scholars have delineated in Europe. Indeed, the belief in supernatural danger on May Eve and May Day, and the need for fire and rowan rituals to ward it off, seems absent from just those western areas which fall within it upon the Continent. Instead, they were found, powerfully, further north and east, in Denmark, Sweden, Norway, Saxony, Silesia, Moravia, Bohemia, and Austria.[42] This is not a map of ethnic or linguistic divisions, but a chart of those areas of Europe which, like Ireland and western and northern Britain, had a pastoral economy involving seasonal transhumance. Elsewhere on the Continent the opening of summer was far less fraught, and its rituals far more celebratory and less defensive. Most of England, in historic times at least, fell into that latter category, and it is to those other rites that this book must now turn.

THE MAY

~~~✤~~~

A ROUND the year 1240 the reforming bishop of Lincoln, Robert Grosseteste, complained to his archdeacons of priests who demeaned themselves by joining 'games which they call the bringing-in of May'.[1] In the early 1420s the corporation of New Romney, a port in Kent, gave money to the men of neighbouring Lydd 'when they came with their May'.[2] In the 1430s the east Cornish market town of Launceston had expenses 'about le May', and the city council of Exeter provided a platform and ribbons for one. In 1441 'the May' at Exeter needed two men to carry it, while in 1446 the number had risen to eight.[3] In 1492 Henry VII gave ten shillings 'to the maidens of Lambeth for a May'.[4] Seven years later St Mary's parish in the Wiltshire chalkland town of Devizes paid 'for the making of May'.[5] The mayor of Nottingham led the young men of the town 'to bring in May' in 1541.[6] Gloucester corporation paid 'Master Arnold's servants' to do the same in 1552, and mention has been made of the one which accompanied St George at York in 1554. At the other end of the social order, the prisoners in Gloucester gaol were allowed to make a 'May pyramid' in 1618,[7] and at the end of the seventeenth century, the poet John Dryden could laud 'the merry crew who danced about the May'.[8] What exactly was meant in some of these cases is unclear, but in each the term was a shorthand for flowers and young foliage fetched to celebrate the coming of summer, named after that season's first month.

References to this custom in England begin with Grosseteste's grumble, cited above. They multiply as soon as English literature became sufficiently developed to include lush background detail for narratives, which was in the fourteenth century. As Chaucer towers over the other writers of the period, so does he furnish the largest number of descriptions. In his *Court of Love*, 'Forth goeth all the Court, both most and least | To fetch the flowers fresh and branch and bloom'. His heroine Emelie goes out at sunrise 'to do May observance' by gathering 'flowers pretty white and red | To make a subtle garland for her head'. The Knight, Arcite, in 'The Knight's Tale', rides out to a wood 'To maken him a garland of the greves, | were it of woodbine or of hawthorn leaves'.[9] A hundred years later the major literary work of that age included a similar scene, when Queen Guinevere, in Malory's *Morte D'Arthur*, goes in cavalcade to the May woods dressed in green silk and comes homeward with her whole party 'bedashed with herbs, mosses and flowers, in the best manner and the freshest'.[10] At about the same time Scottish letters achieved the same degree of rich descriptiveness, and William Dunbar could portray

> every one of thir, in grene arrayit,
> On harp and lute full mirrely they play it,
> And sang ballatis with michty nottis cleir;
> Ladies to danss full sobirly assayit,
> Endlang the lusty rever so they mayit.

In the following century Gavin Douglas and Alexander Scott treated of the same theme.[11]

By then, if not before, real monarchs were acting out these roles. Henry VII's support of Maying seems to have been vicarious, as described, but Henry VIII, and Catherine of Aragon, rode out of Greenwich Palace to feast in the woods of Shooter's Hill on May Day 1515, in one of the best-publicized and most self-conscious pieces of royal pageantry of the age.[12] Edward VI, Mary I, James I, and Charles I all seem to have been in different ways too prim for such activity. Elizabeth, however, loved to dance at country houses on May Day, and did so up to the last years of her life.[13] Charles II, taking his place in the fashions of a more sophisticated period, joined the new custom among the social élite of promenading in Hyde Park on that date, with 'an innumerable appearance of the gallantry on rich coaches'. Pious women had been scandalized to learn of ladies who joined this assembly to ride 'round and round, wheeling of their coaches about and about, laying of the naked breast, neck and shoulders over the boot, with lemon and fun-shaking' to entice 'vain roisterers on horseback'.[14]

Examples of municipal and parochial celebrations have been given above. To them may be added the annual 'reception of May' funded by the churchwardens of Snettisham on the Norfolk coast from 1475 to 1536, the early Tudor expeditions of the bailiffs of Newport, in the Isle of Wight, to the woods on the first Sunday of May,[15] and the tradition of the tutors and students of the university of St Andrews, of 'bringing in May' disguised as monarchs. This was forbidden in 1432, as 'useless and dangerous', but over 200 years later at Aberdeen a burgess, bellman, and drummer still felt able to go through the streets 'by open voice to convene the whole community to pass to the wood to bring in summer'.[16] It should be stressed, however, that even in the aggregate these entries represent only a small minority of English parishes and towns, and Scottish burghs, from which fifteenth- and sixteenth-century records survive. In the second half of the latter century they vanish altogether, arguably under the impact of Protestant disapproval.[17] They must always have represented no more than the official peak of a mountain of private observance of the custom to which sixteenth-century writers amply attest. In the first years of the period Polydor Vergil commented upon the way in which the English of all ages went out on May morning for garlands to set upon houses, gates, and (occasionally) churches.[18] John Stow recalled how in the reign of Henry VIII Londoners would try to spend that morning in 'the sweet meadows and green woods, there to rejoice their spirits with the beauty and savour of sweet flowers and with the harmony of birds'.[19] The schoolboys of Eton were allowed out at 4 a.m. to find greenery to adorn the classrooms.[20] As the feast of the Apostles Philip and James the Less, it was a public holiday.

Under Elizabeth, the custom was attacked by some evangelical Protestants, as empty frivolity carrying a risk of debauchery. Edmund Spenser did so most elegantly, evoking the joy and beauty of the scene when

> Youth's folks now flocken in everywhere
> To gather May baskets and smelling brere
> And home they hasten the posts to dight
> And all the Kirk pillars ere daylight,
> With hawthorn buds and sweet eglantine,
> And garlands of roses and sops in wine,

before condemning it as self-indulgence and idleness.[21] Christopher Fetherston, the most obscure and unpleasant of these writers, told a story of 'ten maidens who went to set May, and nine of them came home with child'.[22] This cautionary tale was echoed by the much more famous Philip Stubbes, save that the number of maidens was 'forty, three-score or a hundred', of whom 'scarcely the third part of them returned home again undefiled'.[23] The theme was taken up again in the next reign by the anonymous author of *Vox Graculi*, to whom May Day was a time when 'divers dirty sluts' wandered the countryside, getting into clinches with their lovers in ditches.[24] Some critics of the tradition translated their feelings into action, such as the labourer of St Aldates parish, Oxford, who was regarded as a 'Puritan' and who got into a fight on May Day 1633 by trying to stop the annual 'bringing in the garland' at nearby St Peter's church.[25]

During the same period, some authors referred to the May morning merry-making in completely straightforward and benevolent terms, as an acceptable fact of life.[26] Others, in the early seventeenth century, went further and extolled those very aspects of it which drew the worst criticism. *A Pleasant Countrey Maying Song*, probably published in 1629, gleefully portrayed the courting of a young couple among the flowers and blossoming thickets on May Day, ending with a hint that the girl got pregnant and the chorus:

> Thus the Robin and the Thrush,
> Musicke make in every bush.
> While they charm their prety notes
> Young men hurle up maidens cotes.[27]

This was the bawdy popular equivalent to Robert Herrick's masterpiece 'Corinna's going a Maying', probably written in the 1630s. Once again the fetching of foliage was juxtaposed with youthful love-making, though the latter was partially rescued from impropriety by the mention of forthcoming marriage:

Come, my Corinna, come, and comming, marke
How each field turns a street, each streed a Parke
Made green, and trimm'd with trees: see how
Devotion gives each House a Bough,
Or Branch: Each Porch, each doore, ere this,
An Arke a Tabernacle is
Made up of white-thorn neatly enterwove
As if here were those cooler shades of love...
There's not a budding Boy, or Girle, this day,
But is got up, and gone to bring in May.
A deale of Youth ere this, is come
Back, and with White-thorn laden home.
Some have dispatcht their cakes and creame,
Before that we have left to dreame:
And some have wept, and woo'd, and plighted Troth,
And chose their Priest, ere we can cast off sloth:
Many a green-gown has been given;
Many a kisse, both odde and even:
Many a glance too has been sent
From out the eye, Loves Firmament:
Many a jest told of the Keyes betraying
This night, and Locks pickt, yet w'are not a Maying.[28]

The behaviour of young people on May Eve and May Day had thus become a cliché of scandal and of titillation alike. It took until the late twentieth century, and the patient labours of demographic historians, to reveal that there was in fact no rise in the number of pregnancies at this season, in or out of marriage. The boom in conceptions came later in the summer.[29] In practice early modern people seem to have found the night of the 30 April generally too chilly, and the woods generally too damp.

In the more relaxed social atmosphere of the Restoration period references to 'Maying' become largely accidental. We know that at Manchester on 1 May 1667 the citizens got up soon after midnight to 'ramble abroad, make garlands, strew flowers, etc.', because they kept awake a dissenting minister, who grumbled to his diary.[30] A May Day procession carrying a garland in north Kent in 1672 is known to history because it was ambushed by a press gang, and some of the men in it found themselves taken off to fight the Dutch.[31] Later that day over in Bedfordshire an apprentice charged with theft provided the alibi that he and other youths had been receiving hospitality at houses outside which they had earlier stuck May bushes.[32] Around this time John Aubrey was told of a division of gender roles at Oxford on May morning, whereby boys 'do blow cows horns and hollow caxes all night', while 'the young maids of every parish carry about their parish Garlands of Flowers, which afterwards they hang up in their churches'.[33] The dawn expeditions of youth to bring in greenery and flowers are recorded in detail in eighteenth-century Oxfordshire, Cornwall, and Northumberland. Their pecuniary side remained as strongly developed around the capital as it had been in the reign of Henry VII. Almost exactly three hundred years after 'the maidens of Lambeth' had coaxed a reward from that monarch, the antiquary John Brand was met by two separate May Day parties of girls on the road between Hounslow and Brentford, asking for money with the words 'Pray sir, remember the garland' and showing the one which they had made. Back in his home town of Newcastle upon Tyne, women went singly around the streets at sunrise, offering woven flowers for sale with a song.[34]

The impulse to celebrate the arrival of summer in Europe's northlands, by bringing home blooms and leaves, is probably ageless. It is certainly recorded from Ireland eastwards to the Ural mountains, at least wherever people were not more concerned with the hopes and perils of the migration to the summer pastures.[35] The English and Welsh folklore collections of the nineteenth century are rich in material for it and permit detailed treatment of certain aspects and developments. One is the effortless way in which the custom was continued in the burgeoning industrial areas and in occupations not normally associated with the countryside. In Victorian Manchester and Preston ribbons were used for decoration on May Day when foliage could no longer be obtained.[36] Iron-working communities in the west Midland Black Country had the rallying-cry 'Waaken chaps and wenches gay, | An' off t'country to gather May'.[37] Edinburgh craftspeople, set amid a countryside not very plentiful in blossoms and flowers at that season, climbed instead to the extinct volcano of Arthur's Seat. There they held a wild dance at daybreak, attired in the newly fashionable national costume of the kilt, before dispersing to work.[38] Sussex fishermen who put to sea that day decorated their masts with blooms.[39] At Devonport, a community built up to support a naval dockyard, a model of an old-fashioned warship resting on a bed of flowers was carried through the streets by four men. A band marched in front and people wearing garlands walked behind it and collected money.[40] When 'Maying' waned towards the end of the century, it did so in town and country alike, as part of a general change in attitude to holiday, festivity, and community.

A second important aspect of the activity for which good nineteenth-century information survives concerns the choice of foliage. Across most of England, flowering hawthorn, or whitethorn, was the favourite kind, being indeed the most spectacular that the season could offer. It was subject, however, to pronounced local variations of taste. In one district of western Somerset, people living on the Brendon hills believed that to bring home the thorn was lucky, while in the vale of Taunton Deane they thought that it tempted disaster.[41] The Cornish often preferred sycamore, while birch was the favoured tree in Wales and its Marches.[42] To all of these the term 'May' was indiscriminately applied, being most closely associated with hawthorn because of the frequency with which the latter was used. Those who brought back the greenery, however, could also employ it to express all the attractions and animosities of a locality; to compliment, admonish, and abuse. At Waterbeach in the Cambridgeshire Fens, young men put sloe blossom by the doors of popular girls, while 'the girl of loose manners had a blackthorn planted by hers; the slattern had an elder tree planted by hers; and the scold had a bunch of nettles tied to the latch of her cottage door'.[43] In Northamptonshire hawthorn was the token of favour, and sloe joined elder, crab-apple, nettle, and thistle as marks of insult.[44] Lancashire lads employed a rhyming slang: most kinds of thorn meant scorn, rowan signified affection, holly declared folly, briar marked a liar, and a plum in bloom proclaimed 'married soon'. Absolved from this were hawthorn, the normal gift of respect, and salt, conveying real hatred.[45] All over Wales, disapproval was signified by the cruder token of a horse's head.[46] Most areas, indeed, had their stock of symbols.[47]

As well as a means of comment, 'Maying' could be one of profit. The female aspect of this, 'garlanding', will be considered below. The male version was most fully developed in the east Midlands, from Leicestershire down to Hertfordshire. It is recorded earliest in the case of the Bedfordshire lad accused of theft during 1672, mentioned above: the bringing of (complimentary) gifts of greenery to the doors of householders at dawn and the return later to receive a reward. The first of these was accompanied in the nineteenth century by the 'Night Song', the second by the 'Day Song'. In 1962 the Leicestershire and Rutland Federation of Women's Institutes appealed to its members to write down as many local May songs as they could remember, and send them in. Sixty were received, from thirty villages, few of them being duplicates. They were studied by E. Ruddock, who decided that most were, from internal evidence, nineteenth-century compositions, but that ten appeared (on grounds that were not stated) to be the older models of which the rest were variations.[48] Robert Gifford has analysed the corpus collected from Bedfordshire and Huntingdonshire, this time for content and function, and suggested that they presented an appeal for food, drink, or money, together with a celebration of love, growth, and the seasonal round, and a reminder of the transitory nature of existence, usually expressed in deeply pious Christian terms.[49] This portrait seems to be true of virtually all the recorded English Mayers' songs, and it is a pointless exercise to attempt to determine the relative age of these components on the ground of likelihood alone. Some may indeed have been added to the songs later than others, but it is at least as likely that all were always present, to suit all tastes in an audience. None features in the relatively large collections of popular song from the seventeenth century, and in nineteenth-century Leicestershire they were certainly learned from printed or written words.[50] The Night Song heard in 1823 in the Hertfordshire chalkland town of Hitchin is representative of the whole genre, containing verses which appear throughout it:

> Remember us poor Mayers all,
> And thus we do begin
> To lead our lives in righteousness
> Or else we die in sin.

We have been rambling all this night
And almost all this day,
And now returnéd back again
We have brought you a bunch of May.

A bunch of May we have brought you,
And at your door it stands,
It is but a sprout,
But it's well budded out,
By the work of our Lord's hands.

The hedges and trees they are so green,
As green as any leek,
Our heavenly father he watered them
With his heavenly dew so sweet.

The heavenly gates are open,
Our paths are beaten plain,
And if a man be not too far gone,
He may return again.

The life of man is but a span,
It flourishes like a flower,
We are here today, and gone tomorrow,
And we are dead in an hour.

The moon shines bright, and the stars give a light,
A little before it is day,
So God bless you all, both great and small
And send you a joyful May.[51]

Day Songs were practically identical to those of the night, only omitting the nocturnal references and substituting lines about May. The only substantial variant not found at Hitchin is an opening verse identical or similar to

All in this pleasant evening, together come are we,
For the summer springs so fresh, green and gay;
We'll tell you of a blossom and buds on every tree,
Drawing near to the merry month of May.[52]

Apart from the east Midland region,[53] May songs (of this sort) were also found in rural Lancashire and Cheshire,[54] and in Cornwall.[55] Wales had its own separate tradition of *Carolau Mai* (May carols), also known as *Carolau haf* (summer carols), *canu haf* (summer singing), or *Canu dan y pared* (singing under the wall). Its popularity in the late seventeenth and early eighteenth centuries is indicated by the number written then by Huw Morus of Llansilin, on the eastward slopes of the Berwyn mountains. Although widespread in the principality at that time, it lasted longest in Morus's area. Many were very pious in tone, having been written by clergymen; they were performed by small groups of young men who were rewarded with food and drink.[56] The plough-boys of the east Midlands, however, were not only the most numerous and best-recorded of the Mayers, but the most colourful. At Great Gransden on the Huntingdonshire clay plateau they wore ribbons in their hats and carried a handkerchief tied to a pole, while at Hitchin they included two men with blackened faces, one in female attire, as 'Mad Moll and her husband'. Some in Bedfordshire villages paraded a youth in a white wedding dress.[57]

In the industrial towns of the Lancashire, Derbyshire, and Yorkshire Pennines, the custom evolved into an altogether different form, which still endures. It is first recorded in Lancashire, at Middleton in the 1790s. Foliage was still left on doorsteps on May Eve or May Morn to flatter or to praise, but in addition the young men would pay off grudges by playing pranks; pulling up fences, trampling gardens, upsetting carts, and setting cattle astray. 'The general observation in the morning would be "Oh, it's nobbut th'mischief-neet" '.[58] By the twentieth century the greenery had vanished but the trickery remained, and still flourishes today in western Yorkshire.[59] The joyous tradition of Maying had given rise to a local season of licensed misrule.

All this set of descriptions has, of course, ignored the most spectacular prize of Mayers: the maypole. There is no real evidence to indicate when it first arrived in the British Isles. A charter of King John's reign was long quoted as referring to one as a permanent feature used to mark an estate boundary at Lostock in Lancashire. Unhappily, David George has now discovered that this was an error based upon a misreading.[60] A will of 1373 talks of 'le Poll' near Pendleton, Lancashire, as another landmark, yet a pool may be the feature concerned.[61] Literature provides the only secure identification, and the first example of this consists of a Welsh poem of the mid-fourteenth century, by Gryffydd ap Adda ap Dafydd. Set at Llanidloes in central Wales, it describes the use of a tall birch tree for the pole, around which festivity took place.[62] In the last two decades of that century, Chaucer's poem *Chaunce of the Dice* referred to the permanent maypole which stood at Cornhill in London.[63] Thus by the period 1350–1400 the custom was well established across southern Britain, in town and country and in both Welsh-speaking and English-speaking areas. Before that its history seems to be lost. The distribution of the poles in Ireland and Scotland would appear to argue against the notion that they were found across the ancient British Isles, for they are recorded only in areas of English influence and language:[64] in the Gaelic regions the fire-ceremonies were the focus of attention instead. It might be suggested that the latter were suited to a pastoral economy and the poles to an arable one, but the early appearance and continuing popularity of the poles in the Welsh mountains rules out such a simple determinism. In Europe they are recorded from the Pyrenees to Sweden and Russia, and in regions such as Scandinavia were used in both arable and livestock-herding areas.[65]

What, then, did they signify? Since Freud wrote, there has been a popular tendency to see them as phallic symbols. This was suggested long before, by the political theorist Thomas Hobbes, who declared that they were relics of the worship of the Roman god of male potency, Priapus.[66] Hobbes, however, was bitterly hostile to them, as to all allied popular merry-making. There is no historical basis for his claim, and no sign that the people who used maypoles thought that they were phallic. They were not carved to appear so, and their original stark outline was always concealed by layers of decoration when they were actually in use, as will become obvious. Another possibility is that they were linked to the general north Eurasian belief in a divine tree or column which ran between the human and divine worlds. The pagan Saxons actually venerated a pillar of wood, the Irminsul.[67] Unhappily, there is absolutely no evidence that the maypole was regarded as a reflection of it. In the same category is the suggestion of Wilhelm Mannhardt, copied by Sir James Frazer, that the pole was regarded as the repositing of a fertility-giving tree spirit.[68] If this could not be directly refuted from the data, neither could it be proved. C. W. von Sydow made a close study of Swedish customs (which had been important to Mannhardt) and discovered absolutely no trace of a belief in an indwelling spirit. Instead he found that the poles, like the fetching of green branches, were simply signs that the happy season of warmth and comfort had returned. They were useful frameworks upon which garlands and other decorations could be hung, to form a focal point for celebration.[69] The British material completely bears out his judgement. Instead of speaking about anything as specific as a spirit, it is probably wiser to adopt the more general formulation used by Mircea Eliade in his glance at maypoles, of rejoicing at the returning strength of vegetation.[70]

There are no precise descriptions of the appearance or use of medieval British maypoles, and the best from the early modern period is the famous and much-quoted one by Philip Stubbes, writing in the 1580s:

They have twenty or forty yoke of oxen, every ox having a sweet nose-gay of flowers placed on the tip of his horns, and these oxen draw home this Maypole...which is covered all over with flowers and herbs, bound about with strings, from the top to the bottom, and sometimes painted with variable colours, with two or three hundred men, women and children following it with great devotion. And thus being reared up, with handkerchiefs and flags hovering on the top, they strew the ground around about, bind green boughs about it, set up summer halls, bowers and arbours hard by it. And then they fall to dance about it.[71]

A pole needing that many oxen to drag it would have been a monster, and not many English villages could have mustered hundreds of people for a procession: Stubbes, a Londoner, seems to have been thinking of one of the huge maypoles brought into towns or cities to stand for decades. In general, however, each part of his portrait can be borne out from contemporary sources. In the 1560s the corporation of Plymouth paid for a pole to be set up on the Hoe each May Day, painted and with flags and streamers hung from it and canvas set round it.[72] That brought into the Leicestershire market town of Hinckley, each year from 1586 to 1593, had a minstrel playing before it.[73] There was an ample 'drinking' at the 'bringing home the summer rod' to the parish of Holy Trinity, Exeter, in 1588.[74] The prominent role of young people in the process is indicated at Eltham in south-eastern Kent, where the parish bought a pole from 'boys' in 1562.[75] What is less clear is the nature of the dances performed about early modern maypoles. None before the nine-teenth century seems to have involved holding ribbons. The single early modern illustration (from the late Stuart period) is a crude woodcut showing people of both sexes prancing in a circle facing the shaft.[76] It seems, however, that a common kind of dance about the poles involved amorous play between the young couples who performed it. In 1618 the poet Nicholas Breton could extol 'the may-pole, where the young folks smiling kiss at every turning'.[77] Twelve years later another versifier could show the youth around the pole

> Dance about both in and out,
> Turn and kiss, and then for greeting.[78]

The poles were communal symbols, and their size and weight meant that erecting one was a group activity. John Stow described how at the beginning of the sixteenth century London parishes would form alliances to procure them if they could not do so alone. The largest of all was that mentioned by Chaucer, which stood on Cornhill, overtopping the church of St Andrew Undershaft and set up by its parishioners every year. The obverse of this communality was that the poles could also become associated with group misbehaviour. The huge one at Cornhill was not set up again after the May Day riots in London during 1517, as a result of which the city fell under profound royal displeasure and the celebrations upon that date became much more muted.[79] Rivalry between villages could be expressed by theft of each other's poles, and such raids led to violence in Hertfordshire in 1602 and Warwickshire in 1639.[80] By their very nature, they had to be fashioned from valuable trees, and the owners of woods were not always consulted when their timber was removed: the earl of Huntingdon was furious to find that his estates had been the source of Leicester's maypoles in 1603.[81]

These disquieting associations of the poles could hardly have seemed less important as the sixteenth century wore on and fear of social disorder increased with a growth in population, poverty, and hunger. None the less, it is fairly clear that hostility to them derived principally from those evangel-ical Protestants who sought a radical reform of both Church and society. They first manifested it in the Reformation of Edward VI, when the famous Cornhill maypole, which had been kept in storage, was sawed up and burned after a preacher denounced it as an idol.[82] A new one, painted white and green, was brought into Fenchurch parish, but the same day the Lord Mayor 'by counsel' had it toppled and broken.[83] Under Mary the traditional festiv-ities revived with the traditional religion, and Elizabeth was, as said, fond of them herself. Despite this, Protestant pressure upon them returned in her reign and intensified even though it now lacked government support. May-poles were only incidentally attacked, being condemned by a mere three authors (one being Stubbes) out of a large body of literature complaining of popular revelry between 1559 and 1630.[84] None the less, they were an implicit target of all that literature, concerned as it generally was with eliminating mixed-gender dancing, drunkenness, and Sunday merry-making. The poles were associated with all those, and in addition rang an automatic alarm bell in the minds of people obsessed with scriptural invectives against the veneration of sticks and stones. The impact of these opinions can be seen dramatically at local level, for between 1570 and 1630 maypoles were banned from Doncaster, Lincoln, Banbury, Canterbury, Shrewsbury, Coventry, Leicester, and Bristol.[85] From the beginning of this period, too, there is no more trace of them in London, revellers resorting to those still standing outside the city limits, notably to the one in the Strand.[86] Between 1588 and 1610, three out of the four Berkshire villages which have left parish accounts covering the period, sold their poles.[87] Yet in 1612 a fifth defiantly invested in a new one,[88] and during the early Stuart period the custom found literary defenders in Nicholas Breton, Robert Herrick, and the author of *Pasquils Palinodia*.[89] All emphasized its beauty and its contribution to communal joy and peace, and James I and Charles I lent support by explicitly allowing maypole dancing on Sundays[90]. By the 1630s there are still many records of the continued use of the poles in rural areas at least.[91]

In Scotland the much more radical Reformation had apparently swept them away already. In the 1580s and 1590s maypoles are recorded in a few places across the Central Lowlands, being the first mention of them in a nation much less well supplied with evidence. In each case the people who set them up were in trouble with the local corporation or presbytery, and after that they are heard of no more.[92] In England and Wales toleration of them ended in 1644, with the famous ordinance of the Long Parliament which directed the removal of them. The royal attachment of them to the issue of Sunday observance had doomed them as soon as the opponents of Charles I seized power, and the measure which condemned them was principally concerned with Sabbatarianism.[93] The only recorded breach of it was at Henley in Arden, Warwickshire, in 1655, when the local JPs moved to stop the erection of poles for traditional games.[94] How much connivance is concealed by this silence is impossible to say, but the prohibition certainly turned the poles, like the celebration of Christmas, into a symbol of resistance to the Long Parliament and the succeeding republic.[95] As such, they sprang up across England, as is well known, as soon as the restoration of the monarchy seemed likely.[96] Spontaneous revival of them in 1660 was followed in the next two years by official sponsorship, led by the aid given by the heir apparent, James, duke of York, to plant a new giant specimen in the Strand.[97] Urban corporations and parishes alike followed the princely example across England,[98] and some poles subsequently reappeared in the Scottish Lowlands, although they seem to have been very rare.[99]

During the eighteenth century maypoles seem to have been both very common and taken for granted in the English and Welsh countryside. Descriptions from then and the early nineteenth century suggest that their appearance and function had not altered since the Tudor period; they were still painted, still decorated with flags and garlands, still a focal point for dancing, still the target of raids by rival villages, and still occasionally a source of friction with landowners upon whose property they had been cut without permission. All that was novel was the absence of controversy over their existence, as they had become so firmly associated with the restoration of the traditional order in Church and State.[100] None the less, from the end of the eighteenth century a new theme enters records of them, which intensifies during the next one; of abandonment and neglect. The accounts speak increasingly of poles rotting away, or blowing down and not being replaced, or standing disused. The last in the environs of London was removed during 1795. In Sussex innkeepers maintained them for some decades after villages had ceased to do so, but by the later Victorian period they too had decided against making the effort. Young people were finding other entertainments, and no longer turned spontaneously to the old focuses of merry-making.[101] The process began long before the depopulation of the countryside, covered a period in which the village community was still seeking seasonal expression (for example, in club walks and harvest homes), and when local youth fought tenaciously for customs such as Guy Fawkes bonfires. The poles were simply going out of fashion at last. They were rescued, to a limited extent, by a self-conscious and institutionalized movement which commenced during Victoria's reign; and which will be the subject of a later chapter.

This one must turn from the 'traditional' maypole to another outgrowth from 'Maying' which was to achieve an apogee even as the poles declined. As shown above, there are good records from the fifteenth century onward for the propensity of women, especially young women, to make money by selling or displaying May garlands. By the early nineteenth century this was still going strong, but the custom seems to have become confined mainly to small girls. In Leicestershire and Rutland mothers commonly arranged the flowers and then handed them over to their little daughters for display.[102] There, as in all other places where the custom prevailed in its nineteenth-century form, the garlands were taken from door to door of the wealthiest households, and money, sweets, or refreshments solicited. Roy Judge, who has made the finest study of it, has given a solid basis of research to what would otherwise be a very powerful impression: that it increased dramatically in popularity in the course of the century, in both town and country. From the 1860s it was being mentioned with growing frequency, and approval, in the local press, and it was institutionalized from the 1880s by becoming organized by schools, especially in small villages.[103] Peter Robson has supplied a case study of the same process, by showing how what commenced as a means of raising cash among the children of fishing families on Dorset's Chesil coast was taken over by the village schools of the district.[104] In 1896 the folklorist Charlotte Burne suggested that the tradition would be both preserved and controlled by school or parish competitions, adults giving prizes and impounding the proceeds of the collections to provide a tea for the children or divide them equally between the latter.[105] This was precisely what was occurring. None the less, unofficial 'garlanding' also seems to have carried on increasing, right up to the 1890s when the schools became dominant and the independent parties of children began to diminish in the face of hostility from the local social élite, often articulated through the press.[106]

One of the strongholds of the custom was the east Midlands, where it was the juvenile female equivalent to 'Maying'.[107] Its range was nevertheless much larger than the latter activity, for it was equally important in Oxfordshire,[108] and in the coastal towns of Devon.[109] It overlapped the Victorian centres of Maying to the east, taking in Lincolnshire, Norfolk, and Essex,[110] and was found (more thinly) across the west Midlands as well.[111] 'Garlanding' was also represented in the three south-eastern counties,[112] in Berkshire and Hampshire,[113] in south-eastern Wiltshire,[114] and on the Dorset coast (as described). This distribution still left some notable gaps: all Scotland and northern England, all Wales (despite its own vigorous tradition of Maying), most of the interior of the West Country, and Cornwall with the exception of Saltash (which faces Devon).[115] It did, however, include northern Leinster and south-eastern Ulster, areas of Ireland where English influence was strong,[116] and there were parallels to it in the north of England. There the Christmas 'vessel box' was probably a transference of one aspect of garlanding, while in early twentieth-century Manchester an aggrieved commentator could say that 'May Day processions of young children are so numerous that their begging amounts to a racket'.[117] They carried nothing, but still had a sense that something was due to them.

The most famous description of a May garland is that furnished by Flora Thompson, purporting to describe the sort made by the schoolchildren of Juniper Hill, on the Oxfordshire–Northamptonshire border, in the 1880s. It consisted of a bell-shaped wooden frame four feet tall, covered in primroses, violets, cowslips, wallflowers, oxlips, and currant flowers. A knot of especially fine blooms was placed on top and a china doll, termed 'the lady', hung in the centre. White muslin was draped over it and it was hoisted on a broomstick. Made in the schoolroom, it was collected at six o'clock on May Morning by all the parish children aged 7 to 11, the girls in white or light frocks and the boys in bright ribbon knots and bows and sashes worn crosswise. They formed a procession led by a boy with a flag and a girl carrying a money-box. Then came the garland, between two bearers, and a May Queen and King, the former crowned with daisies and wearing a white veil and gloves. The royal couple were followed by two maids of honour, a lord and lady with maids of their own, a footman and his lady, and then the remaining children. They made a seven-mile circuit of the district, singing outside the more prosperous houses and collecting money, which was shared out in school the next day. At times on their tour they sighted other such processions, at which they jeered.[118]

As befits what is essentially a literary description, this is uniquely elaborate, combining features of garland processions found across the region but never combined as portrayed here. Queens and Kings, and lords and ladies, were alternatives to each other, and either couple only recorded in garlanding processions at six Oxfordshire communities.[119] Villages in Warwickshire, Huntingdonshire, Northamptonshire, and Rutland produced May Queens alone to lead the processions; elsewhere such regal figures were missing in the tradition. Participation by boys, although found across the whole range of the custom, was always rare. White dresses for the girls were, likewise, widespread but occur only in a minority of descriptions from each region. The same is true of the draping of a cloth over the garland (to be raised when the customer paid up, to display the decorations). The bell-shaped structure is certainly recorded elsewhere—for example in Dorset—but very rarely. Most commonly the garland was mounted on a hoop, or two, or three, or a bent branch. Sometimes the staff upon which most garlands were hoisted was itself turned into the focus of decoration, being covered in flowers and ribbons and termed 'the maypole', although it was carried and displayed in just the same manner. A cross-shaped frame was also occasionally used. At times garlands could take very striking local forms, such as the pyramid of green boughs six feet high, tied with ribbons, crowned with eleven varieties of flower, and hung with a gaily dressed doll, which appeared at Glatton in the Huntingdonshire Claylands in 1854;[120] in this, surely, there was an echo of the huge 'Mays' of late medieval urban parades. This east Midland region had, also, an unusual tradition in commonly hoisting the garland on a line over a street after the procession was over.

In that same area, and also in Devon, the dolls were often prominent enough to become the focus of the display in themselves, being known as may-dolls, may-babies or may-ladies. In some places in those counties the garlands had vanished altogether by the late nineteenth century and the children carried the doll in a box reposing on a bed of flowers. The little figures were found across the whole range of 'garlanding', although by no means essential to the custom, and Sir James Frazer, according to his habit of trying to reduce all Maying traditions to survivals of tree-spirit worship, declared that they were 'obviously' personifications of that spirit.[121] Against this can be argued the fact that they seem to have been a late addition, not recorded in garlands before the end of the eighteenth century. They seem, rather, to have been one of the more obvious decorations that a small girl of the period concerned could provide, and it is possible to extend to the full range of the custom the conclusion which Michael Pickering drew for north Oxfordshire: that the dolls represented the May Queens who appeared in reality in the most elaborate garlanding processions.[122]

The songs sung upon procession were very often versions of those used by the 'Mayers', while some of the more erudite (or heavily prompted) sets of children offered verses of Tennyson.[123] There were also, however, regional preludes which were particularly associated with the garlands, and have been mapped out by Roy Judge.[124] North of the Thames the most common was (or was similar to):

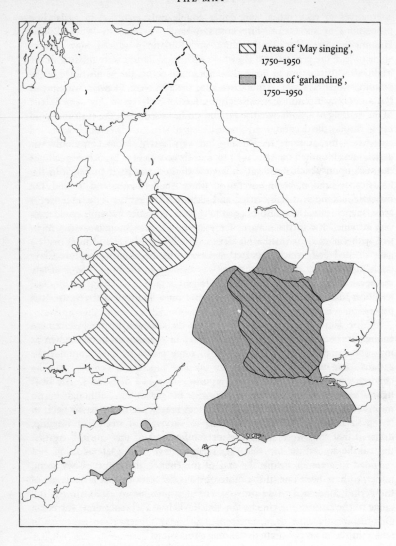

Areas of 'May singing',
1750–1950

Areas of 'garlanding',
1750–1950

MAP 4. Range of 'May singing' and 'garlanding'

Good morning ladies and gentlemen,
I wish you a happy May.
I've come to show you my garland
Because it is May Day.

This introduction would be followed by verses from the Mayers' carols. South of the Thames the preface tended to be either 'The first of May is Garland Day, so please remember the garland', or 'Today, today's the first of May', but there were several local compositions, drawn from all over the range.[125]

Here, then, was an extremely important custom, developed by rural children and taken over by schools and other local institutions as a means of controlling or monitoring it as its popularity grew. The latter peaked in the last third of the nineteenth century, when a single gentleman's house in Devon could be visited by as many as thirty such processions on a single May Day.[126] From the 1900s it began to decline, at an even greater speed than that at which it had risen. Part of the cause was that the village schools to which the custom had often become tied were being closed down, one by one.[127] Nevertheless, although independent garlanding had been increasingly the object of disapproval, it had never been completely replaced. What struck at this was the general rise in standards of living during the twentieth century, which meant that many children were receiving pocket money instead of having to solicit cash or treats from richer neighbours. In this situation, garlanding could be more easily stigmatized as begging and a disgrace to the parents of those who engaged in it, and it finally ended in the affluent 1950s.[128] Two vestiges of it remain, at Charlton on Otmoor in the custom's former stronghold of Oxfordshire, and at Abbotsbury near the Dorset coast. At the former, children take wooden crosses covered with flowers to church and hang a garland on the rood screen. At the latter (now on 13 May) the youngsters parade with the garlands on poles and lay them on the war memorial. In the first case the custom has survived by being absorbed into parish religion, in the second by being rededicated to the communal dead, a process much assisted by the enthusiasm of the local dignitary, the earl of Ilchester.

There remains one further development of the May Day foliage-gathering tradition to be discussed: the Jack in the Green. This was (and is) a wood or wicker frame covered in woven greenery and flowers and worn around the upper half of a man walking or dancing in May Day processions, especially those associated with chimney-sweeps. As such, it is well recorded in the nineteenth and early twentieth centuries. In 1939 a member of the Folklore Society, Lady Raglan, suggested that this figure could be linked to the mysterious heads carved in late medieval churches, which have foliage entwined about them and often sprouting from mouth and nostrils. She attached to these the name 'the Green Man', taken from a popular pub sign displaying a forester, and suggested that both the May Day character and the carved heads were representations of pre-Christian deities or spirits of nature and fertility.[129] This supposition was not based upon any research into the history of either: it was, rather, an extension of Sir James Frazer's preoccupation with tree-spirits encouraged by the proposal of another member of the Society and follower of Sir James, Margaret Murray, that some of the more enigmatic images in medieval churches were representations of pagan deities in which much of the population still believed.[130] This notion was itself equally devoid of any research into medieval sources, but it so perfectly reflected what mid-twentieth-century folklorists wished to believe that it became an orthodoxy.

This remained the case until 1979, when Roy Judge published his monograph upon the Jack in the Green, a turning-point in folklore studies which showed how much could be learned from a systematic investigation of historical evidence.[131] He discovered that the origins of the custom lay in the mid-seventeenth century, when London milkmaids began to dance in the streets upon May Day with their pails and heads crowned with flowers. The display earned them money, and was also symbolic in that the fresh new grass of late spring and early summer formed the basis for the year's first large yields of milk. One of the delights of May Day and of the whole ensuing month was to eat the cream from it, spread on cakes.[132] By the 1690s the maids were leaving their pails behind for the occasion, and instead danced between customers' doors bearing on their heads a pyramid of light wood adorned with ribbons, flowers, and borrowed silver plate. During the mid-eighteenth century they were imitated by the women who picked rags and by the city's chimney-sweeps. The latter had an especial claim upon sympathy at this time, for as fires were no longer needed in homes with the coming of summer, their work and earnings would fall off.

Near the end of the century, the milkmaids and rag-pickers abandoned the custom, and some sweeps began to employ a frame of green boughs, which were much more easily obtained than the silverware. By 1830 this had become standard, and the custom reached its apogee between then and 1880, attracting much attention in London and spilling over from it into the south-eastern counties and up the Thames valley. In all, it was recorded in eighty-one places up to 1941, including isolated examples as far afield as Cheshire, Bristol, Plymouth, and Hereford. The standard appearance of it was that of a tall cone of evergreens with flowers on top, set around a walking or dancing man, and accompanied by a finely dressed 'Lord and Lady', the latter usually played by a boy. After 1880 the custom went into rapid decline as the public got bored with it and found the 'capering' of the performers merely squalid, while the sweeps were forbidden to employ the young boys who had attracted most affection and sympathy. By 1900 it was only recorded in Oxford and London, and vanished soon after. By that time, however, the cone of greenery had been appropriated, like the maypole, for nostalgic 'revivals' of a Maying practices.[133] It was there that Lady Raglan encountered it thirty years latter and, being ignorant of its true context, connected it to the medieval heads. Thus a metropolitan tradition less than two centuries old got linked to decorations which had ceased to be made over four hundred years before, within a vague theory of worship of primeval rural deities.

The carved faces, still popularly known by Lady Raglan's nickname, remain enigmatic. In 1978 Kathleen Basford provided the first (and only) proper study of them,[134] and proved two points. The first was that they virtually all date from the period 1300–1500, and it is most unlikely that pagan gods would be more openly venerated in the later Middle Ages than the earlier, especially without leaving a trace in the relatively abundant local records of the time. The second was that the faces usually appeared anguished or menacing; demonic images of evil rather than visages of respected nature-spirits. She argued, therefore, that they had nothing to do with celebrations of springtime, summer, and rebirth, and they need not, accordingly, have any further place in a consideration of those themes.

Blossoming foliage, maypoles, and garlands were all associated specially with May Day, but played a major role in festivity throughout the following month and indeed in the whole summer season. It is to the contexts of that festivity that this book will now turn.

24

MAY GAMES AND WHITSUN ALES

COMMONERS, unlike royalty and the aristocracy, lacked large buildings in which communal festivities could comfortably be held in bad weather. During the darker and colder seasons, it was the alehouse or the private dwelling which formed the focus of merriment, and neither could accommodate crowds. The church could indeed be employed, but apart from the practical detail that it was not easily heated, there were always scruples about putting a sacred building to secular use, especially that which might conduce to inebriation and irreverence. Thus, the obvious setting for most communal celebration was the open air, or a barn or temporary structure which did not require a fire. The same considerations applied with less force to the 'church house', the permanent building acting as the forerunner of the modern village hall which became relatively common in the late Middle Ages. Nevertheless, to heat it still involved both extra cost and a risk of fire. The coming of summer, therefore, ushered in not merely a season in which the flowering of nature led minds naturally to rejoicing but one in which the clemency of the air made the implementation of that desire most practicable. The English climate usually warms appreciably during the middle and latter part of May, to the point at which outside gatherings or an unheated hall become comfortable. It was therefore in that period that the people of pre-industrial England gave themselves up to communal merry-making with particular frequency, a tendency reinforced by the fact that it lay conveniently between the heavy work of ploughing and sowing, and that of hay-making. The warm weather, and the ability to feast, dance, and play games freely, would last until September, but even for those who could spare the time from agricultural work later in the summer, this part of May offered a joyful inauguration of festive gatherings. Such gatherings were held with special frequency in the two days after the religious feast of Whit Sunday, set aside helpfully for them by the Church and known as the Whitsun holidays. They occurred, however, at any time from May Day onward, and in the early modern period were known variously as May games, summer plays, summer games, ales, or feasts. Some were also called revels or wakes, being names for a specific institution, the church dedication feast, which was much more common later in the summer and will be considered there. Under one or another of these names, however, communal celebrations are recorded in most parts of southern England during the month of May by the late Middle Ages.

Doubtless their comparative scarcity in records before then is simply a matter of surviving evidence. There is every reason to believe that they predate history, answering as they did to such an obvious human need. From 1220 to 1364, and especially in the mid-thirteenth century when reform movements led by bishops were most prevalent, episcopal orders repeatedly forbade the holding of them in churches or the attendance of clergy (who might compromise their dignity at such events).[1] To this period also belong expressions of concern by individual preachers that the seasonal frolics might lead people into sin. Robert Brunne, writing in 1303, could warn:

> Dances, cards, summer games,
> Of many such come many shames.[2]

At about the same time, the Dominican John Bromyard could present at length a picture of May games as devices set by the Devil to recapture souls withdrawn from his grasp by the abstinence of Lent. He spoke of women coming to them 'in their wanton array, frolicking, dancing', and of the whole company feasting and singing love songs while a flute player performed.[3]

It seems to be significant that such admonitions are apparently missing from the fifteenth century, in which communal meals and games became linked, like Plough Monday and Hocktide gatherings, to parish finance. The result was the institution of the church ale, which achieved prominence in the latter two-thirds of that century: a feast made by churchwardens for the express purpose of raising money for their funds. In several villages the records show them replacing levies or gatherings as a more enjoyable way of raising money, often being held in a newly constructed church house.[4] During the century 1450–1550 they are mentioned in the overwhelming majority of parishes for which accounts or other information survive. In many, especially in the countryside, they were the largest single source of revenue. Nevertheless, Norwich, Coventry, Lincolnshire, Lancashire, and all the far northernmost counties apparently did not have them, although all are either relatively or severely lacking in evidence. In London and Bristol they seem to have been very occasional.[5] The wardens of All Saints, Derby, seem to have resorted to them only in the year 1532–3, when they were desperate for money to complete a rebuilding of the tower. They did not provide any in the town itself, but made a tour of three nearby villages, holding an ale in each and returning with the profits.[6] It may be, to judge from later evidence, that in much of the north and the north Midlands the focus of parish celebration was always the late summer wake, or dedication feast, and income continued to depend upon rates, burials, and alternative types of seasonal gatherings such as Plough Monday and the hobby-horse.

Across most of southern England and the south Midlands, however, the ales were very common, being found equally in small villages, market towns, and major urban centres such as Oxford, Reading, Salisbury, Worcester, and Plymouth. They were also held in the city of York and the surrounding shire. Even where they were common, they were by no means universal: Nettlecombe in Somerset, St Aldates in Oxford, and Dartmouth in Devon are all examples of parishes set in districts notable for such events, which none the less do not seem to have adopted them.[7] Furthermore, where they did occur, they varied considerably in frequency. Most parishes which held ales or games did not do so every year, using them instead as occasional events designed to generate a large quantity of money for a particular purpose. Annual ales did occur at Wimbourne Minster in Dorset, Stogursey in the coastal marshes of Somerset, and Thame in Oxfordshire, while Brundish and Denton, on opposite sides of East Anglia's Waveney valley, had an average of three per year.[8] In many districts a rota may have operated, whereby villages held them in turn. Thus, the churchwardens of Yatton, in the north Somerset marshland, were regular guests at the feasts of four other parishes and made donations of money to them. Tintinhull, in the south Somerset arable country, had a reciprocal arrangement of contributions to the ales of three other villages.[9] Individuals could go on 'ale-crawls', thus the convivial or conscientious Sir Henry Willoughby, a Warwickshire gentleman, patronized them in three different villages in May 1526.[10] In 1537 the people of Wing, Crofton, Ascot, and Burcot, in northern Buckinghamshire, attended each other's celebrations.[11] The prior of Worcester dutifully made donations during 1533 to ales in two parishes in the city and two more in villages where the cathedral acted as a landlord.[12] Sometimes private persons would hold such feasts for their own needs, hiring church property for the purpose. At Cratfield, Suffolk, lying like Brundish in the rich arable country south of the Waveney, two out of the five held in 1490 were of this sort.[13]

Most of these early Tudor church ales were held at Whitsun, and most of the rest at some other time during May; but they could be found at any time between Easter and the end of August. Their physical location is rarely specified. At Saffron Walden in Essex, Eltham near the coast of Kent, and St Lawrence, Reading, they were definitely held in the church, but at the first this was discontinued in 1490, and at the second 'put down' in 1511, suggesting disapproval.[14] At St Edmund, Salisbury, at Winterslow, Wiltshire, and at Yatton, the setting was the church hall.[15] In the Dorset market town of Sherborne posts were set up in the churchyard for the ale in 1525, perhaps as the framework for a temporary shelter.[16] Occasionally a menu survives from one of these events. Ale itself was, of course, always brewed, and sometimes, as at Snettisham on the Norfolk coast, only bread added to it.[17] By contrast, the village of Bramley in the north Hampshire woodland also bought veal, mutton, chicken, butter, and cheese for its Whitsun feast in 1530.[18] One of the largest such events on record was held at Huntingfield, next to Cratfield in that same Suffolk farmland above the Waveney, in 1534. Eight parishes pooled their resources to provide beer, milk, cream, bread, eggs, honey, spices, veal, and mutton.[19] Specific entertainments featured at some of these occasions. Music seems to have been fairly common, often played by an individual piper, drummer, or harper hired for the day.[20] Dancing should, as the medieval literary sources suggest, have been a regular feature. Usually the proceeds went straight to the general needs of the parish church, but some Yorkshire communities used part of them to maintain a special 'summer game light'.[21]

A frequent feature of the summer games was the crowning of a mock-king or lord to preside over them. Such figures are mentioned at eighteen of the 104 parishes in which such ales or games are recorded for the period 1450–1550 (17 per cent): they are scattered all over England.[22] At a further twenty-one (20 per cent) the character of the 'King' at the centre of the revels was replaced by Robin Hood, a development to be discussed later. Over a third of these events in the early Tudor period, therefore (but not, apparently, more) were associated with these temporary sovereigns. Earlier in history the dearth of parish records makes evidence very thin, but they were certainly around by the year 1240, when Walter de Cantelupe, bishop of Worcester, condemned clerics who attended 'games to be made of a King and Queen'.[23] They may have existed for centuries before that. In 1303, Robert of Brunne, writing against unseemly games upon a Sunday, could admonish that

> if thou ever in field, ever in town,
> Didst flower garland or crown
> To make a woman gather there
> To see which that fairer were;
> This is against the commandment
> And the holy day for thee is shent;
> It is a gathering for lechery,
> And full great pride, and hearty lye.[24]

This may be another reference to summer queens, instead of merely to local beauty contests. Less equivocal are two accounts, in a monastic chronicle and a poem or song, of the crowning of Robert the Bruce, King of Scots, in 1306.[25] They are apparently contemporary to, or only slightly later than, this event, and the former compares the new monarch to a 'summer king', the latter to a 'king of summer'.

The late medieval and early Tudor sources permit some insight into the activities of these figures. In the 1460s at Wistow, in the vale of York, a village king and queen were elected by the youth, who gathered for this in a 'summerhouse', a converted barn or some other temporary structure. The couple processed in, attended by a seneschal, a guard, and two soldiers, and presided all afternoon over such theatrical and musical entertainments as their elders considered to be 'appropriate and respectable'. The whole gathering numbered over a hundred, and presumably consisted either of the entire village community or of its young people with many guests.[26] In the parish of St Edmunds, Salisbury, a queen and king were also chosen, and fined 8d. each if they refused to serve. Their responsibilities were clearly important, and therefore onerous, for in 1461 their various 'plays' raised over £23, a colossal sum by the standards of parish collections.[27] Communal pride as well as profit was invested in the office, and in 1536 the court leet of Guildford echoed the tone of the Salisbury parish by declaring that if any young men were chosen 'by the whole commontie of this town...to be summer kings, princes and sword-bearers' they would have to do the job or pay a forfeit to parish funds.[28] At St Lawrence, Reading, and Henley, a little further down the Thames, the early Tudor 'king plays' were also specifically 'of the young men',[29] and they may everywhere have been a special concern of local youth. If so, the institution very neatly harnessed their energies, and gave them a seasonal importance, to the benefit of their communities.

Sir James Frazer, it is true, attributed a yet more profound significance to their office. Using mainly nineteenth-century evidence, including some from areas of western and central Europe in which the young mock-monarchs were also found, he argued that they had originally represented spirits of vegetation in a pagan rite, and that the crowning of the summer queens and king in May was originally a sacred marriage intended to make the crops grow.[30] Against this ingenious idea can be lodged two objections from the medieval and early modern English evidence. The first is that there is absolutely nothing to indicate that the young 'monarchs' ever were, or ever had been, regarded in this way. The second is that they were not required to make up a couple, 'queens' or 'ladies' always being much rarer than 'kings' or 'lords'; indeed those at Wistow, Kingston upon Thames, and Salisbury are the only cases (out of the eighteen) where a female counterpart is known to have accompanied the male focal figure. Certainly the events were associated with greenery. A late fourteenth-century life of St Anne portrays a procession of children, 'each a green branch in his hand, even like a summer play'.[31] At St Lawrence, Reading, in the early sixteenth century, a bough or sapling was regularly set up in the market-place as a focus for the 'king game', and presumably decorated.[32] This, however, need signify nothing more than a natural impulse to adorn the gathering-place with seasonal foliage and flowers. It is abundantly evident that the local 'lords' and 'kings' represented not spirits or deities so much as earthly royalty or aristocracy: hence the guard and seneschal at Wistow or the sword-bearers at Guildford. Hence, also, the way in which those at the larger local centres handed out 'liveries' to people attending the games in the manner of late medieval magnates identifying supporters. At the major Surrey market town of Kingston, a painter was paid to make up twenty-four 'great liveries', and up to 2,000 'small' versions; David Wiles has deduced that the former were paper or cloth costumes and the latter badges, handed out to those who gave to the parish funds. In addition, 2,000 pins were also ordered, presumably for those who made small donations.[33] The Leicestershire market town of Melton Mowbray issued arrows to its Whitsun 'lord' in the 1540s either as part of his costume or for a display of archery.[34] The mock-monarch of Kingston took his entourage on visits to another important local centre in the country, Croydon,[35] while a Leicestershire May King was bold enough to call upon the real Queen Mother, Lady Margaret Beaufort, at her palace of Colyweston in 1502, and was well rewarded.[36]

The term 'Lord of Misrule', applied to the mock-rulers at royal and aristo-cratic midwinter revels, does not seem to have been used of the village sovereigns in this period. Nevertheless, Scotland possessed figures who, in the formality of their office and length of their rule, were fairly exact summer equivalents of the Lords of Misrule. They existed in burghs, and were termed 'abbots'. At Aberdeen the title was 'Abbot of Bon Accord' (joviality), some-times supported by a 'prior'. At Edinburgh it was, mysteriously, 'Abbot of Narent'. At Borthwick, Haddington, Peebles, and Linlithgow it was 'Abbot of Unreason'. In other towns the function of these figures was supplied by Robin Hood, to be discussed in the next chapter of this work. The Abbot of Bon Accord was active at Aberdeen by 1440, when the corporation received complaints of 'divers enormities' committed during his time of rule; whatever they were, they were not sufficient to inhibit the custom, which flourished steadily there for over a century. At Peebles, it had been instituted by 1472, and at Edinburgh by 1493. The duties of these individuals are rarely defined in the records but, to judge from the archive of Aberdeen, they consisted broadly of devising entertainments for the town during a period which could last from Easter till late summer. In 1440 and 1445 the 'Abbot' supervised religious plays, in 1492 and 1552 he organized shows for visiting royalty, and in 1523 he acted as Master of Artillery. In 1553 his responsibilities were summed up as holding 'the whole town in gladness with dances, farces, plays and games'. In 1501 Linlithgow's Abbot of Unreason danced before the King (James IV) at the latter's command, and was lavishly recompensed. Scottish communities also appointed Queens of May, chosen presumably for their beauty: James IV gave money in 1505 to one of these at the gate of Holyrood abbey and another at Ayr. In England the only comparable figure to the Scottish mock-clerics was at Shrewsbury, where an 'Abbot' was appointed every May after 1521, with robe, sandals, liveries, and minstrels.[37]

In both parts of Britain, the summer games and their monarchs ran during the mid-sixteenth century into the major obstacle of the Reformation. In England they survived the reign of Henry VIII well enough but, like so many ecclesiastical ceremonies, they fell foul of that of Edward. No governmental or episcopal order was ever issued against them, but the team of royal visitors (local Protestant worthies) sent to enforce religious injunctions in the West Country during 1547 certainly did so. They prohibited church ales, on the grounds that 'many inconveniences' arising from them had been reported.[38] The term was vague enough to obscure their motive, and we can only surmise that it might have been religious (a desire to separate holy places from profane revelry) or practical (a fear of assemblies which might breed rebellion). A complete lack of data prevents us from determining whether those upon other circuits behaved differently. If most did not, this would explain why, of eighteen parishes which were regularly holding such ales in the early 1540s and which have also left good accounts for the reign of Edward, sixteen gave them up in the period 1547–9.[39] The remaining two are both villages in one district of central Oxfordshire, where there is also evidence for ales at a third in the early 1550s: which may reflect a different policy on the part of local visitors.[40] In addition, one Somerset village was holding them at the same time,[41] but there is no trace of any other in the whole body of rural accounts preserved from the last years of the reign. By sharp contrast as soon as Catholic Mary came to the throne, church ales reappeared all over the half of England south and west of the line drawn between London and Chester, in county towns, markets, ports, and (above all) villages. Over most of this huge region they feature in the majority of surviving rural accounts, although noticeably rarer in the three southeastern shires.[42] North and east of the line, they were apparently seldom held, the only recorded cases being at Liverpool, Melton Mowbray, and the market town of Long Melford in Suffolk.[43] These events had always been less popular in the North and north Midlands than elsewhere, but the failure to revive them on the old scale in East Anglia is noteworthy. At four places where they were revived (12 per cent), they included mock-kings, queens, or lords,[44] while Robin Hood featured in at two more ales in the group.[45] There is no evidence that Mary's government encouraged the traditional festivities, and indeed it actually banned May games in Kent in the aftermath of Wyatt's rebellion there, on the grounds that 'lewd practices...are appointed to such assemblies' (by which it meant treasonable, not lascivious, behaviour).[46] Nevertheless, the ales and revels seem to have become so bound up with the old religion that they returned naturally with it, while the heavy expense of restoring Catholic worship produced a need for fund-raising events.

It does not seem as if church ales ever appeared in Scotland, but the fate of that nation's summer games was both well documented and dramatic. By the middle of the sixteenth century the office of 'Abbot' had become controversial in some places. One at Borthwick, just south of Edinburgh, caused understandable offence in 1547 by first ducking a man and then making a priest eat some letters which had just been delivered to him. At Haddington, a short distance to the east, people proved to be increasingly unwilling to serve in the role, until it was abolished in 1552. Even up at Aberdeen, where no such difficulty existed, the Abbots of Bon Accord were criticized in 1553 for 'sumptuous and superfluous banqueting', and ordered to curtail their expenditure. None of this, however, is sufficient to account for the thunderstroke of the Act passed by the Scottish Parliament in 1555. It 'ordained that in all times coming no manner of person be chosen Robert Hude nor Little John, Abbot of Unreason, Queens of May nor otherwise neither in Burgh nor to landward'. The penalties were stiff: loss of the freedom of the town for those who assisted in the choice in burghs, and banishment from the realm for those who accepted the office. In the countryside, they were fining and gaol respectively. The Parliament was not a Protestant one, and the purpose of the statute does not seem to have been moral; rather, it was a political measure taken by the deeply insecure Government of the Queen Regent, Mary of Guise, determined to deny her Protestant enemies rallying-points for ribaldry and rebellion.[47]

Nevertheless, it became convenient to later, Protestant, regimes in Scotland which were equally afraid of sedition and imbued with a dislike of traditional revelry, the latter trait strengthening as the former waned. In 1577 the General Assembly of the reformed Kirk petitioned another regent, the Earl of Morton, to enforce the law upon Sundays at the least. The following year it asked the royal council for a proclamation against 'all kinds of May plays', 'either by bairns at the schools or others'. The result was a hard struggle. Edinburgh complied at once by reiterating the terms of the Act of 1555. The citizens seem to have obeyed it, but only because they could still find such entertainments in the surrounding countryside; in 1588 the burgh drummer was imprisoned for performing at 'May plays' in Kirklistown. During that decade, the presbyteries of the central Lowlands imposed excommunication and penance upon those who frequented them, and towns further north such as Stirling and Perth added their prohibitions to the campaign. None the less, 'May plays, as Robin Hood, abbot unreason etc.' were still held in the Lothians in 1590, and after then they persisted in the southern uplands. In 1610 the presbytery of Kelso was still summoning local lairds for supporting 'the May plays used by them called lord or abbot of unreason'. Only after this date, a general silence falls upon the issue, and the rulers of the revels vanish at last from Scottish history.[48]

In England their fate, and that of the feasts at which they presided, was more complex and part of a much longer story. Church ales and summer games were not, apparently, targets of Elizabeth's Reformation, and their revival under Mary was sustained into the 1560s. The ales are recorded then in accounts from forty-seven parishes, across the same range as during the previous decade.[49] At Northill, Bedfordshire, ten parishes gathered for a feast at Whitsun 1561 which consisted of bread, baked meats, fresh roast veal, fruit, spices, and beer. The entertainment was provided by a minstrel, two fools, six morris dancers, and some fireworks.[50] Five years later the parish of Holy Trinity in the Suffolk town of Bungay, one of the most important along the river Waveney, held the first of three successive annual 'church ale games'. These also seem to have attracted participants from the whole district, and the fare included eggs, butter, currants, pepper, saffron, veal, lamb, honey, cream, bread, custards, pasties, and eight firkins of beer. Plays were presented on a scaffold by parishoners, some wearing masks and some robes lent by the earl of Surrey, heir to the town's patron the duke of Norfolk.[51] These were unusually elaborate events, most ales making do with food and drink alone, or with a musician, a morris side (the technical term for a morris team), a clown, or a maypole or two.[52] Seven parishes in this sample (15 per cent) crowned summer kings of lords.[53] The 'lord' at Melton Mowbray in 1563 had four footmen and two butlers, and raised money not just for the needs of the church but also to repair the local roads. Mere, on the southern Wiltshire chalk downs, had the unique system of an annual 'Cuckoo King', assisted by a 'Cuckoo Prince' who was made King in the next year.

Elizabethan literary works supply better pictures than those before of the parish festivities and of the presiding figures at some. Philip Stubbes, the fierce enemy of many popular pleasures, published in 1583 the most famous of all portraits of a summer king, misleadingly described as a Lord of Misrule: a 'grand captain (of mischief)' chosen by 'the wild heads of the parish conventing together'. He is crowned and annointed, and selects up to a hundred 'lusty guts' of his retinue, whom 'he investeth with his liveries of green, yellow or some other light wanton colour'. He then leads these to the church, to interrupt the service and amuse the parishoners, before going

forth into the churchyard, where they have commonly their summer-halls, their bowers, arbours, and banqueting houses set up, wherein they feast, banquet and dance all that day and (peradventure) all the night too... these they give to everybody that will give money for them... And who will not be buxom to them, and give them money for these their devilish cognizances, they are mocked and flounted at not a little... some give bread, some good ale, some new cheese, some old, some custards, and fine cakes.[54]

Stubbes also provided some further details of the organization of a church ale

the churchwardens of every parish, with the consent of the whole parish, provide half a score or twenty quarters of malt, whereof some they buy off the church stock, and some is given to them of the parishoners themselves, everyone conferring somewhat according to his ability, which malt being made into very strong ale or beer, is set to sale, either in the church or some other place assigned to that purpose.[55]

The invasion of the church portrayed by Stubbes seems to have been a disorderly version of a custom whereby summer kings and queens attended a service, in their regalia and with their retinue, before commencing their rule over the revels. Shortly after this date, William Warner could write 'lord and lady gang till kirk with lads and lasses gay: Fra Mass and Evensong fa good cheer and glee on every green'.[56] At Wootton parish church, just west of Oxford, 'the youth were somewhat merry together in crowning of lords' during the service on Midsummer Day 1583, and got into trouble with the archdeacon because of it.[57] Elizabethan bishops generally tried to prohibit the entry of the mock-monarchs to churches, while in their role as leaders of festivity, because of the irreverence which could result; between 1571 and 1600 a total of nine incorporated this in their visitation articles, led by Edmund Grindal, successively archbishop of York and Canterbury.[58]

Another good view of a summer lord comes from the end of Elizabeth's reign, in 1601, at South Kyme on the edge of the Lincolnshire Fens. There the games lasted much longer than the norm, right until the end of August. They included reciprocal visits of young men between villages, led by their own elected 'lords' and involving a tour of the alehouses in each. The leader of the Kyme lads was the son of a prosperous yeoman and rode with an escort of about a dozen, including flag-bearers, drummers, and six guards carrying reeds with painted paper heads to simulate spears. The season ended on the last Sunday in August, with a maypole being erected and a play performed on the village green after evensong. Over a hundred people attended, from the whole district.[59] A fine image of the procession of a Queen of May comes from Oxford in 1598, where she was described as decked in garlands and brought into town by the militiamen, together with morris dancers, drummers, and men attired in female dress.[60] Sometimes summer queens were carried triumphantly in chairs; the Protestant preacher Stephen Batman compared the Pope, transported in this manner, to 'whitepot queens in western May games' (whitepot being a cream custard).[61]

None of this should be allowed to give the impression that the Elizabethan period was a golden age for the traditional parish revels: on the contrary, they underwent a considerable decline. This commenced in the middle of the 1560s and remained steady beyond the end of the reign, although it does seem as if the 1570s were a decisive period in it. It was then that church ales seem to have vanished from East Anglia, Kent, and Sussex, and to have shrunk considerably in number over the rest of their former range. In many of the parishes in which they had been the mainstay of funding they now became an occasional contribution to it. By the end of the reign they were confined to the West Country and to the valleys of the Thames and its tributaries.[62] This did not mean that they had retreated into remote rural districts, for the Thames valley was the most densely populated and frequently travelled part of the realm. Church ales still abounded on the western outskirts of London and at Oxford, where about half the males of the ruling class went to university.

The reasons for this decline have been discussed elsewhere.[63] It did not result from hostility on the part of the government. The queen herself enjoyed May games, and commanded a personal performance at Greenwich palace of one held around London in the first summer of her reign, which included a giant, drummers, the Nine Worthies of Christendom, St George and the dragon, Robin Hood, Little John, Maid Marian, Friar Tuck, and morris dancers.[64] Her Privy Council intervened in 1589 to declare that the summer games were perfectly lawful in Oxfordshire, where local opposition to them had developed.[65] Likewise the most powerful churchman of the reign, Archbishop Whitgift, enjoyed a pageant provided to end a summer season spent at his rural residence of Croydon in 1592 or 1593, which included scenes of 'Maying' and 'country dances'.[66] Of all the Elizabethan episcopacy, only two showed any hostility to the parish feasts: Cox of Ely, who denounced 'wanton dancing' and 'lewd may games' in 1579, and Coldwell of Salisbury, who condemned the holding of church ales upon Sunday in 1595. Neither seems to have made much local impact.[67]

The decisive role in the discouragement of the traditional festivities seems, therefore, to have occurred at a local level, and it has been argued elsewhere that it stemmed primarily from radical Protestantism, gradually reinforced by a more general fear of social disorder at a time of growing population pressure and poverty.[68] One such was the fervent evangelist William Kethe, who was appointed to a living in north-east Dorset in the early 1570s and immediately made himself unpopular by denouncing church ales: to him, dancing, drinking, and blood sports were all 'disorders' in themselves, whereas to the local people a gathering was orderly if it did not involve violence.[69] Of the same stamp were Humphrey Roberts, at King's Langley in Hertfordshire, who condemned games in general in 1572, and the Essex rector William Harrison, who commented with satisfaction on the dramatic decrease in church ales.[70] During that and the following three decades, a score of other clergymen wrote against feasting and dancing.[71] The most intemperate of all such authors, however, Christopher Fetherston and the much-quoted Stubbes, were laymen, and these were to prove most directly influential in ending the old revelry. John Bruen, a Cheshire gentleman who had got religion, conducted a successful campaign to extirpate summer games from the north-west of the county.[72] The Devon JPs had already forbidden ales upon Sundays by 1595; in that year they abolished Sunday May games also and directed that ales could only take place in daylight, without music or dancing, and with drink provided by licensed alehouse keepers. This was because they caused 'the dishonour of Almighty God, increase of bastardy and of dissolute life and very many other mischiefs'. In 1600 another order banned them altogether, a ruling repeated in 1615 with the comment that two ales during that summer had ended in manslaughter.[73] In 1594 and 1596 the bench of neighbouring Somerset also prohibited them outright, a ruling resulting from the combination of a pronounced religious zeal among some members with the fact that one gentleman, at Dulverton, had been holding them lavishly to raise money to defend himself against a charge of poaching. It was reissued four times during the next twenty years.[74] A similar ban was frustrated in Oxfordshire when opponents of it successfully appealed to the Privy Council,[75] but one upon Sunday ales was passed by the Lancashire justices in 1587.[76]

The frequent repetition of the West Country bans would argue for the fact that they were either difficult to enforce or were always intended to provide a means of regulation rather than abolition; although that in Devon in 1595 did seem to halt a number of traditional church ales permanently.[77] Their tone, also, seems misleading, for social and legal historians seem to be agreed that violence or fornication rarely occurred at them during this period and that patterns of conception, in or out of wedlock, have little relationship to seasonal revelry.[78] Serious fighting certainly did break out at a few parish feasts, as was mentioned in the county orders. It is described in detail in the occasional entry in a legal archive, such as the ugly incident at Goodrich, in the Wye valley in Herefordshire, at the traditional Whit Monday 'mirth, music and dancing' in 1610. As usual about a hundred people were present, including many from neighbouring villages, and an old quarrel between two sets of them ended in a stabbing.[79] Such occurrences would, however, have been written off as rare disturbances of usually pacific events (as they must have been in the early Tudor period), if local élites did not now contain individuals already disposed against them. The result was a continuing decline in their number and frequency during the Jacobean period, although many still continued in the Thames valley and the West.[80] Furthermore, as church ales became rarer, they also tended to be more spectacular when they were held. Wootton St Lawrence, in the woodland of northern Hampshire, followed a long local history of 'king ales' with a three-day one in 1603.[81] In 1611 Seal, in southern Surrey, hosted a five-day extravaganza requiring musicians, a fool, silk points and laces as emblems for guests, ten barrels of beer, a quarter of wheat, three calves, eleven lambs, and a fat sheep.[82] All this was surpassed by the churchwardens of St Cuthbert's, Wells, who badly needed funds for repairs in 1607, and joined forces with the bishop's bailiff, who wanted to attract traders to the town and levy tolls upon them. They presented a May game every Sunday evening from 3 May until the end of June, which included 'morris dancers, loving dancers, men in women's apparel, new-devised lords and ladies', drummers, trumpeters, pipers, ensign-bearers, pikemen, musketeers, Robin Hood, St George, and other heroes of fiction. At times over 3,000 people spectated.[83]

The Jacobean evidence also furnishes a better impression of the sort of people who supported and opposed the feasts. Among the opponents were John Geare, minister of Lyme Regis, who campaigned to end the annual ale to raise funds to repair the breakwater, and the curate of Winsley, in the northwest Wiltshire claylands, who described all women who danced or sang at summer games as whores. There was also the vicar of Iron Acton at the southwest end of Gloucestershire, who permitted the congregation of Rangeworthy chapel to hold their usual Whitsun revel in 1611 only if they moved it to the Monday and attended a three-hour sermon first. Up at Longdon in Worcestershire's vale of Severn, the constable tried to stop the May games in 1616 and 1617 because louts from other villages had taken to frequenting them and brawling.[84] Upon the other side were Christopher Windle, vicar of Bisley in the centre of the Cotswold hills, who had his son made the Whitsun lord in 1610, and the south Devon gentleman Walter Woolton, who told the villagers of Harberton in 1606 that he would get them a church ale and Whitsun lord and lady again, plus a 'fool with his horns'. In the same year Sir Edward Parham of Poyntington in southern Somerset both promoted the ale there and danced in the morris himself, while at nearby Odcombe the courtier and wit Thomas Coryate got himself made summer lord in 1611, and marched with his retinue to Yeovil to advertise the church ale.[85]

Their efforts were supported by a new development in national literature. During the 1570s and early 1580s the attacks upon the summer games had gone virtually unanswered, but from the second half of the 1580s a reaction began to set in. At first it took the form of a celebration of the country revelry in poetry, often by grafting it onto the flourishing genre of pastoral verse. The most famous writer to do so, and the least important in this context, was Sir Philip Sidney, who portrayed one of his imaginary Grecian shepherds as being crowned with a garland 'For he then chosen was the dignity | Of village lord that Whitsuntide to bear'.[86] Of much more consistent significance to the development of this theme were William Warner, Michael Drayton, and Nicholas Breton, the first pioneering it and the last two returning to it far into the Stuart period. In the 1610s Drayton gathered round him in the capital a group of young poets—William Browne, George Wither, John Davies, and Christopher Brooke—who followed his example. Their work was essentially that of Londoners celebrating the pleasures of the countryside, and something of their difference in priorities from genuine rustics is shown in their constant description of pretty May Queens in preference to the more common village lords. Nevertheless, their work at times combined realism and romance very effectively, such as in Drayton's exquisite description of a king ale in a summer bower woven with flowers, published in 1619: the participants feast upon plums, cherries, cheese, curds, clotted cream, spiced syllabubs, and 'cider of the best' before piping and singing.[87] Realism was still more to the fore in other literary treatments of the subject which appeared around 1600. The Cornish gentleman Richard Carew provided a defence of church ales in an account of his county, as promoters of good neighbourliness while raising more money than compulsory levies. He suggested that they be inserted between a church service and sports, and be provided with only moderately strong beer, the elders supervising the young.[88] London playwrights also increasingly portrayed the festivities of youth in the city's suburbs, which reached their most exuberant expression in Francis Beaumont's *The Knight of the Burning Pestle*, finished in 1613. Among its characters was a May Lord chosen by his fellow lads, 'with scarves and rings and posy' and 'gilded staff'.[89]

Such positive images were given support by the land's highest authority in 1618, when (even as May games were finally wiped out in his native Scotland) James I explicitly sanctioned church ales, not merely in general but upon Sundays. The royal declaration to this effect, commonly called the Book of Sports, caused both controversy at a local level and bad feelings in parliaments. The expression of the latter seems to have emboldened the Somerset JPs to repeat their own ban at the Easter sessions in 1624. Three years later, and into the reign of Charles I, their counterparts in Dorset tried to bolster themselves against the Book of Sports by getting a royal assize judge to endorse a similar order. This example was copied in Devon and Somerset, and repeated there successfully until 1633, when the judge concerned overreached himself by requiring the Somerset clergy to publish the order. The result was one of the century's most famous episodes, involving a division of the county gentry over the issue, the apparent rallying of the majority of its clergy to the support of the ales, the intervention of the archbishop of Canterbury against the judge, and the reissue of the royal Book of Sports.[90] The village feasts were now proof against further local prohibitions as long as royal authority itself was unchallenged, and this period came to an end in 1640. Upon convening at the end of that year, the Long Parliament's House of Commons immediately labelled the Book of Sports a grievance, and on 1 September 1641 it formally condemned the provisions in it. Although unsupported by the House of Lords, let alone the King, these rulings had a devastating effect in practice. Of all the surviving churchwardens' accounts, only two show takings from church ales by the summer of 1641: at little South Newington in Oxfordshire and remote St Ives in Cornwall.[91] Both ended then. As an institution, these ales were effectively dead before the Puritan Revolution proper commenced, and they never recovered. After the Restoration only one parish in the whole country, out of over 700 which have left accounts from the late Stuart period, revived them. This was Williton in Somerset, a large village on the coast behind the Brendon hills, and there it was finally abandoned in 1689 when the church house in which it was held was leased out.[92]

What had happened was that a process which had been effected 200 years before had been reversed, and the tie between the summer games and parish finance broken. In the process the importance of the former seems itself to have been somewhat diminished, and the focus of communal festivity shifted instead to the dedication feasts or wakes, which were themselves now to become the centre of controversy, as will be described. The shift, however, was only relative, as May games and Whitsun feasts long continued to flourish in what may be termed the private sector. The inhabitants of Eling, on Southampton Water, still held a 'dinner at the church house' on most Whitsuns in the 1660s and 1670s, the difference being that now the parish funds made a donation to it instead of receiving the profits.[93] A few other parishes, scattered across the country, helped to subsidize May festivities.[94] During the next two years, the summer festivities can be seen operating upon different levels. At the lowest was the private party, well portrayed in a long song of 1671, which describes how a group of young people paid 2*d.* each to hire a fiddler for the day. They met up with him at the local maypole and danced familiar country measures about it, followed by a feast of ale and cakes in the nearby summer bower, with much kissing, before separating at dusk.[95] The Llansanffraid yn Mechain district of eastern Montgomeryshire is studded with hills, the summits of which were levelled off artificially to leave a small mound in the centre. On summer evenings until the mid-nineteenth century, this was used as a seat for a harpist or fiddler, to accompany dancing in that part of the green, while tennis, bowling, or wrestling could take place in another.[96] In nineteenth-century Lancashire, mills and collieries closed upon Whit Monday and Tuesday, allowing people to attend race-meetings or visit markets. Groups would make their own ale, in what were known as 'main brews', and drink it at a private house.[97]

Above this level came the village feasts, no longer associated with communal fund-raising or possessed of any official status. In the middle of the nineteenth century, villages in the Ross district of Herefordshire held them on successive days of Whitsun week, allowing for reciprocal entertainment and enabling a morris troupe to perform at each.[98] At the same period Whit Monday 'revels' were still common in North Devon, twenty-four surviving in 1896. Certain villagers obtained a licence to sell ale during that day, advertised by the traditional signal of a bush set up outside the door. In the words of one commentator:

All classes joined in the games and sports, wrestling, skittles, boxing, running, cock-fighting, climbing the greased pole, football, dancing and cock-slaying. Women ran for gowns, legs of mutton and other prizes; men wrestled for hats and silver spoons; boys climbed a greased pole on which was mounted the prize; and young men gave their young women fairings, usually a packet of sweets, made of almonds, sugars, and spices, or gingerbread nuts, or Spanish nuts.[99]

By contrast, in the 1760s, the Whitsun entertainment at Weston, Norfolk, consisted of a single race sponsored by the landlord of the pub. He greased a ram or pig, cut off its tail and ears (and in the former case its horns), and allowed whomsoever could catch it to keep it.[100] Between the two in scale were the Cornish feasts, where mock-mayors were elected, from among notable local drunkards. They were expected to be thrown into water or onto the communal rubbish heap at the end.[101] Other village Whitsun celebrations are recorded in these centuries in Buckinghamshire, Berkshire, Bedfordshire, Surrey, Hampshire, and the East Riding of Yorkshire.[102]

Most elaborate of all were the May celebrations of Gloucestershire, Wiltshire, Oxfordshire, and Northamptonshire, which faithfully continued the tradition of medieval king ales. They were usually held every few years, contributions to launch them being made by local landowners or solicited in neighbouring villages. Some of the most famous, such at those at Woodstock and Kidlington, were annual. The setting was generally a barn, although 'bowers' of wood and greenery were still constructed for some. The presiding group was fairly standardized, and had developed slightly since the early modern period. There was still a lord, and often a lady also, chosen from local youth for popularity and good looks. At Longcombe, Oxfordshire, in the 1770s they held opposite ends of a ribbon, and she carried a bouquet, when processing to the bower. More often the 'lord' bore a beribboned mace of office. In Oxfordshire he was commonly preceded by a fool, or 'squire', carrying an inflated bladder and dried ox-tail, and accompanied by a morris side. In Gloucestershire he could have an elaborate retinue, of steward, sword-bearer, purse-bearer, page, fool, and mace-bearer, with their badges of office, plus a piper and tabor-player. In Oxfordshire there was sometimes a sword-bearer, with a cake carried on the end of his weapon which was sliced into pieces and given to bystanders. Most ornate of all were the famous ales at Woodstock and Kidlington. At the former the presiding couple kept an owl in a cage, which was termed a parrot, and flails which were called nutcrackers or bagpipes. A person who gave them their real names, in this time of misrule, was fined. At Kidlington a 'lady' ruled alone, and was chosen by her ability to catch and hold a lamb with her mouth, racing for it in competition with other young women.[103]

In a class of their own were the summer monarchs who presided over ritual combats in two different areas speaking Celtic languages. In the eighteenth-century Isle of Man, the Queen of May was chosen in each large parish from among the daughters of the richest farmers. Her entourage consisted of about twenty maids of honour and a set of young men led by a captain. She was attired in 'the gayest and best manner', and was opposed by a Queen of Winter, a man 'dressed in women's clothes, with woollen hoods, fur tippets, and loaded with the warmest and heaviest habits one upon another'. The latter had 'her' own entourage in similar garb, marching to 'the rough music of the tongs and cleavers' even as the followers of May moved to 'violins and flutes'. The two groups would meet upon a common, and that of Winter fight to take the Queen of May prisoner. If they succeeded, then she was 'ransomed for as much as pays the expenses of the day'. The people of Winter then retired to dance and feast in a barn, while those of May sported on a green before repairing for their own meal.[104] In South Wales in the same period the fight was very similar, save that all the participants were boys or men, and the result was rigged so that summer always won. The company of Winter fought with bare branches, that of Summer with green boughs.[105] At Defynnog in the Usk valley above Brecon, the Kings were crowned with holly and bright ribbons respectively, and were only carried around the farms on May Day while their followers collected money.[106] Nothing like this custom is known in Scotland or Ireland or recorded in old Welsh literature, and it is quite impossible to say which of these two variations inspired the other, and how long either had been carried on. Both died out at the beginning of the nineteenth century.

At that time also, the whole face of the Whitsun festivities was altering across England. Once more they were given an institutional form, this time by the parish benefit clubs and friendly societies which multiplied during the late eighteenth century, providing a basic health insurance for their members. By the 1830s it was common for them to parade in Whit week, to a peal of church bells, 'all arrayed in their best, gay with ribbons and scarves, a band of music sounding before them; their broad banner of peace and union flapping over their heads, and their wands shouldered like the spears of an ancient army, or used as walking staves'. There was a tendency for the men's clubs to process on Whit Monday, and those of the women on the Tuesday.[107] Most of the parades ended at the church for a service, followed by a dinner and then dancing. The meals were held at an inn or in a marquee, and the dances, in a tent or private houses, were usually open to members' families and friends, with games often provided for children. Toasts and speeches lent a formal character to the meal, and the order and dignity of the public proceedings won general support for them from landlords and clergy, who contributed subsidies.[108] Their approval was no doubt strengthened by the manner in which the 'club day' sermons dwelt upon temperance, frugality, and self-improvement,[109] but the pleasure of some of the members was very clearly increased by discounting the first, at least, of those. An observer in central Oxfordshire in 1874 could comment that the dinners were invariably 'scenes of debauchery and drunkenness'.[110] Because of all these varied advantages, they gradually replaced the old-style ales and games in the middle part of the century, becoming standard all across the West Country, south and east Midlands, and Norfolk.

The excesses associated even with the 'club day' events caused a widespread campaign during the same period to provide yet more well-regulated attractions. This was waged by temperance societies and Bands of Hope, usually based in Baptist or Methodist chapels, and consisted usually of public teas with games and races provided for children. The societies also held processions of their own, organized railway excursions, concerts, and operatic recitals, and won support in turn from gentry and evangelical parish clergy. They achieved occasional local victories, such as at Wheatley near Oxford, where drinking and blood sports were completely ended at the Whitsun celebrations, and left an enduring rural institution in the shape of the village fete.[111] What destroyed the 'club days', however, was the convergence of two tremendous national forces. The first was the introduction of national insurance, which made the benefit clubs themselves redundant. The second was the general decline in communal village life. In 1871 the medieval Whitsun feasts had been given statutory recognition by the designation of the Monday as a Bank Holiday. Within sixty years, however, it had become essentially a day upon which people did not stay in the community to make merry, but got out of it, by car, train, bus, or bicycle, to the seaside or to beauty spots. The ancient summer games had become the modern summer vacation.

The local fete is the main vestige of them but there remain a few more self-consciously archaic representations. In 1979, for example, the villagers of Pulloxhill, on the chalk downs of Bedfordshire, revived the institution of a church ale. Most famous of the actual survivals of communal May feasts are two in Cornwall, which have gained their staying power partly from the former remoteness of the county and partly from their possession of customs which provoked particular excitement among folklorists. One is at Padstow, upon May Day, centred upon the hobby-horses described earlier. It retains very much the atmosphere of a traditional summer game, the 'horses' providing the entertainment, the streets being lined with green saplings at daybreak, and the song sung as the horses dance being a version of that performed by the nineteenth-century Mayers. The whole occasion is a formidable display of communal solidarity, symbolized by the passage of the model beasts through the whole of the little port, the closure of the town to all 'foreign' motor vehicles, and the conviction that only natives are allowed to wear white on that day. The other event, further west in the peninsula, is Helston Furry, held on or near 8 May. It is actually a dedication feast or wake, one of a type of celebration more common in late summer and to be described in a later chapter: the name derives from the Cornish *feur*, which in turn echoes the latin *feria*, signifying a holy day. Nevertheless, it has most of the characteristics of a May celebration, including the decorating of streets with greenery and flowers and the singing of a Mayer's carol by young people in the early morning. It was already celebrated as a local festival by 1600, but what has given it a peculiar fame, and a focus, in the last 200 years has been its retention of the last of the Cornish processional dances. During the eighteenth century these varied considerably in form, not least at Helston itself. In the nineteenth, however, the remaining example elsewhere, at Grampound, came to an end,[112] and in the early twentieth, those at Helston were both formalized and became nationally famous. They were held to conform to an ideal of antique integrity, and were regarded by some folklorists, upon no real evidence, as being among the most ancient dances in the British Isles. There are now four in all, two in the morning for adolescents and for children, a general one in the evening, and the Furry dance proper at noon. The latter consists of a long line of couples in late nineteenth-century formal evening dress, led by the mayor. It threads its way through the town, passing right through some houses and shops: a symbolic uniting of the community which, whatever the antiquity of the actual dance, fully represents the spirit of the old summer feasts and ales.[113]

25

MORRIS AND MARIAN

As part of his description of a Tudor 'summer lord', and of his followers, Philip Stubbes included the following details:

they bedeck themselves with scarfs, ribbons and laces hanged all over with gold rings, precious stones and other jewels: This done they tie about either leg 20 or 40 bells with rich handkerchieves in their hands, and sometimes laid across over their shoulders and necks, borrowed for the most part of their pretty Mopsies and loving Bessies, for bussying them in the dark. These things set in order, they have their hobby horses, dragons and other antiques, together with their bawdy pipers and thundering drummers, to strike up the Devil's Dance withal, then march these heathen company towards the church and churchyard, their pipers piping, drummers thundering, their stumps dancing, their bells jingling, their handkerchieves swinging about their heads like madmen, their hobby horses and other monsters skirmishing amongst the throng: and in this sort they go to the church (though the minister be at prayer or preaching) dancing and swinging their handkerchieves over their heads, in the church, like devils incarnate.[1]

The 'Devil's Dance' is, of course, the morris, the most famous of what are commonly termed the 'ritual dances' of England: those that are essentially for performance before an audience. Stubbes's portrait is one of the best from a period rich in literary references to it, including passages from plays, poems, ballads, sermons, and tracts.[2] By the age of Elizabeth I it was already the favourite festival dance of the English populace, and retained that distinction far into the nineteenth century. During the eighteenth, as scholars began to take an interest in popular customs, so they started to speculate upon the origins of this one. Between 1740 and 1807 Francis Peck, Joseph Strutt, and Francis Douce all agreed that the earliest records of it located it in fifteenth-century royal and princely courts.[3] They only differed over its point of origin, Peck and Douce arguing that the name derived from the word 'moorish', referring to the Arabs of Spain, and that therefore it was Spanish in origin. Strutt felt that it did not resemble any known Spanish dance and suggested that it had evolved from a courtly fool's entertainment. The issue was not taken any further until 1903, when Sir Edmund Chambers addressed it in the same work in which he had presented his very influential theories regarding the Mummers' Play and Sword Dance. His treatment of it was of a piece; he was too good an archival scholar to deny that the first records of the dance were from royal and aristocratic contexts, but he simply chose to ignore the implications of this evidence. Instead, once again influenced by the theories of

Sir James Frazer, he declared that it descended from an ancient folk rite to induce fertility. He suggested that the name 'moorish' derived from the use of blackened faces, a common motif in popular festivity, which could be compared to those of Arabs. Indeed, he proposed that the morris and the Sword Dance had once been identical, having come down from the same ancient ritual once found throughout western Europe.[4]

Chambers had very little sense of what morris was actually like, the only real fieldwork having been carried out in Oxfordshire for the Oxford don Percy Manning during the 1890s.[5] This was now to be considerably increased by the major figure in the revival of interest in folksong and dance, the London musician Cecil Sharp. His career will be considered further in Chapter 28 of the present book, but his influence upon perceptions of the history of morris was too important to postpone all discussion of him till then. As is well known, he first encountered the dance when staying with his mother-in-law at Headington near Oxford on Boxing Day 1899. He began to collect specimens of it in the mid-1900s and amassed over 150 different examples during the next twenty years. Initially, he accepted the antiquarian concept of it as a medieval courtly dance taken over by the people. By 1912, however, he had discovered Chambers's theory of it as a primitive folk ritual, and this suited him far better. For one thing it chimed with his own concept of rural popular culture as something communal and timeless. For another, it provided a weapon in his feud with Mary Neal. The latter was his principal partner in the early days of his teaching of morris, running the working-class girls' club in London's East End which provided the first teams to learn the dances. Indeed, he had only started to collect them because she had asked him for them. By 1909, however, they had quarrelled. It was partly a matter of personal jealousies, as each tried to take a due share of credit for the revival as it grew in scale. It was also, however, a question of principle, Neal arguing for development of the form and Sharp 'to conserve the morris in its purity.' His argument was considerably stronger if indeed it was the remnant of an ancient ritual, unchanged in its nature for centuries, and he proceeded to go beyond Chambers to assert that the Mummers' Play as well as the Sword Dance was an aspect 'of the same primitive rite'. If that rite excluded women, then it was even more perfectly suited to Sharp's current preoccupations: it can hardly be a coincidence that during this same period of conflict he emerged as an opponent of female suffrage and Neal as ardently supported it. By 1914 he had won the tussle and emerged as undisputed leader of the new folk-dance movement, while the wretched Mary Neal came to believe that morris had indeed been an ancient all-male ceremony, and that she had 'broken a law of cosmic ritual' by giving it to women.[6]

For the next sixty years the notion of the origins of morris put forward by Chambers and Sharp held sway among the public in general and among folk-dancers and folklorists in particular. The latter two (overlapping) groups carried out a very valuable amount of additional fieldwork and research into the recent history of the dance. It was, however, always interpreted within the same theoretical framework, authors differing only over the precise relationship between the different varieties of ritual dance and drama in their common descent from the religion of the Neolithic.[7] To preserve Sharp's definition of 'purity', upon his death in 1924 the English Folk Dance Society set up a Board of Artistic Control to vet all additions to the repertoire. Although the society was largely female, the board was two-thirds male and the most famous of all English folk-dances gradually became closed to women over the next two decades.[8] The situation achieved one logical result in the early 1950s, when William Everett may have passed off some fine dances of his own composition as the 'traditional' Lichfield morris, there being no other way of having them accepted.[9]

In 1956 Douglas Kennedy, in every other respect a devoted follower of Cecil Sharp, abolished the system of vetting in order to allow dances to evolve.[10] In the following year, Barbara Lowe published the first real attempt for one and a half centuries to examine the earliest records of the Morris.[11] Before 1500 she could find only three in England. The first is probably that in the will of Alice de Wetenhall, a widow of Bury St Edmunds and London. Dated 1458, its bequests included a silver cup 'sculpted with moreys dauns'. It is possible that an earlier one still is in the mid-fifteenth-century English translation of the Norman-French romance *The Knight of the Swan*, which described a royal revel including 'morishes'. In 1494 Henry VII's own court made the first of a series of payments for the performance of the 'Morrice Dance'. Barbara Lowe linked these records to Continental references to the same dance, spanning the same period and also invariably connected with courtly entertainments. She suggested that all reflected the same performance, a miniature romantic drama, in which a set of young male dancers competed for the hand of a lady, who chose instead to give her favours to a Fool. The dancers were distinguished by the wearing of bells and by the extraordinary energy of their movements. This entertainment was portrayed in a series of artistic works from France, the Netherlands, Germany, Austria, and Italy dating from the mid- and late fifteenth century, demonstrating its popularity among the ruling élites of the age.

She went on to document how the morris became one of the favourite court spectacles of the ageing Henry VII, and how the young Henry VIII, characteristically, continued it in a more lavish form. In his Christmas revels of 1515, held at Richmond palace, the 'moresks' were performed by five dancers and a fool, wooing two ladies personifying Beauty and Venus. The men wore a total of sixty bells 'from the King's store', suggesting that a stock had been laid up for the dance. Likewise, for the Christmas parties of the little princess Mary in 1522, her Lord of Misrule ordered nine morris 'coats' and 120 bells. The king also had the dance portrayed upon objects, such as the gold salt-cellar mentioned in an inventory of 1510, engraved with five morris dancers, a tabor-player, and a lady. After 1525 Henry and his entourage became bored with it at last, and dropped it from their seasonal repertoire, but by then it had become popular among his subjects. Lowe noted that it first appears in a municipal spectacle at London in 1504, when individual morris-men danced in the Midsummer Watch. During the same parade in 1521 a full company performed, and this was the pattern thereafter. Its first recorded appearance as a parish entertainment was at Kingston upon Thames, a Surrey market town close to the royal palaces along that stretch of the river (like Richmond), from which it might have been copied. The morris was launched there in 1507, with its full cast of dancers, fool, and lady, and it remained a favourite spectacle until the records of the town give out in the 1530s. During the course of the sixteenth century, Lowe discovered, it spread out to towns and villages across southern and midland England, changing seasons in the process to suit its new audience. Whereas it had featured at court during the winter festivities, it migrated to the summer ales and games which were the principal celebrations of local communities.

Barbara Lowe's essay was written specifically for what had by then become the English Folk Dance and Song Society, but its implications seem to have been utterly ignored. Instead the Cecil Sharp dogma remained paramount until the late 1970s, when it began to founder under the impact of two forces. One was the determination of some folklorists to reintroduce a scholarly rigour to their field, of which Roy Judge's book on the Jack in the Green was one of the first triumphs. The second, and perhaps more potent, was the influx of new participants in folk-dance resulting from the second major 'folk revival', of the 1960s. These people, mostly young and often radical in their politics, were not all disposed to accept without question the limitations imposed by an earlier generation—especially if they were women. A number of female or mixed-gender morris sides were formed in defiance of orthodoxy, and occasioned a debate in the letter columns of *English Dance and Song* in 1979–81. In self-defence, some of those who had breached tradition were themselves starting to appeal to history, pointing out, for example, that mixed and women's morris sides had been known in nineteenth-century Lancashire and Cheshire.

In 1978 Roy Dommett first formally questioned whether the origins of morris as a pagan fertility rite could ever actually be proved, and in 1980 A. G. Barrand opened a full-scale attack on that theory.[12] He drew attention to the apparently demonstrable fact that it had started as a court entertainment and moved out from the palaces to the capital and neighbouring towns before diffusing into the countryside. He also emphasized that it had not originally been attached to any particular season, and pointed out that Cecil Sharp himself had known of female morris dancers in the nineteenth century at Spelsbury in Oxfordshire and Blacknell in Worcestershire. To these examples could now be added three more cases from the same south midland area which Sharp had treated as archetypal in his characterization of the dance. These two thrusts of argument, concerning Sharp's use of evidence and the earliest historical records, were developed further in the 1980s. It was discovered that Sharp had arbitrarily selected certain local traditions of dance as typical. One of these, from Bidford in Warwickshire, turned out to have been created in the 1880s, by the romantic pageant master D'Arcy Ferris.[13] Another, from Winster in Derbyshire, was proved to have been designed in 1873 by the local antiquary Llewellyn Jewitt, who added favourite figures of his from other folk customs.[14] These dances had seemed so 'authentic' to Sharp precisely because they had been produced by nineteenth-century folklorists to represent what an ancient morris might have been. Research into the genuine history of the dance was carried forward considerably by John Forrest, who not only reiterated the evidence in favour of its origin as a courtly entertainment but suggested that its form had continued to evolve steadily over the intervening centuries.[15] At the end of the decade he and Michael Heaney founded the Early Morris Project, which confirmed Barbara Lowe's outline of its development while assembling over 700 references to the dance in England from 1458 to 1700, compared with her ninety records. Although their work awaits full publication, preliminary reports show the morris as being based primarily in royal and noble households from 1458 to 1540, in towns from 1540 to 1600, and in villages from 1600 onward. It was supported first by kingly and aristocratic patronage, then by guild and parish sponsorship, and then by money collected by teams in streets and from houses. It thus moved from the public to the private sphere and dispersed across England from the London area.[16]

Against this growing mountain of research, those who still wanted to believe in the immemorial pagan rite could only set the nineteenth-century argument of comparative data; that the modern English morris has certain features in common with other modern European folkdances and one (badly recorded) ancient Roman religious dance, and that therefore all must derive from a prehistoric ancestor.[17] Such protests could only be supported by comparable archival investigation into the history of the Continental dances, and none was attempted. Instead the proponents of the Cecil Sharp orthodoxy fell silent during the 1980s, at least in the scholarly folk-dance periodicals. Sandra Billington suggested that the morris was a renaming of pre-existing vigorous medieval dances known as routs and reyes but, as she was unable to ascertain the nature of these dances, her argument did not prove influential.[18] To an early modern historian, therefore, it does appear that the critics of the Chambers and Sharp thesis have won the day, at least at this point, having proceeded strictly according to the rules of historical evidence.

What may be emphasized here is the fact that the earliest model of the dance prescribed nothing except the cast of characters, the wearing of bells and elaborate coats by the dancers, and rapid movements in the performance. The first of these was certainly not immutable, as solo dancers were known by 1504, as said, and there is no sign of the fool or lady in the companies which appeared in most urban processions and some parish entertainments. The costumes also varied according to local taste. Michael Heaney has shown how the Kingston team were given special hats, coats, and shoes at the start in 1507, and had silver paper added to them in 1510. Nine years later they were all reclothed in satin, in 1522 they had fustian gold skins sewn on, and in 1538 their coats were specified as being green and white. Over the same period the number of dancers rose from four to six, and perhaps to nine.[19] Green and white had also, significantly, been the colours worn by the morrismen at nearby Richmond Palace in 1515, with many small pieces of copper sewn on their jackets and a total of twenty-nine dozen bells. The fool wore yellow sarsnet.[20] At Great Dunmow, a market town in Essex, the 'morres coat' bought in 1527 was by contrast black, while those acquired by Thame, Oxford-shire, in 1555, were yellow and green.[21] The team engaged by the Drapers Company of London in 1541 was simply to be 'well trimmed after the gorgeous fashion'.[22] Usually the morris coats paid for by Tudor parishes and trade guilds were of unspecified form, but they were clearly expensive pieces of equipment, worth storing carefully and hiring out.[23] During the Eliza-bethan period, as the dance became more commonly performed by teams of local youths hoping for rewards from onlookers, and less commonly spon-sored by institutions, the coats were less characteristic, and often replaced by the cheaper scarves, napkins, and handkerchiefs mentioned by Stubbes and other writers of the period.[24] Nevertheless, the costumes could still be elabo-rate, as demonstrated by a famous description of a morris side at Hereford in 1609. It consisted of four 'whiflers' with white and red staves to clear the way, a fiddler and a tabor-player, and twelve dancers. Musicans and dancers wore 'long coats of the old fashion, high sleeves gathered at the elbows and hanging sleeves behind'. They were red with white stripes, worn with white 'girdles' and stockings and white shoes with red roses. The dancers went in two files, the one in scarlet caps with white feathers, and the other with these colours reversed.[25] From this period around 1600, also, date the first artistic repre-sentations of the morris in England, confirming the impression of great variety within the common format of the energetic team dance, wearing bells.[26]

The comparable fates of the morris in Scotland and Ireland make an interesting contrast. The Scottish royal court took up the entertainment at the time that its popularity peaked at the English one: thus Gavin Douglas could write of courtiers in the 1510s:

> Sum singis, sum dancis, sum tellis storeis
> Sum lait at evin bringis in the moreis.[27]

When they lost interest in it, like their counterparts under Henry VIII, it failed to strike roots among commoners. An echo of it survived in the Glovers' Craft of Perth, who in 1633 performed a dance before Charles I which involved wearing bells on legs. The dancers also, however, carried shears and danced through each other's legs, so the bells are the only point of contact.[28] Otherwise the morris seems to have vanished in Scotland. In Ireland, which had no royal court at this period, there is no record of its performance before the nineteenth century, when a version of it existed in some southern and western districts.[29] Only in England, therefore, did it make the transition directly from an élite to a popular entertainment, and Michael Heaney seems to be correct in locating the crucial stage of that process in the 1560s. It was then that references to it multiply at a great rate in rural parishes across south-eastern England, and teams began to tour the countryside and visit gentry seats. The Port of London recorded the importation of 10,000 morris bells in 1567–8 alone, suggesting that demand was far outstripping native supply. By 1569 a broadside ballad could treat the dance as a customary part of popular celebration.[30]

Proponents of social and religious reform, such as Stubbes, were not therefore attacking an immemorial rural ritual when they denounced the morris. They were opposing a new fashion which was sweeping the nation's youth. Already in 1541 the evangelical Protestant writer Miles Coverdale could call it devilish, and associate it with vice,[31] and after 1570 its performers were increasingly prosecuted in both secular and ecclesiastical courts.[32] The charges tended to be for operating in the churchyard, or in service time, or for disturbing the peace, rather than for the dancing in itself.[33] None the less, respectable opinion turned against it to the extent that parishes or guilds increasingly gave up sponsorship of it during the later reign of Elizabeth. Instead, it continued to burgeon in popularity among independent teams, usually of young men. Elizabethan and Jacobean drama repeatedly makes the point that those from London and the surrounding villages competed with each other for a greater share of profits from the public and the honour of their communities. They did so by displaying the remarkable physical stamina and dexterity which the dance demanded, and sometimes by feats which have long since died out, such as using bells of different tones which could be rung in a melodious sequence as the wearers leaped.[34] Morris was never banned in England and, although it did become scarcer at the apogee of godly reform during the Interregnum,[35] there are certainly records of it during this period.[36] With the Restoration, it passed out of the realm of controversy.

During the early nineteenth century, the dance vanished from the London area much as the maypoles had done,[37] and by the middle of that century it persisted as four distinctive regional traditions. By far the most famous and best-studied was that centred upon northern Oxfordshire and found also in the neighbouring parts of adjacent counties. It should best, perhaps, be called 'South Midland', as the term 'Cotswold', attached to it by the morris revival, is geographically inaccurate. It was especially associated with the week after Whitsun, when teams toured villages, gentry seats, and fairs. The traditions of dance were passed down through artisan and labouring families; a small rural community such as Adderbury fielded as many as three teams at once. Music was provided by a pipe and tabor, and dancers tended to wear black box hats, white shirts, bells, and cord breeches or black or white trousers. The hats were decorated with flowers and ribbons, and the shirts with brightly hued ribbons and rosettes, often in team colours. The performers generally numbered from six to twelve, and their performances were extremely varied, some using sticks and some handkerchiefs, while solo jigs were also common. Around 1850 there were perhaps eighty teams in the south Midlands. By 1900, six existed, and of those only one (at Bampton) had survived continuously. Rural depopulation and the end of many traditional village revels played a large part in this decline, but Sharp's informants thought that the decisive factor had been the loss of rich patrons; the gentry had finally got tired of the morris.[38]

In Lancashire and Cheshire, by contrast, it became associated with the late summer custom of rush-bearing. The linkage was already made at Whalley in 1617, and became general in the eighteenth century, turning the dance into one performed as part of a procession. At Manchester in the 1830s between fifty and a hundred morrismen were seen at once, 'all in uniform white dress decorated with ribbons'. Later in the nineteenth century costume tended to become more elaborate, some teams sporting straw hats, black breeches, diagonal sashes, white shirts and stockings, and black shoes or clogs, and carrying wands with coloured streamers, or handkerchiefs, or 'slings' of white cotton. Music was generally provided by bands. A minimum of twenty out of the forty-eight teams recorded in Cheshire 1880–1914 definitely included women, a higher proportion than any recorded elsewhere. The dances them-selves were extremely varied, belonged to individuals rather than localities, and evolved continually. All were traditionally in figures of four, so teams had to be in multiples of that number. During the mid-nineteenth century they successfully broke loose from the dying tradition of rush-bearing, and sur-vived relatively well through the medium of local competitions until they were absorbed into the national revival of folk-dancing. This both ensured the preservation of the tradition and petrified it, for in the 1920s judges imposed a single style.[39]

Another notable region for survival of the dance was comprised by Wor-cestershire, Herefordshire, and Shropshire, across all of which it is recorded in the nineteenth century. Today this tradition is called 'Welsh Border Morris', another partial misnomer as it was rarest near the border itself. The perfor-mances here were unusual in that they were most common at Christmas, especially in hard winters when the labourers who produced them badly needed extra money. Another distinction was that the dancers generally had blackened faces and carried sticks. Instead of ribbons, gaudy rags were usually employed to decorate shirts, while the few teams who carried it on in the early twentieth century took to wearing fancy dress.[40] Nineteenth-century Wales had its own flourishing tradition of *dawnsio haf* (summer dancing) or *dawns y fedwen* (dance of the birch branch) in May and early June. The performers often wore ribboned shirts and hats, black velvet breeches, and grey stockings, and held handkerchiefs. In Denbighshire and Flintshire they went on their circuits carrying borrowed silverware hung upon a frame of white linen fixed to a pole, like the decorated rush-carts of neighbouring Cheshire and Lanca-shire.[41] In addition, the morris clearly influenced the costume of some parti-cipants in the Plough Monday celebrations in East Anglia, discussed in Chapter 11.

All this has been to ignore the addition of one other long-established character to the morris dance: the man–woman. 'She' came out of a parallel entertainment in the early Tudor May games, the plays about Robin Hood. From the beginning of scholarly investigation into the legends about the outlaw, it had been obvious that at the end of the Middle Ages he had been celebrated in these plays as well as in ballads. Two very different approaches to research into his legend were proposed in response. The first, by Joseph Ritson in 1795, assumed that Robin had been a real human being; the second, started by Thomas Wright in 1837, opined that he was originally a woodland spirit, or god, honoured in the May revels.[42] This latter argument gained more support in the early twentieth century. Douglas Kennedy and Lord Raglan suggested that he had been the dying and returning god of vegetation postu-lated by Sir James Frazer as a universal focus of devotion in ancient religion. Margaret Murray, copied by Robert Graves and Pennethorne Hughes, hailed him as the high priest of a coven of pagan witches, representing the horned god of nature worshipped by the 'witch cult' which she believed to have existed in medieval Europe. Maid Marian, according to this view, was the 'maiden' of his coven. These writers made scme impact, among folklorists in particular, until 1955, when the magnificent Barbara Lowe pointed out that they were quite incompatible with a study of the earliest plays and ballads. In these the outlaw rarely had twelve companions (making a coven), wore more colours than green, was a faithful attender of mass, had a devotion to the Virgin Mary, and died old and sordidly. Maid Marian did not appear in his tales until a relatively late stage, and Robin's medieval and Tudor representa-tions were of a thoroughly human character, wielding the favourite national weapon. Medieval historians subsequently endorsed these arguments, and departed upon an exciting quest for the 'real' Robin Hood and an ultimately more practicable one for the audience at which his tales were aimed.

As part of this work it was argued that the ballads seemed to predate the plays, the surviving examples of which were based upon them, and the latter were not studied in their own right until 1981, when David Wiles produced the standard account.[43] He found evidence of them at twenty-seven communities between 1474 and 1588, most of them market towns in southern England, from Kent to Cornwall and (more thinly scattered) in the Midlands.[44] They seemed to be missing from the northern counties in which the action was set, perhaps (he considered) because there it was too close to reality. He found an early occurrence of one at Exeter in 1427, and a very late one, at Enstone in the fringe of the Oxfordshire Cotswolds, in 1652. In general, however, they flourished in the late fifteenth and early sixteenth century, were in full decline under Elizabeth, and had become a memory by the early Stuart period. He attributed this fate to the hostility of Protestant churchmen, and also to changing fashion as the morris replaced the plays as the centre-piece of the May games. David Wiles also made the point that the outlaw always had his own 'company', separate from the morris dancers, and that its principal function was to raise money, in most recorded examples for parish funds. At Kingston upon Thames the 'Robin Hood game' lasted five days. Village Robins tended to make tours of the surrounding district instead; one from Tewkesbury got fifteen miles, to Worcester, in 1519. Dr Wiles also emphasized that the character's fund-raising activities were effective precisely because he was so closely associated with summer, greenery, and careless pleasure. He made an ideal summer lord, and his 'companies' were likewise made up of a community's young men. Certain stock characters were often represented in it: Little John (from the beginning) and Friar Tuck and Maid Marian (after 1500). In small parishes the 'game' seems simply to have been a procession, but elsewhere it was clearly a full-blown play. At Chagford, on the fringe of Dartmoor, the performers spent heavily upon bows and arrows and borrowed the little town's militia armour.

Subsequent research, including that for the present book, has served to confirm most of David Wiles's findings, and to extend them in the following ways. First, concerning origins. It is now known that the outlaw was already famous by 1262 and that the earliest surviving ballads were composed in the fourteenth century, most probably in its second half.[45] By contrast, the first date for a play is still 1427,[46] so it is difficult to support, if also absolutely to refute, the idea that the ballads arose from the games. What can be said with certainty is that the latter became linked to parish finance in the 1470s, very much like Hocktide bindings, and rapidly became adopted for this end over a very wide area. The theme also seems to have become more fashionable altogether at this time, so that in the early part of the decade servants played Robin and the sheriff of Nottingham in Sir John Paston's household near the Norfolk coast.[47] Curiously enough, the plays never feature in the surviving records of East Anglian parishes, and are equally absent from those of cities and of large towns, with the exception of Exeter and Bristol. Additions to David Wiles's sample of material extend his picture of a fashion for them which began in the Thames valley, and spread across to the West Country before the end of the fifteenth century.[48] They reached a peak of popularity in the period 1500–30, when they were found across southern England, but they continued to burgeon in the western and midland counties through the middle of the century, and they reached Lancashire during this period.

Interest in the outlaw spread socially as well as geographically. If the morris travelled outwards from royal and aristocratic households, so Robin Hood plays made the opposite journey. Having appeared in parishes and the homes of country gentry, they reached the court of Henry VIII in 1510, when Robin and Marian both featured in an entertainment. In 1515, when Henry and his

Reports of Robin Hood plays

1 1470–1500
2 1500–1550
3 1550–1600

MAP 5. Range of reports of Robin Hood plays

queen made their celebrated May Day excursion to Shooter's Hill, they were met by 200 of the royal guard, dressed in green as the Merry Men. They fired a salute of arrows and led off their sovereign (as King Edward was led in the most famous tale) to feast with Robin in the woods, within an arbour of branches decorated with flowers and aromatic herbs. The company included Lady May and her retinue, Little John, Friar Tuck, and Maid Marian. Kingston's 'game' had all of these except Lady May. Its Robin and Little John always wore special coats, the friar a russet habit, and Marian a hooded cloak and gloves. In 1520 Robin and John had satin jackets lined with canvas, while their fourteen followers were in dark green coats. They seem to have handed out 'liveries', like a May lord's retinue, to those who gave them money: in most years between 3,000 and 4,000 of these had to be provided, so the crowds drawn by them, even spread over five days, must have been large. Villages, on the other hand, not only had to send their Robins on tour, but sometimes needed to pool their resources to equip one and his band. Thus in 1498 three in Staffordshire did so in order to raise money for their churches at a local fair. Unhappily, the venture ended in a riot which cost lives, and this illustrates the drawback of the plays; that they could encourage serious misbehaviour. In 1509 the corporation of Exeter banned them altogether, and the Lord Warden of the Cinque Ports of Kent and Sussex did the same in 1528. There is no sign, however, that these orders affected their overall popularity, and that at Exeter was blatantly flouted within seven years.[49]

The fashion for Robin Hood entertainments got to Scotland, naturally enough, rather later. There is no mention of the stories until the 1420s, almost two centuries after the first reference to Robin in England, and the earliest record of a play is at Edinburgh in 1492. In the following decade they became a craze, of an intensity apparently exceeding the response in England because it took in most of the major towns. At Aberdeen in May 1508 the corporation excitedly ordered all able men to process behind Robin and Little John 'with their arrayment made in green and yellow, bows, arrows, and all other convenient things'. Ten years later the mighty earl of Arran stiffly refused an invitation from Edinburgh to accept the office of 'Litiljohn' and 'make sports and jocosities in the town'. During the next forty years Robin and his cronies presided over the summer revels at these towns and at Ayr, Dumfries, Dundee, Peebles, and Perth. He also appeared at the royal court. In 1555, however, he and John occupied places in the list of summer festivities forbidden by a nervous Parliament. The result was a prolonged struggle. During the 1560s the Crown and corporations had to issue orders, and the watch be called out, to prevent the appearance of the hero in Edinburgh and Aberdeen. After then he was confined to smaller towns such as Dumfries, Dalkeith, Cranston, Haddington, and St Andrews, but into the 1590s the General Assembly of the Kirk had to keep denouncing his revels. His last recorded appearance was at Linton in the Tweed valley, in 1610, when he was played by a local gentleman, indicating that the provincial social élite still lent him some support. After that the forces of government and clergy seem finally to have triumphed over him, as over the May games in general.[50]

In England there was no such proscription. In the late 1530s one of the government's propagandists and reformist intellectuals, Sir Richard Morison, suggested that the king issue one because the plays celebrated resistance of royal officials, but he was ignored.[51] They certainly suffered from the general hostility to revelry manifested by godly Protestants, but maypoles, morris, and wakes all came through that and the plays did not. It seems that entertainments devoted to the deeds of a single hero had a limited life and were especially vulnerable to changes of taste. The royal court forgot him after 1515, his presence along the Thames was thinning during the next decade, as said, and he faded from the scene almost completely two generations later. Not every community took to him even in his heyday: the village of Tintinhull, Somerset, lying in the arable lowlands of a county where the plays were very popular, attempted one 'only this once' in 1513.[52] When he made his departure, he left behind him Maid Marian, to the morris dance.

She was not, strictly speaking, his to bequeath: rather, they both seem to have come together in the May games. Sir Edmund Chambers traced her to thirteenth-century French pastoral lyrics, in which Robin and Marian were conventional names for shepherd and shepherdess lovers. Before the end of that century an Arras troubadour had turned their story into a play, and Sir Edmund suggested that this, or a successor, was eventually carried to England and blended with the Robin Hood tales in the May games.[53] There she was not necessarily Robin's lady, for she is partnered with the friar in a play designed for the games and printed by Copland in the 1550s.[54] Nevertheless, Chambers's theory has not been challenged by any more likely explanation, and it may well lie behind the undoubted fact that Robin Hood and Marian appear together for the first time in the lavish entertainments at Kingston in 1509. This was two years after Robin and the morris had been recorded there, and Marian may already have been present then as the 'lady' noted as being among the performers; her costume, of Kendal green fringed with satin, was hired in 1508.[55] By 1519 she and Robin both danced with the morris there, and if she slowly came thereafter to be associated with the hero in the ballads, she also came to supply the place of the nameless 'lady' in the original morris, till by the late sixteenth and early seventeenth centuries she was an almost indispensable part of it.[56]

Why, then, did Robin depart from the dance and Marian remain? Apparently because she became a comic figure, providing light relief to the performance together with the fool who survived from the original entertainment. At Kingston until 1516 she was played by a real woman, but thereafter a man took the role. Elizabethan Marians were invariably male, and moreover generally beefy lads thoroughly unconvincing as transvestites, providing a rough and boisterous humour. A tract of 1589 depicted 'the Maid-Marian, trimly dressed up in a cast gown, and a kercher ... his face handsomely muffled with

MORRIS AND MARIAN ·

a diaper napkin to cover his beard, and a great nose-gay in his hand', while the fool 'dances round him in a cotton coat, to court him with a leathern pudding and a wooden ladle'.[57] The ladle was to collect money from the crowd;[58] to this horseplay the gallant courtly dance had come. Likewise, at Redbourne in central Hertfordshire, the Marian would come into church at service time to kiss people and make them laugh.[59] David Wiles suggested that the change of gender of the 'original' festival Marian at Kenilworth may have been because it was considered improper for a woman to dance in a male troupe as the character was now required to do.[60] This is quite possible; it is also so that both the lady of the court morris and the Marian of the French pastoral were swiftly assimilated to a very old popular tradition of festive transvestism, manifested (perhaps) in the 'old woman' of the ancient mid-winter celebrations.

Both the fool and the Marian, at any rate, had a long career in the history of the dance but, whereas the latter was the more prominent in the Elizabethan and early Stuart periods, the former was much more so by the nineteenth century. As the 'squire', he presided over Oxfordshire morris teams, carrying a leather sandbag and dried oxtail with which he cleared a way through the crowds.[61] As the 'Cadi' he was orator and buffoon of the north-east Welsh *dawnsio*, dressed in male coat and waistcoat and female petticoats, with face masked or painted black and red.[62] In the west midland and Welsh Marcher counties he also had a painted face, plus a furry hat, a bell on his back, an inflated bladder on a stick, and a collecting ladle.[63] Only in the processional morris of the north-west was his role largely redundant and his presence rare.[64] By contrast, the man–woman (not now called Marian) was only found in the south Midland and north-western sides, and was not universal there. He was, however, much more prominent in some other customs such as Plough Monday gatherings, to which perhaps he had migrated from the morris.

During the period in which this book was being written, research into the history of the morris has continued at a faster pace than ever before, and two major contributions to it have appeared. One comprises a part of Georgina Boyes's study of the twentieth-century 'folk revival', being a scorching por-trayal of the class and gender prejudices embodied by many of the leading figures of the phenomenon, including Sharp. She has proved that although he went a great way towards doing so, Sharp himself never decisively repudiated the participation of women in the morris. This was left to one of his disciples, and a moving spirit behind the propagation of the dance in the 1920s and 1930s, Rolf Gardiner. He was an advocate of the renewal of Britain through charismatic male leadership, who initially applauded the progress of the Nazi party in Germany. His writings frequently expressed a contempt and distaste for women, and to him the morris was 'the dance of men, sworn to manhood, fiery ecstasy, ale, magic and fertility'. It was under his influence that the dancers became, for the first time, commonly known as 'morris men'.[65] The other important recent addition to the history of the dance is Keith Chandler's survey of its development in the south Midlands since 1660. It was associated with the Early Morris Project, and contributed the information that, as the cup mentioned in the will of 1458 might have been imported, the first certain reference to the dance in England comes in an account of a Christmas entertainment in the household of Sir John Arundell, at Lanherne, Cornwall, in 1466. In the eighteenth and nineteenth centuries it was very much an entertainment provided by the poorer members of the rural working class (carters, shepherds, woodmen, and, above all, 'labourers', a term which could cover many tasks), to raise extra money. Aristocrats, gentry, farmers, tradesmen, and clergy were all valuable sponsors, and any communal festivity was likely to attract a side of dancers. The latter arose in all sizes of communities but, even where there was a family tradition of dancing, few people performed annually and teams were often put together as need and inclination arose. Most were male, but some composed entirely of women are recorded. Groups tended to pass on their own dances, while keeping to a fairly standard size, of six dancers with one in reserve, plus fool, collector, and musician with pipe and tabor drum in the eighteenth century and fiddle thereafter. The core costume of white shirt, breeches or trousers, and stockings, was also a constant, white trousers replacing black kneebreeches after 1800. The dance declined rapidly after the middle of the nineteenth century, partly because of growing social divisions, but also because both patrons and performers increasingly regarded it as outmoded.[66]

It may be concluded, therefore, that down to the twentieth century the story of the morris dance in England has been one of constant evolution and adaptation, according to period, region, and social class. It is hard to argue from all this that it has ever possessed an 'authentic' form, still less that it represents an unchanging and ancient rite. The tale of the dance is, rather, one of a triumph of versatility.

ROGATIONTIDE AND PENTECOST

᠆ᢍ᠅᠍ᢒᢍ᠊

As the secular rejoicing of early summer got under way, so the religious calendar proceeded. By the year 305 the Church in the western Roman empire had started to celebrate an annual commemoration of Pentecost, the inspiration of Christ's apostles by the Holy Ghost. It had become a major event by the opening of the fifth century, being held upon the seventh Sunday after Easter, while the sixth Thursday was set aside to mark the ascension of Christ into heaven. Both were joyous occasions for a lovely season, and before the end of that century the clergy at Vienne in Gaul had begun to tie their activities still more tightly to the agricultural year by processing around the fields on the days before the feast of the Ascension to bless the growing crops.[1] The latter rite was regulated in England by canons passed at the ecclesiastical council of Cloveshoo in 747, one of the most important meetings of the young English Church. They gave the processions the name of Rogations, from the Latin *rogare*, 'to ask', and fixed them as belonging to the Monday, Tuesday, and Wednesday before Ascension Day. They also ordered that the people who processed should fast until noon, and should not accompany the ceremony 'with games, and horse races, and great banquets', as hitherto, but to walk 'with fear and trembling, with the sign of Christ's passion and of our eternal redemption carried before them, together with the relics of saints'.[2] The walking and blessing of the fields had a clear pagan progenitor, in the festival of the Ambarvalia at Rome which had followed exactly this pattern.[3] It may be that there was an Anglo-Saxon equivalent, which is suggested by the tradition of sports and feasts, or it is possible that the Ambarvalia were Christianized and introduced to Britain, where they rapidly became popular.

During the next 700 years occasional glimpses are caught of the development of these feasts and ceremonies. By the eleventh century Pentecost had already acquired its enduring English nickname of Whit Sunday or Whitsun, which has baffled scholars ever since. The most likely explanation is that the festival was a notable time for baptisms, and white was the customary colour of baptismal robes.[4] Medieval writers made their own guesses; thus the four-teenth-century monk John Mirk suggested that the name came from the giving of wit to the disciples by the Holy Ghost.[5] Reference to parish processions at Whitsun or in the preceding week abound in the statutes and mandates of reforming prelates between 1200 and 1320.[6] In that period, too, the boundaries of parishes were fixed, all over England, making it possible for the Rogation processions to become a communal perambulation of them as well as a blessing of the crops.[7] In the 1230s Robert Grosseteste, bishop of Lincoln, complained to his archdeacons of the manner in which they had become so much an expression of parochial pride, the people marching behind their local church's cross and banners, that they were being attacked by members of rival communities.[8] It was perhaps this problem that had caused the corporation of London, in the middle of the previous century, to proclaim that the Crown itself would prosecute anybody who caused disorder on Rogation Days 'as soon as the crosses are out of church'.[9] By the next generation after Grosseteste, the Rogation rituals were certainly carried out even in remote upland regions: the church of Gisburn, in the centre of the Pennines, was burned down in 1288 by a fire started when a plumber heated his tools while all the clergy were away in the fields singing the litanies.[10]

As parish records multiply during the fifteenth and early sixteenth centuries, so a much better picture of the custom emerges. The Rogation Days were now also known as Cross or Gang Days, the former from the carrying of the cross and banner and the latter signifying 'going', in the sense of going round. Urban churchwardens' accounts, such as those of London, Bristol, Reading, Chester, Oxford, Salisbury, Dover, and Tavistock, and some from villages in Norfolk, Cambridgeshire, Lincolnshire, Essex, and Worcestershire, record charges for ringing the bells during the processions, payments in cash or food to those who carried the holy objects, and sometimes the cost of a meal for all who took part.

Most of the rural accounts, however, do not, although religious law made the rites compulsory and John Mirk could claim that to avoid going on the processions was as bad a sin as avoiding church. A quick glance at diocesan records reveals very few cases of alleged neglect of them: three in the largest diocese of all, that of Lincoln, during the years 1517–20. The Norwich consistory court heard just one report of a fault in the processions between 1499 and 1530, and that was a denunciation of some building work which had blocked the route of one. This may, of course, be evidence not of widespread implementation of the ceremony but of widespread indifference to it, and reluctance to report neglect. The evidence of wills is inconclusive, for in contrast with the hundreds of bequests to the Easter sepulchre in early Tudor Northamptonshire, there survive only seven in that county (from five parishes) for entertainment of Rogation processions. None the less, the custom is very widely recorded in rural parishes after the Reformation, when better sources for its distribution exist, and then refreshments for those on the walk were commonly provided by those who lived along the way, leaving no charge to the common fund. It seems most probable that this had always been the case, and that villages were the more ready to offer hospitality because they, unlike townspeople, had crops to be blessed.[11]

There are a few unusually clear representations of the ritual in progress during the reigns of the first Tudors. At St Edmund, Salisbury, parishioners carried seventeen banners depicting saints and scenes from the life of Christ. The people in the procession were described as being boys and men, and they were rewarded in some years with bread and ale and in others with cash.[12] At Durham the monks of the cathedral filed, singing, to one of the town's parish churches upon each of the three days, and one of their number delivered a sermon.[13] Richard Taverner provides a contemporary account of a rural perambulation, with 'certain gospels read in the wide field amongst the corn and grass, that by the virtue and operation of God's word, the power of the wicked spirits which keep in the air may be laid down, and the air made clean, to the intent the corn may remain unharmed'.[14]

Upon the Thursday, Ascension Day, the early Tudor records show that church bells were rung again, while the paschal candle, which had burned through the services of Easter week and upon all the holy days since, was lighted for the last time and then removed as a sign that Christ had now gone up to heaven. London churches were decked with garlands, a custom not recorded elsewhere. At Durham the cathedral clergy processed around the town carrying gold and silver crosses and the relics of saints. They wore copes, or mantles, that of the Prior being golden. Other processions upon this feast are recorded in parishes at Oxford, Salisbury, and Bungay.[15]

Ten days later, at Whitsun, more people paraded. Many of them belonged to parish churches appropriated by cathedrals or religious houses, who were expected at this time to journey with their priests to these parent institutions, and make offerings. The latter, normally in money, were commonly called 'Pentecostals', or 'smoke farthings', the latter term deriving from the fact that they were due from parishioners who possessed at least one chimney.[16] In some cathedrals and parish churches, the Holy Ghost itself appeared at the services, in the form of a white dove let through a hole in the ceiling. The records do not make clear whether it was a model bird or a real one, although common sense favours the former idea. It seems to have been a rare custom, but one widely scattered across the eastern part of the country, being recorded at Lincoln cathedral, the tiny fishing port of Walberswick in Suffolk, the prosperous Lincolnshire market town of Louth, and the London church of St Mary at Hill.[17]

This afternoon, and the two days following, were (as said) the favourite time for the holding of church ales and May games. Processions were less common, being held much more widely at Rogationtide, just past, and at Corpus Christi and Midsummer Eve, to come. In four county towns, however, Whitsun became the occasion for some of the most splendid of all. At Leicester in the early sixteenth century the parishioners of St Mary le Castro and of St Martin made their way to the town's third church, of St Mary Magdalen. The former carried the image of the Virgin, richly robed and crowned, beneath a canopy supported by four of them. She was preceded by minstrels and followed by statues of the twelve Apostles, or perhaps by people dressed to represent them, their names fixed to their bonnets. Then came the unmarried young women, and fourteen men carrying banners. The parishioners of St Martin naturally carried their own patron, and another set of Apostles. Both processions made offerings at the altar of St Mary Magdalen, and then were paid or feasted by their respective churchwardens. At Exeter in the fifteenth century a 'May' and a model elephant were carried through the streets; how far these festivities continued into the early Tudor period is concealed by the failure of the sequence of accounts. The Chester Corpus Christi play was moved to Whit Monday at some time after 1474, and by 1519 had grown into a cycle of biblical pageants provided by the craft guilds. Between 1521 and 1532 these evolved further, into a sequence of twenty-four different subjects requiring the two following days in addition. Norwich in the same period had a Whitsun cycle of eleven subjects, spread over the Monday and Tuesday. They ranged from 'The Creation' to 'The Holy Ghost', and included an 'Ark' and a view of hell. That of the Grocers was mounted upon a cart hung with cloths and drawn by four horses. At both Norwich and Chester the pageants made a wide circuit of the city and seem to have included some spoken drama. At Norwich it is recorded that crowds poured in from the countryside to enjoy the spectacle, and upon the Tuesday the corporation appointed a Lord of Misrule to devise further festivities.[18]

There are no comparable records to prove how far the same complex of early summer rituals existed in Scotland. That in England survived the Reformation of Henry VIII easily enough, but fell foul of the far more Protestant one of the duke of Somerset. To committed followers of the reformed faith the blessing of material objects, even crops, was a perversion of religion, while the use of crosses as parochial boundary marks, at which the Rogation processions halted to sing and pray, could make the perambulations seem almost as much rituals of idolatry as the carrying of saints' images at Whitsuntide. No formal decree abolished the processions at either time, but they withered in the face of official disapproval. Payments for the Rogation processions vanish from churchwardens' accounts in the years 1547–9. The Greyfriars Chronicle states that the perambulations in London were stopped in 1548 because of the government's hostility, while Robert Parkyn, a curate serving in rural south Yorkshire, stated that none took place in his district either during that May, because the crosses at which they halted were being thrown down. Only at Long Sutton in the Lincolnshire Fens is there any record of them during that year, and after then they ceased there as well. In the next three years many parishes, in both town and country, sold off the banners which had been carried on them. In 1548 the same expression of official feeling stopped the Whitsun processions at London, and one of the most elaborate of those recorded in the provinces, at Leicester, was also abandoned; the images of saints carried in them had been prohibited by a royal order in February. The pageants or plays at Norwich went into abeyance in 1547, and only the Chester cycle, shorn of passages offensive to Protestant ears, survived as a memorial to the religious rites of early summer.[19]

Then came the accession of Mary, who encouraged a general revival of the processions in 1554, and sent many of her own clergy to bless London at Rogationtide, carrying garlands and followed by banners, torches, musicians, choristers, and the sacrament carried under a canopy. The garrison of the Tower accompanied its priests around St Katherine's Fields. Bishop Bonner insisted that all the City churches have their banners ready for the processions, and this is faithfully reflected in their surviving records for 1554. The Rogation Day ceremony is also recorded during Mary's reign at Westminster, Chester, Leicester, Bristol, Salisbury, and eighteen market towns and villages scattered across southern England and the Midlands. As before, it is very likely that in most rural communities participants did not require material reward and parish funds were not needed to provide refreshment. Whitsun processions are likewise recorded in the same measure as before, being found at York, Leicester, Bristol, and London. It is notable, however, that the famous Leicester examples were revived only with greatly reduced expenses. At Norwich the pageants were restored in 1556, while the Chester plays were rewritten, apparently to include Catholic material once more.[20]

The process was, of course, reversed as soon as Elizabeth acceded. At the first Whitsun of her reign, 1559, there was 'no solemnity' at Norwich. In 1563, however, having apparently realized that her Reformation was somewhat more moderate than that of Edward, the Grocers' Company agreed to set forth its pageant. To play safe, this was presented not at the usual feast but to mark the retirement of the current mayor. Emboldened by this, the City assembly decided the next year to relaunch the full Whitsun cycle; but at that point something went wrong, and thereafter the pageants never seem to have appeared again.[21] What might have happened is abundantly documented at Chester, where the trick of rewriting the play scripts to suit a new religious regime was repeated yet again. This won the co-operation of the dean and chapter of the cathedral, who continued the customary gift of beer to the players. It was not enough, however, for the zealous Protestants of the ecclesiastical commission of the province of York, led by Archbishop Grindal. From the moment of its formation in the early 1570s this attempted to obtain the suppression of the plays, and in 1575 it succeeded, by the crude tactic of having the mayor summoned before the Privy Council to explain himself.[22] This put a complete end to traditional Whitsuntide ceremonial, the purely religious processions having been forbidden by the government in its initial set of injunctions, during 1559.[23]

Those same injunctions made a classic Elizabethan compromise in the matter of the Rogation Day perambulations; they ordained that these could continue, but only as a tour of the parish boundaries to keep the latter maintained and fixed in mind. The minister was to wear secular dress, and neither hand-bells nor cross nor banners were to be carried. Subsequent visitation articles issued by leading churchmen required parish clergy to make an annual inspection of the bounds, with, in the instruction by Grindal, 'none other ceremony than to say in English the two psalms beginning "Benedic anima mea Domino…" and such sentences of scripture as shall be appointed by the Queen's Majesty's Injunctions, with the litany and suffrages following the same, and reading one Homily already devised and set forth for that purpose'.[24] Grindal's formulation was the most common under Elizabeth, but by no means universal. All bishops agreed that the clergy and leading men of the parish should be present, and say the psalms and prayers. Some, however, omitted the litany and suffrages, and some specified that the churchwardens and parish clergy, or local youth, should attend.[25] The tradition thus created was deeply ambiguous, for the walk was now supposed to be practical in its nature and ends, and yet the presence of the minister and the use of a liturgy (still, moreover, one of blessing) preserved its nature as a sacred occasion.

Some of the confusion immediately created was illustrated in the tribulations of an Essex minister, Richard Kechyn, who observed the new forms in his benefice, including with them the local customs that women joined the walk and that all participants ended it with a dinner at which the poor were entertained. Then, in 1564, a 'hotter' sort of Protestant cleric visited to preach from nearby Bocking, and claimed that the presence of women was against the law and that the meal was a 'feast of Bacchus'. Poor Kechyn had to appeal to his superiors for advice.[26] In the same year the wardens of the parish of Stanford, in Berkshire's White Horse vale, were in trouble with the archdeacon because they had taken a streamer on perambulation and were told that this could fall into the interdicted category of a banner.[27] After the middle of the decade, 'conservative' infringements of the rulings seem to have vanished, but Protestant objections continued from time to time. In Cheshire, Essex, Nottinghamshire, and Cambridgeshire, parsons or laity thought that the perambulation was in itself too 'popish' to be acceptable. The most outspoken was the parishioner at Westlebury in Essex during the 1565 procession, who pointed to a boundary marker and asked: 'Is there an idol here to be worshipped that you have a drinking?' Such incidents, however, were very rare, numbering one or two per county in this little sample over the whole reign. More common was neglect, resulting from squabbles between the minister and the parish élite, or the blocking of the route by a new hedge or ditch, or because of a lack of interest on the part of cleric, or laity, or both. The situation was worst in towns, where parochial boundaries were often badly defined. Three Colchester parishes threw up accusations more often than any others in Essex. Likewise, in 1597 some twenty-five out of 542 questioned in a visitation of Norfolk were slack in perambulating, but eight of these were in the city of Norwich. East Suffolk seems to have had exceptionally severe problems, even in rural areas, for out of 260 parishes which responded to the same visitation, thirty-five had ceased to keep the custom, while in sixteen more the minister did not take part. Such a situation seems, even given the lack of comparable source material for the earlier period, to have been a creation of the Reformation, undermining support for the old ceremony. None the less, the fact that so many people were prepared to report breaches, and that they apparently did not occur in the great majority of parishes, indicates that it was still widely respected.[28]

This pattern underwent significant developments under the early Stuarts. Diocesan records reveal many cases of neglect, some of it derived from principle. In 1631, for example, William Brudenell was appointed to the northern Oxfordshire parish of Deddington. He was horrified to find that his new flock expected him to wear his surplice while on the walk (contrary to the Elizabethan regulations), and to read the gospel at the customary mark of a cross cut in the earth. Subsequently he refused to go at all. Clergy such as he, however, were very scarce. In the archdeaconry of Lewes (most of East Sussex) between 1581 and 1641, only a single parson is recorded as refusing to go on perambulation. In the diocese of Bath and Wells (most of Somerset), eight failed to do so in the period from 1625 to 1640, but of these one was ill, one lame, one under arrest, and one prevented by a boundary dispute. Examples of damage to boundary markers or the withdrawal of traditional hospitality, although much more common, are still not very numerous. The archdeaconry of Chichester (most of West Sussex) threw up fourteen complaints of any kind regarding the custom during the 1620s. Of fifty-five Cambridgeshire parishes which made visitation returns in 1638, every single one claimed to observe it. No early Stuart diocesan archive yet studied reveals anything like the degree of neglect documented in Elizabethan Suffolk. In Essex, where excellent comparable records for the two periods exist, they indicate better performance in the latter one.[29]

This impression is substantiated by churchwardens' accounts. In 1590 none, across the whole nation, seems to show regular payments for celebrations associated with the processions. In the following decade a London church, St Bartholomew the Less, and one in Westminster, St Martin in the Fields, began to make them. By 1639 they feature in the records surviving from every City parish except one, St Mary Aldermanbury. It had become a tradition for the boys in each to be taken around the boundaries every Ascension Day by the minister and leading inhabitants, and to be given some reward as part of the experience. In many cases this consisted of ribbons ('points') to pin or tie upon their clothing; a large parish such as St Mary Woolnoth ordered ten dozen of these each year. Often the children received cakes, fruit, bread, nuts, or beer instead of, or in addition to, these trophies. The boundary markers were regularly touched up with paint as part of the tour, and the adults concerned frequently treated themselves to a dinner or supper on the parish funds. The major growth of the custom was in the reign of James, when it was adopted by thirty parishes, but ten more followed under Charles I. It was developed with equal enthusiasm by clergy of the different views of theology and ritual to be found within the contemporary Church; in the 1620s Henry Burton, one of the most bitter enemies of innovations which seemed to him to be a backsliding towards Catholicism, was to be found leading the perambulation of the bounds of St Matthew Friday Street, while the wardens distributed figs, almonds, and raisins to the boys. In the same span of years the processions also began to be marked by parish feasts and bell-ringing at other Westminster churches and in Bristol, Canterbury, Cambridge, Hereford, Ipswich, Chester, Stafford, Norwich, Warwick, Winchester, York, Gloucester, and Reading.[30]

The same development occurred in a scatter of villages and small towns across southern England and the Midlands, though there the major development was after 1625.[31] Most rural communities still obtained their food and drink from parishioners *en route*, according to the tradition documented in the diocesan court records; in West Sussex the majority of householders in this category were expected to give cakes, with a full meal provided by the local 'great farm'.[32] Northern towns such as Durham, and some in the south such as Oxford and Exeter, apparently did not invest parish funds in increasing the attraction and the importance of the processions.[33] None the less, there remains copious evidence of the large number of communities which did so. The ceremony itself still had a deeply ambiguous quality. There seems no reason to doubt that for somebody like Burton it was solely a means of keeping the parish's boundaries (and therefore its dues) clearly fixed, and fostering a spirit of parochial community. In the countryside, however, it may well have retained more arcane associations. The poet George Wither dealt with both aspects of it. In *Emblems* he described it as intended to preserve property rights, 'That Ev'ry one distinctly knew his own', and to prevent demarcation disputes.[34] In *Haleluiah*, however, he represented the principal aim as being to ensure the safety of the crops.[35]

In view of the clear utility of the custom, and its acceptability to archetypal 'Puritans' such as Burton, there can be little surprise in the fact that it survived the reforms of the 1640s with only a slight contraction. Of the sixty-two London parishes which have left accounts from the Interregnum, forty-two (68 per cent) kept on perambulating. So did some in Oxford, Cambridge, Bristol, York, Winchester, Westminster, Ipswich, Norwich, and Chester. The fact that the processions could be preserved at St Margaret's, Westminster, next to the seat of government at Whitehall and at the door of the House of Commons, indicates how little animosity the successive republican regimes must have felt towards them.[36] In some communities there are signs of momentary hesitation concerning the tradition. At Norwich, for example, none of the parishes which have left records seems to have been perambulated in 1648. The next year, however, three out of four did so and at St Peter Mancroft, held by a noted Presbyterian minister, the wine bill alone came to £6 3s. Thereafter, in the 1650s, the custom was regular and usually the occasion of a fine dinner.[37] As ever, rural parishes do not often record payments, as traditional hospitality still probably provided the costs. But the widespread distribution of those which did feature them indicates a comparable survival of the custom in villages.[38]

Once the Restoration occurred, its slight measure of diminution was reversed and expansion resumed. The rector of Clayworth, Nottinghamshire, noted how the perambulation was reintroduced in his parish with much rejoicing and lavish provision of hospitality along the route; he added sourly that 'when this hot fit was over the charity began to wax cold'. None the less, the processions are recorded more frequently in late Stuart churchwardens' accounts than in early seventeenth-century equivalents. Only ten out of seventy-five London parishes which have left such accounts do not mention them, and in some of these inadequate bookkeeping is apparent. Parishes in every corporate town observed them, and once again they are mentioned in a scatter of villages across the country from one end to another, most commonly in East Anglia and Kent: probably those in which informal hospitality had 'waxed cold'.[39]

The ample evidence from the Restoration period furnishes insight into the further development of the procedure. London parishes began to pay for wands or rods (usually specifically white in colour), with which the children would beat the boundary markers and so increase their chances of committing them to memory. At the fishing port of St Ives in western Cornwall, it was the boys who were beaten at the marks instead, to the same end. At Gateshead, on the Tyne, the parishioners were accompanied by Northumbrian pipers. Those of North Petherton, in Somerset's Parrett valley, had to hire a boat to follow the boundary accurately. Entertainment of the walkers had a tendency to become more elaborate: thus by the 1670s the wardens of one London parish were ensuring that the children in the Ascension Day procession were getting almonds, raisins, ribbons, and silk points, while the adults had bottles of wine. At Whiston, in south-western Yorkshire, the church funds provided bread, beer, tobacco, pipes, and a bonfire at the end of the walk. At Cuckfield, a large parish in the Sussex Weald, the perambulation took three days and so was held very irregularly; when it was decided to do so, the curate, parish clerk, and boys stayed the whole course, but adult parishioners tended to come along for only one of the days, along the section closest to their homes. They all chanted psalms as they walked.[40]

No comparable detailed research into parish records exists for the eighteenth and nineteenth centuries, and the historian is reliant instead upon incidental comment and the increasingly abundant surveys of folklorists. The overall impression is that the popularity of the perambulations came to a peak in about 1700, was maintained for the first half of the eighteenth century, and then entered a long and slow decline which lasted for about a hundred years. They tended to become less frequent, and then irregular, and then to end altogether. Where reasons are given for the loss of enthusiasm, they tend to fall into two categories: enclosure and expense. The former certainly has much relevance in the countryside, for it was during this period that the majority of England's open fields were broken up into smaller holdings, and the proliferation of fences and hedges would doubtless have made many traditional routes more difficult to follow. The complaint of expense, however, is clearly a symptom rather than a cause and, as the processions declined as steadily in towns as in the countryside, there must have been other factors at work. Two may be proposed here: the increasing availability of detailed maps, and the waning of the residual belief that the rite conferred some benediction upon the community. The first robbed it of practical benefit, the second of a spiritual one.[41] Towards the end of the period, also, endowments and bequests which had supported the processions were sometimes reallocated by the Charity Commissioners. At Bovey Tracey on the edge of Dartmoor, in Devon, the latter reduced the 'bounders' from riding horses decked with flowers and enjoying a substantial banquet afterwards, to trudging round on foot and consuming 'ginger bread and buns'.[42] A comparable story of neglect and diminution is found among the perambulations over the same time in Wales[43] and the Isle of Man.[44]

Some of these later perambulations are none the less notable, for being recorded in a detail absent for most of those in previous centuries. A variety of devices were used to impress the boundaries upon the parish youth, the most common being a distribution of fruit, nuts, or halfpennies. At St Cuthbert's, Wells, in 1752, 'selected' boys were whipped at the markers instead.[45] A lad was placed in each of the holes which acted as marks at Huntingdon in 1892, and hit with a spade.[46] In eighteenth-century Scopwick, on the Lincolnshire Wolds, the same system of markers was used, and the youngsters had to stand upon their heads instead.[47] Sometimes the whole procession underwent an ordeal, unwillingly. In 1854 that led by the curate of All Saints, Worcester, had to pass under a bridge over the river Severn when following that part of their boundary by boat; a crowd of unruly townspeople drenched them with mud and water.[48] The same fate befell that of St John the Baptist's parish, Oxford in 1876, at the hands of the undergraduates of Corpus Christi. The president of that college did provide bread, cheese, and ale by way of compensation, and the kinder students of Oriel threw biscuits, old top hats (for use as footballs), and pennies to the children.[49] In the Cornborough district of Devon during the late eighteenth century there were worse hazards, as the fierce inter-parochial rivalry already obvious in the Middle Ages manifested itself still in battles between Rogation parties which collided on the boundary.[50] The same thing happened at Shrewsbury, until the middle of the next century. The return of many old ritual trappings to the Church had permitted the carrying of banners once more, and the poles of these proved to be very useful weapons in the fights, which ended only when 'one side or another was driven off the field. The struggle was often fierce; stones were thrown and serious hurts sometimes received'. Indeed, the violence became the reason for the suppression of the custom.[51]

The general attrition of it underwent a momentary reversal in the 1860s, when the Anglo-Catholic movement brought about a revival in many parishes.[52] Others followed locally in the twentieth century, as pieces of self-conscious antiquarianism, but nothing could halt the overall long-term disappearance of the perambulations, powerfully reinforced by the collapse of the parish as an important unit of local society.[53] At the present day several revivals or survivals persist. The most dedicated of those in an urban setting are probably those of central Oxford, where each Ascension Day schoolchildren can be seen filing behind their clergyman, carrying white wands to beat the markers. The district in which rural perambulations are still most frequent seems to be eastern Devon, where a dozen have held them in the last twenty years. Belstone and Colyford do so annually or almost annually, while at the others they occur at longer intervals or are irregular. Most adventurous of all is probably that of Chudleigh, near Exeter, which takes place every seven years. The route is twenty-one miles long, and at one point a volunteer swims the river Teign while the rest of the party makes a detour by road. Another detour, by bus, is needed to get the whole of it from one side of a busy dual carriageway to another.[54]

In the past few generations, however, Rogationtide has seen a revival in popularity which has brought it closer to its ancient spirit than at any time since the Reformation, a result, perhaps, of a combination of a further waning of Protestant inhibitions with a growing veneration for nature. In the eighteenth century it was already noticed that, to compensate for the lack of the old ecclesiastical blessing of crops, youths in north-west Kent had transferred the rite of 'wassailing' the apple orchards from midwinter to the Rogation Days.[55] Since the Second World War, a large number of country churches, in the south and west of England, have instituted Rogation Sunday services intended specifically to pray for the year's crops, even as the harvest festival gives thanks for them. In Devon not merely fields but the sea and rivers are blessed to protect their yields, and ministers from all the local churches gather at Kingswear and Dartmouth to call down grace upon the fisheries of the river Dart. At Newington in north Kent, the vicar processes with the churchwardens, choir, and congregation, a cross carried before them, to do the same for the cherry orchards. Wiltshire congregations march between churches or chapels for services, stopping at selected stations for prayers and hymns. One church in a farmyard at Foxley in the north-west of the country, the smallest currently used in Britain, was reopened in the 1950s specifically for the blessing of the fields upon this day. The impulse that lay behind the Roman Ambarvalia has survived the millennia better than most other religious rites, in a blend of ancient agricultural need and modern romantic kinship with the natural world.

27

ROYAL OAK

❧

AFTER more than a thousand years in which the propensity to rejoice in early summer had served the interests of both local communities and the Church, it was utilized in the developing cult of the English State. Owing to accidents of fortune, political anniversaries had first appeared in the winter, as will be described. In 1660, however, one was installed in May, to provide an annual thanksgiving for the restoration of the monarchy after eleven years of republican rule. This was coupled with a day of fasting and mourning upon 30 January, anniversary of the execution of Charles I. The May date, the 29th, was not that of the formal proclamation of the Restoration, which had occurred three weeks earlier, but of the 'completion' of the process by Charles II's formal entry into London. More to the point, it was also his birthday, just as the date of the regicide was of course his accession day. Thus two royal anniversaries which had come, since the reign of Elizabeth, to be celebrated as a matter of course, would as long as Charles lived be neatly taken up with rites of passage out of the traumas of the Interregnum. After his death, there would be a new pair of royal days to be loyally remembered, but the religious services upon 30 January and 29 May were intended to remain in perpetuity, followed by public gloom on the former and public rejoicing on the latter. Both were secured by a statute of the Convention Parliament, passed so swiftly and enthusiastically that it is apparently impossible to tell how this measure originated.[1] The winter fast, though it produced thousands of notable sermons, made understandably little impact upon popular custom.[2] The summer festival, equally naturally, had a considerable effect.

To assess the extent of its adoption is admittedly difficult. The statute did not prescribe any penalties for failing to observe it, and in the first visitation of the restored episcopal Church, only four bishops enquired after the matter. It may be significant that returns have survived from two of the dioceses concerned, Salisbury and Ely, and only one parish, Alton Barnes in the Wiltshire chalk downs, confessed that it had forgotten the day. Some of the others, however, may have been dishonest. The only source which provides even an approximate answer to the problem consists of churchwardens' accounts, and these only record the ringing of bells upon the date concerned, the absence of which does not necessarily indicate a lack of observation. Nevertheless, there is still some value in using this evidence as an indication of enthusiasm, and it is notable that of 616 parishes which have left itemized payments to ringers from the reign of Charles II, 233 (39 per cent) rang bells on 29 May. They included, unsurprisingly, all large churches in towns, but also a great many in villages, spread across the country. Some of these rural communities were very small, so that mere wealth was not a vital factor in the distribution. Individual parishes went to further efforts: the west Cornish fishing port of St Ives provided a blazing tar barrel and a drummer, two Oxford parishes lit bonfires, and the wardens of Ashby Folville, on the Leicestershire chalk wolds, treated 'the neighbours'. Mildenhall, on the west Suffolk heathland, had firework displays, and Dallinghoo, in the east of the same county, held a communion. So did St Oswald's church in Durham town. These parochial records are paralleled by an occasional notice of municipal celebration. At Cambridge in 1669, for example, the corporation filed out of church in their scarlet gowns and went off to the town hall for a dinner of salt fish, mutton, veal, bacon, beef, lamb, salads, capons, rabbits, and claret, at the public expense. Cathedral clergy added to the merriment, those of Worcester kindling a huge fire in the Close each year.[3]

Although some of the smaller parishes failed to ring every year, observation of the new festival was remarkably consistent, and hardly responded to the political tensions which emerged as it turned out that the Restoration had not, after all, stabilized the nation. All Saints' parish in Dorchester did, it is true, stop the ringing when feeling began to turn against the government in the Exclusion Crisis of 1678–81. Neighbouring Holy Trinity, however, never faltered, and at the town of Ludlow and the villages of Munslow, Alderbury, and Milton Regis, in Shropshire and Kent respectively, the parish actually took up the custom during that crisis, as if rallying to the Crown. None the less, there is circumstantial evidence that elsewhere enthusiasm for the festival ebbed even though it was not wholly neglected. Samuel Pepys noted a 'very solemn observation' of it in London in 1662, with bonfires in the evening, but by the next year feeling was already running so strongly against the regime that although no shops were open 'hardly ten people' attended some churches, and the general atmosphere was 'ill'. By 1666 the date was still kept as a holiday, and bells rang all over the city at dawn, but there were few fires lit there later although Westminster was full of them. Out in Kent John Evelyn noticed nothing amiss until the Exclusion Crisis, in 1679, when suddenly his local church had so 'thin a congregation' that the minister did not bother to preach. The attendance, however, recovered. In the next year of that crisis, 1680, Anthony Wood recorded that the shops were still closed at Oxford, but business was being done as usual in London, as a blatant insult to the King. This was, however, partly due to royal policy, for the Privy Council had prohibited all fires and fireworks for fear of disorder. Certainly the holiday atmosphere was restored by 1682, Whigs and Tories holding rival demonstrations with burning of effigies, and the defeat of the former left the way clear for loyal commemoration.[4]

This increased rather than diminished in the reign of James II, as it ceased to be the royal birthday and the form of prayer for the service was revised accordingly. Of 565 parishes which have left itemized expenditure upon ringing in these years, 261 (46 per cent) swung bells on 29 May. Once again they included most of those in towns but also many in the countryside, representing every county. Anthony Wood noted 'bonfires, bells, gaudies' at Oxford in 1687, and comparable celebrations probably occurred in other communities. This apparent continued growth in popularity was dealt a serious blow by the revolution of 1688 and the flight of James, presumably because the festival had been so strongly identified with the main branch of the royal family. John Evelyn went to only two services on that date in the 1690s, and at one of those found that the traditional office for it was not used and no attention was paid to its historic significance. At Oxford sermons were a more regular occurrence, but bonfires were few and not heard of after 1693. Of 537 sets of churchwardens' accounts from that decade, only sixty (11 per cent) record ringing on that day, and most were major urban parishes probably dutifully obeying the statute which still called for observation.[5]

No detailed study of parish records exists for a comparable survey of Restoration Day's popularity after 1700. Casual comment, however, suggests that it was no greater in the reign of Anne when even leading Tories, heads of the party most closely identified with the restored monarchy and Church of the 1660s, paid little attention to it.[6] What altered its status, yet again, was another change of dynasty, this time the accession of the Hanoverians in 1714 and the ensuing long supremacy of the Whig party. Almost immediately, 29 May became one of the principal rallying-points of the Jacobite supporters of the exiled Stuarts, the disempowered Tory party into which they blended, and an exuberant, if episodic, popular unrest which could ally with either or both. In 1715 the bells at Norwich rang for the whole of Restoration Day, the streets were strewn with flowers, and sprigs of oak were worn by most people in hats or bosoms. Oak leaves were hung all over houses at Bristol and Manchester, and religious dissenters, identified especially with the Whig party, were attacked at Oxford. The following year the Oxford Whigs tried to avoid attack by wearing oak themselves on the streets; but squibs were thrown at them anyway. The year after that a rural Restoration Day celebration attracted notice, at Watton at Stone in central Hertfordshire, where a large crowd romped with flags in their hands, sprays of foliage on hats, and (in mockery of the government) horns on heads. So the pattern of celebration was established, and sustained in the following decades.[7] The oak was worn in memory of the tree in which Charles II had hidden after the battle of Worcester, so evading his republican pursuers and making possible his restoration as a ruling monarch nine years later. It had no prominence in May festivities before then, and, whatever its archaic associations with Druidry, it scores low on a checklist of trees with arcane properties assembled from the nineteenth-century folklore collections; ash, hazel, birch, rowan, and hawthorn all feature more prominently. On the other hand, it was abundant, and its use as a decoration for persons and buildings fitted perfectly into the old and important May tradition of fetching home greenery.

The problem was that it was being grafted onto a festival which had been established as a celebration of national reunification and had now become an expression of national division. Notices from the remainder of the Georgian period drive home the point. At Newcastle upon Tyne in the 1720s, boys with oak leaves in their hats would taunt those lacking them on Restoration Day by shouting 'Royal Oak; the Whigs to provoke'. Their rivals wore twigs of plane, and chanted 'Plane tree leaves; the Church-folk are thieves'.[8] From 1717 onward the Government banned the sporting of any leaves on that date in London. In 1747 the same prohibition was imposed upon Manchester, one of the centres of a recent Jacobite rebellion, and enforced by dragoons.[9] Three years later celebrations on that day at Walsall, in Staffordshire's Black Country, developed into a riot in which an image of George II was used as a shooting target.[10] Only in the second half of the century did tension subside at a national level, and reports of commemoration concentrate more upon harmless local festivity, an extension of the old Maying and summer games. At Sheffield in the 1780s the cry was 'Down with the Rump', attacking the safe old target of the last republican regime of the 1650s, and a garland of flowers and silver plate upon a light wooden frame was hung over Scotland Street.[11] The villagers of Nuneham Courtenay, just south of Oxford, were observed to set oak boughs at their doors in that decade, and those of Normanton, next to Derby, danced round a maypole on 29 May 1789.[12] For all this, in some communities it remained an opportunity for rancour; at Lyme Regis most doorways were decked with oak each year, but religious nonconformists refused to display it and their doors were given bunches of nettles instead by the church-goers.[13]

It was for this sort of reason that the statute which had imposed the holiday was repealed, along with all which had instituted permanent political anniversaries, in 1859. One obvious and immediate consequence of this was that a day of festivity was turned into one of work. For a century after, schoolchildren in northern England would chant

> Twentieth-ninth of May
> Royal Oak Day;
> If you don't give us a holiday
> We'll all run away.

In the schools at Windermere and Heversham, in Westmorland, and Great Ayton, in northern Yorkshire, the holiday was actually granted for the rest of the century, after the pupils had barred out the master, as had traditionally happened at Christmas. After that time, however, the chant became as ineffectual there as everywhere else, although it remained as a playground habit.[14] For adults, the abolition resulted in a natural drastic diminution in the scale of celebration on that date. During the early nineteenth century this could still be lavish. At Tiverton in the east of Devon a lad dressed as Cromwell would exact money from passers-by, threatening to smear them with dirt; he was, however, worsted in a duel with another, wound about with oak branches and representing Charles II. At Tavistock in the west youths representing the two factions fought with buckets of water. In both towns, and at Exeter, church bells were rung and houses decorated with oak.[15] In Dorset gamekeepers accorded a unique tolerance to people found trespassing in their woods on that morning, if they were gathering oak leaves.[16] Ritual combats between boys representing Civil War parties were also fought out in south-west Staffordshire,[17] while at several settlements in Herefordshire and the neighbouring part of Gloucestershire the streets were hung with garlands and maypoles set in them for dances.[18] In addition, to judge from later comment, the decking of houses and carts with oak, and the wearing of it, must have been very common all over the nation. The date was still called Restoration Day at times, but Royal Oak Day, Oak Apple Day, or Yak Bob Day (meaning the same) were all now more widely used.

Once the public holiday was gone, observance was mostly limited to the decoration of houses and persons, and first the former and then the latter waned everywhere throughout the second half of the nineteenth century and into the early part of the twentieth.[19] The most tenacious manifestation of the custom, however, was among children, and consisted of the habit of wearing oak leaves or 'apples' to school or in the street upon 29 May, and persecuting those who did not; the usual punishment consisted of flogging with nettles, but it could also take the form of pelting with eggs or dirt, pinching, spitting, hair-pulling, and all the other torments which youngsters can inflict upon each other. Between 1860 and 1960 this tradition was recorded in every part of the country, except East Anglia and the counties bordering London, and Wales, where Restoration Day never seems to have penetrated popular culture.[20]

Occasionally, some of the old political rancour was preserved: thus, the Newcastle chant of the 1720s was heard among Somerset children in the 1900s, and victims beaten at Kendal, Westmorland, in the 1880s were termed 'Tom Painers', after the famous republican of the late eighteenth century. Between Herefordshire and Hampshire, the date was generally known as 'Shickshack' or 'Shigshag' Day, a name sometimes accompanied by the rhyme

> Shig—Shag, penny a rag,
> Bang his head in Cromwell's bag,
> All up in a bundle.

This seems to have been nonsensical even to those who used it, although always understood to be a chant of abuse; a Dorset alternative was 'Shicsack, shicksack! lousy back! lousy back!' The name itself has no clear point of origin, the only plausible explanation suggested so far being that it derives from the biblical villain Shishak, king of Egypt, who might have been equated with Cromwell; but this rests upon no evidence.[21] In virtually every case there was no question of a factional fight between the children who had oak and those who had not; the custom was more of an opportunity for the former to gang up on, and bully, the latter. In this rather squalid, and miniaturized way, the celebration of 29 May did return to being, as the Convention Parliament intended, that of a society reunited against a tiny minority of nonconformists. As such it was still noted in playgrounds scattered thinly across the north and north Midlands of England in the years between 1950 and 1980,[22] and may well survive today. In addition, it is possible that a few church towers are still decked with oak boughs.

Much more famous are the communal celebrations of the date retained at two most unusual rural communities. One is Great Wishford in the Wylye valley of Wiltshire, built around the annual celebration of a right to gather wood in nearby Groveley Forest. The festivities there include processions, a unique local women's dance, and a fete, but perhaps the most remarkable and archaic feature is the communal rising just before dawn, to walk singing to the forest and gather oak: one of the most striking modern survivals of an old-fashioned 'Maying'. Yet more spectacular is the pageantry at Castleton in Derbyshire's Peak District. Its centre-piece is the 'garland', a wooden frame three feet high, bound with straw and tied all over with knots of wild flowers and leaves, crowned by a small wreath of choice garden flowers, known as 'the queen'. This is carried on the shoulders of 'the king', a rider in the costume of the Stuart period, accompanied by a human 'queen' in a female attire from the same age. They are followed by young women in white, bearing flowers, who perform another local dance. The procession ends at the church, where the garland is hung upon the tower for a week.

This, at any rate, is the form which the ceremony has taken during the twentieth century, and by the 1960s it was established wisdom among folklorists that it represented an ancient rite of nature-worship.[23] In 1977 an expert upon pagan Celtic Britain visited the little town and confidently informed its people that their procession was the remnant of a ritual of human sacrifice carried out by the local tribe; this was duly repeated to the press.[24] It thus became ripe, in the academic mood of the 1980s, for a classic piece of scholarly deconstruction, and received it at the hands of Georgina Boyes. She demonstrated from the local records that it had developed out of the very different custom of rush-bearing (to be considered later in this book) during the late eighteenth or early nineteenth century. In the former period the bell-ringers had formed the essential element in a parade which had involved both the garland and a rush cart, and which called at the houses of wealthy townspeople for hospitality. By the nineteenth century the cart had gone and the procession was led by a man in ribbons and another, representing a lady in a bonnet, and consisted principally of a morris performed by the ringers. In the 1890s the growing interest of city-dwellers in the countryside turned the event into a tourist attraction, and it was duly prettified. The morris was replaced by the schoolgirls in white, 'king' and 'queen' were given historic costumes, and the traditional drunkenness was forbidden. Thus the custom was fixed in a form which made it an acceptable piece of 'folk' pageantry, and the only subsequent change was that in 1955 the 'queen' turned from the transvestite of old-style festivity into a real woman.[25] None the less, it incorporates very accurately one of the last of the frameworks of flowers which descend directly from the 'Mays' once carried through the streets of late medieval towns.

A MERRIE MAY

꜅⟨⟩꜆

I T has always been appreciated by social historians that Christmas was, as
said earlier, substantially recreated by the Victorians. What has been far
less well understood till recently is that the old May games underwent a
parallel transformation. This was because, whereas nobody pretended that the
Christmas tree or Christmas card were anything other than innovations, the
alteration in the summer festivities was presented as a revival, a self-conscious
quest for authentic tradition. Like the redevelopment of the great winter
festival, it was a response to the emotional needs of its age; but the summer
merry-making became far more bound up with the politics of nostalgia, which
have remained a potent force in national culture until the present. Only from
the 1970s onward did a combination of a new rigour in folklore studies, and a
new sensitivity among intellectuals to what has been termed 'the invention of
tradition', make possible an objective consideration of what had occurred; in
this development the work of Roy Judge has been pre-eminent.

Whereas Christmas was essentially redefined as the supreme festival of the
family, the May games were viewed as an expression of the community, and
especially of the village community. An acute anxiety about the weakening of
traditional social bonds first seems to have manifested itself in the 1810s, when
the end of the Napoleonic wars left England prey to economic difficulties
which brought to the surface tensions long developing from changing patterns
of industry and trade. One form in which it was expressed was a hankering
after an idealized past, characterized by order and harmony; a sentiment
which bonded easily with the new interest in the natural, the primitive, the
organic, and the creative associated with what is vaguely termed the Romantic
Movement.[1] This impulse could feed upon the burgeoning scholarly interest
in traditional popular customs, itself largely a product of the widening gulf
between classes and between town and country, exemplified by the work
published between 1800 and 1815 by Joseph Strutt, Francis Douce, John Brady,
and John Brand.[2]

Of the writers who worked with it in the early nineteenth century, the most
popular and influential was probably Sir Walter Scott, who characterized the
Middle Ages as a time of aristocratic chivalry and a strong bond between
rulers and ruled. He lauded its feasts and festivals as a means of bringing all
ranks of society together in celebration, and giving a 'happy holiday to the

monotony of a life of labour'; to him a revival of this spirit would be a means 'to resolve the difficulties and distractions' of his own times.[3] Such sentiments were also articulated between 1805 and 1830 by other major literary figures, including Wordsworth, Coleridge, Southey, William Cobbett, Thomas Love Peacock, and Washington Irving.[4] It may well have been under the influence of them that the squire of Necton on the Norfolk clay plateau, a Colonel Mason, inaugurated a 'traditional' Whit Monday festival in 1817. It included a may pole, with twelve youngsters performing a set dance about it, and 'maskers or morris dancers, fancifully attired', and was open to Mason's tenantry and the local Friendly Societies.[5] In 1821 Horace Smith appealed for the revival of May Day as a national festival, to symbolize a 'cheerful and cordial intercourse with nature' and to provide an answer to 'Mammon madness'.[6] The following year Cyrus Redding lauded it as a symbol of harmony and goodwill between classes,[7] and in 1830 the century's most popular English poet both drew upon these feelings and inspired them still further, when Tennyson wrote 'The May Queen'. Another example of this circular process was provided in 1836, by J. T. Haines's romantic drama *Richard Plantagenet* at the Victoria Theatre in London. It included the first known example in England of a maypole dance with ribbons suspended from the top of the pole, held by the dancers, and plaited in a pattern. This was an excellent spectacle and reappeared thereafter on the London stage. It was also employed to lend additional colour to the traditional well-dressing ceremony at Buxton in the Derbyshire Peak District in 1840, and thereafter diffused from there through the north-western counties. During the 1850s the custom was starting to appear at southern English fetes, and by the 1880s it had replaced the older maypole dances across the country.[8]

The central decades of the century accentuated the developments of the first four: educated nostalgia for the old summer games intensified even while they declined steadily as genuine aspects of popular culture. It did not feed primarily upon observation of the remaining customs, but upon Tudor and Stuart literary references to the May games, which were presumed in that earlier period to have been more 'pure' and 'authentic', and still retaining something of the social function which they were supposed to have enjoyed in the Middle Ages. Indeed, to those who had reservations about late medieval England because of what Protestants regarded as the corruption of its Church, the time of Elizabeth could appear to have the best of both worlds: a reformed religion and a traditional society united in festivity.[9] This enthusiasm rebounded in turn upon literary taste: Robert Herrick, the finest poet of early Stuart rural celebration, now came to enjoy his first real popularity.[10] It was in 1842 that George Daniel published a work upon the presumed spirit of the medieval and early modern periods which was to be more influential in its title than in its contents: *Merrie England in the Olden Time*. The most prominent author to address the subject in that decade was Lord John Manners, one of the 'Young England' group of Conservative politicians which included Benjamin Disraeli. He led them in calling for a revival of traditional festivals to restore both health and loyalty to the common people; to Manners, the maypole was the premier symbol of social unity and harmony.[11] By no coincidence, it was in 1843–5 that scenes of morris, maypoles, and May Queens reached their peak of popularity in London theatres and fetes, no fewer than eight featuring them in those years. From these settings they migrated easily to burlesque, pantomimes, and pleasure-gardens, being staple fixtures at the Cremorne Gardens from 1858 to 1863 and at the North Woolwich Gardens between 1860 and 1863. In the 1850s the scholar William Husk, librarian to the Sacred Harmonic Society, assisted in the recreation of a Tudor May game at the Crystal Palace.[12]

Ultimately more important, however, were the rural equivalents. During the 1840s a number of country gentry began to act as Colonel Mason had done and sponsor 'revived' summer games at their seats. The most prominent were Lord Campden and Rowland Eyles Egerton-Warburton; the latter, an almost classic Victorian 'improving landlord' and the embodiment of benevolent paternalism, instituted one at Arley Hall in northern Cheshire which lasted until 1866. Centred upon a maypole dance and the coronation of a May queen, and essentially a children's event, it was abolished because the crowds of unruly visitors attracted to it became large enough to disrupt it.[13] Just before its demise, however, it was copied by the minister of Cheetwood parish, a suburb of Manchester,[14] and by a committee at the small town of Knutsford to the south. The latter event, adding a morris and a Jack in the Green to the children's procession and the crowning of the 'queen', became nationally famous and was dubbed 'royal' after the Prince of Wales visited it in 1887. During the 1870s it inspired a set of imitations in Lancashire and Cheshire, and by the 1890s little May queens were found all over those counties. The Cheshire games seem also to have inspired John Ruskin, the philosopher and art critic who was one of the writers to eulogize the social cohesion of the Middle Ages. He visited the county in the 1860s, and in 1881 he joined forces with one J. P. Faunthorpe, principal of Whitelands, a training college for schoolmistresses run by the Church of England, to design a May queen ceremony there. As its pupils graduated, they took it with them to their schools, all across the country, and by 1913 Whitelands could claim to be 'the fostering mother of all May Days'.[15] Even when applied solely to school events this was an exaggeration, for some May queens had probably survived as local traditions from before the time of revivals, while others were products of that same initial period of romantic antiquarianism which had engendered the Arley event: a schoolgirl 'queen' had been crowned regularly at Avington, in the Kennet valley of Berkshire, since as early as 1815, while another was chosen at Albrighton, a Shropshire village, from 1833 onward. Teachers who were never trained at Whitelands still instituted the custom in the time of its greatest growth in the last quarter of the century, parallel to the one of 'garlanding', described earlier.[16] The dainty girls, tricked out in white dresses and flowers, were what the dream of the 'Olden Time' required; in the same period the old-fashioned summer kings were allowed finally to die out.

Independently of the Arley May games, other revivals were taking root and shedding seeds. At Winster, in the Peak District, the antiquarian Llewellyn Jewitt put together a morris dance in 1873, conflated with figures from the Mummers' Play and other folk customs, which (as said above) was later mistaken for an ancient tradition.[17] In the 1880s a professional musician based at Cheltenham, Ernest Richard D'Arcy Ferris, set out to revive the old summer games to improve the social condition of the common people. As he 'could not find any programme extant of the fifteenth-century date', he cheerfully devised his own, mixing lords of misrule, morris, mummers, wassailers, and Highland Scottish dances to provide entertainments sponsored by local magnates, especially in Warwickshire. By 1885 he had decided to send on tour his own variety of morris, put together using costumes from the Betley stained-glass window and from illustrations in the work of the anti-quary Francis Douce, incorporating a fool and a hobby-horse, and set to sixteenth- and seventeenth-century tunes. It became entrenched in the south Warwickshire villages from which the performers were recruited, and ac-cepted later as an important old tradition. Ferris's morris was also taken as 'authentic' by the national press when it was presented at Gray's Inn for Victoria's Golden Jubilee in 1887.[18] For three years in the early 1890s, the mill-owner Edmund Joyson put on a display of customs from 'Merrie England', performed at St Mary Cray, where London ran into Kent. It included a morris, devised by a London ballet master. In 1894 the antiquarian clergyman Francis Galpin provided a similar set of 'Olde Englyshe Pastimes' at Hatfield Broad Oak in western Essex, relying upon literary sources.[19] These were only some of the most spectacular and best-recorded of such events enacted during this period. As they diffused, they became more popular in all senses, the initial domination by gentry sponsors giving way to a more pronounced activity on the part of local scholars, clerics, and teachers.[20] It may well be that this enthusiasm helped to kill the surviving manifestations of the very tradition which was ostensibly being revived; as remarked earlier, the south Midland morris collapsed in the late nineteenth century because of a loss of support by the wealthier classes, who were now devoting themselves to the more glamorous and malleable business of historic 're-creation'.

That devotion was being powerfully reinforced by further social and ideo-logical changes. The rhetoric of 'Merrie England' had begun, and was long maintained, mainly as a conservative one: a hankering after hierarchy, defer-ence, and order in a past dominated by rural landowners. In the second half of the century this began to wane, or to be sublimated, as the importance of gentry in the phenomenon declined. Individuals like Manners and Egerton-Warburton seem in any case to have been more interested in social harmony than social control, and this language became more pronounced in succeeding generations. May games and rituals also fitted neatly into an increasingly influential educational philosophy which called for regulated play, as well as study, in school curricula.[21] Their popularity, in a revived and supposedly antique form, was enormously increased by the cult of rural England which burgeoned from the 1880s and has been the subject of a number of recent studies.[22] It can be related with almost mathematical precision to one phenomenon: in 1800, one-fifth of the population of England lived in towns, while by 1911 the proportion had risen to four-fifths. The balance was tipped towards urban living in mid-century, by which time a distinctively different rural society was ceasing to exist. During the 1870s English agriculture collapsed, and the countryside began to depopulate; by 1900 it seemed possible that the whole land would become one vast conurbation. An almost desperate reaction set in, spreading across art, letters, music, and architecture between 1890 and 1914 to produce a ruralist vision of essential Englishness, in which the traditional May customs could seem to function as sacred rites.

Indeed, there was a growing propensity to regard them as just that, in a historic as well as a symbolic sense. Since Polydor Vergil, at the opening of the sixteenth century, writers had suggested that the May games derived ultimately from pagan rituals. Having begun as a piece of antiquarian speculation, the notion was rapidly developed as a polemical weapon which could be deployed against the traditional communal festivities by Protestant reformers.[23] By the late seventeenth century the campaign of repression had flagged but the association remained, Maying being at first vaguely linked to the Roman Floralia and then to the Druids.[24] The linkage was, however, given at once a much greater scholarly importance and a much higher public profile at the end of the nineteenth century by the work of Sir Edward Tylor, Sir George Laurence Gomme, and Sir James Frazer. The first two proposed, and the last popularized, an idea inspired by geological discoveries of the mid-century and the allied theory of evolution: that folk rituals, like fossils embedded in rock, might be survivals of old religions which could be reconstructed from a close comparative study of them. Frazer was also influenced in turn, as said before, by the German folklorist Wilhelm Mannhardt, into viewing the primary focus of ancient religion as being upon vegetation-spirits which promoted fertility, and May customs were naturally cited prominently by both as evidence. Neither Tylor nor Frazer were themselves enthusiastic about ceremonial; on the contrary, both had come out of a radically Protestant upbringing (the former a Quaker, the latter a Scottish Presbyterian) and had a strong aversion to all forms of religious ritual and display. Both had shaken off religion themselves, and regarded this step as an essential part of general human progress; their books were intended in great measure to further the emancipation of humanity from religious belief. They did not, however, seem to have this effect. Instead, the immense readership of Frazer in particular, consuming the successive editions of his work from 1890 to 1924, seems often to have found a romantic *frisson* in the notion that apparently harmless or meaningless English rural pastimes were in fact remnants of ancient ritual. This bonded closely with the new reverence for the countryside, its people, and its ways, to lend an enhanced solemnity to the revived May games; indeed the relationship was at times very close because, by one of those ironies now abundant in the process, some of the customs used by Frazer in evidence had themselves (unknown to him) been products of the revival.[25]

During the same period, Merrie England became part of a distinctively left-wing discourse. There had always been an element of one there, as evinced by the presence of Coleridge and Cobbett among the earliest proponents of the concept, but it had been a minor theme beside that of an ageless benevolent paternalism. Then, in the central decades of the century, a new enthusiasm arose among English intellectuals for the idea that the landscape, the law, the constitution, and popular culture had all been fashioned by generations of anonymous, collective endeavour. It fused many strands of thought, the most important being an attempt by German writers, from the late eighteenth century onwards, to foster the idea of a communal and ancestral racial culture, both to emancipate their people from French cultural models and to oppose political centralization. To this the Victorians added a romantic sympathy for the humble and obscure, and the new understanding of geological, economic, and industrial processes in which the individual being was subsumed in the mass. A theoretically timeless rural world, and its festivities, was particularly susceptible to idealization in this way, and by the last quarter of the century English liberal thought was, in the words of John Burrow, marked by a 'cult of the concept of a primitive Teutonic freedom, tinged with social democracy' and expressed in the medieval village community.[26] By a wholly fortuitous coincidence, the strike which became the symbol of the American Labor Movement began upon 1 May, and so that became its favourite date. To show solidarity with comrades in the USA, the International Socialist Congress held in Paris in 1889 adopted it as International Labour Day.[27]

The effect of these developments upon English socialist thought was palpable by the 1890s: William Morris, in *A Dream of John Ball* (1888), portrayed one of the ends of the Peasant Revolt of 1381 as having been to preserve the festivals which kept the medieval work-force joyful and free.[28] In 1894 the journalist Robert Blatchford made *Merrie England* the title of a book which called for a return to rural living, a revival of handicrafts, and a general simplification of daily life; it sold over a million copies.[29] It helped to inspire the Guild of Handicraft and the Peasant Arts Fellowship, which explicitly linked the new dreams of a socialist utopia with the traditional revelry of rural England.[30] When the Guild moved from London to the Cotswolds in 1902, it immediately set about sponsoring May games, May queens, and Jacks in the Green in its new locality.[31] Some of the leading figures of the revival of interest in folk music were members of either the Fabian Society, or the Labour Party, or both, and, a Vic Gammon has put it, perceived the rural singer as 'a sort of musical noble savage, in a way apart from the modern world'.[32] Most prominent of them, of course, was Cecil Sharp, who was convinced that collectivism was necessary in society, had a passionate belief in the essentially unchanging and communal nature of country living (he was himself a Londoner), and set himself the task of redeeming the working class from what he regarded as a degenerate and vulgar urbanized mass culture; in the last analysis his view of the masses was as patronizing as that of Lord John Manners. As described earlier, he set about systematically documenting and reviving the morris in the 1900s, at first in partnership with, and later in opposition to, Mary Neal. The latter was also a mystical socialist, dedicated to improving the lives of the masses.[33] Like Frazer, they made no attempt to ascertain the relative antiquity of the material which they collected, and so (again, as described before) inadvertently picked up compositions of Jewitt and Ferris.

The cumulative impact of all these forces upon early twentieth-century culture was considerable. During the 1920s the folk-dance revival really took off, with the morris as its principal showpiece,[34] and in 1934 six clubs formed a separate organization for it, the Morris Ring.[35] In 1907 Joseph Deedy compiled a register of local May queen coronations and (while missing a number) discovered a total of eighty-one. This was clearly not enough for him, and so he founded the Merrie England Society in 1911, with the intention of instituting more, especially around the capital. By 1930 the society could register a hundred such events,[36] the largest being at Hayes Common, Bromley, on the Kentish side of the London suburbs. Hundreds of schools competed, and little girls brought along May-dolls, of the nineteenth-century sort, in prams.[37] The most spectacular addition to those in the provinces was made at Elstow, near Bedford, where in 1925 the headmaster of the village school revived an event which had itself been a product of the first boom in such spectacles, in the 1880s. The 'queen' processed in a carriage, accompanied by train-bearers, maids, a fool, a hobby-horse, and people carrying the maypole. The children performed two dances around the latter.[38] In the north-west 'Rose queens' (at midsummer) and 'Harvest queens' (at the new-style harvest festival) were already starting to supplement the May events before the end of the nineteenth century. In the next few decades they proliferated further, and school-girl monarchs spread across Scotland also as the centre-pieces of local summer festivals. All preserved the standard Arley Hall and Knutsford format: the coronation, the procession, the 'folk' dances.[39]

After 1930 the impetus behind the revived May games faltered, as a result of the weakening of many of the communities which had supported them and, in particular, of the closure of local schools. Nevertheless, several still flourish to the present, including those at Knutsford and Elstow, and other notable examples at Montrose, Wick, and Eyemouth in Scotland, at Ickwell Green to the east of Elstow, and at Ossett in western Yorkshire (where the procession involves a three-mile motorcade). Maypole dancing is still carried on annually at Chiselhurst and Offham in western Kent, Kingsteignton and Lustleigh in eastern Devon, Welford on Avon in southern Warwickshire, Temple Sowerby in the Eden valley of Cumbria, and Barnet in Elmet in western Yorkshire, to name only the most celebrated centres. The Kent town of Rochester stages a spectacular May Day procession including all the figures beloved of the Victorian revivalists, most notably an elaborate Jack in the Green. Alongside these 'traditional' gatherings, the 1960s and early 1970s provided a further full-blown recrudescence of May customs and other 'folk' pastimes, this time based upon clubs (often linked to pubs) and private social groupings meeting at festivals, rather than on great houses, schools, or parishes. All the themes prominent in the Edwardian cult of Merrie England were restated triumphantly: pagan origins, associations with primitive communality and with nature, and an idealized rusticity. The child-queens were shed, but the other products of the earlier 'revival'—the beribboned may pole, the ruralized Jack in the Green, the morris dances and folk-songs standardized by Sharp and his followers, the circular hobby-horse—were taken up enthusiastically. What was distinctive about this second revival was that it had a pronounced counter-cultural atmosphere, being a part of that assault upon prevailing social norms which may perhaps be termed the Second Romantic Movement. By the 1980s it was waning in turn, but left an observance of May customs still much higher than that around 1960: in 1984 the Morris Ring included 160 clubs, and scores more exist which never joined it. From 1980 onward, also, the dance sides began to innovate on a large scale; the revival of the 1960s, while allied to a movement which was ostensibly opposed to the Victorian in every other aspect of British life, had been far more deferential to the nineteenth-century élite's notion of what a May game should be than that élite itself had been to previous models.

In 1975, some 335 years after May Day had last been effectively enforced as a public holiday, it was re-established as one by the reigning Labour Government. The major distinction was that, to conform to the requirements of the working week established in the early twentieth century, the holiday was granted upon the Monday following. The arguments for its institution were almost an exact reproduction of the attitudes of Edwardian socialists: that it was primarily a celebration of International Labour Day, but that it also had important associations with communal values, popular celebration, and a suspension of a normal, hierarchical social order. In the words of one prominent member of the Government, Michael Foot, 'the may-pole, then, is the English Tree of Liberty'.[40] His phrase was a self-conscious echo of Coleridge, and so the left-wing rhetoric of Merrie England was continued to the present by careful reference to its earliest beginnings. It also invited a riposte by the succeeding, Conservative, administrations, which developed into a proposal to abolish the new holiday in 1993: May Day had become a contentious partisan issue for the first time since the Restoration. The party which was largely the creation of Disraeli had (apparently unwittingly) turned its back upon the principles which he had enunciated with the rest of the 'Young

England' group. Likewise, having proudly associated itself with Victorian and Edwardian values in other respects, it was now opposed, in large public demonstrations, by people representing the full panoply of festival characters and entertainers lovingly assembled during those periods. It was the latest irony in the development of the theme of Merrie England; it is hardly likely to be the last.

29

CORPUS CHRISTI

꙳꙳꙳

THE sequence of late medieval religious festivals, which began in the darkness and cold of Advent and the promise of Christmas, and swelled again into the celebration of natural and divine rebirth at Easter, rose to a triumphant climax in June. The second half of the year was not empty of ecclesiastical feasts, for in addition to a host of local holy days it contained those of six apostles (James the Great, Bartholomew, Matthew, Simon the Less, Jude, and Andrew), an evangelist (Luke), and a succession of very popular saints. None the less, it was strikingly lacking in the dramatic communal rituals which were enacted in and around churches at such frequent intervals in the period between the winter and summer solstices. The last of this sequence, in the feast of Corpus Christi, was a joyous affirmation of a central point of Christian doctrine, performed in the open air and thus perfectly suited to a season of warmth, light, and celebration.

It was also a relatively late arrival in the calendar of Church festivals, having been proclaimed in 1317 by Pope John XXII in order to draw greater attention to the sanctity of the Eucharist and to the Real Presence of Christ in the consecrated host. His bull prescribed a liturgy to this end, to be performed on the second Thursday after Pentecost. Within one year this had been implemented across Catholic Europe, being recorded in England at St Peter's abbey, Gloucester, and at Wells cathedral. In 1322 the archbishop of York ordered it to be kept all over his province, and in 1325 a Corpus Christi guild was founded at Ipswich with responsibility for providing a procession of the host through the streets to complement the service. Another appeared at Louth, on the Lincolnshire coast, in 1326, and a further one at Leicester in 1343. A guild was founded at Coventry in 1348, and one was processing through Cambridge in the following year. The adoption of the custom was none the less a slow one, for most of the surviving English missals composed before the mid-fourteenth century do not contain the liturgy for the feast, and most of those kept in the archdeaconry of Norwich around 1360 still omitted it. The guilds only began to exist in large numbers in the middle decades of that century, and by 1388 had multiplied to the point at which a royal enquiry identified forty-two in existence, making Corpus Christi the third most popular dedication for such fraternities after the Virgin and the Trinity.[1] By the early fifteenth century every town corporation and urban parish which has left records was observing the processions, and the same is true of large Scottish burghs as their archives commence during the same century. Over the same period existing processions were being embellished further, notably by the addition of torches and banners.[2]

By the early Tudor period these urban processions were splendid affairs of which detailed descriptions survive. The host, consecrated for the occasion, was enclosed within a shrine and carried upon the shoulders of clergy, protected from rain and birds by a canopy. The populace were required to kneel bareheaded as it passed, and the councillors and craft guilds marched behind the priests in the main procession of each town. Crosses as well as banners and large wax torches were borne by those processing, and the latter sang hymns as they walked. At Leicester the mayor and other leading officers always carried the canopy. At York the shrine was of silver and crystal, and the house-fronts along the processional route were hung with tapestries and the doorways strewn with rushes and flowers. The banners carried at Coventry were of damask and velvet worked with gold. At Durham the shrine was gilded, and kept at the parish church of St Nicholas, from which it was paraded up to the cathedral for the service and then back again. The cathedral's own clergy went before it and behind it came the guilds, carrying torches on the east side of their line and banners upon the west.[3]

At London the largest procession was supplied by the Skinners' Company, and contained 200 clergy and 100 candles. Around this the individual parishes of the metropolis provided their own celebrations, decorating their churches with roses which were sometimes mixed with sweet white woodruff. Garlands were also carried in the parish processions, so that in 1521 the wardens of St Mary at Hill paid for thirty-six portable bunches of roses and lavender, and for another twenty-four of greenery. At Bristol, St John's church paid for candles to be carried by children behind the shrine, while the sexton rang the bells and a quart of muscatel wine was made ready to refresh all who participated.[4] The rite is recorded in every English and Scottish town for which good early sixteenth-century parochial, municipal, or guild documents survive.[5] In the countryside, however, it is much more difficult to find, and it may well be that village communities, lacking large populations with a complex social hierarchy and competing parishes and guilds, did not usually enact it. It is represented only in the churchwardens' accounts of market towns, themselves local centres, such as East Dereham and Swaffham in Norfolk, Saffron Walden and Great Dunmow in Essex, and Ashburton in Devon.[6] On the other hand, there is evidence that it was carried on in the village of Streatham upon the Isle of Ely, not by the parish itself but by the local Corpus Christi guild. The destruction of the records of most of these rural fraternities has left little possibility of knowing how many of them held the annual processions.[7]

At the present day the principal fame of the feast of Corpus Christi in the English-speaking world derives not so much from its religious significance as from the place which it occupies in the development of drama. By the early sixteenth century the theatrical productions of the day occurred at various levels. Upon the lowest, in some market towns, they consisted of a single play, performed after the procession. This was the case at Ashburton, where the participants performed in tunics, with crests on heads and staves in hands, against a background of painted cloths. Productions of this sort also featured regularly at Great Dunmow and at Sherborne in Dorset, and were occasional at St Lawrence, Reading, and in several east midland and East Anglian towns such as Louth, Sleaford, Stamford, Peterborough, Great Yarmouth, Eye, Ipswich, King's Lynn, Bungay, and Bury St Edmunds. In 1500 the library attached to the parish church of St Dunstan, Canterbury, contained a set of texts described as suitable for staging at Corpus Christi. All were biblical.[8]

These fixed performances need to be distinguished from the pictures of saints and of scriptural stories, and models of beasts, which were often carried in the processions. Thus East Dereham in Norfolk paraded a 'monster' on Corpus Christi Day 1493, while nearby Swaffham more demurely set forth an angel in 1515 or 1516.[9] A development from these was to draw full-scale pageants, with actors, upon carts. At York in 1415 the Coopers' Company presented 'Adam and Eve with the tree between them, the serpent deceiving them with an apple; God speaking to them and cursing the serpent, and an angel with a sword expelling them from paradise'.[10] At Dumfries in 1520 the procession included angels with wings and crowns, St Thomas, St John, St Katherine, and St Andrew carrying his cross; wigs were ordered for all the saints.[11] The first records of the carrying of such images or drawing of such tableaux are from Yorkshire: at York itself in 1376 and at Beverley in 1377. The people of King's Lynn, Norfolk, began to perform plays in 1384 and to carry 'tabernacles' in 1388. The archives at Lynn and York are so full that there can be little doubt that these are genuine testimonials to the inception of these entertainments.[12] At Coventry the earliest such records are in 1392, at Exeter in 1413, at Chester in 1422, and at Newcastle upon Tyne in 1427; all in these cases refer to a practice already established, although in the Exeter case it had been so for only a short while.[13] The first appearances in other municipalities are all later, and there a much worse survival rate of documents prevents us from determining whether their tableaux or images also originated at the end of the fourteenth century or afterward. What is certain is that some towns were still taking up the custom in the early sixteenth century, such as prospering Louth in Lincolnshire, where an annual Corpus Christi play was instituted in the 1510s and pageants in 1520.[14]

By the reigns of Henry VIII of England and James V of Scotland, it was very widespread: towns known to have adopted it by then also include Bungay, Bury St Edmunds, Doncaster, Hereford, Ipswich, Kendal, Lancaster, Preston, Shrewsbury, Worcester, Aberdeen, Edinburgh, and Perth. In every case the tableaux seem to have been the responsibility of the craft guilds, sometimes individually and sometimes grouped together; hence in 1536 the Goldsmiths,

Glaziers, Plumbers, Pewterers, and Painters of Newcastle united to provide 'The Three Kings of Cologne'. The total number of spectacles varied widely between places, so that there were fourteen at Ipswich in the 1520s, twenty-seven at Hereford in 1503, and thirty-five at Beverley in about 1520. The order in which they moved was carefully prescribed by municipal ordinance, and was quite frequently the subject of bitter competition and dispute despite this. Contributions were often levied from freemen or from the producers of cheaper pageants in order to pay for the most elaborate. In many places, also, a very light rate was laid upon the whole community to help defray expenses.[15]

A generation after the processional tableaux developed, some in a few English cities made a further evolution, into cycles of proper plays. At Coventry the latter took form rapidly in the 1440s, while at York the process occurred at some point between 1433 and 1460. The Chester cycle expanded much later, from a single play in 1474, which was subsequently moved to Whitsun, into the first three-day sequence, which evolved between 1521 and 1532.[16] The Coventry plays were the most famous in their time, the most frequently cited in literature and visited by royalty. They were also the first to be subjected to something like a scholarly study (by Thomas Sharp in 1825). The city's crafts spent lavishly on costumes and musicians, and the wagons which carried the performers must have been very large if all were like the Cappers', which had to be moved by twelve men. The performances were true plays, probably no more than ten in number and both lengthy and elaborate, so that only the richest guilds could stage them single-handed. All were biblical, and two have survived. York, by contrast, had fifty-two, each much briefer and covering between them the whole of Christian cosmic history from Creation to Doomsday. They also were performed upon wheeled vehicles, apparently with a screened lower chamber for a changing-room, and although short they required trained players. The texts for most of them have come down to the present and, together with the two from Coventry and two cycles which have no clearly identified place of origin, they represent our total collection of Corpus Christi cyclical drama and the most celebrated products of the medieval English stage. They were, indeed, arguably the most popular theatrical events of all time, staging the largest action ever attempted by any drama in the Western world. The prevailing mood in most of the plays was one of celebration, a triumphant review of Christian belief provided at the end of the 'ritual half' of the year at the season when open-air performances were most practicable.[17]

Despite almost two centuries of study, the Corpus Christi drama remains mysterious in important aspects. One, pointed out fairly recently by Alan Nelson, is that we do not know exactly how it was produced. Sharp had suggested that the wagons were hauled between 'stations' at which performances took place. This might have worked at Coventry, but the enormous length of the York cycle, and the wildly variant length of its individual components, would make it impossible for sequence and order to be maintained in such a progression. It would, furthermore, have required at least twenty-one hours and over 300 actors (unless some doubled in other roles). These problems have provoked the suggestions that only some of the cycle was presented each year or else that the whole thing took place in an open space at the end of the procession. Either or neither may be correct.[18] The second puzzle is that several towns which have left good records, including London itself, Bristol, Nottingham, Leicester, and Salisbury, did not provide pageants or plays at Corpus Christi. The question of why they failed to do so has been confronted by Mervyn James, who suggested that the cycles developed in urban centres which contained a tension and free play of political and social forces, and required a constant affirmation of unity, order, and degree. Those towns always dominated by a self-co-opting élite, he argued, never experienced the need for them.[19] The argument is ingenious, and may well be correct, but is not susceptible of proof in the existing condition of the evidence. As Professor James himself noted, conflicts over precedence in the procession could be an occasion for division in themselves. More important is the fact that we do not yet know enough about the political arrangements of most late medieval English towns to tell whether the distinction holds up. At London the point is not that the craft guilds failed to parade with pageants but that they chose to do so at Midsummer (as will be shown) and not at Corpus Christi. At issue was not a difference in social mechanisms but in favoured festivals, based apparently upon local whims or accidents which have not been recorded.

The same whims resulted in what were effectively the same entertainments appearing in other major urban centres upon other feasts. At Chester and Norwich, as said, the play cycles ended up at Whitsun. Canterbury's parade was held on 6 July, the eve of the feast of its principal local saint, Thomas Becket. It included the militia, torch-bearers, the aldermen in scarlet gowns, model giants, gunners, and musicians. The floats were supplied by the town's wards, one always being 'The Martyrdom of St Thomas', with children playing the murderous knights, and a liberal splashing of pigs' blood. At Lincoln the churches and priory lent religious ornaments for use in pageants upon the feast of St Anne, 26 July, and each alderman contributed a silk gown to dress the actors representing kings.[20]

The essential involvement of the feast of Corpus Christi with the doctrine of the medieval Church made it a prime target of early Protestants.[21] As a 'Catholic' reformer, Henry VIII inflicted no damage upon its activities, and a full-scale assault was left to the regime of his son. In the autumn of 1547 an Act of Parliament empowered that government to seize the endowments of the religious guilds upon which so many of the processions had depended.[22] In parishes where it was not coupled with any such body, they could in theory have continued, but in practice the royal ministers discouraged it so strongly at London in 1548 that no clergy dared to perform the processions there. Some priests still held services, and many citizens kept the day as a holiday, but the new liturgy of 1549 expunged it altogether.[23] Official disapproval apparently reached out also to provincial towns, because there likewise the processions with the host, held as lavishly as ever in 1547, did not appear the next year.[24] With them went both the pageants carried in them and the village plays, neither featuring in any records from the rest of Edward's reign. The principal relics of this luxuriant seasonal culture of ritual and entertainment were now the celebrated cycles of plays at Coventry and York, stripped of passages which offended Protestant sensibilities.[25]

Then came the reign of Mary, and in 1554 the former liturgy and the processions were commanded again by royal proclamation. In that year it was neglected by some London parishes, and a Protestant joiner tried to snatch the sacrament from one crossing Smithfield.[26] From 1555, however, it is recorded in all the surviving sets of City churchwardens' accounts except one,[27] and in all those still existing at Bristol. Mary herself, and her consort Philip, led the progress of the host around their palace.[28] The ritual was also definitely revived at York, Chester, Lincoln, Norwich, Newcastle upon Tyne, Canterbury, Cambridge, and Coventry. At Norwich the corporation set up a tree hung with 'flowers, grocery and fruit', and the Grocers' guild paid for a carved and gilded griffin (its emblem) carried by three ladies, a pennant-bearer in a yellow wool coat, a 'crowned angel', and flowers bound in coloured thread.[29] Other Corpus Christi processions made their way through the towns of Dover, Bungay, Ludlow, Sherborne, Ashburton, and Louth, and through several market towns and villages in Buckinghamshire, Kent, and Surrey. Just as before Edward's reign, they seem to have been mainly an urban phenomenon, although obviously also present in some rural communities in the south-east.[30]

This renaissance was, naturally, halted by the Elizabethan Reformation, and in 1559 the liturgy was altered, and the processions prohibited, yet again. The following year the same process occurred in Scotland. There, some long-term resistance did result. In Perth as late as 1577 some townspeople defied both magistrates and minister to perform a play and carry a host at Corpus Christi: their punishment was excommunication, and they had to repent to get their children baptized. In England the processions vanished at once. There, just as under Edward, it was the drama which remained at what was no longer in itself a feast of the Church, purged afresh of passages offensive to the reformed religion.[31] Even so, the proponents of the latter only tolerated it for a time. In the 1570s the celebrated play cycles at Coventry, York, and Wakefield were all abolished, and that at Newcastle was reduced to selections. At Coventry the craft guilds performed productions at midsummer instead, with new, Protestant, texts. The Newcastle plays were banned completely in the 1580s, as were those at Doncaster, Ipswich, and (apparently) Lancaster and Preston. By 1600 only the cycle at Kendal survived, and this was despite much anxiety on the part of the corporation. Wherever the records are good enough to reveal the driving force behind this process, it is found to consist of evangelical Protestantism. The northern play-cycles were systematically repressed between 1572 and 1576 by the ecclesiastical commission of churchmen and magnates established at York to reform the whole region after the defeat of the Rebellion of the Northern Earls. Its impact upon the Chester Whitsun cycle has been described. These men also forbade the Wakefield plays on the grounds that they degraded the life of Christ by representing it on stage. At York itself one of the pioneers of the new religion in the city, the Dean, Matthew Hutton, had threatened the corporation in 1568 with the displeasure of 'the learned' and 'the state' if the Corpus Christi drama continued. In 1570 he was joined by an archbishop of similar hue, Edmund Grindal, who subsequently confiscated the texts. In 1579 the city council asked if the latter might be 'corrected' to the churchmen's satisfaction but, although whole sections were indeed ripped out, no performances were, in the end, permitted. This process was made possible by the collaboration of a few enthusiastic Protestants in the corporation, whom the commission had helped into power. At Coventry the demise of the plays was ascribed to a parallel alliance of new parish ministers and city councillors, to the marked disappointment of most of the populace. The head burgesses of Kendal, apologizing to the northern commission for the continued existence of their cycle of drama, pleaded that they had been forced to permit it because of vociferous public demand. Perhaps because the situation of this little town is secreted among the Westmorland fells, a long way from the commission's seat at York, its plays were allowed to continue for the rest of the reign of Elizabeth. Then the accession of James brought with it a desire for a clean sweep: in 1605 the town council of Kendal received an order for representatives to attend the commission once again, and after that all references to the plays cease.[32] After nearly three hundred years of adoption, elaboration, and repression, the story of the feast of Corpus Christi in Britain had been closed.

For proponents of revelry in general, and medieval seasonal revelry in particular, there was one consolation. The latest date on which Corpus Christi could have fallen in the year, produced by an unusually late Easter, was 24 June. That was also Midsummer Day, part of a round of often frenetic festivities which were older than the doctrine of the Real Presence, than the papacy, and, indeed than Christianity itself. They were also to prove a great deal more durable in Britain than the feast of the Body of Christ. It is to these that this book must turn.

THE MIDSUMMER FIRES

꧁⚜꧂

I N the fourth-century *Acts* of the martyr St Vincent is a description of how the pagans of Aquitane, south-western France, celebrated a festival by rolling a flaming wheel downhill to a river. The charred pieces were then reassembled in the temple of a sky god.[1] The time of the festival was not specified, but just over a thousand years later a monk of Winchcombe, on the Cotswold Edge of Gloucestershire, referred again to the rolling of the wheel, and ascribed it to Midsummer Eve, the evening before the Christian Feast of St John the Baptist upon 24 June.[2] In the sixteenth century the Protestant writer Thomas Naogeorgus described it in detail, implying that it was common in northern Europe on that night.[3] This is certainly borne out by nineteenth-century folklore collections. For a comparable portrayal in Britain, we have to wait until 1909, when a folklorist published the following description of the custom in the Vale of Glamorgan during the 1820s:

People conveyed trusses of straw to the top of the hill, where men and youths waited for the contributions. Women and girls were stationed at the bottom of the hill. Then a large cart wheel was thickly swathed with straw and not an inch of wood was left in sight. A pole was inserted through the centre of the wheel, so that long ends extended about a yard on each side. If any straw remained, it was made up into torches at the top of tall sticks. At a given signal the wheel was lighted and set rolling downhill. If this fire-wheel went out before it reached the bottom of the hill, a very poor harvest was promised. If it kept lighted all the way down, and continued blazing for a long time, the harvest would be exceptionally abundant. Loud cheers and shouts accompanied the progress of the wheel.[4]

At Buckfastleigh, on the fringe of Dartmoor in Devon, the wheel lit at sunset on Midsummer Eve in the mid-nineteenth-century was guided by sticks as it rolled in the hope that it would reach a stream. If it did so, good luck would be due to the community: the action exactly paralleled that in ancient Aquitane.[5] On that Eve in 1954 the villagers of Widdecombe, deeper inside the moor, revived the custom, which had also obtained there a century before.[6] The wheel, however, was not lit, and the revived tradition does not seem to have held. With its failure seems to have passed the last vestige, in Britain at least, of a custom which has a recorded history of almost two millennia, stretching back into the pagan past.

Its longevity was typical of the intensity of the manner in which this festival was celebrated, as were its association with fire and its widespread nature. The feast of St John, commonly known as Midsummer Day, occupied much the same relationship with the solar cycle as Christmas Day; it represented the end of a solstice, the period in which the sun ceased to move for a short period, but rose and set at the same points on the horizon at the extreme end of its range. Now, however, it was at the height of its strength, and light at its longest, and Midsummer Eve represented the culmination of that period of apogee, just before the days began to shorten again as the sun moved southward. In response to the swelling of heat and light, foliage and grasses were now likewise at their fullness, before the time of fruiting approached. No wonder that it seemed to be a magical time to ancient Europeans. The late twelfth-century penitential of Bartholomew Iscanus declared that 'He who at the feast of St John the Baptist does any work of sorcery to seek out the future shall do penance for fifteen days',[7] and indeed rites of divination remained very common on this night far into the modern period. An eleventh-century Anglo-Saxon medical text, the *Lacnunga*, prescribed vervain gathered on Midsummer Day for liver complaints,[8] and the later folklore collections are full of similar plant magic associated with the feast. This book is, however, concerned with communal customs, and those of midsummer revolved mostly around fire. The lighting of festive fires upon St John's Eve is first recorded as a popular custom by Jean Belethus, a theologian at the University of Paris, in the early twelfth century;[9] as appropriate sources before then are so sparse, there is no reason to doubt that the tradition was much older. During the nineteenth century it was found in the whole of Europe and in the north-west part of Africa as well.[10] In the northern half of the continent the festival was generally the most important one of the whole year.[11] It was frequently celebrated in two instalments, upon the eve of the feast of St John, and upon that of the joint one of two other major saints, Peter and Paul, placed five days later upon the 28th. This system afforded an opportunity both to repeat especially effective festivities and to cancel one set in case of bad weather.

In England the earliest references to this merry-making are from the thirteenth century, effectively the time at which the sort of records likely to reveal it first occur. One is an agreement between the lord and tenants of the manor of East Monckton, Wiltshire, in the reign of Henry III, by which the former promised to provide a ram for a feast by the latter if they carried fire around his cornfields on Midsummer Eve. The other is in the *Liber Memorandum* of the church at Barnwell in the Nene valley in Rutland, for the year 1295; it stated that the parish youth would gather at a well that evening for songs and games.[12] The first record in Ireland is from New Ross, a town of English settlers, on St Peter's Eve 1305, when the inhabitants 'stayed up at night and made fire in the streets'.[13] Later in that century a monk of Lilleshall, in Shropshire, wrote that 'In the worship of St John, men waken at even, and maken three manner of fires: one is clean bones and no wood, and is called a bonfire; another is of clean wood and no bones, and is called a wakefire, for men sitteth and wake by it; the third is made of bones and wood, and is called St John's Fire'. The stench of the burning bones, he added was thought to drive away dragons.[14]

From the early sixteenth century come three splendid descriptions of the same celebrations. The famous one is by John Stow of London:

there were usually made bonfires in the streets, every man bestowing wood or labour towards them: the wealthier sort also before their doors near to the said bonfires, would set out tables on the Vigils, furnished with sweet bread, and good drink, and on the festival days with meat and drinks plentifully, whereunto they would invite their neighbours and passengers also to sit, and be merry with them in great familiarity, praising God for his benefits bestowed on them. These were called bonfires as well of good amity amongst neighbours that, being before at controversy, were there by the labour of others reconciled, and made of bitter enemies, loving friends, as also for the virtue that a great fire hath to purge the infection of the air. On the vigil of St John Baptist and St Peter and Paul the Apostles, every man's door being shadowed with green birch, long fennel, St John's Wort, Orpin, white lilies and such like, garnished upon with garlands of beautiful flowers, had also lamps of glass, with oil burning in them all the night, some hung out branches of iron curiously wrought, containing hundreds of lamps lit at once, which made goodly show.[15]

Most parts of this account can be supported from other evidence. In 1400 German merchants in the city paid to hang out lamps upon these nights,[16] while in the early Tudor period the churches there were decorated with birch, and sometimes fennel too, for midsummer.[17] There is also our second description, from the corporation journal for 1526, consisting of a royal order for a celebration 'after the manner of Midsummer', with bonfires in the street, children sitting round them wearing garlands of flowers, and minstrels playing.[18] Up in Suffolk around this time, at the prosperous cloth-working town of Long Melford, one of the wealthiest inhabitants had a fire lit before his house on both evenings, and gave a tub of ale and one of bread to the poor. He also set a table near the blaze himself and called to it 'some of the friends and more civil poor neighbours'.[19]

It is difficult to prove that such rejoicing was universal in medieval and early Tudor England, for it did not require systematic payment and so account books, the one 'objective' source for these periods, is of little help in the matter. Every subjective indication is, none the less, that it was very widespread. Literary commentators took this for granted.[20] Henry VII and Henry VIII had their own bonfires, made in their great hall by its pages and grooms on either eve or both, suggesting a national custom.[21] There are also casual references such as the notes by the Warwickshire gentleman Sir Henry Willoughby, who supplied bread and ale for bonfire parties upon Midsummer and St Peter's Eves in 1521, and gave a penny to a maiden who presented him with a garland at the latter event.[22] There is also the testimony of urban archives. Some early Tudor towns paid directly for the bonfires, such as Sandwich, or for music in the streets on the same nights, such as Newcastle upon Tyne.[23] More invested in the spectacular 'marching watches'. The first of these seems to have begun at London in 1378, when the corporation ordered that the watchmen set in each ward to guard against disorder on festival nights should henceforth process behind their local aldermen on Midsummer and St Peter's Eve. They were to wear splendid costumes and carry 'cressets', pails of fire hung from poles. The order was repeated in 1386,[24] and by the early sixteenth century the local parades had grown into one grand consolidated procession 4,000 strong, including the corporation and the livery companies and featuring morris dancers, model giants, and pageants.[25] They carried so many torches that, according to a later writer, they released

> A thousand sparks dispersed throughout the sky
> Which like to wandering stars about did fly,
> Whose wholesome heat, purging the air, consumes
> The earth's unwholesome vapours, fogs and fumes.[26]

In 1521 the Lord Mayor was a Draper, and so his livery company made a particularly elaborate contribution to the Midsummer Eve entertainments. It included five pageants: 'the Castle of War', 'the story of Jesse', 'St John the Evangelist', 'St George', and 'Pluto', the last of these including a serpent that spat fireballs. All were carried on platforms. There was also a model giant called 'Lord Marlinspikes', a morris team, naked boys dyed black to represent devils, armoured halberdiers, and a King of the Moors clad in black satin robes, with silver paper shoes and a turban crowned with white plumes. He walked or was carried under a canopy, and 'wild fire' went with him. Twenty years later, when a 'watch' was planned, the Drapers projected another morris dance, and giant, and more pageants. This time the pageants were to be 'the Assumption of the Virgin Mary', 'Christ disputing with the Doctors', 'the Rock of Roche', and 'St Margaret'. Sixteen porters were needed to haul these displays. Margaret was to be accompanied by four children dressed as angels, all in yellow wigs and two with wings of peacock feathers. Christ had a black wig, and the Doctors long hair and beards. In addition there were to be twelve 'mummers with visors and hats', eight 'players with two handed swords', banner-bearers, and a dragon with 'aqua vitae' burning in its mouth.[27]

The equivalent display at Coventry seems to have been provoked by a complaint from the Prior of the city's abbey, about the violence which had broken out among the revellers on Midsummer and St Peter's Night in 1421, and had led to deaths. He asked for proper watches to be settled upon those dates, and by the early sixteenth century these had developed, as at London, into a mighty parade by all crafts. It included men in splendid armour, banners, and minstrels, and bearers of torches (in stands called Judases) and of cressets burning resin-soaked rope.[28] Another spectacular display was at Chester, where by 1564 the 'Midsummer Show' traditionally included four giants, a unicorn, two camels, a lynx, a dragon, six hobby-horses, and sixteen 'naked boys'.[29] 'Marching watches' of armed men, torch-bearers and musicians are also recorded during the early sixteenth century at

Nottingham, Exeter, Bristol, Liverpool, Barnstaple, and Totnes. At Gloucester, Plymouth, Carlisle, Salisbury, and Kendal, they appear as soon as municipal archives begin in the later Tudor period, and had almost certainly survived from before then.[30] They were not universal, as York, Norwich, and Leicester are among the major urban centres of the age which have left good records and do not seem to have instituted these parades. None the less, they rank as one of the splendours of late medieval municipal pageantry.

Like so much of that pageantry, it struck a reef in the shape of the Reformation. At first sight, the midsummer revels should not have been vulnerable to that process, being hardly connected to the rites of the old Church; and indeed no statute, proclamation, injunction, or set of visitation articles ever condemned them. Nevertheless, they still offended zealous Protestants. They were associated with the feasts of saints, howbeit important, and scriptural, figures. The notion of magical properties associated with the fires, indicated in some of the sources cited above, was obnoxious to reformers already set on getting rid of holy water, ashes, candles, and 'palm crosses'.[31] Furthermore, the regular assembly of large numbers of armed citizens was disquieting to governments who feared rebellion against the religious changes which they were trying to impose. At the very beginning of those changes, in 1533, Henry VIII's Council was already seeking a pretext to abolish at least some of those parades. It did get rid of the most famous in 1539, by suppressing the London march as what was supposed to be a temporary economy measure. This turned out to last for the rest of the reign, and the plans of the Drapers in 1541 came to nothing. Lord Protector Somerset did revive the procession in 1548, as a compensation for having discouraged those of Corpus Christi, but the favour was not repeated. Thereafter, despite some talk of it, the midsummer 'watch' was never seen again in the city.[32] Elsewhere they lasted longer, but their story in the hundred years between 1540 and 1640 is one of steady attrition; of reductions in scale and in frequency, of controversy and opposition, and eventually, of lapse or abolition.[33] Only those at Chester and Nottingham survived until the Civil War, which naturally enough put paid to them. Chester restored its 'show' when the monarchy returned, but abolished it again in 1678, and this time it never reappeared.[34]

The story of the bonfires was a longer and more complex one. Royal support for the custom was withdrawn in 1541, when Henry VIII cancelled the traditional payment to make one in his hall.[35] After then, also, there is no more mention of any at London. They do not seem to have been an issue in the Edwardian Reformation, but in the first decade of that of Elizabeth there was an outburst of Protestant hostility to them in the dioceses of Canterbury and Winchester.[36] A typical case, among several, was that of a priest at Birchington, in the Isle of Thanet, who was reported to a church court for lighting a St Peter's Eve fire.[37] Most spectacular was the confrontation at Canterbury itself in 1561, between the corporation and citizens, and the

Protestant clergy newly installed in the cathedral. The latter held the bonfires to be 'in contempt of the Christian religion, and for upholding the old frantic superstitions of papistry'. They were answered with the kindling of a larger number than usual, culminating in an outsize specimen on the evening of St Peter's Day, made with the help of the sheriff and a constable. A character called 'Railing Dick' led a procession of boys around it, carrying birch branches and singing bawdy songs.[38] After 1570 there is no more trace of the midsummer pyrotechnics in East Anglia, south-east England, or the whole corridor of the Thames valley up to, and including, Gloucestershire: an area corresponding with uncanny precision to that which Geoffrey Dickens has identified as the heartland of early English Protestantism.[39] Outside it, the traditional spirit portrayed by Stow lasted a little longer, exemplified by the citizen at Warwick in 1571 who bequeathed a sum to pay for four fires to be made in his ward on the two festive eves every year.[40] A late Elizabethan ballad could still portray how

> When midsomer comes, with bavens and bromes they do bonefires make,
> and swiftly, then, the nimble young men runne leapinge over the same.
> The women and maydens together do couple their handes.
> With bagpipes sounde, they daunce a rounde; no malice among them standes.[41]

Just as typical of the age, however, was John Tomkyns, minister of St Mary's at Shrewsbury, who after years of campaigning persuaded the bailiffs to ban summer bonfires in the town (along with may poles) in 1591.[42] After the reign of Elizabeth the festive blazes are not described at any urban centre in the Midlands. They were recorded at Dorchester and nearby Lyme in the 1630s, at the latter community being described as 'for the christening of apples'.[43] A similar phrase, signifying the blessing of the trees, was also used by John Aubrey later in the century, to describe the function of the fires in Somerset and Herefordshire.[44] After 1700, however, there is no further mention of them in those two counties or in Dorset.

The waning of the custom was none the less a slow process, and it showed considerable vitality in other regions. During the late eighteenth century it still flourished in the south-western peninsula, Northumberland, Country Durham, and the Wolds and Pennine foothills of Yorkshire. It is a pattern which no longer bears any resemblance to religious beliefs. In addition the fires were made occasionally in Derbyshire and Nottinghamshire and survived in two pockets further south in the Midlands, on Cannock Chase and Dunstable Downs.[45] These were communal festivities, and the tradition of the beneficial nature of midsummer flames also found echoes in private practice, such as that of the old farmer at Holford in the Quantock hills of Somerset in 1900. Each Midsummer Eve he would pass a burning branch over and under all his cattle and horses.[46] Most exuberant, and most frequently recorded, of all these later revels were those in western Cornwall. At Penzance on both St John's and St Peter's Eves in the years around 1800, 'a line of tar barrels, relieved occasionally by large bonfires' was kindled along the centre of each of the main streets. The young people passed on either side of these, swinging torches of tarred canvas nailed to sticks three to four feet long. At the end of the evening they would link hands and dance 'thread the needle' over the embers. Inland from the port, on the rocky hills of Penwith Hundred, the rural youth danced wildly around their own blazes, hands linked in a circle. At the close they pulled each other over the glowing remnants 'that they might extinguish the fires by treading them out, without breaking their chain, or rather ring'. As at Penzance, this procedure was held to be lucky.[47]

For all this, there is an air of marginalization surrounding the fires by this stage. Apart from Penzance, Sunderland was the only town which still lit them. They were really now the preserve of rural youth, rather than of whole communities, and a focus for fun and games rather than a source of beneficial magic. It is not surprising that their disappearance during the nineteenth century was rapid and ubiquitous. By 1900 only one remained, at the isolated village of Whalton in the Blyth valley of Northumberland. Having thereby acquired the status of a relic, it has been preserved as such, being still lit upon Old Midsummer's Eve, which has fallen on 4 July after the calendar change of 1752.[48] The focus of the celebration is very much upon the local children, who dance round it and scramble for sweets at the close of the festivities. Very different is the atmosphere surrounding the chain of bonfires along the Cornish peninsula, kindled by the Federation of Old Cornwall Societies since the 1920s, representing a revival of the custom about forty years after it had died out in the county. In place of the exuberant adolescents of the eighteenth- and nineteenth-century celebrations, the people who light and watch the fires are mostly adults, motivated by local patriotism and reverence for tradition. The lighting is performed according to an order of service, including a Christian blessing in the Cornish language (itself re-created in the 1920s). Wild flowers are cast into the flames as symbols of prosperity, to become one with the fire, while weeds are burned with a malediction. At the bonfire above St Cleer, a witch's broom and hat are placed on the top, to be destroyed as symbols of evil. It is a sustained and imposing effort of evocation, not of the historic Cornwall of 200 years ago, but of a shadowy Cornish past about four centuries older than that.

The story of the fires in Scotland is superficially similar. They emerge into recorded history, like so many Scottish customs, with the coming of the Reformation and an attack upon them by the new Protestant Kirk. In the 1580s they were forbidden by Kirk sessions and presbyteries at Edinburgh and Stirling, apparently with success. From the next decade, however, the struggle was centred upon the north-east, in the hinterlands of Aberdeen, Elgin, and Dingwall, and it continued for a hundred years.[49] Its tenacity was due to the fact that many people there still believed that the flames of Midsummer and St Peter's Nights had protective properties: they carried them round cereal fields and fixed them in their cabbage patches. This was, of course, precisely why the devout ministers and elders wanted to stop them. In the end, it was the Kirk that lost, a defeat neatly signalled in 1745, when the Reverend J. Bisset of Aberdeen made a bonfire at his own gate, with a table spread near it for the local youngsters.[50] In 1799 a Scottish merchant living in London, Alexander Hogg, left a bequest for an annual Midsummer Day fire, and for ale, bread, and cheese around it, in his native parish of Durris, a few miles up-river from Aberdeen.[51] In the eighteenth century the midsummer fires were found also in Moray, Perthshire, and Ayrshire, in the Border districts around Kelso and Hawick, and on the shores of Loch Ness.[52] In the lowland districts named, they were (by then) merely a focus for enjoyment, but in those further north the flames were still carried three times sunwise around flocks, herds, and fields to protect and bless them. The distribution is still, none the less, a curious one, for it is confined to parts of the Lowlands and adjacent districts of the Highlands; the fires do not seem to feature in contemporary accounts (or later reminiscences) of the central and western Highlands where a more completely Gaelic culture persisted.

This impression is dramatically borne out by a consideration of the Scottish islands, for there is absolutely no evidence of the custom in the Hebrides, but it was abundantly recorded in the Northern Isles, where a Scandinavian rather than a Gaelic influence prevailed. 'Johnsmas' fires in early nineteenth-century Shetland were built on piled stones, with a foundation of 'bones of fish and animals, peats, straw, seaweed, flowers, feathers, even a tet o'oo [tuft of wool]. To these would be added the ornals [broken remains] of any household article with pell [rags]. On top of all was set a small kap [wooden bowl] containing a little fish oil. A glorious blaze would rise'.[53] In Orkney during the same period the Johnsmas flames were kindled of heather set about a core of peat, and danced about and jumped from sunset to sunrise, which in those latitudes is a matter of a few hours. They were lit with an ember carried specially from a homestead; and youths kindled torches from them 'so that in the grimlins [faint light] of midnight the face of the hill was aglow with fiery haloes'. At that time farmers were just ceasing to carry the brands around fields and into byres to bring their land and livestock good fortune.[54] It was in these 'fringe' areas of Scotland that the traditions lasted longest. By 1896 it was described as 'long since died out' in the Highlands and north-east.[55] The fire at Tarbolton in Ayrshire was kept up by boys until the 1900s,[56] those in Shetland persisted as centre-pieces for family parties until the Second World War,[57] and the people of Durris finally ceased to keep faith with Alexander Hogg in 1945.[58] What seems to have doomed the custom was the attrition of the belief that it actually brought protection; after that the effort of keeping it up appears to have caused its demise in most places long before community links and old-style farming practices themselves started to disintegrate.

In Wales the tradition is barely represented, being confined to the heavily Anglicized vale of Glamorgan and a small area of the centre including Darowen in the Dovey valley and Trefedryd in Montgomeryshire. The fires in the latter zone were small affairs. Those in the former could be quite elaborate, built of three or nine different kinds of wood and having fragrant herbs and posies of flowers thrown into them.[59] Even there, however, they were far surpassed as a focus for midsummer merry-making by the ubiquitous may pole, known in this context as *y fedwen haf*, 'the summer birch'. Those in eighteenth- and nineteenth-century Glamorgan were magnificent specimens, decorated with wreaths, ribbons, and sometimes 'pictures' and a crowning weathercock. Fierce rivalry between settlements was expressed in attempts to steal each other's poles, and at midsummer 1768 that at St Fagans had to be guarded all night with guns against hundreds of assailants from three other villages, who had obtained reinforcements from Cardiff. The poles were centres for June merry-making all over the principality.[60]

A survey of the British evidence therefore might suggest that the midsummer fires were not a 'Celtic' custom at all, being found in Wales and in the Scottish Highlands and Islands only where an English or Scandinavian influence was strong. This would fit nicely into a portrait of ancient Celtic festivals as devoted to the opening of seasons (like Beltane) rather than to the cardinal points of the sun. Such a surmise, however, is resoundingly contradicted by the data from Ireland and that outpost of Irish folk culture, the Isle of Man. In the latter during the eighteenth century, the islanders lit midsummer fires on the windward side of every cornfield, so that the smoke would blow over the growing crops, and carried torches around their cattle pens.[61] In Ireland it is true that Peter's Eve fires were only recorded in the east, from County Monaghan to County Wexford, and inland to Westmeath, and so may easily be ascribed to English settler influence. In the eighteenth and nineteenth centuries, from which the first good sources date, the Midsummer Night fires were, however, found almost everywhere in the island, with the belief that smoke, ashes, embers, or torches from them would bless humans, animals, and crops alike. The kindling was often performed with prayers. They were much more common then than those upon May Day, the famous Beltane, and indeed much more so than at any other time of the Irish year.[62] It is in Ireland, more than in any other part of the British Isles, that they persist to the present day, being fairly common focuses for social events in the west. Unsurprisingly, the descriptions of them in the past are more detailed than any British equivalents. Even during the mid-nineteenth century, when the religious element had diminished, it was still very prominent, as in this portrait by Lady Wilde:

When the fire has burned down to a red glow the young men strip to the waist and leap over or through the flames; this is done backwards and forwards several times, and he who braves the greatest blaze is considered the victor over the powers of evil, and is greeted with tremendous applause. When the fire burns still lower, the young girls leap the flame, and those who leap three times back and forward will be certain of speedy marriage and good luck in the after-life, with many children. The married women then walk through the lines of the burning embers; and when the fire is nearly burnt and trampled down, the yearling cattle are driven through the hot ashes, and their back is singed with a lighted hazel twig. These rods are kept safely afterwards, being considered of immense power to drive the cattle to and from the watering places. As the fire diminishes the shouting grows fainter, and the song and dance commence; while professional story-tellers narrate tales of fairy-land, or of the good old times long ago . . . When the crowd at length separate, every one carries home a brand from the fire, and great virtue is attached to the lighted *brone* which is safely carried to the house without breaking or falling to the ground. Many contests also rise amongst the young men; for whoever enters his house first with the sacred fire brings the good luck of the year with him.[63]

It is possible that many of the touches in this picture are specifically Irish, but it is equally so that here we have precisely those 'frantic suppressions of papistry' against which the clergy of Elizabethan Canterbury had fulminated; the records do not permit a decision. The importance of the midsummer flames in Gaelic Irish tradition and their absence from Gaelic Scotland raises a further problem for those who would believe in a single 'Celtic' cultural province of festivals. One resolution of it would be to suggest that the fires of St John, as well as those of St Peter, were brought to Ireland by medieval English settlement which the Scottish Gaels did not experience; but this is, again, unprovable.

So what did the custom signify? Here linguistics cause more confusion than resolution, for the definition of the English term 'bonfire' is itself a matter of considerable difficulty. From the remarks of the Shropshire monk, and other sources cited earlier, it may be surmised that it simply denoted a fire in which bones were burned. The antiquary John Brand, however, pointed out yet other early commentators who derived it from 'boon', a gift or mark of (neighbourly) goodwill.[64] Alternatively, it could be descended from the Danish or Norse word *baun*, meaning a beacon, or from 'bane-fire', as it was the bane of evil things. If it really does come from 'bone', then this is unique in Europe, where most terms for the festive blazes signify 'fire of joy'.[65]

It is possible to get much further with the question of what the fires meant by looking at how they were used. Here Sir James Frazer moved from one sort of explanation to another, beginning by suggesting that their point in the calendar indicated that they were ceremonies of sun-worship, and later em-phasizing them more as rites of protection and blessing.[66] Alan Gailey has recently pointed out how very much more evidence the folklore collections supply for the latter interpretation than the former, indeed to the point of eclipsing any other.[67] The quantity and force of that evidence must, indeed, be obvious from the sample provided above, which can be enormously extended in space and time. Frazer found examples all over Europe of the use of the midsummer blazes to ward off evil, witches being the prime traditional targets. Almost two thousand years before, the Roman writer Pliny had advised farmers to make bonfires around their fields in summer to protect the crops from disease.[68] At the far end of the Old World, in eastern Siberia, the Buryat tribe customarily leaped fires to shield themselves from harm.[69]

The concept of this element as the one which purifies and protects seems to be natural to humanity. It is also obvious to a historian of medieval or early modern Europe why late June would be a particularly important time at which to employ it. It preceded the season at which crops would be most vulnerable to weather or blight, and livestock to their diseases. It also ushered in the months in which insects multiplied most widely and in which, therefore, humans were most likely to contract bubonic plague, typhus, and malaria. The fires of St John and St Peter were therefore deployed against serious dangers, and anxieties.

On the other hand, the two forms of explanation are wholly compatible, for it would have made perfect sense to use the flames when the greatest fire in the traditional cosmos, the sun, was putting out most strength. In this connection, the burning wheels which featured at the opening of this chapter bear a particular significance. As Miranda Green has recently emphasized,[70] the spoked wheel was one of the most widespread and popular images of the sun in prehistoric Europe. It remained the standard symbol for it, or for the whole heaven, in the north-west provinces of the Roman Empire, including Britain. The use of the wheel, wreathed in flames, as an ancillary device in the midsummer ceremonies, reinforces the argument for an essential solar component in those rites. With that in place, the dossier seems to be complete enough to speak confidently of a pre-Christian seasonal ritual of major importance, documented for at least eight and a half centuries and (if one accepts the wheel-rite in ancient Aquitane as connected) for perhaps fifteen or more.

31

SHEEP, HAY, AND RUSHES

AROUND the important ecclesiastical, municipal, and popular ceremonies of June were undertaken a pair of major agricultural tasks which in some districts were so central to the economy that they involved their own formalities of organization and celebration. The first was sheep-shearing, of which a late Elizabethan ballad-writer could declaim:

> At sheering of sheepe, which they do keepe,
> good lorde! What sporte is than.
> What great good cheire, what ale and beare, is set to every man.
> With beefe and with baken, in wooden brown platters, good store,
> they fall to their meate, and merrily eate:
> they call for no sauce therfore.[1]

Just over a hundred years later, another ballad could describe the shearer's feast in almost identical terms,[2] and in its essentials it hardly altered down to the middle of the nineteenth century, its most famous literary portrayal being in Thomas Hardy's *Far from the Madding Crowd*. Other records of Hardy's Dorset bear out most of its details and set them in a geographical and chronological perspective. It is plain that the suppers were partly a local tradition, being much more common in the south of the county than in the north. Until the middle of the nineteenth century the shearing in Dorset was performed by mutual aid between farmers, all converging with their own complements of hands to assist a particular neighbour on a given day. The meal which closed the process was their reward, and their families and friends were invited. Thereafter the process was commercialized, itinerant bands of men who were normally thatchers, hurdle-makers, and hedgers going from farm to farm hiring out their labour. They too got a substantial supper, but one which lacked the invitation to families and thus most of the festive elements which had been attached to the old feasts. Singing remained a feature of them, many of the favourite numbers being taken from corn harvest suppers, but a few designed specially for the occasion, such as

> Here's health unto the shepherd,
> His clip and his dog,
> Thinking on the dumb creatures
> While they feed in the field;
> With other dumb creatures

Their fruit they do yield.
For their dung serves the corn ground,
And the wool clothes the poor.
So drink up your liquor
And fill up some more.[3]

All that was unusual about Dorset was that its southerly climate meant that the work commonly began there in May; otherwise the details provided above can be applied nation-wide wherever sheep were kept in large number.[4] In Sussex and East Anglia the employment of itinerant bands began earlier and was more highly developed, as each group elected a 'captain' to negotiate deals with farmers and set up an itinerary. In the former county he wore a gold band or gold stars in his hat. These groups no longer received suppers from the farms, but each held its own celebration at an inn when the season of work ended. The songs adapted accordingly, as in this one from Sussex:

When all our work is done, and all our sheep are shorn,
Then home with our captain to drink the ale that's strong;
'Tis a barrel of hum-cup, which we calls the Black Ram;
And we do sit and swagger, and swear that we are men,
But yet afore this night I'll stand you half a crown
That if you don't have special care, this Ram'll knock you down![5]

Alongside this work the hay harvest was proceeding but, unlike that of cereals, it seems to have been little attended by ritual. Only in the nineteenth-century Warwickshire Cotswolds was any such recorded, the mowers going to work with a posy of flowers pinned to the smock of each by a wife or sweetheart. Around Ilmington and Whitchurch in this region the last clump of grass was twisted into the shape of a cock's head and cut by flung sickles, while about Brailes a live cock was thrown at instead; in this fashion a very widespread corn-harvest custom was blended with a celebrated Shrovetide one.[6]

As summer wore on, another sort of harvest commenced in most areas, and was conducted annually in July and August until the nineteenth century: of fresh rushes, to carpet the floors of churches and poorer dwellings. In the north-west of England alone, the procedure was developed into a procession to the church, carrying some of the rushes woven with flowers to be hung within the building as decorations. The parade was accompanied by music, if only a piper, and the ensuing religious service was followed by a parish feast, the local equivalent of an ale or revel. The region of this ceremonial 'rush-bearing' comprised essentially the western and central Pennines and the Cumbrian mountains, representing parts of Westmorland, Lancashire, Derbyshire, and Cheshire, and the western extremes of Yorkshire. It must have developed before the end of the Middle Ages, but the paucity of early records in those upland areas is such that it emerges into history, already firmly established, only with the Elizabethan Reformation. After the northern Catholics were crushed, in 1571, the new archbishop of York, the zealous Edmund Grindal, forbade the custom as irreverent.[7] His direction was subsequently seconded by the orders of the JPs of Lancashire, and two spinsters of Goose-nargh were subsequently prosecuted for carrying the garlanded rushes in 1590.[8] In 1617, however, James I himself arrived in the neighbourhood and gave the tradition his support, personally watching a rush-bearing, with piping, at Houghton Tower on a Sunday in August 1617.[9] It was henceforth explicitly legalized in the controversial royal 'Books of Sports', and therefore, predictably, banned by the Westminster Assembly of Divines which reformed the Church as royal power was broken in the Civil War.[10] No evidence survives to resolve the question of whether the prohibition was effective, and it lapsed in 1660. Symbolically in that year the rush-bearing in the Pennine valley of Dent was revived with a pageant of Cromwell, Rebellion and War being worsted by 'Peace and Plenty, and Diana with her nymphs, all with coronets on their heads'.[11] After then the custom was certainly very much alive, for churches in late Stuart Cheshire and Westmorland rang bells to celebrate the arrival of the processions,[12] and in 1682 a clergyman in the Halifax district completely failed in an attempt to stop them there. His objection was that they attracted large crowds from outside the parish con-cerned, which would then 'eat and drink and rant in a barbarous heathenish manner', and his only achievement was to get his doors broken and to be abused verbally.[13]

By the early seventeenth century, and perhaps from the beginning, the practice was diverging into what were to become two very different forms, corresponding to the northern and southern parts of its range. In Cumbria and north Lancashire it was essentially the preserve of young women, like the unfortunate 'spinsters' of Goosenargh and the happy 'nymphs' of Dent. At eighteenth-century Warton, Lancashire, the rushes were tied in bundles with 'fine linen, silk ribbons, flowers etc.' and the maidens bore them to 'music, drums, ringing of bells and all other expressions of joy'. The bundles were placed in the church and the ornaments removed, after which all attending shared a collation and danced round the maypole if the weather was good.[14] This description is paralleled by others from different parts of the region in the next century, with the additional details that the girls wore white dresses and that their floral chaplets were hung on the chancel rails.[15] The colourful and innocuous nature of the custom ensured its survival in Westmorland even as churches became paved and the practical aspect of the procedure redun-dant. A visitor to early twentieth-century Ambleside described the approach up the main street of

four hundred children, all bearing flowers. There were rushes in triangles and spires, fine bouquets from the local nurseries and little nosegays from the fields. As they marched they sang

> Our fathers to the house of God,
> As yet a building rude
> Bore offerings from the flowery sod
> And fragrant rushes strewed.

At the head of the procession walked four girls in green, bearing lilies and rushes. They were followed by tableaux, representations on carts of the Parable of the Sower, Moses in the Bullrushes and David's Harp...the procession winds its way up the hill towards the church, those taking part in it laying their offerings in the grey and purple chequered light of St. Mary's. The children of Ambleside no longer strew the sweet rushes on the floor of the church, they bring instead posies from the hedgerows and fellside, and each child receives a gingerbread cake.[16]

In brief, the custom had been preserved by making it into one focused firmly upon youngsters, and bonded to local patriotism and Anglican piety in an area heavily visited by tourists at this time of year. As such, it still obtains at Ambleside and in the other Westmorland villages of Grasmere, Musgrave, and Warcop.[17]

Further south, rush-bearing developed into a more spectacular form, and one that has been particularly well studied. At Whalley, in the Lancashire Pennines, the rushes were recorded as arriving in a cart as early as in 1617. Rush-carts seem, however, to have burgeoned as a feature of the procession in south-east Lancashire and adjacent parts of Derbyshire, Yorkshire, and Cheshire, during the mid-eighteenth century; and as the communities of the region became steadily more industrialized, so the carts grew more elaborate. By the 1790s they were magnificent physical expressions of a communal pride and confidence which had swelled with the boom in textile-making. An example from Holmfirth, Yorkshire, which appeared around 1768, was already very ornate, the rushes being covered with 'all the flowers the season and the surroundings gardens can supply, arranged with all the ingenuity and taste the builder is master of: the whole being sprinkled with tinsel ornament'. It was drawn by young men in shirts decorated 'with ribbons of every shade and colour', preceded by riders and drummers.[18] The carts in Lancashire reproduced all these details, with the additional few that the rushes were built into a pyramid (and in Derbyshire a haystack shape) ten to twelve feet high, with green boughs on top and one or more men riding upon it. The sides of the structure were covered in a sheet upon which were displayed silverware lent by members of the parish concerned. The Yorkshire specimens had unique triangular frames of flowers at their crowns. Many also had one or more garlands carried in front, and behind each commonly came a band, morris-dancers, more flowers carried by young women, a banner, and sometimes a maiden or young couple walking under a flowery canopy. The triumphal procession made a tour of local inns and wealthy houses, and sometimes of a nearby large town such as Manchester, collecting money.[19]

Building the carts was a truly communal effort: young men made the arrangements, constructed the display, and hauled it, children helped to collect the rushes, womenfolk worked on costumes for the procession, older men lent advice on the rush-plaiting, and everybody could lend silver trinkets and turn out to watch the fun. The value of the ornaments was a source of considerable local reputation and competition: the reported worth of those on a cart sponsored by a Failsworth factory-owner in 1845 exceeded £600. Other industrial employers acted as patrons, as did individual local clergy and gentry. Where upper-class support was strong, as at Radcliffe and Prestwich, pageants (such as Adam and Eve) were added. At times the carts were used to affirm support for the Church and the Tory party, but they were fundamentally not a political symbol. Nor were they used to mock and insult unpopular local figures, being essentially an affirmative spectacle, and their imagery had nothing to do with pagan religion. Essentially, they depended upon the enthusiasm of working-class males, at first handloom weavers and later factory employees. A concomitant of the fierce sense of community which the carts embodied was the violence which regularly broke out when different parties of rush-bearers collided in a street or highway: the silver was hastily stripped away for safe keeping and the youths would then fight to defend their own carts and to wreck those of rivals.[20]

There seems to be no evidence that churches in rural Lancashire and Cheshire were any less in need of rushes than those in the cotton-making districts, or that rushes were harder to obtain there.[21] It seems, rather, that those parishes which were submitted to the social and economic strains of industrial growth were precisely those which developed the carts as a rallying-point for communal identity.[22] They reached their apogee in the years 1800–25, more or less on the heels of the cotton boom, but even in this heyday they were subject to criticism from members of the social élite who deplored the violence and drunkenness often associated with them. This was heavily reinforced by a growing chorus of radical middle-class or working-class hostility which coupled the same objections to the further charge that the custom reinforced a traditional social and religious order. In the 1830s and 1840s these attacks were articulated by the press, the Sunday schools, and the new police forces, even while economic recession was corroding the basis of the custom. Furthermore, rushes were becoming scarcer as more and more land was drained to accommodate the spreading towns, and the paving of churches broke the religious links at last. The carts correspondingly diminished in number and quality, began to carry coal or butter at times instead of rushes, and relied increasingly for sponsorship upon publicans and morris teams. What killed them off, however, was a shift in local leisure patterns during the late nineteenth century. They were associated with the main local summer holiday, the wakes, which will be the subject of a later chapter of the present work: the transformation of these completely removed their context. By the 1890s they were gone, to reappear on occasion as self-conscious pieces of cultural nostalgia at municipal jubilees. Since 1975 one has been paraded regularly at Saddleworth near Manchester, revived very much in this spirit by a local morris side based on a network of pubs.[23] After about four hundred years of coexistence, it was the older and more demure form of the custom, of the procession of young women, which survived the transition to the modern world.

FIRST FRUITS

꙼ᱠᱠᱠᱠ

THE last of the cycle of four feasts mentioned in *Tochmarc Emire* was 'Bron Trogain, earth's sorrowing in autumn'. To keep measure with those before, this would fall upon 1 August, which was indeed the beginning of the autumn season in the medieval British Isles. 'Bron' means 'wrath', but there seems to be no agreement upon the identity of Trogain, to whom this anger is credited.[1] Uniquely, the feast is called in the *Tochmarc* by a name other than that by which it is known in most other sources. There it is Lughnasadh, Lugnasa, or Lughnasa, the festival of the god Lugh, one of the most prominent deities in early medieval Irish literature. It features as this in texts at least as old as *Tochmarc Emire*, so that both terms appear to be traditional.[2] As such, it is the only major ancient Irish feast to be named after a known deity, and it is by no means obvious why this one should be associated with Lugh, who was neither apparently a god of the harvest nor of the sun:[3] he was, rather, the patron of all human skills, with an especial interest in kings and heroes. For decades he has also been represented by scholars as the most widely venerated of all 'Celtic' deities, upon the grounds that the prefix 'Lug' was found in the names of the Roman cities which became Carlisle, Lyons, Leiden, Laon, and Liegnitz, while the plural form 'Lugoves' is found in an inscription in France and a few more in Spain.[4] In view of this it is worth posing the question of why not a single one of the hundreds of other dedications to gods found in what was Roman Gaul, or any of the many recovered from the former 'Celtic' provinces of Britain, Germania, or Noricum, refers to him. In view of this apparently surprising silence, the possibility ought at least to be raised that the prefix 'Lug', like 'Bel', had a more general significance in the world of ancient Celtic languages and that the city names and the 'Lugoves' are not connected with the Irish deity at all.

This point matters in the context of the present book because the same generations of scholars who believed in pan-Celtic deities also tended to accept the concept of pan-Celtic festivals. This notion helped to inspire the finest book ever written about a traditional Irish feast, Máire MacNeill's study of Lughnasadh, which combined medieval literature with folklore surveys from all over the British Isles. Her conclusion was that the evidence testified to the existence in the ancient Celtic world of a festival on 1 August which incorporated the following rites:

a solemn cutting of the first of the corn of which an offering would be made to the deity by bringing it up to a high place and burying it; a meal of the new food and of bilberries of which everyone must partake; a sacrifice of a sacred bull, a feast of its flesh, with some ceremony involving its hide, and its replacement by a young bull; a ritual dance-play perhaps telling of a struggle for a goddess and a ritual fight; an installation of a head on top of the hill and a triumphing over it by an actor impersonating Lugh; another play representing the confinement by Lugh of the monster blight or famine; a three-day celebration presided over by the brilliant young god or his human representative. Finally, a ceremony indicates that the interregnum was over, and the chief god in his right place again.[5]

What underpinned this remarkable set of suggestions was her careful documentation of open-air gatherings held by the country people of Ireland to celebrate the opening of the cereal or potato harvest, on 1 August or a Sunday near to it. Drawing mainly upon eighteenth- and nineteenth-century records, she found examples of seventy-eight of these on hills, most in Ulster but also scattered throughout the rest of the island. There were another thirteen in the North Midlands which were held beside lakes or rivers, and a further eighty connected with holy wells. It was from the legends and folklore associated with these places that Máire MacNeill chose the motifs which she assembled into the sequence of rites cited above. Her process of reasoning was both legitimate and fascinating, but remains speculative until two vital comparisons are provided. First, it would be helpful to know if the tales concerned were confined to the sites of these gatherings, or found in other places as well. Secondly, we need similar studies of the other great festivals of the ancient Irish year, to isolate what appear to be the distinctive traits of each.

It may be suggested, therefore, that Máire MacNeill's reconstruction of pagan ritual is as yet not proven for Ireland itself, and thus can be even less securely applied to Britain. A more immediate concern here is whether the Irish pattern of a first-fruits celebration on hills and by water, which she has amply documented, can be detected in the British world. In the case of the Isle of Man there is no doubt that it can, and this is a matter of small surprise as it belongs so much more obviously to the Irish cultural province: the feast is called Laa'l Lhuanys, echoing the Irish name, and people gathered on hills for it.[6] MacNeill found less conclusive but still arguable parallels in South Wales. In Cardiganshire shepherds held celebrations in the upland pastures at this time of year, while on the first Sunday in August crowds would climb the Brecon Beacons, the highest mountains in the region.[7] She stretched the imagination a little further to include Cornwall in her dossier, where all that she could find was a fair held at Morvah at the correct time of year, and a legend of a giant-slaying located in the same community.[8] The evidence becomes really complex and problematic, however, on turning to Scotland. On first sight the Hebrides ought to be as promising a ground for the festival as Man, being imbued with the same Irish culture and in places hardly touched by the Reformation. Indeed, upon Barra the opening of the harvest was celebrated in the early nineteenth century at the Catholic feast of the Assumption of the Virgin Mary, La-Feill Máire, on 15 August. Allowing for the calendar change of twelve days in 1752, this would put an original festival very close to Lughnasa. The rites, however, were not very similar to the Irish set. People would rise early to pick the first of the newly ripened corn and make it into the *Moilean Máire*, the fatling-of-Mary bannock. Each of the family would then take a piece and walk sunwise around the household fire, singing *lollach Mhaire Mhathas*, the Paean of Mother Mary. The embers of the fire were then put in a pot, and the procession was repeated around the house and farmland, singing the paean again:

> On the feast-day of Mary the fragrant,
> Mother of the Shepherd of the flocks,
> I cut me a handful of the new corn,
> I dried it gently in the sun,
> I rubbed it sharply from the husk,
> With mine own palms.
> I ground it in a quern on Friday,
> I baked it in a fan of sheep-skin,
> I toasted it to a fire of rowan,
> And I shared it with my people.
> I went sunways round my dwelling,
> In the name of the Mary Mother,
> Who promised to preserve me,
> Who did preserve me,
> And who will preserve me,
> In peace, in flocks,
> In righteousness of heart,
> In labour, in love,
> In wisdom, in mercy,
> For the sake of Thy Passion.
> Thou Christ of Grace
> Who till the day of my death
> Will never forsake me![9]

Neither bannocks nor fire, nor indeed dwellings, are prominent in the Irish customs. Bonfires were lit at some of the outdoor gatherings in four of the counties of Ireland, but even there were very rare and incidental to the basic tradition of the open-air feast.[10] Nor is anything like the Catholic ritual of the Outer Hebrides found elsewhere in Scotland. Magnus Spence claimed to have found a 'faint trace' of fires made on 1 August in early nineteenth-century Orkney, but he did not specify what this might be.[11] A big August Eve bonfire was certainly kindled during the same period, by youths in Ayrshire, yet this seems to have been purely a local custom.[12] In general, Highlanders appear to have treated these dates as an opportunity to renew the rites of protection accorded to their homes and cattle at the opening of summer, in readiness for the new, autumn, season: rowan crosses were put over doors, or a ball of cow's hair put in the milk pail, or tar daubed upon the ears and tails of beasts, or blue or red threads tied to tails, or incantations spoken over udders.[13] The absence of fire in these activities, in sharp contrast to those of May Day, is so consistent that it must be deliberate. Most are also essentially individual and low-key. Indeed the only early August custom recorded elsewhere in Scotland which matches the flamboyance of that at Barra is from the Lothians, culturally and geographically at the opposite end of the country. Until the 1790s young herdsmen there used to mark the new season by banding together about a hundred strong and building towers of turves some seven to eight feet high, with flagstaves bearing napkins and ribbons. They would sally forth from these citadels to fight each other with cudgels; those who had no local rivals would march to the local village at noon and hold foot-races.[14] The practice seems to have been a thoroughly localized and idiosyncratic one, and there seems to be no obvious connection between the mock-fortresses of these brawling youths and the hills upon which some of the Irish feasting took place.

Indeed, apart from the special case of the Manx, the only really convincing parallel for the Irish celebrations is the annual climbing of the Brecon Beacons, so that it may be suggested that Máire MacNeill's thesis of a pan-Celtic seasonal ritual, like her reconstruction of pagan rites, is so far unproven. A major difficulty, as she at once recognized, is that the Anglo-Saxons held their own feast of the opening of harvest upon 1 August, the 'hlaef-mass', or 'loaf mass', from which derived its medieval English and Scottish name of Lammas. As such it appears regularly in the Anglo-Saxon Chronicle, explicitly (in 921) as 'the feast of first fruits'. The same name and title are echoed in another early English text, the Red Book of Derby.[15] It was clearly by then the custom to reap the first of the ripe cereals and bake them into bread which was consecrated at church upon that day: a book of Anglo-Saxon charms advised the division of this holy bread into four pieces and the crumbling of each one in the corner of a barn in order to make it a safe repository for the grain about to arrive there.[16] The festival was also known in medieval times as the Gule of August, a term which has always vexed linguists, who have only been able to suggest that it signifies the 'Yule' of August, a period of rejoicing equivalent to that in December.[17] The difficulty evaporates if it is simply an Anglicization of the Welsh gwyl, meaning 'feast', the Welsh name for 1 August being gwyl aust, 'the feast of August'. Certainly the arrival of the time when the first of the harvest could be gathered would have been a natural point for celebration in an agrarian society, and the importance of the first day of August was already so well established by 673 that Archbishop Theodore of Tarsus decreed that the annual synod of the newly established Church in England should be held then.[18] It would seem very likely, therefore, that a pre-Christian festival had existed among the Anglo-Saxons on that date, and Máire MacNeill suggested that this was none other than the Celtic Lughnasadh.[19] Her reasoning was that the early English must have adopted it from the ancient British, because there is no sign of a Continental festival on 1 August: in the medieval Church calendar, indeed, it was given only the minor feast of St Peter ad Vincula. Her case is much strengthened if 'Gule' was indeed a version of *gwyl*. To prove her point directly, however, would involve a detailed knowledge of the religious calendar of the Anglo-Saxons before they arrived in England, which is impossible. To establish it by analogy would require a proper comparative study of early August festivals and customs in Europe; this is certainly practicable but has not yet been attempted.

All that is certain is that across Britain Lammas remained an extremely important date throughout the Middle Ages, for holding of fairs, payment of rents, election of local officials, and opening of common lands.[20] A few of the fairs survive, at Exeter, Chulmleigh, and Honiton in Devon, and at South Queensferry near Edinburgh. From the 1940s Young Farmers' Clubs in southern England revived the custom of a presentation of the first sheaf of harvest at church on the initial Sunday of August.[21] These things, and the occasional remaining payment of fixed dues and appointment of municipal officers on Lammas Day, serve as a reminder of the excitement which once attended the ripening of the corn across the ancient British Isles.

33

HARVEST HOME

⊱❦⊰

I N pre-industrial British society, the cereal harvest, whether of wheat, oats, barley, or rye, represented the most important and most concentrated period of labour in the entire year. It was carried on through the month of August until the early nineteenth century, when an increase in production pushed it both backwards into July and forwards into September.[1] Arrangements for it feature in the first surviving records to provide a detailed view of local economic life, the manorial papers of the high Middle Ages. Earlier than that nothing substantial is known. Bede commented that September was known to the pagan Anglo-Saxons as Haleg-Monath, 'Holy Month', and it can be surmised that this was derived from religious ceremonies following the harvest; but of these apparently no testimony remained by the time of Bede himself.[2] The manorial records (virtually all thirteenth-century) were primarily concerned with the problems of which tenants were required to reap the lord's corn, and what reward they would receive. In most cases the recompense took the form of food and drink given during the process, while certain estates also had the custom of a communal meal at the end, as well as, or instead of, the refreshments at the time. On the east midland estates of Ramsey Abbey, for example, a tenant who was obliged to bring his whole family to the reaping, excepting his wife, was rewarded with a repast at the end consisting of a loaf, ale, meat, and cheese.[3] This system may well have existed ever since substantial landowners first emerged, back in prehistory: the Roman writer Macrobius noted that farmers feasted their field-hands at the end of harvest.[4]

During the early modern period, information upon harvesting increases, and most of it is summed up in three different sets of verses, spread across the span between 1570 and 1650. The earliest is Thomas Tusser's famous rhyming treatise on farming, the first edition of which appeared in 1573. He described how a good employer gave gloves to his field-hands, how the latter cried for 'largesse', and how a 'harvest lord' was appointed to lead and supervise the work. Tusser attached especial importance to the food and drink given during the reaping and the entertainment at the end:

> In harvest time, harvest folke, servants and all,
> should make all togither good cheere in the hall:
> And fill out the black boule of bleith to their song
> and let them be merie all harvest time long.

Once ended thy harvest, let none be begilde,
please such as did helpe thee, man, woman and childe.
Thus dooing, with alway such helpe as they can,
thou winnest the praise of the labouring man.

He added that on departure each 'ploughman' should be presented with a 'harvest home goose'.[5]

The author of the late Elizabethan ballad 'The Mery Life of the Countriman', which has been much quoted earlier in this book, was as concerned to celebrate the process as Tusser was to give practical advice upon it:

When corne is ripe, with tabor and pipe, their sickles they prepare;
and wagers they lay how muche in a day they meane to cut downe there.
And he that is quickest, and cutteth downe cleanest the corne,
a garlande trime they make for him, and bravely they bringe him home.

And when in the barne, without any harme, they have laid up their corne,
In hart they singe high praises to him that so increast their gaine.
And unto the parson, their pastor and teacher also,
With harts most blyth, they give their tyth—their duties full well they knowe.[6]

The standpoint of this writer, detached, external, and preoccupied with hierarchy and obligation, was occupied in the early seventeenth century by a genuine poet, in a famous piece of literature. Robert Herrick's 'The Hock-cart, or Harvest home', was pointedly dedicated to an earl and so concerned with the dues to a secular lord rather than to a clergyman. It depicts the cart carrying the last load from the fields, 'dressed up with all the country art', and followed by adults crowned with ears of corn and a whooping 'rout of rural younglings'. A piper accompanies a harvest-home song. 'Some bless the cart, some kiss the sheaves; some prank them up with oaken leaves'. The landowner has prepared a feast at his seat for them, of beef, mutton, veal, bacon, custard, pies, boiled wheat, and beer. The people drink first to his health, and then to 'maids with wheaten hats' and to a succession of agricultural tools. The poem ends with a homily in favour of social deference and against drunkenness at the feast.[7]

The young women with 'wheaten hats' in the toast may have been harvest queens. In 1614 William Browne could describe them as crowned with chaplets of blooms which they themselves had made.[8] Half a century later Milton, in *Paradise Lost*, could write of how Adam made for Eve

Of choicest flowers a garland to adorn
Her tresses, and her rural labours crown
As reapers oft are wont their harvest queen.[9]

Perhaps significantly, there is no mention of such autumn 'queens' outside these literary sources, and they are scarce in later centuries. Instead a different sort of crowned female figure features very commonly in the nineteenth-century records, and it was noticed at Windsor in 1598 by the German traveller Paul Hentzer:

we happened to meet some country people celebrating their Harvest home; their last load of corn they crown with flowers, having besides an image richly dressed, by which perhaps they would signify Ceres; this they keep moving about, while men and women, men and maidservants, riding through the streets in the cart, shout as loud as they can till they arrive at the barn.[10]

Perhaps it is this doll, and not a live woman, that Milton's reference signified, or was indicated in the pageant presented to Queen Elizabeth at Kenilworth castle in 1575, of Ceres (the Roman corn-goddess) riding in a cart 'like a harvest queen'.[11]

Most of the other early modern references to harvesting merely reproduce all this information.[12] A few, however, extend it, such as the rhyme 'Upon the Norfolk Largess', published in 1673, which explains the reference in Tusser:

> Our harvest men shall run ye cap and leg'
> And leave their work at any time to beg.
> They make a harvest of each passenger,
> And therefore have they a lord-treasurer.[13]

The bulk of the records in this category serve to show the considerable variety of practice which obtained in the payment and entertainment of workers. The wealthy Sir Patricius Curwen of Workington on the Cumberland coast provided not just money and food but also a piper to play in the fields for the nine to seventeen days which the harvest required in each year between 1628 and 1643.[14] Over in Anglesey at the same period, the gentleman farmer Robert Bulkeley paid his hands but gave them no food,[15] while at Bishopston in the chalk hills of Wiltshire the tenants went up to the manor house when their work was completed to receive four pounds of bread, a pound of cheese, and a cup of beer each, just as their medieval predecessors had done.[16]

It is time to turn to the development of these practices in the late eighteenth and nineteenth centuries, and the appearance of others in the much more detailed sources for that period. The organization and remuneration of the corn harvest remained as varied as before. In parts of Devon in 1816, no money was given to the reapers. Instead a crowd of labourers would converge upon a farm which required their work. They would be served a large lunch, a 'drinking' of beer or cider in late afternoon, and a supper at the farmhouse, followed by more alcohol until two or three in the morning. The next day, if the job was done, they would search for another farm with standing corn. Unsurprisingly, many were already inebriated before the end of the afternoon, and an observer said sourly that their behaviour at supper 'may be assimilated to the frolics of a bear-garden'.[17] In 1776 the parson of Weston Longeville, on the Norfolk clay plateau, rewarded field-hands borrowed from other farmers with money, but provided his own with a dinner.[18] During the decades around 1800 unlimited beer or cider was provided in the fields of Worcestershire and South Devon; Shropshire farmers were unusual in giving no more than five to eight quarts per head each day.[19] By the late nineteenth century in eastern Suffolk the ration was down to seventeen pints.[20]

In Victorian East Anglia the usual system was for extra labour to be hired for each harvest, often from itinerant Irishmen. In Cambridgeshire men hoping for work would scrape their scythes in the farmyard; if successful they were given a shilling and a pint of beer.[21] In east Suffolk, both regular and temporary hands would then band together to negotiate a contract with the farmer, laying down rates of pay and conditions of work. The workers then elected a harvest lord of the old sort, usually the farm foreman, who supervised the process; now he also chose a 'lady' as his second in command. His main task was to lead the mowing, but he also demanded 'largesse' from people passing by, and as this traditional custom became more disreputable during the century he took to collecting money from tradesmen who did business with the farmer. The proceeds were used to subsidize the supper which employers still provided at the end.[22] In Fife and Kincardineshire during the same period cash was also demanded from those passing harvesters at work, on pain of being grabbed by limbs and bumped on the ground,[23] but the custom does not seem to be known elsewhere. In the Midlands and southern England physical punishment was meted out as well, but to members of the harvest team who had created problems for the others: in Northamptonshire, Warwickshire, Hampshire, and Suffolk there are records of men being formally thrashed by their fellows in the field.[24]

When the reaping was done, by tradition the gleaning began, a task as dominated by women as the former was by men. In the nineteenth-century east Midlands, this was organized under the leadership of a 'queen', elected by the womenfolk. The best portrait of one derives from Rempstone on the southern fringe of Nottinghamshire, in 1860:

The village crier, having 'proclaimed the Queen', nearly a hundred gleaners assembled at the end of the village. Women with their infant charges, boys with green boughs, and girls with flowers, the whole wearing gleaning-pockets; children's carriages and wheelbarrows, dressed in green and laden with babies etc were in requisition...[A] royal salute was shouted by the boys, and the crown brought out of its temporary depository. This part of the regalia was of simple make; its basis consisting of straw-coloured cloth, surrounded with wheat, barley, and oats of the present year. A streamer of straw-coloured ribbon, dependent on a bow at the crown, hung loosely down; a leaf of laurel was placed in front, while arching over the whole was a branch of jessamine...The ceremony of crowning was now performed; after which the Queen, enthroned in an arm-chair decorated with flowers and branches moved...[to] the first field to be gleaned.

There her proclamation was read, announcing that the gleaning bell would be rung each morning at 8.30, to call everybody together to be led to the fields by her.[25] The Rempstone ceremony was, however, a self-conscious revival, and proceedings elsewhere may have been nowhere like as elaborate.

If social and economic historians have been primarily interested in the labour patterns of nineteenth-century harvesting, folklorists have been far more concerned with the customs which ended the reaping. These have been the focus of a major debate, both parts of which were first propounded outside the British Isles. It commenced with the pioneering work of the German scholar Wilhelm Mannhardt, who in the 1860s became the first investigator to collect folklore systematically, community by community. He proved conclusively that there was a close correspondence between the agricultural customs of the Graeco-Roman world and those of his own time, and went further to argue that, as primitive peoples thought that trees were animate, then they ought to have regarded the spirits of crops as animate likewise, functioning as fertility demons. He used as part of his evidence for this the widespread northern European custom of treating the last bunch of corn to be reaped as especially significant, perhaps meaning that the spirit of the whole field had been driven into it.[26] These ideas were partly inspired by the work of a British academic, Sir Edward Tylor, who had argued that modern folk customs were often survivals of ancient religion. They were given a much greater popularity by another, Sir James Frazer, who adopted Mannhardt's arguments wholesale and reinforced them with further data, drawn partly from the British Isles. There were three stages to Frazer's case. First, that the last sheaf of corn was often given a nickname personifying it as an animate being, in these islands being recorded as the Cailleach, Chailleach, Carline, Carley, or Wrack (all meaning, in Gaelic or Welsh, the old woman), the Old Witch, the Queen, the Maiden, the Mare, the Hare, or the Gander. Secondly, that the reapers often displayed fear of it, cutting it by throwing sickles from a distance or wielding scythes blindfold, and celebrating its fall with a formal ceremony of acclamation and display. Thirdly, that even after its reaping it was treated as retaining a peculiar potency, being delivered to a rival as a token of bad luck, or fed to animals, or ploughed into a field as a bringer of good fortune, or made into a human figure and given a place of honour in the home.[27]

Buoyed up on the tremendous readership of Sir James's work, the animist theory received no determined challenge from folklorists until 1934, when the Swedish scholar Carl von Sydow commenced an attack upon it which he and his pupils were to develop during succeeding decades. He began with the observation that animist beliefs were only sporadic, not universal, among tribal peoples, and that traces of them were proportionately patchy in Europe and Asia. He then proceeded to argue forward, not from any general theory of primitive religion but from the object of the last sheaf itself. This, he suggested, invariably signified the end to a period of heavy and important work, provoking both levity and serious thought. It could be used as an omen for the next harvest or (often jokingly) for the destiny of the person who cut it. It was often carried home in triumph as the visible symbol of the end of labour; once there, it was put to a variety of uses. Nowhere in Europe did von Sydow find an explicitly declared belief that a spirit was present in the sheaf. The association of the corn with a witch or aggressive animal, the spirit of which was caught in the last tuft, was, he suggested, a device to discourage children from playing in the crop and damaging it. The acclamation on finishing the harvest was to him essentially a way of communicating this success to neighbours. He reminded his readers that tribal peoples are noted for concocting humorous fictions to explain their actions.[28] These arguments were more or less completely accepted by social historians concerned with harvesting.[29] Of the two folklorists in these islands who have subsequently made a particular study of last sheaf customs, Calum Maclean agreed that there was no persuasive evidence of a fertility cult, and Alan Gailey concurred that the practical basis for the customs was absolutely plain, whereas any religious derivation was speculative, if not itself susceptible of disproof.[30] It must therefore be concluded that the Mannhardt and Frazer theory of belief in an animating corn spirit is now effectively discounted.

What, then, is the present body of British evidence upon the matter? Its distribution upon the map shows a consistent pattern: 'last sheaf' customs are recorded all over Scotland, including the Hebrides and Northern Isles,[31] in all the arable districts of Wales, its marches, and north-west Worcestershire,[32] in the four westernmost English counties,[33] in north Cumberland and on the Yorkshire and Lincolnshire Wolds,[34] and in east Kent and Hertfordshire.[35] They are also prominent on the Isle of Man,[36] and well scattered across Ireland, although especially common in areas of the north where Scottish influence was strong.[37] By contrast, they seem to be missing from most of England, and most strikingly so from the east Midlands and East Anglia, the main bread-baskets of the Victorian English. Essentially, by the time that these customs were recorded they belonged to what from a metropolitan point of view were the fringes of agriculture, the less commercialized cereal-producing districts. This in itself would suggest that they had formerly been more general, as would the wider distribution of the related tradition of the corn dolly, to be discussed below. The beliefs did not begin to be noticed until the eighteenth century, and not in detail until its very end: none of the early modern observers who wrote of harvest customs portrayed the scene in a field at the end of the reaping. The special naming of the last sheaf was first mentioned in early eighteenth-century Wales,[38] and traditions regarding it first appear in accounts of Scotland in the 1790s.[39] Those from England do not feature in the record until the 1820s, and some were noted down just as they were in the process of dying out.

As Frazer pointed out, the naming of the sheaf went according to strongly marked local traditions, governed most obviously by whether the possession of it was regarded as a liability or an asset. In the first category were 'the Cailleach' in most of the Hebrides and parts of the western Highlands, 'the Ghobbar Bhacach' (Lame Goat) on Skye, 'Yr Wrach' in south-west and north-west Wales, 'the Bitch' in the Orkneys, and 'the Witch' in Yorkshire. In the second were 'the Clyach' or 'Gliack' (which could derive from *cailleach*) in the

'The Cailleach' and 'the Maiden', from Argyll, *c.*1895. Drawn by Lisa Hutton from photographs in the *Folk-Lore Review*, 6.

eastern Highlands and around Aberdeen, 'the claidheag' (perhaps from *claidheamh*, a sword) in Easter Ross, and 'the Maiden' everywhere else in Scotland. Where there was neither a pronounced stigma nor a pronounced virtue attached to the sheaf, more neutral terms were used, such as 'the neck' in Devon, Cornwall, West Cheshire, and the Englishry of Pembrokeshire, 'the Old Sow' in Lincolnshire, 'the Frog' in Worcestershire, 'the Mare' (in Welsh, 'Y Fedi') in Hertfordshire, Shropshire, Herefordshire, and most of Wales, 'the Winter' or 'the Hare' in Galloway, and 'the gander's neck' in parts of Shropshire.[40] There was, however, no perfect correspondence, for in one district of Lewis the Cailleach' was given a place of honour at the feast, whereas in one upon Islay 'the Maiden' was used as a taunt. In general Von Sydow's explanations for the names could stand up well for these British examples, and yet one account of the Hebrides insisted that in some places the fear of the sheaf was palpable enough to go beyond any device to scare children. Nobody wanted to cut it, for it was held to contain an unlucky spirit, and sometimes on common land a whole section of crop was left untouched to avoid confronting this problem.[41] It is possible that in this remote region a respect for pagan tutelary goddesses still lingered.[42] On the other hand it may be that the disgrace which was attached to being the last to harvest in this same region (to be discussed below) was fed backwards into the sheaf: nobody seems to have left crops untouched on land which was not held in common. Furthermore there was no consistency, even within the Hebrides, of attitudes to the sheaf, which could vary from fear to celebration to jest, even upon the same island. In Aberdeenshire it might have different names within a single parish, and be treated in different ways even within one township.

The same considerations apply to the ceremony of cutting. That recorded by Frazer, of the competition to throw sickles at it (sometimes blindfolded), is recorded across most of Wales and southern Scotland, and in Somerset, Shropshire, and Herefordshire. It seems to be missing from south-western England and from all of the Scottish Highlands and islands except Glencoe, Bute, and Kintyre. Wherever it was recorded the atmosphere of the contest was light-hearted, nobody seeming to have any awe of the tuft of cereal concerned. All that altered over time was that during the nineteenth century the sickle was replaced by the scythe as the main harvest tool in most areas, and the custom either lapsed or was transferred to the new implement, the competitors being blindfolded or turned around.

In Devon and Cornwall the energy put elsewhere into the competitions was invested instead in the acclamation, the famous ceremony of 'crying the neck' which was observed all over these two counties in the nineteenth century. It was first noticed in the 1770s, when Lord North, crossing east Devon, was frightened by the shouting which he mistook for demonstrations against the new cider tax.[43] Its basic pattern was for the reapers to complete their work and then to form a circle or group with one holding aloft the ears of the last stalks of corn, or else some chosen from that lying in the field. The company would bow, and then shout 'a neck, a neck, a neck, we have one' a certain number of times, and cheer. The last phrase was often shortened to 'we have 'un', or still further to 'way-en'. This format was subject to a number of local refinements. Near Hartland, in North Devon, the words were sung in a prolonged and beautiful harmony, on a rising scale. Near Kingsbridge, in the south of the county, it was combined with a standard harvest-home cry, of the sort to be described below. At an unnamed place in Cornwall the reapers would call to each other from opposite sides of a small valley, making the exchange: 'I've gotten it. What hast gotten? I've gotten the neck'. In western Dorset, the chant 'We have'en' was performed in the farmyard, without using a tuft of corn.[44]

Other regions had their own traditions of acclamation. County Durham and East Yorkshire usually had just a great cheer at the end of reaping. If the master or steward was present in the Durham fields, the womenfolk would toss him in the air and kiss him. In Cleveland, however, there was a customary shout as the last stalks were cut:

Weel bun and better shorn,
Is Master ————'s corn;
We hev her, we hev her,
As fast as a feather.
Hip, hip, hurrah![45]

Manx reapers bound the last sheaf with ribbons and took it to the nearest hilltop, where the Queen of the 'Mheillea' (Harvest Home) held it over her head while all cheered.[46] Hertfordshire and Shropshire harvesters (by some trick of history) had a virtually identical custom, of 'Crying the Mare'. They would gather, like the Manx, on the highest available ground, and yell (in the Shropshire version):

I 'ave 'er, I 'ave 'er, I 'ave 'er!
What 'ast thee, whad 'ast thee, whad 'ast thee?
A mar'! A mar'! A mar'!

The verse usually ended with a taunt to a farm as yet still reaping. The latter was the main point of the Cheshire custom of 'shutting' (shouting), in which a ringleader would yell from a local high-point:

'Oh yes! Oh yes! Oh yes! this is to give notice
That Meester ———— 'as gen th' seck a turn (turned the tables)
And sent th'owd hare into Meester ———— 's standing corn',

and his mates would cheer. The 'old hare' here may be taken as a quite literal symbol, as hares would flee from fields under reaping into those still untouched.[47]

Mocking rival farmers and their teams, who were lagging behind in the harvesting, was one of the main uses of the last sheaf—or of another bunch of corn—in the Hebrides, Argyll, Orkneys, and west Wales.[48] At times this was supposed to be light-hearted, and in Welsh-speaking Pembrokeshire a boy sent to drop 'Yr Wrach' into another farmhouse was made to shine all the shoes in it if he was caught.[49] In other parts of the same county however, and in the Hebrides, a messenger hurling the demeaning tuft into a rival house, yard, or field, would be badly hurt if the occupants caught him, for it was regarded as a serious insult.[50] Taunts at harvest-time resulted in a murder on South Uist, in the Outer Hebrides, in the sixteenth century, and an attempted one on the same island two hundred years later.[51] Even in the nineteenth century there were people in those islands who watched all night for fear that 'the Cailleach' would be put upon them; some (though these were few) had come to regard it as a curse as well as a slight.[52] Something of this bitter spirit obtained in the same period in areas of Shropshire and Staffordshire, where a farmer who had finished work often sent a gaily decorated horse to a less fortunate neighbour as a mocking offer of help; a boy had to ride it as a man would have been beaten up.[53] In most of Scotland, Wales and its Border, the south-west of England, and Cumberland, however, the last sheaf was regarded as a valued trophy, and taken home in triumph. In parts of west Wales, Galloway,

Cornwall, and Devon, this process was made into a game, whereby one reaper (often the man who had cut it) was expected to smuggle it into the farmhouse while the servant girls watched for him with pails of water. The test was to see if he could get it to the table dry.[54] In south-east Scotland the victor in the sickle-throwing contest was able to give it to the woman of his choice.[55] Most commonly, the sheaf was hung in the house until the next harvest: occasionally it was made into bread after the celebration supper,[56] and in a sprinkling of neighbourhoods across Scotland it was fed to horses, either at once, at Christmas, or at the ploughing of the fields.[57] None of these paragraphs of description, however, does justice to the sheer luxuriant variety of local practices concerning the last sheaf, especially in Scotland. Around Longforgan, Perthshire, 'the Maiden' was committed to 'one of the finest girls in the field', who carried it in a procession to the farmhouse.[58] In Fife two sheaves were gathered and called respectively 'the Old Woman' and 'the Maiden', the former representing the harvest of the past year, and the latter that of the year to come.[59] On some farms in the Gareloch district of Dumbartonshire and in Perthshire and Aberdeenshire, the last stalks were severed by either young boys or young girls.[60] To select a handful of examples from this tremendous range of responses to the end of harvest, and to bind them together in a general theory of primitive religion, as Sir James Frazer did, was as much a triumph of artistry as of scholarship.

From bearing home in triumph a last sheaf decorated with ribbons, it was but a short step to dressing it up or weaving it into a rough human figure like that seen at Windsor in 1598. Such images, not necessarily made out of the last stalks themselves, are recorded in the late eighteenth and nineteenth centuries over much of Britain. They do not, however, seem to have been really common. Either they were an annual tradition in a particular district, such as the Gareloch, or a particular community such as Balquhidder in the Perthshire Highlands, Duns in Berwickshire, or Werrington in east Cornwall, or else they were made occasionally. In the Highlands, Hebrides, and Devon, they shared the name of the last sheaf: klyack, maiden, cailleach, or neck respectively.[61] In County Durham and perhaps in other parts on northern England, they were called mell dolls, and in Man *yr mheilla*—both from the Scandinavian *mele*, meaning corn[62] They were 'kirns', 'kerns', or 'kern babies' (again apparently from 'corn') in southern Scotland, north-east England down to Lincolnshire, and Norfolk.[63] In Cambridgeshire and west Somerset apparently 'corn dollies';[64] and in Kent 'Ivy Girls'.[65] Few regions, however, had an absolutely standard name: in Northumberland, for example, they could be 'harvest dolls', 'kern babies', or 'harvest queens'; in Yorkshire 'kerns', 'mell dolls', or 'harvest dolls', and in Berwickshire 'the kirn' or 'the queen'.[66] The treatment of the figures varied in proportion. In eighteenth-century Northumberland one could be 'attired in great finery, crowned with flowers, a sheaf of corn placed under her arm, and a sickle in her hand', and fixed on a pole to reside over the end of reaping.[67] In nineteenth-century Galloway it could be dressed in a child's long white frock, with a ribbon around its waist, a wooden ladle for its head and neck, a clay face, and bead eyes. It was fastened to a pitchfork and carried home from the last field by workers singing:

> ————'s corn's weel shorn,
> Bless the day he was born!
> Kirny, Kirny, oo,
> Kirny, Kirny, oo![68]

During the same period the 'Maiden' or 'Cailleach' of western Argyll and Perthshire could be dressed in a sleeved bodice and a shirt sewn with flounces of silk, muslin, or tissue paper.[69] Sometimes, as at Longforgan, Perthshire, and in the Isle of Man, it was associated with a young woman, who carried it and became herself the 'harvest queen' or 'queen of the feast'.[70] At Cambridge in the decades around 1800 the festival tradition of transvestism was occasionally utilized to produce a 'queen' pulled through the streets in a cart and consisting of a man in female dress and face-paint, crowned with ears of corn.[71]

Sheaves, dolls, and shouting were appropriate mechanisms to demonstrate the end of reaping in areas of small agricultural units. Where farms were larger, the most obvious and enduring symbol of harvest home was that portrayed by the German at Windsor and by Herrick: the decorated cart carrying the last load homeward. In the late eighteenth and nineteenth centuries this was recorded all over England, but especially in those parts of the Midlands, East Anglia, and South from which last sheaf and 'crying customs' were missing; suggesting that the difference was simply one of scale of agriculture.[72] In general it was decorated with green boughs, flowers, and ribbons, drawn by beribboned horses, and had children, or womenfolk, or a chosen man, or (in East Anglia) the 'Harvest Lord', sitting on top. Those who rode on it, drove it or ran beside it would shout or sing, usually a variant on

> We have ploughed, we have sowed,
> We have reaped, we have mowed,
> We have brought home every load,
> Hip, hip, hip, Harvest home!

or

> Harvest home! harvest hum! harvest home!
> We've ploughed, we've sown,
> We've reaped, we've mown.
> Harvest home! harvest home!

though there were of course several purely local rhymes.[73] In the south and east Midlands the chant was often followed by the challenge 'We want water and can't get none', a reference to a game, found across this whole region, whereby either fellow villagers or female relatives of the harvesters would try to throw water over the cart while the driver avoided them or urged on the horses so fast that the pailfuls missed their target. It was a further achievement, and rite of passage, to be made before the celebrations began.

Those celebrations still centred upon the feast which had featured so prominently in the medieval and early modern accounts of harvest. Around 1800 it was known generally as the harvest supper, harvest feast, or harvest home, in much of East Anglia and the east Midlands as the 'horkey', 'horkey supper', 'largesse spending', or 'harvest frolic', in the Isles of Scilly as 'Nicla Thies', in northern England as the 'mell supper', 'cream pot', 'kern supper', 'churn supper', or 'inning goose', in Cornwall as the 'gooldize' (feast of ricks), in the Isle of Man as the *mheillea*, in southern Scotland as the 'kirn' or 'kirn supper', in northern Scotland as the 'maiden feast', the 'kirn', or the 'bere-barrel' (bere being barley), and in Orkney as the 'heuk butter', 'cuttin butter' or (on a larger scale) 'muckle supper'.[74] They were absent from large areas of Wales, the Highlands, the Hebrides, and north-western England, in which arable farming was marginal to the economy or else units of production were very small.[75] The basis of the event was an ample meal, to the limit that the farmer could reasonably provide: thus, the most common components in southern England were beer, beef, and plum pudding, and in Scotland beer, bread and cheese, or else gruel, and oatmeal with cream, but there were naturally many local specialties. The same is true of the entertainments, usually involving toasts, drinking-games, singing, and dancing, but also at times charades and short dramatic sketches. In north-eastern England teams of guisers or sword-dancers would sometimes call. The normal setting was the farmhouse kitchen, but for larger companies a barn would be decorated with sheaves and flowers. A study of nineteenth-century harvest supper songs would probably provide a valuable addition to the history of popular culture. As with other seasonal rhymes and songs at that period many were remarkably standardized. The most widespread, or perhaps simply the most cheerfully remembered by educated observers because of its impeccable sentiments, was a variant on:

> Here's a health to our master,
>   The lord of the feast;
> God bless his endeavours
>   And send him increase;
> May all his crop prosper
>   So we reap them next year;
> Here's the master's good health, boys,
>   Come drink off your beer!
>
> Now harvest is ended
>   And supper is past,
> Here's the mistress's health, boys,
>   So fill up your glass;
> For she's a good wife
>   And has give us good cheer,
> Here's the mistress's health, boys,
>   Come drink off your beer![76]

Another favourite was 'The Barley Mow', of which a standard version ran:

> Here's a health to the barleymow,
> Here's a health to the man who very well can
> Both harrow and plough and sow.
>   When it is well sown,
>   See it is well mown,
> Both raked and gravelled clean.
>   And a barn to lay it in,
> Here's a health to the man who very well can
> Both thrash and fan it clean.[77]

There were of course characteristic regional examples, such as that from the East Riding of Yorkshire of which the Hornsea version went:

> We hev her, we hev her,
>   A cod iv a thether;
> At oor toon end
>   A yew an a lamb,
> A pot an a pan
>   May we get seeaf in,
> Wiv oor hahvest yam,
>   Wiv a up o'good yal,
> An sum hawpence ti spend.[78]

In general, what is impressive about the recorded songs is their eclecticism. Many were clearly learned from the chapbooks in which they are still often preserved, and which explain the wide distribution of some. Several, in turn, had literary origins: one was from a play by Dryden (*King Arthur*), another an imitation of Ariel's song in Shakespeare's *The Tempest*, another mentioned the Roman goddess Ceres, and yet another was based upon the Christmas carol 'God Rest You Merry Gentlemen'.[79] By the later nineteenth century a standard harvest home repertoire would also include Gilbert and Sullivan, patriotic naval shanties, and popular romantic melodies.[80] Even a cursory inspection of the genre reinforces a sense of how permeable the world of rural popular culture was, by the eighteenth century at the latest, and how closely literature and oral tradition were intermixed. The historian has also lost a whole aspect of it, consisting of the songs which were considered too indecent to be collected by folklorists.[81]

During the eighteenth century the harvest supper was a virtually indispensable part of the system of rewards for the work wherever a farmer employed more than a few hands.[82] During the nineteenth, it was clearly in serious decline, although the process was uneven and at times partially reversed in certain areas.[83] The key period in it was the first half of the century, which was precisely that in which the London-based *Every-Day Book* edited by William Hone idealized the suppers as a model of harmonious social relations. To Hone 'Harvest time is as delightful to look on to us who are mere spectators of it, as it was in the golden age' (an epoch which he did attempt to locate).

A contributor described a Gloucestershire supper as 'pomp without pride, liberality without ostentation, cheerfulness without vice, merriment without guilt, and happiness without alloy'.[84] At a time of increasing social tensions and divisions, when war between classes seemed possible, writers like these were reaching for the suppers as a reassuring symbol of old-style harmony. What was removing them in the same period was an increasing disposition among agricultural employers to commute the traditional entertainment for extra money. As has been noted,[85] this tendency predated both the large-scale mechanization of English agriculture and its recession in the face of foreign competition: it resulted, rather, from the erosion of a close relationship between farmers and workers and the introduction of individual piece-work, as farming became more commercialized. Social historians have tended to sound an elegiac note when describing this pattern,[86] echoing both Hone and the late Victorian folklorists. Farm-workers themselves, however, do not seem to have shared these feelings, for the commutation of payment in kind for payment in cash provoked no recorded disturbances and rarely featured in the complaints articulated by agricultural employees.[87]

As is well known, the traditional feasts were replaced by the new, and very successful, institution of the harvest festival, a remarkable reversion to the late medieval pattern whereby parochial organization was blended with popular entertainment.[88] It is probable that the idea of a harvest thanksgiving service was first devised by the celebrated romantic clergyman R. S. Hawker of Morwenstow, in north Cornwall, in 1843, when he invited his congregation to receive the sacrament 'in the bread of the new corn'. Either by transference from there or by independent evolution, the services also appeared at Elton near Peterborough in the 1850s. By the end of that decade they were spreading across the east Midlands, with occasional occurrences as far afield as Somerset, and had been instituted at St Paul's Cathedral. In 1862 Convocation recommended a form of service for the occasion, with latitude left to individual clergy to develop it according to local tastes. Initially it was taken up by High Church clerics, but by 1870 those of evangelical tastes were turning to it as well, and twenty years later it was almost universal. The most common format was for villagers to process to their church for a morning service and communion, and then to hold a feast followed by dancing and games and sometimes an evening service as well. These events were normally held upon a weekday, to avoid incurring any sabbatarian disapproval of the celebrations. From the beginning, the church was decorated for the occasion with harvest motifs, such as sheaves, fruit, and the occasional corn dolly. In 1898 J. Arthur Gibbs praised the 'delightful manner' of these adornments, 'such huge apples, carrots and turnips in the windows and strewn about in odd places; lots of golden barley all around the pulpit and font; and perhaps there will be bunches of grapes, such as grow wild on the cottage walls, hung round the pulpit'.[89]

The same impulse which has led social historians of those developments to rue the decline of the harvest suppers has caused them generally to disparage the new festivals, as mechanisms for control of workers by the social élite, mirrors of hierarchy, and exercises in 'labour relations'.[90] These observations are legitimate enough, even though they presuppose a particular set of political attitudes; almost by definition, right-wing historians tend not to be interested in popular culture. What perhaps ought to be suggested as well is that the festivals could not have taken off had not huge numbers of ordinary people been in favour of them; the push towards them from below must have been at least as important as any manipulation from above. As James Obelkevitch has pointed out, they permitted parishioners to decorate a church lavishly with their own ornaments for the first time since the Reformation.[91] The dinners, whether paid for jointly by employers and limited to field-hands with a tea for their families later, or supported by communal contributions and including virtually the whole village, filled a gap left by the snapping of the old social bonds within agriculture. If they were less drunken and violent than the old suppers, and the speeches and toasts stressed a civic and national consciousness instead of the old identity with the farm and the harvesting band, then these developments possessed certain advantages to compensate for a loss of the former informality and rough vigour. The smugly approving tone in which local newspapers and dignitaries often described them[92] may well grate upon a modern reader, but it seems to have reflected a very widespread contentment.

In the twentieth century most of them passed into history in turn, as village communities themselves eroded, leaving the church services and decorations to be widely maintained, howbeit often by shrunken congregations. A revival of the festivals occurred across the Somerset levels at the end of the 1950s, led by East Brent, and they are still maintained there and at Wedmore and East Huntspill. The Brent celebration, held in a marquee in early afternoon, is given a magnificent touch of ostentation by the production of a ten-foot loaf of bread and a cheddar cheese carried by six men. The traditional triumphing rituals at the end of reaping on the other hand, have been removed by the changing processes of production. Bob Bushaway has charted how to harvest and thresh a six-quarter wheat crop at ten acres a day required 130 men in the 1840s, thirty-three in the 1870s when the horse-drawn mechanical reaper was introduced, and three in the 1940s when combine harvesters had come into use.[93] A hundred years had destroyed the spirit and practice of thousands, and the new mechanized harvesting made traditions such as the taking of the last sheaf difficult to enact in practice, as well as depriving them of social context.[94]

It is ironic, then, that the present ritual celebration of harvest consists principally of a Christian religious service which is itself much less than two centuries old. None the less, the feeling persists in different forms that the season belongs to older deities as well, and this is a belief which predates Tylor, Mannhardt, and Frazer. Elizabethan observers of English harvest customs, after all, instinctively recalled the Roman worship of the corn-goddess

Ceres. In 1836 a lady observing the 'crying of the neck' in west Devon could conclude that it was a relic of 'Druidry'.[95] Nobody has doubted that Mannhardt was correct in his demonstration that nineteenth-century European peasant harvest rites had much in common with those in classical antiquity. The point of more recent scholarly discussions is that they fulfilled certain obvious social needs, two thousand years ago as much as in Mannhardt's time, and that these can be proved whereas their religious antecedents may not. The confident interpretation of them as survivals of pagan religion, made by the nineteenth-century folklorists, achieved wide acceptance largely because it was in harmony with presuppositions. That interpretation not only remained pre-eminent for half a century, but retains much popularity. In the 1960s a non-academic folklorist of considerable distinction, George Ewart Evans, could still confidently describe both the last sheaf and the 'harvest queen' as representing 'the old pagan Corn Goddess'.[96] Customs connected with that sheaf were abandoned in late nineteenth-century Wales, not just because of changing reaping methods but because proponents of the contemporary evangelical revivals stigmatized them as heathen.[97] Likewise, in some western Somerset churches in the twentieth century, corn dollies were refused a place among the harvest festival decorations because of a similar belief.[98] Such an assumption, reinforced considerably by Frazer, also helped to account for the opposite phenomenon, of the boom in the weaving of the dollies at Evening Centres and Women's Institutes, especially in the eastern counties, during the 1940s.[99] To be sure, the dolls are now works of art requiring creative talent and technical expertise, but the attraction of making them would not be so great were it not for the feeling that they have an ancient numinous significance.[100] The same feeling has also been primarily responsible for the self-conscious retention of certain last-sheaf ceremonies long after the new technology had made them difficult to perform as a matter of course. The 'neck' was still 'cried' on the Exmoor coast of Devon in 1950, and the Federation of Old Cornwall Societies deliberately revived the custom at five farms in the two decades after the Second World War.[101] At Balquhidder in the southern Highlands west of Loch Earn, the 'maiden' was ritually gathered in 1958 (and may be yet) just as it was seen and described there by Sir James Frazer himself.[102] Whether or not the view of these practices as religious survivals is correct, it has certainly helped to preserve some semblances of them, where 'functional' interpretation would not have done.

34

WAKES, REVELS, AND HOPPINGS

THE four months between July and October may have been full of hard agricultural work—weeding, reaping, binding, and threshing—but they also contained some of the finest weather of the year and therefore some of its best potential for outdoor festivity. In most of Scotland this took the form of fairs, sports, and dances, lacking any ritual structure. Only in the northern Hebrides, where religious reformation had been least effective, did something of the latter obtain; at Michaelmas, the feast of St Michael the Archangel upon 29 September. He was regarded locally as patron saint of the sea upon which the islanders partly or wholly depended for survival, and his day was marked by a set of customs first recorded in their outline in the 1690s, when the region began to be studied by outsiders.[1] On Michaelmas Eve the womenfolk of a household would make the *struan*, a huge bannock including all the varieties of grain grown on the farm. In the morning all would attend church, and then the family would share a meal consisting of *struan* and lamb, opened in Catholic communities with a hymn to St Michael. The remains of the food were given to the local poor, and next everybody except the very young and the very old mounted horses and formed a procession with the other islanders, led by the local minister or priest. It rode sunwise around the local burial ground, repeating the hymn in Catholic areas: an annual tribute to the dead, near the end of the sailing and fishing season and after the harvest. There followed horse races and other sports, and in the evening each townland gathered in the largest house, for an exchange of gifts between the young people and dancing to hired musicians. The cavalcade and feasting was held during the eighteenth century in Catholic and Protestant communities alike upon Skye, Coll, and Tiree, and in all of the Outer Hebrides. It lingered longest among the Catholics of the latter, being last recorded on North Uist in 1866. The *struan* was still baked in the Outer Hebrides in the early twentieth century, and may be yet, but only as a private, and irregular, family treat. The early part of the nineteenth, therefore, saw the decisive decline of a custom which had been the largest and most dramatic communal rite of the early modern Hebridean year: it seems to have collapsed with the progressive depopulation and loosening of the island communities.[2]

In mainland Britain, Michaelmas was a day for holding courts, paying rents, and enjoying a good meal—traditionally of goose. Instead of having a single date in late summer or autumn for communal feasting and celebration, early modern England enjoyed festivity at that season in three localized forms. One consisted of harvest suppers, as described. Another was provided by fairs. The third consisted of the dedication feasts of parish churches and chapels, celebrations held annually to commemorate the foundation of these institutions and to honour their patrons. By the sixteenth century they were popularly known as 'wakes', a term which has no proved derivation but is probably the same as that employed by John Mirk for the midsummer 'wake fires', signifying that people stayed awake late to make merry. In the seventeenth century Sir Henry Spelman drily suggested that it derived from the Anglo-Saxon 'wak', signifying drunkenness, but there is no evidence to support this.[3] The dedication feasts could hardly have been a widespread custom until the parish system settled down in the thirteenth century, and it is not clear how far they were observed in the later Middle Ages. Records tend to be few and incidental before the late Tudor period, such as the payments by the Prior of Worcester to a minstrel 'upon our dedication day' in 1519 and 'to singers in the dedication day in the morning' in 1532.[4] All that can be said with certainty is that the feasts must have been very frequent by 1536, when Henry VIII took drastic measures to curtail them in his first set of articles to reform the Church which he had just taken over. It had obviously been a powerful criticism of them that by staggering their timing across a region the various parishes in it could provide an opportunity for a long process of reciprocal entertainment. In 1532 the House of Commons had complained to the king that holy days in general had become far too numerous, encouraging idleness and diluting piety; Henry now responded by directing that all churches hold their dedication feasts upon the same day, the first Sunday in October.[5] Of all the various directives of the English Reformation, this seems to have been the only one which was almost completely ignored, unless clergy and parishioners obeyed it for a period and then, in some fashion not apparent to history, backslid. That particular Sunday may have been chosen by the king and his advisers because it was in any case a favourite time for wakes: certainly in the nineteenth century they tended to occur in the period from June to October, with a minor cluster before harvest work and a major one after it.[6]

Henry was certainly following practice by directing that the dedication feasts be held on a Sunday, not only because it was (as has often been stressed) the day of leisure but because a religious commemoration could be followed by a communal celebration. This was precisely the connection which was to get them into trouble later in the Reformation, for they trampled over two of the principal sensitivities of Protestants: they were originally bound up with the cult of saints, and they were an occasion for drinking, dancing, and other secular self-indulgence upon the Lord's Day. A bill to prohibit them on Sundays was passed by both Houses of Parliament in 1584, only to be vetoed by Queen Elizabeth as an infringement of her control over the Church.[7] In Lancashire a knot of 'Puritan' JPs immediately compensated by enacting the same measure locally upon their own authority,[8] and once the queen was dead and James I on the throne, a parliamentary sanction was attempted again. In 1606 a bill almost identical to that of 1584 was passed by the Commons but stuck, for unknown reasons, in the Lords, while another which failed for lack of time in the 1614 Parliament was probably along the same lines.[9] Once again, effective action was left to local initiatives, such as that of the parishioners of Buxted in the Sussex Weald, who entered their decision in the register in 1613 to move the wake from Sunday 'as we desire to keep this day in holiness after the example of Nehemiah and his people'.[10] It could be argued that wakes, like ales and May games, were in any case illegal on the Lord's Day under the declaration put out by James at his succession, which banned 'disordered or unlawful exercises' then. An anonymous high official in the east Midlands, who immediately ordered constables to stop Sunday ales under its provisions, included wakes in the prohibition.[11]

It must therefore have seemed significant to many that the king did not name them among the festivities permitted after evening prayer on Sundays in his so-called Book of Sports in 1618. They were therefore included in sabbatarian bills intended to give the force of statute law to the royal declaration of 1603, which passed both Houses of Parliament in 1621 and again in 1624. On both occasions, notoriously, James surprised and annoyed MPs by using his veto against it, just as Elizabeth had done, because it seemed to him to usurp his authority to regulate the national religion with his own, prerogative, powers.[12] Charles I, like his father, opened his reign with a conciliatory gesture upon this issue, by passing in 1625 an Act of Parliament which incorporated most of the material in those rejected by his father. It did not, however, mention wakes, talking instead of the need to confine Sunday recreations to such as were 'lawful', without trying to define the latter. The result was an inevitable confusion leading to the famous church ales controversy and the reissuing of James's Book of Sports, this time with an explicit declaration that wakes were lawful upon Sundays.[13] This history made it absolutely inevitable that they would be prohibited upon it by the same ordinance of the Long Parliament in 1644 which banned church ales on the Lord's Day and ordered the destruction of maypoles. As part of the same process they were condemned in principle, and at any time, by the Westminster Assembly of clergy later that same year.[14] There is no record of any during the rest of the 1640s nor in the Interregnum, but when the legislation of the Long Parliament and Westminster Assembly lapsed at the Restoration, they reappeared in large areas of the country.

Despite this history of controversy, there are very few sources which indicate what Tudor or Stuart wakes actually looked like. It may be presumed that they involved feasting, dancing, and sports like the ales and revels with which they were generally classed in the period. None the less, they had only the slightest links with parish finance, and so have left little trace in churchwardens' accounts. They made small impact upon the imagination of poets, in comparison with the more glamorous May games and King ales. It is possible, also, that there is a simple semantic problem: that the term 'wake' obtained chiefly in the northern and midland counties, which attracted the notice of fewer commentators in early modern England and from which fewer local records survive. Further south the dedication days were known more as 'parish feasts', and as 'revels', a name which overlapped with the early summer celebrations. In the far north of England they were called 'hoppings', a name derived from the dances which were a feature of them. A poem of 1686 provides a portrait of some of the diversions obtainable at one of the latter:

> To horse-race, fair or hoppin go
> There play our cast among the whipsters,
> Throw for the hammer, lowp [leap] for slippers,
> And see the maids dance for the ring,
> Or any other pleasant thing;
> Fart for the pig, lie for the whetstone
> Or choose what side to lay our bets on.

This may be compared with a southern English equivalent from the previous generation and a much more famous pen: that of the early Stuart poet Robert Herrick. His verses 'The Wake' begin with an invitation to a companion to join him there for 'tarts and custards, cream and cakes'. For entertainments he promises:

> Morris-dancers shalt thou see,
> Marian too in Pageantrie:
> And a mimick to devise
> Many grinning properties.
> Players there will be, and those
> Base in action as in clothes:
> Yet with strutting they will please
> The incurious villages.

At evening there is cudgel play,

> But the anger ends all here,
> Drenched in ale, or drowned in beer.
> Happy Rustics, best content
> Withe the cheapest merriment:
> And possesse no other feare
> Than to want the wake next year.[15]

Few other commentators were as benign. Wakes, although apparently comparable with other early modern village celebrations, seem to have had, at times, a particularly bad reputation for debauchery. Thomas Tusser, not usually a censorious author, could write in 1573:

> Tomorrow thy father his wake day will keepe:
> Then every wanton may dance at her will,
> Both Tomkin with Tomlin, and Jankin with Gill.[16]

The ballad *The Country Wake*, published in 1707, dwelt upon the drunkenness and fornication for which it held these events to be reputed, with lines intended to disgust an urban readership, such as:

> Then did you not hear of a Country Trick?
> They say that Tuskin's no Dastard:
> For when Country Gillians do play with their Dicks
> Then London must Father their Bastards.[17]

The West Country 'revels' are, by contrast, well recorded for the early Stuart period, mostly in the local legal archives which have been so well investigated for this subject by David Underdown.[18] From these sources he identified them in twenty-one communities in Wiltshire, Somerset, and Dorset between 1608 and 1640, though it is by no means clear that all of these were dedication feasts. By their very nature, they featured only in such records when they were connected with some crime or disorder. Most of the latter were incidental, but there was a fight at Tockenham Wick in north Wiltshire during 1620 when a group of louts arrived from nearby Wooton Bassett to break up the feast, while another occurred at Coleford in northern Somerset during 1634, when constables tried to stop the revel and an alehouse keeper maintained that it was lawful under King Charles's new Book of Sports. This region, and Professor Underdown's patient research, also provides copious evidence for the survival of the feasts during the Interregnum; though they may have conformed to parliamentary law by being held upon a day other than Sunday, those in Somerset certainly flouted an outright ban made by the county bench in 1649. The next year the people of Langford Budville in the vale of Taunton Deane held one with 'fiddling and dancing and a great rout of people'. A tithingman bringing the justices' ruling was chased away by a group of Wellington men shouting, 'We will keep revel in despite of all such tithing calves as thou art'. In 1653 there was a fight between two blacksmiths and a soldier at the 'wonted revel or wake day' at Kingsweston in the centre of Somerset, while at Holwell in Blackmore vale, a tithing man and churchwarden organized one on a national fast day, 'with great rejoicing and feasting'. Two years later a woman confessed to the bench that she had got pregnant after the revel at Staple Fitzpaine in Taunton Deane, and in 1656 one was held at Timsbury, south of Bristol, which attracted 'a great concourse' and produced 'many disorders and abuses'.

This sort of popularity in the face of the strongest possible official disapproval helps to explain the continuing vitality of these events in the late seventeenth and eighteenth centuries. Of 290 Northamptonshire parishes investigated by John Bridges between 1719 and 1724, 198 had an annual feast. Of a group of twenty-eight in northern Buckinghamshire, exactly half maintained one in 1755, while four years later seven out of a set of fifteen Berkshire parishes did so. In the region around Stamford, in the east Midlands, 118 wakes were recorded in 1846. During the mid-eighteenth century, ninety-four were counted in 193 Oxfordshire parishes. In that century, indeed, parish feasts were found in every part of England except East Anglia and the counties bordering London.[19] In those areas, and in communities elsewhere which did not have feasts, the same role was fulfilled by fairs, most of which also occurred in late summer and in autumn and which themselves often derived from old dedication day celebrations.[20] The latter still abounded in North Wales during September, being known as the *gwylmabsant*, or 'saint's festival'. They were 'mostly confined to the lower order',[21] and the dancing at them was famous, musicians travelling between them to accompany it. Young people would save money to be well-dressed at them.[22] In Scotland a much more thorough religious reformation had left only a few traces of them, but these existed. At Sandwick, in Orkney, parishioners did no work on the consecration date of the kirk, although there was no merry-making.[23] During the earlier eighteenth century, those of Culross on the Firth of Forth still assembled on the morning of their patron saint's feast, 'and carried green branches through the town, decking the public places with flowers, and spent the rest of the day in festivity'. In the later part of the century, however, this celebration was transferred to the king's birthday.[24]

Although no further attempt was made to regulate them by national legislation, wakes became controversial again as soon as the preoccupations of magistrates and clergy switched back from religious nonconformity to public morals at the end of the seventeenth century. At the Epiphany Quarter Sessions in 1710 the Gloucestershire bench issued an order to prohibit them. It renewed this at Easter on the petition of the 'ministers and principal inhabitants' of Coaley, Frocester, and Nympsfield in the centre of the county, who felt that they occasioned 'rioting and drunkenness, lewdness, and debauchery and other immoralities' on Sundays. In 1776 it was the turn of the justices of the north-east division of Somerset to ban revels, while those of Nottinghamshire threatened to refuse licences to publicans who promoted wakes. The feasts were also attacked in print, William Somerville complaining in 1740 that at rural wakes he saw 'nothing but broken heads, bottles flying about, tables overturned, outrageous drunkenness, and eternal squabble'.[25] The same condemnations echoed down the century. In 1778 William Hutchinson, considering the village feasts of County Durham, lamented that 'the Sabbath is made a day of every dissipation and vice which it is possible to conceive could crowd upon a villager's manners and rural life'.[26] In 1791 a local antiquarian wrote of Nottinghamshire that 'with the lower sort of people, especially in manufacturing villages, the return of the wake never fails to produce a week, at least, of idleness, intoxication and riot: these ... render it highly desirable to all the friends of order, of decency and of religion, that they were totally suppressed'.[27]

Local evidence, and the comments of more even-minded observers, bear out most of these complaints. In 1765 the curate of Roborough, in North Devon, told the Exeter consistory court that for nine years running Revel

Sunday in his village had been marked by 'fightings, bloodshed, drunkenness, riots', and the very services in his church interrupted by jocularity and brawling occasioned by 'the young, giddy and most abandoned creatures of all the neighbouring parishes'.[28] In County Durham wake day was popularly (and cheerfully) called 'Wicked Sunday'.[29] An advertisement at Newcastle upon Tyne in 1758 read: 'On this day the annual diversions at Swallwell will take place, which will consist of dancing for ribbons, grinning for tobacco, women running for smocks, ass races, foot courses by men, with an odd whim of a man eating a cock alive, feathers, entrails, etc'.[30] The last 'whim', fortunately, was indeed 'odd', but the other sports were all standard. A smock was the usual prize for a female foot-race, and 'grinning' consisted of pulling comical or repulsive faces, often through a horse-collar. In the same year William Borlase could defend the Cornish parish feasts, at which the distinctive entertainments were matches between the young men, of wrestling or hurling (the ball game with the ball encased in silver). He none the less admitted to their unfortunate 'frolicking and drinking', and advocated their reform. Two steps had already been widely taken to improve matters: to ban competitions between villages and to restrict Sunday activities to worship and hospitality, with festivities on the next two days.[31] Despite all this, eighteenth-century observers could describe wakes without appending criticisms or reservations: The Spectator printed a portrait of 'a green covered with a promiscuous multitude of all ages and both sexes, who esteem one another more or less the following part of the year according as they distinguish themselves at this time. The whole company were in their holiday clothes, and divided into several parties, all of them endeavouring to show themselves in those exercises wherein they excelled' (in this case cudgel-fighting, football, and wrestling).[32] In 1736 both the Daily Gazetter and the London Magazine published a piece which argued that without wakes common people 'would become dull and spiritless' and 'addict themselves to less warrantable pleasures'.[33]

It is clear that by the eighteenth century the dedication feasts had come to occupy precisely the same ground of controversy as church ales had done in the early seventeenth. Unlike the ales, however, they were not vulnerable to institutional change, and continued with undiminished vigour and notoriety into the nineteenth century, from which much more numerous and detailed descriptions survive. At its opening, the Northamptonshire poet John Clare could provide a long and warm portrait of a village feast in his neighbourhood, with stalls vending gingerbread, ribbons, bows, and bonnets, ballad-singers hawking wares, a sailor showing his scars, telling tales of naval battles, and being given money, soldiers swaggering about, enjoying the fun, and recruiting drunken youngsters, and people dancing to gipsy fiddlers. Everybody wears their best clothes, and relatives from other villages join parishioners for dinners with songs and drinking of healths. The games include sack-racing, hunting a greased pig, badger-baiting, cock-fighting, horse-racing, running by girls for a smock, and wrestling. Couples embrace on the grass upon their way home.[34] William Hone's *Every-Day Book* included in 1832 a very similar description of a midland event, including such details as the joyful peal of bells on the Sunday, the gathering of guests from outside the village in the church gallery to hear the service, and the setting up of swings and roundabouts for children in the following few days, with 'bowls, quoits and nine-pins for the men; and the merry dance in the evening, for the lasses'. Nevertheless, it still felt obliged to add that it was 'in reality productive of greater evil than good', poor people being encouraged to overspend, and men to get drunk and fight.[35]

These negative aspects, as before, impressed many educated observers most strongly. A local newspaper, the *Voice of the People*, could declare in 1831 of the famous Stalybridge Wakes, near Manchester, 'Those who derive amusement from hurdy-gurdy grinders, cat-gut scrapers; drums and gingerbread; noise and dirt, gin and penny-whistles, beef and pudding, ale and spice-cake, broken heads and bloody noses, terminating in empty pockets, head-aches, black eyes and comfortable lodgings in the lock-ups, may have ample means of gratification'.[36] During the 1840s a commentator in the same area wrote bitterly of the encouragements provided by some factory-owners

at the fag end of an annual wake. When the bulk of the people had spent their money in fun and fury, and riotous living, these gentry and publicans would subscribe for sack-races, for eating boiling porridge, for eating hot rolls dipped in treacle, suspended on a line of string, eight or ten competitors for a prize standing with gaping mouths, swaying bodies, and their hands tied behind their backs. Then, as dusk came on, and the excitement flagged, these "gentlemen", with their glasses of whisky, sitting at the second-storey windows of the hotel or "the Lamb", threw shovelfuls of hot coppers among the frantic crowds'.[37]

Village feasts were still common in Cornwall during this early part of the century, but in the rest of the West Country the surviving 'revels' were isolated, though celebrated, events.[38] Only six are recorded in the whole of Dorset. Some had distinctive competitions among the customary set, such as wheeling barrows blindfolded at Cattistock in the Dorset chalk downs. More common were special foodstuffs, served publicly or privately: in central Gloucestershire, Bisley was noted for pig's cheek and parsnips, Nympsfield for plum dumplings, Haresfield for mutton and turnips, and Painswick for pies with china dogs baked in them. The denser concentration of the events in that county was due to its proximity to the Midlands, where they abounded in villages from the Welsh Marches across to Cambridgeshire and Lincolnshire.[39] They were almost equally common in the rural north-east, still known as wakes, hoppings, or feasts in most places, but also as 'the tides' or 'thumps' in the West Riding of Yorkshire.[40] In Herefordshire wakes were held even in little hamlets where no church had ever existed to make one technically possible. Across in Lincolnshire they were far more a feature of large 'open' parishes which were not controlled by a gentry family. The thickly scattered feasts of the Welsh Border counties, like those of Gloucestershire, had their characteristic dishes: for example in Herefordshire the roast duck and green peas of Blakemere or the rice pudding and currants of Peterchurch; or in Shropshire the fig cakes at Norton in Hales and the eel pies at Shrewsbury.

Activities were proportionately varied, and ranged from the County Durham pattern whereby men played football or quarterstaves or just sat drinking beer, to the chaotic delights of Bunbury Wakes in central Cheshire, where a master of ceremonies in 1808 had to be competent to judge.

pony and donkey-racing; wheelbarrow, bag, cock, and pig racing; archery, singlestick, quoits, cricket, football, cocking, wrestling, bull and badger baiting, dog-fighting, goose-riding, bumble-puppy... dipping, mumbling, jawing, grinning, whistling, jumping, jingling, skenning, smoking, stalling, knitting, bobbing, bowling, throwing, dancing, snuff-taking, pudding-eating, etc.[41]

One competitive activity which required no judge was brawling. Local people often considered the continuing violence at wakes to be therapeutic. Sometimes it was internal, such as in Herefordshire where on 'the evening of the feast it was usual to settle by fighting all the quarrels of the past year... one beating wiped off the score'. More common elsewhere were contests between communities with traditional rivalries, such as Soham and Wicken in the Cambridgeshire Fens, and Castleton and Bradwell in the High Peak of Derbyshire. The people of the last two villages 'fought with knobsticks in the fields between'.[42] In view of all this it is noteworthy how seldom any really serious injury seems to have occurred: incidents such as the one at Newland Wake, Oxfordshire, in 1843, when a publican killed a young carpenter,[43] were very rare indeed. The violence was thus controlled, and to those involved it was, like the intoxication, a cathartic release which helped put the world to rights rather than to disrupt it. None the less, to describe it as 'ritualized' may carry a danger of misleading, for the animosity involved, once a grudge was nursed or a feud up and running, was real enough, and so was the pain inflicted.

One of the most striking features of the early part of the century was the way in which, as villages industrialized and were sucked into conurbations, their feasts gained strength instead of losing it. They became all the more important as focal points for communities in the throes of social and economic adaptation, buoyed up on the prosperity which was often an initial consequence of the changes. At this period they abounded in the suburbs of Sheffield and around Bradford, Huddersfield, and Halifax.[44] They were equally common in the west midland Black Country, and multiplied in Birmingham as the city grew, formally attached to new churches or chapelries but sponsored by publicans. As the suburbs sprouted in turn, so wakes appeared there, lacking even notional ecclesiastical connections and focused directly upon public houses.[45] Most flamboyant, and best-studied, were those of the Lancashire textile-manufacturing area, which have been made the subject of theses by Robert Poole and Theresa Buckland.[46] They combined the traditional festivities of the feasts with the more recently evolved local entertainments of the rush-cart and the north-western morris, to produce an elaborate spectacle reflecting the pride of the various communities and often sponsored by local gentry and employers as well as publicans. Just as elsewhere in a region which contained several such events, they were spread over the late summer and autumn to permit reciprocal visiting and entertainment between the parishes. Friendship, rivalry, individual or communal prowess, and personal gain (through the prizes offered at competitions) could all be gratified at them. The largest were spread over almost a week, commencing with the Sunday of the church service, but Monday and Tuesday were always the most important part of that period. The self-employed had no difficulty in attending, and factory-owners were often expected to give holidays if a wake were occurring in the vicinity. From supporting the event directly, they could gain personal entertainment, reinforce communal solidarity and personal popularity, and advertise their wares.

It must be stressed, however, that most educated commentators upon the feasts, as may be surmised from those quoted above, were not supportive. Outsiders were especially appalled by the drunkenness and violence, and even the local élite was seldom convinced of the value of these aspects as a safety-valve within society. Two developments from the late eighteenth century increased this hostility. One was the growth of the population in general and of urban centres in particular, which increased the size of the crowds at the festivities. They were swelled further by improved communications: at Ilkley Feast, in the West Riding, in 1870, so many strangers arrived by train that they easily overpowered the local police force which tried to control them when they got drunk.[47] The second was a growth in humanitarian sentiment which deplored the blood sports—baiting of bulls, bears, and badgers, and fighting of dogs and cocks—which were an important traditional part of the celebrations. Indeed, cruelty, as well as drunkenness and brawling, was considered to be an important part of their cathartic value by many who attended. All through the first half of the nineteenth century the barrage of criticism and complaint, expressed in books, letters, speeches, sermons, and (especially) newspapers, remained constant.[48] Where a local ruling class had direct power over the holding of a feast, the result could be fatal to it. Stixwould feast, in the Lincolnshire chalklands, was suppressed because the landlord withdrew his support.[49] In the 1770s the Birmingham Street Commission successively banned the various entertainments of wakes from public places within the city, while a hundred years later the authorities at Wednesbury in the Black Country obtained an order from the Home Secretary to forbid them within their precincts.[50] Such power was, however, rarely disposed of and had narrow limits. Most rural feasts were in 'open' parishes, as said, while the Birmingham revellers just moved out to the wakes multiplying in the suburbs and the Wednesbury event relocated on private land.

Interference from above was more effective in abolishing specific entertainments which the élite found particularly offensive. They included the nude races for adult men at Birmingham, which the city magistrates halted after three prosecutions.[51] Most commonly and dramatically, they consisted of the blood sports in which animals were tormented. A string of orders by county magistrates and town councils in the late eighteenth century developed into a national campaign of considerable intensity in the early nineteenth, culminating in parliamentary legislation in the 1830s. This could be made effective by the newly established police forces. The net result of all this effort was that by 1840 the baitings had withdrawn into a few wakes in the suburbs of Birmingham, in the Black Country, and in industrial Lancashire, and were wiped out in most of these by the middle of the next decade. Their last stronghold was in the mining district west of Manchester, where the ringleaders of the bull-baiting at Chowbent Wakes had to be imprisoned in successive years during the 1840s, and the final attempt to provide it was in 1851.[52] This still, however, left legal blood sports such as coursing of hares, and shooting of sparrows and pigeons, and the perennial violence between humans. In the form of single combats, this could be an entertainment in itself. At Shaw wakes in 1846 people were surprised that 'there was only one genuine Lancashire up-and-down fight in the whole week'. 'Up and down' meant with fists and clogs; at Turton head-butting was also allowed in one year, but the Rochdale fighting champion, a pork-butcher, shattered a cast-iron oven door with his head during the warm-up and so frightened off all opponents.[53]

Most of the feasts were therefore not, in their essence, amenable to control from above in society or outside their community: to be transformed or destroyed they could only respond to changes within their own clientele. One force for this consisted of the impact of evangelical religion upon the working classes, especially transmitted by Nonconformist denominations such as Baptists and Methodists which had no sympathy for wakes as a relic of the old Church as well as occasions for vice. It overlapped with, and was reinforced by, the temperance movement, and the growth of a political radicalism which tried to foster ideals of sobriety, education, and self-improvement in the populace. This combination of developments seems to have been decisive in bringing about the decline of the parish festivities in Wales and Cornwall,[54] and in eradicating some elsewhere, such as that at Eccles in Lancashire.[55] Elsewhere in the Lancashire textile area, however, the evangelists and reformers could put forth immense efforts of concerted condemnation and the provision of rival attractions such as pageants, meals, and excursions, to very little effect.[56] It took fundamental shifts in loyalty, taste, and opportunity to destroy the feasts. One such was the continuing growth of urban areas, eliminating the space needed for the traditional celebrations, while another was represented by the increasing occupational and social divisions among the populace, fracturing a sense of community. As wakes grew larger and more invaded by strangers, the element of reciprocal hospitality became ever less obvious and more a private matter. Conversely, the commercial elements—shows and rides—grew more important and more elaborate, touring round the various events so that one became increasingly like another. As such, they were particularly vulnerable to the competition of alternative forms of leisure activity which developed in the late nineteenth century, such as fairgrounds powered by steam and electricity, organized games, races at stadiums and courses, circuses, and (above all) family excursions to the seaside or rural beauty spots. All represented more exciting ways of spending a holiday.[57] Robert Poole expressed the change neatly when speaking of Lancashire: 'At the beginning of the nineteenth century, wakes time meant a crowded town; by the end of the century, it meant a deserted town'.[58]

Marshamchurch, near the north coast of Cornwall, still preserves its revel, on the Monday after the feast of its patron saint Marwenne. It has been retained as a self-conscious piece of archaism and is centred upon a schoolgirl 'queen' borrowed from Victorian May festivities; but its traditional entertainments of wrestling, country dancing, and foot-racing provide a good enough representation of a Georgian village feast, fostered by and fostering a genuine communal pride. Otherwise only the annual arrival of a travelling fun-fair in some villages and towns stands as a memorial to the former existence of one of the most popular and long-lived of British calendar customs.

35

SAMHAIN

Hallowe'en developed from the Celtic feast of Samhain (pronounced 'sow-in'), which marked the end of summer and the beginning of winter. For the Celts, Samhain was the beginning of the year and the cycle of the seasons. Samhain was a time when the Celts acknowledged the beginning and the ending of all things. As they looked to nature, they saw the falling of the leaves from the trees, the coming of winter and death. It was a time when they turned to their Gods and Goddesses seeking to understand the turning cycles of life and death. Here, on the threshold of the cold barren winter months, it was also a time of feasting and celebration as the weakest animals were culled to preserve valuable foodstuffs and provide food to last until the following spring...For the Celts, Samhain was a time when the gates between this world and the next were open. It was a time of communion with the spirits of the dead, who, like the wild autumnal winds, were free to roam the earth. At Samhain, the Celts called upon their ancestors, who might bring warnings and guidance to help in the year to come.

Samhain was a time of change and transformation where both the past and the present met with the uncertain tides of the future yet to come. It was a time for magic and divination, when Druids and Soothsayers would forecast the events of the coming year. The high Kings of Ireland held a week long feast for this purpose, where seers foretold the coming pattern of farming and hunting, the times of eclipses and storms, and whether neighbouring Kings were plotting warfare. For the Celts, Samhain was both an end-of-summer feast and a time of communion with the realms of the spirit.

When Christianity became established in Britain, the Pagan Goddesses and Gods were said to have fallen under the rule of all the saints. All Hallows Day (November 1st), now known as 'All Saints Day', celebrates this take over. The old Pagan traditions, however, were not eradicated and lived on in the guise of Hallowe'en—the eve of All Hallows Day or All Saints Day. It should not be surprising that Christianity should seek to suppress the Pagan celebration of Samhain. To the new religion, the deities of the old faith seemed like evil spirits. The natural 'uncanniness' of Samhain was interpreted as a time of danger for the Christian soul. The spirits of the dead and the spirits of the Otherworld, which the Celts called to at this time, were confused with the evil demons of the Christian religion...

Christianity not only suppressed old Celtic celebrations, but replaced them with Christian festivals. If we look closely, it is not difficult to see that All Souls' Day (November 2nd) is a continuation in a Christian form of the older Pagan practices of Samhain. This is a time when on the continent Catholic families will visit the family tomb, say prayers for the dead, light candles and even picnic at the graveside. Just as their Pagan ancestors did, they are communing with the dead.

T HESE extracts are taken from the leaflet issued by the British Pagan Federation for Hallowe'en 1993, to defend the festival against attacks upon its celebration made by some radical Christians. They have been chosen simply because they represent the most concise and eloquent summary in recent years of a century of assertions repeated in popular works of folklore all through the twentieth century. Some of them are certainly correct, while most may be so. The purpose of the next three chapters is to make a re-examination of all the evidence for the development of the feast and of its associated days of All Saints and All Souls, and to show how intractable and ambivalent much of it seems to be.

Samhain, 1 November, was the major festival which marked the opening of winter in early medieval Ireland; it is sometimes spelt Samain or Samuin, although the pronunciation was the same. In *Tochmarc Emire* it is the first of the four quarter days mentioned by the heroine Emer; 'Samhain, when the summer goes to its rest'.[1] To the writer of this text, probably working in the tenth century, it was therefore the opposite to the time of Beltane, being the period at which the livestock had been gathered in from the summer pastures and the cold and confined season was setting in for human and farm animal. The cereal harvest would likewise have long been completed and the time of warfare and of trading was at an end. It was therefore an ideal moment for the convention of the year's most important tribal assemblies, and indeed 'the *feis* of Samhain', at which local kings gathered their people, is a favourite setting for early Irish tales. In *Serglige Con Culaind*, which exists in a twelfth-century version, it is stated that the *feis* of the Ulaid (Ulstermen) lasted 'the three days before Samuin and the three days after Samuin and Samuin itself. They would gather at Mag Muirthemni, and during these seven days there would be nothing but meetings and games and amusements and entertainments and eating and feasting'.[2] These activities (together with a great deal of boasting and brawling) are precisely those portrayed at the *feis* in this and other accounts of it.[3] No doubt there were religious observances as well, but none of the tales ever portrays any, and a text like *Sanas Chormaic*, which is so informative on Beltane, furnishes nothing for the winter festival. Indeed, the only such reference is in the work of the thoroughly unreliable seventeenth-century Irish antiquary Jeffrey Keating, who states that the Druids of Ireland used to assemble on the hill of Tlachtga on 'the night of Samain' and kindle a sacred fire. From this 'every householder in the country' relit his own domestic fire, which had been extinguished that night.[4] His source is unknown, and the story implies an extremely unlikely degree of religious and political centralization in pagan Ireland; it may be that it is a mistaken transference of the custom of Beltane. When Keating's story is put aside, a considerable suspicion arises that the rites of Samhain do not feature in medieval Irish literature simply because by the time that it was written, centuries after Christianization, the authors did not know what they had been.

Jeffrey Gantz, author of one of the most accurate and accessible translations of that literature, has suggested that Samhain was regarded as a time of unusual supernatural power, because of the number of stories set at that feast in which humans are attacked or approached by deities, fairies, or monsters.

He also draws attention to the number of legendary kings who were slain at that time.[5] The same evidence has caused Proinsias MacCana to call Samhain 'a partial return to primordial chaos...the appropriate setting for myths which symbolise the dissolution of established order as a prelude to its recreation in a new period of time'.[6] Both may be correct, but their point cannot be proved from the tales themselves; it could just be that several narratives are started, set, or concluded at this feast because it represented an ideal context, being a major gathering of royalty and warriors with time on their hands. In the same way, many of the Arthurian stories were to commence with a courtly assembly for Christmastide or Pentecost. The same sort of consideration applies to gatherings of Otherworld beings at this part of the year, such as the 'bright folk and fairy hosts' believed by the fourteenth century to hold games and feast upon nuts each Samhain at the prehistoric mounds of the Bruigh na Boinne.[7] They may just have been visualized as counterparts to the human assemblies at this time.

Heavy Irish immigration into the Scottish Highlands and Isles in the early Middle Ages carried the name Samhain there, in local variations, but to the Welsh the day was 'Calan Gaeaf', 'the first day of winter', and the night before was termed 'Nos Galan Gaea', 'winter's eve'. Perhaps significantly, the earliest Welsh literature attributes no arcane significance to these dates (in sharp contrast to May Eve) and describes no gatherings then (in sharp contrast to New Year). It must be concluded, therefore, that the medieval records furnish no evidence that 1 November was a major pan-Celtic festival, and none of religious ceremonies, even where it was observed. An Anglo-Saxon counterpart is difficult either to prove or to dismiss completely. Bede, in his work on the calendar, stated that September had been called 'Haleg-monath', while October was 'Vuinter-fylleth' and November 'Blod-monath'. He knew that 'Haleg-monath' meant 'holy month', but not why, and therefore neither can we; it is possible, as said before, that it derived from rites connected with the end of the grain harvest. The name for October signified the coming of winter, while that for November meant 'blood month'; and here Bede had some important information to offer. He stated that it derived from the annual slaughter of livestock in early winter to reduce the number that had to be kept through the lean months, and that the victims were dedicated to the gods as sacrifices.[8] There may here be a record of a festival, of equivalent importance and even of simultaneous timing to Samhain; or it may be that the passage describes an agricultural process rather than an event. Pagan Scandinavia had its own major festival of the opening of winter, the 'Winter Nights'; which began on the Saturday in the week between 11 and 17 October. It features prominently in the saga literature, as a time when each substantial farmer held a feast and a sacrifice.[9] Unhappily for our purposes, however, it is debatable how far the Christian authors of the sagas were accurately remembering heathen practices, and doubtful whether this festival was introduced into Britain.

At the end of the nineteenth century, two distinguished academics, one at Oxford and the other at Cambridge, made enduring contributions to the popular conception of Samhain. The former was the philologist Sir John Rhŷs, who suggested that it had been the 'Celtic' New Year. He had not documented this from early records, but inferred it from contemporary folklore in Wales and Ireland, which he felt to be full of Hallowe'en customs associated with new beginnings. To reinforce these he cited Keating's entry about Tlachtga, which he believed to fall into the same category, and 'corrected' the wording of a passage in *Sanas Chormaic* to support his view.[10] He thought that it was vindicated when he paid a subsequent visit to the Isle of Man and found that its people sometimes called 31 October New Year's Night ('Hog-unnaa') and practised customs then which were usually associated with 31 December.[11] In fact, the flimsy nature of all this evidence ought to have been apparent from the start. The divinatory and purificatory rituals on 31 October could be explained either by a connection to the most eerie of Christian feasts (All Saints) or by the fact that they ushered in the most dreaded of all the seasons. The many 'Hog-unnaa' customs were also widely practised on the conventional New Year's Eve, and Rhŷs was uncomfortably aware that they might simply have been transferred, in recent years, from then to Hallowe'en, to increase merriment and fund-raising on the latter. He got round this problem by asserting that in his opinion (based upon no evidence at all) the transfer had been the other way round.

This issue can only properly be addressed using the data of the medieval sources, and this is not sufficient to conclude the matter. The fundamental problem is that writing, Christianity, and the Roman calendar all entered Wales and Ireland as parts of the same process. Therefore, by definition, the earliest records are going to commence the year on 1 January or 25 March according to the Roman fashion. This is certainly true of every surviving medieval Welsh calendar.[12] None the less, there are possible traces of an earlier system in the Irish records. *Tochmarc Emire*, after all, reckoned the year around the quarter-days which commenced the seasons, and put Samhain at the beginning of those. If it was the principal annual assembly of at least some of the Irish kingdoms, then it would make sense to calculate some sort of transaction from it. What seems to be insoluble is the crucial problem of whether 1 November was once the only date observed, or whether it had always run side by side with January, being used for different sorts of reckoning.

Rhŷs's theory was further popularized by the Cambridge scholar, Sir James Frazer. At times the latter did admit that the evidence for it was inconclusive,[13] but at others he threw this caution overboard and employed it to support an idea of his own: that Samhain had been the pagan Celtic feast of the dead. He reached this belief by a simple process of arguing back from a fact, that 1 and 2 November had been dedicated to that purpose by the medieval Christian Church, from which it could be surmised that this had been a Christianization of a pre-existing festival. He admitted, by implication, that there was in fact no actual record of such a festival, but inferred the former existence of one from a number of different propositions: that the Church had taken over other pagan holy days, that 'many' cultures have annual ceremonies to honour their dead, 'commonly' at the opening of the year, and that (of course) 1 November had been the Celtic New Year. He pointed out that although the feast of All Saints or All Hallows had been formally instituted across most of north-west Europe by the emperor Louis the Pious in 835, on the prompting of Pope Gregory IV, it had already existed, on its later date of 1 November, in England at the time of Bede. He suggested that pope and emperor had, therefore, merely ratified an existing religious practice based upon that of the ancient Celts.[14]

The story is, in fact, more complicated. By the mid-fourth century Christians in the Mediterranean world were keeping a feast in honour of all those who had been martyred under the pagan emperors; it is mentioned in the *Carmina Nisibena* of St Ephraem, who died in about 373, as being held on 13 May. During the fifth century divergent practices sprang up, the Syrian churches holding the commemoration in Easter Week and those of the Greek world preferring the Sunday after Pentecost. That of Rome, however, preferred to keep to the May date, and Pope Boniface IV formally endorsed it in the year 609. By 800 churches in England and Germany, which were in touch with each other, were celebrating a festival dedicated to all saints upon 1 November, instead. The oldest text of Bede's Martyrology, from the eighth century, does not include it, but the recensions at the end of the century do. Charlemagne's favourite churchman Alcuin was keeping it by then, as were also his friend Arno, bishop of Salzburg, and a church in Bavaria. Pope Gregory, therefore, was endorsing and adopting a practice which had begun in northern Europe. It had not, however, started in Ireland, where the *Felire* of Oengus and the *Martyrology of Tallaght* prove that the early medieval churches celebrated the feast of All Saints upon 20 April.[15] This makes nonsense of Frazer's notion that the November date was chosen because of 'Celtic' influence; rather, both 'Celtic' Europe and Rome followed a Germanic idea. The origins of that idea are lost; it may be simply that some northern churchmen felt the need of a spectacular feast at the opening of winter, at a time when some form of merriment was badly needed.

The dead arrived later. In 998 Odilo, abbot of Cluny, ordered a solemn mass for the souls of all Christian dead in his monastery and its daughter houses. The date which he chose was in February. When his example was followed, in other networks of churches during the next two centuries, it gradually became the norm to hold the feast of All Souls upon 2 November, which not only suited the sombre nature of the season but could be conveniently linked to the preceding festival, as saints were increasingly seen as intercessors upon behalf of departed souls facing judgment or suffering it. Indeed, by the high Middle Ages both festivals had become primarily a time at which to pray for dead friends or family members, when the withering of flowers and leaves, and the coming of frosts, directed human attention to death and decay.[16] If the season was peculiarly appropriate to the rite, the latter was made ever more necessary by the developing Christian theological emphasis upon the terrors of hell, which in turn gave rise to the doctrine of purgatory. It remains possible that northern European pagans had honoured their dead at this time, but not only is the evidence still utterly wanting but Frazer's chain of reasoning completely breaks down.

To hazard any guess about the ancient religious significance of Samhain and Calan Gaeaf, therefore, we are left completely dependent upon inferences projected backward from folklore collected in the last few centuries; and it has already been suggested that this can be a difficult business. Nevertheless, it can be taken further. It seems to be proved, from both medieval and modern evidence, that May Eve and May Day, at the opening of summer, was regarded in the pastoral areas of the British Isles as a time when fairies and witches were especially active, and magical devices required to guard against them. Logically, the opening of winter, with the reoccupation of the home pastures and the byres, ought to have been another such, and so it seems was the case. In nineteenth-century Wales Nos Galan Gaea was the year's most frightening *Ysbrydnos*, a night when spirits were abroad, and churchyards, stiles, and crossroads were all to be avoided as particular gathering-places for them.[17] The same reputation attended Samhain Eve, *Oiche Shamhna*, in Ireland, where another name for it was 'Puca' (or Goblin) Night.[18] In Scotland the sixteenth-century poet Alexander Montgomerie could write:

> In the hindered of harvest, on alhallow evin,
> Quhen our gude nychbouris rydis if I reid rycht
> Sum buklit on one bwnwyd and some on ane bean
> Ay trippard in troupes fra the twilycht;
> Sum saidlit on a scho-aip graithit in grene,
> Sum hobland on hempstalkis hovand on hicht,
> The King of Phairie and his court with the elph-quene,
> With mony elrich incubus was rydand that nycht.[19]

> (At the hind-end of harvest, on Hallowe'en,
> When our 'good neighbours' ride if I think right
> Some mounted on a ragweed and some on a bean,
> All tripping in troupes from the twilight;
> Some saddled on a she-ape all arrayed in green,
> Some riding on hempstalks rising on high,
> The King of Faerie and his court with the Elf-queen
> With many a wierd incubus was riding that night.)

Lest it be thought that these beliefs were confined to Celtic regions of the 'upland' zone, it should be noted that in the nineteenth-century Shetland Isles, where a Norse culture prevailed, it was thought that at 'Hallowmas' 'the trows [trolls] came out from their fastnesses and wreaked havoc among cattle and crops in the yard'.[20] At Longridge Fell, in the Lancashire Pennines, people would walk the hillsides on Hallowe'en until the early part of that century, between 11 p.m. and midnight. Each carried a lighted candle, and if one went out the holder would know that an attack from a witch was impending and would thus be warned to take precautions. The custom was called 'lating' (hindering) the witches.[21] In all likelihood a prehistoric belief in the danger from supernatural forces at the turning of the pastoral seasons was much reinforced by the arcane associations of the Christian feast of the dead. Nevertheless, the analogy with the May Eve and May Day is so strong that it seems hardly plausible that all the dread of the night came from the Christian festival. It is this that lends credence to the characterization of the ancient Samhain as a particularly numinous time, made by Jeffrey Gantz and Proinsias MacCana, despite the lack of clear evidence in the early literature alone.

It must now be asked whether the folklore records provide any insight into the rituals which might have been employed at the pagan festival. Frazer certainly believed that he had found one, in the precise seasonal equivalent to the rite of Beltane: the use of fire as protective magic. He believed, indeed, that he had uncovered so much data for this that he could term Hallowe'en one of the 'Celtic' fire-festivals, and his information can now be much increased. As in the case of Beltane, the custom really only began to be recorded in detail when it was in advanced decline. In 1589 'hallowmas fires' were forbidden by the presbytery at Stirling. In 1648 the same order was made with respect to Fife by a Kirk Assembly and at Slains, also in Scotland, by the local kirk sessions.[22] A writer in Anglesey during 1741 noted that Hallowe'en 'coelcerths' (bonfires) were 'upon the decline'.[23] It was in the last third of that century that Thomas Pennant, the travel writer, drew the attention of the educated public to the custom in both Scotland and Wales. He described how in the eastern Highlands as soon as night fell on Hallowe'en, 'a person sets fire to a bush of broom fastened around a pole; and attended with a crowd, runs round the village. He then flings it down, heaps great quantity of combustible matters in it, and makes a great bonfire. A whole tract is thus illuminated at the same time, and makes a fine appearance'.[24] In North Wales he heard of how families built a fire each, and, when it burned down, left a marked white pebble in the ashes for each one of them. If any stone was missing in the morning, then the person whom it represented would die within the year.[25]

Shortly after Pennant wrote, William Owen published a similar reference to the Welsh custom,[26] and John Ramsay of Ochtertyre recorded a very full account of the Scottish one, starting with a description of how after dusk the young people of every settlement had 'assembled on some eminence near the houses'. They had made a fire,

Which from the feast was called *Samh-nag or Savnag*. Around it was placed a circle of stones, one for each person of the families to whom they belonged. And when it grew dark the bonfire was kindled, at which a loud shout was set up. Then each person taking a torch of ferns or sticks in his hand, ran round the fire exulting; and sometimes they went into the adjacent fields where, if there was another company, they visited the bonfire, taunting the others if inferior in any respect to themselves. After the fire was burned out they returned home, where a feast was prepared, and the remainder of the evening was spent in mirth and diversions of various kinds. Next morning they repaired betimes to the bonfire, where the situation of the stones was examined with much attention. If any of them were misplaced, or if the print of a foot could be discerned near any particular stone, it was imagined that the person for whom it was set would not live out the year. Of late years this is less attended to, but about the beginning of the present century it was regarded as a sure prediction. The Hallowe'en fire is still kept up in some parts of the Low Country; but on the western coasts and in the Isles it is never kindled, though the night is spent in merriment and entertainments.[27]

A further hundred years of records filled out the details of the fire-rites in both countries. In Perthshire they flourished all through the nineteenth century, being repeatedly noted for their number and the exuberance with which they were maintained.[28] Another of their strongholds was in the north-east, from the Moray to the Braemar districts. There each member of a family carried a torch of fir wood around their fields, sunwise, to protect them. At Corgarff in the upper Don valley, these were thrown into the bonfire at the end, with the words 'Brave bonefire, burn á, Keep the fairies á awá'.[29] In Moray boys begged fuel for their fires from each householder in their village, commonly with the words 'Ge's a peat t' burn the witches'. Once the blaze was started, 'One after another of the youths laid himself down on the ground as near to the fire as possible so as not to be burned, and in such a position as to let the smoke roll over him. The others ran through the smoke, and jumped over him'.[30] This may have been an echo of the rite of the 'Beltane carline', or (more probably) the smoke was regarded as having protective powers. At Hallowe'en 1874 Queen Victoria herself paid tribute to the traditions of the region by having an 'immense' bonfire made in front of Balmoral Castle, upon which the effigy of a witch was burned after being escorted thither by people costumed as fairies.[31] By that time, however, the custom was dying in the Grampians, and nowhere did it seem to survive the end of the century. Indeed, despite this very marked popularity all along the Highland Line and in the districts on either side, it seems to be recorded nowhere else, save at Paisley on the Clyde, which is not far away, and on one single Hebridean island, Skye, in 1923.[32] It may be that it had never been a tradition in the Western Highlands and the Isles; Ramsay was in doubt about the matter, and earlier observers in the Hebrides, such as Martin, and later folklorists there, such as Carmichael, do not mention it. The Skye exception may have been a later addition. There was a slightly wider distribution, apparently also covering the Highland borderlands but extending further into the lowlands, for the belief that all household fires should be extinguished and relit on the morning of All Saints' Day.[33] It is a clear parallel to the custom of Beltane, and an interesting echo of that described by Keating, but again does not seem to have been universal.

Likewise, the coel earth on Nos Galan Gaea was apparently confined to north and central Wales, and the divinatory rite with the stones was found only in the north-west. What was ubiquitous throughout the Welsh areas in which the fires were lit was the belief that the most fearsome spirit abroad in the night took the form of a tail-less black sow, *yr Hwrch Ddu Gwta*. In north-western Denbighshire, children running home from the fire would scream 'the tail-less black sow take the hindermost'. In Anglesey they had a rhyme:

> A Tail-less Black Sow
> And a White Lady
> Without a head
> May the Tail-less Black Sow
> Snatch the hindmost.
> A Tail-less Black Sow
> On Winter's Eve,
> Thieves coming along
> Knitting stockings.

It was said that menfolk on the island would pretend to be the pig, grunting in the darkness, to get the youngsters home faster. All across the north of the principality during the nineteenth century, down to and including Montgomeryshire, *yr Hwrch Ddu* was said to sit on stiles upon this night, waiting for victims.[34] Who this being might have been is a complete puzzle. Romano-British iconography and inscriptions, and medieval Welsh literature, are alike devoid of clues; the eleventh-century tale of Math, son of Mathonwy, certainly features a sow, but there is nothing supernatural about it. The modern notion of Ceridwen as a (white) sow-goddess, popularized by Robert Graves in *The White Goddess*, entirely lacks any supporting evidence. Such a figure seems to be wholly missing from the earlier Welsh records, and may have been a folk-devil evolved from the early modern period onward. In general, the fires in Wales seem to have been associated with divinatory rather than purificatory purposes, although the Denbighshire boys did run sunwise around theirs and believed that it was lucky to pass over the embers.[35] The Winter's Eve blazes survived with diminishing frequency across their full range for most of the nineteenth century, and lasted in Merionethshire until the 1930s.[36]

There is an exact parallel to the Scottish and Welsh customs on the Isle of Man, where in 1845 it was recorded that fires called 'Sauin' had been kindled each 31 October 'till a late period' to fend off fairies and witches.[37] They were also known in Ireland, but only, it seems, in two places. One was in the Protestant districts of north-eastern Ulster, which had been heavily settled from Scotland, and the other in Dublin itself—and there only from the mid-twentieth century! Alan Gailey, discussing the distribution of the fires in Ulster, noted the striking lack of any ritual activity or solemnity associated with them, and suggested that they might represent a recent innovation.[38] There is, indeed, a remarkable absence of them in the rich folklore collections for the rest of nineteenth-century Ireland, something which puzzled Frazer.[39] This pattern does harmonize with the parallel lack of them in the more Gaelic regions of Scotland, the western and central Highlands and the Hebrides.

They are also not recorded in those other 'Celtic' areas of Britain, Cornwall and Cumbria, and at this point the whole notion of a 'Celtic fire festival' begins to break down. What we have instead is a powerful local tradition in three different areas: the districts on either side of Scotland's Highland Line, north and central Wales, and the Isle of Man. The custom of the stones in or by the fire, found in the first two, must have migrated from one to the other by one of those strange and hidden processes by which identical popular practices (including some which are plainly late developments) can be found in widely separated places. Fires were indeed lit in England on All Saints' Day, notably in Lancashire, and may well ultimately have descended from the same rites, but were essentially part of a Christian ceremony (as will be described), and could have a separate origin.

On the other hand, the use of bonfires was only one aspect of a genuinely widespread feeling that the night of 31 October to 1 November was an especially numinous and dangerous one, requiring protective measures, found all over Ireland, Wales, and Scotland. Instead of employing flames, many of the southern Irish relied upon the *parshell*, a cross of sticks woven with straw which was placed over the inside of the entrance to a home. On the coasts of Connacht some householders preferred what is described, rather mysteriously, as 'a charm of fire, iron and salt against the puca', or goblin. On the Hebridean island of South Uist, boys would carry a burning peat around their house and outbuildings to protect them.[40] Elsewhere in the Hebrides, people were more concerned to propitiate the powers of the sea, at the opening of the season of the worst storms; and they did so with one of the most blatant examples recorded in the British Isles of a pagan rite surviving into the Christian epoch. On Lewis in the seventeenth century fishermen would go down to the shore at Hallowe'en, kneel at the edge of the waves, and repeat the Paternoster. One of them then waded in up to his waist, poured out a bowl of ale, and asked a being called Shoney (Johnny) for a good catch over the next year. Then they all went up to St Malvey's chapel and sat in silence for a while before making merry in the fields for the rest of the night. The ceremony was ended in the 1670s after a determined campaign against it by two ministers,[41] but it simply migrated to, or resurfaced upon, the midnight before Maundy Thursday at the opening of the sailing season. It survived on Iona until the late eighteenth century and on Lewis until the early nineteenth, at which time the chant of the man pouring the bowl was (in Alexander Carmichael's translation):

> O God of the sea
> Put weed in drawing wave
> To enrich the ground,
> To shower on us food.[42]

Thus, there seems to be no doubt that the opening of November was the time of a major pagan festival which was celebrated, at the very least, in all those parts of the British Isles which had a pastoral economy. At most, it may have been general among the 'Celtic' peoples. There is no evidence that it was connected with the dead, and no proof that it opened the year, but it was certainly a time when supernatural forces were especially to be guarded against or propitiated; activities which took different forms in different regions. Its importance was only reinforced by the imposition upon it of a Christian festival which became primarily one of the dead, and it is to the development of that festival that this book must turn.

SAINTS AND SOULS

By the end of the Middle Ages, the Christian feast of the dead, known as Hallowtide, Hollontide, or Allantide, had developed into a spectacular affair, for which there are ample records in England. The book of ceremonial for the court of Henry VII specified that upon All Saints' Day the monarch would dress in purple and his attendants in black, the colours of mourning.[1] For that evening, as the parish accounts indicate, many churches laid in extra supplies of candles and torches, to be carried in procession and to illuminate the building. Some in London arranged unusually elaborate entertainments as part of the service on that night; one such was St Mary Woolnoth which in 1539 paid five maidens wearing garlands to play harps by lamplight. Each mayor of Bristol in the 1470s was expected to entertain the whole council and other prominent citizens and gentry, to 'fires and their drinkings with spiced cakebread and sundry wines', before they dispersed to their respective parish churches for evensong. There they presumably prepared for the most famous ritual of the night, the ringing of church bells to comfort the souls in purgatory after the congregation had offered prayers for them. In the chapel of the fifth earl of Northumberland, in the 1510s, the peals rang out from the moment that the liturgy ended until midnight, and so it probably was in the parishes. In a few places the rites were repeated, or took place on the following evening, the feast of All Souls.[2] In this way the opening of the season of darkness and cold had been made into an opportunity to confront the greatest fear known to humans, that of death, and the greatest known to Christians, that of damnation.

The concept of purgatory, the belief that the living could assist the condition of the dead by praying for them, and the notion that saints could function as intercessors between humans and Christ or the Christian god, were all doctrines condemned by Protestants, and so this complex of rituals was bound to run into trouble as soon as the latter took control. It precariously survived the reign of Henry VIII, the ringing for the dead being one of a number of ceremonies which Archbishop Cranmer tried to abolish in January 1546. He actually drafted a letter for the royal signature, but Henry refused to provide it, apparently because a more conservative adviser, Stephen Gardiner, warned him that to do so would imperil a hoped-for *rapprochement* with the Catholic powers of France and the Empire.[3] The custom was therefore unlikely to survive long under the more Protestant government of the young Edward VI; and although it was not prohibited in any surviving royal injunction or proclamation, or episcopal article, it was forbidden by at least one of the commissions of royal visitors sent to enforce the injunctions of 1547.[4] If the other commissions behaved in the same way, then this would explain why the ringing was absent in 1548 from virtually all the parishes in which it was recorded till then. The exceptions were Halesowen at the north end of Worcestershire, North Elmham in central Norfolk, and the market town of Thame in eastern Oxfordshire. At Thame, a very conservative community, the ringers went to work again in 1549, but after that all payment to them ceased.[5]

With the accession of Mary, of course, the custom could be restored, and it is recorded in her reign in the accounts of twenty parishes, representing both urban and rural settlements from Devon to Lincolnshire.[6] This is about the same proportion of the whole body of surviving evidence as that in which it was represented before the Reformation and, as the Elizabethan material indicates a very widespread popularity, the most plausible conclusions are that it had a general revival under Mary and that in many parishes the ringers did not need to be paid for their work. If either or both is true, the restored ritual met a final and fatal check in the Elizabethan Reformation, when it was dropped from the new liturgy of 1559. The feast of All Saints was officially retained, but as a day upon which to commemorate saints as outstandingly godly human beings, and not as semi-divine intercessors; the prayers for the dead were, of course, abolished once more. The result was the longest and hardest struggle waged by the Elizabethan reformers against any of the traditional ecclesiastical rituals, partly no doubt because of a profound fear for the fate of the family dead and partly because the ringing upon All Saints' Night was a ceremony which could be carried on without the use of (now illegal) ornaments or the participation of a priest, and after dark. People were being cited in church courts for performing it all through the 1560s, in both villages and towns and in all regions. The custom continued to be condemned in the visitation articles of bishops of Lincoln, Chester, and Hereford in 1580s, and prosecutions for it also persisted into that decade, in the dioceses of York and Oxford. The most dramatic was that of certain men at Hickling in the Nottinghamshire part of the vale of Belvoir, who, upon All Saints' Day 1587, 'used violence against the parson at that time to maintain their ringing'. This also seems to be the latest such case on record, but more may be uncovered in the 1590s as other ecclesiastical archives are explored.[7]

Once people were thwarted in their attempts to bring comfort to the dead within churches, they developed different strategies to provide prayers in a ritual framework outside them. In the Lancashire parish of Whalley, where the Ribble flows out of the Pennines, Catholic families still assembled at the midnight before All Saints' Day in the early nineteenth century. Each did so on a hill near its homestead, one person holding a large bunch of burning straw on the end of a fork. The rest knelt in a circle around and prayed for the souls of relatives and friends until the flames burned out. The author who recorded this custom added that it gradually died out in the latter part of the century, but that before that it had been very common and at nearby Whittingham such fires could be seen all around the horizon at Hallowe'en. He went on to say that the name 'Purgatory Field', found across northern Lancashire, testified to an even wider distribution, and that the rite itself was called 'Teen'lay'.[8] The word is puzzling in its derivation, though certainly archaic, as it could be related either to the Old English *tendan*, to kindle (hence dialect words for a bonfire, *tearle* or *tend*, and firewood, *tennle*), and to the Old Irish *tenlach*, a hearth.[9] Another observer recalled how in the first half of the same century he had journeyed along the Ribble at Hallowe'en and, 'under the name of Teanla fires', he had 'seen the hills throughout the country illuminated with sacred flames'. He added that they were 'connected with superstitious notions concerning purgatory'. None the less, he added information which indicated that the fires were also employed for older purposes of protection and purification, like those in Wales and Scotland; for in the low-lying Fylde district at the mouth of the Ribble, a farmer would circle his fields 'with a burning wisp of straw at the point of fork...to protect the coming crop from noxious weeds'.[10] Even in the Fylde, however, as other witnesses made plain, the primary purpose of the bonfires was as focuses for prayers for the dead.[11]

Northern Lancashire was the most notable stronghold of popular Catholicism in post-Reformation England, and it is quite possible that all who practised the 'teen-lay' there were of the old faith. The villages around Derby, however, were not an area of Catholic survival, and yet in November 1768 a contributor to the *Gentleman's Magazine* could note that every year people would go out to common land on All Saint's Day and light small fires which they called 'tindles'. He added that it was something to do with purgatory and the dead, going on to say that enclosure would soon put a stop to the practice.[12] So it might have done there, but 'tindles' were still being made elsewhere in Derbyshire on All Souls' Night 1868.[13] It is still more of a surprise to discover that the name of Purgatory Field at Gosmore, in the chalk hills at the north end of Hertfordshire, was said to derive from former midnight assemblies of men there at Hallowe'en to pray for the souls of the departed until a fire burned out.[14] Finally, a possible reference to the custom in an area between these occurs in a note made at the end of an almanac in 1658 by the antiquary Sir William Dugdale: that at Hallowe'en the master of a family 'used to' carry a burning bunch of straw around a field, saying

Fire and Red low
Light on my teen low.[15]

The location of this ritual was most probably Dugdale's own county of Warwickshire, to which his writings usually referred, and it seems to be the same as those described above; but neither suggestion is provable.

The 'teen-lay' rite was, therefore, one response to the end of official ceremonies to care for the dead; it provided them directly. Another obtained them
indirectly, by adapting a separate tradition which was itself old by the time of
the Reformation. The tract *Festyvall*, published in 1511, has the entry: 'We read
in old time good people would on All Hallowen Day bake bread and deal it for
all Christian souls'.[16] It did not explain how, or to whom, it was 'dealt', but
Thomas Blount's *Glossographia*, published in 1674, provides the passage:

All Souls Day, November 2d: the custom of Soul Mass cakes, which are a kind of oat
cakes, that some of the richer sorts of persons in Lancashire and Herefordshire (among
the Papists there) use still to give the poor upon this day; and they, in retribution of their
charity, hold themselves obliged to say this old couplet:

> God have your soul,
> Bones and all[17]

Near the end of the same century, John Aubrey noted that it was a custom
in Shropshire and neighbouring counties, and not just among 'Papists', for a
'high heap of soul cakes' to be set on a household table upon All Souls' Day.
Visitors were expected to take one, with the rhyme, 'A soule-cake, a soule-
cake, Have mercy on all Christen soules for a soule-cake'.[18]

These early references leave open the question of whether the souls of the
dead or of the living were being prayed for in the transaction, although
neither would recommend itself to a Protestant. The issue is resolved by the
much greater quantity of evidence from the nineteenth century, by which time
the custom of 'souling' or 'soul-caking' was carried on by groups of poor
people, usually children, going from door to door on All Saints' or All Souls'
Day. Its epicentre was still in the counties from Lancashire southward to
Monmouthshire, but it extended into Wales upon one side and Derbyshire,
Staffordshire, and Yorkshire on the other, and was also found in Somerset and
Hertfordshire. In other parts of Yorkshire, and in Warwickshire, the cakes
were still made even though visitors did not call for them.[19] There was hardly
any connection with actual surviving Catholicism, but in many cases the
descent from a means of praying for the dead was absolutely plain. One name
for the custom in Wales was *hel bwyd cennady meirw*, 'collecting the food of
the messenger of the dead', and bread and cheese given to the poor in
Caernarvonshire on All Souls' Day was called 'food of the letting loose of the
dead'.[20] In Lancashire the cakes were, like the teen-lay, 'connected with
superstitious notions respecting purgatory'.[21] The 'lower classes' of Monmouthshire were recorded as 'begging bread for the souls of the dead'.[22] A
Staffordshire soulers' song contains the lines

> Peter stands at yonder gate
> Waiting for a Soul Cake.[23]

To the author of the single study devoted to the songs, the fundamental
derivation from a means of praying for the departed seemed obvious, and he

further observed that the most common tune bore a resemblance to sixteenth-century church music.[24] There is also a stray Scottish reference to an identical custom, from Aberdeen, where 'dirge loaves' were given to callers on All Souls' Day.[25]

On the other hand, the nineteenth-century collections also make it clear that after three hundred years this purpose to the custom had largely disappeared. Instead it had become the first of that sequence of old holy days, stretching through the early winter, upon which poor members of the community (and particularly their children) could legitimately go the rounds of their wealthier neighbours and ask for food or money. Not that they often pressed their luck by treating it as a sequence for, as Charlotte Burne has shown, the areas in which 'Souling', 'Clementing', and 'Catterning' took place (the last two having been dealt with earlier in this book) tended to be mutually exclusive.[26] As so often the songs employed by the late nineteenth century had become remarkably standardized. In Wales and the west Midlands, the usual one was, or was similar to:

> Soul! Soul! For a soul-cake
> I pray good misses, a soul-cake!
> An apple or pear, a plum or a cherry,
> Any good thing to make us merry.
> One for Peter, two for Paul
> Three for Him who made us all.
> Up with the Kettle and down with the Pan,
> Give us good alms and we'll be gone.[27]

This was also used in Hertfordshire.[28] Another and less common variety, found in Staffordshire, was:

> Soul, Soul for an apple or two,
> If you've got no apples, pears will do;
> If you've got no pears ha'pennies will do,
> If you've got no ha'pennies God bless you.[29]

The Somerset one was distinctive:

> A soul, a soul for a soul cake
> One for Jack Smith,
> And one for Tom White
> And one for myself and I'll bid you goodnight.
> My clothes are very ragged
> My shoes are very thin
> I've got a little pocket
> To put three halfpence in
> And I'll never come a souling
> Till another year.[30]

The custom was dealt a serious blow by the educational reform of 1870, which meant that henceforth all but very small children were confined to school during the daylight hours when it was most easily carried on.[31] Nevertheless, it proved to be remarkably resilient in rural Cheshire, northern Shropshire, and the adjoining part of Staffordshire, where youngsters still carried it on in the 1950s; although they were given fruit, biscuits, or coins, they continued faithfully to refer to these as 'soul-cakes'.[32] It may still survive there today, and certainly does at Sheffield, where children use the 'caking' rhyme while now lacking any knowledge of its former meaning.[33]

Central Cheshire was also unusual in that many of the 'soulers' who went about there in the nineteenth century were young men, with their own distinctive songs. That from Halton went:

> Kind gentlemen of England we hope you will prove kind;
> With ale and strong beer.
> And we will come,
> And we will come,
> No more a souling
> Until this time next year...
> God bless the master of this house, the mistress also,
> Likewise the little children that round your table go;
> Likewise your men and maidens, your cattle and your store;
> And all that lies within your house, we wish you ten times more.[34]

In keeping with their greater age and prowess, they often provided an entertainment in return for their 'soul cakes' and beer. At its least elaborate it consisted of the romping of a hobby-horse similar to that used in midwinter on the Derbyshire–Nottinghamshire border. At its most highly developed, it integrated the horse into a local version of the usual English Mummers' Play, linking it to a Cheshire legend of a steed which ran a record race. Otherwise the characters, and the combat and resurrection, were standard, save the Beelzebub carried a clog rather than a club and Little Devil Doubt had been corrupted into 'Dairy Doubt' or 'Jerry Doubt'. By the end of the century the 'Soulers' Play' was still performed by groups of men moving between private houses in and around eight villages, at the lower end of the river Weaver.[35] In all of these it subsequently became moribund, but was restored at one, Antrobus, by the efforts of a retired army officer, and has been maintained there as a pub performance. As such, it has been made the subject of some of the best recent studies of a folk-play, and also of the sociology of a revived seasonal custom.[36]

The Antrobus play certainly has made a remarkable transition, from an entertainment provided, primarily for profit, by members of an agricultural community, to one maintained by men mostly working outside the village, and in industry, from a sense of tradition: in this sense it has turned, in the twentieth century, into a genuine 'ritual', like some Christmas Mummers' Plays. Its action is characterized by a very powerful internal logic; weak on narrative and social or moral sense, it depends upon the fielding of an increasingly outrageous set of characters who evoke laughter, but also fear, surprise, and questioning. All are peripheral to the community, all economically unproductive; they are either menacing outsiders or internal misfits, all the more unsettling for the fact that they are so highly stylized and the action is deliberately not naturalistic. In this context the misbehaviour of the Wild Horse makes a perfect climax to the presentation, being literally bestial in character and yet acted by a human, and so the end-product of a continuous deliberate disharmony between jest and earnest. The overall impact is, perhaps, the better definition, and so reinforcement, of the community. This is something now all the more important, as Antrobus sits upon the edge of an expanding industrial area, and such communal identity is increasingly achieved by the continued existence of the play in itself.

At Antrobus, as in the backstreets of Sheffield, it is possible to see how much the changing needs of communities can remodel customs which originated as one means of seeking comfort for the dead in the aftermath of the Elizabethan Reformation. Traces of others are occasionally recorded locally—for example, in nineteenth-century Derbyshire it was noted that 'formerly' people had strewn flowers on their family graves upon All Saints' Day[37]—and probably some initially resorted to domestic prayers and other private practices which have left no trace in the records. All had long outlived their original purpose by 1928, when the Church of England restored the feast of All Souls as a commemoration of the dead, and provided a service for it in the Book of Common Prayer.[38]

The readoption of it was the less controversial in that it was by that date overshadowed by a much greater national festival of the dead, lacking any specific denominational association, in the form of Armistice Day, 11 November. The latter sprang from the need to honour the enormous sacrifice in the First World War of men whose families had not expected them to be soldiers; it seemed most natural to do so upon the date at which the war ended. Initially, it was by no means clear what the mood of that commemoration would be; an annual festival of patriotic celebration, of victory in the greatest of Britain's wars, seemed to some to be the most natural form. In 1920, however, the government decided firmly against a public holiday, in Lord Curzon's words because it would be 'an occasion for public rejoicing, and is therefore hardly suitable for a day on which so solemn and impressive a ceremony is to take place'. In that year also the practice of a two-minute silence, to be observed all over the nation annually at the time of the armistice, was made permanent. In 1925 the Charity Ball which had become a regular feature of the date was replaced, at the urging of the vicar of St Martin in the Fields, with a solemn 'Festival of Remembrance'. By then the overwhelming majority of religious services to mark the armistice were characterized by a tone of mourning, sacrifice, and redemption, and by 1928 the last traces of patriotic bombast had been expunged from the liturgy employed upon the Sunday closest to the date.[39] A general mood of revulsion against war was responsible for this development, but it was admirably suited to a sombre season, which has natural associations with death. The association was strengthened with the abolition of the two-minute silence on the coming of the Second World War, concentrating the commemoration upon the church services of 'Remembrance Sunday' which now had the dead of yet another tremendous conflict to honour.

The accidents of history have ensured that it is these rather than the revived liturgy upon All Souls' Day, which now reflect something of the intensity of feeling which once informed the prayers and the peals of bells upon All Saints' Night.

THE MODERN HALLOWE'EN

I T is time now to examine the joint legacy of a shadowy pagan festival and a Christian feast of the dead in the various communities of the British Isles, as manifested in the past couple of hundred years. The first and most obvious aspect of it is the keeping of All Hallows' Eve as a feast, or time for socializing. In nineteenth-century Ireland, where most of the population had remained Catholic, the two traditions of origin were perfectly fused. Most families prepared an unusually good communal meal for the evening, the poor going about in the day 'collecting money, bread-cake, butter, cheese, eggs, etc., etc.' from the wealthier homes, 'repeating verses in honour of solemnity, demanding preparations for the festival in the name of St Columb Kill'. When all was ready, candles would be lit and prayers formally offered for the souls of the dead. After this the eating, drinking, and games would begin.[1] In the Highlands of Scotland during the early part of the century, the night was regarded as 'the most important occasion' for family celebrations in the year.[2] Household parties were also the rule in the Western and Northern Isles, with local variations such as separate suppers for boys and girls upon Lewis and a special 'Hallowmas cake' in the Shetlands.[3] As was natural in a predominantly Protestant country, these occasions usually differed from the Irish in the absence of prayers for the dead. The same pattern obtained in Wales, with the occasional ritual which blurred the boundaries of belief, such as in Caernarvonshire, where a piece of bread was placed on the window-sill as the household ate inside, with the words

> May'st thou bless thy whole family,
> This is what I give thee this year.

The term 'thy' implies that the recipients were ancestral spirits. Elsewhere customs normally associated with Christmas were given a first airing, such as in Carmarthenshire, where the wassail bowl was brought out for the evening.[4]

In England and the southern half of Scotland, by contrast, there is little trace of feasting and of merry-making until the present century, while (in the provinces at least) the season was as characterized by fear as it was in the 'Celtic' areas. In the Lancashire cotton towns in the 1790s, it was believed that All Saints' Night and All Souls' Night were 'especially set apart for spiritual appearances'.[5] In the remoter parts of the Cambridgeshire Fens during the nineteenth century, people employed a range of precautions on Hallowe'en. 'These included the placing of food on the doorstep to appease any witch who might approach the house; the putting of salt in the key-holes; the safe locking up of all the domestic and farmyard animals; the killing of a cockerel and hanging of its tail feathers on stable doors; and the strewing of osiers on all the exterior thresholds'.[6] It should be noted that the action which was intended in Caernarvonshire for the family dead was designed in Cambridgeshire wholly to propitiate forces of evil. Perhaps (and no stronger expression can be used) the combination in England and southern Scotland of the lack of an underlying ancient festival, and the presence of a thorough religious reformation, had created a vacuum at Hallowtide. There existed the powerful memory of a connection of the season with the dead, and the vestigial customs based upon attempts to propitiate or comfort them. The sense of the uncanny hung over the time, and yet there was no agreed set of communal rituals—such as bonfires, libations, woven crosses, or feasting—with which to respond to it.

A common feature of the household festivities in Ireland, northern Scotland, Man, and Wales is that they involved a large number of practices intended to divine the future of the individuals gathered there, especially with regard to death or marriage.[7] Hallowe'en had this in common with other festive nights—New Year's Eve, May Eve, and Midsummer Eve were all notable examples—and this is an area of activity which, for reasons of space, has been specifically excluded from this book. None the less, it is remarkable that Hallowe'en was more celebrated for divination than any other night of the year, at least in these 'Celtic' areas of the archipelago. Some methods were particularly associated with it; the stones in or near the bonfire was one of them, and the burning or casting of nuts was another. The latter was, indeed, found over almost the whole of the island of Britain, being equally well known in Northumberland, Sussex, and Welsh-speaking Carmarthenshire in the years around 1800, while the presbytery at Elgin in north-east Scotland could reprove a man for selling nuts for divination at dusk upon Hallowe'en 1641. In the north of England the date was, until recently, popularly known as 'Nut-Crack Night'.[8] The only distinction of such activities among the English was that they tended to be rarer and upon a smaller social scale, reflecting the lack of a tradition of general festivity of the sort found in the western and northern regions. Most of the purpose of the enquiries upon that night seems to have been to determine when people would die, an enterprise at once suited to the opening of the most lethal of seasons and to a date associated with those already dead.

Hallowe'en was also notable for the activity of mummers or guisers, figures found at winter festivals in general but particularly appropriate to a night upon which supernatural beings were said to be abroad and could be imitated or warded off by human wanderers. In Ireland costumes were sometimes associated with the people who went about before nightfall collecting for the feast; youths in one district of County Cork brought the Lair Bhan or White

Mare, a man covered in a white sheet holding a wooden horse's head like some of the midwinter mock-beasts known in England.[9] In Shetland the 'skeklers' were abroad again as at Christmas, while Man had its own groups of young men who went about villages singing and declaiming rhymes outside houses and receiving rewards.[10] Orkney boys in the early twentieth century went about dressed in female clothes, while those on Skye in the same period wore old clothes and blackened their faces. The latter were traditionally allowed to 'exercise the greatest licence', sitting where they pleased in a kitchen, singing, conversing, and ignoring the inhabitants of the house which they had entered and who were expected to set scones, cakes, and fruit before them.[11] Sooty, painted, or masked faces were also important on the Scottish mainland, as was odd dress of almost any kind. A common rhyme among Scots Hallowe'en guisers was:

> Tramp, tramp, tramp, the boys are marchin'
> We are the guisers at the door,
> If ye dinna let us in
> We will bash yer windies in
> An ye'll never see the guisers any more.[12]

It is difficult to judge how far all of this activity in the Lowlands was indigenous and how much it was increased by the time of recording (mostly twentieth-century) by Irish and Highland immigration, and later on by American influence. There is no doubt, by contrast, concerning the traditional nature of the equivalent in Wales. In late nineteenth-century Glamorgan the young people cross-dressed as the opposite gender and went from house to house singing verses such as:

> Winter's Eve; Biting of apples.
> Who is coming out to play?
> On the top of the tree
> Whittling an umbrella stick;
> It is one o'clock, it is two o'clock,
> It is time for the pigs to have dinner.

At least some of these lines were riddles; the being whittling on top of the tree, for example, was one of the spectres of the night, the 'White Lady'. Unlike the 'black sow', she has definite antecedents in medieval literature and may well have been a pagan goddess. In Montgomeryshire during the middle part of the century 'the lower order of working men' used to dress themselves 'in sheeps' skins and old ragged clothes and mask their faces, going about the houses and streets'. They called themselves *gwrachod*, 'hags', which were ancient figures of fear in Wales, featuring as monsters in the medieval tales *Culhwch ac Olwen* and *Peredur*. They often frightened children and were sometimes 'impertinent' to adults, and so were 'put down to a great extent by the police'. *Yr gwrachod* were also active in north Wales in the 1790s.[13] Nothing comparable to them, or to any of the other traditions of Hallowe'en fancy dress, can be found in England until the twentieth century; although when they did take root there they drew on a much older local experience of mummery at other festivals.

When imitating malignant spirits it was a very short step from guising to playing pranks, and young people often took it in the same areas. In many parts of Ireland they banged on doors or turned animals round in shafts; in County Waterford Hallowe'en was *oidhche na h-aimléise*, Mischief Night.[14] In northern Scotland the custom is recorded as far back as 1736, when the Kirk session of Canisbay, almost at the tip of Caithness, condemned local lads for battering doors with stolen cabbages.[15] Down in nineteenth-century Cromarty youths worked exactly the same trick, and sought for a lone woman to seize so that they could drag her in a cart, 'over the rough stones, amid shouts, and screams and roars of laughter'.[16] Perhaps she represented a witch, or perhaps it was just a nasty piece of male bonding. On the east coast of Sutherland, lying between, children at the end of the century had a varied repertoire of tricks, including blocking as well as thumping doors, blowing the smoke of burning cabbage-stalks through key-holes, stopping up the tops of chimneys with turves, letting horses out of stables, and pretending to break windows by smashing bottles against adjacent walls.[17] Similar practical joking and vandalism was known in the Hebrides.[18] Once again, it may be noted that the date became 'Mischief Night', with this sort of misbehaviour, in parts of lowland Scotland and in Yorkshire; but only, it seems, during the twentieth century.

The traditional illumination for guisers or pranksters abroad on the night in some places was provided by turnips or mangel wurzels, hollowed out to act as lanterns and often carved with grotesque faces to represent spirits or goblins. They were common in Ireland[19] and found in Sutherland[20] in the late nineteenth century, but by that time were also a well-established local custom in southern and western Somerset.[21] They were known as 'spunkies' or 'punkies', being the common Somerset name for the balls of ignited marsh gas sometimes seen upon the levels. Children in the Brendon hills would sing outside farms and cottages:

> It's Spunky Night, it's Spunky Night,
> Gie's a candle, Gie's a light.
> If 'ee don't, 'ee'll have a fright.

The carved faces, outlined by the candle within, were taken in that district as warnings of death, and used to scare unpopular people. This association must be borne in mind when considering the allied custom in the south of the county, whereby youngsters would parade the streets of towns and villages with their 'punkies', and compete to make the finest. This procedure is recorded at Langport, Long Sutton, and Lopen, and still exists at Hinton St George on the last Thursday of October, where the carved vegetables are judged in the village hall after the procession; they now cover a full range of patterns rather than just representing faces, and are often of considerable beauty. The most common story at Hinton is that the custom developed because the village's menfolk used the mangel-lanterns to light their way home for Chiselborough Fair. Only a heretical minority (when I visited represented only by one woman) follows the folklorist Kingsley Palmer in maintaining that the lanterns are symbols of the dead, the little flames in the marshes being traditionally regarded as the souls of unbaptized babies. The latter belief, however, is certain and this may be a case in which the common-sense explanation is less reliable than the more romantic one; a suggestion supported by the evidence from Brendon.

The lanterns made from vegetables were known elsewhere in the very early twentieth century, for example at Wyke Regis, on Dorset's Isle of Portland, and Whitwell in central Hertfordshire.[22] In eastern England they became generally known as Jack o'Lanterns, another name for marsh flames which has been recorded since the sixteenth century.[23] It is striking, however, that they are so little mentioned in English folklore collections before 1900, and indeed the celebration of Hallowe'en in any fashion was very muted in the country before this time. It was proportionately little observed in England's American colonies, commemoration being restricted to an Episcopalian celebration of All Saints' Day and an extremely varied pattern of divinatory practices. What altered this situation, dramatically, was large-scale Irish immigration into the USA during the nineteenth century, bringing an intensive observation of the festival with it. In the first half of the twentieth, Hallowe'en developed steadily into a national festivity for Americans, guising becoming a ubiquitous tradition of fancy dress to represent ghosts, goblins, and witches, pumpkins replacing Irish vegetables as cases for lanterns, and mischief-making and house-to-house calls combining in the custom of trick-or-treat.[24] The same process occurred in Britain, partly as a result of a parallel massive influx of Irish under Victoria but mainly also because of increasing American cultural influence from that period onward. By the middle of the twentieth century Hallowe'en was established as a major festival in areas of England where Irish influence was strong, or which had a tradition of festive guising or of existing customs of the night, such as punkies. In other words, it flourished in the north, the north-west Midlands, and the West Country, the aspects of fancy dress and of mischief being given differences of emphasis according to local taste.[25] By then also it had spread across the rest of Scotland,[26] and during the later twentieth century it increased in popularity throughout England, very much on the American model. It has now at last gained an equivalent status, as a truly national feast, with a unique preoccupation with traditionally menacing supernatural forces.

It might have been expected that this very novelty, combined with the arcane associations of the night, would create strains, and they have been increased by the fact that today almost every national festival is by definition one for the children, the family having replaced every other social unit as the essential community of the British. An attack upon the celebration of Hallowe'en, especially in schools, correspondingly developed in the late 1980s, and continues at the time of writing. It has not, however, taken the form of a chauvinist reaction against an alien feast, but has been inspired (like the celebration) from America and has been given a specifically Christian rhetoric. It has been organized by evangelical groups in Protestant denominations, usually operating through youth clubs, parent organizations, school boards of governors, and media campaigns, and rests upon two arguments. The first is that Hallowe'en is a glorification or glamorization of evil powers. The second is that it is essentially unchristian; in the words of the organizers of a youth-group campaign against it in 1993, it leaves young Christians feeling 'disenfranchised'.[27]

To a historian (or at least to this historian), a number of comments upon this situation seem pertinent. The first is to note with interest that, in a supposedly modern and pluralist society, some Christian groups should find it unpalatable that there should be a single national and public festival which does not (in contrast to every other traditional seasonal celebration and every seventh day) have an apparent Christian component. The second is to emphasize, once again, that a Christian feast of the dead is thoroughly embedded in the history of Hallowe'en and that its legacy is usually impossible to distinguish from that of paganism in the practices and associations of the night. It is of course maintained by what is still by far the largest of the world's churches, the Roman Catholic. To describe the feast as fundamentally unchristian is therefore either ill-informed or disingenuous. Such an attitude could be most sympathetically portrayed as a logical development of radical Protestant hostility to the holy days of All Saints and All Souls; having abolished the medieval rites associated with them and attempted to remove the feast altogether, evangelical Protestants are historically quite consistent in trying to eradicate any traditions surviving from them. If so many of those traditions appear now to be divorced from Christianity, this is precisely because of the success of earlier reformers in driving them out of the churches and away from clerics; the relative negativity of nineteenth-century English attitudes to Hallowe'en has already been suggested. Nevertheless, it is also possible to interpret some of the objections to the festivities in a specifically modern context.[28] The fun consists principally of parodying or evoking two phenomena with which present-day industrial society is profoundly uneasy: the supernatural, and death. The existence of the former, at least below the level of divinity, has been officially denied, and yet it still exerts a hold upon the imagination of very many people, in many different ways. The latter remains universal, and mysterious, but direct contact with the dying and the dead is a rarer and rarer experience within the contemporary developed world; it is increasingly left to a sequence of specialists without any ritual function. In the secularized and sanitized condition of contemporary Britain, death functions essentially as a negative and disharmonious action; an interruption or omission, bearing no relation to any of the other workings of society.

This three-part consideration of the history of All Hallows commenced with a lengthy quotation from the 1993 factsheet upon the subject issued by the British Pagan Federation. That quotation was employed to elucidate, and sometimes to question, commonly held attitudes concerning the origins of the festival. It seems fair, therefore, to conclude with a summary of what that same document has to say about its modern significance:

Dressing up as monsters at Hallowe'en allows children to come to terms with the unseen and sometimes frightening world of dreams. This is a recognised form of play therapy which helps balance the developing personality. For adults as well, it is a time when conventions relax a little. Adults too can dress up and 'play' at fancy dress parties and can take pleasure in firework displays and other childhood delights. It is a time when tricks and games can be played. It is a time when both adults and children can reach out to touch the realms of myth and imagination, which are so important for the maintenance of mental health and creative well being.

Hallowe'en has many faces and means many things. Rooted in a Celtic Pagan past, it preserves the age old custom of an end of summer feast. It should not be feared, but welcomed as a time to help children and adults come to terms with their fears of change and death. It should also be a time for celebrations, stories and games; a time for laughing in the face of adversity and for challenging the darkness of winter.

That seems, at least, to be an argument worth making.

BLOOD MONTH AND VIRGIN QUEEN

$\approx$ ❧ $\approx$

'BLOD-MONATH', Bede had called November, and it retained its character until the opening of the modern period as the time when livestock which could not be fed through the winter was slaughtered and salted down. The process was usually accomplished in the first half of the month, around the medieval feast of St Martin upon 11 November. 'Martinmas', or 'Martlemas', therefore acquired the reputation of a time of feasting and jollity, its grimmer associations of killing overlaid by the pleasure of eating the meat products which were not to be preserved: the last taste of unsalted meat until spring. To William Warner, in the reign of Elizabeth, 'At Martlemas we turned a crab, thilke told of Robin Hood'; a 'crab', in this context, was a roasting apple.[1] Another early modern rhyme ran:

> It is the day of Martlemas,
> Cupps of ale should freely pass;
> What though winter has begun
> To push down the summer sun,
> To our fire we can betake
> And enjoy the crackling brake,
> Never heeding winter's face
> On the day of Martlemas.[2]

In Ireland until the nineteenth century the feast remained tinged with the ritual connotations mentioned by Bede, for in most of the west of the island, and some places in the east, it was considered lucky to kill an animal upon this day and to sprinkle its blood on the threshold of the home. A cock was the most convenient victim, but a sick sheep or goat was often chosen instead.[3] Nothing like this seems to be recorded in Britain, where the annual immolation was kept up for purely practical reasons and pleasures until the development of root crops enabled farmers to feed whole herds and flocks through the winters.

After Martinmas the medieval winter unfolded for many people without further celebration until Christmas, although some would be involved with the rite of the Boy Bishop on St Nicholas's Day and others, then and later, would be making merry upon the feasts of Catherine or Clement. For a large part of the early modern period, however, the mid-part of November was occupied, at least in the metropolis, by a festival of a completely novel kind, setting a precedent for others to come. It was Queen Elizabeth's accession date upon 17 November, representing a Protestant holy day slowly evolved to replace the traditional ecclesiastical rites abolished at the Reformation.

Its importance was first stressed at the four hundredth anniversary of the queen's accession, in 1958, by her biographer Sir John Neale and (more especially) by the art historian Sir Roy Strong.[4] Sir John noted that a few London parishes rang bells upon that day from the tenth anniversary, in 1568, but that the custom became national as a result of an upsurge of feeling towards the queen provoked by the rebellion of 1569 and the papal bull excommunicating her in 1570. He showed that it was added to the calendar of Anglican holy days in 1576, and illustrated its celebration at Bridgnorth in the Severn valley in Shropshire (where the corporation sometimes had a bonfire), at Ipswich in Suffolk (where the schoolmaster presented pageants in 1583), and at St Andrew Holborn in London (where the parish instituted a dole to poor women in 1584). He quoted a commentator upon the last official celebration, in 1602, who remarked that the day passed 'with the ordinary solemnity of preaching, singing, shooting and running'. Sir Roy endorsed this account of the feast's origins and added that at court it was celebrated by a ceremonial tournament at which the queen received the homage of nobles and gentry, who often rode there in ornate carriages accompanied by allegorical figures who addressed the sovereign.

He also provided a much more detailed study of its civic and parochial festivity, covering eleven towns and twenty-six parishes. In this he showed that bells had been rung at Worcester as well as at London in 1568, and that, although the custom spread across most of southern and central England in the 1570s, it reached Norfolk and Suffolk only in the next decade and some Durham parishes only in the 1590s. He illustrated the same range of municipal display for the occasion as Neale had done, across his wider sample, and also showed how it could evolve over time. Thus Oxford corporation paid for a sermon in 1571, and added organ music in 1572, fireworks in 1573, music and almsgiving in 1585, a drummer in 1587, and bonfires in 1590. Maidstone had bell-ringing, and at various times fireworks, a militia review, an open-air venison roast, and a pageant carried through the town by child players. In 1589 Northampton built a model castle on its conduit, which was besieged, taken, and burned. Sir Roy suggested that the festival provided Protestant England with its first holiday, and allowed a revival of the civic display which had been dampened down by the Reformation. The official prayer book for the day was published in 1576 and enlarged in 1578, with Thomas Bentley publishing a set of private prayers and meditations for the date in 1582 and Edmund Bunny, subdeacon of York, adding some commentaries in 1585. These prayers stressed the sacred nature of godly monarchy and hailed Elizabeth as the restorer of peace, liberty, and the true religion. The service also gave an opportunity to clergymen from Archbishop Whitgift downwards to preach and publish sermons on the same theme, usually treating the queen as spiritual heiress of the righteous sovereigns of the Old Testament. Sir Roy also showed that observation of the day was attacked by the occasional radical Protestant, like Robert Wright, chaplain to Lord Rich, who thought that the praise that was given to Elizabeth was idolatrous. It was nevertheless, he added, far more the target of Catholic polemicists, who were angered by the unprecedented dedication of a holy day to a living human being.

Strong's essay remains the basic study of the subject, but in 1975 Frances Yates added further details upon the royal jousts and in 1989 David Cressy devoted a chapter to the feast in his book upon Protestant festivity.[5] The former established that the tilts are first recorded in 1581 and were in large measure the responsibility of Sir Henry Lee, himself a formidable competitor. He last took part in 1590, wearing gilt armour with crowns upon the caparison to indicate that he was the queen's champion. Her favourite courtier at that time, the earl of Essex, was armoured in black, and the decorations of the tiltyard included a pavilion representing the Temple of the Vestal Virgins (a compliment, of course, to the Virgin Queen) and a crowned pillar written with verses extolling the sovereign. Earlier costumes for retainers had included those of native Americans and Gaelic Irish. The surviving speeches drew upon the imagery of medieval chivalry, full of knights, hermits, shepherds, and fairies, linking the world of Protestantism with that of the Middle Ages. Professor Cressy amplified and reworked Sir Roy Strong's material, looking at more sermons and more parochial and municipal celebrations. He drew attention to the role of official sponsorship in spreading the celebrations, by local leaders such as the bailiff of Ludlow, the mayors of Oxford and Liverpool, and the chancellor of the bishop of Gloucester. He also noticed that in parts of the east Midlands parishioners called the day by its pre-Reformation name, the feast of St Hugh of Lincoln, the popular local patron. Lincoln College, Oxford, tactfully rang for both the queen and the saint. Professor Cressy traced observation of the day back to 1567, at Lambeth, and found it at a second London church in 1568. He established that it not only became general in southern England during the 1570s but spread into the north in the middle of the decade. He also suggested that it was never a true holy day, like those still maintained in the reformed Church for Christ and the apostles, because no rest from work was enjoined, and so the bell-ringing and services took place in the evening.

Further research has added nothing to knowledge of the royal jousts, and little to that of the municipal celebrations, but has contributed some more suggestions about the early observation of the day at parish level.[6] For one thing it may have answered Professor Cressy's question concerning whether the propagation of it depended more upon local enthusiasm or pressure from the central government. It reveals a spontaneous expression of loyalty to the queen on the part of a few parishes in the late 1560s, greatly swelled by the rebellion and plots of the years 1569–71. Official recognition of this did not come until almost a decade had passed and bells were being rung for 17 November in virtually all southern counties, most of those in the Midlands, and in Chester and York. Doubtless accidents in the survival of records conceal a still wider distribution. The pattern of appearance was for major urban centres to take it up first, followed by market towns and villages, and the effect of official recognition was to push observation into more rural communities and additional urban parishes in the south, and into the countryside and lesser towns in the north. There was, however, no neat movement from major to minor settlements, and parishes with the most illustrious patronage were not necessarily the first to get involved. St Margaret, Westminster, at the gate of the monarch's principal winter residence, did not ring bells until 1570, and St Martin in the Fields, near the other gate of the palace, began in 1572. The university church of Cambridge trailed four years behind a less distinguished parish in that town, and no Oxford church seems to have done anything until the official prayers were issued. The process of adoption clearly depended greatly upon local whim. In the City of London, the church of St Botolph Bishopsgate was already ringing for 'the queen's day' when its records begin in 1568. Another London parish commenced in that year, and another in 1569, after reading the royal homily issued against rebellion. Nineteen more started in the 1570s, one in the 1580s, and one more in the 1590s, while St George Botolph Lane and Holy Trinity Minories never seem to have bothered. By the time that Elizabeth died her accession day was honoured in every country in her realm for which records survive, but in twenty-one parishes which have left records for the last decade of her reign, from every region, the celebration was only commenced in that final ten years. And there are another forty-nine, again from every region, which had still not taken notice of it. Most were small villages or poorer urban parishes, but then so were many of those where the bells were rung. At the market towns of Cranbrook in Kent, and Dursley in Gloucestershire, and in the Suffolk arable village of Cratfield, observation was commenced and then abandoned.

Thus, to describe the festival of the queen's accession as a 'national' one is both accurate and misleading; the complex of communities which made up the nation adopted or ignored it at will. The tendency to call it 'St Hugh's Day' was also a matter of local caprice. As Professor Cressy remarked, it was chiefly found in the huge territory of the pre-Reformation diocese of Lincoln with which the saint's cult had especially been associated. On the other hand, not only did it overspill this territory, to reach out as far as Hertfordshire, Warwickshire, Nottinghamshire, and Derbyshire, but within that great area only a minority of communities which have left records in each county opted for that piece of pious nostalgia. Generally, the earlier entries for celebration of the event, between 1568 and 1576, went to some lengths to make clear exactly what it commemorated, the queen's accession. Later, however, it was known simply by its date, or as 'the queen's day', 'the queen's night', 'the queen's holy day', or (especially common among those churches which took it up after 1585) 'Coronation day', an error which indicates that many parish officials had forgotten exactly what they were celebrating.

Nor is it clear that there was, indeed, much celebration. The principal form was to ring the church bells, paying the ringers in cash or in bread and beer. They also usually required candles, as the job was done in the dark hours, and the appearance of the label 'queen's night' for the occasion in several parishes would confirm Professor Cressy's suggestion that the peals rang out in the evening once most people had finished work. None the less, at Mildenhall in the west Suffolk heathlands the bells were busy at daybreak instead, and so it may have been elsewhere. Only a few places held a communion, and some attention must be paid to the statement of the vice-chancellor of Oxford in 1602, while eulogizing the day, that services upon it were thinly attended. Even given the fact that mid-November is not the best time in the English year for outdoor festivities, it is notable that the parish funds were not used to provide any entertainments except the reward to the ringers. And out of the whole sample of surviving records of those funds, only St Lawrence, Reading, managed to supply this reward by a collection among parishioners. At Bishop's Stortford, the Hertfordshire market town, this was attempted, and failed. As no release from work was allowed that day, the various activities described by the writer in 1602 quoted by Sir John Neale referred to clergy, countries, and garrisons such as that of the Tower. At St Oswald, Durham, the churchwardens supplied a tar barrel (for a bonfire), but this does not seem to have happened elsewhere. Even the impressive catalogue of municipal celebration complied by Sir Roy Strong and David Cressy must be viewed with two qualifications. One is that several corporations do not appear to have launched public entertainments for that day, including Newcastle upon Tyne, Plymouth, York, and Marlborough. The other is that those which did, tended to provide them in some years but not in all. When all this is said, however, the commemoration of the royal anniversary was certainly a very widespread, very common, and very important event in the second half of the reign.

Naturally enough, it ceased promptly with the death of Elizabeth, the jousts and bell-ringing transferring to the accession date of the new monarch, James; it seemed that, after all, a new calendar festivity had not been created.[7] This appearance was to be wrong, at least as far as the capital was concerned, and the disproof was to occur as part of the much wider historical process by which the reputation of Elizabeth became a stick with which to beat the new Stuart royal family. As a consequence, a celebration which had commenced as an expression of loyalty to the existing regime could be turned at times into the exact opposite. The development began in the latter half of James's reign, when his own wife converted to the faith of Rome and many of his more zealously Protestant subjects began to press for war with Spain. It was then that a few London churches began to ring bells again on 17 November, while in 1620 a parishioner of St Pancras Soper Lane left money for an annual sermon. That allowance was doubled by the man's son in 1625, upon the arrival of the Catholic queen Henrietta Maria, French wife of the new King Charles I; in that same year sixteen more churches in London and two at

Westminster can be proved to have revived the custom. That still leaves thirty-seven London parishes from which accounts survive but which apparently did not ring bells then, while outside the capital it is recorded only at Lambeth (opposite Westminster), at two parishes in Bristol and one in Cambridge, and at fiercely Protestant Dorchester.

Nevertheless, the minority of metropolitan churches which paid for ringing on 17 November could make quite a din, and the insult was more obvious in that a cruel providence had placed the current queen's birthday on the 16th and the king's on the 19th. In 1630 the contrast between the court's tilts in honour of Henrietta Maria and the City's pealing and lighting fires the next day for Elizabeth was obvious to all. Ben Jonson presented Her Majesty with a poem, complimenting her and suggesting that public celebrations would have been more appropriate. Two days later nothing was prepared in London to mark King Charles's nativity, whereupon the Privy Council summoned the Lord Mayor to demand that this be remedied. He ordered ringing, and the citizens obediently did so and lit more than a thousand fires in the streets. Thereafter twenty-five out of the fifty-five London parishes which have left contemporary records continued to ring for Charles's birthday. Nine managed to ring for Henrietta Maria as well. On the other hand only one of those which had honoured Elizabeth failed to keep up the salute to her; a satisfactory compromise had been reached.[8]

The English Revolution, and the abolition of the monarchy, left the status of the day in confusion. On the one hand, a parish in Bristol and two in the metropolis stopped the ringing for Elizabeth, presumably because honours paid to any monarch might now be dangerous. On the other, one more in Bristol and seven others in London maintained it and a further one in the City actually took it up, apparently because the English Deborah had been a leader whose memory was honoured by Protestants of all shades.[9] The custom thus continued all through the Interregnum, and into the period of the restored monarchy, when it once again became an occasion to embarrass a reigning king and his Catholic wife, in the persons of Charles II and Catherine of Braganza. During the so-called Exclusion Crisis, between 1679 and 1681, the leaders of the Whig party sponsored elaborate processions to Temple Bar after nightfall after 17 November, bearing effigies of the Pope and his minions which were tipped into a huge bonfire. Destiny had, once again, been kind to them and cruel to a living queen, for Catherine's birthday was upon the 15th. The number of churches which now rang for Elizabeth's is concealed by the fact that most London parishes ceased to enter individual payments to ringers during the 1670s; contemporaries, however, recorded that the clamour of bells was general in the City as her day dawned. The ringing and processions were imitated at Salisbury and Taunton. They ebbed, as is well known, with the growing support for the monarchy. In 1682 a Tory corporation had the pageants at London destroyed when still under construction, and the militia tried to put out all bonfires.[10] By 1684 Queen Elizabeth's Day was apparently no longer observed outside London, and there the celebration was once again confined to ringing, still, it is notable that three of the six City parishes which have left itemized payments to ringers in the reign of the Catholic James II continued the custom.[11]

It was destroyed, not by the repression of the principles and the party with which it had become associated, but by the exact reverse. The Revolution of 1688 ensured that England never again had either a Catholic king or a Catholic queen; it also made the Whigs either actually or potentially the party of government. Hence, 17 November was not required any longer as a platform upon which to stage demonstrations intended to admonish an erring regime. It was occasionally utilized for partisan purposes, most notably in 1711 when the Whigs were temporarily out of power following a massive electoral defeat. Then their main political club, the Kit-Cat, spent £200 on preparations for a procession in London of the old sort, to burn effigies of the Pope, the Devil, and the Stuart Pretender. The Tory Secretary of State confiscated the figures on the previous night, fearing that the event would turn into a riot against his administration, but the Whigs managed a smaller parade and burned a 'Pope'.[12] Then, from 1715, their party achieved what was to be a half-century of political supremacy, and they were more concerned with preventing, rather than instigating, such demonstrations. It is in this period that Queen Elizabeth's Day finally falls into oblivion; after more than one and a half centuries, its ideological value was finally at an end.

None the less, it is difficult to believe that its demise would have occurred had it not been first a forerunner and then a supplement to a much more important and dynamic Protestant festival, serving the same ideological needs while incorporating others, placed close to it in early winter, and still flourishing at the present day. It is to the history of this greater celebration that this present study must now turn.

39

GUNPOWDER TREASON

~≈⟨⟩≈~

It was as if these men and boys had suddenly dived into past ages and fetched therefrom an hour and deed which had before been familiar with this spot. The ashes of the original British pyre which blazed from that summit lay fresh and undisturbed in the barrow beneath their tread. The flames from funeral piles long ago kindled there had shone down upon the lowlands as these were shining now. Festival fires to Thor and Woden had followed on the same ground, and duly had their day. Indeed, it is pretty well known that such blazes as this the heathmen were now enjoying are rather the lineal descendants from jumbled Druidical rites and Saxon ceremonies than the invention of popular feeling about Gunpowder Plot.

Moreover to light a fire is the instinctive and resistant act of men when, at the winter ingress, the curfew is sounded throughout Nature. It indicates a spontaneous, Promethean rebelliousness against the fiat that this recurrent season shall bring foul times, cold darkness, misery, and death. Black chaos comes, and the fettered gods of the earth say, Let there be light.

THESE passages are taken from what is probably the most famous description of November the Fifth bonfires in the whole of literature; that at the opening of Thomas Hardy's *The Return of the Native*, first published in 1878. It represents a magnificent early evocation of the view of folk customs which was to possess most writers upon them during the next hundred years. The principal fire in the story is kindled upon a prehistoric tumulus at the highest point of a wild heath, a setting intended to exemplify a timeless rural world conditioned by its close relationship with nature (or, rather, Nature). The custom of kindling it is detached from its conventional (political and historic) connotations, and associated intensely, if vaguely, with a tradition of sacred fires, coming down from prehistory and created by the emotional demands of the season itself.

This impression, or sensation, was given apparent scholarly support by the records of Scottish and Welsh Hallowe'en bonfires collected by antiquaries from the late eighteenth century onward. In a discussion of November the Fifth bonfires published by the periodical *Folk-Lore* in 1903,[1] W. Henry Jewitt boldly proposed (without research) that they were simply the ancient Hallowe'en fires transferred to a new date, and that the effigies (or 'guys') burned upon them were memories of human sacrifice. Sir James Frazer himself, significantly, drew back from such a deduction, but his books did much to confirm the notion of Hallowe'en as a universal Celtic fire-festival.[2] Both popular and learned works upon folk customs produced during most of the remainder of the twentieth century spoke confidently of the fires of Guy Fawkes's Night as descended directly from pagan ritual.[3] The belief was given support as late as 1982 by one of the first writers to relate those customs properly to a historical context, Bob Bushaway. He stated that the 'lighting of what folklorists refer to as need-fires had been a widespread practice, particularly in southern England, and this predated the state service'.[4] He drew attention to the tradition in the Isle of Portland during the early nineteenth century, whereby men jumped bonfires on 5 November with children in their arms, to bring them luck. This, he pointed out, was a magical rite, associated with midsummer fires. Need-fires, however, were not seasonal, but *ad hoc* magical rites, while in the case of the Portland custom Dr Bushaway could not guard against the suggestion that it might well have been transferred from midsummer to November fires which were not themselves an old tradition.

It was left to David Cressy, in his pioneering work upon Protestant festivity published in 1989,[5] to point out that there is absolutely no trace of late autumn or early winter bonfires in medieval or Tudor England, in striking contrast to those at midsummer. The use of fire in rites involving prayers for the dead has indeed been noted here, as recorded from the seventeenth or eighteenth century; but the incidence is local and there is no evidence that it represents a custom older than the period of the Reformation. There is, in brief, nothing to link the Hallowe'en fires of North Wales, Man, and central Scotland with those which appeared in England upon 5 November. It seems inevitable, therefore, to conclude with Professor Cressy that none would have been lit upon that date were it not for the bungled attempt of Guy Fawkes and his fellow conspirators to blow up king, Lords, and Commons in Westminster Palace upon 5 November 1605. The Parliament which had thus narrowly escaped destruction was postponed until early 1606, when the fervently Protestant MP Sir Edward Montagu proposed a perpetual anniversary to give thanks for the foiling of the conspiracy, based upon the ancient Hebrew tradition of days of deliverance. The resulting bill passed the Commons within two days, a reflection partly of sheer relief at a narrow escape, but also of the fact that it satisfied all factions and viewpoints represented in the House. It afforded the same opportunities for preaching and celebration for those who wished primarily to flaunt their loyalty to monarchy, those who were more concerned with Parliament, and those whose most emphatic loyalty was to the reformed religion. The statute which resulted ordered all people to attend church on the morning of each 5 November, when parish clergy would read not only prescribed prayers of thanksgiving but also the Act of Parliament itself, which justified the continuation of laws against Catholic worship.[6]

The new holy day was adopted fairly slowly, despite the unequivocal text of the statute. At Pitstone Green in the vale of Aylesbury, the prayers for it were only acquired in the financial year 1607–8. Chetton, a Shropshire village, initially observed the wrong date. Most parishes which adopted the celebration only did so in the 1610s, with some following in the next two decades. By the 1620s, however, it was the most popular state commemoration in the calendar, far surpassing the royal birthday, accession day, or coronation day. Its predominance was not achieved because of popularity in the London area, where more churches rang bells for James's accession date. It was, rather, the result of the adoption of the festival in market towns and villages, especially in Devon, Somerset, Staffordshire, and Shropshire. By 1625 it was found in all parts of England, and its progress had been occasioned by the whims of parish élites. Some municipal leaders, also, had adopted it with marked enthusiasm, so that in towns as scattered as Canterbury, Norwich, Carlisle, and Nottingham, corporations provided music and artillery salutes and attended church in scarlet robes of office. The most spectacular festivities were probably at Canterbury, with armed parades and volleys, although Bristol's annual twin bonfires and firework display were also notable. Nevertheless, there is no trace of comparable efforts in most urban centres. The statute did not specify a day off work, only attendance at a morning service. The frequency with which ringers were provided with candles may indicate that the bells were often swung before daybreak to fit the prayers in before the opening of business hours, rather than in the evening to encourage merry-making.[7]

After the accession of Charles I, popular interest in the day continued to intensify, and was given a new double edge by the young king's devotion to his Catholic wife Henrietta Maria. It was this which had occasioned the revival of Queen Elizabeth's Day in parts of London, and the multiplication of Gunpowder Treason celebrations was in part another judgement on the marriage. It was during the period 1625–40 that the date became 'Bonfire Night' in some areas, fires and burning tar barrels being paid for by parishes in London, Cambridge, and Durham. Images of the Pope or Devil were burned in unofficial blazes in the capital, and in 1628 an observer recorded 'trumpets and psalms' there as well. None the less, the festival did not become identified with opposition to the Crown, and Charles's favourite churchman, Archbishop Laud, led the bishops in attempting to enforce observation of it. They did, however, issue a new form of prayer to emphasize the sin of rebellion in general as well as the danger from Catholicism.[8]

Those prayers were dropped in turn at the English Revolution, to leave the celebration still in place as a festival of parliamentary government and the Protestant religion, although no longer of monarchy. Its many aspects had saved it yet again, to leave it the only survivor of the pre-war system of religious feasts and State anniversaries. A few parishes did give it up, but more adopted it during the Interregnum. The result was both a greater absolute number of communities and a larger proportion (46 per cent of parishes which have left accounts) keeping up the custom than ever before. Its status as the only legal seasonal festival also resulted in a further penetration of the countryside, even though a few places took a while to realize exactly what was required; the extreme case was Whalley, in the Lancashire Pennines, which rang for six years upon 1 November instead, as its people had done for the dead a century before, until in 1658 they corrected the date.[9]

When the Restoration occurred, and a full cycle of ecclesiastical and statutory festivals was reinstalled, the popularity of 'Gunpowder Treason Day' continued unabated. It was still the most widely celebrated of political anniversaries, far surpassing the new annual festivity of Restoration Day. Bells were rung upon it in 55 per cent of the parishes which have left accessible accounts from the reign of Charles II. They included a large number of villages in every part of the realm, from Grasmere in the middle of the Cumbrian Mountains, where the churchwardens were more concerned with rewarding people for killing ravens which menaced young lambs, to St Buryan near Land's End, one of the last strongholds of the ancient Cornish language. Some in Cambridgeshire provided bonfires, and Darlington, on the Tees in County Durham, paid for tar barrels. At London, Samuel Pepys saw boys flinging 'crackers' in the streets on 5 November 1661, the day having been kept 'very strictly' there, and observed bonfires in the City in 1664, so thick that coaches could not pass. In 1662 a Dutch visitor to the capital noted that 'many bonfires are lit all over the town in celebration, and a great lot of fireworks are let off and thrown amongst the people'. The period's other notable diarist, John Evelyn, regularly attended sermons upon the date. Once again the anniversary flourished because of the flexibility of its message: to some it was still an opportunity to berate Catholics, to others one to eulogize monarchy and condemn rebellion. Just as before, the one theme or the other became more pronounced according to the political situation of the time. During the growth of popular feeling against Catholicism during the 1670s, Londoners developed the tradition of parading effigies of the Pope and burning them at Temple Bar, a piece of street theatre which was enacted every year from the conversion of the royal heir to the faith of Rome in 1673 to the collapse of public opposition to his succession in 1682.[10]

The symbolic ambivalence of the day enabled it to hold its own with perfect ease when the Catholic James did succeed, the official prayers merely being altered once again to remove the invective against Popery and enhance that against treason. Of parishes which have left records accessible to a historian, 59 per cent record ringing upon it under his rule; nor was there any change in the pattern of distribution. The really delightful thing about the festivity was that an exuberant celebration of it under James could conceal a gesture of detestation of his religion within one of loyalty to his person. It is impossible, for example, to tell whether one sentiment or another motivated the churchwardens of Prestbury, on the Cotswold Edge, to purchase a hundred pieces of wood for a gigantic bonfire on the first 5 November of the reign. Sermons delivered on the date under James's rule still included several against Catholicism; indeed at Westminster it was a matter for comment when one fell into this category, but at Oxford it was just as much an oddity when one did *not*. The government did make some attempts to regulate observation, including a ban upon bonfires in the City of London, for fear of more Pope-burnings. In 1686 youths there paraded candles upon sticks instead, to the anger of the King, and the next year the Lord Mayor obediently set a watch to stop further 'disorders' of this sort. The order against fires or fireworks seems to have been extended to cover the whole nation in 1686, for the Yorkshire diarist Adam de la Prynne recorded that in large provincial towns it was circumvented by the placing of candles in windows as a witness against Catholicism. If the order ever was made general, it was spectacularly flouted at Oxford in 1688, when a passionately anti-Catholic sermon at the university church was followed by a record number of fires in streets and colleges, 'in spite to the papists'.[11]

It was upon 5 November 1688, even as the bonfires were flaring up at Oxford, that the army of William of Orange landed at Tor Bay. Within three months William and Mary sat on the throne, and the official prayers for Gunpowder Treason Day 1689 had to be rewritten yet again, to put back the condemnation of Catholicism and to add thanks for another providential delivery, this time from an unpopular royal government. On that day the bell-ringers at St Mildred, Canterbury, refused to accept any payment for their work, while their fellow parishoners paraded with tubs of fire 'in contempt of the sacrifice of the mass'. The new monarchs were occupied at that same moment with a 'splendid ball, and other festival rejoicings'. Of the parishes which have left itemized accounts for ringing from the 1690s accessible to a historian, 57 per cent paid for Gunpowder Treason Day. The figure, though large, is nevertheless not an increase on that under James, and respectable citizens (at least) were soon worrying about the practical dangers of pyro-technics. At Oxford by 1692 bonfires were mostly confined to colleges, and townspeople preferred to light up their windows. The same development had been anticipated at London in 1691, where the night 'was celebrated with illuminations, that is, by setting up innumerable lights and candles in the windows towards the street, instead of squibs and bonfires, much mischief having been done by squibs'. Whereas fires had been banned under James for political reasons, they were suffering the same fate under William as a safety measure. None the less, the date remained by far the most important political anniversary in England.[12]

Official, and 'respectable', commemoration of it remained constant throughout the eighteenth century, most corporate towns having a municipal provision of drink, bonfire, and fireworks, while groups of tradesmen often held tavern dinners, sometimes preceded by a procession.[13] In some places corporations continued to sponsor celebrations into the early nineteenth century, notably at Exeter, where until the 1830s the mayor and councillors marched to the cathedral for the thanksgiving service and had the guildhall illuminated. After the service the cathedral clergy had a huge bonfire built in the churchyard, while the mayor gave an oyster supper to the city officers.[14] Villages could also celebrate lavishly and formally. At Weston Favell, North-amptonshire, an enormous fire was made annually in the late eighteenth century, and revelry began several days before. At the Lancashire textile-making community of Middleton, the lord of the manor presented a two-horse load of coal to the local youths each year in the 1790s, to make another great blaze near the church which would last all night and into the next day.[15]

Nevertheless, it is also true that in the course of the eighteenth century official enthusiasm for the anniversary became more muted. Party rivalry ceased to be concerned with it, while local élites had to reckon with an inflated calendar of royal and princely birthdays produced by the sheer fertility of the Hanoverian dynasty; in 1775 November alone had thirteen State anniversaries. By the middle of the century Gunpowder Treason Day was heavily overshadowed by some of these, by the birthdays of popular politicians and military heroes, and by civic spectacles such as the Lord Mayor's Show in London.[16] This relative waning of official enthusiasm had the effect of throwing into greater prominence the element of popular misbehaviour on the day which had been present from near the beginning, when Pepys and the Dutchman noticed fireworks being thrown around the London streets. The latter activity was steadily maintained; at Lincoln in 1818 every parish had its bonfire, while some people baited bulls and others hurled squibs and 'serpents'.[17] The formal junketings at Exeter were accompanied by the kicking of tar barrels around the streets and raucous parades, one of which carried effigies of priests, friars, and nuns, and of a pope in a wire cage seven feet high. A band accompanied it with discordant music.[18] Up at Middleton the lads stole gates, fences, and plantation timber to augment the lord's gift of fuel, and fired off guns.[19] In the last decades of the eighteenth century, by 'ten o'clock, London was so lit up by bonfires and fireworks, that from the suburbs it looked in one red heat'. Amid the flames, a great deal of brawling was always going on; the butchers traditionally had a fire in Clare Market, and fought around it using the sinews of bulls as flails.[20] At Kettering, in Northamptonshire, a serious fire was started by boys throwing squibs on 5 November 1766, and a farmer whose ricks were burning was taunted by bystanders with the high price of his grain. It was also becoming relatively common for the Pope to be replaced by other effigies carried to the fire, often of prominent national politicians or of unpopular local figures, such as the justice whose image was incinerated at Castle Cary, Somerset, in 1768.[21] Increasingly, however, Guy Fawkes himself was becoming the universally acceptable villain for burning, represented as a carnival grotesque devoid of partisan associations.

All this being so, it is not surprising that, from mid-century onward, occasional complaints should be voiced against the festivities. A contributor to the Gentleman's Magazine in 1751 urged that something should be done to stop the casting of fireworks into crowds and the breaking of windows and burning of fences by masked revellers.[22] In 1785 the East Sussex market town of Lewes, which had kept up a particularly vigorous tradition of Pope-burning ever since the 'Exclusion Crisis', was the scene of a major riot; it began when some householders called in magistrates to prevent a fire being kindled next to their homes. There was another at Southampton three years later, when the mayor tried to ban bonfires from the streets.[23] In the 1790s *The Times* was calling for action against the 'greasy rogues', 'blackguards', and 'idle fellows' who rampaged in London on this night in every year.[24] Thus the stage was set for the prolonged struggle between local authorities and merry-makers which took up the early and middle part of the nineteenth century, a process which has now been well studied by David Cressy, Robert Storch, Robert Gifford, and D. G. Paz. The crucial element in its development was the novel degree of radical unrest and of official repression which developed in England in the wake of the French Revolution. In this tenser social atmosphere upper-class patrons increasingly withdrew their support from the celebrations which could lead to disorder, and in some counties their place was taken by a new phenomenon: the bonfire boys.

These gangs or societies were secret associations of youths, usually aged around 20, which appeared in old-fashioned small towns in Sussex, Surrey, and Devon between 1815 and 1830 and in Essex during the 1850s. Guildford, Chelmsford, and Exeter had just one gang each, while several operated within Lewes and Rye. They were mostly composed of artisans and labourers from a cross-section of trades, although shipwrights formed their own societies at Harwich and Maldon, shoemakers in Horsham and Crediton, and clay-cutters at Kingsteingnton. At Exeter and Lewes young men from wealthy middle-class families were among the leadership. They were usually masked and carried bludgeons to discourage interception. In Guildford they had 'fantastic costumes', at Exeter white jackets and trousers, sou'wester hats and high boots, and at Little Waltham coats turned inside out, hats elongated, and faces blackened, while the Lewes societies sported striped shirts. These groups were rarely drawn from more modern industries, or from communities affected by Chartism or trade unionism; they essentially expressed traditional notions of popular rights, patriotism, and hostility to Catholicism. As such they had a more natural alliance with local Tories, but never seem to have been manipulated by politicians or a party. In general their functions were to keep the fire festival going, if possible at traditional points in the town, and to mock malefactors. At times these were foreign enemies, such as the Russian Tsar or the Indian ruler Nana Sahib, and unpopular policies were also occasionally derided, such as the new licensing laws at Farnham in 1872 and free trade at Boreham, Essex, in 1887. Mostly, however, targets were local people who had offended the community because of their religion or their morals; in this sense the bonfire celebrations merged with the old custom of the charivari.[25]

In general, all the characteristics of the gangs or societies were equally true of promoters of Guy Fawkes festivities elsewhere in this period, without the element of organization and costume. On 5 November 1828 a masked crowd threw stones and fireworks at the house of an unpopular employer at Luton in the Bedfordshire chalk hills, while two years later the duke of Manchester became the target at his seat of Kimbolton castle in Huntingdonshire. He had led a drive against poaching, and was rewarded by losing his fences and gateposts to the local bonfire.[26] In 1831 the festival was for once harnessed by the populace in many places for a liberal cause, with the burning in effigy of certain bishops who had voted against the Great Reform Bill in the House of Lords.[27] Two years after that East Enders paraded the image of a police spy through Bethnal Green, beheaded it, and smeared the head with red ochre before setting it up on a stake while the body burned.[28] Whether formally mobilized by gangs or not, the demonstrations were, like the traditional brawling, remarkably restrained; nobody was ever actually killed or crippled, and nobody's home burned down.

None the less, the potential for either was now enough to scare local governors, and in the new police forces of the 1830s they possessed instruments suited to the task of repression, although their campaigns predated these. Their first priority was to get the fires out of public streets and highways, their second, to clear away the crowds. Both were accomplished in the City of London by the early 1830s.[29] At Lymington, on the Hampshire coast, they were achieved after a three-year campaign in 1827, while at Basingstoke in the north of that county the mayor secured them in 1830 with the aid of 300 armed vigilantes.[30] At the market town of Stroud, on Gloucestershire's Cotswold Edge, the custom of rolling tar barrels down the high street was stopped in 1824.[31] The street fires at Chipping Campden, further north in the Cotswolds, were halted by police after a fierce fight with a crowd in 1840.[32] In other parts of the West Country and the Welsh Marches, the process was only carried out more than a generation later. It was in the 1880s that soldiers were called in to accomplish the work at Dorchester and that a series of arrests managed it at Ludlow.[33] The tar-barrel rollers at Chepstow, where the Wye runs into the Severn, fought the local constables stubbornly from 1863 to 1892; when some were arrested for stoning an officer, a public subscription paid for their lawyers.[34] At Bridport and Lyme Regis, on the Dorset coast, the barrels carried on flaming until 1909, when the police finally got their way.[35]

The most spectacular struggles, of course, took place where the bonfire gangs had taken charge. At Witham, in the arable lands of north-east Essex, the local one opposed the constabulary from 1859 to 1890, and eventually wore it out; more strenuous efforts by the police only produced worse violence. At Chelmsford the gang hung on to the town centre every year between 1860 and 1888.[36] The Lewes revellers gave up tar barrels and fire balls under police pressure in 1841 but, when the justices banned celebration altogether six years later, a pitched battle involving a hundred constables was required to clear the streets. The result was only a tighter organization by the bonfire societies.[37] The forces of law had more success in Surrey, where the merry-making was put down at Godalming, Chertsey, Farnham, and Croydon between 1860 and 1880. Most ferocious was the contest at Guildford, where the magistracy tried unavailingly to stop Guy Fawkes festivities from the 1820s to the 1850s. When two men were fined for promoting them in 1843, their payments were provided by public subscription and they were escorted from prison by a cheering crowd. In the 1850s masked 'Guys' demanded money from passers-by, and blew horns to summon reinforcements when the local police tried to intervene. This state of affairs no longer seemed tolerable in the town by the next decade; the new and wealthy people who were moving in, attracted by its booming economy, had little sympathy for the old popular licence. The police force was increased and augmented both by 'specials' and by detachments of the army. In 1865 the power of the Guildford 'Guys' was finally broken; but not before one constable had died of his wounds.[38]

During this same period the legal basis of the celebrations was completely removed at a national level. The traditional church service caused an increasing amount of trouble to tender consciences during the early nineteenth century. Some Tories disliked it because it eulogized a revolution (that of 1688), while liberal opinion was offended by its abuse of Roman Catholicism. A student at Oriel College, Oxford, refused to attend it in the chapel and was punished by the Provost with the loss of a testimonial on graduation. Bishop Blomfield of London was faced with a curate who claimed that 'it is not a church service but a state service'. Queen Victoria herself felt that her Catholic subjects were justified in complaining of its language.[39] The issue was brought to a head in 1850, when the Pope appointed a full hierarchy of archbishops and bishops for England. At first it looked as if the action would produce a renascence of Gunpowder Treason Day as a fete of anti-Catholicism. There was a record number of guys and fires around London that year, towards which the police showed an unusual tolerance. At Battle, in Sussex, the local gentleman, Sir Godfrey Webster, renewed his patronage of that town's bonfires, while at Lewes the authority came to terms with the gangs. 'Young Exeter' was allowed to burn the Pope and his officials in the cathedral yard once again. At Northampton and the nearby towns of Towcester and Kettering, crowds demonstrated furiously against Catholicism, and in succeeding years Tories and Anglicans encouraged a repetition of this with Whigs and dissenters as targets. By 1856, however, so much violence and crime had resulted in the area that the local ruling class reunited to set the police upon the revellers and drive them from the streets into the fields.[40]

This process was reproduced in Parliament in the summer of 1858, when Earl Stanhope moved that the queen be formally requested to abolish the forms of prayer prescribed for the day, upon the grounds that they were politically obsolete and were grossly unfair to Catholics. He was supported by the archbishop of Canterbury and the bishop of London, as well as by several secular peers. The Tory duke of Marlborough proposed that the service be rewritten rather than abolished, but he received little support and Victoria gladly assented to the the address which the Lords sent to her. With the church commemoration now gone, it was a small step, in March 1859, for Parliament to repeal the statute which had enjoined it.[41] Celebration was, therefore, left to local initiative and custom, deprived of any national and official framework at all. Local initiative had, however, proved to be all too fruitful, and it was in the next decade that some of the most savage struggles took place. The issue was to be resolved ultimately not by straightforward repression but by two different developments, which were to preserve the Guy Fawkes festivities while altering them profoundly in character.

The first seems to have been pioneered at the Hertfordshire town of Hitchin in the 1870s, when its Bonfire Club organized a torchlit parade of over 400 masqueraders, instead of the traditional chaotic exuberance. The beauty and order of the spectacle attracted enthusiastic upper-class support, Lord Allington and the local MP providing £50 between them for a firework display and a set of costumed 'guys' to be carried to music played by the town's band. During the 1880s similar parades were instituted across southern England. At Horsham 'most of the chief families of the town and district' sponsored one. The Winchester equivalent was led by the city's fire brigade, while the mayor of Salisbury lit the bonfire which concluded the one there. At Lewes the traditional societies organized the processions, and *The Times* commented upon the 'good order and temper' of the latter. The corporation of Chelmsford seized upon the device to end almost thirty years of warfare with the local bonfire boys, organizing 400 torchbearers with blackened faces to march up to a gigantic bonfire; the gangs co-operated and the event was a total success. The same procedure was instituted at Lewisham, Hampstead, Hastings, Rye, Folkestone, and most of the towns of Dorset, and in the 1890s at Battle, Reigate, Dorking, Nutley, Walton, Eastbourne, Bridgwater, and Teignmouth. Robert Storch, who has made the finest study of the bonfire gangs, has characterized this development as a means by which the local élites regained control of the populace—essentially as an exercise in subjugation. Though such an element may have been present, it is also worth remarking that the processions would not have been so successful had they not been so acceptable to the local community as a whole, including, crucially, the surviving gangs and societies. They represented a more or less ideal resolution of everybody's wishes, and put an end to the tensions which had come to cluster around the night.[42] As such they lasted into the twentieth century, in most places to metamorphose slowly into the municipal firework display. In several West Country towns, such as Bristol, Bridgwater, Wells, and Glastonbury, they evolved instead into processions of carnival floats brightly lit with electricity. The modern, winter, equivalent of the medieval summer pageants, they now take place upon different nights in early or mid-November, and often synchronize with the illumination of public Christmas decorations; what began as an anniversary for Protestant rejoicing has become a regional rite of passage into the festive season *par excellence*.

The second Victorian development in the observation of the day was less spectacular but more fundamental: that in most places it moved out of the public into the private sphere and from the centre of a community to its margins. In the physical sense this was quite literal, as the fires migrated from streets and squares into gardens and wastelands; they also tended to become, even more than before, the business of working-class children and youths. The latter often solicited firewood, money, food, or drink for the night from wealthier neighbours, with a set song or rhyme. The one recorded in 1903 at Charlton on Otmoor, in the marshy basin north-east of Oxford, contains lines found in most of the other known versions:

> The fifth of November, since I can remember,
> Was Guy Faux, Guy, Poke him in the eye,
> Shove him up the chimney-pot, and there let him die.
> A stick and a stake, for King George's sake,
> If you don't give me one, I'll take two,
> The better for me, and the worse for you,
> Ricket-a-racket your hedges shall go.[43]

All the standard components of the jingle are there: the appeal to traditional celebration of the day; the denigration of Guy Fawkes, as the universal enemy, the patriotism and monarchism (with King George substituted for King James to stand for the brave days of old); and the threat of misrule if wood is not given. The most usual opening was:

> Remember, remember, the fifth of November,
> Gunpowder Treason and Plot,

and Fawkes was occasionally portrayed as 'Poor Old Guy', the subject of comic misadventures related with some sympathy, as if his real identity had been forgotten.[44] In the earliest of these rhymes to be noted,[45] the King concerned is still James, while Victoria herself was sometimes invoked later in the nineteenth century. The most exuberantly individualist of all the local equivalents was heard in Berkshire in the 1890s:

> Remember, remember, the Vifth of November,
> Gunpowder, trason and plot,
> Pray tell me the reason why Gunpowder trason,
> Should iver be vorgot.
> Our Quane's a valiant Zawlger,
> Car's her blunderbus on her right shawlder,
> Cocks her pistol, drays her rapier,
> Praay gie us zummit vor her zaayke yer,
> A stick, an' a styaake vor Quane Vickey's zaakye,
> If'e wunt gie on I'll taayke two,
> The better vor we an' the wus vor you.[46]

Such small-scale celebrations among youngsters were almost ubiquitous in the late nineteenth-and early twentieth-century English countryside. They virtually always involved fireworks, and usually included bonfires, although the burning of 'guys' and other effigies was much rarer and represented a set of local, though very widely scattered, traditions, most commonly observed in southern seaside towns, in Lancashire, and in Oxfordshire.[47] In the same period they spread into north and central Wales, replacing the older Hallowe'en bonfires in that region.[48]

As the rhymes suggested, the long association of the festival with misbehaviour and disorder continued very easily in its new incarnation. In the North Riding of Yorkshire the establishment of a strong rural constabulary was required to stamp out a local custom of stealing brooms to make torches; which was accomplished in the later years of Victoria.[49] The same activity persisted in south-eastern Wiltshire in the 1930s, carried on by boys who believed that all law was suspended upon that night.[50] In the same decade youths at Botley, near Southampton, were fined for adding cars to their bonfire in the village square.[51] Doors were routinely pelted in several Devonshire settlements.[52] Most spectacular were the disturbances which developed at Cambridge in the mid-twentieth century, when town lads, reinforced by many from the villages, took to rampaging through the streets, throwing fireworks, brawling, and overturning cars. University students responded by fighting them, and the local constabulary became regarded as legitimate targets by both groups. Indeed, the licence of undergraduates upon this night was later regarded as 'amazing', and the Chancellor of the Exchequer at the time of writing, Kenneth Clarke, was one of many otherwise respectable and ambitious students who treated policemen's helmets as prized trophies upon 5 November. The situation was only brought under control by more ruthless and concerted official action in the later 1960s.[53]

In most of Lancashire and Yorkshire, a formal separation was made in the twentieth century between the bonfire celebrations and misrule, the latter being moved backwards to the 4th and being given the nickname of Mischief Night already applied in the same area to May Eve. By the 1950s it was especially popular in the industrial towns, where on 4 November it was observed that 'youngsters bent on mischief roam the streets in happy warfare with the adult world'.

Householders' front doors are repeatedly assaulted with bogus calls, their window panes daubed with paint, their doorknobs coated with treacle or tied 'sneck to sneck', their evening newspapers (projecting from letter boxes) exchanged, their milk bottles placed so that they will be tripped over, their house-numbers unscrewed and fixed onto other houses, their windows tapped, their backyards turned upside down and possibly ransacked for tomorrow's bonfires, their drainpipes stuffed with paper and set alight, and their porchlight bulbs considered legitimate targets for catapults.

Adults were seen to endure all this 'with admirable fortitude', although local newspapers often expostulated.[54] This situation still seems to obtain, although many of the pranks now appear to have been shifted forward the few days to Hallowe'en.

Everywhere in the twentieth century the festival adapted easily to the two great forces of mass production of consumer goods and the relocation of communal life in the family unit. By 1908 one company alone, Paine, was selling 500 tons of fireworks annually. The following year, *The Times* commented upon the growing fashion for back-garden fireworks parties in the suburbs, limited to the family and invited friends. By the 1920s the groups of children going about wealthier homes were usually asking for pennies to buy commercially produced fireworks.[55] Bonfires, on a small scale, survived as focal points for the parties, and the formerly patchy distribution of effigy-burning became much more general, a figure in human clothes, still loosely called a 'guy', being a prized ornament for a fire. Many were made by children, and instead of the 'stick and a stake' demand, the solicitation 'a penny for the guy' became standard on public streets, the effigy destined for burning being displayed for admiration. It was noticed by the 1950s, however, that few children had any idea who the ubiquitous 'Guy' had been. The chants and rhymes, too, continued to evolve, producing such pieces of local idiosyncrasy as this, from Northampton:

> Guy Fawkes, Guy,
> Hit him in the eye,
> Hang him on a lamp-post
> And leave him there to die.
> Umbrella down the cellar
> There I saw a naked fella
> Burn his body, save his soul,
> Please give me a lump of coal;
> If a lump of coal won't do,
> Please give me a halfpenny,
> Then up and down the Drapery
> Round and round the Market Square,
> Till I get to Marefair,
> Where I'll spend my ha'penny,
> Guy Fawkes, Guy.[56]

Despite the new familial setting, a muted disorder, with throwing of 'bangers', often for weeks before the night, continued even in areas with no 'Mischief Night' tradition. It was possible also for customary violence to appear in areas formerly relatively quiet. Cambridge was one example of this, and another was the north-eastern industrial town of Sunderland, where rioting invariably broke out in the working-class Southwick district on 5 November in the late 1970s. The community halted the disorder in the early 1980s by employing the same stratagem used by so many others a century before: a spectacular public display. In this case it consisted of a powerful set of fireworks and a huge bonfire with an effigy of the Prime Minister, Margaret Thatcher (blamed for the local high rate of unemployment), as the 'guy'. The same devices were being increasingly used, in any case, to counter the perceived danger of private parties. By the 1960s increasing affluence meant that commercial fireworks were being bought in unprecedented numbers, and the resulting accidents were running at an average rate of 1,400 per year. In 1970 a national Firework Code was employed to reduce this, and succeeded in halving it during the rest of that decade, although in 1980 the British still burned up £14 million in bangs and sparks on or before Guy Fawkes's Night.[57] Despite the increasing safety of the back-garden display, however, it was in the 1980s that this began to go out of fashion in turn, to be replaced by the grandiose municipal and society equivalents with paid admission. The latter provided a more impressive spectacle, for less expense. After about a hundred years, the pendulum has started to swing back again from private to com-munal celebration, although with the community now firmly relegated to spectators.

In addition there remain survivals of an older mode of celebration, providing in their own way much more dramatic, if disturbing, experiences. The torchlit procession, guy-carrying, and great fire at Battle in Sussex, revived under the patronage of Sir Godfrey Webster, still hold out against attempts to relocate or abolish them. More secure, and even more spectacular, are the equivalents further west in the country at Lewes, where the bonfire societies have survived to the present by becoming based upon particular areas of the town or upon institutions such as schools. Archaic touches are provided by the carrying and burning of a pope, with references in placards and advertisements to the execution of Protestant martyrs under Mary Tudor; by the dragging of tar barrels upon sledges, which are later rolled blazing into the river Ouse; and by the presence of both a gigantic communal bonfire and of many smaller blazes, on hills and by the river, which light up the landscape like the Beltane, Midsummer, and Hallowe'en fires of old. Each society provides its own fancy dress, native Americans, pirates, Cavaliers, and Arabs being old favourites, and it marches carrying effigies (again varied) and torches, all destined for the great bonfire. Upon a windy night, the latter portions of the processions have to reckon with both burning lumps of tow upon the road and sparks flying at head height, representing two almost continuous streams of fire. The town fills up with visitors, and the pubs do a roaring trade, but the sheer interest of the spectacles generally prevents any violence.

Less well-known, and even more exciting, is the celebration at Ottery St Mary at the east end of Devon. It incorporates a motorized evening carnival procession of the West Country sort, mentioned above, and another huge communal bonfire upon which a guy is burned, usually dressed to resemble a Victorian plutocrat; much of the crowd manifests a gruesome enthusiasm as it catches fire. The distinctive feature of 5 November at Ottery, however, is the tar-barrel running, representing a surviving pocket of the custom suppressed elsewhere in the nineteenth century. Until about 1870 the barrels were rolled, using staves but, in the face of police opposition, it became the custom to carry them by hand, limiting their size and providing better control.[58] Neither restriction, it must be said, is more than relative. The capacity of the barrels now ranges from ten gallons, which are carried by children from 6 years upward, before dusk, to sixty gallons, left to adult men, at midnight. The larger specimens are provided by pubs, outside which they are lighted, and the number and identity of those who carry each is determined beforehand by the Tar Barrel Society. The trick is to wear old clothes, with a cap and gloves of sacking drenched in water, and to run with the barrel held upon the back of the neck, fast enough to make the flames shoot out of the open end, safely behind you. The catch is that the running is done through crowded streets, and that each cask is picked up and borne away by the first person brave enough to attempt this, whereupon the other runners in the group then chase and fight him, or her, for possession of it. Serious injuries are unknown, but minor burns, cuts, and bruises routine, the latter especially common among spectators stampeding out of the way. It is rather awe-inspiring to see parents in Ottery actively encouraging their young and adolescent children to feats from which adults elsewhere would attempt desperately to restrain their off-spring. The skill and courage involved are a source of pride both to individuals and to the whole community.

At Ottery in 1990, assisting a laughing 'barrel girl' whose hair, coat, and gloves were all on fire, I asked her why she took part. She chose to make a general interpretation of the question, and said that it was to chase evil spirits away from her community at the beginning of winter. At Battle the 'bonfire boys' had told me that their procession came down directly from the fire rituals of the 'Celtic New Year'. In both cases the reality of the Gunpowder Treason had receded into oblivion, to be replaced by the speculative theories of Victorian and Edwardian folklorists. Thomas Hardy's dream of how the English past ought to have been had become accepted as historical truth by some, at least, of the people who continued the customs which he had incorporated into fiction. Nevertheless, it is worth making the suggestion that Guy Fawkes's Night would never have continued to the present, with such popularity, as the surviving British fire festival, because of its historical significance alone. It is arguable, at the least, that, as faith in the magical and protective powers of fire waned, and with it the need to kindle those made at the ancient feasts of May and June, so the simple value of it as a comfort in gathering darkness remained, in early November. With a potent symbol of excitement, heat, light, and celebration, the new Bonfire Night occupied a neat point between the end of the warm, green, months and the major midwinter festival, at precisely the moment when the onset of cold, darkness, and decay are most apparent. In this sense Hardy's portrait of the fires on Egdon Heath may come very close to explaining the perpetuation of the festival, if not its origin.

40

CONCLUSIONS

⚜

THIS is not a book which works up to any obvious conclusion through systematic argument; the contents have been too diffuse and self-contained. It may be that readers will have extracted portions of them which relate to interests of their own and formed them into patterns which would not have been obvious to the author. If so, then in terms of the book's aims such a result would be regarded as a success. What follows here is a series of personal reflections, representing notions and concerns which arose during the writing of the work and which are as discontinuous as the rest of its contents. If many are themselves inconclusive, and point to further research, then part of the purpose of the work has been to draw attention to such lines of enquiry.

I

The first concerns the history of the ancient British and Irish year. This has never been made the subject of a sustained study by any expert in early Irish or Welsh literature, and what has been written upon it has consisted of a paragraph or two provided almost by default, usually in the works of scholars who were not primarily expert in literary sources at all. Nevertheless, this has sufficed to build up a powerful impression of an 'ancient Celtic year', probably uniform from Ireland to Gaul, consisting of the four quarter-days of Samhain, Imbolc, Beltane, and Lughnasadh (in various spellings), and commencing on the first of those festivals. The importance of the quarter-days in medieval Irish literature was noticed in the first systematic treatment of those texts, such as the works of Charles Vallancey in the eighteenth century. By the second half of the nineteenth, it had become assumed by English folklorists that they were observed in ancient Britain as well. One of these writers, Charles Hardwick, either borrowed, or made himself, a misreading of the description of the fire rite of Beltane in *Sanas Chormaic* which caused him to believe that it was carried out upon all four feasts.[1] From this error sprang the characterization of them as 'the fire festivals', which was never taken into academe but has persisted in popular works until the present day.

Most of the academic books upon the Celts produced for a general readership in the 1950s and 1960s made no reference to the subject.[2] Two important publications in 1967 did turn to it, but only briefly and cautiously. One was Anne Ross's splendid pioneering work on pagan Celtic Britain, which only suggested that Beltane and Samhain might have been generally observed in the Celtic world.[3] The other was a joint survey of Celtic civilization by Nora Chadwick and Myles Dillon, which just stated that Celts (in general) observed the four festivals.[4] Then came 1970, with a boom in works for a popular market upon all things Celtic, and two of those authors contributed to it with books which were decidedly less restrained upon the subject. Nora Chadwick declared that the four festivals (and no others) were celebrated by the whole Celtic world, that Samhain was the New Year, and that most were concerned with fertility.[5] Anne Ross said much the same, save that she suggested that each was connected to a particular deity. She did, however, also state that it was only 'probable' that the Celts in general had these feasts, that they might have been distinctively Irish, and that the Irish themselves seemed to have others as well.[6]

During the next twenty-five years, the subject was once again ignored by some of the standard textbooks upon ancient Celtic culture.[7] On the other hand, those by Anne Ross and Nora Chadwick were reprinted, in the latter case twenty years after the author's death. In 1979 Lloyd Laing produced one which repeated the usual information about the four festivals, though he added rather confusingly that while Imbolc and Lughnasadh may not have been celebrated in Iron Age Britain 'they certainly had their equivalents'.[8] Another apparent muddle of ideas appeared in 1986, in the first of a series of very successful books by Miranda Green. On one page she told readers that Beltane and Samhain, being suited to a pastoral society, may never have been celebrated in lowland Britain and Gaul. On another, however, the usual four feasts were casually described as 'the great Celtic festivals'.[9] In the same year Graham Webster supplied by far the most detailed consideration of the subject in any textbook of the past forty years, amounting to almost four pages. It was also unusual in that it provided footnotes to support its information. It started from the presupposition that the Celts in general only celebrated the four festivals, with the New Year at Samhain, and went on to suggest what the characteristics of those feasts might have been. None of his references was to original sources, save to well-known Irish tales in popular translations; most were to Anne Ross, Máire MacNeill, and Sir James Frazer. Frazer's ghost, in fact, hangs over the whole description.[10] This is hardly surprising. Nora Chadwick never carried out any research into the matter, and Anne Ross, Lloyd Laing, Miranda Green, and Graham Webster could not, for all are not historians but archaeologists (and very distinguished archaeologists at that). They are experts in material remains, not literature, and as their works give only a tiny amount of space to consideration of this question it would be unfair to cite them at all were it not for the fact that they have provided the staple texts upon the matter which colleagues, and everybody else, read. In other words, nobody has carried out any general survey of it since Sir John Rhŷs and Sir James Frazer, about a hundred years ago. John Carey is at present working upon the Irish observation of Samhain, and producing valuable results,[11] but that is a consideration of one festival in one country.

There is, in fact, only one material remain from the pagan Celtic world (as conventionally defined) which bears upon the matter, and that is the famous bronze calendar from Roman Gaul, found at Coligny in what is now south-eastern France. It is totally unlike the Irish system, being a very complex sequence of sixty-four divisions with no equivalent names. Nor, as it is now in fragments, does it indicate when the year begins. None of the prehistoric monuments of the British Isles can be said with perfect confidence to be aligned upon movements of the sun at any of the quarter-days. On the other hand, most of the greatest, from the fourth, third, and second millennia BCE, are alligned with remarkable precision upon the midwinter or midsummer solstice. The Coligny calendar suggests that we give up either the traditional notion of a uniform Celtic system of reckoning the year, or the traditional notion of the extent of a Celtic cultural province. The monuments suggest that we either accept that the Iron Age British and Irish celebrated the solstices as well, or else (which is perfectly arguable) that the ritual year in these islands altered fundamentally between the second and the first millennia BCE. What can be suggested is that there is nothing in the material remains to support the fourfold division accepted by the archaeologists. The early Irish literature, on the other hand, certainly does testify abundantly to the importance of the quarter-days, but the Welsh equivalent only mentions one of them (May Eve), and consistently places its favourite feast in midwinter. Even the Irish literary sources, moreover, include references to Christmas, and every time a medieval Irish document marks the opening of a calendar year, it does so either from then or from 1 January or 25 March. The medieval Welsh ebulliently celebrated their New Year at a time identified with the Roman Kalendae, upon 1 January. This apparent practice, of marking the opening of a year at the winter solstice, simply puts these Celtic peoples at one with the rest of ancient northern and western Europe. Even the Irish seem therefore to have operated a dual system, of reckoning time both from midwinter and from the opening of seasons. This is not so different from the medieval English practice, whereby the year was commenced in January or March, and yet rents and other dues were paid quarterly at either the cardinal solar points of Christmas, Lady Day, Midsummer Day, and Michaelmas, or else as the seasons opened at Candlemas, May Day, Lammas, and All Saints' Day.

There is, therefore, absolutely no firm evidence in the written record that the year opened on 1 November in either early Ireland or early Wales, and a great deal in the Welsh material to refute the idea.[12] Nor can it confidently be concluded that even the Irish only celebrated the four quarter-days. The whole argument for a 'Celtic New Year' was originally based upon conclusions drawn from relatively recent folklore, and it has been suggested that these were flawed. What the folklorists' collections portray is a general Irish celebration of the quarter-days, midwinter, and midsummer. Midsummer bonfires, with much the same rituals, are recorded all over England, Wales, Ireland, Lowland Scotland, and the Northern Isles, with complete irrelevance to boundaries between Celtic areas and others; but they are apparently not mentioned in the Gaelic-speaking parts of Scotland. Since records begin, the New Year (on 1 January) was marked by rituals and merry-making of equal intensity in the Gaelic world of the Hebrides and the Anglicized one of the Lothians. The Irish feast of Imbolc, rededicated to St Brigid, was kept with the same rite all over Ireland, and also in Man and the Hebrides; but not anywhere on the British mainland. There its role was taken by the universal Christian holy day of Candlemas. It embodied a parallel tradition of honouring a divine woman, often through women, and lasted longest in the Celtic land of Wales; but the two traditions may have converged, and medieval Catholic rituals in general survived in Welsh popular culture. The Irish way of celebrating Lughnasadh, by contrast, was found in Man but not anywhere in Scotland, including the Hebrides. Elsewhere in Britain it has only one, isolated, parallel, in South Wales. The same feast was, however, celebrated in different ways and under different names all over Celtic, Saxon, or Norse Britain. The ritual of Beltane was found in all the Celtic areas of the British Isles, but also in pastoral regions of Germanic and Scandinavian Europe. A feast with ritual practices at the other end of the herding season was equally well known in both ancient Ireland and ancient Scandinavia, and represented by folk practices in the uplands of Wales and Scotland. There was, however, no common rite as there had been at Beltane. The people of north and central Wales, Man, and the southern and eastern Highlands used fire again, but apparently not those of Ireland and the Hebrides.

Perhaps it may seem unreasonable to expect that prehistoric tribal peoples would employ identical seasonal ceremonies across the whole of the British Isles, let alone the whole of north-west Europe. This is, none the less, the assumption which underpinned traditional scholarly approaches to the subject, from Sir James Frazer to Máire MacNeill and, in the case of the purification by fire or rowan at the opening of the summer pastures, it is actually justified. That does, however, seem to be a unique case. What the folklore record portrays as a rule are strongly marked regional traditions of festivity which bear no strict relationship to nineteenth- and twentieth-century notions of Celtic and Germanic cultural provinces. It may therefore be suggested as a proposal worthy of testing, that the notion of a distinctive 'Celtic' ritual year, with four festivals at the quarter-days and an opening at Samhain, is a scholastic construction of the eighteenth and nineteenth centuries which should now be considerably revised or even abandoned altogether.[13]

II

Records of seasonal customs in Britain during the early and high Middle Ages do exist, but are so rare that their appearance can really be described as incidental. Anything like a systematic account of such customs only becomes possible in England in the fourteenth century when different types of source material—household accounts, literary works, corporation documents, and the first parish records—begin to occur in sufficient quantity to provide cross-comparison. The same stage is not reached in lowland Scotland until the sixteenth century, and in Wales, Man, and the Scottish Highlands and islands, until the eighteenth. For England at least, however, the late medieval evidence is rich enough to allow conclusions to be drawn, and a major one was proposed in the book which acted as a stepping-stone to this.[14] It was that the period between 1350 and 1530 produced not merely a greater quantity of records of communal customs and seasonal rites, but an actual increase in both, representing a continual elaboration of religious, municipal, and courtly ritual. It was also proposed in that book that it was much more difficult to account for this development than to demonstrate that it occurred, and that the form of explanation most easy to test, the economic one, proved to be inadequate by itself. It was therefore suggested that the true reasons would probably lie in a mixture of economic stimulants, religious needs, and intangible developments of taste, varying from place to place. In settling for that, I had faced a choice. Would I select one possible chain of causation out of the options, argue for it as dramatically as I could, create a more exciting and polemical book, and leave it to my colleagues to contest my argument and make a case for alternatives? Or would I prefer the apparent truth that the research which I had undertaken had revealed a historical phenomenon and created a set of questions about it which I could not determine myself without further work? The second seemed to me to be the more honest response and better suited to the facts of the case; it did, however, lay me open to an immediate charge of being too cautious, hesitant, or 'lame'.

That charge was indeed made occasionally in reviews, but a good deal more gently than I might have expected. The most detailed and helpful discussion of the issue was by Keith Wrightson,[15] who endorsed the notion that interpretation had to be 'flexible and multi-faceted', and proposed some more possibilities: that patterns of neighbourly co-operation in a period of labour shortage encouraged collective participation in festivity as well as work; that the financing of ritual provided a means of enhancing status for the prosperous and defused potential tensions arising from social differentiation; and that parishes and towns engaged in competition to express identity through a generally approved cultural fashion. All were exciting suggestions, but none actually moved the questions closer to solution. That communities competed, and used culture as an expression of that competition, is self-evident; but why that culture? It is equally obvious that ritual was employed to enhance status and defuse tension; but why ritual, and why so much of it? It is not obvious, by contrast, that the fifteenth-century world of independent smallholders and artisans demanded more neighbourly co-operation than the more over-crowded and highly organized one of the thirteenth-century manor. What is absolutely clear is that these issues are best approached through an intensive study of local English communities by social historians of the late Middle Ages. Several of these exist, but none to date has taken this problem into account, being concerned primarily with economic and political aspects of society and failing to integrate matters of ceremonial, festivity, and religious belief, as opposed to ecclesiastical structure.

Nevertheless, a fresh examination of my own body of late medieval and early Tudor material, during the writing of this book, has made me more impressed than before by the importance of a particular sort of religion. The researches of Eamon Duffy at the national level and Clive Burgess at the local one have recently brought this into clearer focus,[16] and the parish, guild, and municipal records employed in my own work bear out their suggestions. These sources testify overwhelmingly to a faith based upon communion, intercession, and penance (in this world and the next), all provided through increasingly elaborate, and very popular, structures of ritual. Penance was most easily expressed through holy works, not merely in the beautification of the parish church itself and of the rites which took place in it, but through service to the parish and the strengthening of its institutions. In a very real sense, salvation occurred through ceremony, in a close co-operation of clergy and all ranks of laity which meant that the social benefits were also obvious. It may well be argued that these developments were themselves the result of demographic and social forces, such as a constant fear of plague and a more independent and well-paid labour force. This, however, would require more substantiation than seems at present to be possible, while it could be argued with some strength that the same developments were the logical results of a system of Christian belief and practice which had been evolving steadily ever since the high Middle Ages, through a succession of different demographic and economic conditions. In the same manner I would agree that the parish replaced the manor as the basic unit of local life during the later Middle Ages, and that its enhanced importance was reflected in the new elaboration of its activities and financial arrangements. Once again, however, it may be asked whether this enhanced importance had necessarily to take this form. After all, the parish continued to accumulate responsibilities until it reached an apogee of power in the seventeenth century; but it did so then with a very different sort of religion and attitude to festivity.

If I would emphasize the independent power of ideology more than before, and so forfeit the safety of my earlier position, then I would also now draw attention to a particular historical development which was only implicit in my earlier work upon this subject. During the period up to about 1450, clergy and corporation leaders alike had a grudging attitude towards popular pastimes.

The former were concerned mainly to ensure that priests did not attend them, that they did not take place in or around sacred places, and that they did not lead people into sin. The latter were determined to control them and to ban those which had proved disorderly. During the mid-fifteenth century, however, there was a general movement towards employing seasonal festive customs as a means to raise money for the parish church. This included some, like Hocktide bindings, May games, and Robin Hood plays, which had previously been specific objects of censure by local lay and religious leaders. This remarkable and very widespread development seems to have been both spontaneous and silent, for no published work of the time refers to it and it was neither precipitated nor endorsed by official action. The result, however, was very neat, because activities which might have been considered before to be a potential way to damnation now became tied, through fund-raising, to a system of salvation. As soon as that system was scrapped, at the Reformation, the merry-making automatically began to be regarded once more as a liability by social and religious élites. If this picture is correct, then it was the evolution of a religious ideology which produced a society imbued with a general taste for ceremony and acted as a means to endorsement of secular festivity. In other words, Merry England was inspired by the fires of hell.

The same material, and that from the later Tudor and the Stuart period, gives rise to one further suggestion. In what is by far the best survey to date of adolescence in early modern England,[17] Ilana Krausman Ben-Amos refuted the view that there was any such thing as a youth culture, or subculture, at this time. She demonstrated that 'most youths had few values that truly distinguished them from adults, and they had few, if any, institutions which were wholly theirs, separating them from society at large.' Thus, religious and sexual attitudes reflected those of that broader society, recreation and leisure time were shared by adults, and the mobility of most youngsters prevented the formation of strong and durable alliances. What all this proves, beyond doubt, is that there was no cohesive subculture of the sort associated with young people in the modern developed world. What perhaps needs to be stressed here (leaving aside the question of whether the modern youth subculture actually is that cohesive) is the existence in late medieval and early modern England of a particular festive role for youth. It was institutionalized in the pre-Reformation period in the number of Plough Monday gatherings, King games, and Robin Hood plays which were specifically 'by the young men'; perhaps all were. It is also clear from the data provided in this book that the youths often, and perhaps generally, organized themselves for these activities without the supervision of adults. The fact that they were acting on behalf of a wider community, and with its full co-operation, does not alter the significance of the freedom and responsibility which they were able to take for their actions. In this manner they both served the community and acted as its benefactors; their age-group was both institutionalized and dignified for these purposes. The subsequent religious Reformation and the 'Reformation of

Manners' removed much of this system, but they recreated the role in a different form in the vigilante operations of the metropolitan apprentices at Shrovetide—in this sense seizing the process of reform and making it their own within a framework of seasonal ritual. Similarly, the evidence presented in this book indicates that, although adults frequently watched or joined in summer games and dances, they were essentially the business of the young, often operating independently. They could hire their own musicians, make their own meeting times, buy their own food and drink, and indulge in customs ideally suited to their age-group, such as the kissing dance around the maypole. In a largely rural society, lacking a mass media or commercialized leisure pursuits, this is the closest thing to a youth culture which we should expect to find, and the modern comparison may not be very helpful. None of this is to challenge the case which Professor Ben-Amos was actually making, merely to suggest that in the making of it something important may have been lost.

III

The implications of this book for Reformation studies are far more straightforward.[18] During the past ten years the English Reformation has become the subject of an exciting, informative, and somewhat artificial debate. Its outline is familiar to anybody with even a cursory knowledge of the area. Upon the one hand are those who have portrayed the relationship between Protestantism and the mass of the people as essentially adversarial, and the Reformation as a process imposed from above, very slowly, upon a populace which had on the whole been content with the old Church and reacted to the new one with a mixture of confusion, demoralization, and hostility. These writers tend to argue that the long-term legacy of the changes was a much greater alienation of common people from the established religion.[19] Upon the other are a number of scholars less well defined as a group and sometimes less overtly polemical in their style, who have stressed the early appeal of Protestantism to sections of the populace and the manner in which, from the reign of Elizabeth onward, the new religion made a profound impact upon popular culture.[20]

To describe the debate as artificial is not to belittle any of the scholars who have promoted it; rather, the characterization arises from a sense that the disputes are largely the result of individual concentration upon different aspects of what is fundamentally the same picture. By contrast, the portrait of the English Reformation which was presented in most schools and universities until the 1970s was in such obvious need of revision by then, in the light of recent work in diocesan and parochial archives, that a vigorous polemical attack on it was wholly appropriate. This revisionist polemic has apparently called forth an equivalent tone of controversy from colleagues who accept, implicitly or explicitly, most of its criticisms of the traditional historiography and seem more to be engaged in a process of adding depth, sensitivity, and complexity to the new picture which has emerged as a result. Arguments at present seem to arise essentially from differences of emphasis, in part a consequence of the use of differing source material; thus those who have stressed the popularity of the old Church and widespread hostility to reform have tended to make more use of churchwardens' accounts, ecclesiastical court books, and visitation returns, while their critics often attached more importance to wills and printed works.

In this context, Tessa Watt's recent monograph may be particularly significant.[21] It draws upon a hitherto relatively neglected body of evidence— ballads, broadsides, and other cheap printed material—and suggests that this supports both and neither of the two positions characterized above. These popular wares incorporated both a Bible-centred Protestantism and a traditional visual piety in a fashion which repressed a sense of confrontation between new and old forms and emphasized instead a continuing interest in death, salvation, miracles, prodigies, heroic action, and moral behaviour, which transcended religious reform. Alterations of emphasis did occur, such as the partial replacement of saints as protagonists by historical or Biblical figures, but in general the elements of continuity with the past were stronger, and the changes incorporated painlessly into traditional forms. Those issues which most obviously divided the rival Churches, and different varieties of Protestant, were usually ignored. The works concerned concentrated instead upon broadly consensual values, based upon simple behavioural rules and expressed in a form which was intended to entertain. They reveal a remarkably resilient popular culture which was at once deeply permeable to religious change and able to absorb it.[22]

In *The Rise and Fall of Merry England* I provided my own judgements upon the nature and pace of the English Reformation(s), and much of the evidence is reproduced in this book. What I have added here is the testimony of the later folklore collections. The employment of these for early modern history was pioneered, like so much else, by Sir Keith Thomas back in 1971,[23] and in this case his lead was not followed up. By pursuing it now, and asking whether traces of the practices and beliefs of the late medieval Church may be found in more recent popular culture, I have tried to recover some further evidence of the qualitative nature of the process of the Reformation in England. The result is effectively a full-blooded reapplication of the theory of 'survivals' to folk customs which has recently become so unpopular amongst folklorists. The distinction here, however, is that the 'Old Religion' which is being sought in this exercise is not a putative one concealed in the shades of pagan antiquity, but a well-documented one which was brought to an end only four to five centuries ago. One well-known folklorist, Theo Brown, has already made such a study, in a book published almost twenty years ago which, although completely ignored by historians, strikingly presaged some of the conclusions of Tessa Watt.[24] It was essentially an analysis of West Country ghost stories, designed to reveal popular attitudes to death and the afterlife. Some certainly displayed a thoroughgoing Protestantism, but in the main they were very hard to relate to the reformed faith. Instead, they embodied a powerful sense of the efficacy of works and of penance in achieving salvation, and also of the local priest as a conjuror, employing spells in ancient languages, and consecrated objects. Theo Brown summed all this up as 'a mixture of ancient pagan belief, half-remembered old Catholic teaching and later Puritan doctrine possibly distorted as a result of misleading sermons'.[25] Her analysis seems to be a perfectly accurate one, and it seems here that we have exactly that sort of popular religion which drove evangelical Protestants in Elizabethan and Jacobean England to despair and rage.

The material provided in *Merry England* testified abundantly to a rapid reformation in external matters, imposed from above upon a population which, on the whole and especially outside of the south-east and of the Thames valley, took considerably longer to acquire any positive enthusiasm for them. What it failed to explain, in the main, were the processes by which the changes were eventually absorbed and internalized. It is suggested here that the folklore collections of the eighteenth, nineteenth, and twentieth centuries do indeed provide a novel insight into those processes. They reveal that in the case of the most famous and popular ceremonies—the hallowing of candles at Candlemas and of foliage and wooden crosses on Palm Sunday, the Easter sepulchre, and prayers for the dead on All Saints' or All Souls' Day—the proscription within the churches was followed in some places and amongst some people by a transference of the rite into private practice. In every case what was being provided by the Church was a ritual which imparted an enhanced sense of blessing and personal well-being. In the first four the beneficiaries were the living, and in the last the deceased were helped instead. The first four ceremonies also hallowed objects which were believed thereafter to possess especial virtue. All were more strongly imported into popular custom in Wales (especially) and the north and west of England, those regions which have always been recognized as less responsive to early Protestantism. None the less, the total area concerned is very large. In the case of Candlemas customs it comprised most of Wales, Dorset, and the Trent valley; in that of Palm Sunday foliage it took in virtually the whole of England and Wales; in that of 'palm crosses' it was the north of England; in that of Good Friday bread (held here to be descended from the consecrated wafer in the sepulchre) it again took in most of the realm; and in that of prayers for the dead in early November, the various devices covered between them large areas of the North, the Midlands and Wales, with some parts of the West Country and Home Counties as well.

Two aspects of this process seem to be particularly remarkable. The first is that, although in a few places they were associated with areas of enduring popular Catholicism, in most they were not. Wales provides notable examples both of the success of the reformed faith and of the transference of forbidden ceremonies from the church to the home; indeed, it is distinctly possible that the two were linked. The other remarkable aspect of the process is that the counterfeiting of Catholic ritual in popular pastime does not seem to have attracted animosity at any level of reform. What we seem to have here is one of the significant silences of history, an apparent instinctive assumption upon the part of Protestants that the folk practices were essentially harmless. At times in other cultures these assumptions were articulated, and one of the most fluent of those who did so was Diego Duran, a Dominican friar working among the natives of Mexico in the late sixteenth century. He wrote of the importance of a distinction between genuine survivals of the pre-Christian religion, which had to be extirpated, and practices from it which had been transmuted into games, entertainments, and social habits, and could be tolerated.[26] A parallel process has been explored by R. A. Markus in his consideration of the conversion of the Roman world to Christianity. He suggested that many phenomena in the Christianized empire which historians now recognize as 'pagan survivals' were simply taken for granted as part of the fabric of existence and of a common inherited culture. Christians were conscious of their origins but did not consider these to be very significant.[27]

The data employed in this book could quite legitimately be pressed into the service of the debate over the nature of the English Reformation which was characterized above. If people felt so strongly for the forbidden ceremonies of the old Church that many of them found it necessary to imitate them outside the new religious structure, then this reinforces the impression that for a proportionate number of them the reforms were alien and unwelcome. It is proposed here, however, that a different sort of conclusion may perhaps be more helpful to an understanding of the process of reformation. The early Tudor Church had, clearly, provided parishioners with certain services, and experiences, not obtainable from its Protestant successor. One apparently widespread popular reaction to this difficulty was to set about providing them for one's self, through the medium of what was later to be dubbed folk ritual. In general the reformers seem to have accepted this transposition as unimportant, and so allowed it to occur without molestation. The result was not so much an episode in the history of resistance to the Reformation as a part of the process of acceptance of it, easing the transformation of a Catholic to a Protestant society. Once transferred to sections of the laity, these rites remained there until their final demise, not as part of an alteration of religion, but as part of the greater and much more gradual phenomenon of 'the decline of magic'. The matter may perhaps be summed up by the Newcastle clergyman Henry Bourne, who stands at once at the end of the line of evangelical clergymen who complained of popular pastimes and near the beginning of the succession of scholarly observers who systematically recorded them and gave birth to the discipline of folklore. Writing in 1725, he commented that some 'vulgar antiquities' were 'the produce of heathendom' and others 'the inventions of indolent monks', but that all ought to be judged by the single criterion of whether they were 'sinful or wicked' in practice. His definition of wickedness comprised anything which led to crime, drunkenness, brawling, malice, or fornication; none of the relics of religion cited above came into those categories.[28] If earlier generations of Protestant ministers had shared his view, which is perfectly compatible with the Elizabethan and early Stuart 'complaint literature', then perhaps we have recovered another part of the complex experience of religious alteration in early modern England and Wales. If so, it is one which reflects well on popular culture for its toughness and adaptibility, but also upon reformers who are too easy to characterize from the present day as zealots, for displaying a canny sense of priorities.

IV

In the writing of the passages of this book concerning the period from 1550 to 1900, a number of limitations of evidence became clear which the author was not qualified to amend. One was referred to in the text, being the apparent lack of research into the impact of the Scottish Reformation upon ritual observances. It is allied to a relative lack of work upon Scotland's equivalent of the early modern 'Reformation of Manners' in England. The image of the stool of repentance looms very large in the popular imagination (usually with Robert Burns seated upon it), yet despite a large body of source material, even in publication, work upon this function of early modern presbyteries and kirk sessions has hardly begun. Instead, research into the Scottish Reformation has concentrated upon matters of politics, ecclesiastical government, doctrine, and sociology. An identical statement could be made about the study of eighteenth- and nineteenth-century Anglicanism. There seems to be very little research into the ornaments and ceremonies used in parish churches during that period, and the wider ritual concerns of the clergy such as perambulations, harvest festivals, the observation of 'political' holy days, and attitudes to local feasts and games. This is despite the existence of relevant sources, such as parish records, visitation returns, and tracts, in very large quantity. Either of those areas, however, would require ample funding and a large book to themselves, and a scholar specializing in the field.

The sources used most prominently for the later periods covered by this book have, of course, been the collections made by folklorists. Even within the limitations imposed upon them by the interests of the collectors, which generally excluded ecclesiastical and civic ritual, and most customs and beliefs of the urban proletariat, they have serious shortcomings. What they tell us about most, of course, are the preoccupations and prejudices of the individuals who made them.[29] Popular customs were almost always observed from outside, and recorded flatly and briefly with no attempt to comprehend what they meant to the people by whom they were carried on or articulated. When the emotions or opinions evoked by them were recorded at any length, they were almost always those of the observer, not the performers. This is a phenomenon entirely understandable, given the spirit of the observation. In earlier decades popular practices were recorded mainly to afford entertainment or disgust to an educated readership, but also to provide raw material for theorizing about the nature of earlier society and religion; and it was this preoccupation which later came to predominate. The truly pernicious consequence of the view of folk customs as survivals from an archaic world, and of an obsessive quest for their origins, has been the subject of much recent comment;[30] the populace was regarded simply as a vector for practices which it no longer properly understood and had long been divorced from their true context. The opinions of the 'folk' themselves were therefore at best irrelevant and at worst a distraction to the scholar. This attitude is now a cause of frustration not merely for social historians but for those of literature and the performing arts; for example, collections of folk-plays very rarely contained any impression of what they were actually like as performances. Furthermore, the politics of nineteenth-century folk traditions were usually studiously ignored, especially in the late Victorian and Edwardian periods. The impression given by most of the collections is that the traditions concerned were in inevitable slow decline because of their incompatibility with modern industrialized society; very seldom is it admitted that some were wiped out after years of struggle between their practitioners and police reinforced by soldiers. This was no doubt partly because of a scholarly preoccupation with the remote past, but also seems to have been due to a genteel distaste. It was much more attractive to folklorists of that period to speculate that Guy Fawkes bonfires might have been derived from pagan human sacrifice than to mention the recent desperate battles between bonfire boys and special constables. Too often, the study of folklore could be used as a doorway into a never-never land, attractive because it seemed so remote from the world of class conflict.

When all this is said, the collections remain extremely valuable. Their sheer bulk and range is impressive, and the preoccupations behind them do make them very relevant when dealing with the question of whether popular customs were indeed survivals from old religions—which is not always answered in the negative. Their utility to historians of all periods must have been repeatedly demonstrated in the preceding pages. They can also be said usually to have been accurate observations, a conclusion which is easily reached through the cross-comparison made possible by their profusion. Indeed, when this exercise is complete, there are only two which stand out as odd, across the whole of the British Isles: that for the Outer Hebrides by Alexander Carmichael,[31] and that for Wales (overwhelmingly for the south of the principality) by Marie Trevelyan.[32] Both are relatively late, and yet describe customs with a colour and an elaboration unknown in other works upon the same regions, including those made earlier. Each, in fact, includes some rites which appear remarkably archaic, are portrayed in considerable detail, and yet occur in the collections of no other scholar, even though they are also characterized as being extinct by the time of writing. Both authors tend, in fact, to be somewhat vague as to the location and the period of the customs which they describe. Both have enjoyed an enormous popularity and influence among general readers upon folklore. For these reasons they have already aroused serious misgivings among scholars,[33] but have been accepted in this present work for lack of any positive refutation of them, and a belief that Carmichael in particular might indeed have known his chosen communities exceptionally well.

The virtues and shortcomings of the early folklorists find an almost perfect reversal in the works of social historians publishing between 1970 and 1990, such as E. P. Thompson, Robert Malcolmson, Robert Storch, and Bob Bushaway.[34] These were the writers who commenced the work of integrating popular customs into mainstream history, and did so from a full range of contemporary (essentially eighteenth- and nineteenth-century) records. In the process they pushed class conflict to the forefront of the picture. To a large extent their technique consisted of inverting the sympathies of their sources. The latter were virtually all produced by a social élite, who frequently expressed dislike and contempt for the masses, either in general or with regard to particular moments and activities. The historians concerned reacted with varying degrees of intensity by taking the viewpoint of the populace and treating landlords and employers as people who violated a customary law and a traditional sense of reciprocal obligation for their own selfish ends. At its most extreme, in the cases of Bob Bushaway and the great Edward Thompson, this attitude embodied a sense that individuals who possess a disproportionate amount of private wealth and political power, in a society in which poverty is widespread, are innately guilty of misconduct. In that respect their writings can be viewed as much as cultural artefacts as those of the Victorian and Edwardian folklorists. Even more than in the case of the folklore collections, however, this does not necessarily make their perceptions inaccurate; in many respects they seem to have been objectively correct and indeed morally just. In others, however, the material represented in this book suggests that their analysis needs more fine-tuning. Very often, they tended to treat the working classes as relatively homogeneous in their identity and interests, ignoring the variety in both which prevailed especially before the mid-nineteenth century. The hostility displayed towards traditional customs by religious nonconformists and political radicals in those classes were often glossed over. Sometimes in the writings of these authors, labourers, the poor, and those who availed themselves of traditional doles and hospitality, are regarded as being synonymous. The disengagement of the social élites from communal festivity and traditional generosity was often regarded as simply an act of will, rather than as one consequence of a general increase in social tension as the population grew, labour relations became more commercialized, economic actions became more sophisticated and diverse, and revolutionary armies fanned out across Europe. On the other hand, the price of that disengagement was certainly paid by the poorer members of society and, had it not been for the feelings entertained by these scholars for them, then a lot of work in this field would never have been undertaken at all.

The greatest problem of perspective in studying British folk customs, however, remains the gulf between specialists in modern and in early modern history. In the work of the social historians cited above, the practices which were eroded in their period were treated as literally immemorial. They were regarded as originating in a timeless society which was wholly transformed in the centuries between 1700 and 1900. Historians of the Tudor and Stuart periods, however, do not notice most of the same customs; the few who have dealt with popular festivity have been concerned with different practices. What may be suggested here is that the customs might actually have been different. There was, of course, a great deal of continuity in many seasonal traditions, but it can be argued that there were some important qualitative and quantitative changes. During the period between 1660 and 1800 the morris and hobby-horse dances seem to have ceased to be national institutions and to have broken into a set of localized forms. During the same span of time, a host of ritualized begging customs apparently sprang up, including the outright requests for money or food upon old winter and early spring festivals (Souling, Catterning, Clementing, Gooding or Thomasing, Lucky Birds, Valentining, and Shroving or Lent-Crocking) and the Mummers' Play, Plough Play, Pace-Eggers, and Sword Dance. Traditions of this sort had existed before, as local troupes of players, hobby-horse and morris dancers, wassailers, and mummers moved between the local big houses. So had paupers and vagrants, seeking Christmastide generosity. None the less, what the sources suggest is both an overall expansion of these sorts of activity and a much more pronounced formalization into regional traditions. This process reached its apex in the late eighteenth and early nineteenth centuries and went into decline thereafter. Perhaps such a picture is illusory, being based on deceptive evidence, but I suggest that it is now for social historians of the 'long eighteenth century' to prove it so. If, on the other hand, their work turns out to support my suggestion of a genuine development of considerable importance, then they have the task of explaining why the society of this period should have produced it. Hitherto those of them who have dealt with such issues have worked from the assumption of a static, customary, traditional England, destroyed by industrialization, urbanization, and capitalism. In this respect they are identical with the old-fashioned folklorists from whom they differ in every other way.

V

In 1994 the periodical of the Folklore Society included an article entitled 'Margaret Murray: Who Believed Her, and Why?', by its president, Jacqueline Simpson.[35] Dr Murray was a former president, whose principal field had been Egyptology but who had become more widely known among historians for her theory about the nature of the Great Witch Hunt. This, expressed in a series of works between the 1910s and the 1950s, suggested that its victims had actually been practitioners of the ancient pagan religion of western Europe. Although always controversial, this won quite wide acceptance among specialists in medieval and early modern studies, and a much greater popularity among the general public. It only collapsed in the world of academic scholarship in the 1970s, a comfortable span of years after her death in 1963, partly because her own treatment of sources was examined and found to be faulty, and partly because a series of carefully researched local studies into the Witch Hunt failed to bear out her ideas. This story was summed up with admirable concession in Dr Simpson's piece, one purpose of which was to knock a few more nails into the coffin of the Murray thesis by showing how hopelessly flawed her methods were from the point of view of a folklorist as well as of a historian.

Another, however, was to clear the reputation of the Folklore Society, in which Margaret Murray had been so prominent, from any guilt by association. To this purpose, she pointed out that Dr Murray's books had always received critical reviews in the society's periodical, and that its only member who had accorded her views unequivocal support seems to have been Gerald Gardner. This gentleman in many ways deserves a place in history ahead of all his colleagues, being the only one who has been claimed as the founder of a new religion (Wicca, arguably the most important modern pagan tradition). He was, however, regarded by the society as its most eccentric and disreputable member,[36] and his approval was the reverse of a recommendation. Dr Simpson's article can therefore be viewed as part of a process by which current scholars of folklore are putting their own house in order. They are applying rigorous new standards to their discipline and so bidding for (and deserving) the attention of historians, archaeologists, and anthropologists once again. This process does, inevitably, often involve the castigation of predecessors in their field and in their institutions.[37]

The present book has been a beneficiary of this new approach, and in many ways may claim to carry it on. Its author is, moreover, in no position to defend the Murray thesis, being one of those writers singled out for praise by Dr Simpson for his criticisms of it. Despite all these considerations, it may now be suggested that the true context for Margaret Murray's work is becoming lost from view and that it would be unhelpful as well as unjust to begin to regard her as, in this respect, an isolated crank. She was, after all, not the first scholar to propose the idea that a pagan religion was persecuted in the Witch Hunt; that was put forward in the nineteenth century by at least three historians, including the celebrated Jules Michelet, and by a folklorist, Charles Godfrey Leland. Dr Murray merely seemed to document it properly for the first time.[38] Furthermore, her opinions upon the subject developed steadily over five decades and became less and less credible. It was in the 1930s that she began to suggest that English royalty had been members of the witch religion, and in the 1950s that some of them, and of the aristocracy, had been made human sacrifices according to a systematic tradition, up to the sixteenth century.[39] From 1930 onwards her new books ceased to be published by university presses, and it is easy to believe that by the 1940s and 1950s there was almost nobody in the Folk-Lore Society, any more than inside academe, who fully endorsed her opinions.

It was her work of the 1910s and 1920s, concerning the existence of a pagan 'witch cult' in medieval and early modern Europe, which continued to convince respected historians of those periods (although not those expert in the Witch Hunt) until the 1960s.[40] At that earlier time, also, her position in the Folk-Lore Society seems to have been different. It was to the society that she first aired her ideas upon the subject, in a series of lectures and papers between 1917 and 1920. Her first presentation was followed by a letter to its journal from one of its most prominent members, Charlotte Burne, who stated that she had been unable to attend herself, but was very excited by what she had heard reported of it, and thought that it sounded wholly convincing. It is true that when Dr Murray's first book upon the theme did appear, in 1921, it was sent by the same journal to a specialist, and (as Dr Simpson has pointed out) had its shortcomings relentlessly laid bare. This does not, however, mean that her colleagues in the society necessarily accepted the criticisms, and Margaret Murray's own reviews of publications upon the Witch Hunt which did not endorse her theory, in the same periodical, were just as negative (and much ruder). Contributions to that journal which did favour her ideas, usually expressed in the form of unfavourable comment upon the work of others, continued into the 1950s.[41] Furthermore, she made a separate, and equally influential, contribution towards historical debate in 1934, when she suggested that the spread-legged female figures called *sheela na gigs*, carved in medieval churches, were images of pagan fertility goddesses. She went on to opine that this proved the continued vitality of pagan folk religion in England throughout the Middle Ages.[42] This provided the direct inspiration for Lady Raglan to link the carved medieval foliate heads with the Jack in the Green and so invent the notion of the Green Man. Neither idea was seriously questioned until the 1970s and 1980s.[43]

Most important, however, is the issue raised by Charlotte Burne's admiring letter of 1917, sent, after all, upon nothing more than a report of the first public airing of Margaret Murray's views. She said that the latter made perfect sense because they fitted well into the account of ancient religion and its folkloric survivals provided by Sir James Frazer, of which Charlotte Burne herself was wholly convinced.[44] Here indeed is the key to the matter: that Margaret Murray's picture of a pagan nature religion, surviving furtively in the countryside throughout the Middle Ages and beyond, was absolutely in harmony with the view of rural British culture taken, with equal confidence and equally little regard for the proper conduct of historical research, by Charlotte Burne and also by Cecil Sharp, Violet Alford, Mary Macleod Banks, and, indeed, the vast majority of the luminaries of the Folk-Lore Society and the English Folk Dance and Song Society until the 1970s. It was of a timeless and sealed world, in which the Old Religion and the Old Ways long endured, at first literally and then subsumed into a shadow-world of legends, dances, plays, rites, and superstitions. The question must now be confronted of why this myth—for such it was—had such a potency for so many people in this country between about 1880 and about 1980. The trite answer is, of course, the influence of *The Golden Bough*, but to make this is to beg the question of why Frazer's work should have had such an enormous impact. A second easy reply, which at least gets us further, is to point to the cult of the countryside, referred to earlier in this book, which burgeoned in England after 1880 as it became a predominantly urbanized nation employing most people in commerce, industry, or public services. This is surely closer to the heart of the matter, but still leaves a large problem. Why did folklorists not focus upon images of a green and ordered land centred upon the manor house, the parish church, the common fields, and the village feast, as the proponents of Merrie England had done? Why did they turn instead to evocations of pagan deities and archaic rites?

The question, although not its resolution, becomes considerably plainer when the writings of Frazer, Murray, Alford, and their colleagues and followers are treated as not a branch of scholarship but as one of creative literature. Helen Law's *Bibliography of Greek Myth in English Poetry*, published in 1955, revealed not only that Pan was far and away the most popular deity of English poets, but that his considerable lead over all the other immortals was the result of a spate of verse produced between 1895 and 1914. This poetry was devoted to the countryside and the natural world but, even given that the authors were determined to see these in pagan terms (itself something which requires explanation), there was no need to turn to the goat-footed god. The rural landscape might easily have been populated with nymphs, dryads, ondines, and other picturesque and benign spirits, or else with the more familiar and polite Olympians, who after all stood for aspects of nature as well as of civilization. Pan, however, was not a 'safe' deity. As Patricia Merivale has pointed out, in her study of his image in modern literature, he could stand as much for the savagery in nature as for its comforting aspects. He was also very much a sexual being.[45] Margaret Murray was only one of many writers in her time to be dreaming about a horned god, served by exciting and disturbing rites, in the familiar English landscape. She just took the extra step of trying to make the dream into a historical reality; Gerald Gardner helped to turn it into a contemporary one. Sir James Frazer and the English folklorists of the early twentieth century were working with images which were alien not just to the conventional religion of their time but to the conventional morality. In that lay their attraction, and power.

Instead of shunting the Murray thesis and Frazerian folklore into an academic cul-de-sac, therefore, it would seem more appropriate to put them in a high road of modern British culture. There is obvious need now for a proper study of the treatment of the themes of paganism and witchcraft in the English-speaking world during the last couple of centuries. Only when that work is complete can the significance of early twentieth-century British folklore studies be properly understood.

VI

It is one of the arguments of this book that the rhythms of the British year are timeless, and impose certain perpetual patterns upon calendar customs: a yearning for light, greenery, warmth, and joy in midwinter, a propensity to celebrate the spring with symbols of rebirth, an impulse to make merry in the sunlight and open air during the summer, and a tendency for thoughts to turn towards death and the uncanny at the onset of winter. It is another, however, that those customs have altered perpetually in form since records began and are still evolving. This is true at every level of society, popular cultures being as dynamic in this respect as those of the élite. Certain periods seem to have been particularly fruitful for the proliferation of seasonal rites and festivities, because of particular combinations of circumstance; the late Middle Ages and the eighteenth century are two of these. None, however, was perfectly static, so that the mid- and late Tudor age, which destroyed the traditional seasonal ceremonies of the Church, also saw the growth of morris into a national craze and (arguably) created a set of rituals designed to transfer the proscribed ceremonies into private practice. It is apparent, also, that calendar customs were created around social units which altered significantly over time: in ancient Britain the household, clan, and kingdom, in the high Middle Ages the household and the manor, and in the late Middle Ages the household, the municipality, and the parish. The church produced its own institutional rituals during this whole span of time, often overlapping or blending with the others. These were greatly diminished after the Reformation, and from the seventeenth century the festive role of the parish and great household was also much reduced. Instead the principal unit of celebration became the local community, much less formally defined and growing ever more complex with time. During the past 150 years it has been replaced, almost universally, by the family.

What is also plain is that the last couple of centuries, in this as in every other aspect of British life, have produced a completely unprecedented amount of change. The vast majority of the population have been moved out of not only all direct contact with farming processes but any direct dependency upon their rhythms, as international trade has virtually abolished seasonal limitations on foodstuffs. A holiday has ceased to consist of a celebration within the community, and become an escape from it to a completely different sort of surroundings. No amount of nostalgia or anxiety for a rapidly diminishing and deteriorating natural environment can alter the essential irrelevance which it now possesses for the daily lives and seasonal habits of most of the British; however, this very fact may cause it to play an ever greater part in religious symbolism. The provision of a national social security system and a tremendous rise in standards of living have removed a culture in which poor people can legitimately solicit charity by going between the houses of wealthier neighbours offering entertainment, despite the persistence of poverty and the return of widespread begging. The collapse of a belief in magic among the bulk of the population has destroyed the need for rituals of blessing, purification, and protection. It is possible that some of these will be recreated, drawing on old examples and images; that greater social polarization will make begging customs again prevalent; that ostensibly magical rites will be seen as important aspects of psychotherapy; and that a revived paganism will make a pattern of regularly spaced festivals, to honour the seasonal processes, habitual among large numbers of the population. None of this, however, is certain at present.

When all is said, a vigorous seasonal festive culture survives and continues to develop among the British. This is partly because those fundamental emotional demands of daylight hours and climate are still very much in operation. It is also, however, because of a recasting of the meaning of the ritual year, which becomes plain when considering the identity and observation of those festivals which are flourishing: Christmas, New Year, St Valentine's Day, Mother's Day (and, increasingly, Father's Day also), Easter, spring and summer Bank Holidays, Hallowe'en, Guy Fawkes's Night. The list is one of family festivals, children's festivals, parents' festivals, lovers' festivals, festivals of adult friendship, festivals of responsibility and obligation, and festivals of irresponsibility, both adult (New Year's Eve) and juvenile (Hallowe'en). The ritual calendar, in an age in which most kinds of community have been atomized by central government and the mass media, is becoming a celebration of private relationships and the individual lifecycle. Humanity has come to replace the natural world at the centre of the wheel of the year.

✥ NOTES ✥

The following Abbreviations have been used

BL	British Library
Bod. L	Bodleian Library, Oxford
EETS	Early English Text Society
JEFDSS	*Journal of the English Folk Dance and Song Society*
HMC	Historical Manuscripts Commission
L	Library
RO	Record Office
TRHS	*Transactions of the Royal Historical Society*

It may be helpful to repeat here that the name of the periodical *Folk-Lore* was altered to *Folklore* in 1960, in keeping with the change in that of its parent society.

All titles published in London unless otherwise stated.

CHAPTER 1

1. For a concise summary of current thinking, see E. P. Sanders, *The Historical Figure of Jesus* (1993), 85–9.
2. For desperate and futile attempts to get round this problem, see the next chapter.
3. The sources are listed in E. K. Chambers, *The Medieval Stage* (Oxford, 1903), i. 241 n. 1.
4. Ibid. i. 242–3; John Dowden, *The Church Year and Kalendar* (Cambridge, 1910), 27–8; J. G. Frazer, *Adonis, Attis, Osiris* (1907), 255; *Corpus Inscriptionum Latinarum*, I. i. 278.
5. This text is considered by Gaston H. Halsberghe, *The Cult of Sol Invictus* (Leiden, 1972), 174; and Frazer, *Adonis*, 255.
6. Sources as at n. 5, plus Franz Cumont, *La Natalis Invicti* (Paris, 1911), *passim*; H. Usener, *Das Weihnachtsfest* (Bonn, 1911), 348–50.
7. Quoted in Frazer, *Adonis*, 256, save for Maximus of Turin, *Sermo* 61. a. 1.
8. Pliny, *Natural History*, xviii. lix. 221; Columella, *De Re Rustica*, ix. 14. 12.
9. Ovid, *Fasti*, iii. 135–47.
10. H. H. Scullard, *Festivals and Ceremonies of the Roman Republic* (1981), 205–6.
11. Lucian, *Saturnalia*, 4. See also Tacitus, *Annals*, xiii. 15, and Arrian, *Discourses*, I. 25. 8.
12. Ovid, *Fasti*, I. 1–20; Alexander Murray, 'Medieval Christmas', *History Today* (Dec. 1986), 33; David Miller, 'A Theory of Christmas', in Miller (ed.), *Unwrapping Christmas* (Oxford, 1993), 8.
13. Chambers, *Medieval Stage*, i. 238–44; Geoffrey Grigson, 'The Three Kings of Cologne', *History Today* (Dec. 1954), 28–34.
14. Chambers, *Medieval Stage*, i. 243–6; Dowden, *The Church Year*, 34–5.
15. Michael J. O'Kelly, *Newgrange* (1982), 123–5.
16. George Eogan, *Knowth and the Passage Tombs of Ireland* (1986), 178.
17. For the most optimistic interpretation, see T. O'Brien, T. Jennings, and D. O'Brien, 'The Equinox Cycle at Cairn T. Loughcrew', *Riocht Na Midhe*, 8 (1987), 3–15; for a cautionary word, see Jean McMann, 'Forms of Power: Dimensions of an Irish Megalithic Landscape', *Antiquity*, 68 (1994), 537.

18. Colin Richards, 'Barnhouse and Maeshowe', *Current Archaeology*, 131 (Oct. 1992), 451–4.

19. Richard Bradley, 'A New Study of the Cursus Complex at Dorchester on Thames', *Oxford Journal of Archaeology*, 7 (1988), 271–90.

20. Aubrey Burl, 'By the Light of the Cinerary Moon', in C. L. N. Ruggles and A. W. R. Whittle (eds.), *Astronomy and Society in Britain during the Period 4000–1500 BC* (British Archaeological Reports, British series, 88; 1981), 256.

21. Aubrey Burl, 'Pi in the Sky', in Douglas Heggie (ed.), *Archaeoastronomy in the Old World* (Cambridge, 1982), 150–66.

22. Julian Richards, *English Heritage Book of Stonehenge* (1991), 68.

23. G. A. Wait, *Religion and Ritual in Iron Age Britain* (British Archaeological Reports, British series, 149; 1985), 154–77.

24. Ronald Hutton, *The Pagan Religions of the Ancient British Isles* (Oxford, 1991), 156.

25. *The War of the Gaedhil with the Gaill*, ed. J. H. Todd (Rolls series, 1867), 112.

26. Pliny, *Natural History*, XVI. XCV. 250.

27. *Bede*, Works, ed. J. A. Giles (1843), vi. 178.

28. Alexander Tille, *Yule and Christmas* (1889), 147–56.

29. *A Collection of the Laws and Canons of the Church of England*, ed. John Johnson (Oxford, 1850), i. 328. Ibid. i. 137 has the earliest reference which can be found to 'midwinter', in the law code of Ine of Wessex, 693.

30. Tille, *Yule and Christmas*, 147–9.

31. Clement A. Milnes, *Christmas in Ritual and Tradition* (1912), 25.

32. *Ynglinga Saga*, ch. 8.

33. *The Saga of Hakon the Good*, ch. 13.

34. *Svarfdaela Saga*, ch. 12.

35. In *The Medieval Stage*, volume ii. appendix N.

36. Ibid. i. 244–5, and appendix N.

37. *Councils and Synods…871–1066*, ed. D. Whitelocke, B. Brett, and C. N. L. Brooke (Oxford, 1981), i. 319–20.

38. *Medieval Handbooks of Penance*, ed. John T. McNeill and Helcra M. Gamear (New York, 1938), 349.

39. *Mirk's Festival*, ed. T. Erbe (EETS, 1905), 44–5.

40. *Dives and Pauper*, ed. P. H. Barnum (EETS, 1976), 5, 29.

41. Sir Ifor Williams, *The Beginnings of Welsh Poetry*, ed. and trans. Rachel Bromwich (1972), 163.

CHAPTER 2

1. Daniel Rock, *The Church of our Fathers* (1904), iv. 248–9

2. Ronald Hutton, *The Rise and Fall of Merry England* (Oxford, 1994), 6.

3. Ibid. 6–7.

4. George Caspar Homans, *English Villagers of the Thirteenth Century* (Cambridge, Mass., 1942), 357–8; Nathaniel J. Hone, *The Manor and Manorial Records* (1906), 94; N. Neilson, *Customary Rents* (Oxford Studies in Social and Legal History, 2; 1910), 30–2.

5. *A Roll of the Household Expenses of Richard de Swinfield, Bishop of Hereford*, ed. John Webb (Camden Society, 59; 1853), 22–31.

6. Anna Jean Mill, *Medieval Plays in Scotland* (Edinburgh, 1927), 308.

7. Fitts I–III.

8. Hutton, *Merry England*, 305–6 nn. 2–5.

9. J. M. Golby and A. W. Purdue, *The Making of the Modern Christmas* (1986), 26; William Sandys, *Christmastide* (1853), 45.

10. Ibid. 48.

11. *Household Accounts from Medieval England*, ed. C. M. Woolgar (Oxford, 1992), 414–19.

12. *The Household Book of Dame Alice de Bryene*, ed. Vincent B. Redstone (Suffolk Institute of Archaeology and Natural History, 1931), 25–9.

13. Hutton, *Merry England*, 7–8.

14. Enid Welsford, *The Court Masque* (Cambridge, 1927), 30–61; Mill, *Medieval Plays*, 15.

15. Welsford, *Court Masque*, 36; Hutton, *Merry England*, 9.

16. Welsford, *Court Masque*, 38.

17. Mill, *Medieval Plays*, 30.

18. U. Lambert, 'Hognel Money and the Hogglers', *Surrey Archaeological Collections*, 30 (1917), 54–60; Hutton, *Merry England*, 12–13, 50.

19. Hutton, *Merry England*, 13, 58.

20. *The Diary of Henry Machyn*, ed. J. Nichols (Camden Society, 1848), 99.

21. *Festive Songs and Carols*, ed. W. Sandys (Percy Society, 23; 1847), 19–20.

22. Hutton, *Merry England*, 14, 58; F. Marian McNeill, *The Silver Bough* (Glasgow, 1961), iii. 78–9; Richard Leighton Greene, *The Early English Carols* (Oxford, 1935), chs. 1–5.

23. Hutton, *Merry England*, 15, 51.

24. Sandys, *Christmastide*, 47.

25. Hutton, *Merry England*, 16.

26. BL Add. MS 4843, fo. 423.

27. Hutton, *Merry England*, 15.

28. G. Huelin, 'Christmas in the City', *Guildhall Miscellany* NS 3 (1977–9), 164–5.

29. McNeill, *Silver Bough*, iii. 81.

30. Hutton, *Merry England*, 15.

31. Ibid. 15–16; Alan H. Nelson, *The Medieval English Stage* (Chicago, 1974), ch. 6; Leslie Hotson, *The First Night of Twelfth Night* (1954), 176–7; Mary Macleod Banks (ed.), *British Calendar Customs: Scotland* (Folk-Lore Society, 1939), ii. 127–8.

32. Hutton, *Merry England*, 16.

33. Ibid. 97.

34. Swansea University L, Corporation Records D2.

35. Hutton, *Merry England*, 248.

36. Clwyd (Denbighshire) RO, PD/101/1/133.

37. D. Roy Saer, 'The Christmas Carol-Singing Tradition in the Tanad Valley', *Folk Life*, 7 (1969), 16–17.

38. Ibid. 15–25.

39. Ibid. 15–42; Peter Roberts, *The Cambrian Popular Antiquities* (1815), 133–4; William Howells, *Cambrian Superstitions* (1831), 182; Jonathan Ceredig Davies, *Folk-Lore of West and Mid-Wales* (Aberystwyth, 1911), 60; Trefor M. Owen, *Welsh Folk Customs* (St Fagans, 1974), 28–33; E. J. Dunnill, 'Monmouthshire', *Folk-Lore* 24 (1913), 108; Enid Pierce Roberts, 'Hen Garolau Plygain', *Transactions of the Honourable Society of Cymmrodorion* (1952), 50–71; Roy Saer, 'A Midnight Plygain at Llanymawddwy Church', *Folk Life* 22 (1983–4), 99–107; J. Fisher, 'The Religious and Social Life of Former Days in the Vale of Clwyd', *Archaeologia Cambrensis*, 6th ser. 6 (1906), 155–6.

40. Howells, *Cambrian Superstitions*, 182.

41. J. Fisher, 'Two Welsh-Manx Christmas Customs', *Archaeologia Cambrensis*, 84 (1929), 308–14; Joseph Train, *An Historical and Statistical Account of the Isle of Man* (Douglas, 1845), ii. 127–8.

42. See the account of what was done at Middleton, Lancashire, in the 1790s, in *The Autobiography of Samuel Bamford*, ed. W. H. Chaloner, (1967), i. 132.

43. Hotson, *Twelfth Night*, 176–7.

44. John Brady, *Clavis Calendaria* (1812), i. 154; Robert Chambers, *The Book of Days* (1864), 64; A. R. Wright, *British Calendar Customs*, ed. T. E. Lones (Folk-Lore Society, 1936), i. 79–80.

45. Hotson, *Twelfth Night*, 176–7; Albert Feuillerat, *Documents Relating to the Office of the Revels in the Time of Queen Elizabeth* (Materialienzur Kunde des Alteren Englischer Dramas; 1908), *passim*; R. Chris Hassel, jun., *Renaissance Drama and the English Church Year* (Lincoln, Nebr. 1979), 1–3.

46. Hassel, *Renaissance Drama*, 5–60; Hutton, *Merry England*, 154, 197.

47. *The Diary of John Evelyn*, ed. E. S. de Beer (Oxford, 1955), iii. 308, 350, iv. 30; *The Diary of Samuel Pepys*, ed. Robert Latham and William Matthews (1970), iv. 120, viii. 193.

48. Sandys, *Christmastide*, 146; William Hone, *The Every Day Book and Table Book* (1832), i. 40.

49. 'The Journal of Lady Mildmay', ed. Rachel Weigall, *Quarterly Review*, 215 (1911), 134.

50. Philip Lee Ralph, *Sir Humphrey Mildmay* (New Brunswick, 1974), 106–8.

51. [Edward Fisher], *A Christian Caveat to the Old and New Sabbatarians* (1649), 10–11.

52. John Taylor, *The Complaint of Christmas and the Tears of Twelfthtyde* (1631), 22–3, and *Christmas In and Out* (1652), 12.

53. *Christmas His Masque* (1616), in Ben Jonson, *Works*, ed. C. H. Herford Percy and Evelyn Simpson (Oxford, 1941), vii. 437–45; Thomas Nabbes, *The Springs Glorie* (1638), sig. A; Taylor, *Complaint of Christmas*, 22–3, and *The Complaint of Christmas* (Oxford, 1646), 19; Fisher, *Christian Caveat*, 10–11; J. A. R. Plimlott, *The Englishman's Christmas* (Hassocks, 1978), 68–9.

54. Hutton, *Merry England*, 164–5, 167, 177; *The Roxburghe Ballads*, ed. William Chappell (Ballad Society, 1871), i. 154–8.

55. Felicity Heal, *Hospitality in Early Modern England* (Oxford, 1990), 71–7, 148–9, 173–5, 219, 280–1, 293–4.

56. Ibid.

57. Sandys, *Christmastide*, 135–42.

58. *The Old and Young Courtier* (1670); *Round about our Coal-fire* (n.d.), *Times Alteration* (n.d.).

59. *The Pepys Ballads*, ed. Hyder Edward Robbins (Cambridge, Mass., 1929–32), iii. 51–5.

60. Heal, *Hospitality*, 297.

61. Hutton, *Merry England*, 241–2.

62. Bob Bushaway, *By Rite* (1982), 128–30, 158, 240–1; and see also Robert W. Malcolmson, *Popular Recreations in English Society 1700–1850* (Cambridge, 1973), 26–7, 57–8.

63. Hutton, *Merry England*, 87, 100, 114, 163, 189, 205–6; Somerset RO, DD/SAS SE 14.

64. Jonson, 'Christmas His Masque', 440.

65. K. E. Wrightson, 'The Puritan Reformation of Manners with Special Reference to the Counties of Lancashire and Essex 1640–1660' (Cambridge Ph.D. thesis, 1973), 210.

66. HMC MSS In Various Collections, i. 130.

67. E. A. B. Barnard, *A Seventeenth Century Country Gentleman* (Cambridge, 1944), 41, 72.

68. *Quarter Sessions Records for the County of Somerset*, ed. E. H. Bates-Harbin (Somerset Records Society, 1912), iii. 324.

69. Henry Bourne, *Antiquitates Vulgares* (Newcastle, 1725), 147–50.

70. William Henderson, *Notes on the Folk-Lore of the Northern Counties of England and the Borders* (Folk-Lore Society, 1879), 70.

71. Malcomson, *Popular Recreations*, 27, 57.

72. Sandys, *Christmastide*, 185.

73. e.g. *The Roxburghe Ballads*, ed. J. Woodfall Ebsworth (Ballad Society, 1893), vii. 774–814.

74. Jonson, 'Christmas His Masque', 440; John Brand, *Observations on the Popular Antiquities of Great Britain*, ed. Sir Henry Ellis (1908), i. 191, 240; Nicholas Breton, *Olde Mad-Cappes New Galley-Mawfrey* (1602), Sig D4; Taylor, *Complaint of Christmas* (1631), 22–3.

75. Doris Jones-Baker, *The Folklore of Hertfordshire* (1977), 123; Malcolmson, *Popular Recreations*, 57.

76. *Gentleman's Magazine*, 54 (1784), 98.

77. 'Account of New Year's Gifts, Presented to Queen Elizabeth 1584–5', ed. Bishop Lyttleton, *Archaeologia*, 1 (1770), 9–12.

78. Sandys, *Christmastide*, 133–4; Pepys, Diary, iv. 57; *British Calendar Customs: Scotland*, ii. 104.

79. Jonson, 'Christmas His Masque', 440.

80. *The Dairy of Samuel Newton*, ed. J. R. Foster (Cambridge Antiquarian Society, 1890), 7–8

81. Pepys, *Diary*, v. 1, ix. 405.

82. Bourne, *Antiquitates Vulgares*, 142–5.

83. Plimlott, *Englishman's Christmas*, 74–6; Malcolmson, *Popular Recreations*, 27.

84. e.g. John Brady, *Clavis Calendria* (1812), i. 143; Robert Chambers, *The Book of Days* (1864), 31.

85. John Ashton, *A Righte Merrie Christmasse* (n.d.), 201–4; Fisher, *Christian Caveat*, 10.

86. Ashton, *Merrie Christmasse*, 203–4; Pepys, *Diary*, viii. 589.

87. Plimlott, *Englishman's Christmas*, 72–3.

88. Newton, *Diary*, 7–8.

89. *The Household Account Book of Sarah Fell*, ed. Norman Penney (Cambridge, 1920), 25–6, 167–8, 239.

90. Plimlott, *Englishman's Christmas*, 75–6, 120–2.

CHAPTER 3

1. *Statutes of the Realm* (1819), IV. i. 132–3.

2. In the Prayer Book of 1559 and the calendar of feasts of 1560.

3. Ian B. Cowan, *The Scottish Reformation* (1982), 155.

4. Ibid. 155–6.

5. Ibid. 155–6.

6. F. Marian McNeill, *The Silver Bough* (Glasgow, 1961), ii. 59; *British Calendar Customs: Scotland*, ed. Mary Macleod Banks, iii (Folk-Lore Society, 1941), 234, 238; Anna Jean Mill, *Medieval Plays in Scotland* (Edinburgh, 1927), 162.

7. McNeill, *Silver Bough*, ii. 59, *British Calendar Customs: Scotland*, iii. 239–40; Mill, *Medieval Plays*, 243, 245, 253.

8. Mill, *Medieval Plays*, 163–5, 238–40, 245.

9. *British Calendar Customs: Scotland*, iii. 234–5.

10. For the most recent discussion of James's policy, see Julian Goodare, 'Scotland', in Bob Scribner, Roy Porter, and Mikuláš Teich (eds.), *The Reformation in National Context* (Cambridge, 1994), ch. 6.

11. Mill, *Medieval Plays*, 242.

12. McNeill, *Silver Bough*, 59; *British Calendar Customs: Scotland*, iii. 239, 242.

13. For examples from Elgin, Culross, Slains, and St Andrews, *see British Calendar Customs: Scotland*, iii. 226, 241–2.

14. Ibid. iii. 226, 241.

15. William Harrison, *The Description of England*, ed. Georges Edelen (Ithaca, NY, 1968), 36; Henry Burton, *A Tryall of Private Devotions* (1628), *passim*; William Prynne, *Histrio-Mastix* (1632), 233–63.

16. 'Christmas His Masque.'

17. *The Records of a Church of Christ in Bristol*, ed. Roger Hayden (Bristol Record Society, 1974), 85.

18. W. H. Summers, 'Some Documents in the State Papers Relating to Beaconsfield', *Records of Bucks.*, 7 (1897), 98–9, 108.

19. W. Mepham, 'Essex Drama under Puritanism and the Commonwealth', *Essex Review*, 58 (1949), 181.

20. Conrad Russell, *The Fall of the British Monarchies 1637–1642* (Oxford, 1991), 183–4.

21. Ibid.

22. 'Lords of Misrule', *History Today* (Dec. 1985), 7–20.

23. Ronald Hutton, *The Rise and Fall of Merry England* (Oxford, 1994), ch. 6.

24. Durston, 'Lords of Misrule', 7–13; Hutton, *Merry England*, 207–9, 215.

25. *Minutes of the Westminster Assembly of Divines*, ed. A. F. Mitchell and John Struthers (Edinburgh, 1874), 3–11.

26. *Acts and Ordinances of the Interregnum*, ed. C. H. Firth and R. S. Rait (1911), i. 598–606, 854.

27. Hutton, *Merry England*, 215.

28. Durston, 'Lords of Misrule', 14; Alan Everitt, *The Community of Kent and the Great Rebellion* (Leicester, 1966), 231–4; Hutton, *Merry England*, 210–11.

29. Hutton, *Merry England*, 213–25.

30. *The Kingdomes Weekly Intelligencer* (14–21 Dec. 1647 and 21–8 Dec. 1647).

31. Hutton, *Merry England*, 215–16.

32. D. Roy Saer, 'The Christmas Carol-Singing Tradition in the Valley', *Folk Life*, 7 (1969), 15.

33. Hutton, *Merry England*, 217.

34. Durston, 'Lords of Misrule', 19.

35. *British Calendar Customs: Scotland*, iii. 240.

36. McNeill, *Silver Bough*, iii. 73.

37. James R. Nicolson, *Shetland Folklore* (1981), 145–7.

38. Ibid. 146; *British Calendar Customs: Scotland*, iii. 206–9.

39. *British Calendar Customs: Scotland*, iii. 223.

40. William Grant Stewart, *The Popular Superstitions and Festive Amusements of the Highlanders of Scotland* (Edinburgh, 1823), 241–4.

41. Walter Gregor, *Notes on the Folk-Lore of the North-East of Scotland* (Folk-Lore Society, 1881), 156–6; Sir John Sinclair, *The Statistical Account of Scotland*, v (1793), 48.

42. *British Calendar Customs: Scotland*, iii. 226.

43. Robert Chambers, *The Book of Days* (1864), 28–9.

44. William Hone, *The Every-Day Book and Table Book* (1832), i. 21.

45. For the general background to this, see Hugh Trevor-Roper, 'The Invention of Tradition: The Highland Tradition of Scotland', in Eric Hobsbawm and Terence Ranger (eds.), *The Invention of Tradition* (Cambridge, 1983), ch. 2.

46. *The Oxford English Dictionary*, 2nd edn. (1989) vii. 290.

47. Ibid.

CHAPTER 4

1. Alexander Tille, *Yule and Christmas* (1889), 103; John Brand, *Observations on the Popular Antiquities of Great Britain*, ed. Sir Henry Ellis (1908), i. 519–20.

2. Ronald Hutton, *The Pagan Religions of the Ancient British Isles* (Oxford, 1991), 271–2, 274, 279, 337.

3. For this and the above, Ronald Hutton, *The Rise and Fall of Merry England* (Oxford, 1994), 5–6.

4. Richard Leighton Greene, *The Early English Carols* (Oxford, 1935), p. xcix.

5. Hutton, *Merry England*, 6.

6. Ibid. 88, 100–1, 120.

7. *St Martin in the Fields: The Accounts of Churchwardens*, ed. John V. Kitto (1901), 185 ff.; Westminster Public L. St Margaret, Westminster, E5–E6.

8. Albert Feuillerat, *Documents Relating to the Office of the Revels in the Time of Queen Elizabeth* (Materialien zur Kunde des Älteren Englischer Dramas; 1908), *passim*.

9. Hutton, *Merry England*, 174–5, 182.

10. *The Poetry of George Wither*, ed. Frank Sidgwick (1902), 178.

11. John Parkinson, *Paradisi in Sole, Paradisus Terrestris* (1629), 606.

12. *The Poems of Robert Herrick*, ed. L. C. Martin (Oxford, 1965), 285.

13. Coles, *Knowledge of Plants*, quoted in T. F. Thiselton Dyer, *British Popular Customs* (1876), 459.

14. 'Old Christmas Returned', in *The Pepys Ballads*, ed. Hyder Edward Rollins (Cambridge, Mass., 1929–32), iii. 51.

15. John Aubrey, *Remaines of Gentilisme and Judaisme*, ed. James Britten (Folk-Lore Society, 1881), 89.

16. *Round About our Coal Fire*, quoted in Dyer, *British Popular Customs*, 459.

17. Hutton, *Merry England*, 214, 342.

18. Quoted in T. G. Crippen, *Christmas and Christmas Lore* (1923), 26.

19. R. P. Chope, '31st Report on Devonshire Folk-Lore', *Transactions of the Devonshire Association*, 63 (1931), 134; T. Brown, '51st Report', Ibid. 86 (1954), 298–9; John Nicholson, *Folk Lore of East Yorkshire* (1890), 19–20; P. H. Ditchfield, *Old English Customs Extant at the Present Time* (1896), 18; Mrs Gutch and Mabel Peacock (eds.), *County Folk-Lore*, v. *Lincolnshire* (Folk-Lore Society, 1908), 218–19; Ella Mary Leather, *The Folk-Lore of Herefordshire* (Hereford, 1912), 91–3; Mabel Peacock, 'The Calenig, or Gift', *Folk-Lore*, 13 (1902), 202–3; M. A. Courtney, *Cornish Feasts and Folklore* (1890), 7; Thomas Ratcliffe, 'A Derbyshire Christmas Kissing Bunch', *Notes and Queries*, 8th ser. 2 (1892), 506–7; William Hone, *The Every-Day Book and Table Book* (1832), i. 1629–30; J. M. Golby and A. W. Purdue, *The Making of the Modern Christmas* (1896), 63.

20. Peter Roberts, *The Cambrian Popular Antiquities* (1815), 132.

21. For a sample spanning the years 1672–1801, see Frederick William Hackwood, *Staffordshire Customs, Superstitions and Folklore* (Lichfield, 1924), 49.

22. A. Clark, 'Some Wiltshire Folk-Lore', *Wiltshire Notes and Queries*, 1 (1893–5), 151.

23. Kevin Danaher, *The Year in Ireland* (Cork, 1972), 264; Sidney Oldall Addy, *Household Tales with other Traditional Remains* (1895), 106; Marie Trevelyan, *Folk-Lore and Folk-Stories of Wales* (1909), 30; Charlotte Sophia Burne, *Shropshire Folk-Lore* (Hertford, 1922), 397.

24. T. Brown, '52nd Report', *Transactions of the Devon Association*, 87 (1955), 355; Leather, *Herefordshire*, 91–3; Burne, *Shropshire*, 397–8.

25. A. R. Wright, *British Calendar Customs*, ed. T. E. Lones (Folk-Lore Society, 1936), i. 10.

26. Cuthbert Bede, 'Mistletoe Superstition', *Notes and Queries*, 2nd ser. 3: 343.

27. Danaher, *Year in Ireland*, 234.

28. *British Calendar Customs: Scotland*, ed. Mary Macleod Banks, i. (Folk-Lore Society, 1937), ii (1939), 28; and iii (1941), 217.

29. Henry Bourne, *Antiquitates Vulgares* (Newcastle upon Tyne, 1725), 126–7.

30. R. T. Hampson, *Medii Aevi Kalendarium* (1841), 90; John Nicholson, *Folk Lore of East Yorkshire* (1890), 18; James R. Nicolson, *Shetland Folklore* (1981), 147; Clement A. Miles, *Christmas in Ritual and Tradition* (1912), 351–60; Brand, *Observations*, i. 467; William Brockie, *Legends and Superstitions of the County of Durham* (Sunderland, 1886), 97; 'Christmas Candles', *Folk-Lore*, 28 (1917), 106–7; Wright, *British Calendar Customs* i. 212, 215; Courtney, *Cornish Feasts*, 7; *British Calendar Customs: Scotland*, iii. 218.

31. Brand, *Observations*, i. 467–8; Danaher, *Year in Ireland*, 235; R. L. Tongue, *Somerset Folkore*, ed. K. M. Briggs (Folk-Lore Society County Folklore, 8; viii; 1965), 176–7; Brockie, *Durham*, 97; Addy, *Household Tales*, 103–4; John Nicolson, *Folk-Lore of East Yorkshire* (1890), 18; Roberts, *Cambrian Popular Antiquities*, 132; Mrs Gutch (ed.), *County Folk-Lore*, vi. *East Riding of Yorkshire* (Folk-Lore Society, 1912), 114; Mrs Gutch (ed.), *County Folk-Lore*, ii. *North Riding of Yorkshire, York, and the Ainsty* (Folk-Lore Society, 1901), 273; Northcote W. Thomas (ed.), *County Folk-Lore*, iv. *Northumberland* (Folk-Lore Society, 1904), 79; Mrs Gutch (ed.), *County Folk-Lore*, v 216–19; Dyer, *British Popular Customs*, 446; Trefor M. Owen, *Welsh Folk Customs* (St Fagans, 1974), 34, 47–8; Llewellynn Jewitt, 'On Ancient Customs and Sports of the County of Nottingham', *Journal of the British Archaeological Association* 1st ser. 8 (1853), 237; Burne, *Shropshire*, 397; Leather, *Herefordshire*, 109; Thomas Sternberg, *The Dialect and Folk-Lore of Northamptonshire* (1851), 186; James Britten, 'Warwickshire Customs, 1759–60', *Folk-Lore Journal*, 1 (1883), 352; F. Marian McNeill, *The Silver Bough*, iii (Glasgow, 1961), 72–3; J. B. Partridge, 'Folklore from Yorkshire (North Riding)', *Folk-Lore*, 25 (1914), 376; Wright, *British Calendar Customs*, i. 210–12, 234; Courtney, *Cornish Feasts*, 7; *British Calendar Customs: Scotland*, iii. 208–9, 217–18; Jacqueline Simpson, *The Folklore of the Welsh Border* (1976), 173; BL Add. MS 41313, fo. 84 (letter from Cornworthy, Devon, 1806); George Morley, *Shakespeare's Greenwood* (1900), 142.

32. Herrick, *Poems*, 263, 285.

33. BL Add. MS 41313, fo. 84.

34. Aubrey, *Miscellanies*, 5.

35. Bourne, *Antiquitates Vulgares*, 126–7.

36. J. G. Frazer, *Balder the Beautiful* (1914), i. 247–58.

37. Alexander Tille, *Yule and Christmas* (1889), 92–3.

38. Frazer, *Balder*, i. 247–9; E. O. James, *Seasonal Feasts and Festivals* (1961), 294–5.

39. C. W. von Sydow, 'The Mannhardtian Theories about the Last Sheaf and the Fertility Demons from a modern critical point of view', *Folk-Lore*, 45 (1934), 299.

40. Sources at n. 31.

41. Tongue, *Somerset Folklore*, 176–7.

42. Owen, *Welsh Folk Customs*, 47–8.

43. Addy, *Household Tales*, 103–4.

44. *British Calendar Customs: Scotland*, iii. 205–6, 217–18.

45. Courtney, *Cornish Feasts*, 7.

46. Kingsley Palmer, *The Folklore of Somerset* (1976), 96; R. P. Chope, 'Devonshire Calendar Customs. Part II. Fixed Festivals', *Transactions of the Devonshire Association*, 70 (1938), 345; Tongue, *Somerset*, 153; Dyer, *British Popular Customs*, 446–7; Wright, *British Calendar Customs*, i. 214; Peter Robson, 'Calendar Customs in Nineteenth and Twentieth Century Dorset' (Sheffield M.Phil. thesis, 1988), 24–5.

47. Romaine Joseph Thorn, 1795, quoted in Brand, *Observations*, i. 470; and Robert Studley Vidal, 1806, in BL Add. MS 41313, fo. 84ᵛ.

48. T. Brown, '48th Report on Folklore', *Transactions of the Devonshire Association*, 83 (1951), 75, and '67th Report', ibid. 102 (1970), 270.

CHAPTER 5

1. James R. Nicolson, *Shetland Folklore* (1981), 145–7.
2. *A Tour in Scotland* (1769), i. III.
3. F. Marian McNeill, *The Silver Bough* iii (Glasgow, 1961), 113; *British Calendar Customs: Scotland*, ed. Mary Macleod Banks, ii (Folk-Lore Society, 1939), 95–7; T. F. Thiselton Dyer, *British Popular Customs* (1876); Walter Gregor, *Notes on the Folk-Lore of the North-East of Scotland* (Folk-Lore Society, 1881), 159.
4. *British Calendar Customs: Scotland*, ii. 35–7.
5. E. J. Guthrie, *Old Scottish Customs* (1885), 233.
6. McNeill, *Silver Bough*, iv. 224–5.
7. Venetia Newall, 'The Allendale Fire Festival in Relation to its Contemporary Social Setting', *Folklore*, 85 (1974), 93–103.
8. Venetia Newall, 'Up-Helly Aa: A Shetland Fire Festival', in Theresa Buckland and Juliette Wood (eds.), *Aspects of British Calendar Customs* (Folklore Society Mistletoe Series, 22; Sheffield, 1993), 57–74.
9. *British Calendar Customs: Scotland*, ii. 37–40, 95; McNeill, *Silver Bough*, iii. 100, 226; Dyer, *British Popular Customs*, 506–7.
10. Joseph Train, *An Historical and Statistical Account of the Isle of Man* (Douglas, 1845), ii. 124.
11. *Johnson and Boswell in Scotland*, ed. Pat Rogers (New Haven, 1993), 237–9.
12. John Ramsay, *Scotland and Scotsmen in the Eighteenth Century*, ed. Alexander Allardyce (Edinburgh, 1888), ii. 438–9.
13. Alexander Carmichael, *Carmina Gadelica* (Edinburgh, 1900), i. 149.
14. Hector MacIver, quoted in McNeill, *Silver Bough*, iii. 94.
15. Margaret Fay Shaw, *Folksongs and Folklore of South Uist* (1955), 13, 25–7.
16. J. G. Campbell, *Witchcraft and Second Sight in the Highlands and Islands of Scotland* (Glasgow, 1902), 230–2.
17. *British Calendar Customs: Scotland*, ii. 59–66.
18. J. G. Frazer, *The Golden Bough* (1890), i. 145–6, and *Spirits of the Corn and of the Wild* (1914), ii. 322–4.
19. I owe this reference to Dr James Gibson, who will be publishing it in his edition of the *Records of Early English Drama* for Kent.
20. *The Poems of Robert Herrick*, ed. L. C. Martin (Oxford, 1965), 264.
21. F. Sawyer, 'Sussex Folklore', *Sussex Archaeological Collections*, 33 (1883), 256; R. W. Blencowe, 'Extracts from the Journal and Account Book of the Rev. Giles Moore', ibid. i, (1850), 72–3.
22. John Aubrey, *Remaines of Gentilisme and Judaisme*, ed. James Britten (Folk-Lore Society, 1881), 40.
23. Quoted in John Brand, *Observations on the Popular Antiquities of Great Britain*, ed. Sir Henry Ellis (1908), i. 28–9, and R. P. Chope, 'Devonshire Calendar Customs. Part II. Fixed Festivals.', *Transactions of the Devon Association*, 70 (1938), 353.
24. BL Add. MS 41313, fo. 85 (Robert Studley Vidal to John Brand).
25. Anna Eliza Bray, *A Description of the Part of Devonshire bordering on the Tamar and Tavy* (1836), i. 335; F. Sawyer, 'Sussex Folklore and Customs Connected with the Seasons', *Sussex Archaeological Collections*, 33 (1883), 254; Robert Hunt, *Popular Romances of the West of England* (1881), 38; P. H. Ditchfield, *Old English Customs Extant*

at the Present Time (1896), 47; A. R. Wright, *British Calendar Customs*, ed. T. E. Lones (Folk-Lore Society, 1936), ii. 64–7, 236–7, 287; Peter Robson, 'Calendar Customs in Nineteenth and Twentieth Century Dorset' (Sheffield M.Phil. thesis, 1988), 22–4; M. A. Courtney, *Cornish Feasts and Folklore* (1890), 9–10; Jacqueline Simpson, *The Folklore of Sussex* (1973), 102–3.

26. Robson, 'Calendar Customs', 22–4.

27. R. P. Chope, '31st Report on Devonshire Folk-Lore', *Transactions of the Devonshire Association*, 63 (1931), 131.

28. Wright, British Calendar Customs, i. 35.

29. Sources at nn. 25 and 27, plus Brand, *Observations*, i. 29; R. L. Tongue, *Somerset Folklore*, ed. K. M. Briggs (Folklore Society County Folklore, 8; 1965), 176; *Illustrated London News* (12 Jan. 1860); 12. J. Rendel Harris, 'The Origin and Meaning of Apple Cults', *Bulletin of the John Rylands Library*, 5 (1918–19), 29–74; Ralph Whitlock, *The Folklore of Devon* (1977), 135–7; F. W. Mathews, *Tales of the Blackdown Borderland* (Somerset Folk Series, 13; 1923), 120–9; W. G. Willis-Watson, *Calendar of Customs... Connected with the County of Somerset* (Taunton, 1920), 24–30; R. W. B., 'Wassailing Orchards in Sussex', *Notes and Queries*, 1st ser. 5 293.

30. Simpson, *Sussex*, 102–3.

31. Bob Pegg, *Rites and Riots: Folk Customs of Britain and Europe* (Poole, 1981), 15–17.

32. T. Brown, '51st Report on Folklore', *Transactions of the Devonshire Association* 86 (1954), 299; T. Brown, '54th Report', ibid. 89 (1957), 84–5; T. Brown, '71st Report', ibid. 106 (1974), 266.

33. Ella Mary Leather, *The Folk-Lore of Herefordshire* (Hereford, 1912), 93.

34. Thomas Pennant, *A Tour in Scotland* (1776), i. III.

35. Brand, *Observations*, i. 30.

36. Sources at nn. 33–4, plus Brand, Observations, i. 238, 33; L. M. Eyre, 'Folklore Notes from St. Brivael's', *Folk-Lore*, 13 (1902), 174; Leather, *Herefordshire*, 93–5; John Noake, *Notes and Queries for Worcestershire* (1856), 220; Thomas Hyde, *Historia Religionis Veterum Persarum* (Oxford, 1700), 257; Jacqueline Simpson, *The Folklore of the Welsh Border* (1976), 135; Wright, *British Calendar Customs*, i. 85.

37. Information collected from Mrs Spurway, of Linton, Herefordshire, 1984.

38. Wright, *British Calendar Customs*, i. 85.

39. Aubrey, *Remaines*, 9, 40.

40. Marie Trevelyan, *Folk-Lore and Folk-Stories of Wales* (1909), 29.

41. Bushaway, *By Rite*, 157–8; 'Scraps of English Folklore', *Folk-Lore*, 39 (1928), 387.

42. Wright, *British Calendar Customs*, i. 237; Simpson, *Sussex*, 104; Doris Jones-Baker, *The Folklore of Hertfordshire* (1977), 123.

43. E. Estyn Evans, *Irish Folk Ways* (1957), 280.

44. Joseph Train, *An Historical and Statistical Account of the Isle of Man* (Douglas, 1845), ii. 115.

45. J. Weld, *A History of Leagram* (Chetham Society, 1913), 134; David Clark, *Between Pulpit and Pew* (Cambridge, 1982), 92–3; Tongue, *Somerset*, 152; William Brockie, *Legends and Superstitions of the County of Durham* (Sunderland, 1886), 96–7; John Nicholson, *Folk Lore of East Yorkshire* (1890), 19; Mrs Gutch (ed.), *County Folk-Lore*, ii. *North Riding of Yorkshire, York and the Ainsty* (Folk-Lore Society, 1901), 230–1; Mrs Gutch (ed.), *County Folk-Lore*, vi. *East Riding of Yorkshire* (Folk-Lore, Society, 1912), 85–6; *County Folk-Lore*, ii. 3. *Leicestershire and Rutland*, ed. Charles J. Billson (Folk-Lore Society, 1895), 70; Northcore W. Thomas (ed.) – , *County Folk-Lore*, iv. *Northumberland* (Folk-Lore Society, 1904), 63–4; Mrs Gutch and Mabel Peacock (eds.), *County Folk-Lore*, v. *Lincolnshire* (Folk-Lore Society, 1908), 169; William Henderson,

Notes on the Folk-Lore of the Northern Counties of England and the Borders (Folk-Lore Society, 1879), 73; T. F. Thiselton Dyer, *British Popular Customs* (1876), 7; Frederick William Hackwood, *Staffordshire Customs, Superstitions and Folklore* (Lichfield, 1924), 3; Leather, *Herefordshire*, 90; John Rhys and T. W. E. Higgens, '"First Foot" in the British Isles', *Folk-Lore*, 3 (1892), 253–71; G. Hastie, 'First-Footing in Edinburgh', *Folk-Lore*, 4 (1893), 309–14; James E. Crombie, 'First-Footing in Aberdeenshire', *Folk-Lore*, 4 (1893), 315–21; E. S. Thompson, 'First Foot in Lancashire', *Folk-Lore*, 11 (1900), 220; Trefor M. Owen, *Welsh Folk Customs* (Cardiff, 1974), 42; John Harland and T. T. Wilkinson, *Lancashire Folk-Lore* (1807), 214; Llewellyn Jewitt, 'On Ancient Customs and Sports of the County of Nottingham', *Journal of the British Archaeological Association*, 1st ser. 8 (1853), 231; L. M. Eyre, 'Folklore Notes from St Brivael's', *Folk-Lore*, 13 (1902), 174; Charlotte Sophia Burne, *Shropshire Folk-Lore* (1883), 314–15; Edward W. B. Nicholson, *Golspie* (1897), 100–3; Ethel H. Rudkin, 'Lincolnshire Folklore', *Folk-Lore*, 44 (1933), 281; Wright, *British Calendar Customs*, ii. 2–15; Hunt, *Popular Romances*, 382; *British Calendar Customs: Scotland*, ii. 76–89; Iona and Peter Opie, *The Lore and Language of Schoolchildren* (Oxford, 1959), 291–2; Roy Palmer, *The Folklore of Warwickshire* (1976), 155; Simpson, *Welsh Border*, 132–3.

46. Clark, *Between Pulpit and Pew*, 92–3.

47. Burne, *Shropshire*, 314–15.

48. Owen, *Welsh Folk Customs*, 42.

49. J. B. Partridge, 'Cotswold Place-Lore and Customs', *Folk-Lore*, 23 (1912), 443.

50. Henderson, *Folk-Lore*, 72–3.

51. Mrs Gutch (ed.), *Lincolnshire*, 169.

52. Mrs Gutch (ed.), *North Riding*, 231.

53. *British Calendar Customs: Scotland*, ii. 86–9; Rhys and Higgens, 'First Foot', 270–1.

54. Wright, *British Calendar Customs*, ii. 15.

55. Ruskin, 'Folklore', 281; Hunt, *Popular Romances*, 382; Hackwood, *Staffordshire*, 3.

56. Palmer, *Warwickshire*, 155.

57. Brockie, *Durham*, 96–7.

58. Clark, *Between Pulpit and Pew*, 92–3.

59. Wright, *British Calendar Customs*, ii. 9–10, 15; Opie and Opie, *Lore and Language*, 291–2; Crombie, 'First-Footing in Aberdeenshire', 315–21; Hastie, 'First-Footing in Edinburgh', 309–14.

60. Opie and Opie, *Lore and Language*, 291.

61. I personally knew several families who observed it in the London area during the 1960s.

62. Thompson, 'First Foot', 220; Harland and Wilkinson, *Lancashire*, 214.

63. Wright, *British Calendar Customs*, ii. 9–10.

64. Hastie, 'First-Footing', 310–13.

65. *British Calendar Customs: Scotland*, ii. 95–7.

66. *The Athenaeum* (5 Feb. 1848); Jonathan Ceredig Davies, *Folk-Lore of West and Mid-Wales* (Aberystwyth, 1911), 65; Owen, *Welsh Folk Customs*, 43; M. S. Clark, 'Pembrokeshire Notes', *Folk-Lore*, 15 (1904), 194–8; Opie and Opie, *Lore and Language*, 234.

67. Henderson, *Folk-Lore*, 72; Hackwood, *Staffordshire*, 3; Harland and Wilkinson, *Lancashire*, 214; Burne, *Shropshire*, 400; James Napier, *Folk Lore: Or, Superstitious Beliefs in the West of Scotland* (Paisley, 1879), 159.

CHAPTER 6

1. Bob Bushaway, *By Rite* (1982), 248–9.

2. Jacqueline Simpson, *The Folklore of Sussex* (1973), 131–3.

3. Ella Mary Leather, *The Folklore of Herefordshire* (Hereford, 1912), 106–7.

4. Robert Plot, *The Natural History of Staffordshire* (Oxford, 1686), 430.

5. C. S. Burne, 'Staffordshire Folk and their Lore', *Folk-Lore*, 7 (1896), 374.

6. Wirt Sikes, *British Goblins* (1880), 284–5.

7. G. P. G. Hills, 'Notes on some Blacksmiths' Legends', *Papers and Proceedings of the Hampshire Field Club*, 8 (1917–19), 65; F. Sawyer, 'Sussex Folklore and Customs Connected with the Seasons', *Sussex Archaeological Collections*, 33 (1883), 252, and '"Old Clem" Celebrations and Blacksmiths Lore', *Folk-Lore Journal*, 2 (1884), 321–9; Simpson, *Sussex*, 138.

8. Hill, 'Notes', 71.

9. Ibid. 69–70; John Brand, *Observations on the Popular Antiquities of Great Britain*, ed. Sir Henry Ellis (1908), i. 408–9; Bushaway, *By Rite*, 186; E. P. Thompson, *Customs in Common* (1991), 5.

10. T. F. Thiselton Dyer, *British Popular Customs* (1876), 426–8.

11. Ibid. 427–8; A. R. Wright, *British Calendar Customs*, ed. T. E. Lones (Folk-Lore Society, 1936), ii. 178–9; Doris Jones-Baker, *The Folklore of Hertfordshire* (1977), 168–70.

12. Dyer, *British Popular Customs*, 430; Thomas Sternberg, *The Dialect and Folk-Lore of Northamptonshire* (1851), 183; Bushaway, *By Rite*, 187.

13. Dyer, *British Popular Customs*, 425; G. F. Northall, *English Folk-Rhymes* (1892), 222–3.

14. J. Langford, 'Warwickshire Folk-Lore and Superstitions', *Transactions of the Birmingham and Midland Institute Archaeological Section* (1875), 21; Roy Palmer, *The Folklore of Warwickshire* (1976), 158–9.

15. Charlotte S. Burne, 'Souling, Clementing, and Catterning', *Folk-Lore*, 25 (1914), 285–94; Wright, *British Calendar Customs*, i. 168–72; *County Folk-Lore*, i (Folk-Lore Society, 1895), 3. Leicestershire and Rutland, ed. Charles J. Billson, 95; *Folklore*, 77 (1966), 141.

16. Burne, 'Souling, Clementing, and Catterning', 285–7, 294–5.

17. Wright, *British Calendar Customs*, i. 173, 180–5.

18. For other examples, see Northall, *English Folk-Rhymes*, 225–8.

19. Simpson, *Sussex*, 140–1; Sawyer, 'Old Clem', 321–9.

20. C. T. Lawley, *The Midland Weekly News Supplement* (21 July 1894), p.1, col. 5.

21. Palmer, *Warwickshire*, 169–70.

22. Ruth Tongue, *Somerset Folklore*, ed. K. M. Briggs (Folklore Society County Folklore, 8; 1965), 173.

23. Charlotte Sophia Burne, *Shropshire Folk-Lore* (1883), 392–3.

24. P. H. Ditchfield, *Old English Customs Extant at the Present Time* (1896), 25–7.

25. Sources at nn. 20–4 above; R. T. Hampson, *Medii Aevi Kalendarium* (1841), 83; Sawyer, Sussex Folk-'Lore', Brand, *Observations*, i. 455–7; William Hone, *The Every-Day Book and Table Book* (1832), i. 253; 1587; Enid Porter, *Cambridgeshire Customs and Folklore* (1969), 126; Leather, *Herefordshire*, 108; John Symonds Udal, *Dorsetshire Folk-Lore* (Hertford, 1922), 49; W. B. Gerish, *The Folk-Lore of Hertfordshire* (Bishops Stortford, 1911), 6; John Noake, *Notes and Queries for Worcestershire* (1856), 215–16; J. B. Partridge, 'Cotswold Place-Lore and Customs', *Folk-Lore*, 23 (1912), 455; 'Scraps of English Folklore', *Folk-Lore*, 24 (1913), 237; Bruce McWilliams, 'Begging on St Thomas's Day', *Folk-Lore*, 28 (1917), 450; Ethel H. Rudkin, 'Lincolnshire Folklore', *Folk-Lore*, 44 (1933), 287–8; Wright, *British Calendar Customs*, i. 200–7; M. A. Courtney, *Cornish Feasts and Folklore* (1890), 6; Jones-Baker, *Hertfordshire*, 171–9; Simpson, *Sussex*, 220; James Obelkevitch, *Religion and Rural Society: South Lindsey 1825–1875* (Oxford, 1976), 269; Bushaway, *By Rite*, 187–8; BL Add. MS 24544, p. 350 (note concerning Sheffield).

26. Udal, *Dorsetshire*, 49; Peter Robson, 'Calendar Customs in Nineteenth and Twentieth Century Dorset' (Sheffield M.Phil. thesis, 1988), 130–1; L. M. Eyre, 'Folklore Notes from St Brivael's', *Folk-Lore*, 13 (1902), 173–4; Frederick William Hackwood, *Staffordshire Customs, Superstitions and Folklore* (Lichfield, 1924), 47; George Morley, *Shakespeare's Greenwood* (1900), 133, 137; Wrighty, *British Calendar Customs*, i. 200–4.

27. Bushaway, *By Rite*, 187–8.

28. Simpson, *Sussex*, 142–3.

29. Burne, *Shropshire*, 392–3.

30. Wright, *British Calendar Customs*, i. 171.

31. Burne, 'Souling, Clementing, and Catterning', 295–7.

32. Bushaway, *By Rite*, 38–44.

33. 'The Household Book of Sir Miles Stapleton, Bt', ed. J. C. Cox, *The Ancestor* (1903), 150–9.

34. Robson, 'Calendar Customs', 132; Michael Pickering, *Village Song and Culture* (1982), 18–49; Mrs Gutch (ed.), *County Folk-Lore*, ii. *North Riding of Yorkshire, York and the Ainsty* (Folk-Lore Society, 1901), 269–70; Porter, *Cambridgeshire*, 127; T. F. Thiselton Dyer, *British Popular Customs* (1876), 465; John Harland and T. T. Wilkinson, *Lancashire Folk-Lore* (1867), 257.

35. Robson, 'Calendar Customs', 132–6; Tony Deane and Tony Shaw, *The Folklore of Cornwall* (1975), 187; A. Clark, 'Some Wiltshire Folk-Lore', *Wiltshire Notes and Queries*, 1 (1893–5), 150–1; Bushaway, *By Rite*, 38; Pickering, *Village Song*, 18–49; Leather, *Herefordshire*, 109; Udal, *Dorsetshire*, 32–3; Sternberg, *Northamptonshire*, 186; Morley, *Shakespeare's Greenwood*, 138–9; 'Scraps of English Folklore', *Folk-Lore*, 36 (1925), 82; Simpson, *Sussex*, 145.

36. Tongue, *Somerset Folklore*, 175.

37. Bushaway, *By Rite*, 159.

38. Kevin Danaher, *The Year in Ireland* (Cork, 1972), 241–3.

39. F. Marian McNeill, *The Silver Bough* (Glasgow, 1961), iii. 88–9; Alexander Carmichael, *Carmina Gadelica* (Edinburgh, 1900), i. 126.

40. Table Talk, quoted in Brand, *Observations*, i. 3.

41. James Britten, 'Warwickshire Customs, 1759–60', *Folk-Lore Journal*, 1 (1883), 352.

42. Hone, *Every-Day Book*, ii, 10–11; Wright, *British Calendar Customs*, i. 286; Llewwllyn Jewitt, 'On Ancient Customs and Sports of the County of Nottingham', *Journal of the British Archaeological Association*, 1st ser. 8 (1853), 230.

43. Brand, *Observations*, i. 7–8.

44. J. Stephens, 'Cornish Wassailing', *Journal of the Royal Institute of Cornwall*, 24 (1933–6), 101–10; Bushaway, *By Rite*, 20; Tongue, *Somerset Folklore*, 176; E. E. Balch, 'In a Wiltshire Village', *Antiquary* NS 4 (1908), 381; Leather, *Herefordshire*, 109–10; Partridge, 'Cotswold Place-Lore', 465–6; Wright, *British Calendar Customs*, i. 237, 284–6; Robson, 'Calendar Customs', 153–4.

45. *The Oxford Book of Carols*, ed. Percy Dearmer, Ralph Vaughan Williams, and Martin Shaw (Oxford, 1928), 37.

46. e.g. ibid. 38 (from Somerset); Roy Palmer, *The English Country Songbook* (Dent, 1979), 217–18 (from Somerset); Stephens, 'Cornish Wassailing', 106–11; Elizabeth Lamb, 'Cornish Wassailing Today', *English Dance and Song* (Winter, 1971), 132–3.

47. Ditchfield, *Old English Customs*, 43–4; Wright, *British Calendar Customs*, i. 32, 87; Northall, *English Folk-Rhymes*, 229; Palmer, *Warwickshire*, 171–2.

48. Sources at n. 44.

49. Brand, *Observations*, i. 6.

50. Sidney Oldall Addy, *Household Tales with Other Traditional Remains* (1895), 103; Hackwood, *Staffordshire Customs*, 4; Wright, *British Calendar Customs*, i. 194, 237–8; Simpson, *Sussex*, 149.

51. William Howells, *Cambrian Superstitions* (1831), 181.

52. Trefor M. Owen, *Welsh Folk Customs* (St Fagans, 1974), 58.

53. Ibid. 61; 'Gloucestershire Songs', *Folk Song Society Journal*, 8 (1927–31), 231–2; T. Gwynn Jones, *Welsh Folklore and Folk-Custom* (Cambridge, 1979), 159; Jonathan Ceredig Davies, *Folk-Lore of West and Mid-Wales* (Aberystwyth, 1911), 67.

54. John Nicholson, *Folk-Lore of East Yorkshire* (1890), 17; Addy, *Household Tales*, 108–10; Ditchfield, *Old English Customs*, 16; William Henderson, *Notes on the Folk-Lore of the Northern Counties of England and the Borders* (Folk-Lore Society, 1879), 65–6; Mrs Gutch (ed.), *County Folk-Lore*, ii. 273; Mrs Gutch (ed.), *County Folk-Lore*, vi. 273; Jewitt, 'Ancient Customs', 238; E. Wright, 'A Yorkshire "Wassail Box" ', *Folk-Lore*, 17 (1906), 349–51; Wright, *British Calendar Customs*, i. 239–41.

55. Stephens, 'Cornish Wassailling', 110.

56. Brand, *Observations*, i. 14, 457–8; Mrs Gutch (ed.), *County Folk-Lore*, ii. 281–3; Northcote W. Thomas (ed.), *County Folk-Lore*, iv. *Northumberland* (Folk-Lore Society, 1904), 88; Dyer, *British Popular Customs*, 505; Northall, *English Folk-Rhymes*, 181–2; Henderson, *Folk-Lore*, 177; Walter Gregor, *Notes on the Folk-Lore of the North-East of Scotland* (Folk-Lore Society, 1881), 161–2; Iona and Peter Opie, *The Lore and Language of Schoolchildren* (Oxford, 1959), 290; *British Calendar Customs: Scotland*, ed. Mary Macleod Banks, ii (Folk-Lore Society, 1939), 443.

57. Maria J. MacCulloch, 'Folk-Lore of the Isle of Skye', *Folk-Lore*, 34 (1923), 88–90; *British Calendar Customs: Scotland*, ii. 47.

58. Alexander Carmichael, *Carmina Gadelica* (Edinburgh, 1900), 157–9; Allan McDonald, *Gaelic Words and Expressions from South Uist and Eriskay*, ed. J. L. K. Campbell (Dublin, 1958), 61; F. Marian McNeill, *The Silver Bough* (Glasgow, 1961), iii. 94; *British Calendar Customs: Scotland*, ii. 50–1, 56–7.

59. Ernest W. Marwick, *The Folklore of Orkney and Shetland* (1975), 102–3; Dyer, *British Popular Customs*, 19; James R. Nicolson, *Shetland Folklore* (1981), 148; Brand, *Observations*, i. 9.

60. Joseph Train, *An Historical and Statistical Account of the Isle of Man* (Douglas, 1845), ii. 114–15.

61. Jones, *Welsh Folklore*, 157; Davies, *Folk-Lore*, 63–4; R. Williams, 'History of the Parish of Llanbrynmair', *Montgomeryshire Collections*, 22 (1888), 321.

62. Opie and Opie, *Lore and Language*, 234.

63. Sykes, *British Goblins*, 252–6; Eyre, 'St Brivael's', 174; F. W. Baty, *Forest of Dean* (1952), 27; Owen, *Welsh Folk Customs*, 44–5; Leather, *Herefordshire*, 90.

64. Jewitt, 'Ancient Customs', 231.

65. Dyer, *British Popular Customs*, 7. See also Langford, 'Warwickshire Folk-Lore', 21; Henderson, *Folk-Lore*, 75; Burne, *Shropshire*, 317; 'Yorkshire Custom', *Folk-Lore Journal*, 5 (1887), 74–5; Noake, *Notes and Queries*, 220–1; Morley, *Shakespeare's Greenwood*, 146; Michael M. Rix, 'More Shropshire Folk-Lore', *Folk-Lore*, 71 (1960), 185; Wright, *British Calendar Customs*, i. 35; *British Calendar Customs: Scotland*, ii. 56–7; Opie and Opie, *Lore and Language*, 233.

66. Jones-Baker, *Hertfordshire*, 178.

67. e.g. Hackwood, *Staffordshire*, 3; David Clark, *Between Pulpit and Pew* (Cambridge, 1982), 93; Lucy E. Broadwood and J. A. Fuller-Mairland (eds.), *English Country Songs* (1893), 14–15; Bushaway, *By Rite*, 159.

68. C. Burne, 'The Collection of English Folk-Lore', *Folk-Lore*, 1 (1890), 321.
69. Brand, *Observations*, i. 7–8.

CHAPTER 7

1. R. J. E. Tiddy, *The Mummers's Play* (Oxford, 1923), 73.
2. E. K. Chambers, *The English Folk-Play* (Oxford, 1933).
3. Ivor Allsop, 'Reminiscences of a Plough Stot', *English Dance and Song*, 39: 3 (1977), 110.
4. Robert W. Malcolmson, *Popular Recreations in English Society 1700–1850* (Cambridge, 1973), 165.
5. 'A Battle amongst the Christmas Mummers', *Roomer*, 1: 1 (1980), 1–2.
6. T. F. Ordish, 'The Morris Dance at Revesby', *Folk-Lore Journal*, 7 (1889), 220–31, and 'Folk Drama', *Folk-Lore*, 2 (1891), 253–71.
7. *The Medieval Stage* (Oxford, 1903), 2 vols.
8. For which see, *inter alia*, Robert Ackerman, *J. G. Frazer: His Life and Work* (Cambridge, 1987); Robert Frazer, *The Making of 'The Golden Bough'* (New York, 1990); Robert Frazer (ed.), *Sir James Frazer and the Literary Imagination* (1990); Joseph Fontenrose, *The Ritual Theory of Myth* (Berkeley, 1971); Edmund R. Leach, 'Golden Bough or Gilded Twig?', *Daedalus* (Spring 1961), 371–87.
9. For criticisms of Chambers's methods, see Georgina Boyes, 'Excellent Examples: The Influence of Exemplar Texts on Traditional Drama Scholarships', *Traditional Drama Studies*, 1 (1985), 21–3; Craig Fees, 'Christmas Mumming in a North Cotswold Town' (Leeds University Ph.D. thesis, 1988), 1–10; Theresa Buckland, 'English Folk Dance Scholarship: An Overview', in Theresa Buckland (ed.), *Traditional Dance* (Crewe, 1982), i. 3–10.
10. Cecil Sharp, *Sword Dances of Northern England. Part I* (1911), *Part II* (1912), *Part III* (1913); A. H. Fox Strangways, *Cecil Sharp* (Oxford, 1933), 100–3.
11. The quotation is from Theodore H. Gaster, *Thepsis: Ritual, Myth and Drama in the Ancient Near East*, 2nd edn. (New York, 1966), 436. See also Arthur Bernard Cook, *Zeus*, (5 vols.; Cambridge, 1914–25); Jane Ellen Harrison, *Themis*, 2nd ed. (New York, 1927); Francis Macdonald Cornford, *The Origin of Attic Comedy* (Garden City, NY, 1914); Arthur Pickard-Cambridge, *Dithyramb, Tragedy and Comedy* (Oxford, 1927); Theodore Gaster's foreword to his edition of Cornford, *Origin of Attic Comedy* (New York, 1961).
12. Alice B. Gomme, 'Mummers' Plays, Some Incidents In', *Folk-Lore*, 41 (1930), 195–8; Maud Karpeles, 'English Folk Dances: Their Survival and Revival', *Folk-Lore*, 43 (1932), 123–43.
13. Chambers, *English Folk-Play*, 225.
14. Violet Alford, *Sword Dance and Drama* (1962), 13–28, 201–16.
15. This is the main theme of Alan Brody, *The English Mummers and their Plays* (Philadelphia, 1969).
16. E. T. Kirby, 'The Origin of the Mummers' Play', *Journal of American Folk-Lore*, 84 (1971), 275–88.
17. Lucille Armstrong, 'Ritual Dances', *Folk Music Journal*, 3: 4 (1978), 297–315; Alex Helm, *The English Mummers' Play* (Folklore Society, 1981).
18. e.g. Rogan Paul Taylor, 'Shamanism, Popular Entertainment, and the Faust Myth' (Lancaster University Ph.D. thesis, 1987), 70–1.
19. Alford, *Sword Dance*, 73–6.
20. E. C. Cawte, Alex Helm, and N. Peacock. *English Ritual Drama: A Geographical Index* (Folk-Lore Society, 1967).

21. Alan Gailey, *Irish Folk Drama* (Cork, 1969).

22. Peter Robson, 'Calendar Customs in Nineteenth and Twentieth Century Dorset' (Sheffield University M.Phil. thesis, 1988), 148–53.

23. Simon Lichman, 'The Gardener's Story and What Came Next: A Contextual Analysis of the Marshfield Paper Boys' Mumming Play' (Pennsylvania University Ph.D. thesis, 1981), 1–2, 213–15.

24. Craig Fees, 'Christmas Mumming in a North Cotswold Town' (Leeds University Ph.D. thesis, 1988), ch. 1.

25. Robson, 'Calendar Customs', 153.

26. Barry James Ward, 'A Functional Approach to English Folk Drama' (Ohio State University Ph.D. thesis, 1972), 30; Boyes, 'Excellent Examples', *passim*.

27. Georgina Smith, 'Chapbooks and Traditional Plays: Communication and Performance', *Folklore*, 92 (1981), 208–17; E. C. Cawte, '"It's an Ancient Custom"—But How Ancient?', in Theresa Buckland and Juliette Wood (eds.), *Aspects of British Calendar Customs* (Folklore Society Mistletoe Series, 22; Sheffield, 1993), 41–3.

28. Trinity College, Dublin, MS 1206, ch. 9, pp. 11–12. I am very grateful to Daniel Beaumont for sending me a copy of these pages from Dublin. For other comments upon their worth, see Cawte, '"It's an Ancient Custom"', 41–3.

29. Chambers, *English Folk-Play*, 174–92.

30. F. Marian McNeill, *The Silver Bough* (Glasgow, 1959), ii. 77; Cawte, '"It's an Ancient Custom"', 43–4.

31. T. Gibson, 'Some Old Country Sports—from the Crosby Records', *Transactions of the Lancashire and Cheshire Historic Society*, 33 (1881), 19–20.

32. Alford, *Sword Dance*, 79–198; Cawte, '"It's an Ancient Custom"' 43–4; E. C. Cawte, 'A History of the Rapper Dance', *Folk Music Journal*, 4: 2 (1981), 79–116; Boyes, 'Excellent Examples'.

33. Violet Alford, letter in *Folk-Lore*, 58 (1947), 247–8.

34. Ead., 'The Mummers' Play', *Proceedings of the Scottish Anthropological and Folklore Society*, 4 (1949), 21–33; *Sword Dance*, 79–198.

35. Tiddy, *Mummers' Play*, 104–5.

36. Chambers, *English Folk-Play*, 155–94.

37. Arthur Brown, 'Folklore Elements in the Medieval Drama', *Folk-Lore*, 63 (1952); Margaret Dean-Smith 'Folk Play Origins of the English Masque', *Folk-Lore*, 65 (1954), 74–86, and 'The Life-Cycle Play or Folk-Play', *Folk-Lore*, 69 (1958), 237–53; P. Happe, 'The Vice and the Folk Drama', *Folklore*, 75 (1964), 161–93; Thomas Pettitt, 'The Folk Play in Marlowe's "Doctor Faustus"', *Folklore*, 91 (1980), 72–7. Also see Margaret Dean-Smith, 'An Un-Romantic View of the Mummers' Play', *Theatre Research*, 8: 2. (1966), 89–99. One of the largest red herrings trailed by Chambers turned out to be the suggestion (at the time certainly worth while) that the famous poem of *Sir Gawain and the Green Knight* embodied ancient pagan traditions such as the death-and-resurrection ritual. After long repetition and elaboration, this was convincingly rejected by C. S. Lewis, Morton Bloomfield, and Charles Moorman in the 1960s. It has been revisited and rejected anew by Frederick B. Jonassen, 'Elements from the Traditional Drama of England in "Sir Gawain and the Green Knight"', *Viator*, 17 (1986), 221–54, and Bella Millett, 'How Green is the Green Knight?', *Nottingham Medieval Studies*, 38 (1994), 138–51. Like the Knight himself, however, the theory seems certain to rise again, at least in popular works.

38. 'Mummers' Play', 25.

39. 'Pull Out Your Purse and Pay', *Folklore*, 79 (1968), 176–201, and 'British West Indian Folk Drama and the "Life Cycle" Problem', *Folklore*, 81 (1970), 241–57.

40. P. S. Smith, 'Collecting Mummers' Plays Today', *Lore and Language* (July 1969), 5–8.

41. A. E. Green, review of Alan Brody, *English Mummers*, in *English Dance and Song*, 34: 3 (1972), 118–19.

42. Gareth Morgan, 'Mummers and Momoeri', *Folklore*, 100 (1989), 84–7 and 'The Mummers of Pontus', *Folklore*, 101 (1990), 143–51; Craig Fees, 'Mummers and Momoeri': A Response, *Folklore*, 100 (1989), 240–7.

43. E. C. Cawte, '"It's an Ancient Custom"', 41–4; Georgina Smith, 'Chapbooks and Traditional Plays', *Folklore*, 92 (1981), 208–17; Craig Fees, 'Towards Establishing the Study of Folk Drama as a Science', *Roomer*, 4: 5 (1984), 41–51; Boyes, 'Excellent Examples'.

44. *Lark Rise to Candleford* (Oxford, 1945), 229–30.

45. Ward, 'Functional Approach to English Drama', 13.

46. Stuart Piggott, 'The Character of Beelzebub in the Mummers' Play', *Folk-Lore*, 40 (1929), 193–5; Alice B. Gomme, 'The Character of Beelzebub in the Mummers' Play', *Folk-Lore*, 40 (1929), 292–3.

47. J. H. Bettey, 'The Cerne Abbas Giant: The Documentary Evidence', *Antiquity*, 55 (1981), 118–196.21; Ronald Hutton, *The Pagan Religions of the Ancient British Isles*, paperback edn. (Oxford, 1993), p. xi.

48. Hutton, *Pagan Religions*, 150–1, 328.

49. Lichman, 'The Gardener's Story', 252–71; Fees, 'Christmas Mumming', *passim*; Ward, 'English Folk Drama', 21–4, 1, and 4–90. Recent studies of Plough, Pace-Egg, and soulers' plays, to be considered later, are also highly relevant here.

50. Ward, 'English Folk Drama' ch. 3.

51. Lichman, 'The Gardener's Story', 98–180.

52. Fees, 'Christmas Mumming', *passim*.

CHAPTER 8

1. M. M. Banks, 'The Padstow May Festival', *Folk-Lore*, 49 (1938), 392–4.

2. Joseph Fontenrose, *The Ritual Theory of Myth* (Berkeley, 1966), ch. 2.

3. E. C. Cawte, *Ritual Animal Disguise* (Folklore Society, 1978), 157–68; Roy Edmund Judge, 'Changing Attitudes to May 1844–1917' (Leeds University Ph.D. thesis, 1987), 410–11. I am very grateful to the Prideaux-Brune family for my entertainment upon my visit.

4. J. G. Frazer, *The Magic Art and the Evolution of Kings* (1911), 68.

5. Cawte, *Ritual Animal Disguise*, 168–77.

6. Violet Alford, 'Some Hobby Horses of Great Britain', *JEFDSS*, 3: 4 (1939), 221–407 and 'The Hobby Horse and other Animal Masks', *Folklore*, 79 (1968), 123–33; Cawte, *Ritual Animal Disguise*.

7. Cawte, *Ritual Animal Disguise*, 26–9; Albert Fevillerat, *Documents Relating to the Office of the Revels in the Time of Queen Elizabeth* (Materialien zur Kunde des Alteren Englischer Dramas; 1908), *passim*; Christopher Bagshaw, *A True Relation* (1601), 18.

8. Cawte, *Ritual Animal Disguise*, 41, 62.

9. Ibid. 85–93. For the revival, I have drawn upon the note in *Folk-Lore*, 64 (1953), 363, and personal acquaintance with the Ancient Order.

10. Cawte, *Ritual Animal Disguise*, 94–109. Information on the revival was gained from friends at St Fagans and Caerphilly, notably Mr John Crosby, and from Mick Tems, 'The Mari Lwyd', *English Dance and Song* 53: 4 (1991), 12–13.

11. Trefor M. Owen, *Welsh Folk Customs* (St Fagans, 1974), 49–55.

12. Mona Douglas, 'Folk Dance and Song in Mann', *Proceedings of the Scottish Anthropological and Folklore Society*, 4: 1 (1949), 53.

13. Cawte, *Ritual Animal Disguise*, 153–6.

14. Iorwerth C. Peate, 'Mari Lwyd—Lair Bhan', *Folk Life*, 1 (1963), 95–6.

15. Cawte, *Ritual Animal Disguise*, 117–24.

16. Mick Tems, 'A Welsh Christmas', *English Dance and Song*, 43: 4 (1981), 15.

17. Cawte, *Ritual Animal Disguise*, 110–17.

18. Ian Russell, 'A Survey of Traditional Drama in North-East Derbyshire 1970–78', *Folk Music Journal*, 3: 5 (1979), 399–478.

19. Cawte, *Ritual Animal Disguise*, 142–8.

20. Ibid. 125–53.

21. See the next chapter.

22. H. Dewar, 'The Dorset Ooser', *Proceedings of the Dorset Natural History and Antiquarian Field Club* (1962), 178–80.

23. 'The Ooser', *Somerset and Dorset Notes and Queries*, 2 (1891), 288.

24. *Folklore, Myths and Legends of Britain* (1973), 164.

25. Cawte, *Ritual Animal Disguise*, 153.

26. Peter Robson, 'Calendar Customs in Nineteenth and Twentieth Century Dorset' (Sheffield University M.Phil. thesis, 1988), 145–6.

27. E. Carrington, 'On Certain Ancient Wiltshire Customs', *Wiltshire Archaeological and Natural History Magazine*, 1 (1854), 88–9.

28. M. Ingram, 'Ridings, Rough Music and the "Reform of Popular Culture" in Early Modern England', *Past and Present*, 105 (1984), 82–7.

29. Alford, 'Some Hobby Horses', 235–40.

30. S. Addy, 'Guising and Mumming in Derbyshire', *Journal of the Derbyshire Archaeological and Natural History Society*, 29 (1907), 31–44; Theo Brown, 'Tertullian and Horse-Cults in Britain', *Folk-Lore*, 61 (1950), 31–4; Brian W. Rose, 'A Note on the Hobby Horse', *Folk-Lore*, 66 (1955), 362–4.

31. Cawte, *Ritual Animal Disguise*, 215; Luke Lyon, 'Hobby-Horse ceremonies in New Mexico and Great Britain', *Folk Music Journal*, 4: 2 (1981), 142.

32. Iorwerth Peate, 'Mari Lwyd: A Suggested Explanation', *Man*, 63 (1943), 53–5.

33. Owen, *Welsh Folk Customs*, 50–6, 62.

34. J. G. Frazer, *The Golden Bough* (1890), i. 261–2.

35. E. K. Chambers, *The Medieval Stage* (Oxford, 1903), vol. ii, appendix N.

36. Arthur West Haddan and William Stubbes, *Councils and Ecclesiastical Documents Relating to Great Britain and Ireland* (Oxford, 1871); iii. 189–90 covers the section later rewritten by the Pseudo-Theodore.

37. J. M. Kemble, *The Saxons in England* (1876), i. 525; Alexander Tille, *Yule and Christmas* (1889), 98.

38. Chambers, *Medieval Stage*, ii. 305; Cawte, *Ritual Animal Disguise*, 79.

39. e.g. Aubrey Burl, *Rites of the Gods* (1981), 27–8; an error the more influential for being part of a deservedly popular book by a distinguished archaeologist.

40. Chambers, *Medieval Stage*, iii. 302. The latest translators, Michael Lapidge and Michael Herren, render *ermulus* as 'snake': *Aldhelm: The Prose Works* (Ipswich, 1979), 160–1.

41. Robert Plot, *The Natural History of Staffordshire* (Oxford, 1686), 434.

42. Cawte, *Ritual Animal Disguise*, 79.

43. Michael Heaney, 'New Evidence for the Abbots Bromley Hobby-Horse', *Folk Music Journal*, 5: 3 (1987), 359–60.

44. Theresa Buckland, 'The Reindeer Antlers of the Abbots Bromley Horn Dance: A re-examination', *Lore and Language*, 3: 2A (1980), 1–8.

45. 'The Abbots Bromley Horn Dance', *Antiquity*, 7 (1933), 206–7.

46. *Ritual Animal Disguise*, 79.

47. Ibid. 13–23, lists St Mary Stafford and Seighford (Staffordshire), Culworth (North-amptonshire), and Holme Pierrepont (Nottinghamshire), to which I can only add Yoxall: Staffordshire RO, D1851/1/13/20. These three Staffordshire parishes represent three-quarters of those in the county from which early Tudor parish accounts survive, directly or indirectly, to which the manorial record from Abbots Bromley in 1532 can now be added to make a fourth. In addition, Cawte lists a payment from St Mary's, Reading, in 1556, but this is for a hobby-horse as part of a May game, and a one-off.

48. William Salt L, Stafford, Salt MS 366 (i); Staffordshire RO, D1323/E/1.

49. Northamptonshire RO, 94P/21.

50. Nottinghamshire RO, PR 547.

51. Cawte, *Ritual Animal Disguise*, 17–8, 22, states that the Seighford dance was at Easter, following the information given by an antiquarian vicar in 1710; but the original accounts to which the clergyman referred are lost, and he could have been misled by the fact that the annual accounting was done ('collected') at Easter, as was usually the case, rather than that the money from the dance was itemized as collected then.

52. Ronald Hutton, *The Rise and Fall of Merry England* (Oxford, 1994), 87–8.

53. Ibid. 201–2.

54. Cawte, *Ritual Animal Disguise*, 11–13, 23.

55. Data from Cawte, *Ritual Animal Disguise*, 23–64, 79–82, and sources given there, although the arguments made are my own.

56. Tom Pettit, 'An Early Tup?', *Roomer*, 4: 1 (1984), 1–2.

57. Cawte, *Ritual Animal Disguise*, 217.

58. Ibid. 224–5.

59. Ibid. 218.

CHAPTER 9

1. James R. Nicolson, *Shetland Folklore* (1981), 147.

2. David Rorie, 'New Year's Day in Scotland', *Folk-Lore*, 20 (1909), 481–2; Mary Macleod Banks (ed.), *British Calendar Customs: Scotland* (Folk-Lore Society, 1939), ii. 66, 69–70; F. Marian McNeill, *The Silver Bough* (Glasgow, 1961), iii. 9708.

3. Edward W. B. Nicholson, *Golspie* (1897), 99–103.

4. A. Jeffrey, *The History and Antiquities of Roxburghshire* (1857–64), iii. 241.

5. Doris Jones-Baker, *The Folklore of Hertfordshire* (1977), 175–6.

6. Personal communication from Mark Rowe, of Burton on Trent, 11 Jan. 1989.

7. Robert D. Storch, 'Introduction' to Storch (ed.), *Popular Culture and Custom in Nineteenth-Century England* (1982), 1–2.

8. Sybil Marshall, *Fenland Chronicle* (Cambridge, 1967), 199–200; Russell Wortley, 'A Penny for the Plough Boys', *English Dance and Song*, 36: 1 (1974), 23.

9. M. A. Courtney, *Cornish Feasts and Folklore* (1890), 10–11.

10. Robert Hunt, *Popular Romances of the West of England* (1881), 394–5.

11. John Troutbeck, *A Survey of the Ancient and Present State of the Scilly Isles* (1796), 172. See also Robert Heath, *A Natural and Historical Account of the Isles of Scilly* (1750), 125, and R. L. Bowley, *The Fortunate Islands*, 7th edn. (1980), 102.

12. J. G. Frazer, *The Golden Bough* (1890), ii. 140–1.

13. *Sanas Chormaic: Cormac's Glossary*, trans. John O'Donovan and ed. Whitley Stokes (Calcutta, 1868), 60.

14. *Golden Bough*, ii. 143–4, and *Spirits of the Corn and of the Wild* (1914), iii. 317–22.

15. Kevin Danaher, *The Year in Ireland* (Cork, 1972), 243–50, and 'Some Distribution Patterns in Irish Folk Life', *Bealoideas*, 26 (1957), 108–23.

16. Thomas Crofton Croker, *Researches in the South of Ireland* (1824), 233.

17. 'Irish Folk-Lore', *Folk-Lore Journal*, 6 (1888), 54; Leland L. Duncan, 'Further Notes from County Leitrim', *Folk-Lore*, 5 (1894), 197; Hugh J. Byrne, 'All Hallows Eve and other Festivals in Connacht', *Folk-Lore*, 18 (1907), 438–9; Bryan L. Jones, 'Wren Boys', *Folk-Lore*, 19 (1908), 234–5; Thomas J. Westorpp, 'A Folklore Survey of County Clare', *Folk-Lore*, 22 (1911), 206–7; Iona and Peter Opie, *The Lore and Language of School-children* (Oxford, 1959), 288–9; Alan Gailey, *Irish Folk Drama* (Cork, 1969), 80–4.

18. Trefor M. Owen, *Welsh Folk Customs* (St Fagans, 1974), 63.

19. Ibid. 59–60, 63–6; J. Fisher, 'Two Welsh-Manx Christmas Customs', *Archaeologia Cambrensis*, 6th ser. 84 (1929), 314–16; Jonathan Ceredig Davies, *Folk-Lore of West and Mid-Wales* (Aberystwyth, 1911), 65; T. F. Thiselton Dyer, *British Popular Customs* (1876), 35–6; M. S. Clark, 'Pembrokeshire Notes', *Folk-Lore*, 15 (1904), 197; Bertram Lloyd, 'Notes on Pembrokeshire Folk-Lore', *Folk-Lore*, 56 (1945), 309.

20. G. Waldron, *Description of the Isle of Man* (Manx Society, 1865), 49–50; Joseph Train, *An Historical and Statistical Account of the Isle of Man* (Douglas, 1845), ii. 124–6; A. W. Moore, *The Folk-Lore of the Isle of Man* (1891), 139; Frazer, *Spirits of the Corn*, ii. 319.

21. *British Calendar Customs: Scotland*, ii ed. Mary Macleod Banks (Folk-Lore Society, 1939), 102.

22. T. Brown, '69th Report on Folklore', *Transactions of the Devonshire Association*, 104 (1972), 266–8.

23. A. R. Wright, *British Calendar Customs*, ed. T. E. Lones (Folk-Lore Society, 1939), ii. 145.

24. William Henderson, *Notes on the Folk-Lore of the Northern Counties of England and the Borders* (Folk-Lore Society; 1879), 125.

25. Peter Robson, 'Calendar Customs in Nineteenth and Twentieth Dorset' (Sheffield M.Phil. thesis, 1988), 139.

26. E. K. Chambers, *The Medieval Stage* (Oxford, 1903), chs. 13–14; Peter Burke, *Popular Culture in Early Modern Europe* (1978), 192.

27. Chambers, *Medieval Stage*, i. 321–3; *Dean Cosyn and Wells Cathedral Miscellanea*, ed. Aelred Watkin (Somerset Records Society, 1941), 20. *Records of Early English Drama: Devon*, ed. John M. Wasson (Toronto, 1986), 319–26.

28. For general accounts, and most of what follows, see Chambers, *Medieval Stage*, i. 336–71; C. H. Evelyn-White, 'The Boy Bishop (*episcopus puerorum*) in Medieval England', *Journal of the British Archaeological Association*, NS II (1905), 30–48, 231–56; S. E. Rigold, 'The St Nicholas tokens', *Proceedings of the Suffolk Institute of Archaeology*, 34, Pt II (1978), 87–101; R. L. de Molen, '*Pueri Christi imitatio*: The Festival of the Boy Bishop in Tudor England', *Moreana*, 40 (1975), 17–29; Neil Mackenzie, 'Boy into Bishop: A Festive Role Reversal', *History Today* (Dec. 1987), 10–16; Ronald Hutton, *The Rise and Fall of Merry England* (Oxford, 1994), 10–12.

29. Chambers, *Medieval Stage*, i. 352, 353, 356; R. T. Hampson, *Medii Aevi Kalendarium* (1841), 79; Anna Jean Mill, *Medieval Plays in Scotland* (Edinburgh, 1927), 18.

30. Sources at n. 28, plus Mill, *Medieval Plays*, 18; Hampson, *Medii Aevi Kalendarium*, 79; Arthur F. Leach, 'The Schoolboys' Feast', *Fortnightly Review*, NS 59 (1896), 134–5; *Household Accounts from Medieval England*, ed. C. M. Woolgar (British Academy; Oxford, 1992), 418.

31. Leach, 'Schoolboys' Feast', 139.

32. Chambers, *Medieval Stage*, i. 364–6; Mill, *Medieval Plays*, 155–6.

33. Hutton, *Merry England*, 11–12.

34. Mill, *Medieval Plays*, 18–19.

35. Hutton, *Merry England*, 12.

36. *The Medieval Records of a London City Church (St Mary at Hill) 1420–1559*, ed. Henry Littlehales (EETS, 1905), 126.

37. E. G. C. Atchley, 'On the Medieval Parish Records of the Church of St Nicholas, Bristol', *Transactions of the St Paul's Ecclesiological Society*, 6 (1906), 11–13; Robert Ricart, *The Maire of Bristowe Is Kalendar*, ed. Lucy Toulmin Smith (Camden Society, 1872), 80–1.

38. BL Stowe MS 871, fos. 32–3.

39. *Boxford Churchwardens' Accounts 1530–1561*, ed. Peter Northeast (Suffolk Records Society, 1982), p. xiv.

40. 'Boy Bishops', *Transactions of the Shropshire Archaeological and Natural History Society*, 3rd ser. 6 (1906), p. xiii.

41. Hutton, *Merry England*, 12, and sources cited there.

42. Mill, *Medieval Plays*, 18–19.

43. *The Courts of the Archdeaconry of Buckingham 1483–1523*, ed. E. M. Elvey (Buckinghamshire Record Society, 1975), 261.

44. *Tudor Royal Proclamations*, ed. Paul L. Hughes and James F. Larkin (New Haven, 1964), vol. i., no. 202; Hutton, *Merry England*, 77–8.

45. Hutton, *Merry England*, 97–8; Hampson, *Medii Aevi Kalendarium*, 81. The quotation is from Henry Machyn.

46. *Remaines of Gentilisme and Judaisme*, ed. James Britten (Folk-Lore Society, 1881), 40–1.

47. Christina Hole, *English Custom and Usage* (1941), 19.

48. John Brand, *Observations on the Popular Antiquities of Great Britain*, ed. Sir Henry Ellis (1908), i. 441–50; J. Weld, *A History of Leagram* (Chetham Society, 1913), 133–4; K. V. Thomas, *Rule and Misrule in the Schools of Early Modern England* (Reading, 1976), 21; Rex Cathcart, 'Festive Capers?', *History Today* (Dec. 1988), 49–52.

49. Sandra Billington, *Mock Kings in Medieval Society and Renaissance Drama* (Oxford, 1991), 30–2, which is the standard work upon the subject. I only differ from her in failing to find any firm evidence of midwinter mock-rulers in Britain between 1335 and 1414. The reference to a 'Christen King' which she identifies in William Langland, *The Vision of Piers Plowman . . . together with Richard the Redeless*, ed. Walter W. Skeat (Oxford, 1886), passus IV. i. 1, seems to me to translate better as 'Christian King' than 'Christmas King'.

50. Billington, *Mock Kings*, 32.

51. Alan H. Nelson, *The Medieval English Stage* (Chicago, 1974), 123.

52. Hampson, *Medii Aevi Kalendarium*, 117; *British Calendar Customs: Scotland*, ii. 66, 127, iii. 235.

53. St John's College, Cambridge, MS D91/19 fos. 59 and 121. I owe these references to Michael K. Jones.

54. *Letters and Papers, Foreign and Domestic, of the Reign of Henry VIII*, ed. J. S. Brewer (1864), II. ii. 1444–80, *passim*.

55. *Records of Early English Drama: Cumberland, Westmorland and Gloucestershire*, ed. Audrey Douglas and Peter Greenfield (Toronto, 1986), 335.

56. Hutton, *Merry England*, 90.

57. Ibid. 90–1; Billington, *Mock Kings*, 38–42.

58. Hutton, *Merry England*, 101.

59. *British Calendar Customs: Scotland*, ii. 127; T. F. Thiselton Dyer, *British Popular Customs* (1876), 28.

60. John Stow, *A Survey of London*, ed. Charles Lethbridge Kingsford (Oxford, 1908), i. 97.
61. Chambers, *Medieval Stage*, i. 418; William Sandays, *Christmastide* (1853), 65.
62. Lincolnshire RO, Ancaster MSS HC/23/40.
63. Billington, *Mock Kings*, 35; and in the same decade see the Barrington household accounts, Essex RO, DD/Ba/A/2, Dec. 1635, for a 'Puritan' gentleman who kept a Lord of Misrule.
64. Polydor Vergil, *Works*, trans. John Langley (1663), 194–5; *Table Talk of John Selden*, ed. Sir Frederick Pollock (1927), 28. See also Nicholas Breton, *Fantastickes* (1626), 22; John Webster, *The Duchess of Malfi*, III. ii. 9.
65. *Records of Early English Drama: Devon*, ed. John M. Wasson (Toronto, 1986), 403.
66. Chambers, *Medieval Stage*, i. 418; BL Harleian MS 6388, fo. 28v.
67. *Cumberland, Westmorland and Gloucestershire*, ed. Douglas and Greenfield, 71.
68. Ibid. 296; David Underdown, *Revel, Riot and Rebellion* (Oxford, 1985), 46.
69. *Letters and Papers*, IV. i. 170.
70. Hutton, *Merry England*, 10, 100, 114, and sources there. They are attested at Swaffham, Great Witchingham, Shipham and Snettisham (Norfolk), Dennington, and Mildenhall (Suffolk), and Great Dunmow, and Harwich (Essex).
71. PRO, SP 1/99, fos. 203–4.
72. Hutton, *Merry England*, 100, 114.
73. Richard L. Greaves, *Society and Religion in Elizabethan England* (Minneapolis, 1981), 423–4.
74. Hutton, *Merry England*, 90, 128, 179; Griffin Higgs, *The Christmas Prince*, ed. Frederick S. Boas (Malone Society, 1922).
75. *The Black Book of Lincoln's Inn*, ed. J. W. Walker (1897), i. 181–90.
76. Hutton, *Merry England*, 114–14; Billington, *Mock Kings*, 45–8.
77. Hutton, *Merry England*, 179–80.
78. Aubrey, *Remaines*, 122.
79. *The Diary of Samuel Pepys*, ed. Robert Latham and William Matthews (1970), iii. 2; *The Diary of John Evelyn*, ed. E. S. De Beer (Oxford, 1955), iii. 307–8, 504.
80. Brand, *Observations*, i. 22–3; Barnaby Googe, *The Popish Kingdom* (1570), 45–6.
81. Ben Jonson, *Works*, ed. C. H. Herford Percy and Evelyn Simpson (Oxford, 1941), vii. 437–8; Brand, *Observations*, i. 24, 27.
82. Seldon, *Table-Talk*, 28.
83. Pepys, *Diary*, ix. 409.
84. Robert Chambers, *The Book of Days* (1864), 64.
85. Brand, *Observations*, i. 25.
86. Mrs Gutch and Mabel Peacock (eds.), *County Folk-Lore*, v. *Lincolnshire* (Folk-Lore Society, 1908), 170; William Hone, *The Every-Day Book and Table Book* (1832), i. 51–3.
87. Hone, *Every-Day Book*, i. 47–50; BL Add. MS 41313, fo. 80 (information from Devon); John Brady, *Clavis Calendaria* (1812), i. 155; Laurence Whistler, *The English Festivals* (1947), 77; Chambers, *Book of Days* 64; Owen, *Welsh Folk Customs*, 48; Robert Hunt, *Popular Romances of the West of England* (1881), 388; M. A. Courtney, *Cornish Feasts and Folklore* (1890), 15.
88. Wright, *British Calendar Customs*, ii. 83–4.

CHAPTER 10

1. J. A. R. Plimlott, *The Englishman's Christmas* (Hassocks, 1978); J. M. Golby and A. W. Purdue, *The Making of the Modern Christmas* (1986); Gavin Weightman and Steve

Humphries, *Christmas Past* (1987); David Miller (ed.), *Unwrapping Christmas* (Oxford, 1993); Geoffrey Rowell, 'Dickens and the Construction of Christmas', *History Today* (Dec. 1993), 17–24.

2. Goldby and Purdue, *Modern Christmas*, 12–13, 43; Plimlott, *Englishman's Christmas*, 82.

3. Plimlott, *Englishman's Christmas*, 77, 81.

4. Ibid. 78–80.

5. Trefor M. Owen, *Welsh Folk Customs* (St Fagans, 1974), 28; Flora Thompson, *Lark Rise to Candleford* (Oxford, 1945), 229–30; Rowell, 'Dickens', 24.

6. Rowell, 'Dickens', 20; Weightman and Humphries, *Christmas Past*, 12–15.

7. Rowell, 'Dickens', 17–19; Golby and Purdue, *Modern Christmas*, 45–51; David Miller, 'A Theory of Christmas', in Miller (ed.), *Unwrapping Christmas*, 19; Plimlott, *Englishman's Christmas*, 88–9.

8. Golby and Purdue, *Modern Christmas*, 52; Weightman and Humphries, *Christmas Past*, ch. 3; Plimlott, *Englishman's Christmas*, 90–5.

9. Rowell, 'Dickens', 22; Laurence Whistler, *The English Festivals* (1947), 32; Plimlott, *Englishman's Christmas*, 97–101; Weightman and Humphries, *Christmas Past*, 104–21.

10. Whistler, *English Festivals*, 48–51; George Buday, *The History of the Christmas Card* (1954); Mary Searle-Chatterjee, 'Christmas Cards and the Construction of Social Relation Today', in Miller (ed.), *Unwrapping Christmas*, 176; Plimlott, *Englishman's Christmas*, 101–7.

11. Plimlott, *Englishman's Christmas*, 104–5; Searle-Chatterjee, 'Christmas Cards', 177–81.

12. Whistler, *English Festivals*, 33; Weightman and Humphries, *Christmas Past*, ch. 8; Plimlott, *Englishman's Christmas*, 12–30.

13. Weightman and Humphries, *Christmas Past*, ch. 3.

14. Whistler, *English Festivals*, 34–5; Searle-Chatterjee, 'Christmas Cards', 184–6.

15. Ben Jonson, *Works*, ed. C. H. Herford Percey and Eveline Simpson (Oxford, 1941), vii. 437–45.

16. Thomas Nabbes, *The Springs Glorie* (1638), sig A.

17. Whistler, *English Festivals*, 35–6; Weightman and Humphries, *Christmas Past*; Plimlott, *Englishman's Christmas*, 111–18; Golby and Purdue, *Modern Christmas*, 71–5.

18. Rogan Taylor, 'Who is Santa Claus?', *Sunday Times Magazine* (21 Dec. 1980), 13–17.

19. Ronald Hutton, *The Shamans of Siberia* (Glastonbury, 1993), lists all the known first-hand accounts.

20. Weightman and Humphries, *Christmas Past*, 125–34; Golby and Purdue, *Christmas*, 56–7; Plimlott, *Englishman's Christmas*, 136.

21. Weightman and Humphries, *Christmas Past*, 43–5; Plimlott, *Englishman's Christmas*, 130.

22. Plimlott, *Englishman's Christmas*, 141.

23. Ibid. 108–10, 142, 157–8; Whistler, *English Festivals*, 37–8; Rowell, 'Dickens', 22–3.

24. Whistler, *English Festivals*, 43; Golby and Purdue, *Modern Christmas*, 63; Weightman and Humphries, *Christmas Past*, 47–9, 109–11; Plimlott, *Englishman's Christmas*, 139–40.

25. Golby and Purdue, *Modern Christmas*, 102–3; Weightman and Humphries, *Christmas Past*, 29–30.

26. Plimlott, *Englishman's Christmas*, 151; Golby and Purdue, *Modern Christmas*, 107; Searle-Chatterjee, 'Christmas Cards', 187.

27. Whistler, *English Festivals*, 55; Plimlott, *Englishman's Christmas*, 159.

28. Weightman and Humphries, *Christmas Past*, 29, 37; Plimlott, *Englishman's Christmas*, 149.

29. A. R. Wright, *British Calendar Customs*, ed. T. E. Lones (Folk-Lore Society, 1936), i. 16–17.

30. For thoughts on this, see Adam Kuper, 'The English Christmas and the Family: Time Out and Alternative Realities', in Miller (ed.), *Unwrapping Christmas*, 166.
31. For typical comment, see David Harrison, 'Driven Crackers by the Christmas Crush', *Observer* (19 Dec. 1993), 4.
32. Weightman and Humphries, *Christmas Past*, 35-7, 97, 121.
33. e.g. ibid. 50-2; Golby and Purdue, *Modern Christmas*, 10.
34. Quoted in Golby and Purdue, *Modern Christmas*, 24.
35. Ibid. 13.
36. Lesley Gerard, 'Great Britain plc Has Busy Time on Holiday', *Observer* (2 Jan. 1994), 5.
37. On which see Kuper, 'The English Christmas and the Family', 167.
38. Miller, 'A Theory of Christmas', 3-26.
39. *Libanii Opera*, ed. J. J. Reiske (1784), i. 256.

CHAPTER 11

1. George Caspar Homans, *English Villagers of the Thirteenth Century* (Cambridge, Mass., 1942), 361-3.
2. *Dives and Pauper*, ed. P. H. Barnum (EETS, 1976), 157.
3. 'Leverington Parish Accounts', *Fenland Notes and Queries*, 7 (1907-9), 184-90.
4. H. R. Loraine, *Knapton* (North Waltham, 1952), 6.
5. Ronald Hutton, *The Rise and Fall of Merry England* (Oxford, 1994), 16.
6. *Extracts from the Account Rolls of the Abbey of Durham*, ed. J. T. Fowler (Surtees Society, 99; 1898), i. 224.
7. Hutton, *Merry England*, 17.
8. They are first mentioned at Peterborough in 1467 and at Brundish, Suffolk, in 1475: *Peterborough Local Administration*, ed. W. T. Mallows (Northamptonshire RO, 1939), 4, and East Suffolk RO, FC 89/A2/1.
9. Hutton, *Merry England*, 75, 79-81, 87.
10. *Visitation Articles and Injunctions of the Period of the Reformation*, ed. Walter Howard Frere (Alcuin Club, 1910), ii. 175.
11. Hutton, *Merry England*, 119, 323.
12. Ibid. 100.
13. Ibid. 114; E. C. Cawte, '"It's an Ancient Custom"—But How Ancient?', in Theresa Buckland and Juliette Wood (eds.), *Aspects of British Calendar Customs* (Folklore Society Mistletoe Series, 22; Sheffield, 1993), 52-3.
14. Hutton, *Merry England*, 119, 323.
15. Ibid. 119, 323; W. Palmer, 'Episcopal Visitation Returns, Cambridgeshire', *Transactions of the Cambridgeshire and Huntingdonshire Archaeological Society*, 5 (1930-7), 32; H. Bradshaw, 'Notes of the Episcopal Visitation of the Archdeaconry of Ely in 1685', *Proceedings of the Cambridge Antiquarian Society*, 3 (1864-76), 104; M. W. Barley, 'Plough Plays in the East Midlands', *JEFDSS* 7 (1953), 72; Cawte, '"It's an Ancient Custom"', 53.
16. Thomas Davidson, 'Plough Rituals in England and Scotland', *Agricultural History Review*, 7 (1959), 34.
17. Thomas Tusser, *Five Hundred Points of Good Husbandrie*, ed. W. Payne and S. J. Herrtage (English Dialect Society, 1878), 180.
18. Robert W. Malcolmson, *Popular Recreations in English Society* (Cambridge, 1973), 28; Bob Bushaway, *By Rite* (1982), 168-70; E. K. Chambers, *The English Folk-Play* (1934), 89-90; BL Add. MS 27966, fo. 242V (account of Norwich area); George Hadley, *History of...Kingston upon Hull* (Hull, 1788), 823-6; C. F. Tebbutt, *Huntingdonshire*

Folklore (St Ives, 1984), 52–5; *Gentleman's Magazine* (Dec. 1762), 568; William Brockie, *Legends and Superstitions of the County of Durham* (Sunderland, 1886), 101; John Nicholson, *Folklore of East Yorkshire* (1890), 17; Llewellyn Jewitt, 'On Ancient Customs and Sports of the County of Nottingham', *Journal of the British Archaeological Association*, 1st ser. 8 (1853), 238; J. G. Frazer, 'Plough Monday', *Folk-Lore Journal*, 5 (1887), 161; A. R. Wright, *British Calendar Customs*, ed. T. E. Lones (Folk-Lore Society, 1936), ii. 94–101; Russell Wortley, 'A Penny for the Plough Boys', *English Dance and Song*, 36 (1974), 23.

19. Wright, *British Calendar Customs*, ii. 94–101; M. Walker and Helen Bennett, *Somerset Folklore* (Somerset Rural Life Museum, 1980), n.p.; T. Brown, '49th Report on Folk-Lore', *Transactions of the Devonshire Association*, 84 (1952), 298; Doris Jones-Baker, *The Folklore of Hertfordshire* (1977), 124; Jacqueline Simpson, *The Folklore of Sussex* (1973), 105.

20. *Gentleman's Magazine* (Dec. 1762), 568.

21. Cawte, ' "It's an Ancient Custom" '; 50; Malcolmson, *Popular Recreations*, 165–6.

22. Bushaway, *By Rite*, 251.

23. Ibid. 168; Malcolmson, *Popular Recreations*, 165–8.

24. Idwal Jones, 'Plough Monday and the Primitive Methodists in Leicestershire', *Roomer*, 1: 2 (1980), 7–8.

25. Nicholson, *East Yorkshire*, 17.

26. Malcolmson, *Popular Recreations*, 82.

27. Tebbutt, *Huntingdonshire Folklore*, 52–5.

28. Ibid. 55–6; Enid Porter, *Cambridgeshire Customs and Folklore* (1969), 103–4; J. G. Frazer, *Spirits of the Corn and of the Wild* (1914), ii. 330–1; Sybil Marshall, *Fenland Chronicle*, 200–1.

29. Chambers, *Folk-Play*, 89, 91–100; Barley, 'Plough Plays', 68–77; E. C. Cawte, Alex Helm, and N. Peacock, *English Ritual Drama: A Geographical Index* (Folklore Society, 1967), *passim*; Ruairidh Greig, 'The Kirmington Plough-Jags Play', *Folk Music Journal*, 3 (1977), 233–41; Alun Howkins and Linda Merricks, 'The Ploughboy and the Plough Play', *Folk Music Journal*, 6 (1991), 187–208.

30. Chambers, *Folk-Play*, 89, 91–100, 232–5.

31. C. Baskerville, 'Mummers' Wooing Plays in England', *Modern Philology*, 21 (1924), 225–72; Barley, 'Plough Plays', 68–88.

32. *The English Mummers and their Plays* (Philadelphia, 1969).

33. Cawte, ' "It's an Ancient Custom" ', 39–41.

34. The references are all cited in Paul and Georgina Smith, 'The Plouboys or Modes Dancers at Revesby', *English Dance and Song*, 42 (1980), 7–9; they included Tiddy, Chambers, and Dean-Smith.

35. Barley, 'Plough Plays', 70–1.

36. 'Pleugh Song and Pleugh Play', *Saltire Review*, 2: 6 (1955), 39–44.

37. Paul and Georgina Smith, as at n.34.

38. Barley, 'Plough Plays', 88.

39. Howkins and Merricks, as at n.29.

40. Mabel Peacock, 'The Hood-game at Haxey, Lincolnshire', *Folk-Lore*, 7 (1896), 330–50.

41. E. O. James, *Seasonal Feasts and Festivals* (1961), 299.

42. 'Throwing the Hood at Haxey', *Folk Life*, 18 (1980), 7–24.

43. Joyce Godber, *History of Bedfordshire* (Bedford, 1969), 169, n.56; Tebbutt, *Huntingdonshire Folklore*, 52–5; Wright, *British Calendar Customs*, iii 94–101; Wortley, 'Penny for the Plough Boys', 25.

44. Bushaway, *By Rite*, 273.

45. Jones-Baker, *Hertfordshire*, 123; bulletins in *Folk-Lore*, 60 (1949), 403; 65 (1954), 172–3; and 70 (9159), 340; Alexander Howard, *Endless Cavalcade* (1964), 17–18; Margaret Baker, *Folklore and Customs of Rural England* (Newton Abbot, 1974), 102–3; Lawrence Whistler, *The English Festivals* (1947), 84–5; R. L. Tongue, *Somerset Folklore*, ed. K. M. Briggs (Folk-Lore Society, 1965), 153; Davidson, 'Plough Rituals', 31–2; information from Antonia Galloway of Soham, 20 May 1984.

46. Peter Robson, 'Calendar Customs in Nineteenth and Twentieth Century Dorset' (Sheffield M.Phil. thesis, 1988), 27.

47. Pauline Dennis, 'Whittlesey Straw Bear', *English Dance and Song*, 43 (1981), 21–2.

48. Russell Wortley, 'Plough Monday, 1974, at Balsham, Cambs', *English Dance and Song*, 36 (1974), 109.

49. Information from Antonia Galloway, 20 May and 9 Sept. 1984.

CHAPTER 12

1. Most accessibly translated in *The Tain*, ed. Thomas Kinsella (Oxford, 1970), 27.

2. Eric B. Hamp, '*imbloc, oimelc*', *Studia Celtica*, 14 (1979), 106–13, which also surveys the linguistic arguments outlined above.

3. For different discussions of it, see Kathleen Hughes, *Early Christian Ireland: Introduction to the Sources* (1972), 226–9; Proinsias MacCana, *Celtic Mythology* (1983), 34–5, 90–1; Ronald Hutton, *The Pagan Religions of the Ancient British Isles* (Oxford, 1991), 153–4, 167, 175, 182, 252, 285, 287.

4. Kevin Danaher, *The Year in Ireland* (Cork, 1972), 13–27; Loreto Todd, 'County Tyrone Folk-Beliefs', *Lore and Language*, 7 (July 1972), 7; John C. O'Sullivan, 'St Brigid's Crosses', *Folk Life*, 11 (1973), 60–81; T. H. Mason, 'St Brigid's Crosses', *Journal of the Royal Society of Antiquaries of Ireland*, 75 (1945), 160–6.

5. Danaher, *Year in Ireland*, 24–35; O'Sullivan, 'St Brigid's Crosses', 60–5; E. Estyn Evans, *Irish Folkways* (1957), 270; Alan Gailey, *Irish Folk Drama* (Cork, 1969), 84–6; Mason, 'St Brigid's Crosses', 163–6.

6. Joseph Train, *An Historical and Statistical Account of the Isle of Man* (Douglas, 1845), 116.

7. C. I. Paton, 'Manx Calendar Customs', *Folk-Lore*, 51 (1940), 189–90.

8. M. Martin, *A Description of the Western Isles of Scotland* (1703), 119.

9. *Scotland and Scotsmen in the Eighteenth Century*, ed. Alexander Allardyce (Edinburgh, 1888), ii. 447.

10. *British Calendar Customs: Scotland*, ed. Mary Macleod Banks, ii. (Folk-Lore Society, 1939), 152.

11. *Carmina Gadelica* (Edinburgh, 1900), i. 167–73.

CHAPTER 13

1. E. O. James, *Seasonal Feasts and Festivals* (1961), 232; Mary Clayton, *The Cult of the Virgin Mary in Anglo-Saxon England* (Cambridge, 1990), 25.

2. H. H. Scullard, *Festivals and Ceremonies of the Roman Republic* (1981), 69–70.

3. e.g. Thomas Becon, *The Reliques of Rome* (1563), fos. 158–78, and Joshua Stopford, *Pagano-Papismus* (1675), 237–43. Compare with Scullard, *Festivals*, 70 ff.

4. Bede, *Works*, ed. J. A. Giles (1843), vi. 178–9.

5. *The Use of Sarum*, ed. Walter Howard Frere (Cambridge, 1898), 7–9; Eamon Duffy, *The Stripping of the Altars* (New Haven, 1992), 15–17.

6. Ronald Hutton, *The Rise and Fall of Merry England* (Oxford, 1994), 17–18.

7. Duffy, *Stripping of the Altars*, 20.

8. Anna Jean Mill, *Medieval Plays in Scotland* (Edinburgh, 1927), 116, 124.

9. Hutton, *Merry England*, 18; C. Phythian-Adams, 'Ceremony and the Citizen', in Peter Clark (ed.), *The Early Modern Town* (1976), 116.

10. George Caspar Homans, *English Villagers of the Thirteenth Century* (Cambridge, Mass., 1947), 363.

11. Hutton, *Merry England*, 77, 80, 83, 93, 97, 106.

12. Northcote W. Thomas (ed.), *County Folklore*, iii: *Orkney and Shetland Islands* (Folk-Lore Society, 1903), 195; James R. Nicolson, *Shetland Folklore* (1981), 136–7.

13. Kevin Danaher, *The Year in Ireland* (Cork, 1972), 38.

14. T. F. Thiselton Dyer, *British Popular Customs* (1876), 55.

15. Llewellyn Jewitt, 'On Ancient Customs and Sports of the County of Nottingham', *Journal of the British Archaeological Association*, 1st ser. 8 (1853), 231.

16. *British Calendar Customs: Scotland*, ed. Mary Macleod Banks, ii. (Folk-Lore Society, 1939), 158–9.

17. Trefor M. Owen, 'The Celebration of Candlemas in Wales', *Folklore*, 84 (1973), 238–51, and *Welsh Folk Customs* (St Fagans, 1974), 56–7; Edmund Hyde Hall, *A Description of Caernarvonshire* (Caernarvonshire Historical Society, 1952), 320.

18. Owen, *Welsh Folk Customs*, 70; Marie Trevelyan, *Folk-Lore and Folk-Stories of Wales* (1909), 244.

19. Robert Plot, *The Natural History of Oxfordshire* (Oxford, 1677), 202.

20. A. R. Wright, *British Calendar Customs*, ed. T. E. Lones (Folk-Lore Society, 1936), ii. 130–5; R. P. Chope, 'Devonshire Calendar Customs. Part II. Fixed Festivals', *Transactions of the Devonshire Association*, 70 (1938), 358; Bob Bushaway, *By Rite* (1982), 46; Mrs Gutch (ed.), *County Folk-Lore*, iii. *North Riding of Yorkshire, York and the Ainsty* (Folk-Lore Society, 1901), 233–4; Doris Jones-Baker, *The Folklore of Hertfordshire* (1977), 125.

21. John Brady, *Clavis Calendaria* (1812), i. 201.

22. William Hone, *The Every-Day Book and Table Book* (1832), i. 209–11.

23. Robert D. Storch, 'Introduction', to Storch (ed.), *Popular Culture and Custom in Nineteenth-Century England* (1982), 2.

24. E. P. Thompson, *Customs in Common* (1991), 5.

CHAPTER 14

1. The sources are collected in R. T. Hampson, *Medii Aevi Kalendarium* (1841), 162–3, and A. R. Wright, *British Calendar Customs*, ed. T. E. Lones (Folk-Lore Society, 1936), ii. 138–9.

2. Ronald Hutton, *The Rise and Fall of Merry England* (Oxford, 1994), 18.

3. *John Donne: The Epithalmions, Anniversaries and Epicedes*, ed. W. Milgate (Oxford, 1978), 6–10; *The Poems of Robert Herrick*, ed. L. C. Martin (Oxford, 1965), 149.

4. *The Works of Michael Drayton*, ed. J. William Hebel (Oxford, 1932), ii. 352–4.

5. *British Calendar Customs: Scotland*, ed. Mary Macleod Banks, ii. (Folk-Lore Society, 1939), 172.

6. Robert Plot, *The Natural History of Staffordshire* (Oxford, 1686), 430.

7. Wright, *British Calendar Customs*, ii. 138–9.

8. *The Journal of William Shellinks' Travels in England*, trans. and ed. Maurice Exwood and H. L. Lehmann (Camden Society, 5th ser. 1; 1993), 73.

9. *The Diary of Samuel Pepys*, ed. Robert Latham and William Matthews (1970), ii. 36, iii. 28–9, iv. 35, vii. 42, viii. 62, ix. 67–8.

10. HMC Rutland MSS, ii. 22.

11. *Antiquitates Vulgares* (Newcastle, 1725), 174–5.

12. F. Marian McNeill, *The Silver Bough* (1959), ii. 36.

13. 'Valentines', *Folklore Society Newsletter*, 14 (1992), 14–16; Walter Gregor, *Notes on the*

Folk-Lore of the North-East of Scotland (Folk-Lore Society, 1881), 166; Mrs Gutch (ed.), *County Folk-Lore*, ii. *North Riding of Yorkshire, York and the Ainsty* (Folk-Lore Society, 1901), 236; T. F. Thiselton Dyer, *British Popular Customs* (1876), 109–10; Wright, *British Calendar Customs*, ii. 143, 145; *British Calendar Customs: Scotland*, ii. 170–2.

14. John Brady, *Clavis Calendaria* (1812), i. 222; Anna Eliza Bray, *A Description of the Part of Devonshire Bordering on the Tamar and the Tavy* (1836), ii. 285–6; J. B. Partridge, 'Cotswold Place-Lore and Customs', *Folk-Lore*, 23 (1912), 443; BL Add. MS 41313, fo. 80^V (letter from Devon).

15. Marie Trevelyan, *Folk-Lore and Folk Stories of Wales* (1909), 243–5; Mrs Gutch and Mabel Peacock (eds.), *County Folk-Lore* v. *Lincolnshire* (Folk-Lore Society, 1908), 187–8; Llewellyn Jewitt, 'On Ancient Customs and Sports of the County of Nottingham', *Journal of the British Archaeological Association*, 1st ser. 8 (1853), 231; William Hone, *The Every-Day Book and Table Book* (1832), ii. 222.

16. Bob Bushaway, *By Rite* (1982), 39–40; *County Folk-Lore* (Folk-Lore Society, 1895): 3. Leicestershire and Rutland, ed. Charles J. Billson, 71.

17. C. F. Tebbutt, *Huntingdonshire Folklore* (St Ives, 1984), 57–8; John Brand, *Observations on the Popular Antiquities of Great Britain*, ed. Sir Henry Ellis (1908), i. 60; Sidney Oldall Addy, *Household Tales with other Traditional Remains* (1895), III; P. H. Ditchfield, *Old English Customs Extant at the Present Time* (1896), 55–6; Enid Porter, *Cambridgeshire Customs and Folklore* (1969), 104, and *The Folklore of East Anglia* (1974), 57; C. E. Prior, *Dedications of Churches* (Oxfordshire Archaeological Society Reports, 1903), 34, 41; Dyer, *British Popular Customs*, 105, 108; Ella Mary Leather, *The Folk-Lore of Herefordshire* (Hereford, 1912), 96; W. B. Gerish, 'Valentine's Day Custom at Northrepps', *Folk-Lore*, 5 (1894), 3; Thomas Sternberg, *The Dialect and Folk-Lore of Northamptonshire* (1851), 179; M. L. Stanton *et al.*, 'Worcestershire Folklore', *Folk-Lore*, 26 (1915), 94; Alfred Williams, *Folk-Songs of the Upper Thames* (1923), 303; Doris Jones-Baker, *The Folklore of Hertfordshire* (1977), 127; Wright, *British Calendar Customs*, ii. 146–9.

18. Tebbutt, *Huntingdonshire Folklore*, 136; Ditchfield, *Old English Customs*, 55–6; Porter, *Cambridgeshire*, 104; Dyer, *British Popular Customs*, 105; Jones-Baker, *Hertfordshire*, 127; Iona and Peter Opie, *The Lore and Language of Schoolchildren* (Oxford, 1959), 236.

19. Prior, *Dedications*, 41; Sternberg, *Northamptonshire*, 179; Stanton *et al.*, 'Worcestershire', 94.

20. Brand, *Observations*, i. 60; Dyer, *British Popular Customs*, 108.

21. Porter, *East Anglia*, 57; Williams, *Folk-Songs*, 303; Ditchfield, *Old English Customs*, 55–6.

22. Gerisch, 'Northrepps', 3. For other local oddities, see Porter, *East Anglia*, 57; Prior, *Dedications*, 34; Opie and Opie, *Lore and Language*, 235.

23. *Colburn's Calendar of Amusements in Town and Country* (1840), 35; Ditchfield, *Old English Customs*, 56; Elizabeth James, 'Norwich and St Valentine', *English Dance and Song*, 40 (1978), 35–6, and 'East Norfolk's Valentine Man', *English Dance and Song*, 40 (1978), 96–7.

24. Information from Earl Parfitt, by then of Milton Keynes, 16 Aug. 1994.

25. Opie and Opie, *Lore and Language*, 235–6.

26. Laurence Whistler, *The English Festivals* (1947), 93–4.

27. BL Add. 41313, fo. 80^V (Robert Studley Vidal to John Brand).

28. Whistler, *English Festivals*, 95–6.

29. A case-study being Porter, *Cambridgeshire*, 104.

30. Whistler, *English Festivals*, 96–8; 'Valentines', *Folklore Society Newsletter*, 14–16; Wirt Sikes, *British Goblins* (1880), 259.

31. *The Vigilance Record* (Aug. 1908), 6.

32. Sybil Marshall, *Fenland Chronicle* (Cambridge, 1967), 202–3.

33. *Vigilance Record* (Aug. 1908), 6; George Long, *The Folklore Calendar* (1930), 25–6; John Symonds Udal, *Dorsetshire Folk-Lore* (Hertford, 1922), 21; Richard Blakeborough, *Wit, Character, Folklore and Customs of the North Riding of Yorkshire* (1898), 78–9; Wright, *British Calendar Customs*, ii. 142–4; Jacqueline Simpson, *The Folklore of the Welsh Border* (1976), 137; James Obelkevitch, *Religion and Rural Society: South Lindsey, 1825–1875* (Oxford, 1976), 266; 'Scraps of English Folklore', *Folk-Lore*, 36 (1925), 86; 'Scraps of English Folklore', *Folk-Lore*, 40 (1929), 283.

34. Wright, *British Calendar Customs*, ii. 142.

CHAPTER 15

1. Lists are provided in Ronald Hutton, *The Rise and Fall of Merry England* (Oxford, 1994), 305–6.

2. Ibid. 19, 89, 101, 123, 154, 197; Mary Macleod Banks (ed.), *British Calendar Customs: Scotland* (Folk-Lore Society, 1937), i. 28–9.

3. George Hadley, *History of . . . Kingston-upon-Hull* (Hull, 1788), 823–6; Graham Mayhew, *Tudor Rye* (Falmer, 1987), 58; *Records of Early English Drama: Chester*, ed. Lawrence M. Clopper (Manchester, 1979), pp. li–liii.

4. *Records of Early English Drama: Cumberland, Westmorland and Gloucestershire*, ed. Audrey Douglas and Peter Greenfield (Toronto, 1986), 25.

5. *York Civic Records*, ed. Angelo Raine (1946), v. 117.

6. Hugh Owen, 'The Diary of Bulkeley of Dronwy, Anglesey', *Anglesey Antiquarian Society and Field Club Transactions* (1937), 138.

7. William Kethe, *A Sermon Made at Blandford Forum* (1571), fo. 18.

8. *Albions England* (1586), U. 121.

9. pp. 60–1.

10. *Jack a Lent his Beginning and Entertainment* (1621), sig. B2. For other early Stuart references, see *Pasquils Palinodia* (1619), 20, and Thomas Nabbes, *The Springs Glorie* (1638), sig. B.

11. *Materials for the History of Thomas Becket*, ed. James Craigie Robertson (1877), iii. 9.

12. Henry Thomas Riley (ed.), *Memorials of London and London Life* (1848), 571.

13. Hutton, *Merry England*, 19.

14. Thomas Tusser, *Five Hundred Pointes of Good Husbandrie*, ed. W. Payne and S. J. Herrtage (English Dialect Society, 1878), 180.

15. *The Journal of William Shellinks' Travels in England*, trans. and ed. Maurice Exwood and H. L. Lehmann (Camden Society, 5th ser. 1; 1993), 73.

16. Greater London RO, X56/5.

17. HMC 6th Report, appendix, 567; Joseph Strutt, *The Sports and Pastimes of the People of England*, ed. J. Charles Cox (1903), 224; John Aubrey, *Remaines of Gentilisme and Judaisme*, ed. James Britten (Folk-Lore Society, 1881), 41.

18. Strutt, *Sports and Pastimes*, 94–6; Morris Marples, *A History of Football* (1954), 19–46; Philip Stubbes, *Anatomie of Abuses* (1583), 83.

19. Clopper (ed.), *Chester*, pp. li–liii.

20. Douglas and Greenfield (eds.), *Cumberland, Westmorland, and Gloucestershire*, 25.

21. Anna Jean Mill, *Medieval Plays in Scotland* (Edinburgh, 1927), 11; F. Marian McNeill, *The Silver Bough* (Glasgow, 1959), ii. 40.

22. Marples, *History of Football*, 13.

23. Richard Carew, *The Survey of Cornwall*, ed. F. E. Halliday (1953), 147–50.

24. On which see Hutton, *Merry England*, 89.

25. Ian W. Archer, *The Pursuit of Stability: Social Relations in Elizabethan London* (Cambridge, 1991), esp. 1–3; Keith Lindley, 'Riot Prevention and Control in Early Stuart London', *TRHS* 5th ser. 33 (1983), 109–10; Hutton, *Merry England*, chs. 4–5, and esp. pp. 188–9.

26. John Brand, *Observations upon the Popular Antiquities of Great Britain*, ed. Sir Henry Ellis (1908), i. 88, cites *The Seven Deadly Sins of London* (1606), *The Masque of the Inner Temple* (1613), and *Tottenham Court* (1638), to which can be added Francis Beaumont's *The Knight of the Burning Pestle* (1613), v. 320–1.

27. Considered in Brand, *Observations*, i. 88, and Hutton, *Merry England*, 188–9.

28. John Latimer, *The Annals of Bristol in the Seventeenth Century* (Bristol, 1900), 260–92.

29. Ibid. 353, 434.

30. *Calendar of State Papers, Domestic Series*, 1673, 547; PRO, SP 29/333/89 (canon's complaint).

31. Brand, *Observations*, i. 88, quotes *A Satyre against Separatists* (1675) and *Poor Robin's Almanac* (1707).

32. Guildhall Library, London, MS 1568.

33. Quoted in A. R. Wright, *British Calendar Customs*, ed. T. E. Lones (Folk-Lore Society, 1936), i. 21.

34. J. M. E. Saxby, *Shetland Traditional Lore* (Edinburgh, 1932), 78–9.

35. William Grant Stewart, *The Popular Superstitions and Festive Amusements of the Highlanders of Scotland* (Edinburgh, 1823), 255–7; Walter Gregor, *Notes on the Folk-Lore of the North-East of Scotland* (Folk-Lore Society, 1881), 164–6; McNeill, *Silver Bough*, ii. 42–3; Ernest W. Marwick, *The Folklore of Orkney and Shetland* (1975), 106.

36. McNeill, *Silver Bough*, ii. 45; *British Calendar Customs: Scotland*, i. 3–5.

37. Joseph Train, *An Historical and Statistical Account of the Isle of Man* (Douglas, 1845), 117.

38. Gregor, *North-East of Scotland*, 166; T. F. Thiselton Dyer, *British Popular Customs* (1876), 79; William Henderson, *Notes on the Folk-Lore of the Northern Counties of England and the Borders* (Folk-Lore Society; 1879), 77–8; *British Calendar Customs: Scotland*, i. 12–14, 25–6.

39. Doris Jones-Baker, *The Folklore of Hertfordshire* (1977), 129.

40. F. Sawyer, 'Sussex Folklore and Customs Connected with the Seasons', *Sussex Archaeological Collections*, 33 (1883), 239.

41. Strutt, *Sports and Pastimes*, 227.

42. R. P. Chope, 'Devonshire Calendar Customs. 1: Moveable Festivals', *Transactions of the Devonshire Association*, 68 (1936), 237.

43. Brand, *Observations*, i. 77–9.

44. J. Weld, *A History of Leagram* (Chetham Society, 1913), 124–5; Wright, *British Calendar Customs*, i. 22–3; T. Gwynne Jones, *Welsh Folklore and Folk-Custom* (Cambridge, 1979), 159–60.

45. William Hone, *The Every-Day Book and Table Book* (1832), i. 251–2; Jacqueline Simpson, *The Folklore of Sussex* (1973), 106.

46. J. Fisher, 'The Welsh Calendar', *Transactions of the Honourable Society of Cymmrodorion* (1894–5), 112–13; Edmund Hyde Hall, *A Description of Caernarvonshire* (Caernarvonshire Historical Society, 1952), 321.

47. *Tusser Redivivus*, quoted in Hone, *Every-Day Book*, i. 247–8.

48. Simpson, *Sussex*, 107.

49. Brand, *Observations*, i. 73–4.

50. Wright, *British Calendar Customs*, i. 23.

51. M. D. George, *London Life in the XVIIIth Century* (1925), 17, 326, 351–2; Robert W. Malcolmson, *Popular Recreations in English Society 1700–1850* (Cambridge, 1973), 119–22; R. W. Bushaway, 'Rite, Legitimation and Community in Southern England, 1700–1850', in Barry Stapleton (ed.), *Conflict and Community in Southern England* (New York, 1992), 117; Simpson, *Sussex*, 107; Bob Bushaway, *By Rite* (1982), 6; T. F. Thiselton Dyer, *Old English Social Life* (1898), 205–6; R. L. Tongue, *Somerset Folklore*, ed. K. M. Briggs (Folk-Lore Society, 1965), 157; John Brady, *Clavis Calendaria* (1812), i. 209; Margaret Baker, *Folklore and Customs of Rural England* (Newton Abbot, 1974), 107–8; Hone, *Every-Day Book*, 251; Peter Roberts, *The Cambrian Popular Antiquities* (1815), 112; Jonathan Ceredig Davies, *Folk-Lore of West and Mid-Wales* (Aberystwyth, 1911), 71; *County Folk-Lore*, (Folk-Lore Society, 1895): 3. Leicestershire and Rutland, ed. Charles J. Billson, 72–3; Trefor M. Owen, *Welsh Folk Customs* (St Fagaas 1974), 72–3; Thomas Sternberg, *The Dialect and Folk-Lore of Northamptonshire* (1851), 179–80; D. H. M. Read, 'Hampshire Folklore', *Folk-Lore*, 22 (1911), 323; Wright, *British Calendar Customs*, i. 23–4.

52. M. A. Courtney, *Cornish Feasts and Folklore* (1890), 23.

53. Malcolmson, *Popular Recreations*, 36–7, 79, 83; Brand, Observations, i. 92; George Morley, *Shakespeare's Greenwood* (1900), 102–3; Peter Robson, 'Calendar Customs in Nineteenth and Twentieth Century Dorset' (Sheffield M.Phil. thesis, 1988), 37–9; Mabel Peacock, 'The Hood Game at Haxey, Lincolnshire', *Folk-Lore* 7 (1896), 345–6; Wright, *British Calendar Customs*, i. 27; Matthew Alexander, 'Shrove Tuesday Football in Surrey', *Surrey Archaeological Collections*, 77 (1986), 197–205.

54. Brand, *Observations*, i. 91; Gregor, *North-East of Scotland*, 166; McNeill, *Silver Bough*, iv. 21–3; *British Calendar Customs: Scotland*, i. 16–26.

55. Owen, *Welsh Folk Customs*, 75–6; Davies, *West and Mid-Wales*, 71.

56. Sources at nn. 53–5, plus Malcolmson, *Popular Recreations*, 138–45; Robert O. Storch, 'Remember, Remember The Fifth of November', in Storch (ed.), *Popular Culture and Custom in Nineteenth-Century England* (1982), 80; Hugh Cunningham, *Leisure in the Industrial Revolution* (1980), 78. The case-studies are from Malcolmson and Alexander.

57. Wright, *British Calendar Customs*, i. 27.

58. McNeill, *Silver Bough*, iv. 21–3.

59. Malcolmson, *Popular Recreations*, 140.

60. Jacqueline Simpson, *The Folklore of the Welsh Border* (1976), 138.

61. Tony Deane and Tony Shaw, *The Folklore of Cornwall* (1975), 165.

62. Seemingly for the first time in Robert Studley Vidal's letters to John Brand from Cornborough, Devon, in the 1800s, by which time it was well established: BL Add. MS 41313, esp. fos. 80–1.

63. William Brockie, *Legends and Superstitions of the County of Durham* (Sunderland, 1886), 95–6; Wright, *British Calendar Customs*, i. 3; Jones, *Welsh Folklore*, 159.

64. Source at n. 62.

65. Tongue, *Somerset Folklore*, 156; Dyer, *British Popular Customs*, 77–8; 87; C. E. Prior, *Dedications of Churches* (Oxfordshire Archaeological Society, 1903), 41; Ralph Whitlock, *The Folklore of Wiltshire* (1976), 50–2; Peter Manning, 'Stray Notes on Oxfordshire Folklore', *Folk-Lore*, 14 (1903), 107; D. H. M. Read, 'Hampshire Folklore', *Folk-Lore*, 22 (1911), 323; Wright, *British Calendar Customs*. i. 16–17; G. F. Northall, *English Folk-Rhymes* (1892), 190–1; Wendy Boase, *The Folklore of Hampshire and the Isle of Wight* (1976), 149; Jones-Baker, *Hertfordshire*, 128; Robson, 'Calendar Customs', 182–206.

66. Jones-Baker, *Hertfordshire*, 128.

67. Boase, *Hampshire*, 149.

68. Dyer, *British Popular Customs*, 87–8.

69. Ibid. 77–8.

70. Read, 'Hampshire', 323.

71. Source at n. 62; Robert Health, *A Natural and Historical Account of the Isles of Scilly* (1750), 127.

72. Malcolmson, *Popular Recreations*, 171; Kingsley Palmer, *The Folklore of Somerset* (1976), 98; M. Walker and Helen Bennett, *Somerset Folklore* (Somerset Rural Life Museum, n.d.), n.p.; T. Brown, '53rd Report on Folklore', *Transactions of the Devonshire Association*, 88 (1956), 253–4; T. Brown, '63rd Report', ibid. 98 (1966), 88; R. P. Chope, 'Devonshire Calendar Customs 1: Moveable Festivals', ibid. 68 (1936), 233–6; 'Lent-Crocking', *Somerset and Dorset Notes and Queries*, 5 (1897), 142; Tongue, *Somerset Folklore*, 155; Marie Trevelyan, *Folk-Lore and Folk-Stories of Wales* (1909), 246; Anna Eliza Bray, *A Description of the Past of Devonshire Bordering on the Tamar and the Tavy* (1836), ii. 286–7; P. H. Ditchfield, *Old English Customs Extant at the Present Time* (1896), 167; Stanley Jackson Coleman, *Carmarthenshire Folklore* (Douglas, 1955), n.p.; Ralph Whitlock, *The Folklore of Devon* (1977), 138–40; John Symonds Udal, *Dorsetshire Folk-Lore* (Hertford, 1922), 22; Wright, *British Calendar Customs*, i, 4–7, 17, 20; 'The Folk-Lore of Somerset,' *Folk-Lore*, 31 (1920), 239–40; Northall, *Folk-Rhymes*, 190–1; Robert Hunt, *Popular Romances of the West of England* (1881), 383; Courtney, *Cornish Feasts*, 21–3; W. G. Willis Watson, *Calendar of Customs . . . Connected with the County of Somerset* (Taunton, 1920), 52; Deane and Shaw, *Cornwall*, 163; Robson, 'Calendar Customs', 182–206.

73. Palmer, *Somerset*, 98; Tongue, *Somerset*, 155.

74. Bray, *Tamas and Tavy*, ii. 286–7; Wright, *British Calendar Customs*, i. 4–5; Whitlock, *Devon*, 139.

75. Malcolmson, *Popular Recreations*, 171–2.

76. Wright, *British Calendar Customs*, i. 17; Northall, *Folk-Rhymes*, 190–1; Hunt, *Popular Romances*, 383.

77. Malcolmson, *Popular Recreations*, 172; 'Lent Crocking', 142; Robson, 'Calendar Customs', 202–3.

78. T. Brown, '53rd Report', 253–4; Iona and Peter Opie, *The Lore and Language of Schoolchildren* (Oxford, 1959), 239; Robson, 'Calendar Customs', 182; Tongue, *Somerset*, 155.

79. Trefor M. Owen, *Welsh Folk Customs* (St Fagans, 1974), 72.

80. Again, the literature is vast, being well represented by the relevant sections of Brand and Wright, the Folk-Lore Society County Folk-Lore series, and the country studies by Burne, Leather, Hackwood, Addy, Nicholson, and Brodie.

81. Walker and Bennett *Somerset Folklore*, n.p.; Tongue, *Somerset*, 157; Courtney, *Cornish Feasts*, 23–4; Robson, 'Calendar Customs', 33–4; Deane and Shaw, *Cornwall*, 164

82. Crichton Porteous, *Ancient Customs of Derbyshire* (Derby, 1962), 13–14.

CHAPTER 16

1. *The Oxford English Dictionary*, 2nd edn. (1989), viii. 828–9.

2. Thomas Tusser, *Five Hundred Pointes of Good Husbandrie*, ed. W. Payne and S. J. Herrtage (English Dialect Society, 1878), 87–90.

3. Venetia Newall, *An Egg at Easter* (1971), 179–80.

4. *A Collection of the Laws and Canons of the Church of England*, ed. John Johnson (Oxford, 1850), 475–8, 516.

5. Eamon Duffy, *The Stripping of the Altars* (New Haven, 1992), 41.

6. *Tudor and Stuart Proclamations*, ed. Robert Steele (Oxford, 1910), vol. i, nos. 220–3390, *passim*, and vol. ii. nos. 96–2277, *passim*; John Taylor, *Jack A Lent his Beginning and Entertainment* (1621), sig. B2, *Tudor Royal Proclamations*, ed. Paul L. Hughes and James F. Larkin (New Haven, 1964–9), vol. i, nos. 177, 209, 214, 297, 368, vols. ii–iii, nos. 453–800, *passim; Stuart Royal Proclamations*, ed. James Larkin and Paul Hughes, vol. i (Oxford, 1973), nos. 181, 184, 193; *Stuart Royal Proclamations*, ed. James Larkin, vol. ii (Oxford, 1983), nos. 37, 59, 82, 106, 123, 160, 296.

7. Two different versions of the rite, taken from *Festyvall* (1511) and Nicholas Doncaster, *The Doctrine of the Mass Book* (1554), are reprinted in John Brand, *Observations on the Popular Antiquities of Great Britain*, ed. Sir Henry Ellis (1908 reprint), i. 95–6.

8. Henry John Feasey, *Ancient English Holy Ceremonial* (1897), 1–12, assembles the evidence from inventories.

9. Ibid. 13–49. There seems to be no comparable Scottish data.

10. Ibid. 13–14, 40.

11. *Inventory of Church Goods temp. Edward III*, ed. A. Watkin, (Norfolk Record Society, 19; 1948), *passim*.

12. Steele, *Proclamations*, vol. i, no. 188.

13. Edward Cardwell, *Documentary Annals of the Reformed Church of England* (Oxford, 1884), i. 42; J. Strype, *Ecclesiastical Memorials* (Oxford, 1822), ii. 2. 125.

14. Ronald Hutton, 'The Local Impact of the Tudor Reformations', in Christopher Haigh (ed.), *The English Reformation Revised* (Cambridge, 1987). 121–2.

15. PRO, E. 117, *passim*.

16. Hutton, 'The Local Impact', 134–5.

17. Peter Roberts, *The Cambrian Popular Antiquities* (1815), 112.

18. *The Diary of Henry Machyn*, ed. J. Nichols (Camden Society, 1848), 33.

19. Nash, Jonson, Beaumont, Fletcher, Taylor, and Quarle, quoted in Brand, *Observations*, i. 101, and A. R. Wright, *British Calendar Customs*, ed. T. E. Lones (Folk-Lore Society, 1936), i. 39.

20. Wright, *British Calendar Customs*, i. 39–40; M. A. Courtney, *Cornish Feasts and Folklore* (1890), 24.

21. Wright, *British Calendar Customs*, i. 33–4.

22. Brand, *Observations*, i. 103–6.

23. Ibid. 107.

24. *The Journal of William Shellinks' Travels in England*, trans. and ed. Maurice Exwood and H. L. Lehrnann (Camden Soc. 5th ser. 1, 1993), 75.

25. *The Diary of Samuel Pepys* (ed. by Robert Latham and William Matthews, 1974), viii. 89.

26. *Shellinks' Travels*, 75.

27. Brand, *Observations*, 103.

28. M. D. George, *London Life in the XVIIIth Century* (1925), 118.

29. Prys Morgan, 'From a Death to a View', in Eric Hobsbawm and Terence Ranger (eds.), *The Invention of Tradition* (Cambridge, 1983), 90.

30. *Diary of . . . Richard Symonds*, ed. C. E. Long (Camden Society, 1859), 27.

31. *The Poetical Works of Robert Herrick*, ed. L. C. Martin (Oxford, 1956), 236. For 'simnel', see T. F. Thiselton Dyer, *British Popular Customs* (1876), 115.

32. John Brady, *Clavis Calendria* (1812), i. 245–6; Frederick William Hackwood, *Staffordshire Customs, Superstitions and Folklore* (Lichfield, 1924), 11; Charlotte Sophia Burne, *Shropshire Folk-Lore* (1883), 323.

33. Hackwood, *Staffordshire*, 12; Wright, *British Calendar Customs*, i. 44; George Morley, *Shakespeare's Greenwood* (1900), 103–5; John Noake, *Notes and Queries for Worcestershire* (1856), 210; 'Worcestershire Folklore', *Folk-Lore*, 26 (1915), 24.

34. Brady, *Clavis Calendria*, i. 246 (for Cheshire); Dyer, *British Popular Customs*, 117 (for Monmouthshire); Ella Mary Leather, *The Folk-Lore of Herefordshire* (Hereford, 1912), 96–7; Burne, *Shropshire*, 323–4.

35. P. H. Ditchfield, *Old English Customs Extant at the Present Time* (1896), 68–9; L. M. Eyre, 'Folklore Notes from St. Brivael's', *Folk-Lore*, 13 (1902), 174; J. B. Partridge, 'Cotswold Place-Lore and Customs', *Folk-Lore*, 23 (1912), 444; Katherine M. Briggs, *The Folklore of the Cotswolds* (1974), 21; Kingsley Palmer, *The Folklore of Somerset* (1976), 99; R. P. Chope, 'Devonshire Calendar Customs. I. Moveable Festivals', *Transactions of the Devonshire Association*, 68 (1936), 237.

36. R. T. Hampson, *Medii Aevi Kalendarium* (1841), 175–6; J. Weld, *A History of Leagram* (Chetham Society, 1913), 126–7; Ditchfield, *Old English Customs*, 69; John Harland and T. T. Wilkinson, *Lancashire Folk-Lore* (1867), 222; *The Autobiography of Samuel Bamford*, ed. W. H. Chaloner (1967), i. 136–7.

37. Ditchfield, *Old English Customs*, 68–9; *County Folk-Lore*, i. (Folk-Lore Society, 1895): 3. Leicestershire and Rutland, ed. C. J. Billson, 74.

38. Trefor M. Owen, *Welsh Folk Customs* (St Fagans, 1974), 78–9; Ditchfield, *Old English Customs*, 68–9.

39. Wright, *British Calendar Customs*, i. 47; Burne, *Shropshire*, 323–4; Leather, *Herefordshire*, 96.

40. Whitlock, *Devon*, 140; Iona and Peter Opie, *The Lore and Language of Schoolchildren* (Oxford, 1959), 241–2.

41. Hampson, *Medii Aevi Kalendrium*, 180.

42. Llewellyn Jewitt, 'On Ancient Customs and Sports of the County of Nottingham', *Journal of the British Archaeological Association*, 1st ser. 8 (1853), 232; John Nicholson, *Folk Lore of East Yorkshire* (1890), 12; Mrs Gutch (ed.), *County Folk-Lore*, iii. *North Riding of Yorkshire, York and the Ainsty* (Folk-Lore Society, 1901), 241; Mrs Gutch (ed.), *County Folk-Lore*, vi. *East Riding of Yorkshire* (Folk-Lore Society, 1912), 93–4; 'Scraps of English Folklore', *Folk-Lore*, (1929), 284; Richard Blakeborough, *Wit, Character, Folklore and Customs of the North Riding of Yorkshire* (1898), 76; information concerning Bishop Middleham, County Durham, *c.*1900, and Hartlepool, *c.*1920, from Wyvis Crosby, Aug. 1977; Wright, *British Calendar Customs*, i. 52; William Hutchinson, *A View of Northumberland* (1776), vol ii, appendix 8; *British Calendar Customs: Scotland*, Mary Macleod Banks (Folk-Lore Society, 1937), 29–30. By one of those fascinating caprices of transference and adoption, it was also found at one village in the Vyrnwy Valley of eastern Montgomeryshire, Llansantffraid-ym-Mechain: Owen, *Welsh Folk Customs*, 79.

43. Dyer, *British Popular Customs*, 121–3; Owen, *Welsh Folk Customs*, 79.

44. William Henderson, *Notes on the Folk-Lore of the Northern Counties of England and the Borders* (Folk-Lore Society, 1879), 80.

45. Sources at n. 42.

46. John Aubrey, *Remaines of Gentilisme and Judaisme*, ed. James Britten (Folk-Lore Society, 1881), 10; Brand, *Observations*, i. 132–6; Robert Chambers, *The Book of Days* (1864), i. 462; Wright, *British Calendar Customs*, ii. 173.

47. Brand, *Observations*, i. 135; Aubrey, *Remaines*, 10.

48. Brand, *Observations*, i. 139; R. L. Tongue, *Somerset Folklore* ed. K. M. Briggs (Folklore Society County Folklore 8, 1965), 158; Nicholson, *East Yorkshire*, 13; *County Folk-Lore*, v. *Lincolnshire*, ed. Mrs Gutch and Mabel Peacock (Folk-Lore Society,

1908), 194–5; Leather, *Herefordshire*, 98; Edward W. B. Nicholson, *Golspie* (1897), 109; BL Add. MS 41313, fo 83 (information upon Devon); Blakeborough, *North Riding*, 79; 'Scraps of English Folklore', *Folk-Lore*, 20 (1909), 223; 'Scraps of English Folklore', *Folk-Lore*, 36 (1925), 86; Wright, *British Calendar Customs*, ii. 171–4; Courtney, *Cornish Feasts*, 27; Banks, *British Calendar Customs: Scotland*, ii. 195–6; Kevin Dana-her, *The Year in Ireland* (Cork, 1972), 84.

49. Opie and Opie, *Lore and Language*, 243–7.

50. Sources at n. 48.

CHAPTER 17

1. Venetia Newall, *An Egg at Easter* (1971), 159; John Dowden, *The Church Year and Kalendar* (Cambridge, 1910), 105–17; John T. McNeill, *The Celtic Churches* (1974), 109–18, 196–7.

2. Dowden, *Church Year*, 40–2; T. F. Thiselton Dyer, *British Popular Customs* (1876), 148; E. O. James, *Seasonal Feasts and Festivals* (1961), 208–10; John Brand, *Observations on the Popular Antiquities of Great Britain*, ed. Sir Henry Ellis (1908), i. 143.

3. *A Collection of the Laws and Canons of the Church of England*, ed. John Johnson (Oxford, 1850), 328.

4. Ibid. 249; *Medieval Handbooks of Penance*, ed. John T. McNeill and Helena M. Gamer (New York, 1938), 84.

5. Bede, *Works*, ed. J. A. Giles (Oxford, 1843), vi. 178–9.

6. The historiography of the issue is well discussed in Newall, *Egg at Easter*, 384–6. The case against Bede's interpretation has recently been reasserted with considerable force by Alby Stone, 'Eostre: An Old English Goddess?', *Talking Stick*, 10 (Spring 1993), 2–3.

7. Bede, *Ecclesiastical History*, ii. 9, describes an assassination attempt upon the then still pagan King Edwin of Northumbria on Easter Day 626. N. J. Higham, *The Kingdom of Northumbria* (Stroud, 1993), 81, has suggested that it was 'the pagan festival of Easter' which the king was celebrating. In fact there is nothing to indicate that Bede did not mean the Christian feast, which was being kept at Edwin's court by his Christian queen and her bishop. Muirchu's famous seventh-century *Life of Patrick*, chs. 15–22, contains an account of 'a festival of idolatory, with many conjurations, feats of sorcery and sundry other heathen superstitions' held, at Tara in Ireland by the pagan King Loegaire at the same time as Easter. It is notable, however, that Muirchu himself says that it was not an annual but an irregular event. The whole episode may indeed be a complete fable, or it could be a memory of the *feis*, or inauguration feast, of an Irish monarch: D. A. Binchy, 'The Fair of Tailtu and the Feast of Tara', *Eriu*, 18 (1958), 113–36.

CHAPTER 18

1. *Manuale ad Usum Percelebris Ecclesia Sarisburiensis*, ed. A. Jeffries Collins (Henry Bradshaw Society, 1960), 12–14; Henry John Feasey, *Ancient English Holy Week Ceremonial* (1897), 53–83; Eamon Duffy, *The Stripping of the Altars* (New Haven, 1992), 23; J. Charles Cox, *Churchwardens' Accounts* (1913), 253–4.

2. Feasey, *Holy Week Ceremonial*, 51–5.

3. Ibid. 53–4; Trefor M. Owen, *Welsh Folk Customs* (St Fagans, 1974), 80.

4. Ronald Hutton, *The Rise and Fall of Merry England* (Oxford, 1994), 21.

5. Ibid. 21, 52.

6. D. H. M. Read, 'Hampshire Folklore', *Folk-Lore*, 22 (1911), 325.

7. Tract quoted in William Kelly, *Notices Illustrative of the Drama... of Leicester* (1865), 25–6.

8. *Tudor Royal Proclamations*, ed. Paul L. Hughes and James F. Larkin (New Haven, 1964), vol. i., no. 188.

9. [Anthony Sparrow (ed.)], *A Collection of Articles* (1671), 2–3.

10. Edward Cardwell, *Documentary Annals of the Reformed Church of England* (Oxford, 1884), i. 42.

11. Hutton, *Merry England*, 83; Richard Watson Dixon, *History of the Church of England from the Abolition of the Roman Jurisdiction* (1903), ii. 516; Worcester (St Helen's) RO, 009/1/BA 2636, parcel 11, fos. 155–9 (I owe this reference to Diarmaid MacCulloch).

12. *Narratives of the Days of the Reformation*, ed. J. G. Nichols (Camden Society, 1859), 287; Charles Wriothesley, *A Chronicle of England*, ed. W. D. Hamilton (Camden Society, 1875), ii. 113.

13. Published 1554, quoted in John Brand, *Observations on the Popular Antiquities of Great Briatin*, ed. Sir Henry Ellis (1908), i. 125–6.

14. Hutton, *Merry England*, 97.

15. Ibid. 106.

16. Brand, *Observations*, i. 127; Bob Bushaway, *By Rite* (1982), 150–1; William Brockie, *Legends and Superstitions of the County of Durham* (Sunderland, 1886), 93; John Nicholson, *Folk Lore of East Yorkshire* (1890), 12; P. H. Ditchfield, *Old English Customs Extant at the Present Time* (1896), 70; Mrs Gutch (ed.) *County Folk-Lore*, ii. *North Riding of Yorkshire, York and the Ainsty* (Folk-Lore Society, 1901), 241–3; Northcote W. Thomas (ed.), *County Folk-Lore*, iv. *Northumberland* (Folk-Lore Society, 1904), 69; William Henderson, *Notes on the Folk-Lore of the Northern Counties of England and the Borders* (Folk-Lore Society, 1879), 80; Richard Blakeborough, *Wit. Character, Folklore and Customs of the North Riding of Yorkshire* (1898), 76; A. R. Wright, *British Calendar Customs*, ed. T. E. Lones (Folk-Lore Society, 1936), i. 54–6; Flora Thompson, *Lark Rise to Candleford* (Oxford, 1945). 232: Jacqueline Simpson, *The Folklore of Sussex* (1973), 109–10; 'Scraps of English Folklore', *Folk-Lore*, 36 (1925), 82; William Hutchinson, *A View of Northumberland* (1778), vol. ii, appendix 9.

17. Brockie, *Durham*, 93; Gutch, *County Folklore*, ii. 241–3; Henderson, *Northern Counties*, 80; Wright, *British Calendar Customs*, i. 56.

18. Marie Trevelyan, *Folk-Lore and Folk-Stories of Wales* (1909), 245–6.

19. Owen, *Welsh Folk Customs*, 80–2; L. M. Eyre, 'Folklore Notes from St Brivael's', *Folk-Lore*, 13 (1902), 174; Charlotte Sophia Burne, *Shropshire Folk-Lore* (1883), 330.

20. Cox, *Churchwardens' Accounts*, 249–52, 258–9; *The Use of Sarum*, ed. Walter Howard Frere (Cambridge, 1898), i. 142–3; Feasey, *Holy Week Ceremonial*, 84–92. These authors cite London, Salisbury, and Exeter cases, to which I can only add Rye: East Sussex RO, Rye Corporation Records 147/1, fos. 1–111. For references to the ceremony in sermons see *Speculum Sacerdorale*, ed. E. H. Weatherly (EETS, 1935), 101–2, and *Mirk's Festival*, ed. T. Erbe (EETS, 1905), 117–18.

21. *Two Lives of Saint Cuthbert*, trans. Bertram Colgrave (Cambridge, 1940), 219; Feasey, *Holy Week Ceremonial*, 95–103; Wright, *British Calendar Customs*, i. 62–3; Arnold Kellet, 'King John's Maundy', *History Today* (Apr. 1990), 34–9.

22. W. Lambarde, 'The Order of the Maundy Made at Greenwich, March 19, 1572', *Archaeologia*, 1 (1770), 7–8; John Nichols, *The Progesses... of Queen Elizabeth* (1788), i. 37*–38*.

23. Brand, *Observations*, i. 143–7; Wright, *British Calendar Customs*, i. 62–3.

24. *Rites of Durham*, ed. Canon Fowler (Surtees Society, 107; 1903), 77.

25. Brand, *Observations*, i. 147.

26. Wright, *British Calendar Customs*, i. 64–5; William Hone, *The Every-Day Book and Table Book* (1832), i. 401–2.

27. Feasey, *Holy Week Ceremonial*, 93–113; Duffy, *Stripping of the Altars*, 28–9; H. Owen and J. B. Blakeway, *A History of Shrewsbury* (1825), i. 336; *Select Works of John Bale*, ed. H. Christmas (Parker Society, 1849), 528.

28. Cox, *Churchwardens' Accounts*, 259.

29. Raymond Crawfurd, 'The Blessing of Cramp Rings', in Charles Singer (ed.), *Studies in the History and Method of Science* (Oxford, 1917), 165–88.

30. Ibid. 173; *Gentleman's Magazine*, 64 (1794), 433 and 889.

31. Feasey, *Holy Week Ceremonial*, 114–20; Duffy, *Stripping of the Altars*, 29; both using *Missale ad Usum Insignis et Praeclarae Ecclesiae Sarum*, ed. F. H. Dickinson (1861–83), cols. 316–33.

32. *Rites of Durham*, 11–12.

33. Feasey, *Holy Week Ceremonial*, 114–28; Cox, *Churchwardens' Accounts*, 259; *Dives and Pauper*, ed. P. H. Barnum (EETS, 1976), 2, 26, 87–9; E. K. Chambers, *The Medieval Stage* (Oxford, 1963), ii. 17–19; F. M. Salter, *Medieval Drama in Chester* (Toronto, 1955), 19; *The Earl of Northumberland's Household Book*, ed. Bishop Thomas Percy (1905), 322–3.

34. D. Whitelocke, M. Brett, and C. N. L. Brooke (eds.), *Councils and Synods... 871–1066* (Oxford, 1981), 220.

35. Feasey, *Holy Week Ceremonial*, 119–20; E. O. James, *Seasonal Feasts and Festivals* (1961), 211.

36. Duffy, *Stripping of the Altars*, 29.

37. *Tudor Royal Proclamations*, no. 188.

38. Thomas Cranmer, *Miscellaneous Writings*, ed. J. E. Cox (Parker Society, 1844), 415; John Foxe, *Acts and Monuments*, ed. Stephen Reed Cattley (1938), v. 561–2.

39. See n. 10.

40. Sources at n. 11.

41. Hutton, *Merry England*, 97.

42. Brand, *Observations*, i. 86.

43. Hutton, *Merry England*, 23–4; Duffy, *Stripping of the Altars*, 31–2; T. F. Thistleton Dyer, *Church Lore Gleanings* (1892), 224. The parishes where the sepulchre was apparently not used in the early Tudor period were Bramley, Stoke Charity, Crondall, and Ellingham (Hants); Croscombe, Halse, Banwell, and Nettlecombe (Somerset); Dennington, Metifield, Brundish, Mickfield, and Bardwell (Suffolk); Bolney and Steyning (Sussex); Launceston (Cornwall); Winterslow (Wilts.); Sheriff Hutton (Yorks.); Horley (Surrey); North Elmham (Norfolk); Addlethorpe Ingoldmells (Lincs.); Bassingbourn (Cambs.); Stoke Edith (Herefordshire). The locations of these records are given in the appendix of Hutton, *Merry England*. The larger totals for Hampshire, Somerset, and Suffolk are almost certainly due to the greater survival of rural accounts from those countries, so to plot the sample on a map is valueless.

44. Chambers, *Medieval Stage*, ii. 8–16; A. Heales, 'Easter Sepulchres', *Archaeologia*, 42 (1867), 263–70.

45. *Inventory of Church Goods temp. Edward III*, ed. A. Watkin (Norfolk Record Society, 19, 1948), *passim*.

46. Hutton, *Merry England*, 53.

47. Ibid. 74–5.

48. Ibid. 82, 84.

49. Ibid. 95, 97.

50. Ibid. 105–6.

51. Hone, *Every-Day Book*, i. 402–3; T. F. Thiselton Dyer, *British Popular Customs* (1876), 149.

52. Richard Mason, *Tales and Traditions of Tenby* (1858), 19.

53. F. Sawyer, 'Sussex Folklore and Customs Connected with the Seasons', *Sussex Archaeological Collections*, 33 (1883), 240–1; Jonathan Ceredig Davies, *Folk-Lore of West and Mid-Wales* (Aberystwyth, 1911), 73; Mrs Gutch (ed.), *County Folklore*, ii. 43; Frederick William Hackwood, *Staffordshire Customs, Superstitions and Folklore* (Lichfield, 1924), 12; Mrs Gutch (ed.), *County Folklore*, vi. *East Riding of Yorkshire* (Folk-Lore Society, 1912), 95; Enid Porter, *Cambridgeshire Customs and Folklore* (1969), 108; Ella Mary Leather, *The Folk-Lore of Herefordshire* (Hereford, 1912), 78–9; Ralph Whitlock, *The Folklore of Devon* (1977), 142; L. Salmon, 'Folklore in the Kennet Valley', *Folk-Lore* 13 (1902), 423; John Symonds Udal, *Dorsetshire Folk-Lore* (Hertford, 1922), 30–2; Charlotte Sophia Burne, *Shropshire Folk-Lore* (1883), 333; M. L. Stanton *et al.*, 'Worcestershire Folklore', *Folk-Lore*, 26 (1915), 95; Wright, *British Calendar Customs*, i. 71–3 (for Warwickshire, Cornwall, Hampshire, Wiltshire, Gloucestershire, and County Durham); James Obelkevitch, *Religion and Rural Society: South Lindsey 1825–1875* (Oxford, 1976), 267.

54. Porter, *Cambridgeshire Customs*, 108.

55. Thomas Sternberg, *The Dialect and Folk-Lore of Northamptonshire* (1851), 189.

56. *Poor Robin's Almanac*, quoted in Brand, *Observations*, i. 154–7.

57. Hone, *Every-Day Book*, i. 403–4.

58. Brand, *Observations*, i. 154–7; Brockie, *County of Durham*, 105; Marjorie Rowling, *The Folklore of the Lake District* (1976), 113; Owen, *Welsh Folk Customs*, 83; *British Calendar Customs, Scotland*, i. 36.

59. *British Calendar Customs, Scotland*, i. 36.

60. James, *Seasonal Feasts*, 211; Feasey, *Holy Week Ceremonial*, 179–80.

61. J. G. Frazer, *Balder the Beautiful* (1914), i. 131–41.

62. A point noted by Duffy, *Stripping of the Altars*, 23.

63. *Rites of Durham*, 10.

64. Hutton, *Merry England*, 24.

65. Feasey, *Holy Week Ceremonial*, 179–82; *Councils and Synods...1205–1313*, ed. F. M. Powicke and C. R. Cheney (Oxford, 1964), 56, 178, 318, 513, 715–16, 1006, 1123.

66. Listed in the appendix to Hutton, *Merry England*.

67. Feasey, *Holy Week Ceremonial*, 179–234; Cox, *Churchwardens' Accounts*, 54–60; *Sarum Manual*, ed. Collins, 19–25; *Rites of Durham*, 10–11.

68. Hutton, *Merry England*, 81, 84.

69. Ibid. 95–6, 106.

70. *Rites of Durham*, 12–13.

71. Duffy, *Stripping of the Altars*, 30.

72. Feasey, *Holy Week Ceremonial*, 130–78; *Records of Plays and Players in Norfolk and Suffolk 1330–1642*, ed. D. Galloway and J. Wasson (Malone Society, 1980), 16.

73. *Northumberland Household Book*, 333; *Henley Borough Records*, ed. P. Briers (Oxfordshire Record Society, 1960), 129–99; Hugh R. Watkin, *Dartmouth* (1935), i. 62; Surrey (Kingston upon Thames) RO, KG/2/2. years 1509 and 1519; Charles Kerry, *History of the Municipal Church of St Lawrence, Reading* (Reading, 1881), 237; Cox, *Churchwardens' Accounts*, 35 (for St Martin in the Fields, Westminster).

74. *Sarum Manual*, ed. Collins, 64–81; Cox, *Churchwardens' Accounts*, 240.

75. William H. Hale, *A Series of Precedents and Proceedings in Criminal Cases* (1847), 7, 208–9.

76. *A Collection of the Laws and Canons of the Church of England*, ed. John Johnson (Oxford, 1850), ii. 261.

77. Duffy, *Stripping of the Altars*, 93.
78. Devon RO, Exeter St Petrock PW4; Berkshire RO, DIP 97/5/2.
79. Hutton, *Merry England*, 120–1, 176–7.
80. Ibid. 177, 182.
81. Ian B. Cowan, *The Scottish Reformation* (1982), 155–6.
82. *Minutes of the Westminster Assembly of Divines*, ed. A. F. Mitchell and John Struthers (Edinburgh, 1874), 3–11.
83. *Certain Queries Proposed by the King* (27 Apr. 1647); *Acts and Ordinances of the Interregnum*, ed. C. H. Firth and R. S. Rait (1911), i. 854.
84. Hutton, *Merry England*, 213–14.
85. *The Diary of John Evelyn*, ed. E. S. de Beer (Oxford, 1955), iii. 150, 169, 211–12.
86. Hutton, *Merry England*, 214.
87. Ibid. 246–7.
88. Norman Sykes, *Church and State in England in the Eighteenth Century* (1934), 250; John Walsh, Colin Haydon, and Stephen Taylor (eds.), *The Church of England, c.1689–c.1833* (Cambridge, 1993), 11; Cox, *Churchwardens' Accounts*, 238–9; Jacqueline Simpson, *The Folklore of the Welsh Border* (1976), 146.

CHAPTER 19

1. Venetia Newall, *An Egg at Easter* (1971), esp. 159, 204, and ch. 11.
2. Ibid. 263.
3. William Kethe, *A Sermon Made at Blandford Forum* (1571), fos. 18–19; Bale, quoted in Henry John Feasey, *Ancient English Holy Week Ceremonial* (1897), 126.
4. *The Great Diurnal of Nicholas Blundell*, ed. F. Tyres and J. J. Bagley (Lancashire and Cheshire Record Society, 110; 1968), 132, 207, 248, 280.
5. George Casper Homans, *English Villagers of the Thirteenth Century* (Cambridge, Mass., 1942), 365.
6. John Aubrey, *Remaines of Gentilisme and Judaisme*, ed. James Britten (Folk-Lore Society, 1881), 161–2.
7. P. H. Ditchfield, *Old English Customs Extant at the Present Time* (1896), 79–80; Trefor M. Owen, *Welsh Folk Customs* (National Museum of Wales, 1974), 86.
8. Iona and Peter Opie, *The Lore and Language of Schoolchildren* (Oxford, 1959), 252.
9. William Hone, *The Every-Day Book and Table Book* (1832), ii. 450; Ditchfield *Old English Customs*, 80; *Journal of the Archaeological Association*, 5 (1850), 253; John Harland and T. T. Wilkinson, *Lancashire Folk-Lore* (1867), 228; *The Autobiography of Samuel Bamford*, ed. W. H. Chaloner (1967), 138; Jacqueline Simpson, *The Folklore of the Welsh Border* (1976), 144.
10. *British Calendar Customs: Scotland*, ed. M. Macleod Banks (Folk-Lore Society, 1937), i. 41–3.
11. Bamford, *Autobiography*, 138.
12. Marjorie Rowling, *The Folklore of the Lake District* (1976), 112–13.
13. Charles Hardwick, *Traditions, Superstitions and Folk-Lore* (Manchester, 1872). 73; Harland and Wilkinson, *Lancashire*, 228–30; Wright, *British Calendar Customs*, i. 87; Newall. *Egg at Easter*, 365–70.
14. E. C. Cawte, *Ritual Animal Disguise* (Folk-Lore Society, 1978), 140–2.
15. R. J. E. Tiddy, *The Mummers' Play* (Folcroft, 1923), 234–6; Hardwick, *Traditions*, 73; Harland and Wilkinson, *Lancashire*, 236–7; Wright, *British Calendar Customs*, i. 87; Rowling, *Lake District*, 115–16; Mary Danielli, 'Jollyboys, or Pace Eggers, in Westmorland', *Folk-Lore*, 62 (1951), 463–7: Simpson, *Welsh Border*, 145; John Brennan, 'Pace-

Egging in the Calder Valley', *English Dance and Song*, 38: 2 (1976), 50–1; E. C. Cawte, Alex Helm, and N. Peacock, *English Ritual Drama: A Geographical Index* (Folk-Lore Society, 1967), 41, 48–9, 61, 64–5; William T. Palmer, *Lake Country Rambles* (1902), 318–34; Alexander Pearson, *Annals of Kirby Lonsdale and Lunesdale in Bygone Days* (Kendal, 1930), 185–94; 'Peace Egg', *Yorkshire Folk-Lore Journal*, 1 (1888), 131; Alex Helm, *Five Mumming Plays for Schools* (Folk-Lore Society, 1965).

16. Barry James Wood, 'A Functional Approach to English Folk Drama' (Ohio State University Ph.D. thesis, 1972), chapter 3; Brennan, 'Pace-Egging', 50.

17. Nicholas Blundell, *Great Diurnall*, cx. 132, 207, 248, 280; William Hutchinson, *A View of Northumberland* (Newcastle, 1778), vol, ii, appendix 10.

18. Opie and Opie, *Lore and Language*, 250–1.

19. Brand, *Observations*, i. 172; J. Weld, *A History of Leagram* (Chetham Society, 1913). 127; David Clark, *Between Pulpit and Pew* (Cambridge, 1982). 102; Hone, *Every-Day Book*, 426–7, ii. 450–1; William Brockie, *Legends and Superstitions of the County of Durham* (Sunderland, 1886), 93–4; T. F. Thiselton-Dyer, *British Popular Customs* (1876), 157; Llewellyn Jewitt, 'On Ancient Customs and Sports of the County of Nottingham', *Journal of the British Archaeological Association*, 1st ser. 8 (1853), 233; Harland and Wilkinson, *Lancashire*, 230; Newall, *Egg at Easter*, 365–70.

20. *British Calendar Customs: Scotland*, i. 37–41; James R. Nicolson, *Shetland Folklore* (1981), 138; Robert Chambers, *The Book of Days* (1864), i. 425.

21. Kingsley Palmer, *The Folklore of Somerset* (1976), 100–1; Wright, *British Calendar Customs*, i. 91.

22. 'Irish Folk-Lore', *Folk-Lore Journal*, 6 (1888), 60.

23. Information from Wyvis Crosby, by then of Bournemouth, given in Aug. 1977.

24. Brand, *Observations*, i. 172; Hone, *Every-Day Book*, 450–1; Wright, *British Calendar Customs*, i. 90–1; Rowling, *Lake District*, 113–14; Opie and Opie, *Lore and Language*, 253–4; 'Scraps of English Folklore', *Folk-Lore*, 40 (1929), 284.

25. Opie and Opie, *Lore and Language*, 253–4.

26. Ethel H. Rudkin, 'Lincolnshire Folklore', *Folk-Lore*, 44 (1933), 285; Frederick William Hackwood, *Staffordshire Customs, Superstitions and Folklore* (Lichfield, 1924), 14; Opie and Opie, *Lore and Language*, 253–4.

27. Chambers, *Book of Days*, i. 425; *British Calendar Customs: Scotland*, i. 37–45; Opie and Opie, *Lore and Language*, 253–4; Nicholson, *Shetland Folklore*, 138.

28. Dyer, *British Popular Customs*, 178; R. H. Buchanan, 'Calendar Customs', *Ulster Folklife*, 8 (1962), 22–3; Opie and Opie, *Lore and Language*, 254; 'Irish Folk-Lore', *Folk-Lore Journal*, 6 (1888), 60.

29. Hackwood, *Staffordshire Customs*, 14.

30. Opie and Opie, *Lore and Language*, 252–3; Clark, *Pulpit and Pew*, 102; information from Wyvis Crosby of Hartlepool in the 1920s, provided in Bournemouth Aug. 1977.

31. R. L. Tongue, *Somerset Folklore*, ed. K. M. Briggs (Folk-Lore Society County Folklore, 8; 1965), 161.

32. Information from Wyvis Crosby, as above, n. 30.

33. Doris Jones-Baker, *The Folklore of Hertfordshire* (1977), 133.

34. Laurence Whistler, *The English Festivals* (1947), 125.

CHAPTER 20

1. George Caspar Homans, *English Villagers of the Thirteenth Century* (Cambridge, Mass., 1942), 365; Samuel Denne, 'Memoir on Hokeday', *Archaeologia*, 7 (1785), 244–68.

2. *Statutes of the Realm* (1819), iv. i. 132–3.

3. To judge from Nicholas Breton, *Fantastickes*, quoted in John Dover Wilson, *Life in Shakespeare's England* (Cambridge, 1939), 23.

4. *Mirk's Festival*, ed. T. Erbe (EETS, 1905), 129.

5. Wilson, *Shakespeare's England*, 24.

6. *Inter alia*, John Brand, *Observations on the Popular Antiquities of Great Britain*, ed. Sir Henry Ellis (1908), i. 161–3.

7. Homans, *English Villagers*, 365.

8. *Records of Early English Drama: Chester*, ed. Lawrence M. Clopper, Manchester (1979), 253–4, 434.

9. *County Folk-Lore*, i (Folk-Lore Society, 1895), 3 Leicestershire and Rutland, ed. Charles J. Billson, 76; William Kelly, *Notices Illustrative of the Drama ... of Leicester* (1865), 168–74.

10. Charles Deering, *Nottinghamia Vetus et Nova* (Nottingham, 1751), 125.

11. William Hone, *The Every-Day Book and Table Book* (1832), i. 430.

12. HMC Middleton MSS, 354: *Records of the County of Wilts.*, ed. Howard Cunnington (Devizes, 1932), 91.

13. Cf. William Warner, *Albions England* (1589), book 5, p. 121, 'At Paske begun our Morrice'; *British Calendar Customs: Scotland*, ed. Mary Macleod Banks (Folk-Lore Society, 1937), 44, for 'Robin Hood, abbots unreason etc.' at Cranston 1590, and a maypole in Lanarkshire, 1625.

14. Henry Bourne, *Antiquitates Vulgares* (Newcastle upon Tyne, 1725), 196–7.

15. *The Autobiography of Samuel Bamford*, ed. W. H. Chaloner (1967), i. 138.

16. Hone, *Every-Day Book*, i. 436–8.

17. T. F. Thiselton Dyer, *British Popular Customs* (1876), 171–2.

18. Ibid. 178; Hone, *Every-Day Book*, i. 430; Robert W. Malcomson, *Popular Recreations in English Society 1700–1850* (Cambridge, 1973), 29.

19. Jacqueline Simpson, *The Folklore of the Welsh Border* (1976), 146–7.

20. Leicestershire RO, DE 36/140/9–12.

21. Richard Carew, *The Survey of Cornwall (1602)*, ed. F. E. Halliday (1953), 212.

22. J. G. Frazer, *The Golden Bough*, abridged ed. (1925), 287.

23. Bamford, *Autobiography*, i. 138–43; David Rollinson, *The Local Origins of Modern Society* (1992), 199–218.

24. Denne, 'Hokeday', 244–50.

25. Henry Thomas Riley, *Memorials of London and London Life* (1868), 561–71.

26. E. K. Chambers, *The Medieval Stage* (Oxford, 1963), i. 155 n. 3.

27. Ibid. i. 156.

28. ll. 1210–11.

29. Denne, 'Hokeday'. loc. cit.

30. Records of Hocktide gatherings in the period 1450–1550 can be found in the following sources: 'Churchwardens Accounts of the Parish of St. Andrew, Canterbury', ed. C. Cotton, *Archaeologia Cantiana*, xxxii. 212–43, xxxiii. 3–59, xxxiv. 1–27 (1485–1540); 'Accounts of the Churchwardens of St. Dunstan, Canterbury', ed. J. Cowper, *Archaeologia Cantiana*, xvi. 297–319, xvii. 93–100 (1490–1538); *The Churchwardens' Account Book for the Parish of St. Giles's, Reading*, ed. W. L. Nash (Reading, 1881), 1–29 (1518–29); Charles Kerry, *History of the Church of St. Lawrence, Reading* (Reading, 1883), 239 (1498–9, 1501, 1546–7); *Churchwardens' Accounts of St. Mary the Great, Cambridge*, ed. J. Foster (Cambridge Antiquarian Society, 1905), 34 (1516–18); *Records of Early English Drama: Cambridge*, ed. Alan H. Nelson (Toronto, 1989), 105–112, 1081–1103 (covers 1469–1536); 'The Churchwardens' Accounts of the Parish of St. Mary, Thame', ed. J. P.

Ellis, *Berks, Bucks and Oxon Archaeological Journal*, 10 (1904–5) 19; Oxfordshire RO, MS. DD. Par Thame b. 2, f. 77 (1546); Oxfordshire RO, MS. DD. Par. St. Michael, Oxford, a. 1–2 (1471, 1475–1547); Oxfordshire RO, MS. DD. Par. St. Mary the Virgin, Oxford, c. 33 (1510); *Lambeth Churchwardens' Accounts*, ed. C. Drew (Surrey Record Society, 1940, 2–56 (1504–22); *Churchwardens' Accounts of the Parish of Badsey*, ed. E. A. B. Barnard (1913), 9–10 (1525–9); *The Medieval Records of a London City Church: St. Mary at Hill*, ed. Henry Littlehales (EETS, 1905), 228–90 (1497–1515); *Churchwardens' Accounts of S. Edmund and S. Thomas, Sarum*, ed. H. J. F. Swayne (Wiltshire Record Society, 1896), 47–85 (1497–1541), 273–5 (1545–8); 'Churchwardens' Accounts, All Saints' Church, Walsall', ed. G. P. Mander, *Collections for a History of Staffordshire*, 52 (1928), 186–7 (1462); Cambridgeshire RO, P11/5/1–2 (Bassingbourn, 1497–1538); *Henley Borough Records*, ed. P. Briers (Oxfordshire Record Society, 1960), 75–204 (1474–1532); Surrey RO (Kingston upon Thames), KG/2/2, years 1508–39; 'Parish Records of Amersham', *Records of Buckinghamshire*, 7 (1890), 44 (1529–30); Buckinghamshire RO, PR234/5/1, fos. 39, 44 (Wing accounts for 1543–5). There is a probable reference to the custom at Shrewsbury in 1548–9: H. Owen and J. B. Blakeway, *A History of Shrewsbury* (1825), i. 559.

31. Sources at n. 39.

32. Sources at n. 30.

33. *Boxford Churchwardens' Accounts*, ed. Peter Northeast (Suffolk Records Society, 23; 1982), 1–40; Buckinghamshire RO, PR234/5/1, fos. 6–47 (ale at Crofton); *Churchwardens' Accounts of Marston, Spilsbury, Pyrton*, ed. F. Weaver and G. Clark, (Oxfordshire Record Society, 1925), 13; Churchwardens' Accounts of Croscombe etc., ed. Bishop Hobhouse (Somerset Record Society, 1890), 158: Oxfordshire RO, MS. DD. Par. St. Michael, Oxford a. 2, years 1547–8; W. B. Gerish, *The Hock-Tide Observance at Hexton in Hertfordshire* (Bishop's Stortford, 1910), 1–8; *The Records of St. Michael's Parish Church, Bishop's Stortford*, ed. J. Glasscock (1882), 1–37. BL Add. MS 6223, f. 13 (Wassair at Barton, Herts.).

34. Ronald Hutton, *The Rise and Fall of Merry England* (Oxford, 1994), 87.

35. Ibid. 100, 114. Records of Hocktide gatherings in the period 1550–1640 can be found in the following sources: 'St. Andrew, Canterbury', cccib. 45–50 (years 1554–9); Oxfordshire RO, MS. DD. Par. St. Michael, Oxford a. 2–3 (1556–1640); *Lambeth Churchwardens' Accounts*, 68 (1554–7); *S. Edmund and S. Thomas, Sarum*, 102–31 (1556–85), 279–91 (1557–82); Hampshire RO, 63m70/PWI, years 1554–63, 1586, 1596 (Bramley); *The Early Churchwardens' Accounts of Hampshire*, ed. John Foster Williams (Winchester, 1913), n.p., for Stoke Charity, years 1555–62; Hampshire RO, 88M81/PWI, years 1554–9 (St John, Winchester); *The Churchwardens' Accounts of the Parish of St. Mary, Reading*, ed. F. and A. Garry (Reading, 1893), 25–49 (1555–75); J. Silvester Davies, *A History of Southampton* (Southampton, 1883), 372 n. 3 (1568–80); Surrey RO (Kingston upon Thames), KG/2/3, years 1561–76; Gerish, *Hexton*, 1–8; John Symonds Udal, *Dorsetshire Folk-Lore* (Hertford, 1922), 33 (for Blandford, 1607 and 1616); Wiltshire RO, 1899/65 years 1567–80 (St Martin, Salisbury); Oxfordshire RO, MS. DD. Par. St Mary the Virgin, Oxford, c. 33, years 1566–1602; Oxfordshire, MS. DD. Par. St Martin, Oxford a. 1, years 1560–1640; Oxfordshire RO, MS. DD. Par. St Peter in the East, Oxford, a. 1–2, d. 1, years 1580–1631, Hampshire RO, 29M84/PWI, years 1625–6 (Alton); Daniel Lysons, *The Environs of London* (1792), ii. 55, 145 (for Brentford 1618–40 and Chelsea 1594, 1606–11); John George Taylor, *Our Lady of Battersey* (1925), 52 (1566–5). The 'wives' gathering' for Holy Trinity, Bungay, in 1558 may be another such, but there is nothing to connect it with Hocktide: East Suffolk (Lowestoft) RO, 115/E1/1, p. 3. The many Gatherings at Dursley, Gloucestershire, recorded as Hocktide revenue by A. R.

Wright, *British Calendar Customs*, ed. T. E. Lones (Folk-Lore Society, 1936), i. 126–7, seem to me to be from hoggling not hocking: Gloucestershire RO, P124/CW/2/4.

36. Hutton, *Merry England*, 119–20, 164, 189.

37. Ibid. chs. 4–5.

38. Samuel Byrd, *A Friendlie Communication* (1580), fos. 15–16.

39. Thomas Sharp, *A Dissertation on the Pageants or Dramatic Mysteries . . . of Coventry* (Coventry, 1825), 11–12, 36–7, 50–77, 126–9, 133, 221–5; John Nichols *The Progresses, Processions, etc. of Queen Elizabeth* (1823), iii. 135.

40. Sources at n. 35.

41. Oxfordshire RO, MS. DD. Par. St Peter in the East d. 1, years 1664–77; and MS. DD. Par. St Cross, Oxford e. 6, years 1661–7.

42. Robert Plot, *The Natural History of Oxfordshire* (1677), 201.

43. Wright, *British Calendar Customs*, i. 127, says that it was 'once' observed commonly in Dorset, but gives neither a date nor a reference for the observation.

44. Iona and Peter Opie, *The Lore and Language of Schoolchildren* (Oxford, 1959), 241.

45. John Nicholson, *Folk Lore of East Yorkshire* (1890), 13.

46. At Walsall and Badsey: sources at n. 30.

47. Owen and Blakeway, *Shrewsbury*, i. 559; John Brand, *Observations on the Popular Antiquities of Great Britain*, ed. Sir Henry Ellis (1908), i. 182–3; J. Weld, *A History of Leagram* (Chetham Society, 1913), 127–8; J. M. Pearson, 'Montgomeryshire Folklore', *Montgomeryshire Collections*, 37 (1915), 197–8; Hone, *Every-Day Book*, i. 425; Charles Hardwick, *Traditions, Superstitions and Folk-Lore* (Manchester, 1872), 74; Sidney Oldall Addy, *Household Tales with other Traditional Remains* (1895), 115; Peter Roberts, *The Cambrian Popular Antiquities* (1815), 125; Robert Chambers, *The Book of Days* (1864), i. 429; Frederick William Hackwood, *Staffordshire Customs, Superstitions and Folklore* (Lichfield, 1924), 13; Dyer, *British Popular Customs*, 177; Ella Mary Leather, *The Folk Lore of Herefordshire* (Hereford, 1912), 100; Trefor M. Owen, *Welsh Folk Customs* (St Fagans, 1974), 89–91; John Harland and T. T. Wilkinson, *Lancashire Folk-Lore* (1867), 233–4; Charlotte Sophia Burns, *Shropshire Folk-Lore* (1883), 336–740; George Morley, *Shakespeare's Greenwood* (1900), 105–6; John Noake, *Notes and Queries for Worcestershire* (1856), 211–12; M. L. Stanton *et al.*, 'Worcestershire Folklore', *Folk-Lore*, 26 (1915), 96; Wright, *British Calendar Customs*, i. 108–9; Roy Palmer, *The Folklore of Warwickshire* (1976), 158–9; Simpson, *Welsh Border*, 148; Bob Bushaway, *By Rite* (1982), 172–4; 'Scraps of English Folk-Lore', *Folk-Lore*, 36 (1925), 86.

48. *Gentleman's Magazine* (1784), quoted in Bushaway, *By Rite*, 174; and Harland and Wilkinson, *Lancashire*, 233–4.

49. Hackwood, *Staffordshire*, 13; Hone, *Every-Day Book*, i. 425; Bushaway, *By Rite*, 174.

50. Simpson, *Welsh Border*, 148.

51. Morley, *Shakespeare's Greenwood*, 106.

52. Burne, *Shropshire*, 339–40.

53. Hackwood, *Staffordshire*, 13.

54. Leather, *Herefordshire*, 100.

55. Weld, *Leagram*, 128; Harland and Wilkinson, *Lancashire*, 233; Burne, *Shropshire*, 340; Wright, *British Calendar Customs*, i. 109; Palmer, *Warwickshire*, 158–9.

56. Addy, *Household Tales*, 115.

CHAPTER 21

1. Laurence Whistler, *The English Festivals* (1947), 130; David Fox, *St George* (1983), 1–18.

2. Fox, *St George*, 17–18; H. F. Westlake, *The Parish Guilds of Medieval England* (1919), *passim*.

3. *Records of the Guild of St George in Norwich*, ed. M. Grace (Norfolk Record Society, 9; 1937), 1–112; *Records of Early English Drama: Norwich*, ed. David Galloway (Toronto, 1982), 13–15.

4. *Records of Early English Drama: Newcastle-upon-Tyne*, ed. J. J. Anderson (Toronto, 1982), 13–15.

5. William Kelly, *Notices Illustrative of the Drama... of Leicester* (1865), 37–9.

6. Thomas Sharp, *A Dissertation on the Pageants or Dramatic Mysteries... at Coventry* (Coventry, 1825), 161; Alan H. Nelson, *The Medieval English Stage* (Chicago, 1974), 51.

7. *The Earl of Northumberland's Household Book*, ed. Bishop Thomas Percy (1905), 333.

8. Sharp, *Coventry*, 161; *The Church Book of St Ewen, Bristol* (Bristol and Gloucester Archaeological Society, 1967), 46–158; Bristol RO, P/asts/Ch W, years ?1446–1542; *Churchwardens' Accounts of Croscombe* etc., ed. Bishop Hobhouse (Somerset Record Society, 1890), 32–6; *Records of Plays and Players in Norfolk and Suffolk 1330–1642* (Malone Society, 1980), 76–7; Robert Whiting, 'For the Health of my Soul', *Southern History*, 5 (1983), 80.

9. Westminster Central Library, St Margaret E1 (V), year 1491; Somerset RO, D/P/gla.j. 4/1, year 1498; Somerset RO, D/P/stogs 4/1/1, year 1507–8; *Churchwardens' Accounts*, ed. Hobhouse, 32; *Churchwardens' Accounts of S. Edmund and S. Thomas, Sarum*, ed. Henry J. F. Swayne (Wiltshire Record Society, 1896), 64; East Yorkshire RO, DDHE/ 29/A, year 1531–2; *History of the Municipal Church of St Lawrence, Reading*, ed. Charles Kerry (Reading, 1883), 45.

10. Patrick Collinson, *The Birthpangs of Protestant England* (1989), 50.

11. e.g. *The Accounts of the Wardens of the Parish of Morebath, Devon*, ed. J. E. Binney (Exeter, 1904), 164; Leicestershire RO, DE 1564/1384, year 1547–8; *Churchwardens' Accounts of St Mary the Great, Cambridge*, ed. J. Foster (Cambridge Antiquarian Society, 1905), 119–24; *Churchwardens' Accounts of Ashburton*, ed. A. Hanham (Devon and Cornwall Record Society, 1970), 121; 'Ancient Churchwardens' Accounts of a City Parish', *British Magazine* 34 (1847), 675; *S. Edmund and S. Thomas, Sarum*, 274–5; *Churchwardens' Accounts of the Town of Ludlow*, ed. T. Wright (Camden Society, 1869), 36; BL Add. MS 32243, of. 46; Devon RO, 1718A add./PW12.

12. 'An Account of the Company of St George in Norwich', *Norfolk Archaeology*, 3 (1852), 341–2; *Records of Early English Drama: Norwich*, 26–30.

13. *York Civic Records*, ed. Angelo Raine (Yorkshire Archaeological Society Record Society, 1946), v. 3–4.

14. Kelly, *Leicester*, 50–1.

15. *Acts of the Privy Council*, ed. J. R. Dasent, ii. 186; John Foxe, *Acts and Monuments*, ed. Stephen Reed Cattley (1838), vi. 351–2.

16. *The Diary of Henry Machyn*, ed. J. Nichols (Camden Society, 1848), 60, 85.

17. *York Civic Records*, ed. Raine, v. 105.

18. Kelly, *Leicester*, 50–1; 'Account of the Company of St George', 343; Alan Nelson, *The Medieval English Stage* (Chicago, 1974), 51; *Records of Early English Drama: Chester*, ed. Lawrence M. Clopper (Manchester, 1979), 55, 57.

19. *Parish of Morebath, Devon*, 185; North Devon RO, 1677A/PWI, year 1557–8; Essex RO, DIP 94/5/1, year 1558–9; Worcestershire RO, 850/1284/1, p. 12.

20. *Records of Early English Drama: Norwich*, 47–102; David Underdown, *Revel, Riot and Rebellion* (Oxford, 1985), 259.

21. Underdown, *Revel, Riot and Rebellion*, 259.

22. 280; F. M. Salter, *Medieval Drama in Chester* (Toronto, 1955), 28.

23. 'Account of the Company of St George', 354–74; Kelly, *Leicester*, 48–50; Enid Porter, *The Folklore of East Anglia* (1974), 60–1.

24. Whistler, *English Festivals*, 132; A. R. Wright, *British Calendar Customs*, ed. T. E. Lones (Folk-Lore Society, 1936), ii. 181–2.

CHAPTER 22

1. J. G. Frazer, *The Golden Bough* (1890), ii. 254–5.
2. *Sanas Chormaic*, most accessibly trans. John O'Donovan and ed. Whitley Stokes (Calcutta, 1868), 19, 23, 26.
3. Definitively ed. A. G. van Hamel, in *Compert Con Culainn and other stories* (Dublin Institute for Advanced Studies Medieval and Modern Irish series, 3; 1956). Most accessible to English readers in *The Tain*, ed. Thomas Kinsella (Oxford, 1970), 27.
4. e.g. Anne Ross, *Pagan Celtic Britain* (1967), 57 and n. 3.
5. Proinsias MacCana, *Celtic Mythology* (1970), 32; Ross, *Pagan Celtic Britain*, 57, 376.
6. As Dr Ross made plain, in her work at n. 4.
7. D. A. Binchy, 'The Fair of Tailty and the Feast of Tara', *Eriu*, 18 (1958), 113. On 128–31 he convincingly disposes of the notion that Muirchú's *Life of Patrick* refers to a Beltane ceremony either.
8. Most easily read in English in *The Mabinogion*, trans. Jeffrey Gantz (1976), 61–3, 130–3.
9. Kevin Danaher, *The Year in Ireland* (Cork, 1972) 95–6; William Hone, *The Every-Day Book and Table Book* (1832), ii, 595–6; G. H. Kinaham, 'County Donegal, May Eve', *Folk-Lore Journal*, 2 (1884), 90–1; Alan Gailey, 'The Bonfire in Northern Irish Tradition', *Folklore*, 88 (1977), 12–13.
10. Thomas Crofton Croker, *Fairy Legends and Traditions of the South of Ireland* (1825), 71–2.
11. Gailey, 'The Bonfire', 12–13.
12. Sir William R. Wilde, *Irish Popular Superstitions* (Dublin, 1852), 39–40, 47–9.
13. Lady Jane Francesca Wilde, *Ancient Cures, Charms and Usages of Ireland* (1890), 99–100; Leland L. Duncan, 'Further Notes from County Leitrim', *Folk-Lore*, 5 (1894), 193; William Camden, *Britannia*, ed. Richard Gough (1779), ii. 659; A. H. Singleton, 'Dairy Folklore, and other notes from Meath and Tipperary', *Folk-Lore*, 15 (1904), 457; R. H. Buchanan, 'Calandar Customs', *Ulster Folklife*, 8 (1962), 29.
14. Thomas Pennant, *A Tour in Scotland* (1776), i. 110–11.
15. *British Calendar Customs: Scotland*, ii, as Mary Macleod Banks, 219.
16. M. Martin, *A Description of the Western Islands of Scotland* (1703), 105.
17. John Ramsay, *Scotland and Scotsmen in the Eighteenth Century*, ed. Alexander Allardyce (Edinburgh, 1888), ii. 439–45.
18. Sir John Sinclair, *The Statistical Account of Scotland* (1791–9), v. 84, xi. 620, and xv. 517 n. 1.
19. Lachlan Shaw, *The History of the Province of Moray* (1775), 241.
20. F. Marian McNeill, *The Silver Bough* (Glasgow, 1959), 62.
21. *British Calendar Customs: Scotland*, ii. 226–30.
22. Alexander Carmichael, *Carmina Gaedelica* (Edinburgh, 1900), i. 182–3.
23. Walter Gregor, *Notes on the Folk-Lore of the North-East of Scotland* (Folk-Lore Society, 1881), 167.
24. *British Calendar Customs: Scotland*, ii. 231.
25. Walter Gregor, 'Notes on Beltane Cakes', *Folk-Lore*, 6 (1895), 2–5; McNeill, *Silver Bough*, 81.
26. McNeill, *Silver Bough*, 60–2; J. M. E. Saxby, *Shetland Traditional Lore* (Edinburgh, 1932).
27. Carmichael, *Carmina Gaedelica*, i. 183–91.

28. *British Calendar Customs: Scotland*, ii. 222; McNeill, *Silver Bough*, ii. 64; William Henderson, *Notes on the Folk-Lore of the Northern Counties of England and the Borders* (Folk-Lore Society, 1879), 72.

29. Allan Macdonald, *Gaelic Words and Expressions from South Uist and Eriskay*, ed. J. L. Campbell (Dublin, 1958), 46; McNeill, *Silver Bough*, ii. 62, 67–8; *British Calendar Customs: Scotland*, ii. 217–18, 232; Gregor, 'Beltane Cakes', 2–5; William Grant Stewart, *The Popular Superstitions and Festive Amusements of the Highlanders of Scotland* (Edinburgh, 1823), 261; I. F. Grant, *Highland Folkways* (1961), 66, 297.

30. Joseph Train, *An Historical and Statistical Account of the Isle of Man* (Douglas, 1845), i. 328.

31. C. I. Paton, 'Manx Calendar Customs', *Folk-Lore*, 51 (1940), 279.

32. *Victorian History of the County of Nottingham* (1906), i. 186; Mrs Gutch and Mabel Peacock (eds.), *County Folk-Lore Lincolnshire* (Folk-Lore Soceity, 1908), 202–3.

33. A. R. Wright, *British Calendar Customs*, ed. T. E. Lones (Folk-Lore Society, 1936), ii. 198; Marjorie Rowling, *The Folklore of the Lake District* (1976), 121; A. Craig Gibson, 'Ancient Customs and Superstitions in Cumberland', *Transactions of the Historic Society of Lancashire and Cheshire*, 10 (1857–8), 105.

34. M. A. Courtney, *Cornish Feasts and Folklore* (1890), 28; Anna Eliza Bray, *A Description of the Part of Devonshire Bordering on the Tamar and the Tavy* (1836), i. 325–6.

35. Marie Trevelyan, *Folk-Lore and Folk-Stories of Wales* (1909), 22–4.

36. R. U. Sayce, 'A Survey of Montgomeryshire Folklore', *Montgomeryshire Collections*, 47 (1942), 21, and 'The Seasonal Bonfires', *Montgomeryshire Collections*, 50 (1948), 190–1.

37. Croker, *Fairy Legends*, 71; Duncan, 'Leitrim', 193; Lady Jane Francesca Wilde, *Ancient Legends, Mystic Charms and Superstitions of Ireland* (1887), i. 196 and *Ancient Cures*, 99–101; Camden, *Britannia*, ii. 659; Sir W. Wilde, *Superstitions*, 56, 55, 58; E. Estyn Evans, *Irish Folk Ways* (1957), 272–3; Buchanan, 'Calendar Customs', 37.

38. Pennant, *Tour*, i. 169; Stewart, *Popular Superstitions*, 260; J. G. Campbell, *Witchcraft and Second Sight in the Highlands and Islands of Scotland* (1900), 270; Ramsay, *Scotland and Scotsmen*, ii. 454; *British Calendar Customs: Scotland*, ii. 235.

39. Wright, *British Calendar Customs*, ii. 198; Train, *Isle of Man*, ii. 117–18; R. L. Tongue, *Somerset Folklore*, ed. K. M. Briggs (Folk-Lore, Society County Folklore 7; 1965), 161–2; William Howells, *Cambrian Superstitions* (1831), 178; Ella Mary Leather, *The Folk-Lore of Herefordshire* (Hereford, 1912), 18; Gibson, 'Ancient Customs', 105.

40. Trevelyan, *Folk-Lore*, 261; Jacqueline Simpson, *The Folklore of the Welsh Border* (1976), 149–50.

41. Kingsley Palmer, *The Folklore of Somerset* (1976), 62.

42. J. G. Frazer, *Balder the Beautiful* (1914), i. 159–60, and *The Magic Art and the Evolution of Kings* (1911), 54.

CHAPTER 23

1. *Councils and Synods . . . 1205–1313*, eds. F. M. Powicke and C. R. Cheney (Oxford, 1964), 480.

2. HMC New Romney, 540–1.

3. Richard Peter and Otho Bathurst Peter, *The Histories of Launceston and Dunheved* (Plymouth, 1885), 124; *Records of Early English Drama: Devon*, ed. John M. Wasson (Toronto, 1986), 361–75.

4. William Chappell, *Old English Popular Music*, ed. H. Ellis Woodbridge (New York, 1961), i. 33.

5. Wiltshire RO, 189/1, year 1499.

6. *Records of the Borough of Nottingham* (Nottingham, 1885), iii. 382.

7. University College London, Alex Helm Collection. A3/12; Christopher Windle, *A Book, for a Buck with a Parke* (1618), 417.

8. *The Flower and the Leaf*, ll. 610–12.

9. The Chaucerian references are collected in R. T. Hampson, *Medii Aevi Kalendarium* (1841), 231–2.

10. Sir Thomas Malory, *Le Morte D'Arthur*, xix. 1–2.

11. The references are collected in *British Calendar Customs: Scotland*, ed. Mary Macleod Banks, ii (Folk-Lore Society, 1939), 207.

12. Edward Hall's Chronicle, quoted in John Stow, *A Survey of London*, ed. Charles Lethbridge Kingsford (Oxford, 1908), i. 98–9.

13. Richard L. Greaves, *Society and Religion in Elizabethan England* (Minneapolis, 1981), 429, 457.

14. *The Diary of John Evelyn*, ed. E. S. De Beer (Oxford, 1955), iii. 285: W. B., *The Yellow Book* (1 May 1656), 3.

15. *Records of Plays and Players in Norfolk and Suffolk 1330–1642*, ed. D. Galloway and J. Wasson (Malone Society, 1980), 87–93; P. G. Stone, 'The Ledger Book of Newport'. *Antiquary*, 48 (1912), 183.

16. Anna Jean Mill, *Medieval Plays in Scotland* (Edinburgh, 1927), 19–20, 152–3.

17. As is plain at Aberdeen, above, and argued for England in Ronald Hutton, *The Rise and Fall of Merry England* (Oxford, 1994), 3–4.

18. Polydor Vergil, *Works*, trans. John Langley (1663), 194.

19. Stow, *Survey*, 98.

20. *The State of Eton School* (1560), quoted in John Brand, *Observations on the Popular Antiquities of Great Britain*, ed. Sir Henry Ellis (1908), i. 217.

21. Edmund Spenser, *Poetical Works*, eds. J. C. Smith and E. de Selincourt (1926), 436.

22. In *A Dialogue against... Dauncing* (1582), n.p.

23. In *Anatomie of Abuses* (1583), ed. Frederick J. Furnivall (New Shakespeare Society, 1879), 149.

24. *Vox Graculi* (1622), 62.

25. Oxfordshire RO, MS Diocesan Papers c 27, f. 46.

26. Such as Francis Beaumont and John Fletcher, *The Two Noble Kinsmen*, Act iii; Thomas Nashe, *Works*, ed. R. B. Mckerrow (1910), iii, 240; William Shakespeare, *Midsummer Night's Dream*, i. i. 166–7.

27. *The Pepys Ballads*, ed. Hyder Edward Robbins (Cambridge, Mass., 1929), ii. 8–11.

28. *The Poems of Robert Herrick*, ed. L. C. Martin (Oxford, 1965), 68.

29. Peter Laslett and Karla Oosterveen, 'Long-term Trends in Bastardy in England', *Population Studies*, 27 (1973), 259.

30. Oliver Heywood, quoted in BL Add. MS 24544, p. 179.

31. Eveline Legh, Lady Newton, *The House of Lyme* (1917), 256.

32. Robert W. Malcolmson, *Popular Recreations in English Society 1700–1850* (Cambridge, 1973), 30.

33. John Aubrey, *Remaines of Gentilisme and Judaisme*, ed. James Britten (Folk-Lore Society, 1881), 18.

34. Henry Bourne, *Antiquitates Vulgares* (Newcastle, 1725), 200–1; William Hutchinson, *A View of Northumberland* (Newcastle, 1778), vol. ii, appendix, 13; Brand, *Observations*, i. 212–22.

35. J. G. Frazer, *The Golden Bough* (1890), i. 72–82. One does not, I think, need to postulate Sir James's concept that this was to bring 'the blessings which the tree spirit has it its power to bestow' to account for this simple and natural human desire.

36. Charles Hardwick, *Traditions, Superstitions and Folklore* (Manchester, 1872), 90.

37. Frederick William Hackwood, *Staffordshire Customs, Superstitions and Folklore* (Lichfield, 1924), 15.

38. William Hone, *The Every-Day Book and Table Book* (1832), ii. 609–11.

39. F. Sawyer, 'Sussex Folklore and Customs Connected with the Seasons', *Sussex Archaeological Collections*, 33 (1883), 246.

40. G. Doe, 'Sixth Report of the Committee on Devonshire Folk-Lore', *Transactions of the Devonshire Association*, 15 (1883), 104–5.

41. R. L. Tongue, *Somerset Folklore*, ed. K. M. Briggs (Folklore Society County Folklore 8; 1965), 162.

42. M. A. Courtney, *Cornish Feasts and Folklore* (1890), 29; A. R. Wright, *British Calendar Customs*, ed. T. E. Lones (Folk-Lore Society, 1936), ii. 211–13; Ella Mary Leather, *The Folk-Lore of Herefordshire* (Hereford, 1912), 101; Marie Trevelyan, *Folk-Lore and Folk-Stories of Wales* (1909), 24; Robert Holland, *A Glossary of Words Used in the County of Chester* (English Dialect Society, 1886).

43. Enid Porter, *Cambridgeshire Customs and Folklore* (1969), 113.

44. T. F. Thiselton Dyer, *British Popular Customs* (1876), 254.

45. Wright, *British Calendar Customs*, ii. 195–6.

46. T. Gwynn Jones, *Welsh Folklore and Folk-Custom* (Cambridge, 1979), 163; Trevelyan, *Folk-Lore*, 25.

47. For others, see C. F. Tebbutt, *Huntingdonshire Folklore* (St Ives, 1984), 63–6; Brand, *Observations*, i. 229; Hone, *Every-Day Book*, ii. 57; Dyer, *British Popular Customs*, 235.

48. E. Ruddock, 'May-Day Songs and Celebrations in Leicestershire and Rutland', *Transactions of the Leicestershire Archaeological Society*, 40 (1964–5), 69–71.

49. Robert Gifford, 'Popular Culture in Bedfordshire and Huntingdonshire 1820–1870' (University of London Institute of Education MA thesis, 1982), 25.

50. Ruddock, 'May-Day Songs', 69–71.

51. Hone, *Every-Day Book*, i. 568–9.

52. Roy Palmer, *The English Country Songbook* (1979), 133.

53. For which more data in Percy Dearmer, Ralph Vaughan Williams, and Martin Shaw, *The Oxford Book of Carols* (Oxford, 1928), 61–3; Palmer, *Country Songbook*, 271–2; *English Country Songs*, ed. Lucy E. Broadwood and J. A. Fuller-Maitland (1893), 98–9, 108–9; Iona and Peter Opie, *The Lore and Language of Schoolchildren* (Oxford, 1959), 260; F. B. Hamer, 'May Songs of Bedfordshire', *JEFDSS* 9: (1961), 81–2; Thomas Sternberg, *The Dialect and Folk-Lore of Northamptonshire* (1851), 180–1; Dyer, *British Popular Customs*, 233; Porter, *Cambridgeshire*, 111; W. B. Gerish, *The Mayers and their Song* (1905); Doris Jones-Baker, *The Folklore of Hertfordshire* (1977), 141.

54. Robert Chambers, *The Book of Days* (1864), i. 546–8; Palmer, *Country Songbook*, 133; Holland, *Glossary*, 502–3.

55. Where they are still heard in the Padstow May Day and Helston Furry Day celebrations.

56. Trefor M. Owen, *Welsh Folk Customs* (St Fagans, 1974), 100–1.

57. Dyer, *British Popular Customs*, 217; Hone, *Every-Day Book*, i. 565–7; University College London, Alex Helm Collection, A3/11.

58. *The Autobiography of Samuel Bamford*, ed. W. H. Chaloner (1967), i. 144–5.

59. John Harland and T. T. Wilkinson, *Lancashire Folk-Lore* (1867), 239–40; J. Weld, *A History of Leagram* (Chetham Society, 1913), 128–9; Sidney Oldall Addy, *Household Tales with other Traditional Remains* (1895), 16; Opie and Opie, *Lore and Language*, 255.

60. In *Records of Early English Drama: Lancashire* (Toronto, 1991), 290–1, edited by him.

61. Harland and Wilkinson, *Lancashire*, 241.

62. *A Celtic Miscellany*, ed. Kenneth Hurlstone Jackson (1951), 87–9.

63. Joseph Strutt, *The Sports and Pastimes of the People of England*, ed. J. Charles Cox (1903), 276.

64. Kevin Danaher, *The Year in Ireland* (Cork. 1972), 96–100; Dyer, *British Popular Customs*, 272; Sir William R. Wilde, *Irish Popular Superstitions* (Dublin, 1852), 61–3; R. H. Buchanan, 'Calendar Customs', *Ulster Folklife*, 8 (1962), 26. For the Scottish examples, see below.

65. Mircea Eliade, *Patterns in Comparative Religion* (1958), 309–13.

66. *Leviathan*, ed. A. D. Lindsay (1914), 363.

67. *Translatio S. Alexandri*, ch. 3; Mircea Eliade, *The Sacred and the Profane* (New York, 1959), 35.

68. J. G. Frazer, *The Golden Bough* (1890), i. 72.

69. C. W. von Sydow, 'The Mannhardtian Theories about the Last Sheaf and the Fertility Demons from a Modern Critical Point of View', *Folk-Lore*, 45 (1934), 291–9.

70. Eliade, *Patterns*, 309–13.

71. Stubbes, *Anatomie*, 148–9.

72. *Records of Early English Drama: Devon*, ed. John M. Wasson (Toronto, 1986), 238–64.

73. Leicestershire RO, DE 1225/65.

74. Devon RO, 1718A add/PW4/B.

75. 'Eltham Churchwardens' Accounts', ed. A. Vallance, *Archaeologia Cantiana*, 48 (1936), 121.

76. Illustrating *The May-Day Country Mirth*, published in the period 1671–84, and reprinted in *The Roxburghe Ballads*, ed. William Chappell (Ballad Society, 1871), vii. 79–81.

77. *The Court and Country* (1618), 7.

78. *The May-Day Country Mirth*, as above; it was written in 1630.

79. Stow, *Survey*, i. 98–9, 143, 348–50.

80. *Warwick County Records*, ed. S. C. Ratcliff and H. C. Johnson (Warwick, 1941), vi. 53; *Hertford County Records: Sessions Rolls 1581–1698*, ed. W. J. Hardy (Hertford, 1905), 34.

81. William Kelly, *Notices Illustrative of the Drama . . . of Leicester* (1865), 102–12.

82. Stow, *Survey*, i. 143.

83. *The Diary of Henry Machyn*, ed. J. Nichols (Camden Society, 1848), 20.

84. Stubbes, *Anatomie*, loc. cit.; Hugh Roberts, *The Day of Hearing* (Oxford, 1600); *Vox Graculi* (1622), 63.

85. Hutton, *Merry England*, 121–2, 189.

86. Charles Phythian-Adams, 'Milk and Soot', in *The Pursuit of Urban History*, ed. Derek Fraser and Anthony Sutcliffe (1983), 93.

87. Berkshire RO, D/P 78/5/1. year 1588 (Kintbury); D/P 118/5/1, year 1610 (Stanford in the Vale); and D/P 35/5/1. year 1590 (Childrey).

88. Berkshire RO, D/P 8/5/1 (Ashampstead).

89. Breton, *Court and Country*, 7; Herrick, *Poems*, 230, 239; *Pasquils Palinodia* (1619), sig B3.

90. As the latest contribution to a large literature, see Hutton, *Merry England*, ch. 5.

91. Henry Burton, *A Divine Tragedie Lately Acted* (1641), *passim*; Oxfordshire RO, MS. DD. Par. Oxford St Peter in the East, year 1635; Somerset RO. DD/Cd/81, case concerning Dundry Hay.

92. *British Calendar Customs: Scotland*, i. 44; Anna Jean Mill, *Medieval Plays in Scotland* (Edinburgh, 1927), 224, 262–3, 265.

93. *Acts and Ordinances of the Interregnum*, eds. C. H. Firth and R. J. Rait (1911), i. 420–1.

94. *Warwick County Records*, iii. 271–2.

95. Hutton, *Merry England*, ch. 5.

96. For the latest summary, see ibid. 223–6.

97. Ibid. 225–6.

98. Ibid. 229–30; *County Folk-Lore*, vi: *East Riding of Yorkshire* ed. Mrs Gutch (Folk-Lore Society, 1912), 27; Frank Earp, *May Day in Nottinghamshire* (Wymeswold, 1991), 23; 'Maypole Gazetteer', *English Dance and Song*, 46, 2 (1984), 9; Hackwood, *Staffordshire*, 16–17; Ann Hughes, 'Coventry and the English Revolution', in *Town and Countryside in the English Revolution*, ed. R. C. Richardson (Manchester, 1992), 94.

99. Hone, *Every-Day Book*, ii. 609–11; *British Calendar Customs: Scotland*, ii. 249–50.

100. T. Gwynn Jones, *Welsh Folklore and Folk Custom* (Cambridge, 1979), 154; Brand, *Observations*, i. 237, 241; Bob Bushaway, *By Rite* (1982), 19; Strutt, *Sports and Pastimes*, 281; Robert W. Malcolmson, *Popular Recreations in English Society 1700–1850* (Cambridge, 1973), 55; E. P. Thompson, *Customs in Common* (1991), 75–6; Hone, *Every-Day Book*, ii. 574–7, 597; Trevelyan, *Folk-Lore*, 24; Jonathan Ceredig Davies, *Folk-Lore of West and Mid-Wales* (Aberystwyth, 1911), 74–5; *Journal of the Archaeological Association*, 5 (1850), 254; Richard Mason, *Tales and Traditions of Tenby* (1858), 22; Leather, *Herefordshire*, 101; Percy Manning, 'Some Oxfordshire Seasonal Festivals', *Folk-Lore*, 8 (1897), 312; Owen, *Welsh Folk Customs*, 101–3; Ralph Whitlock, *The Folklore of Devon* (1977), 143; Harland and Wilkinson, *Lancashire*, 243–4; James Britten, 'Warwickshire Customs, 1759–60', *Folk-Lore Journal* 1 (1883), 353; Wright, *British Calendar Customs*, ii. 226–7; Anne Hughes. *The Diary of a Farmer's Wife, 1796–1797* (1980), 34–5; Hugh Cunningham, *Leisure in the Industrial Revolution* (1980), 87–8; *The Early Poems of John Clare*, ed. Eric Robinson and David Powell (Oxford, 1989), ii. 26; Tony Deane and Tony Shaw *The Folklore of Cornwall* (1975), 172; Earp, *Nottinghamshire*, 19; Bourne, *Antiquitates Vulgares*, 201; R. W. Bushaway, 'Rite, Legitimation and Community in Southern England, 1700–1850', in *Conflict and Community in Southern England*, ed. Barry Stapleton (New York, 1992), 112; *The Wentworth Papers*, ed. J. Cartwright (1883), 119–21.

101. Thomas Sharp, *A Dissertation on the Pageants or Dramatic Mysteries... at Coventry* (Coventry, 1825), 179; Tebbutt, *Huntingdonshire*, 66–7; Sawyer, 'Sussex Folk-Lore', 246; T. Brown, '64th Report on Folklore', *Transactions of the Devonshire Association*, 99 (1967), 340; Edward Peacock, *English Church Furniture* (1866), 176–7; Wright, *British Calendar Customs*, ii. 218–23; Davies, *West and Mid-Wales*, 74–5; Anna Eliza Bray, *A Description of the Part of Devonshire bordering on the Tamar and the Tavy* (1836), i. 327; Mrs Gutch (ed.), *County Folk-Lore*, ii. *North Riding of Yorkshire, York and the Ainsty* (Folk-Lore Society, 1901), 54–6; S. Jackson Coleman, *Huntingdonshire Lore and Legend* (Treasury of Folklore 41. Douglas, 1955), n.p.; Harland and Wilkinson, *Lancashire*, 246; John Symonds Udal, *Dorsetshire Folk-Lore* (Hertford, 1922), 39–40; J. G. Frazer, *The Magic Art and the Evolution of Kings* (1911), 68; Charlotte Sophia Burne, *Shropshire Folk-Lore* (1883), 359–60; Hilderic Friend, 'Maypoles', *Folk-Lore Journal*, 2 (1884), 317–18; John Noake, *Notes and Queries for Worcestershire* (1856), 210; D. H. M. Read, 'Hampshire Folklore', *Folk-Lore*, 22 (1911), 296–8; J. B. Partridge, 'Cotswold Place-Lore and Customs', *Folk-Lore* 23 (1912); 451; Katherine M. Briggs, *The Folklore of the Cotswolds* (1974), 25; M. A. Courtney, *Cornish Feasts and Folklore* (1890), 28; Peter Robson, 'Calendar Customs in Nineteenth and Twentieth Century Dorset' (Sheffield M.Phil. thesis, 1988), 56–67; Jones-Baker, *Hertfordshire*, 143; Marjorie Rowling, *The Folklore of the Lake District* (1976), 118; Earp, *Nottinghamshire*, 19–29; University College London, Alex Helm Collection, A3/9, AB/11, A3/12, *passim*; Mrs Gutch and Mabel Peacock (eds.), *County Folk-Lore*, v. *Lincolnshire* (Folk-Lore Society, 1908), 197–202.

102. Ruddock, 'May-Day Songs', 81.

103. Roy Judge, 'Changing Attitudes to May Day 1844–1914' (Leeds University Ph.D. thesis, 1987), 100–23.

104. Peter Robson, 'Dorset Garland Days on the Chesil Coast', in *Aspects of British Calendar Customs*, ed. Theresa Buckland and Juliette Wood (Folklore Society, Sheffield, 1993), 159–66.

105. Bushaway, *By Rite*, 238.

106. Judge, 'May Day', 100–23.

107. Ruddock, 'May-Day Songs', 81–2; Wright, *British Calendar Customs*, ii. 214–17; University College London, Alex Helm Collection A3/12, under Hertfordshire, Huntingdonshire, Northamptonshire, Leicestershire; Tebbutt, *Huntingdonshire Folklore*, 59–67; P. H. Ditchfield, *Old English Customs* (1896), 106–7; Dyer, *British Popular Customs*, 241–54; Hone, *Every-Day Book*, 615–16; University College London, Alex Helm collection A3/9, under Hertfordshire, A3/11, under Northamptonshire; Brand, *Observations*, i. 221; Porter, *Cambridgeshire*, 111–14; Percy Manning, 'May-Day at Watford, Herts', *Folk-Lore*, 4 (1893), 403–4; Jones-Baker, *Hertfordshire*, 141–3; Hamer, 'May Songs', 83–5.

108. Percy Manning, 'Stray Notes on Oxfordshire Folklore', *Folk-Lore*, 14 (1903), 168–70; Ditchfield, *Old English Customs*, 100–2; Michael Pickering, *Village Song and Culture* (1982), 40–2; C. E. Prior, *Dedications of Churches* (Oxfordshire Archaeological Society Reports, 1903), 22–40; Dyer, *British Popular Customs*, 261–2; Percy Manning, 'Some Oxfordshire Seasonal Festivals', *Folk-Lore*, 8 (1897), 307–12; Flora Thompson, *Lark Rise to Candleford* (Oxford, 1945), 201–8; *Oxfordshire Village Life: The Diaries of George James Dew*, ed. Pamela Horn (Abingdon, 1983), 13–89; Roy Judge, 'Fact and Fancy in Tennyson's "May Queen" and in Flora Thompson's "May Day"', in *Aspects of British Calendar Customs*, ed. Buckland and Wood, 167–83.

109. R. J. King, '1st Report on Devonshire Folk-Lore', *Transactions of the Devonshire Association*, 8 (1876), 50; R. P. Chope, '28th Report', ibid. 59 (1927), 170–1; R. P. Chope, '32nd Report', ibid. 64 (1932), 165; R. P. Chope, '33rd Report', ibid. 65 (1933), 132; R. P. Chope, '34th Report', ibid. 66 (1934), 95; R. P. Chope, 'Devonshire Calendar Customs Part II', ibid. 70 (1938), 364–5; C. Laycock, '41st Report on Devonshire Folklore', ibid. 74 (1942), 103–4; Dyer, *British Popular Customs*, 217, 301; Whitlock, *Devon*, 145.

110. University College London, Alex Helm Collection, A3/11 and A3/12, under Lincolnshire, Norfolk, and Essex; *County Folk-Lore*, v. *Lincolnshire*, 195; Dyer, *British Popular Customs*, 237–8; Broadwood and Mason, *English County Songs*, 98–9; Ethel H. Rudkin, 'Lincolnshire Folklore', *Folk-Lore*, 44 (1933), 285–6.

111. Dyer, *British Popular Customs*, 263; Wright, *British Calendar Customs*, ii. 216; Leather, *Herefordshire*, 100–1; Frazer, *The Magic Art*, 88; M. L. Stanton *et al.*, 'Worcestershire Folklore', *Folk-Lore*, 26 (1915), 95; University College London, Alex Helm Collection, A3/11, A3/12 and A3/13 under Derbyshire, Gloucestershire, and Warwickshire.

112. University College London, Alex Helm Collection, A3/11, A3/12 and A3/13, under Kent, Surrey and Sussex; Jacqueline Simpson, *The Folklore of Sussex* (1973), 115–17; Opie and Opie, *Lore and Language*, 260; Jean Shuttleworth, 'Garland Day in West Kent', *English Dance and Song*, 37: 1 (1975), 17; Dyer, *British Popular Customs*, 243.

113. Ditchfield, *Old English Customs*, 102–3; D. H. M. Read, 'Hampshire' *Folk-Lore*, 22 (1911), 296–9; University College London, Alex Helm Collection, A3/9, A3/12 and A3/13, under Berkshire and Hampshire.

114. Ralph Whitlock, *The Folklore of Wiltshire* (1976), 42; J. P. Emslie, 'May Day', *Folk-Lore*, 11 (1900), 210.

115. Ditchfield, *Old English Customs*, 104.

116. Danaher, *Year in Ireland*, 102–3; Buchanan, 'Calendar Customs', 26.
117. Opie and Opie, *Lore and Language*, 261.
118. *Lark Rise to Candleford*, 201–8.
119. Somerton, Bucknell, Marston, Headington, Bampton, and Spelsbury. Sources at n. 108.
120. Tebbutt, *Huntingdonshire*, 59–60. The flowers were tulip, anemone, cowslip, lilac, king-cup, laburnum, meadow orchis, wallflower, primrose, crown imperial, and rose.
121. *The Golden Bough* (1890), i. 83.
122. *Village Song and Culture* (1982), 40–2.
123. Ibid. 40–1.
124. Judge, 'May Day', 100–23.
125. Apart from those mentioned by Roy Judge, see Porter, *Cambridgeshire*, 111; Dyer, *British Popular Customs*, 261–2; Manning, 'Watford', 403–4; Wright, *British Calendar Customs*, ii. 215–16; Hamer, 'May Songs', 83–4.
126. King, '1st Report', 50.
127. See e.g. the situation in Dorset: Robson, 'Dorset Garland Days', 159–66. See also Wright, *British Calendar Customs*, ii. 215–16.
128. Porter, *Cambridgeshire*, 111–12; Tebbutt, *Huntingdonshire*, 59–66; Opie and Opie, *Lore and Language*, 260.
129. Lady Raglan, 'The Green Man in Church Architecture', *Folk-Lore*, 50 (1939), 45–57.
130. Margaret Murray, 'Female Fertility Figures', *Journal of the Royal Anthropological Institute*, 64 (1934), 93–100.
131. *The Jack-in-the-Green* (Folklore Society, 1979).
132. Phythian-Adams, 'Milk and Soot', 86. 95.
133. See Chapter 26.
134. *The Green Man* (Ipswich, 1978).

CHAPTER 24

1. Listed in Richard Vallpey French, *Nineteen Centuries of Drink in England* (1884), 81–4. See also *Councils and Synods 1205–1313* ed. F. M. Powicke and C. R. Cheney (Oxford, 1964), 197, 265, 303, 622, 722, 1044.
2. *Robert of Brunne's Handlyng Synne*, ed. F. J. Furnivall (EETS, 1901), 156.
3. G. R. Owst, *Literature and Pulpit in Medieval England* (Cambridge, 1933), 393–4.
4. *Churchwardens' Accounts of Croscombe etc.*, ed. Bishop Hobhouse (Somerset Record Society, 1890), 81–6, 178–97; East Suffolk RO, FC 185/E1/1, year 1451; Oxfordshire RO, MS. DD, Par. St Michael, Oxford, a. 1, year 1457–8; Richard and Otho Peter, *The Histories of Launceston and Dunheved* (Plymouth, 1885), 356–70; *Churchwardens' Accounts of S. Edmund and S. Thomas, Sarum*, ed. H. J. F. Swayne (Wiltshire Record Society, 1896), 1–13; Somerset RO, D/P/gla.j.4/1, nos.1–7.
5. The sources are listed in the appendix to Ronald Hutton, *The Rise and Fall of Merry England* (Oxford, 1994).
6. *The Chronicles of the Collegiate Church of Free Chapel of All Saints Derby*, ed. J. Charles Cox and W. H. St John Hope (1881), 51–2.
7. Somerset RO, DD/WO/Box 49/1; Oxfordshire RO, MS DD Par. St Aldates e. 15, b. 17–19; Hugh R. Watkin, *Dartmouth* (1935), i. 300–52.
8. Dorset RO, PE/WM/ CW1–12; Somerset RO, D/P/stogs/4/1/1; Oxfordshire RO, MS DD Par. Thame b. 2; East Suffolk RO, FC 89/A2/1; Norfolk RO, PD 136/56.
9. *Churchwardens' Accounts*, ed. Hobhouse, 81–143, 178–88.
10. HMC Middleton MSS, p. 382.

11. Buckinghamshire RO, PR 234/5/1, of. 21.

12. *Records of Early English Drama: Herefordshire and Worcestershire*, ed. David N. Klausner (Toronto, 1990), 521–2.

13. John James Raven, *Cratfield* (1985), 18.

14. Essex RO, D/P 192/5/1, year 1490; S. Robertson, 'Elham, Church of St. Mary', *Archaeological Cantiana*, 10 (1876), 66–7; Charles Kerry, *History of the Municipal Church of St. Lawrence, Reading* (Reading, 1883), 235–6.

15. Sources at n. 4, plus W. Symonds, 'Winterslow Church Reckonings', *Wiltshire Archaeological and Natural History Magazine*, 36 (1909–10), 29–37.

16. 'Sherborne All Hallows Churchwardens' Accounts', *Somerset and Dorset Notes and Queries*, 23 (1939), 331–3.

17. *Records of Plays and Players in Norfolk and Suffolk 1330–1642*, ed. D. Galloway and J. Wasson (Malone Society, 1980), 87–93.

18. Hampshire RO, 63M70/PWI, year 1530.

19. Raven, *Cratfield*, 17.

20. e.g. *Players in Norfolk and Suffolk,* ed. Galloway and Wasson, 191–2; J. Charles Cox, *Churchwardens' Accounts* (1913), 205.

21. Roscoe E. Parker, 'Some Records of the Somyr Play', in Richard Beale Davis and John Leon Lievsay (eds.), *Studies in Honor of John C. Hodges and Aluin Thale* (Knoxville, Tenn., 1961), 19–26.

22. Sources given in Hutton, *Merry England*, 301, n. 78. The communities are Wiston (Yorkshire); Colyweston (Leicestershire); Melton Mowbray (Leicestershire); Henley (Oxfordshire); Andover (Hampshire); Calne (Wiltshire); St Nicholas, Bristol; Bramley (Hampshire); Croscombe (Somerset); St Lawrence, Reading (Berkshire); Steyning (Sussex); St Edmund, Salisbury (Wiltshire); Halesowen (Worcestershire); Sherborne (Dorset); Winterslow (Wiltshire); Deane (Wiltshire); Great Dunmow (Essex); Kingston upon Thames (Surrey).

23. *Councils and Synods*, ed. Pcwicke and Cheney, 313.

24. *Robert of Brunne's Handlyng Synne*, 36.

25. *Flores Historiarum*, ed. H. R. Luyard (Rolls Series, 1890), iii. 130; *Historical Poems of the XIVth and XVth Centuries*, ed. Russell Hope Robbins (New York, 1959), 16.

26. Parker, 'Records of the Somyr Play', 20–1.

27. *Churchwardens' Accounts*, ed. Swayne, 1–13.

28. *Guildford Borough Records, 1514–1546*, ed. E. Dance (Surrey Record Society, 1958), 33.

29. Kerry, *St. Lawrence, Reading*, 235–6; *Henley Borough Records*, ed. P. Briers (Oxfordshire Record Society, 1960), 198.

30. J. G. Frazer, *The Golden Bough* (1890), i. 83–96, and *The Magic Art and the Evolution of Kings* (1911), 85–9, 97.

31. Parker, 'Records of the Somyr Play', 19–20.

32. Kerry, *St. Lawrence, Reading*, 235.

33. Surrey RO (Kingston), KG/2/2; David Wiles, *The Early Plays of Robin Hood* (Cambridge, 1981), 13.

34. Leicestershire RO, DG/36/140/1–2.

35. Surrey RO (Kingston), KG/2/2, years 1506–35, *passim*.

36. St John's College library, Cambridge, D 91/20/f.22. I owe this reference to Dr Michael K. Jones, the biographer of Lady Margaret.

37. Anna Jean Mill, *Medieval Plays in Scotland* (Edinburgh, 1927), 27–8, 131–265, (1825), i. 331–3. *passim*, 317–23; H. Owen and J. B. Blakeway, *A History of Shrewsbury* (1825), i. 331–3.

38. HMC Dean and Chapter of Wells MSS, ii. 264–5.

39. *Boxford Churchwardens' Accounts 1530–1561*, ed. Peter Northeast (Suffolk Records Society, 1982), 46–55; *The Early Churchwardens' Accounts of Hampshire*, ed. John Foster Williams (Winchester, 1913), 113–16 (Crondall); Hampshire RO, 63M70/PWI (Bramley); *The Accounts of the Wardens of the Parish of Morebath, Devon, 1520–1573*, ed. J. E. Binney (Exeter, 1904), 159–64; *Churchwardens' Accounts*, ed. Hobhouse, 158–61 (Yatton); Oxfordshire RO, MS DD Par Oxford St Michael, a. 2, years 1547–9; Oxfordshire RO, MS DD Par Oxford St Martin a. 1, years 1547–9; *Churchwardens' Accounts of Ashburton, 1479–1580*, ed. A. Hanham (Devon and Cornwall Record Society, 1970), 109–24; Symonds, 'Winterslow Church Reckonings', 37; H. Walters, 'The Churchwardens' Accounts of the Parish of Worfield', *Transactions of the Shropshire Archaeological and Natural History Society*, 3rd ser. 7 (1907), 223–40, and 8 (1908), 113–19; Leicestershire RO, DG 36/140/1–5 (Melton Mowbray); Dorset RO, PI55/CW/20–6 (Sherborne); Somerset RO, D/P/hal. 4/1/4 fos. 1–6 (Halse), and D/P/ilm 4/1/1, years 1543–9 (Ilminster); West Sussex RO, Par, 11/a/1, years 1540–50 (Ashurst); *The Churchwardens' Accounts of West Tarring*, ed. W. J. Pressey (1934), years 1546–9; West Suffolk RO, EL 110/5/3, years 1543–9, (Mildenhall).

40. *Churchwardens' Accounts of Marston, Spelsbury, Pyrton*, ed. F. Weaver and G. Clark (Oxfordshire Record Society, 1925), 13–18, 67–70; Oxfordshire RO, MS DD Par Thame b. 2, years 1547–9.

41. Somerset RO, D/P/wins 4/1/1, year 1551 (Winford).

42. In all, thirty-three parishes: in Cornwall (Anthony, Poughill, Stratton); Devon (Morebath, Ashburton, Woodbury, Crediton, Braunton, Dartington, South Tawton); Somerset (Yatton, Halse, Winkleigh); Dorset (Sherborne); Wiltshire (Steeple Aston, Mere, and St Edmund, Salisbury); Berkshire (two Reading parishes and Stanford); Hampshire (Crondall and St John, Winchester); Surrey (Wandsworth); Sussex (Rye); Kent (St Mary, Dover); Oxfordshire (Marston, Pyrton, Thame, and St Michael, Oxford); Warwickshire (St Nicholas, Warwick); Northamptonshire (Norton by Daventry); Worcestershire (Badsey). Sources given in Hutton, *Merry England*, appendix.

43. *Liverpool Town Books*, ed. J. A. Twemlow (1918), i. 51; Leicestershire RO, DG 36/140/ 6–7; West Suffolk RO, FL 509/1/15, years 1555–7.

44. Winchester, Salisbury, Melton Mowbray, Crediton.

45. Melton Mowbray (again) and Anthony.

46. *Acts of the Privy Council of England* v (1554–6), 151.

47. Mill, *Medieval Plays*, 28–30, 150, 249, 53.

48. Ibid. 32, 152–3, 168–70, 221–4, 243–4, 253, 257, 257–8, 278–9.

49. The full list is given in Hutton *Merry England*, 320–1, n. 7. The breakdown by county is Cornwall (2), Devon (9), Somerset (1), Gloucestershire (1), Dorset (1), Wiltshire (5), Hampshire (3), Sussex (1), Kent (1), Warwickshire (2), Shropshire (1), Worcestershire (1), Northamptonshire (1), Leicestershire (2), Bedfordshire (1), Buckinghamshire (3), Oxfordshire (6), Berkshire (3), Hertfordshire (1), Essex (1), Suffolk (1).

50. *Elizabethan Churchwardens' Accounts*, ed. J. Farmilae and R. Nixseaman (Bedfordshire Historical Record Society, 1953), 6–10.

51. East Suffolk (Lowestoft) RO, 115/E1/1, years 1566–8.

52. e.g. *West Tarring*, ed. Pressey, year 1561; Buckinghamshire RO, PR 7/5/1, years 1562–8 (Aston Abbots); Warwickshire RO, DR 87/1, year 1560–1 (St Nicholas, Warwick); Symonds, 'Winterslow Church Reckonings', 42–3; A. Vallance, 'Eltham Churchwarden's Accounts', *Archaeologia Cantiana*, 18 (1936), 121; Leicestershire RO, DE 1564/ 1384, years 1561–6 (St Martin, Leicester).

53. Leicestershire RO, DE 26/140/9 (Melton Mowbray); *West Tarring*, ed. Pressey, year 1566; Symonds, 'Winterslow Church Reckonings', 29; *Early Churchwardens' Accounts*,

ed. Williams, 88 (Stoke Charity); *Elizabethan Churchwardens' Accounts*, ed. Farmilae and Nixseaman, 6–10; Berkshire RO, D/P/ 130/5/1A, years 1560–9 (Thatcham); 'The Churchwardens' Accounts of Mere', ed. T. Baker, *Wiltshire Archaeological and Natural History Magazine*, 35 (1908), 37–43.

54. *Anatomy of Abuses* (1583), ed. Frederick J. Furnivall (New Shakespeare Society, 1879), 146–8.

55. Ibid. 150–1.

56. William Warner, *Albions England* (1602), bk. 5, p. 121.

57. E. Brinkworth (ed.), *The Archdeacon's Court* (Oxfordshire Record Society, 1942), 43–4.

58. *Visitation Articles and Injunctions of the Period of the Reformation*, ed. Walter Howard Frere (Alcuin Club, 1910), iii. 209, 256–7, 271, 291, 383; W. P. M. Kennedy, *Elizabethan Episcopal Administration* (Alcuin Club, 1924), 59, 73, 110, 160, 194, 220, 228, 350.

59. Norreys Jephson O' Conor, *Godes Peace and The Queenes* (Oxford, 1934), 108–25.

60. HMC Cecil MSS, viii. 201.

61. Quoted in Francis Douce, *Illustrations of Shakespeare and of Ancient Manners* (1807), 457.

62. Sources given in Hutton, *Merry England*, 322, nn. 34–5.

63. Ibid. ch. 4.

64. *The Diary of Henry Machyn*, ed. J. Nichols (Camden Society, 1848), 201.

65. Public Record Office, SP 12/224/61.

66. Thomas Nashe, *Works*, ed. R. B. McKerrow (1910), iii. 230–45.

67. Kenneth L. Parker, *The English Sabbath* (Cambridge, 1988), 62–4, 118–19.

68. Hutton, *Merry England*, ch. 4.

69. William Kethe, *A Sermon Made at Blandford Forum* (1571).

70. Humphrey Roberts, *An Earnest Complaint of Divers Vain, Wicked and Abused Exercises* (1572); William Harrison, *The Description of England*, ed. Georges Edelen (Ithaca, NY, 1968), 36.

71. Hutton, *Merry England*, 129–34, 156–7.

72. William Hinde, *A Faithful Remonstrance of the Holy Life... of John Bruen* (1641), 11–12, 89–131.

73. *Records of Early English Drama: Devon*, ed. John M. Wasson (Toronto, 1986), 293–6.

74. Hutton, *Merry England*, 140–1.

75. Public Record Office, SP 12/224/47–87.

76. Hutton, *Merry England*, 140–1.

77. At Chudleigh, Shobrooke, and Braunton: Devon RO, Chudleigh PWI/V and Shobrooke PWI, and North Devon RO, 1677A/PWI.

78. T. Barnes, 'County Politics and a Puritan Cause Célèbre: Somerset church ales, 1633', *Transactions of the Royal Historical Society*, 5th ser. 5 (1959), 107; K. E. Wrightson, 'The Puritan Reformation of Manners with Special Reference to the Counties of Lancashire and Essex 1640–1660' (Cambridge Ph.D. thesis, 1973), 31; Peter Laslett and Karla Oosterveen, 'Long-Term Trends in Bastardy in England', *Population Studies*, 27 (1973), 259; G. R. Quaife, *Wanton Wenches and Wayward Wives* (1979), 84–7.

79. *Records of Early English Drama: Herefordshire and Worcestershire*, ed. David N. Klausner (Toronto, 1990), 74–96.

80. Hutton, *Merry England*, 157–8.

81. Hampshire RO, 75M72/PWI.

82. Surrey RO (Guildford), PSH/SEA/2/1.

83. C. J. Sisson, *Lost Plays of Shakespeare's Age* (Cambridge, 1936), 162–75.

84. David Underdown, *Revel, Riot and Rebellion* (Oxford, 1985), 56–62; HMC MSS In Various Collections, i. 294–5.

85. Underdown, *Revel, Riot and Rebellion*, 59, 63; Thomas Coryate, *Coryats Crambe* (1611).

86. Quoted in John Brand, *Observations on the Popular Antiquities of Great Britain*, ed. Sir Henry Ellis (1908), i. 280.

87. Hutton, *Merry England*, 135-7, 164-7, 169-70.

88. *The Survey of Cornwall* (1602), 141-4.

89. Hutton, *Merry England*, 137, 166-7.

90. Ibid. 168-74, 189-94, represents the latest retelling of this story.

91. Ibid. 201.

92. Somerset RO, DD/WY 37/1.

93. Hampshire RO, 4M69/PWI, years 1661-77.

94. Hutton, *Merry England*, 229-30.

95. *Early Ballads*, ed. Robert Bell (1877), 384-6.

96. Trefor M. Owen, *Welsh Folk Customs* (St Fagans, 1974), 96.

97. John Harland and T. T. Wilkinson, *Lancashire Folk-Lore* (1867), 247; Roger Elbourne, *Music and Tradition in Early Industrial Lancashire* (Folklore Society, 1980), 50; *The Autobiography of Samuel Bamford*, ed. W. H. Chaloner (1967), i. 145-6.

98. Ella Mary Leather, *The Folklore of Herefordshire* (Hereford, 1912). 103.

99. Ralph Whitlock, *The Folklore of Devon* (1977), 47.

100. Robert W. Malcolmson, *Popular Recreations in English Society 1700-1850* (Cambridge, 1973), 31-2; D. H. M. Read, 'Hampshire Folklore', *Folklore*, 22 (1911), 296-7.

101. Tony Deane and Tony Shaw, *The Folklore of Cornwall* (1975), 178.

102. Malcolmson, *Popular Recreations*, 31-2; D. H. M. Read, 'Hampshire Folklore', *Folklore*, 22 (1911), 296-7.

103. 'Morris Dancing and May Day Games', *Walford's Antiquarian*, 9 (May 1886), 198-200; Michael Pickering, *Village Song and Culture* (1982), 32; C. E. Prior, *Dedications of Churches* (Oxfordshire Archaeological Society Reports, 1903), 34; T. F. Thiselton Dyer, *British Popular Customs* (1876), 281; Percy Manning, 'Some Oxfordshire Seasonal Festivals', *Folklore*, 8 (1897), 313-15; *County Folklore*, 1; (Folk-Lore Society, 1895): 1. Gloucestershire, ed. E. Sidney Hartland, 56-7; Percy Manning, 'Stray Notes on Oxfordshire Folklore', *Folk-Lore*, 14 (1903), 171-4; Aluin Hawkins, *Whitsun in 19th Century Oxfordshire* (History Workshop pamphlets, 8 1973), 5-10; Bod. L, MS Top Oxon d. 200, for 27-30, 45 (Percy Manning's notes); Malcolmson, *Popular Recreations*, 31-2; Thomas Blount, *Fragmentata Antiquitatis* (1679), 149; F. Carrington, 'Ancient Ales in the County of Wilts', *Wiltshire Archaeological and Natural History Magazine*, 2 (1855), 192.

104. Waldron, *Description of the Isle of Man*, quoted in John Brand, *Observations on the Popular Antiquities of Great Britain*, ed. Sir Henry Ellis (1908), i. 257-8; Joseph Train, *An Historical and Statistical Account of the Isle of Man* (Douglas, 1845), ii. 117-20.

105. Marie Trevelyan, *Folklore and Folk-Stories of Wales* (1909), 25-6.

106. Wirt Sykes, *British Goblins* (1880), 276.

107. William Howitt, *The Rural Life of England*, 2nd edn., (1840), 444-8.

108. Owen, *Welsh Folk Customs*, 92; Ralph Whitlock, *The Folklore of Wiltshire* (1976), 42-4, and *Folklore of Devon*, 143; John Symonds Udal, *Dorsetshire Folklore* (Hertford, 1922), 59; Bob Bushaway, *By Rite* (1982), 260-4; Malcolmson, *Popular Recreations*, 32-3; James Obelkevitch, *Religion and Rural Society: South Lindsey 1825-1875* (Oxford, 1976), 86-8; Howkins, *19th Century Oxfordshire*, 19-43; Jacqueline Simpson, *The Folklore of Sussex* (1973), 120.

109. C. F. Howkins, *19th Century Oxfordshire*, 25-6.

110. *Oxfordshire Village Life: The Diaries of George James Dew (1846-1928), Relieving Officer*, ed. Pamela Horn (Abingdon, 1983), 51. And see also pp. 41, 51, 58, 70; and David Neave, *Mutual Aid in the Victorian Countryside, 1830-1914* (Hull, 1991), 89-91.

111. Whitlock, *Wiltshire*, 43; Howkins, 19th Century Oxfordshire, 20, 44, 61.

112. University College London, Alex Helm Collection, 3/11; 'Cornwall'.
113. For an early and long description, see William Hone, *The Every-Day Book and Table Book*, (1832), ii. 648–51. Joseph Needham, 'The Geographical Distribution of English Ceremonial Dance Traditions', *JEFDSS* 3: 1 (1936), 26–38, leads those authors who regarded the Furry Dance as 'Romano-British'. Conventional folklorist accounts are found in Roy Christian, *Old English Customs* (Newton Abbot, 1966), 39–41, and Tony Deane and Tony Shaw, *The Folklore of Cornwall* (1975), 173–4. Most valuable of all is the critical analysis in Roy Judge, 'Changing Attitudes to May Day 1844–1914' (Leeds Ph.D. thesis, 1987), 291–5. The basic text, however remains R. M. Nance, 'Helston Furry Day', *Journal of the Royal Institute of Cornwall* NS 4 (1961), 36–46.

CHAPTER 25

1. *Anatomie of Abuses*, 80; Frederick J. Furnivall (New Shakespeare Society, 1879), 146–7.
2. Collected by Barbara Lowe, 'Early Records of the Morris in England', *JEFDSS* 7: 2 (1957), 61–82; E. C. Cawte, *Ritual Animal Disguise* (Folklore Society, 1978), 54–5; Jane Garry, 'The Literary History of the English Morris Dance', *Folklore*, 94 (1983), 219–28.
3. Francis Peck, *New Memories of the Life of John Milton* (1740), 135; Joseph Strutt, *The Sports and Pastimes of the People of England*, ed. J. Charles Cox (1903), 201; Francis Douce, *On The Ancient English Morris Dance* (1807).
4. E. K. Chambers, *The Medieval Stage* (Oxford, 1903), i. 195–201.
5. Percy Manning, 'Some Oxfordshire Seasonal Festivals', *Folk-Lore*, 8 (1897), 307–24.
6. Cecil Sharp and Herbert C. Macilwaine, *The Morris Book. Part 1* 2nd edn. (1912), *Part 2*, 2nd edn. (1919); *Part 3*, 2nd edn. (1924); Roy Judge, 'Mary Neal and the Esperance Morris', *Folk Music Journal*, 5 (1989), 545–90; A. H. Fox Strangeways, *Cecil Sharp* (Oxford, 1933), 26–88.
7. Maud Karpeles, 'English Folk Dances: Their Survival and Revival', *Folk-Lore*, 43 (1932), 123–43; Douglas N. Kennedy, 'The English Morris Dance and its European Analogues', *Proceedings of the Scottish Anthropological and Folklore Society*, 4: 1 (1949), 6–12; Violet Alford, 'Midsummer and Morris in Portugal', *Folk-Lore*, 44 (1933), 218–35, and 'Morris and Morissa', *JEFDSS* 2 (1935), 41–9; Rodney Gallop, 'The Origins of the Morris Dance', *JEFDSS* 1 (1934), 122–9; Joseph Needham, 'Geographical Distribution of English Ceremonial Dance Traditions', *JEFDSS* 3 (1936), 1–45; *English Dance and Song*, 43: 3 (1981), 17–18; E. Phillips Barker, 'Two Notes on the Processional and the Morris Dance', *Journal of the English Folk Dance Society* (1915), 38–4; Reginald Netti, *Folk-Dancing* (Arco Handbook, 1962); Hugh Rippon, *Discovering English Folk Dance* (Shire Publications, Aylesbury, 1975); Russell Wortley, *The XYZ of Morris* (Morris Ring, 1978).
8. K. N. J. Loveless, 'Douglas Neil Kennedy', *English Dance and Song*, 25 (1973), 87–9.
9. Roy Judge, 'The Morris in Lichfield', *Folklore*, 103 (1992), 131–59.
10. Loveless, 'Douglas Neil Kennedy', 87–9.
11. Barbara Lowe, 'Early Records of the Morris in England', *JEFDSS* 8: 2 (1957), 61–82.
12. R. Dommett, 'How it all Began', *Morris Matters*, 1: 4 (autumn 1978), 4–8; A. G. Barrand, 'ABCD Morris', *English Dance and Song*, 42: 3 (1980), 11–13.
13. Roy Judge, 'D'Arcy Ferris and the Bidford Morris', *Folk Music Journal*, 4 (1984), 443–80;
14. Georgina Smith, 'Winster Morris Dance', in *Traditional Dance*, ed. Theresa Buckland (Crewe, 1982), i. 93–108. For earlier expressions of disquiet regarding Sharp's methods, see Roy Dommett's contribution to Lionel Bacon, *A Handbook of Morris Dances* (Morris Ring, 1974), n.p., and Keith Chandler, 'Morris Dancing in the South Midlands: A Social History' (Lancaster University BA dissertation, 1979).

15. *Morris and Matachin* (English Folk Dance and Song Society, 1984).

16. Michael Heaney, 'Kingston to Kenilworth: Early Plebeian Morris', *Folklore*, 100 (1989), 88–104; John Forrest and Michael Heaney, 'Charting Early Morris', *Folk Music Journal*, 6: 2 (1991), 169–86.

17. A. L. Lloyd, 'The Ritual of the Caluz', *Folk Music Journal*, 3: 4 (1978), 316–23; Lucille Armstrong, 'The Ritual of Morris', *English Dance and Song*, 43:3 (1981), 17–18.

18. 'Routs and Reyes', *Folklore*, 89 (1978), 184–203.

19. Heaney, 'Kingston to Kenilworth', 88–93.

20. Lowe, 'Early Records', 62.

21. Essex RO, DP 11/5/1, year 1527; Oxfordshire RO, Par. Thame b.2, year 1555.

22. *A Calendar of Dramatic Records in the Books of the Livery Companies of London*, ed. Jean Robertson and D. J. Gordon (Malone Society, 1954), 1–36.

23. e.g. the Great Dunmow record at n. 21; the Kingston records in Surrey RO (Kingston upon Thames) KG/2/1; 'Morris Coats', *Notes and Queries*, 5th ser. 5 337.

24. Sources at n. 23.

25. Meg Goodwin, *Old Meg of Herefordshire* (1609).

26. This is once again to assign a later rather than an earlier date to the famous window which was formerly set into the manor house at Betley, Staffs. Most of the dancers in it were copied from a copper engraving made by Israhel von Mecheln or Meckenem in the 1460s. This, the absence of beards upon all the men, and the inclusion of the arms of the Audley family, who gave up Betley in 1536, all makes it possible that the window is early Tudor. One expert upon stained glass, Charles Bridgeman, has indeed claimed it for that period. The lettering across the maypole, however, is no earlier than the Elizabethan age, and most authorities upon such glass assign it to then or to the early seventeenth century, when the building in which it is first recorded was erected. I therefore follow this latter view: C. Bridgeman, 'Note on the Betley Morris Dance Window', *Collections for a History of Staffordshire* NS 16 (1923), 1–5; Herbert Read, *English Stained Glass* (1926), 240–9; E. J. Nichol, 'Some Notes on the History of the Betley Window', *JEFDSS* 7: 2 (1953), 59–67. A different problem attaches to the figure playing a pipe and tabor, probably late fifteenth-century, in the window of the Zouche Chapel of York Minster. He has been proposed as a morris dancer because of what could be bells below his knees. The same objects, however, hang on his wrists and the edge of his tunic, and could be rings or other decorations: Philip Underwood, 'Earliest Morris Dancer', *English Dance and Song*, 49: 21 (1987), 17. A carved wooden panel from Lancaster Castle may well be the earliest depiction of the dance, showing three men performing feverishly in short tunics, one with bells on knees. The style of the figures indicates a sixteenth or very early seventeenth-century origin: Anne C. Gilchrist, 'A Carved Morris-Dance Panel from Lancaster Castle', *JEFDSS* 1: 2 (1933), 86–8. The finest Tudor or Stuart representation is therefore in the painting *The Thames at Richmond*, kept in Cambridge's Fitzwilliam Museum and produced by a Flemish artist in the early seventeenth century. Its dancers number four, performing in couples with white shirts, black or red breeches, and identical grey hats with yellow plumes.

27. Anna Jean Mill, *Medieval Plays in Scotland* (Edinburgh, 1927), 12.

28. F. Marian McNeil, *The Silver Bough*, ii (Glasgow, 1959), 77.

29. John Fry and Alan J. Fletcher, 'The Kilkenny Morries, 1610', *Folk Music Journal*, 6: 3 (1992), 381–3; Thomas Crofton Croker, *Fairy Legends and Traditions of the South of Ireland* (1818), 271–2; Sir William R. Wilde, *Irish Popular Superstitions* (Dublin, 1852), 64–5.

30. Heaney, 'Kingston to Kenilworth', 99–102. This material is wholly supported by the parish evidence used in Ronald Hutton, *The Rise and Fall of Merry England* (Oxford, 1994), 113–14.

31. Heaney, 'Kingston to Kenilworth', 96.

32. Forrest and Heaney, 'Charting Early Morris', 175–86.

33. e.g. Frederick Emmison, 'Tithes, Perambulations and Sabbath-breach in Elizabethan Essex', in *Tribute to an Antiquary*, ed. Frederick Emmison and Roy Stephens (1976), 201–2; Peter Clark, *English Provincial Society from the Reformation to the Revolution* (1977), 157: PRO, SP 14/64/66 (deposition from Salisbury); E. R. C. Brinkworth, *Shakespeare and the Bawdy Court of Stratford* (1972), 54–5.

34. See esp. John Marston *et al.*, *Jack Drums Entertainment* (1601) Act I; Francis Beaumont, *The Knight of the Burning Pestle* (1613), IV. 8–60; John Fletcher, *Women Pleased* (n.d.) VI. 85–214; Thomas Dekker, John Ford, William Rowley, *The Witch of Edmonton* (1621), II. i. 1–24, III. IV.

35. Cf. *The Autobiography of Henry Newcome*, ed. Richard Parkinson (Chetham Society, 1852), 121.

36. e.g. Lowe, 'Early Records', 76–7; Henry Reece, 'The Military Presence in England' (Oxford D.Phil. thesis, 1981), 84.

37. The last record seemingly being the performance of a Hertfordshire village team in Clerkenwell in 1826: William Hone, *The Every-Day Book and Table Book* (1832), ii, 792–4.

38. Bod. L. MS Top Oxon d. 200, fors. 27–30 (Percy Manning's notes); Forrest, *Morris and Matachin*, chs. 2–3; Sharp and Macilwaine, *The Morris Book*, Parts 1, 2, and 3; Michael Heaney, 'A New Theory of Morris Origins', *Folklore*, 96 (1985), 29–37; K. Chandler, 'Morris Dancing in the Eighteenth Century', *Lore and Language*, 3: 8 (1983), 31–8; Michael Pickering, *Village Song and Culture* (1982), 30–2; Percy Manning, 'Some Oxfordshire Seasonal Festivals', *Folk-Lore*, 8 (1897), 307–15; E. C. Cawte, '"It's an Ancient Custom"—But How Ancient?', in Aspects of *British Calendar Customs*, ed. Theresa Buckland and Juliette Wood (Folklore Society, 1993), 45–8; 'Morris Dancing and May-Day Games', *Walford's Antiquarian*, 9 (May 1889), 198–200; Alun Hawkins, *Whitsun in 19th Century Oxfordshire* (History Workship Pamphlets 8; 1973), 9–13; R. Wortley, 'The Cotswold Morris: Hey-Day, Decline and Revival', *Ethnic*, 1: 2 (1959), 4–11; Keith Chandler, *Ribbons, Bells and Squeaking Fiddles* (Folklore Society, 1993).

39. Alfred Burton, *Rush-Bearing* (Manchester, 1891), 117; Alex Helm, 'The Rushcart and the North-Western Morris', *JEFDSS* 7: 3 (1954), 172–9; A. G. Gilchrist, 'The Lancashire Rush-Cart and the Morris Dance', *Journal of the English Folk Dance Society*, 2nd ser. 1 (1927), 17–27; Thomas Middleton. 'Rushbearing and Morris Dancing in North Cheshire', *Transactions of the Lancashire and Cheshire Antiquarian Society*, 60 (1948), 47–55; Lesley Edwards and Janet Chart, 'Aspects of Morris Dancing in Cheshire 1880–1914', *English Dance and Song*, 43: 1 (1981), 5–10; Daniel Howson and Bernard Bentley, 'The North-West Morris', *JEFDSS* 9: 1 (1960), 42–55; R. J. P. Poole, 'Wakes, Holidays and Fairs in the Lancashire Cotton District, *c.*1790–1890' (Lancaster Ph.D. thesis, 1985), 100–3; Theresa Jill Buckland, 'Ceremonial Dance Traditions in the South-West Pennines and Rossendale' (Leeds Ph.D. thesis, 1984) 243–68, 757–74.

40. Ella Mary Leather, *The Folk-Lore of Herefordshire* (Hereford, 1912), 130; E. C. Cawte, 'The Morris Dance in Herefordshire, Shropshire and Worcestershire', *JEFDSS* 9: 4 (1963), 197–212; David Jones, 'Morris Dances of the Welsh Border', *English Dance and Song*, 48: 2 (1986), 14–15.

41. Hone, *Every-Day Book*, i, 562–5; Marie Trevelyan, *Folk-Lore and Folk-Stories of Wales* (1909), 249–50; Trefor M. Owen, *Welsh Folk Customs* (National Museum of Wales, 1974), 101–7; Lois Blake, 'The Morris in Wales', *JEFDSS* 9: 1 (1960), 56–7.

42. The historiography of this debate is summarized in Barbara Lowe, 'Robin Hood in the Light of History', *JEFDSS* 7: 4 (1955), 228–38: Maurice Keen, *The Outlaws of Medieval Legend* (1961), appendix 1; J. C. Holt, *Robin Hood*, 2nd edn. (1989), 54–7.

43. *The Early Plays of Robin Hood* (Cambridge, 1981). Pioneering work upon the subject was carried out by W. Simeone, 'The May Games and the Robin Hood Legend', *Journal of American Folklore*, 64 (1951), 265–74.

44. In Berkshire, Abingdon, Finchamstead and St Lawrence, Reading; in Buckinghamshire, Amersham. In Cornwall, St Columb Major, St Columb Minor, St Ives, and Stratton. In Devon, Ashburton, Chagford, and Woodbury. In Kent, Hythe. In Leicestershire, Leicester and Melton Mowbray. At London. In Oxfordshire, at Henley and at Thame. In Shropshire, at Bridgnorth and at Shrewsbury. In Somerset at Croscombe, Tintinhull, and Wells. In Staffordshire, at Wednesbury. In Surrey, at Kingston upon Thames. In Worcestershire, at Cleeve Prior, Ombursley, and St Helen's, Worcester.

45. Colin Richmond, 'An Outlaw and Some Peasants', *Nottingham Medieval Studies*, 37 (1993), 90–101.

46. C. Radford, 'Early Drama in Exeter', *Transactions of the Devonshire Association*, 67 (1935), 367.

47. Holt, *Robin Hood*, 159–60.

48. *Records of Early English Drama: Devon*, ed. John M. Wasson (Toronto, 1986), 42, 57, 207, 383, 393, 397, 410 (for Barnstaple 1559, Chudleigh 1561, Honiton 1572, Farway 1561 Colyton, 1572, and St John's Bow, Exeter 1488–1554); Cornwall RO, DDP/7/5/1 fos. 20–9 (for Anthony 1555–59); E. G. C. Atchley, 'On the Medieval Parish Records of the Church of St Nicholas, Bristol', *Transactions of the St Paul's Ecclesiological Society*, 6 (1906), 67; Somerset RO, D/P/gla.j. 4/1 (St John, Glastonbury, 1498); Graham Mayhew, *Tudor Rye* (Falmer, 1987), 58 (Rye, 1511); Devon RO, 1718A add/PWI (Holy Trinity, Exeter, 1555–88); R. T. Hampson, *Medii Aevi Kalendarium* (1841), 263–4 (for Manchester under Mary Tudor); North Devon RO, 1677/A/U (Braunton, 1560–2); *The Farington Papers*, ed. Susan Maria Farington (Chetham Society, 1856), 128–30 (for Burnley, 1579); *Journal of Prior William More*, ed. Ethel S. Fegan (Worcestershire Historical Society, 30; 1914), 87–332 (for Tewkesbury, Gloucestershire, 1519) BL Add. MS 6223, fos. 11–13 (Hexton, Hertfordshire, 'until the 1560s'); John Symonds Udal, *Dorsetshire Folk-Lore* (Hereford, 1922), 105 (for Bridport, 1555).

49. Hutton, *Merry England*, 31–3.

50. Mill, *Medieval Plays*, 22–32, 137–286 *passim*.

51. Sydney Anglo, 'An Early Tudor Programme for Plays and Other Demonstrations against the Pope', *Journal of the Warburg and Courtauld Institutes*, 20 (1957), 176–9.

52. *Churchwardens' Accounts of Croscombe etc.*, ed. Bishop Hobhouse (Somerset Record Society, 1890), 200.

53. Chambers, *Medieval Stage*, i. 171–6. See also John Brand, *Observations on the Popular Antiquities of Great Britain*, ed. Sir Henry Ellis (1908), i. 255–6.

54. Lowe, 'Robin Hood', 235–6.

55. Heaney, 'Kingston to Kenilworth', 88–91.

56. Forrest and Heaney, 'Charting Early Morris', 176–86.

57. *Pasquil and Marforius* (1589), n.p.

58. As in the painting, 'The Thames at Richmond'. In the panel from Lancaster Castle, it is Marian who does the collecting: see n. 26.

59. William Urwick, *Nonconformity in Herts* (1884), 107–15.

60. *Early Plays of Robin Hood*, 21–3.

61. Sources at n. 38.

62. Sources at n. 41.

63. Sources at n. 40.

64. Sources at n. 39.

65. Georgina Boyes, *The Imagined Village* (Manchester, 1993), 160–7.

66. Keith Chandler, 'Ribbons, Bells and Squeaking Fiddles': The Social History of Morris Dancing in the English South Midlands, 1660–1900 (Folklore Society Tradition Series, 1; 1993).

CHAPTER 26

1. John Dowden, *The Church Year and Kalendar* (Cambridge, 1910), 43–4; John Brand, *Observations on the Popular Antiquities of Great Britain*, ed. Sir Henry Ellis (1908), i. 202; E. O. James, *Seasonal Feasts and Festivals* (1961), 218–22.

2. *Documents Illustrative of English Church History*, ed. Henry Gee (1986), 22–3.

3. H. H. Scullard, *Festivals and Ceremonies of the Roman Republic* (1981), 124–5.

4. A. R. Wright, *British Calendar Customs*, ed. T. E. Lones (Folk-Lore Society, 1936), 149; John Brady, *Clavis Calendaria* (1812), 360–2.

5. *Mirk's Festival*, ed. T. Erbe (EETS, 1905), 159

6. *Councils and Synods . . . 1205–1313*, ed. F. M. Powicke and C. R. Cheney (Oxford, 1964), 3, 205, 274, 328–30, 344, 363–4, 409, 416–18, 520, 652, 1057.

7. Gervase Rosser, 'Parochial Conformity and Voluntary Religion in late Medieval England', *TRHS* 6th series 1 (1991), 174.

8. *Councils and Synods*, ed. Powicke and Cheney, 205

9. *Borough Customs*, ed. Mary Bateson (Selden Society, 1906), ii. 47.

10. Sir Herbert Maxwell, 'Chronicle of Lanercost', *Scottish Historical Review*, 6 (1909), 287–8.

11. Ronald Hutton, *The Rise and Fall of Merry England* (Oxford, 1994), 34–5.

12. *Churchwardens' Accounts of S. Edmund and S. Thomas, Sarum*, ed. Henry J. F. Swayne (Wiltshire Record Society, 1876), 1–85.

13. *The Rites of Durham*, ed. J. Raine (Surtees Society, 1842), 87–9.

14. Richard Taverner, *Postils on the Epistles and Gospels*, ed. E. Carswell (Oxford, 1841), 280.

15. Hutton, *Merry England*, 36.

16. White Kennett, *Parochial Antiquities* (1695), 596–7; Wright, *British Calendar Customs*, i. 149–50.

17. Hutton, *Merry England*, 36; Alan H. Nelson, *The Medieval English Stage* (Chicago, 1974), ch. 6.

18. Hutton, *Merry England*, 36–7, 59.

19. Ibid. 79–85.

20. Ibid. 98–9; R. Fitch, 'Norwich Pageants', *Norfolk Archaeology*, 5 (1859), 28–9; *Records of Early English Drama: Chester*, ed. Lawrence M. Clopper (Manchester, 1979), p. liii.

21. Fitch, 'Norwich Pageants', 29–31; *Records of Early English Drama: Norwich*, ed. David Galloway (Toronto, 1984), 50–3.

22. *Chester*, ed. Clopper, pp. liv–v.

23. Hutton, *Merry England*, 105.

24. Ibid. 105; *Visitation Articles and Injunctions of the Period of the Reformation*, ed. Walter Howard Frere (Alevin Club, 1910), iii. 69, 264.

25. W. P. M. Kennedy, *Elizabethan Episcopal Administration* (Alcuin Club, 1924), P. cx and *passim*.

26. John Strype, *The Life and Acts of Matthew Parker* (Oxford, 1821), i. 303–5.

27. Berkshire RO, D/P 118/5/1, year 1564.

28. Hutton, *Merry England*, 106, 142–3.

29. Ibid. 175–6.

30. Ibid. 176, 182

31. Ibid. 176.

32. *Churchwardens' Presentments (17th Cenury)*, ed. H. Johnstone (Sussex Record Society, 1947–8), *passim*.

33. Hutton, *Merry England*, 1976.

34. Repr. in Wright, *British Calendar Customs*, i. 130.

35. George Wither, *Haleluiah* (Spencer Society, 1879), 274–6.

36. Hutton, *Merry England*, 217–18.

37. Norfolk RO, PD 26/71, PD58/38 (5), COL 3/4, PD 191/23.

38. Hutton, *Merry England*, 218.

39. Ibid. 247.

40. Ibid. 247–8.

41. 'Perambulation of Purton, 1733', ed. T. Maskelyne, *Wiltshire Archaeological and Natural History Magazine*, 40 (1917–19), 119–28; C. F. Tebbutt, *Huntingdonshire Folklore* (St Ives, 1984), 68–9; 'Beating the Bounds, Out Parish of St Cuthbert's, Wells, *Somerset and Dorset Notes and Queries*, 7 (1901), 268–98; J. Weld, *A History of Leagram* (Chetham Society, 1913), 129–30; Bob Bushaway, *By Rite* (1982), 25, 35–40, 83–6; *Journal of the Archaeological Association*, 8 (1853), 233; *British Calendar Customs*, i. 130–4; Robert W. Malcolmson, *Popular Recreations in English Society 1700–1850* (Cambridge, 1973), 58–9; William Brockie, *Legends and Superstitions of the County of Durham* (Sunderland, 1886), 102; John Nicholson, *Folk Lore of East Yorkshire* (1890), 31; Robert Chambers, *The Book of Days* (1864), i. 583–5; P. H. Ditchfield, *Old English Customs Extant at the Present Time* (1876), 116–17; Mrs Gutch (ed.), *County Folklore*, vi. *East Riding of Yorkshire* (Folk-Lore Society, 1912), 99–101; Frederick William Hackwood, *Staffordshire Customs, Superstitions and Folklore* (Lichfield, 1924), 21–6; Enid Porter, *Cambridgeshire Customs and Folklore* (1969), 116; Ella Mary Leather, *The Folk-Lore of Herefordshire* (Hereford, 1912), 149; Charlotte Sophia Burne, *Shropshire Folk-Lore* (1883), 345–9; George Morley, *Shakespeare's Greenwood* (1900), 112–13; John Noake, *Notes and Queries for Worcestershire* (1856), 222–3; J. B. Partridge, 'Cotswold Place-Lore and Customs', *Folk-Lore*, 23 (1912), 452; R. W. Bushaway, 'Rite, Legitimation and Community in Southern England 1700–1850', in Barry Stapleton (ed.), *Conflict and Community in Southern England* (New York), 116–17; Mrs Gutch (ed.), *County Folk-Lore*, ii. *North Riding of York and the Ainsty* (Folk-Lore Society, 1901), 250–1.

42. Bushaway, *By Rite*, 256

43. J. Fisher, 'The Religious and Social Life of Former Days in the Vale of Clwyd', *Archaeologia Cambrensis*, 6th ser. 6 (1906), 170; G Evans, 'Cardiganshire: Its Plate, Records and Register's, *Archaeologia Cambrensis*, 6th ser. 6 (1906), 329–30; T. M. Owen, 'Perambulation of the Boundaries of Churchstoke Parish', *Montgomeryshire Collections*, 34 (190), 197–211; Jonathon Ceredig Davies, *Folk-Lore of West and Mid-Wales* (Aberystwyth, 1911), 83.

44. A. W. Moore, *The Folk-Lore of the Isle of Man* (1891), 117.

45. 'Beating the Bounds, St Cuthberts', 268–71.

46. Tebbutt, *Huntingdonshire Folklore*, 68–9.

47. *Gentleman's Magazine*, 103: 1 (1833), 116–17.

48. Noake, *Worcestershire*, 222–3

49. *Kilvert's Diary 1870–79*, ed. William Plomer (1946), 314–16

50. Bushaway, *By Rite*, 86.

51. Burne, *Shropshire Folk-Lore*, 345–6.

52. Bushaway, *By Rite*, 273.

53. Tebbutt, *Huntingdonshire Folklore*, 68–9; *Folk-Lore*, 60 (1949), 348; R. P. Chope '33rd Report on Devonshire Folk-Lore', *Transactions of the Devonshire Association*, 65 (1933), 128, and '34th Report', ibid. 71 (1934), 84; W. Knight, '64th Report', ibid. 81 (1949), 90; T. Brown, '61st Report', ibid. 96 (1964), 99; and '65th Report', ibid. 100 (1968), 284–7; Wright, *British Calendar Customs*, i. 130–4; R. L. Tongue, *Somerset Folklore*, ed. K. M. Briggs (Folklore Society, 1965), 165; Lawrence Whistler, *The English Festivals* (1947), 156; Gutch (ed.), *Country Folk-Lore*, ii. 99–101; Peter Robson, 'Calendar Customs in Nineteenth and Twentieth Century Dorset' (Sheffield M.Phil. thesis, 1988), 78; Doris Jones-Baker, *The Folklore of Hertfordshire* (1977), 144; G. Peachy, 'Beating the Bounds of Brightwalton', *Berks, Bucks and Oxon Archaeological Journal*, 10 (1904–5), 75–81.

54. The parishes are Belstone, Bickington, Bishopsteignton, Chudleigh, Colyford, Hennock, Honiton, Ilsington, Kinkerswell, South Brent, and South Molton. I am very grateful to Thomas, Baron Clifford of Chudleigh, for additional information.

55. Brand, *Observations*, i. 207.

CHAPTER 27

1. Ronald Hutton, *The Rise and Fall of Merry England* (Oxford, 1994), 249.

2. Ibid. 249, 251, 257.

3. Ibid. 250.

4. Ibid. 250–1.

5. Ibid. 254, 257–8.

6. Paul Kleber Monod, *Jacobitism and the English People 1688–1788* (Cambridge, 1989), 181.

7. Ibid. 181–3.

8. John Brand, *Observations on the Popular Antiquities of Great Britain*, ed. Sir Henry Ellis (1908), i. 274.

9. Monod, *Jacobitism*, 182–3.

10. Bob Bushaway, *By Rite* (1982), 77–8.

11. BL Add. MS 24544, p. 224.

12. Robert W. Malcolmson, *Popular Recreations in English Society 1700–1850* (Cambridge, 1973), 30–1.

13. John Symunds Udal, *Dorsetshire Folk-Lore* (Hertford, 1922), 43.

14. E. M. Wilson, 'Royal Oak Day in Westmorland', *Folk-Lore*, 51 (1940), 114–16; Marjorie Rowling, *The Folklore of the Lake District* (1976), 119; Iona and Peter Opie, *The Lore and Language of Schoolchildren* (Oxford, 1959), 264–5; Richard Blakeborough, *Wit, Character, Folklore and Customs of the North Riding of Yorkshire* (1898), 82.

15. R. P. Chope, 'Devonshire Calendar Customs, Part II. Fixed Festivals', *Transactions of the Devonshire Association*, 70 (1938), 372–7.

16. Margaret Baker, *Folklore and Customs of Rural England* (Newton Abbot, 1974), 124.

17. Frederick William Hackwood, *Staffordshire Customs, Superstitions and Folklore* (Lichfield, 1924), 20.

18. *Illustrated London News*, (30 May 1857), p. 515; Ella Mary Leather, *The Folklore of Herefordshire* (Hereford, 1912), 102.

19. Bushaway, *By Rite*, 79–80: William Brockie, *Legends and Superstitions of the County of Durham* (Sunderland. 1886), 103; P. H. Ditchfield, *Old English Customs Extant at the Present Time* (1896), 120–1; Leather, *Herefordshire*, 107; Charlotte Sophia Burne, *Shropshire Folk-Lore* (1883), 365; John Noake, *Notes and Queries for Worcestershire*

(1856), 209–10; J. H. P. Still, 'Essex' *Folk-Lore*, 20 (1909), 489; D. H. M. Read, 'Hampshire Folklore', *Folk-Lore*, 22 (1911), 297–8; J. B. Partridge, 'Cotswold Place-Lore and Customs', *Folk-Lore*, 23 (1912), 451–2; Wilson, 'Royal Oak Day', 114–16; A. R. Wright, *British Calendar Customs*, ed. T. E. Lones (Folk-Lore Society, 1936), ii. 255–65; Christina Hole, *English Custom and Usage* (1941), 101; Peter Robson, 'Calendar Customs in Nineteenth and Twentieth Century Dorset' (Sheffield M.Phil. thesis, 1988), 74; Jacqueline Simpson, *The Folklore of the Welsh Border* (1976), 153; Mrs Gutch and Mabel Peacock (eds.), *County Folk-Lore*, v. *Lincolnshire* (Folk-Lore Society, 1908), 206.

20. Gutch and Peacock (eds.), *County Folk-Lore*, v. 205–6; Kingsley Palmer, *The Folklore of Somerset* (1976), 102; C. F. Tebbutt, *Huntingdonshire Folklore* (St Ives, 1984), 69; T. Brown, '58th Report on Folklore', *Transactions of the Devonshire Association*, 92 (1961), 113; E. Wilson, 'Some Extinct Kendal Customs', *Transactions of the Cumberland and Westmorland Antiquarian and Archaeological Society* NS 38 (1938), 165; Wright, *British Calendar Customs*, ii. 254–70; R. L. Tongue, *Somerset Folklore*, ed. K. M. Briggs (Folk-Lore Society, 1965), 163–4; John Nicholson, *Folk Lore of East Yorkshire* (1890), 14; Ditchfield, *Old English Customs*, 120–1; Mrs Gutch (ed.), *County Folklore*, ii. *North Riding of Yorkshire, York and the Ainsty* (Folk-Lore Society, 1901), 249; Mrs Gutch (ed.), *County Folklore*, vi. *East Riding of Yorkshire* (Folk-Lore Society, 1912), 97–8; *County Folk-Lore*, i. (Folk-Lore Society, 1895): 3. Leicestershire and Rutland, ed. Charles J. Billson, 93; Hackwood, *Staffordshire*, 19; T. F. Thiselton Dyer, *British Popular Customs* (1876), 304–5; Leather, *Herefordshire*, 102; Ralph Whitlock, *The Folklore of Devon* (1977), 148; Udal, *Dorsetshire*, 43–4; Read, 'Hampshire Folklore', 297–8; Angelina Parker, 'Oxfordshire Village Folklore 1840–1900', *Folk Lore*, 24 (1913), 87–8; Wilson, 'Royal Oak Day', 114–16; Hole, *English Custom*, 101; Tony Deane and Tony Shaw, *The Folklore of Cornwall* (1975), 176; Robson, 'Calendar Customs', 74; Wendy Boase, *The Folklore of Hampshire and the Isle of Wight* (1976), 138; Rowling, *Lake District*, 119; Opie and Opie, *Lore and Language*, 263–5; Jacqueline Simpson, *The Folklore of Sussex* (1973), 118–19; Simpson, *Welsh Border*, 153–4.

21. Stanley Jackson Coleman, *Lore and Legend of Hampshire* (Treasury of Folklore 37; Douglas, 1954), 'Shig Shag Day'.

22. Opie and Opie, *Lore and Language*, 263–5; Simpson, *Welsh Border*, 154.

23. Cf. Crichton Porteous, *The Ancient Customs of Derbyshire* (Derby, 1962), 5–6; Roy Christian, *Old English Customs* (Newton Abbot, 1966), 44–5.

24. Noted angrily by Georgina Boyes, 'Cultural Survivals Theory and Traditional Customs', *Folk Life*, 26 (1987–8), 9.

25. Georgina Boyes, 'Dressing the Past', in Theresa Buckland and Juliette Wood (eds.), *Aspects of British Calendar Customs* (Folklore Society Mistletoe Series, 22; Sheffield, 1993), 105–18.

CHAPTER 28

1. For a general survey of this development, see Alice Chandler, *A Dream of Order: The Medieval Ideal in Nineteenth-Century English Literature* (1971), 1–20.

2. Joseph Strutt, *The Sports and Pastimes of the People of England* (1801); Francis Douce, *Illustrations of Shakespeare and of Ancient Manners* (1807); John Brady, *Clavis Calendria* (1812); John Brand, *Observations on the Popular Antiquities of Great Britain*, ed. Sir Henry Ellis (1813).

3. Quoted in Chandler, *Dream of Order*, 45–51.

4. Ibid. 101–20; J. W. Burrow, *A Liberal Descent: Victorian Historians and the English Past* (Cambridge, 1981), 240–1.

5. William Hone, *The Every-Day Book and Table Book* (1832), ii. 69–76.
6. Roy E. Judge, 'Changing Attitudes to May Day 1844–1914' (Leeds Ph.D. thesis, 1987), 346–9.
7. Ibid. 384–6.
8. Ibid. 175–83.
9. Burrow, *A Liberal Descent*, 264–7.
10. Judge, 'Changing Attitudes', 219.
11. Chandler, *Dream of Order*, 162–6.
12. Judge, 'Changing Attitudes', 155–60.
13. Ibid. 282–7; Roy Judge, 'May Day and Merrie England; *Folklore*, 102 (1991), 131–40.
14. Charles Hardwick, *Traditions, Superstitions and Folk-Lore* (Manchester, 1872), 91.
15. Judge, 'May Day and Merrie England', 131–45; Lesley Edwards and Janet Chart, 'Aspects of Morris Dancing in Cheshire 1880–1914', *English Dance and Song*, 43: 1 (1981), 5–10.
16. Ibid. 135–48; Judge, Changing Attitudes', 284–7, 361–78.
17. Georgina Smith, 'Winster Morris Dance: The Sources of an Oikotype', in Theresa Buckland (ed.), *Traditional Dance* (Crewe, 1892), i. 93–108.
18. Roy Judge, 'D'Arcy Ferris and the Bidford Morris', *Folk Music Journal*, 4 (1988), 443–80, and 'Merrie England and the Morris', *Folklore*, 104 (1993), 124–43.
19. Judge, 'Merrie England', 130–43.
20. Judge, 'Changing Attitudes', 163–5, 384–91.
21. Ibid. 375–95.
22. Raymond Williams, *The Country and the City* (1973), ch. 21; Martin J. Wiener, *English Culture and the Decline of the Industrial Spirit* (Cambridge, 1981), 42–64; Jan Marsh, *Back to the Land: The Pastoral Impulse in England, from 1880 to 1914* (1982), *passim*; Alun Hawkins, 'The Discovery of Rural England', in Robert Colls and Philip Dodd (eds.), *Englishness: Politics and Culture 1880–1920* (1986), 62–88; Gillian Bennett, 'Folklore Studies and the English Rural Myth', *Rural History*, 4 (1991), 77–91.
23. Ronald Hutton, *The Rise and Fall of Merry England* (Oxford, 1994), 144–237, *passim*.
24. Judge, 'Changing Attitudes', 216–17.
25. Edmund R. Leach, 'Golden Bough or Gilded Twig?', *Daedalus* (Spring 1961), 371–87; J. W. Burrow, *Evolution and Society* (Cambridge, 1966), ch. 7; Robert Ackerman, *J. G. Frazer: His Life and Work* (Cambridge, 1987), *passim;* Gillian Bennett, 'Geologists and Folklorists: Cultural Evolution and "The Science of Folklore"', *Folklore*, 105 (1994), 25–38.
26. Burrow, *A Liberal Descent*, 107–22, and '"The Village Community" and the Uses of History in late Nineteenth-Century England', in Neil McKendrick (ed.), *Historical Perspectives* (1974), 255–84.
27. Judge, 'Changing Attitudes', 348–56.
28. Chandler, *Dream of Order*, 224–5.
29. Marsh, *Back to the Land*, 6–7.
30. Judge, 'Changing Attitudes', 353–6.
31. Fiona MacCarthy, *The Simple Life: C. R. Ashbee in the Cotswolds* (1981), 9–10, 117; Craig Fees, 'Christmas Mumming in a North Cotswold Town' (Leeds Ph.D. thesis, 1988), 204–5.
32. Vic Gammon, 'Folk Song Collecting in Sussex and Surrey 1843–1914', *History Workshop*, 10 (1980), 73–85.
33. A. H. Fox Strangways, *Cecil Sharp* (Oxford, 1933), *passim*; Roy Judge, 'Mary Neal and the Esperance Morris', *Folk Music Journal*, 5 (1989), 545–90; David Harker, 'Cecil Sharp in Somerset: Some Conclusions', *Folk Music Journal*, 2: 3 (1972), 220–40.

34. Fox Strangways, *Cecil Sharp*, 182.

35. Walter Abson, 'Fifty Years of the Morris Ring', *English Dance and Song*, 46.2 (1984), 11–12.

36. Judge, 'May Day', 145–8; A. R. Wright, *British Calendar Customs*, ed. T. E. Lones (Folk-Lore Society, 1936), ii. 227–8.

37. George Long, *The Folklore Calendar* (1930), 70–1.

38. Stanley Jackson Coleman, *Bedfordshire Lore* (Treasury of Folklore, 33; Douglas, 1954), n.p.

39. Judge, 'Changing Attitudes', 163; F. Marian McNeill, *The Silver Bough*, iv (Glasgow, 1968), 41.

40. *Independent* (9 Apr. 1993), 21. The first public motion for the holiday came from the radical socialist MP Dennis Skinner, the government itself avoiding the articulation of any ideology in its introduction: which is why Mr Foot's later remarks are of particular interest: *Parliamentary Debates*, 5th ser. 901. 517; 908. 442–3

CHAPTER 29

1. The festival and its inception are the subject of an excellent monograph: Miri Rubin, *Corpus Christi* (Cambridge, 1991). For further details of its early history in England, see John Wodderspoon, *Memorials of the Ancient Town of Ipswich* (1850), 1561–62; *Inventory of Church Goods temp. Edward III*, ed. A. Watkin (Norfolk Record Society, 19; 1948), p. xxxix; Thomas North, *A Chronicle of the Church of St Martin in Leicester* (1846), 184–8; *Records of Early English Drama: Cambridge*, ed. Alan H. Nelson (Toronto, 1986), 5; Alan H. Nelson, *The Medieval English Stage* (Chicago, 1974), chs. 8 and 10.

2. e.g. at Bridgwater torches appeared in 1428–9, and at Nottingham torches in 1473 and banners in the 1490s: *Bridgwater Borough Archives*, ed. T. Dilks (Somerset Record Society 58; 1943), 62–101; and *The Account Books of the Guilds of St George and St Mary in the Church of St Peter Nottingham*, ed. R. Hodgkinson (Thoroton Society Record Series, 1939), 16–23. At St Michael, Oxford, the banners for the parish procession were added in 1434: Oxfordshire RO, MS.DD.Par. Oxford St Michael a. l.

3. James Thompson, *History of Leicester* (1849), i. 149–50; *Records of Early English Drama: York*, ed. Alexandra F. Johnston and Margaret Rogerson (Manchester, 1979), 1–289, 689–839; *Rites of Durham*, ed. Canon Fowler (Surtees Society, 107; 1907), 77; Thomas Sharp, *A Dissertation on the Pageants or Dramatic Mysteries ... at Coventry* (Coventry, 1825), 160–72.

4. *The Medieval Records of a London City Church*, ed. Henry Littlehales (EETS, 1905), 81–305; Guildhall L, MSS 6842, 645/1, 4956/1, 3907/1, 1002/1, 2895/1, 593/1, 4887, and 1297/1; Bristol RO, P/St JB/Ch W/2.

5. *The Church Book of St Ewen's, Bristol*, ed. B. Masters and E. Ralph (Bristol and Gloucester Archaeological Society, 1967), 31–158; Bristol RO, P/AS/ChW/3 and P/xch/ la; *The Records of the City of Norwich*, ed. William Hudson and John Cottingham Tingey (Norwich, 1910), ii. 230; E. K. Chambers, *The Medieval Stage* (Oxford, 1903), ii. 338–99 (for Beverley, Bury St Edmunds, Hereford, Ipswich, Bungay, King's Lynn, Shrewsbury, Worcester, and Great Yarmouth). *Records of Maidstone* (Maidstone, 1926), 2; *Henley Borough Records*, ed. P. Briers (Oxfordshire Record Society, 1960), 199–225; *Account Books of ... Nottingham*, ed. Hodgkinson; *Calendar of the Plymouth Municipal Records*, ed. R. N. Worth (Plymouth, 1893), 29–35; *Records of Early English Drama: Devon*, ed. John M. Wasson (Toronto, 1986), 101–39, 348–85 (for Exeter); Devon RO, Dartmouth Corporation Records, Mayors' Accounts, years 1526–33;

Richard Welford, *History of Newcastle and Gateshead* (1885), ii. 97–508; *Peterborough Local Administration*, ed. W. T. Mallows (Northamptonshire RO, 1939), 82–161; 'Accounts of the Wardens of St Dunstan's, Canterbury', ed. J. Cowper, *Archaeologia Cantiana*, 16 (1886), 304–19, 17 (1887), 93–110; 'Churchwardens' Accounts of the Parish of St Andrew, Canterbury, 1485 to 1625', *Archaeologia Cantiana*, 32 (1917), 208–43, 33 (1918), 3–59; *The First Churchwardens' Book of Louth*, ed. Reginald C. Dudding (Oxford, 1941), 186–98; Charles Kerry, *History of the Municipal Church of St Lawrence, Reading* (Reading, 1883), 234–5; *Churchwardens' Accounts of the Town of Ludlow*, ed. T. Wright (Camden Society, 1869), 22–5; 'Sherborne All Hallows Churchwardens' Accounts', *Somerset and Dorset Notes and Queries*, 23 (1939–42), 209–333; Wiltshire RO, 189/1; Anna Jean Mill, *Medieval Plays in Scotland* (Edinburgh, 1927), 121–30, 172–3, 179–235, 247, 261, 265–73.

6. *Records of Plays and Players in Norfolk and Suffolk 1330–1642*, ed. D. Galloway and J. Wasson (Malone Society, 1980), 2, 100, 159; Essex RO, D/P 11/5/1, and D/P 192/5/1; *Churchwardens' Accounts of Ashburton, 1479–1580*, ed. A. Hanham (Devon and Cornwall Record Society, 1970), 1–114.

7. Miri Rubin, 'Corpus Christi's Fraternities and Late Medieval Piety', in W. J. Sheils and Diana Wood (eds.), *Voluntary Religion* (Studies in Church History, 23; 1986), 97–109.

8. J. Charles Cox, *Churchwardens' Accounts* (1913), 268–70; 'Sherborne All Hallows', 209–333; *Players in Norfolk and Suffolk*, ed. Galloway and Wasson, p. xi; Essex RO, D/P 11/E/1; *Records of Plays and Players in Lincolnshire 1300–1585*, ed. S. J. Karhl (Malone Society, 1969), pp. xxiii–xxxvi; 'St Dunstan's, Canterbury', 47.

9. *Players in Norfolk and Suffolk*, ed. Galloway and Wasson, 2, 100.

10. Nelson, *Medieval English Stage*, ch. 3.

11. Mill, *Medieval Plays*, 172–3.

12. *York*, ed. Johnston and Rogerson, 689; A. Leach, 'Some English Plays and Players 1220–1548', in *An English Miscellany Presented to Dr Furnivall* (Oxford, 1901), 208–9; *Players in Norfolk and Suffolk*, ed. Galloway and Wasson, 38–55.

13. *Records of Early English Drama: Coventry*, ed. R. W. Ingram (Manchester, 1981), 1–12; *Records of Early English Drama: Chester*, ed. Lawrence M. Clopper (Manchester, 1979), 6–7; *Records of Early English Drama: Newcastle upon Tyne*, ed. J. J. Anderson (Toronto, 1982), 3; *Devon*, ed. Wasson, 357–8.

14. *Players in Lincolnshire*, ed. Karhl, 76–84.

15. Chambers, *Medieval Stage*, ii. 338–98; *Players in Lincolnshire*, ed. Karhl, 76–84; Harold C. Gardiner, *Mysteries' End* (New Haven, 1967), ch. 3; V. A. Kolve, *The Play Called Corpus Christi* (1966); Leach, 'Some English Plays', 206–34; Nelson, *Medieval English Stage, passim*; William Tydeman, *The Theatre in the Middle Ages* (Cambridge, 1978), 114–20.

16. *Coventry*, ed. Ingram, 1–174; *York*, ed. Johnston and Rogerson, 1–83; *Chester*, ed. Clopper, 1–43.

17. Sharp, *Dissertation*, 4–75; *Coventry*, ed. Ingram, 1–174; Nelson, *Medieval English Stage*, chs. 3, 8; *York*, ed. Johnston and Rogerson, 1–289, 689–839; Clifford Davidson, *From Creation to Doom* (New York, 1984); Kolve, *Corpus Christi, passim*.

18. Nelson, *Medieval English Stage*, ch. 2; Tydeman, *Theatre in the Middle Ages*, 114–20.

19. Mervyn James, 'Ritual, Drama and Social Body in the Medieval English Town', repr. in his collected essays, *Society, Politics and Culture* (Cambridge, 1986), 17–41.

20. Canterbury Cathedral L, Literary MS C13, fo. 10; *Players in Lincolnshire*, ed. Karhl, 24–69; Nelson, *Medieval English Stage*, ch. 6.

21. See e.g. *John Bon and Master Parson* (printed by Luke Shepherd, 1548).

22. *Statutes of the Realm* (1819), iv. i. 24–33.

23. *Monumenta Franciscana*, ed. Richard Howlett (Rolls Series, 1882), ii. 216–20. The surviving London churchwardens' accounts confirm this chronicle.

24. Cheshire RO, P1/11; 'St Dunstan, Canterbury', 111–12; *Ashburton*, 119–22; *Churchwardens' Accounts of S. Edmund and S. Thomas Sarum*, ed. Henry J. F. Swayne (Wiltshire Record Society, 1896), 89–90; E. G. C. Atchley, 'On the Medieval Parish Records of the Church of St Nicholas, Bristol', *Transactions of the St Paul's Ecclesiastical Society*, 6 (1906), 63; *Ludlow*, 33–9.

25. *York*, ed. Johnston and Rogerson, 291–3; *Coventry*, ed. Ingram, 174–93.

26. *Monumenta Franciscana*, ii. 251; *The Diary of Henry Machyn*, ed. J. Nichols (Camden Society, 1848), 62–3.

27. The very Protestant Parish of St Botolph Aldgate: Guildhall L, 9235/1. For references to the other City accounts, and those of Bristol, see Ronald Hutton, *The Rise and Fall of Merry England* (Oxford, 1994), appendix.

28. Machyn, *Diary*, 139.

29. *York Civic Records*, ed. Angelo Raine, (1953), 105; *Coventry*, ed. Ingram, 205; *Chester*, ed. Clopper, 54–60; Chambers, *Medieval Stage*, ii. 379, 388; *Newcastle-upon-Tyne*, ed. Anderson, 26–7; *Records of Early English Drama: Norwich*, ed. David Galloway (Toronto, 1984), 37, 43–4; 'St Andrew, Canterbury', 42–9; Dorset RO, P155/CW/31–4; *Ashburton*, 123–8.

30. BL, Egerton MS 1912, fos. 62–135; East Suffolk (Lowestoft) RO, 116/E/1/1; *Ludlow*, 55–77; BL Add. MS 36937, fos. 2–9; *Lambeth Churchwardens' Accounts 1504–1645*, ed. C. Drew (Surrey Record Society, 1940–3), 68–76; 'Early Churchwardens' Accounts of Wandsworth', ed. C. Davis, *Surrey Archaeological Collections*, XV (1900), 114–26.

31. Gardiner, *Mysteries' End*, 65–85; Mill, *Medieval Plays*, 275–8.

32. Ibid. 79–87; Sharp, Dissertation, 11–12, 133, 221–5; *York*, ed. Johnston and Rogerson, 365–839; *Newcastle-upon-Tyne*, ed. Anderson; *Records of Early English Drama: Cumberland, Westmorland and Gloucestershire*, ed. Audrey Douglas and Peter Greenfield (Toronto, 1986), 1–27; *Players in Norfolk and Suffolk*, ed. Galloway and Wasson, pp. xiii–xiv; *A Calendar to the Records of the Borough of Doncaster* (Doncaster, 1899–1903), iv. 24–86; John Wodderspoon, *Memorials of the Ancient Town of Ipswich* (1850), 174–5; *Tudor Parish Documents of the Diocese of the York*, ed. J. S. Purvis (Cambridge, 1948), 173; J. S. Purvis, 'The York Religious Plays', in Alberic Stacpoole *et al.* (eds.), *The Noble City of York* (York, 1972), 854; *Records of Early English Drama: Lancashire*, ed. David George (Toronto, 1991), 29, 86–7.

CHAPTER 30

1. J. Zwicker, *Fontes Historiae Religionis Celticae* (Rotterdam, 1934–6), i. 302–3; J. J. Hart, 'Rota Flammis Circumsepta', *Revue Archéologique de l'Est et du Centre-Est*, 2 (1951), 82–7.

2. BL Harl. MS 2345, fo. 496.

3. Translated as Barnaby Googe, *The Popish Kingdom* (1570), 55.

4. Marie Trevelyan, *Folk-Lore and Folk-Stories of Wales* (1909), 27–8.

5. T. Brown, '72nd Report on Folklore', *Transactions of the Devonshire Association*, 107 (1975), 188.

6. T. Brown, '52nd Report on Folklore', *Transactions of the Devonshire Association*, 87 (1955), 356.

7. *Medieval Handbooks of Penance*, ed. John T. McNeill and Helen M. Gamer (New York, 1938), 350.

8. G. Storms, *Anglo-Saxon Magic* (The Hague, 1948), 10.

9. *Patrologiae Cursus Completus*, cii. 141.

10. J. G. Frazer, *The Golden Bough* (1890), i. 272–3, 290–1, ii. 258–68, and *Balder the Beautiful* (1914), i. 163–96, 208–19.

11. Peter Burke, *Popular Culture in Early Modern Europe* (1978), 195.

12. C. Baskerville, 'Dramatic Aspects of Medieval Folk Festivals in England', *Studies in Philology*, 17 (1920), 51–3; Nathaniel J. Hone, *The Manor and Manorial Records* (1906), 98.

13. Kevin Danaher, *The Year in Ireland* (Cork, 1972), 154–5.

14. *Mirk's Festival*, ed. T. Erbe (EETS, 1905), 182–2.

15. *A Survey of London*, ed. Charles Lethbridge Kingsford (Oxford, 1908), i. 101.

16. Ibid. ii. 284.

17. C. Goss, 'The Parish and Church of St Martin Outwich', *Transactions of the London and Middlesex Archaeological Society* NS 6 (1933), 84–90; Guildhall L, 1297/1–2, years 1488–1546; Guildhall L, 645/1, years 1534–46; *The Medieval Records of a London City Church*, ed. Henry Littlehales (EETS, 1905), 81–359; Guildhall L, 4956/1, for 155ᵛ–73; Guildhall L, 3907/1, years 1530–46.

18. Corporation of London RO, Journal 12, fo. 329.

19. Sir W. Parker, *The History of Long Melford* (1873), 73.

20. Polydor Vergil, *Works*, trans. John Langley (1663), 195; William Warner, *Albions England* (1586), bk. 5, p. 121.

21. *Letters and Papers, Foreign and Domestic, of the Reign of Henry VIII*, ed. J. S. Brewer (1864), II. ii. 1446 and III. ii. 1536, 1541: BL Arundel MS 97, fos. 20ᵛ. 76: Sydney Anglo, 'The Court Festivals of Henry VII', *Bulletin of the John Rylands Library*, 43 (1960–1), 28–43.

22. HMC Middleton MSS, p. 333.

23. Peter Clark, 'Reformation and Radicalism in Kentish Towns c.1500–1553', in *The Urban Classes, the Nobility and the Reformation* (Publications of the German Historical Institute, 5; 1979), 111; *Records of Early English Drama: Newcastle-upon-Tyne*, ed. J. J. Anderson (Toronto, 1982), 15, 24.

24. *Memorials of London and London Life*, ed. Henry Thomas Riley (1868), 419–20, 488.

25. Stow, *Survey*, i. 101–4.

26. *London's Artillery* (1616), repr. in John Brand, *Observations on the Popular Antiquities of Great Britain*, ed. Sir Henry Ellis (1908), i, 326–7.

27. George Unwin, *The Guilds and Companies of London* (1925), 269–70; *A Calendar of Dramatic Records in the Books of the Livery Companies of London*, ed. Jean Robertson and D. J. Gordon (Malone Society, 1954), 1–36.

28. Thomas Sharp, *A Dissertation on the Pageants or Dramatic Mysteries...at Coventry* (Coventry, 1825), 180–200.

29. *Records of Early English Drama: Chester*, ed. Lawrence M. Clopper (Manchester, 1979), pp. li–lii.

30. Charles Hoskins, *The Ancient Trade Guilds and Companies of Salisbury* (1912), 171; *Calendar of the Plymouth Municipal Records*, ed. R. N. Worth (Plymouth, 1893), 105; *Records of Nottingham* (1885), iii. 361; *The Great Red Book of Bristol*, pt. 1, ed. E. Veale (Bristol Record Society, 1933), 26–7; J. A. Picton, *Memorials of Liverpool* (1875), 45; *Records of Early English Drama: Cumberland, Westmorland and Gloucestershire*, ed. Audrey Douglas and Peter Greenfield (Toronto, 1986), 301; *Records of Early English Drama: Devon*, ed. John M. Wasson (Toronto, 1986), 132–9, 279–80, 342.

31. See e.g. William Kethe, *A Sermon Made at Blandford Forum* (1571), fo. 19.

32. *Calendar of State Papers Spanish*, iv. ii. 1091; *Letters and Papers* XIV (1539), 1144; Charles Wricthesley, *A Chronicle of England*, ed. W. D. Hamilton (Camden Society,

1875), i. 100; S. Williams, 'The Lord Mayor's Show in Tudor and Stuart Times', *Guildhall Miscellany*, 10 (Sept. 1959)), 4–6; *Harleian Miscellany*, ix. 389–408.

33. A tale told in detail in Ronald Hutton, *The Rise and Fall of Merry England* (Oxford, 1994), 76, 88, 121–2, 163–4, 202.

34. F. M. Salter, *Medieval Drama in Chester* (Toronto, 1955), 28.

35. BL Arundel MS 97, fos. 20ᵛ, 76.

36. A. Hussey, 'Archbishop Parker's Visitation', *Home Counties Magazine*, 5 (1903), 208; Ralph Houlbrooke, *Church Courts and the People during the English Reformation* (Oxford, 1979), 249.

37. Canterbury Cathedral L, MS X/8/6, fo. 37ᵛ.

38. E. J. Baskerville, 'A Religious Disturbance in Canterbury, June 1561', *Bulletin of the Institute of Historical Research*, 158 (1992), 340–8.

39. 'The Early Expansion of Protestantism in England, 1520–58', *Archiv fur Reformationsgeschichte*, 78 (1987), 187–221.

40. William Hone, *The Every-Day book and Table Book* (1832), ii. 869–70.

41. *The Mery Life of the Countriman* (1585–1603), repr. in *The Shirburn Ballads*, ed. Andrew Clark (Oxford, 1907), i. 363.

42. Charlotte Sophia Burne, *Shropshire Folk-Lore* (1883), 358–9.

43. Peter Robson, 'Calendar Customs in Nineteenth and Twentieth Century Dorset' (Sheffield M. Phil. thesis, 1988), 86; David Underdown, *Fire from Heaven* (1992), 64.

44. Ella Mary Leather, *The Folk-Lore of Herefordshire* (Hereford, 1912), 104.

45. R. T. Hampson, *Medii Aevi Kalendarium* (1841), i. 311 (for Westmorland); Brand, *Observations*, i. 318 (for Cornwall); R. L. Bowley, *The Fortunate Islands*, 7th edn., (1980), 102 (for Scilly); Charles Hardwich, *Traditions, Superstitions and Folk-Lore* (Manchester, 1872), 33; John Nicholson, *Folk Lore of East Yorkshire* (1890), 14; William Brockie, *Legends and Superstitions of the County of Durham* (Sunderland, 1886), 106; William Bottrell, *Traditions and Hearthside Stories of West Cornwall* (Penzance, 1870), 8, 54–9; P. H. Ditchfield, *Old English Customs Extant at the Present Time* (1896), 143 (for Cornwall); Mrs Gutch (ed.), *County Folk-Lore*, ii. *North Riding of Yorkshire, York and the Ainsty* (Folk-Lore Society, 1901), 253; Northcote W. Thomas (ed.), *County Folk-Lore*, iv. *Northumberland* (Folk-Lore Society, 1904), 75–6; Mrs Gutch (ed.) *County Folk-Lore*, vi. *East Riding of Yorkshire*, (Folk-Lore Society, 1912), 102; William Borlase, *Antiquities, Historical and Monumental, of the County of Cornwall* (1769), 135–6 (also cites Cumberland evidence); Frederick William Hackwood, *Staffordshire Customs, Superstitions and Folklore* (Lichfield, 1924), 45; Llewellyn Jewitt, 'On Ancient Customs and Sports of the County of Nottingham', *Journal of the British Archaeological Association*, 1st ser. 8 (1853), 235; M. A. Courtney, *Cornish Feasts and Folklore* (1890), 39–43; Worthington Smith, *Dunstable: Its History and Surroundings* (1904), 167; Marjorie Rowling, *The Folklore of the Lake District* (1976), 122; William Huchinson, *A View of Northumberland* (Newcastle, 1778), ii, appendix 15; BL Add. MS 24544, p. 241 (for south Yorkshire); A. R. Wright, *British Calendar Customs*, ed. T. E. Lones (Folk-Lore Society, 1936), iii. 10–25 (for Derbyshire, Yorkshire, Cornwall).

46. R. L. Tongue, *Somerset Folklore*, ed. K. M. Briggs (Folklore Society, County Folklore viii, 1965), 166.

47. Hardwick, *Traditions*, 33; Courtney, *Cornish Feasts*, 40–1; Bottrell, *Traditions*, 54–9.

48. For its enshrinement in the annals of folklore, see J. Walker, 'The Midsummer Bonfire at Whalton', *Archaeologia Aeliana*, 25 (1903), 181–4.

49. *Records of the Presbyteries of Inverness and Dingwall 1643–1688*, ed. William Mackay (Scottish History Society, 1896), 268, 323; Thomas Moresinus, *Papatus seu Depravatae*

Religionis Origo et Incrementum (Edinburgh, 1594), 56; F. Marian McNeill, *The Silver Bough*, ii (Glasgow, 1959), 16, 89; *British Calendar Customs: Scotland*, ed. Mary Macleod Banks, iii (Folk-Lore Society, 1941), 27; Anna Jean Mill, *Medieval Plays in Scotland* (1927), 10.

50. McNeill, *Silver Bough*, ii. 89–90.

51. A. Macdonald, 'Midsummer Bonfires', *Folk-Lore*, 15 (1904), 105–6

52. Sir John Sinclair, *The Statistical Account of Scotland*, iii (1792), 105 and xxi (1799), 145; John Ramsay, *Scotland and Scotsmen in the Eighteenth Century*, ed. Alexander Allardyce (Edinburgh, 1888), ii. 436; Frazer, *Balder the Beautiful*, i. 206–7; Lachlan Shaw, *History of the Province of Moray* (1775), 241; *British Calendar Customs: Scotland*, iii. 15–36.

53. J. M. E. Saxby, *Shetland Traditional Lore* (Edinburgh, 1932), 75–6.

54. McNeill, *Silver Bough*, ii. 90–1; Ernest W. Marwick, *The Folklore of Orkney and Shetland* (1975), 111–12.

55. *Presbyteries of Inverness and Dingwall*, p. xl.

56. *British Calendar Customs: Scotland*, iii. 15.

57. James R. Nicolson, *Shetland Folklore* (1981), 140.

58. McNeill, *Silver Bough*, iv (1968). 75–6,

59. Brand, *Observations*, i. 318; Marianne Robertson Spencer, *Annals of South Glamorgan* (1970 reprint), 61; R. R. Sayce, 'A Survey of Montgomeryshire Folklore', *Montgomeryshire Collections*, 47 (1942), 21; Trevelyan, *Folk-Lore*, 27.

60. Trefor M. Owen, *Welsh Folk Customs* (St Fagans, 1974), 108–10.

61. Joseph Train, *An Historical and Statistical Account of the Isle of Man* (Douglas, 1845), ii. 120.

62. Danaher, *The Year in Ireland*, 134–55; Brand, *Observations*, i. 303–5; T. F. Thiselton Dyer, *British Popular Customs* (1876), 321–2; L. L. Duncan, 'Further Notes from County Leitrim', *Folk-Lore*, 5 (1894), 193; A. C. Haddon, 'A Batch of Irish Folk-Lore', *Folk-Lore*, 4 (1893), 351, 359; Alexander Hislop, *The Two Babylons* (Edinburgh, 1853), 53; Sir John Graham Dalyell, *The Darker Superstitions of Scotland* (Edinburgh, 1834), 195; Sir William R. Wilde, *Irish Popular Superstitions* (Dublin, 1852), 40, 50; 'Irish Folk-Lore', *Folk-Lore Journal*, 5 (1887), 212–13; 'Irish Folk-Lore', *Folk-Lore Journal*, 6 (1888), 54; Bryan J. Jones, 'Irish Folklore from Cavan, Meath, Kerry and Limerick', *Folk-Lore*, 19 (1908), 323; Thomas J. Westropp, 'A Folklore Survey of County Clare', *Folk-Lore*, 22 (1911), 207–8, and 'Folklore on the Coasts of Connacht', *Folk-Lore*, 34 (1923), 324; R. H. Buchanan, 'Calendar Customs', *Ulster Folklife*, 8 (1962), 31; Michael J. Walsh, 'Notes on Fire-Lighting Ceremonies', *Folk-Lore*, 58 (1947), 277–84; Alan Gailey, 'The Bonfire in Northern Irish Tradition', *Folklore*, 88 (1977), 3–38; E. Estyn Evans, *Irish Folk Ways* (1957), 274–5.

63. Lady Jane Francesca Wilde, *Ancient Legends, Mystic Charms, and Superstitions of Ireland* (1887), i. 214–15.

64. Brand, *Observations*, i. 300 n. 1.

65. Gailey, 'Bonfire', 34–7.

66. *The Golden Bough* (1890), i. 158–9, 272–3, ii. 258–89, and *Balder*, i. 329–46.

67. Gailey, 'Bonfire', 26–9.

68. *Natural History* XVIII. 1xx.

69. Maria Czaplicka, *Aboriginal Siberia* (1914), 189.

70. *The Sun-Gods of Ancient Europe* (1991), 56–60, and chs. 4 and 5. This is the latest and best work to remark upon an association first studied by H. Gaidoz, 'Le Dieu Gaulois du soleil et le symbolisme de la roue', *Revue Archéologique* (1884), 7–37.

CHAPTER 31

1. *The Mery Life of the Countriman* (1585–1603), in *The Shirburn Ballads*, ed. Andrew Clark (Oxford, 1907), i. 363.

2. *Merry Songs and Ballads*, ed. John S. Farmer (1897), ii. 162–3.

3. John Symonds Udal, *Dorsetshire Folk-Lore* (Hertford, 1922), 53–7.

4. See e.g. Doris Jones-Baker, *The Folklore of Hertfordshire* (1977), 151–2; Roy Palmer, *The Folklore of Warwickshire* (1976), 48; James Obelkevitch, *Religion and Rural Society: South Lindsey, 1825–1875* (Oxford, 1976), 57; Thomas Sternberg, *The Dialect and Folk-Lore of Northamptonshire* (1851), 175–6.

5. Jacqueline Simpson, *The Folklore of Sussex* (1973), 120–2; George Ewart Evans, *Ask the Fellows Who Cut the Hay* (Oxford, 1965), 45–50.

6. Palmer, *Warwickshire*, 48–9.

7. *Visitation Articles and Injunctions of the Period of the Reformation*, ed. Walter Howard Frere (Alcuin Club, 1910), iii. 256–7.

8. *Lancashire Quarter Sessions Records*, ed. James Tait (Chetham Society, 1917), 11.

9. *The Journal of Nicholas Assheton*, ed. F. R. Raines (Chetham Society, 1848), 41–2.

10. Ronald Hutton, *The Rise and Fall of Merry England* (Oxford, 1994), 168, 191, 208.

11. T. F. Thiselton Dyer, *British Popular Customs* (1876), 367–8.

12. Cumbria RO (Kendal), WPR/83, years from 1681, and WPR/91/W1, years from 1670; Cheshire RO, P66/12/1, years from 1690. Other references from churchwardens' accounts, some apparently lost, are given in Alfred Burton, *Rush-Bearing* (Manchester, 1891), 16.

13. E. P. Thompson, 'Patrician Society, Plebeian Culture', *Journal of Social History*, 7 (1974), 394.

14. Dyer, *British Popular Customs*, 355–6.

15. Robert Chambers, *The Book of Days* (1864), i. 506; P. H. Ditchfield, *Old English Customs Extant at the Present Time* (1896), 133–7.

16. Nancy Price, *Pagan's Progress* (1954), 96.

17. Marjorie Rowling, *The Folklore of the Lake District* (1976), 120–1.

18. Vernon Noble, 'Eighteenth Century Yorkshire Rushbearing', *Lore and Language*, 3: 8 (1983), 77–8.

19. Burton, *Rush-Bearing, passim*; *The Autobiography of Samuel Bamford*, ed. W. H. Chaloner (1967), i. 146–55; Charlotte S. Burne, 'Reminiscences of Lancashire and Cheshire when George IV was King', *Folk-Lore*, 20, 'The Rushcart and the North-Western Morris', *JEFDSS* 7: 3 (1954), 172–9, and (1909), 204; Alex Helm, 'Rushcarts of the North-West of England', *Folk Life*, 8 (1970), 20–31; E. C. Cawte, 'Early Records of a Rushcart at Didsbury', *Folk-Lore*, 72 (1911), 330–7; A. G. Gilchrist, 'The Lancashire Rush-Cart and Morris Dance', *Journal of the English Folk-Dance Society*, 2nd ser. 1 (1927). 17–27: Thomas Middleton, 'Rushbearing and Morris Dancing in North Cheshire', *Transactions of the Lancashire and Cheshire Antiquarian Society*, 60 (1948), 47–55; Bob Schofield, 'As in Days of Yore', *English Dance and Song*, 39: 2 (1977), 51–3.

20. R. J. R. Poole, 'Wakes, Holidays and Fairs in the Lancashire Cotton District, *c*.1790–1890' (Lancaster Ph.D. thesis, 1985), 58–72; Theresa Jill Buckland, 'Ceremonial Dance Traditions in the South-West Pennines and Rossendale' (Leeds Ph.D. thesis, 1984), 155–66.

21. Points considered by Poole, 'Wakes, Holidays and Fairs', 46–9.

22. As suggested by Buckland, 'Ceremonial Dance Traditions', 155.

23. Poole, 'Wakes, Holidays and Fairs', 77–116; Buckland, 'Ceremonial Dance Traditions', 224–55; Schofield, 'Days of Yore', 53.

CHAPTER 32

1. In another Irish text, the fourteenth-century *Colloquy of the Old Men*, August is known, equally enigmatically, as 'the Trogan month'.

2. Máire MacNeill, *The Festival of Lughnasa* (Oxford, 1962), 3. The word is pronounced 'loonasah'.

3. Thomas F. O'Rahilly, *Early Irish History and Mythology* (Dublin, 1946), ch. 15, makes a particular discussion of this last point.

4. Brief and conventional statements on the matter are made in Myles Dillon and Nora K. Chadwick, *The Celtic Realms* (1967), 13, 108, 143–59, and Nora Chadwick, *The Celts* (1970), 152, 170–80; but the most recent and detailed survey has been by a linguist, Antonio Tovar, 'The God Lugus in Spain', *Bulletin of the Board of Celtic Studies*, 29: 4 (1982), 591–9. All the usual evidence of iconography and place-names is listed again, and the comparative rarity of it is tackled by the simple device of regarding all inscriptions to Mercury in Gaul as Romanized dedications to Lugh—even though the same evidence makes it plain that many other Gallic deities were identified with Mercury! It would be hard to understand why such effort is made to press information into a particular mould were it not for Professor Tovar's candid statement that the ubiquity of the worship of Lugh is one of the main props of the traditional scholastic concept of 'the unity of the Celts' as a culture across all their lands. This concept is now in question, and it is linguists who, understandably enough, feature as its most numerous defenders.

5. MacNeill, *Lughnasa*, 426.

6. Joseph Train, *An Historical and Statistical Account of the Isle of Man* (Douglas, 1845), ii. 120–1; MacNeill, *Lughnasa*, 350–5.

7. MacNeill, *Lughnasa*, 381.

8. Ibid. 381–5.

9. Alexander Carmichael, *Carmina Gadelica* (Edinburgh, 1900), i. 196–7.

10. Alan Gailey, 'The Bonfire in Northern Irish Tradition', *Folklore*, 88 (1977), 11.

11. F. Marian McNeill, *The Silver Bough* (Glasgow, 1959), ii. 90.

12. Ibid. ii. 98.

13. Ibid. ii. 97, where the locations of most of these customs are not specified. MacNeill, *Lughnasa*, 356–73, struggles hard to relate all Scottish August fairs and feasts to the same old festival.

14. William Hone, *The Every-Day Book and Table Book* (1832), ii. 1051–4.

15. R. T. Hampson, *Medii Aevi Kalendarium* (1841), i. 332–4; John Brand, *Observations upon the Popular Antiquities of Great Britain*, ed. Sir Henry Ellis (1908), i. 348.

16. *Leechdoms, Wortcunning and Starcraft of Early England*, ed. T. O. Cockayne (Rolls Series, 1866), iii. 291.

17. Hampson, *Medii Aevi Kalendarium*, i. 332–4; Brand, *Observations*, i. 348.

18. *A Collection of the Laws and Canons of the Church of England*, ed. John Johnson (Oxford, 1850), 92.

19. *Lughnasa*, 373–8.

20. To sample a very large number of examples, see Public Record Office, SP 29/263/158 (for Coventry); MacNeill, *Lughnasa*, 373–8; *The Diary of Henry Machyn*, ed. J. Nichols (Camden Society, 1848), 241; T. Brown, '67th Report on Folklore', *Transactions of the Devon Association*, 102 (1970), 269; *Records of Early English Drama: Newcastle-upon-Tyne*, ed. J. J. Anderson (Toronto, 1982), 11; A. R. Wright, *British Calendar Customs*, ed. T. E. Lones (Folk-Lore Society, 1936), iii. 44–5; *Records of Early English Drama: Norwich*, ed. David Galloway (Toronto, 1984), 21.

21. Laurence Whistler, *The English Festivals* (1947), 182–3.

CHAPTER 33

1. David Hoseason Morgan, *Harvesters and Harvesting 1840–1900* (1982), 167.
2. Bede, *Works*, ed. J. A. Giles (1843), vi. 178.
3. George Caspar Homans, *English Villagers of the Thirteenth Century* (Cambridge, Mass., 1942), 371; Joyce Godber, *History of Bedfordshire* (1969), 88–9; *Thirteen Custumals of the Sussex Manors of the Bishop of Chichester*, ed. W. Peckham (Sussex Record Society, 1925), *passim*; *Rentalia et Custumaria*, ed. C. Elton (Somerset Record Society, 1891), *passim*; Andrew Jones, 'Harvest Customs and Labourers' Perquisites in Southern England, 1150–1350', *Agricultural History Review*, 25 (1977), 14–22.
4. John Brand, *Observations on the Popular antiquities of Great Britain*, ed. Sir Henry Ellis (1908), ii. 16.
5. Thomas Tusser, *Five Hundred Pointes of Good Husbandrie*, ed. W. Payne and S. J. Heritage (English Dialect Society, 1878), 129–32, 181, 309.
6. Repr. in *The Shirburn Ballads*, ed. Andrew Clark (Oxford, 1907). 363.
7. *The Poems of Robert Herrick*, ed. L. C. Martin (Oxford, 1965), 101–2.
8. *The Shepherds Pipe* (1614), n.p.
9. Quoted in J. G. Frazer, *The Golden Bough* (1924 edn.), 405.
10. William Brenchley Rye, *England as seen by Foreigners in the Days of Elizabeth and James the First* (1865), III.
11. John Nichols, *The Progresses, Processions... of Queen Elizabeth* (1823), iii. 135.
12. John Dryden, *King Arthur*, v. i; John Aubrey, *Remaines of Gentilisme and Judaisme*, ed. James Britten (1881), 34; Brand, *Observations*, ii. 18–20.
13. From *Norfolk Drollery* (1673), repr. in Brand, *Observations*, ii. 17.
14. Cumbria (Carlisle) RO, Workington Estate Records, Curwen Account Book, fos. 35–200.
15. 'The Diary of Bulkeley of Dronwy, Anglesey', ed. Hugh Owen, *Anglesey Antiquarian Society and Field Club Transactions* (1937), 75.
16. John Aubrey, *Wiltshire: The Topographical Collections*, ed. J. E. Jackson (Devizes, 1862), 311.
17. *Gentleman's Magazine* (1816), repr. in Bob Bushaway, *By Rite* (1982), 128–30; and see William Crossing, *A Guide to Dartmoor* (1912), 92.
18. Woodforde's Diary, repr. in Bushaway, *By Rite*, 39–40.
19. Bushaway, *By Rite*, 119–22.
20. Ronald Blythe, *Akenfield* (1969). 55.
21. Enid Porter, *Cambridgeshire Customs and Folklore* (1969), 119.
22. Blythe, *Akenfield*, 55; *County Folk-Lore* (Folk-Lore Society, 1895): ii, Suffolk, ed. Lady Eveline Gurdon, 69; George Ewart Evans, *Ask the Fellows who Cut the Hay* (Oxford, 1965), 85–92; and see William Hone, *The Every-Day Book and Table Book* (1832), ii. 1165.
23. *British Calendar Customs: Scotland*, i. ed. Mary Macleod Banks (1937), 61–2.
24. Bushaway, *By Rite*, 116–17; Brand, *Observations*, ii. 23.
25. *Notes and Queries* 2nd ser. 10. 285, repr. in Morgan, *Harvesters*, 158–9. For the 'queens', see also Porter, *Cambridgeshire*, 124, and Doris Jones-Baker, *The Folklore of Hertfordshire* (1977), 160–1.
26. See esp. *Antike Wald- und Feldkulte* (Berlin, 1877), but also *Mythologische Forschungen* (Strasburg, 1884), *Die Korndämonen* (Berlin, 1868), and *Roggenwolf and Rogenhund* (Danzig, 1866).
27. *The Golden Bough* (1890), i. 332–408, and *Spirits of the Corn and of the Wild* (1914), i. 142–65.

28. C. W. von Sydow. 'The Mannhardtian Theories about the Last Sheaf and the Fertility Demons from a Modern Critical Point of View', *Folk-Lore*, 45 (1934), 291–309, and *Selected Papers in Folklore* (Copenhagen, 1948), 89–105, 146–65; Albert Eskeröd, *Arets Äring* (Stockholm, 1947).

29. Bushaway, *By Rite*, 127; Morgan, *Harvesters*, 165.

30. Calum I. Maclean, 'The Last Sheaf in the North of Ireland', *Ulster Folklife*, 18 (1972), 23–7.

31. Maclean, 'The Last Sheaf', 193–203; Frazer, *Golden Bough*, i. 339, 334–6, and *Spirits of the Corn*, i. 157–65, 265; R. C. Maclagan, 'Notes on Folklore Objects Collected in Argyleshire', *Folk-Lore*, 6 (1895), 148–52; Malcolm MacPhaill, 'Folklore from the Hebrides', *Folk-Lore*, 11 (1900), 441; Alice B. Gomme, 'A Berwickshire Kirn-Dolly', *Folk-Lore*, 12 (1901), 215–16, and 'Harvest Customs', *Folk-Lore*, 13 (1902), 177–9; F. Marian McNeill, *The Silver Bough*, i (Glasgow, 1957), 120–8; Amy Stewart Fraser, *The Hills of Home* (1973), 198–9; J. A. Fotheringhame, 'Folklore from the Orkney Islands', *Folk-Lore*, 30 (1919), 131; Mary Macleod Banks, 'The Scottish Harvest Feast', *Folk-Lore*, 43 (1932), 418–19, and *British Calendar Customs: Scotland* (Folk-Lore Society, 1937), i. 65–86; Naomi Mitchison, 'A Harvest Experience', *Folklore*, 84 (1973), 252–3; John Gregorson Campbell, *Superstitions of the Highlands and Islands of Scotland* (Glasgow, 1900), 243–4.

32. Charlotte Sophia Burne, *Shropshire Folk-Lore* (1883), 372–4; Marie Trevelyan, *Folk-Lore and Folk Stories of Wales* (1909), 262–3; Morgan, *Harvesters*, 165; Jonathan Ceredig Davies, *Folk-Lore of West and Mid-Wales* (Aberystwyth, 1911), 78–9; Ella Mary Leather, *The Folk-Lore of Herefordshire* (Hereford, 1912), 104; M. S. Clark, 'Pembrokeshire Notes', *Folk-Lore*, 25 (1904), 194–5; Frazer, *Spirits of the Corn*, i. 142–4; Iorwerth C. Peate, 'Corn Ornaments', *Folklore*, 82 (1971), 177–84 and 'Corn Customs in Wales', *Man*, 30 (1930), 151–5; Trefor M. Owen, *Welsh Folk Customs* (St Fagans, 1974), 115–21.

33. Kingsley Palmer, *The Folklore of Somerset* (1976), 104; F. Ellworthy, '"Crying the Neck". A Devonshire Custom', *Transactions of the Devonshire Association*, 23 (1891), 353–70; R. Chope, '31st Report on Devonshire Folk-Lore', ibid. 63 (1931), 131–2: R. Chope, '33rd Report on Devonshire Folk-Lore', ibid. 65 (1933), 131; R. Chope, '34th Report on Devonshire Folk-Lore', ibid. 66 (1934), 87; T. Brown, '48th Report of Devonshire Folk-Lore', ibid. 83 (1951), 76; T. Brown, '52nd Report on Devonshire Folk-Lore', ibid. 87 (1955). 356; Frazer, *Golden Bough*, i. 407; R. L. Tongue, *Somerset Folklore*, ed. K. M. Briggs (Folklore Society, 1965), 168; William Hone, *The Every-Day Book and Table Book* (1832), ii. 1170–1; A. R. Wright, *British Calendar Customs*, ed. T. E. Lones (Folk-Lore Society, 1936), i. 189–90; M. A. Courtney, *Cornish Feasts and Folklore* (1890), 52–3.

34. Marjorie Rowling, *The Folklore of the Lake District* (1976), 125–6; Mrs Gutch (ed.), *County Folk-Lore*, vi. *East Riding of Yorkshire* (Folk-Lore Society, 1912). 105–6; Mrs Gutch and Mabel Peacock (eds.), *County Folk-Lore*, v. *Lincolnshire* (Folk-Lore, 1908), 209–10; 'Scraps of English Folklore', *Folk-Lore*, 40 (1929), 284.

35. Brand, *Observations*, ii. 24; Robert Chambers, *The Book of Days* (1864), ii. 378; H. W. Underdown, 'A Harvest Custom', *Folk-Lore*, 15 (1904), 464.

36. Joseph Train, *An Historical and Statistical Account of the Isle of Man* (Douglas, 1845), ii. 122–3; A. W. Moore, *The Folk-Lore of the Isle of Man* (1891), 121–2.

37. Gailey, 'Last Sheaf', 1–22; Kevin Danaher, *The Year in Ireland* (1972), 190–1; H. W. Lett, 'Winning the Churn', *Folk-Lore*, 16 (1905), 185–6; 'Harvest Rites in Ireland', *Folk-Lore*, 25 (1914), 379–80.

38. By Lewis Morris, quoted in Owen, *Welsh Folk Customs*, 115.

39. *Gentleman's Magazine* (Feb. 1974), 124; Sir John Sinclair, *The Statistical Account of Scotland*, xix (1797), 550.

40. For this and most below, see sources at nn. 31–5.

41. Campbell, *Superstitions*, 243–4.

42. For evidence for the veneration of these in ancient Irish and British religion, see G. A. Wait, *Ritual and Religion in Iron Age Britain* (British Archaeological Reports, British series, 149; 1985), 217–24.

43. Peter Robson, 'Calendar Customs in Nineteenth and Twentieth Century Dorset' (Sheffield M. Phil. thesis, 1988), 93.

44. Sources at n. 33. plus Anna Eliza Bray, *A Description of the Part of Devonshire Bordering on the Tamar and the Tavy* (1836), 330–2: J. Rendel Harris. 'The Origin and Meaning of Apple Cults', *Bulletin of the John Rylands Library*, 5 (1918–19), 73: 'Old Harvest Customs in Devon and Cornwall', *Folk-Lore*, 1 (1890), 280; Bl Add. MS 41313. fo. 86 (concerning Cornborough, Devon); Bushaway, *By Rite*, 128–9: John Symonds Udal, *Dorsetshire Folk-Lore* (Hertford, 1922), 68–71.

45. William Brockie, *Legends and Superstitions of the County of Durham* (Sunderland, 1886), III; John Nicholson, *Folk Lore of East Yorkshire* (1890), 14: William Henderson, *Notes on the Folk-Lore of the Northern Counties of England and the Borders* (Folk-Lore Society, 1879), 89.

46. Train, *Man*, ii. 122–3.

47. Chambers, *Book of Days*, ii. 378; Burne, *Shropshire*, 372–3; Robert Holland, *A Glossary of Words Used in the County of Chester* (English Dialect Society, 1886), 315.

48. Sources at nn. 31–2.

49. M. S. Clark, 'Pembrokeshire Notes', *Folk-Lore*, 15 (1904), 194–8. See also Maclean, 'The Last Sheaf', 194, for a similarly joking approach taken in Skye.

50. Frazer, *Spirits of the Corn*, i. 142–3; McNeill, *Silver Bough*, i. 123.

51. Maclean, 'The Last Sheaf', 195–6.

52. *British Calendar Customs: Scotland*, i. 71.

53. Wright, *British Calendar Customs*, i. 189.

54. T. Gwynn Jones, *Welsh Folklore and Folk-Custom* (Cambridge, 1979). 156–7; T. Brown, '48th Report', 76; Trevelyan, *Folk-Lore*, 262–3; Owen, *Welsh Folk Customs*, 116–17; Courtney, *Cornish Feasts*, 52–3; *British Calendar Customs: Scotland*, i. 84–6.

55. Gomme, 'Kirn-Dolly', 215–16.

56. Maclean, 'The Last Sheaf', 194–7; Frazer, *Golden Bough*, 344–5; Maclagan, 'Argyleshire', 148–52: McPhail, 'Hebrides', 441; McNeill, *Silver Bough*, i. 122; Rowling, *Lake District*, 125–6.

57. *British Calendar Customs: Scotland*, i. 65–84.

58. Sinclair, *Statistical Account*, xix. 550.

59. Joseph Wilkie, *A History of Fife* (1924), 31.

60. Fraser, *Spirits of the Corn*, i. 157–61.

61. *British Calendar Customs: Scotland*, i. 66; McNeill. *Silver Bough*, i. 122; Maclagan, 'Argyleshire', 148–52; Frazer, *Golden Bough*, i. 344–5: Brand, *Observations*, ii. 20.

62. R. T. Hampson, *Medii Aevi Kalendarium* (1841). i. 345; Brockie, *Durham*, III; Henderson, *Northern Counties*, 88–9; Moore, *Man*, 121–2.

63. McNeill, *Silver Bough*, i. 121–2: Henderson, *Northern Counties*, 88–9; Gutch and Peacock (eds.), *County Folklore*, v. *Lincolnshire*, 209; Hone, *Every-Day Book*, ii. 1166; Gomme, 'Kirn-Dolly', 215–16.

64. Porter, *Cambridgeshire*, 123; Tongue, *Somerset Folklore*, 167–8. It may be that this name was imposed by the folklorists who wrote of them.

65. Brand, *Observations*, ii. 21–2.

66. William Hutchinson, *A View of Northumberland* (Newcastle, 1778), ii. appendix 17; Brand, *Observations*, ii. 20; Gutch (ed.), *County Folk-Lore*, vi. *East Riding*, 108; Henderson, *Northern Counties*, 89; Gomme, 'Harvest Customs', 177–9.

67. Hutchinson, *Northumberland*, ii. appendix 17.

68. McNeill, *Silver Bough*, i. 121–2.

69. Ibid., i. 122; Frazer, *Golden Bough*, i. 344–5.

70. Sinclair, *Statistical Account*, xix. 550; Moore, *Man*, 121–2.

71. Brand, *Observations*, ii. 22; Porter, *Cambridgeshire*, 120–1.

72. C. F. Tebbutt, *Huntingdonshire Folklore* (St Ives, 1984), 71–2; Brand, *Observations*, ii. 24; Nicholson, *East Yorkshire*, 14–15; Hone, *Every-Day Book*, ii. 1164; Henderson, *Northern Counties*, 87–8; S. Jackson Coleman, *Huntingdonshire Lore and Legend* (Douglas, 1955), n.p.: Porter, *Cambridgeshire*, 120–2; Burne, *Shropshire*, 374; Ralph Whitlock, *A Calendar of County Customs* (1978), 132; Evans, *Ask The Fellows*, 214; Blythe, *Akenfield*, 56: Thomas Sternberg, *The Dialect and Folk-Lore of Northamptonshire* (1851), 176–7; Underdown, 'A Harvest Custom', 464; Angela Parker, 'Oxfordshire Village Folk-Lore, 1840–1900', *Folk-Lore*, 24 (1913), 85–6: James Obelkevitch, *Religion and Rural Society: South Lindsey 1825–1875* (Oxford, 1976), 58; Ethel H. Rudkin, 'Lincolnshire Folklore', *Folk-Lore*, 44 (1933), 286–7; Ralph Whitlock, *The Folklore of Wiltshire* (1976), 60; Flora Thompson, *Lark Rise to Candleford* (Oxford, 1939), 236–7; Morgan, *Harvesters*, 164; Roy Palmer, *The Folklore of Warwickshire* (1976), 49–50; Jacqueline Simpson, *The Folklore of Sussex* (1973), 127–8; Bushaway, *By Rite*, 133–4; 'Scraps of English Folklore', *Folk-Lore*, 37 (1926), 77; Kingsley Palmer, *The Folklore of Somerset* (1976), 104.

73. A selection of which are printed in G. F. Northall, *English Folk-Rhymes* (1892), 261–3, as well as in the sources above.

74. Jones, *Welsh Folk-Lore*, 155; Tebbutt, *Huntingdonshire*, 71–2; Hone, *Every-Day Book*, ii. 1164–72; J. Rock, 'Old Sussex Harvest Custom', *Sussex Archaeological Collections*, 14 (1862), 186–8; Brand, *Observations*, ii. 25–9; R. L. Bowley, *The Fortunate Islands*, 7th edn. (1980), 102, Robert W. Malcolmson, *Popular Recreations in English Society 1700–1850* (Cambridge, 1973), 55–69; Train, *Man*, ii. 122–3; Chambers, *Book of Days*, ii. 379; Mrs Gutch (ed.), *County Folk-Lore*, ii. *North Riding of Yorkshire, York and the Ainsty* (Folk-Lore Society, 1901), 254–66; Gutch (ed.), *County Folk-Lore*, vi. *East Riding* 104; *County Folk-Lore*, i. *Suffolk*, 70–1; Gutch and Peacock (eds.), *County Folk-Lore*, v. 209; Henderson, *Northern Counties*, 87–8: Robert Heath, *A Natural and Historical Account of the Isles of Scilly* (1750), 52–3; Porter, *Cambridgeshire*, 121–2; Leather, *Herefordshire*, 104–5; Gomme, 'Harvest Customs', 177–9; Udal, *Dorsetshire*, 68–70; Burne, *Shropshire*, 376; J. C. Atkinson, *Forty Years in a Moorland Parish* (1891), 239–45; Sternbery, *Northamptonshire*, 178; Richard Blakeborough, *Wit, Character, Folklore and Customs of the North Riding of Yorkshire* (1898), 85; George Morley, *Shakespeare's Greenwood* (1900), 117–19; D. H. M. Read, 'Hampshire Folklore', *Folk-Lore*, 22 (1911), 326–7; McNeill, *Silver Bough*, i. 125–8; Frazer, *Spirits of the Corn*, i. 156–8; 'Scraps of English Folklore', *Folk-Lore*, 35 (1924) 348; Rudkin, 'Lincolnshire Folklore', 286–7; Wright, *British Calendar Customs*, i. 183–4; Thompson, *Lark Rise*, 236–8; Morgan, *Harvesters*, 166; Anne Hughes, *The Diary of a Farmers's Wife 1796–1797* (1980), 51–3; Rowling, *Lake District*, 126; Paimer, *Warwickshire*, 50–1; Simpson, *Sussex*, 129–30; Ernest W. Marwick, *The Folklore of Orkney and Shetland* (1975), 115; Evans, *Ask The Fellows*, 101; Blythe, *Akenfield*, 56; Bushaway, *By Rite*, 128–37; 'Scraps of English Folk-Lore', *Folk-Lore*, 36 (1925), 250; Tony Deane and Tony Shaw, *The Folklore of Cornwall* (1975), 183.

75. See e.g. Fraser, *Hills of Home*, 198–9, and Clark, 'Pembrokeshire Notes', 198.

76. An Essex rendering printed in Hone, *Every-Day Book*, ii. 1172. See also Porter, *Cambridgeshire*, 121; Northall, *Folk-Rhymes*, 264; Simpson, *Sussex*, 129–30; Jones-Baker, *Hertfordshire*, 159–60.

77. A Sussex variety in Northall, *Folk-Rhymes*, 263. It is mentioned in several of the accounts at n. 74, and compare the rendering in Alfred Williams, *Folk Songs of the Upper Thames* (1923), 289.

78. Nicholson, *East Yorkshire*, 14–15.

79. See the set printed in *Early Ballads*, ed. Robert Bell (1877), 376–84. For a comparable view, See Robson, 'Calendar Customs', 97–102.

80. S. G. Kendall, *Farming Memoirs of a West Country Yeoman* (1944), 171–3, for a harvest supper in north-east Somerset, 1883.

81. Cf. *County Folk-Lore*, i. *Suffolk*, 70–1.

82. Malcolmson, *Popular Recreations*, 55–69.

83. Such as South Lindsey in Lincolnshire: Obelkevitch, *Religion and Rural Society*, 58–9. Otherwise see sources at n. 74.

84. Hone, *Every-Day Book*, 1164, 1181.

85. Morgan, *Harvesters*, 167.

86. Ibid. 166–74; Bushaway, *By Rite*, 133–7, 265–73; Obelkevitch. *Religion and Rural Society*, 58–60; R. W. Gifford, 'Popular Culture in Bedfordshire and Huntingdonshire 1820–1870' (University of London Institute of Education MA thesis, 1982), 16–17.

87. On which see Michael Pickering, *Village Song and Culture* (1982), 66.

88. For this and most below, see C. M. Bouch, *Prelates and People of the Lake Counties* (Kendal, 1948), 425, 440; David Clark, *Between Pulpit and Pew* (Cambridge, 1982), 104–6; Laurence Whistler, *The English Festivals* (1947), 193; D. H. Ditchfield, *Old English Customs Extant at the Present Time* (1896), 149; Porter, *Cambridgeshire*, 123; Morgan, *Harvesters*, 168–73; G. J. Cuming, *A History of the Anglican Liturgy* (1969), 196–7; Robson, 'Calendar Customs', 96; Rowling, *Lake District*, 125; Craig Fees, 'Christmas Mumming in a North Cotswold Town' (Leeds Ph.D. thesis, 1988), ii, 2, 50; Obelkevitch, *Religion and Rural Society*, 158–61; Gifford, 'Popular Cultures', 16–17; Elizabeth M. Lamb, 'Harvest-tide Festivities in the South West', *English Dance and Song*, 36, 3 (1974), 92–4; Bushaway, *By Rite*, 268–73.

89. Quoted in Morgan, *Harvesters*, 173.

90. Thus, ibid. 174; Obelkevitch, *Religion and Rural Society*, 60; Gifford, 'Popular Culture', 16–17; Bushaway, *By Rite*, 268–73.

91. *Religion and Rural Society*, 158–9. I do not find Dr Obelkevitch's characterization of this as 'pagan', as opposed to 'Christian', the most helpful analysis: 'medieval' would be, I suggest, more to the point.

92. Quoted regularly in the sources above.

93. *By Rite*, 108.

94. On which, in particular, see Gailey, 'Last Sheaf', 8.

95. Bray, *Tamar and Tavy*, 332.

96. Evans, *Ask The Fellows*, 214.

97. Peate, 'Corn Customs', 155.

98. Tongue, *Somerset Folklore*, 168.

99. Cf. Porter, *Cambridgeshire*, 124.

100. An impression based upon an acquaintance with twenty-two makers of them in Cambridgeshire and Suffolk in the 1970s.

101. T. Brown, '48th Report', 76; *Folklore*, 65 (1954), 49.

102. Maclean, 'The Last Sheaf', 193.

CHAPTER 34

1. M. Marton, *A Description of the Western Islands of Scotland* (1903), 79–80.

2. Alexander Carmichael, *Carmina Gadelica* (Edinburgh, 1900), i. 200–11; Alan Macdonald, *Gaelic Words and Expressions from South Uist and Eriskay*, ed. J. L. Campbell, Dublin, 1958), 232; F. Marian McNeill, *The Silver Bough*, i (Glasgow, 1957), 104, 115.

3. John Brand, *Observations on the Popular Antiquities of Great Britain*, ed. Sir Henry Ellis (1908), ii. 1.

4. *Records of Early English Drama: Herefordshire and Worcestershire*, ed. David N. Klausner (Toronto, 1990), 461, 517.

5. Anthony Sparrow (ed.), *A Collection of Articles* (1971), 167–8.

6. For example, there is the list of Oxfordshire wakes in C. E. Prior, *Dedications of Churches* (Oxfordshire Archaeological Society Reports, 1903), 22–41. Four were in June, three in August, five in September, and six in October.

7. Kenneth L. Parker, *The English Sabbath* (Cambridge, 1988), 122.

8. *Records of Early English Drama: Lancashire*, ed. David George (Toronto, 1991), 4. 58.

9. Ronald Hutton, *The Rise and Fall of Merry England* (Oxford, 1994), 156 and nn. 16, 19, and 20.

10. T. F. Thiselton Dyer, *Old English Social Life* (1898), 206–7.

11. Hutton, *Merry England*, 154, 157, and nn. 9 and 27.

12. Ibid. 168–9, 171.

13. Ibid. 189–91.

14. Ibid. 207–8.

15. *A Joco-serious Discourse in two Dialogues*, repr. in Brand, *Observations*, ii. 9; *The Poems of Robert Herrick*, ed. L. C. Martin (Oxford, 1965), 255.

16. *Five Hundred Pointes of Good Husbandrie*, repr. in Brand, *Observations*, ii. 3.

17. Repr. in *Merry Songs and Ballads*, ed. John S. Farmer (1897), iv. 162–3.

18. *Revel, Riot and Rebellion* (Oxford, 1985), 67–8, 74–86, 264–70.

19. Felicity Heal, *Hospitality in Early Modern England* (Oxford, 1990), 358–65; Robert W. Malcolmson, *Popular Recreations in English Society 1700–1850* (Cambridge, 1973), 16–19.

20. Ibid. 20–23; Henry Morley, *Memoirs of Bartholomew Fair* (1892), 1–92; R. J. R. Poole, 'Wakes, Holidays and Fairs in the Lancashire Cotton District. c.1790–1890' (Lancaster Ph.D. thesis, 1985), 40.

21. Peter Roberts, *The Cambrian Popular Antiquities* (1815), 128–9.

22. Marie Trevelyan, *Folk-Lore and Folk-Stories of Wales* (1909), 257–8.

23. Sir John Sinclair, *The Statistical Account of Scotland*, xvi (1795), 460.

24. Ibid. xviii (1797), 652.

25. Malcolmson, *Popular Recreations*, 146–7.

26. *A View of Northumberland* (1778), ii. 26.

27. Brand, *Observations*, ii. 12. And see Malcolmson, *Popular Recreations*, 148–9, for other comments of this sort.

28. Arthur Warne, *Church and Society in Eighteenth-Century Devon* (Newton Abbot, 1969), 168–9.

29. William Brockie, *Legends and Superstitions of the County of Durham* (Sunderland, 1886), 98.

30. Brand, *Observations*, ii. 9.

31. John Rule, 'Methodism, Popular Beliefs and Village Culture in Cornwall, 1800–50', in Robert D. Storch (ed.), *Popular Culture and Custom in Nineteenth-Century England* (1982), 53–4.

32. Brand, *Observations*, ii. 8.

33. Malcolmson, *Popular Recreations*, 70.

34. 'The Village Minstrel', in *The Early Poems of John Clare*, ed. Eric Robinson and David Powell (Oxford, 1989), ii. 152–61.

35. *The Every-Day Book and Table Book* (1832), ii. 54–5.

36. Quoted in Roger Elbourne, *Music and Tradition in Early Industrial Lancashire* (Folklore Society, 1980), 34.

37. Hugh Cunningham, *Leisure in the Industrial Revolution* (1980), 66.

38. Peter Robson, 'Calendar Customs in Nineteenth and Twentieth Century Dorset' (Sheffield M.Phil. thesis, 1988), 87–8; T. F. Thiselton Dyer, *British Popular Customs* (1876), 324–5; Ralph Whitlock, *The Folklore of Wiltshire* (1976), 57–8, and *The Folklore of Devon* (1977), 150; John Symonds Udal, *Dorsetshire Folk-Lore* (Hertford, 1922), 108–9; J. B. Partridge, 'Cotswold Place-Lore and Customs', *Folk-Lore*, 23 (1912), 453–5; A. R. Wright, *British Calendar Customs*, ed. T. E. Lones (Folk-Lore Society, 1936), iii. 69–75; M. A. Courtney, *Cornish Feasts and Folklore* (1890), 1–6.

39. *County Folk-Lore*, i (Folk-Lore Society 1895), 3: Leicestershire and Rutland, ed. Charles J. Billson, 96–7; Prior, *Dedications*, 22–41, Ella Mary Leather, *The Folk-Lore of Herefordshire* (Hereford, 1912), 156–7; Charlotte Sophia Burne, *Shropshire Folk-Lore* (1883), 441–9; D. H. M. Read, 'Huntingdonshire', *Folk-Lore*, 23 (1912), 352; T. E. Lones, 'Worcestershire Folklore', *Folk-Lore*, 25 (1914), 370; Ethel H. Rudkin, 'Lincolnshire Folklore, *Folk-Lore*, 44 (1933), 286; Flora Thompson, *Lark Rise to Candleford* (Oxford, 1945), 230–2; James Obelkevitch, *Religion and Rural Society: South Lindsey, 1825–1875* (Oxford, 1976), 84–5; Michael Pickering, *Village Song and Culture* (1982), 109–10; Enid Porter, *Cambridgeshire Customs and Folklore* (1969), 142–5.

40. Brockie, *Durham*, 98, 106–7; Northcote W. Thomas (ed.), *County Folk Lore*, iv. *Northumberland* (Folk-Lore Society, 1904); Dyer, *British Popular Customs*, 333–4; S. O. Addy, 'Garland Day at Castleton', *Folk-Lore*, 12 (1901), 405–6; Richard Blakeborough, *Wit, Character, Folklore and Customs of the North Riding of Yorkshire* (1898), 92–3; Wright, *British Calendar Customs*, iii. 70–6.

41. Brockie, *Durham*, 98; Wright, *British Calendar Customs*, iii. 3–4.

42. Leather, *Herefordshire*, 156; Porter, *Cambridgeshire*, 145; Addy, 'Garland Day', 405–6.

43. Pickering, *Village Song*, 109–10.

44. Hone, *Every-Day Book*, ii. 1260–2; P. H. Ditchfield, *Old English Customs Extant at the Present Time* (1896), 131; 'The Yorkshire Name for Wakes', *Folk-Lore Journal*, 2 (1884), 25.

45. Frederick William Hackwood, *Staffordshire Customs, Superstitions and Folklore* (Lichfield, 1924), 105–7; Douglas Reid, 'Interpreting the Festival Calendar: Wakes and Fairs as Carnivals', in Storch (ed.), *Popular Culture*, 127–35.

46. R. J. R. Poole, 'Wakes, Holidays and Fairs', as in n. 20; Theresa Jill Buckland, 'Ceremonial Dance Traditions in the South-West Pennines and Rossendale' (Leeds Ph.D. thesis, 1984). These have yielded publications as Theresa Buckland, 'Wakes and Rushbearing c.1780–c.1830: A Functional Analysis', *Lore and Language*, 3: 6A (1982), 29–44, and John K. Walton and Robert Poole, 'The Lancashire Wakes in the Nineteenth Century', in Storch (ed.), *Popular Culture*, 102–20.

47. Robert Storch, 'Introduction: Persistence and Change in Nineteenth-Century Popular Culture', in Storch (ed.), *Popular Culture*, I.

48. Expressed in most of the sources in nn. 38–47.

49. Obelkevitch, *Religion and Rural Society*, 85.

50. Reid, 'Interpreting the Festival Calendar', 130–1; Hackwood, *Staffordshire*, 105–6.

51. Reid, 'Interpreting the Festival Calendar', 130–1.

52. Ibid. 134; Malcolmson, *Popular Recreations*, 109–38; Poole, 'Wakes, Holidays and Fairs', 127–9.

53. Poole, 'Wakes, Holidays and Fairs', 130–1.

54. Rule, 'Methodism, Popular Beliefs and Village Culture', 59; Trevelyan, *Folk-Lore*, 257–8.

55. Walton and Poole, 'Lancashire Wakes', 117–18.

56. Poole, 'Wakes, Holidays and Fairs', 144–54.

57. Reid, 'Interpreting the Festive Calendar', 131–3; Walton and Poole, 'Lancashire Wakes', 105, 11–20; Poole, 'Wakes, Holidays and Fairs', 155–211.

58. Poole, 'Wakes, Holidays and Fairs', 117.

CHAPTER 35

1. Most accessibly translated by Thomas Kinsella, in his rendering of *The Tain* (Oxford, 1970), 27. Likewise, in *Tain Bo Cuailnge* itself, the surviving versions of which could date from anywhere between the eighth and the twelfth centuries, it is 'the feast of Samain at the summer's end': ibid. 143.

2. Most accessibly translated by Jeffrey Gantz, in *Early Irish Myths and Sagas* (1981), 155.

3. Compare, for example, those in *Mesca Ulad*, and the episode of Aillen of the Flaming Breath in the Fionn cycle.

4. *Forus Feasa*, ii. 246 (Irish Texts Society, 8), analysed (and dismissed) by D. A. Binchy, 'The Fair of Tailtu and the Feast of Tara', *Eriu*, 18 (1958), 129–30.

5. Gantz, *Early Irish Myths and Sagas*, 12–13.

6. Proinsias MacCana, *Celtic Mythology* (1970), 127.

7. 'The Bodleian Dinnschenchas', ed. W. Stokes, *Folk-Lore*, 3 (1892), 507.

8. Bede, *Works*, ed. J. A. Giles (1843), vi. 178–9.

9. See esp. *Gisli Saga*, ch. 15.

10. *Lectures on the Origin and Growth of Religion as Illustrated by Celtic Heathendom* (1886), 514–15.

11. Sir John Rhŷs, *Celtic Folklore: Welsh and Manx* (Oxford, 1901), i. 316–22.

12. J. Fisher, 'The Welsh Calendar', *Transactions of the Honourable Society of Cymmrodorion* (1894–5), 104–5. Fisher himself accepted Rhys's theory of a 'Celtic New Year' on 1 November, without providing better evidence.

13. *Balder the Beautiful* (1914), i. 224–6.

14. *Adonis, Attis, Osiris* (1907), 301–9.

15. *Butler's Lives of the Saints*, ed. Herbert Thurston and Donald Attwater (New York, 1956), iv, 234–5; John Dowden, *The Church Year and Kalendar* (Cambridge, 1910), 23.

16. Dowden, *Church Year*, 23; Frazer, *Adonis, Attis, Osiris*, 301–9.

17. T. Gwynn Jones, *Welsh Folklore and Folk-Custom* (Cambridge, 1979), 146–51; Trefor M. Owen, *Welsh Folk Customs* (St Fagans, 1974), 131.

18. Kevin Danaher, *The Year in Ireland* (Cork, 1972), 200–8.

19. F. Marian McNeill, *The Silver Bough*, iii (Glasgow, 1968), 13.

20. James R. Nicolson, *Shetland Folklore* (1981), 141–2.

21. R. T. Hampson, *Medii Aevi Kalendarium* (1841), i. 365.

22. *British Calendar Customs: Scotland*, ed. Mary Macleod Banks; iii (Folk-Lore Society, 1939), 173; Anna Jean Mill, *Medieval Plays in Scotland* (Edinburgh, 1927), 10.

23. Owen, *Welsh Folk Customs*, 141.

24. *A Tour in Scotland* (1776), ii. 47.

25. Quoted in John Brand, *Observations upon the Popular Antiquities of Great Britain*, ed. Sir Henry Ellis (1908), i. 389–90.

26. Quoted in Brand, *Observations*, i. 389–90.

27. John Ramsay, *Scotland and Scotsmen in the Eighteenth Century*, ed. Alexander Allardyce (Edinburgh, 1888) ii. 437.

28. Sir John Sinclair, *The Statistical Account of Scotland*, v. (1793), 517; James Napier, *Folk Lore: Or, Superstitious Beliefs in the West of Scotland* (Paisley, 1879), 179–80; E. J.

Guthrie, *Old Scottish Customs* (1885), 67; J. G. Frazer, 'Folk-Lore at Balquhidder', *Folk-Lore Journal*, 6 (1888), 270; *British Calendar Customs: Scotland*, iii. 112, 114.

29. Sinclair, *Statistical Account*, xxi (1796), 145; A. Macdonald, 'Some former Customs of the Royal Parish of Craithie', *Folk-Lore*, 17 (1907), 85; Banks, *British Calendar Customs: Scotland*, iii. 112–13, 115–16.

30. Walter Gregor, *Notes on the Folk-Lore of the North-East of Scotland* (Folk-Lore Society, 1881), 167–8.

31. T. F. Thiselton Dyer, *British Popular Customs* (1876), 401.

32. William Hone, *The Every-Day Book and Table Book* (1832), ii. 1259–60; Maria J. MacCulloch. 'Folk-Lore of the Isle of Skye', *Folk-Lore*, 34(1923), 86–7.

33. Banks, *British Calendar Customs: Scotland*, iii. 111.

34. Jones, *Welsh Folklore*, 147–9; Brand, *Observations*, i. 389–90; Edmund Hyde Hall, *A Description of Caernarvonshire* (Caernarvonshire Historical Society, 1952); Elias Owen, 'Folk-Lore, Superstitions, or What-Not, in Montgomeryshire', *Montgomeryshire Collections*, 15 (1882), 131–2.

35. Jones, *Welsh Folklore*, 148.

36. Ibid. 147–8; Owen, *Welsh Folk Customs*, 124–5: R. Williams, 'History of the Parish of Llanbrynmair', *Montgomeryshire Collections* 22 (1888), 321–2: R. V. Sayce, 'A Survey of Montgomeryshire Folklore'; ibid. 47 (1942), 21; T. Jones, 'History of the Parish of Llansantffraid yn Mochnant', ibid. 4 (1871), 140; R. V. Sayce. 'The Seasonal Bonfires', ibid. 59 (1948), 87.

37. Joseph Train, *An Historical and Statistical Account of the Isle of Man* (Douglas, 1845), ii. 123.

38. Alan Gailey, 'The Bonfire in Northern Irish Tradition', *Folklore*, 88 (1977), 11–12; Danaher, *Year in Ireland*, 209.

39. *Balder*, i. 241.

40. Danaher, *Year in Ireland*, 207–81; 'Omurethi', 'Customs Peculiar to Certain Days', *Journal of the Kildare Archaeological Society*, 5 (1906–8), 450; Thomas J. Westropp, 'Folklore on the Coasts of Connacht', *Folk-Lore*, 34 (1923), 334–5; Allan Macdonald, *Gaelic Words and Expressions from South Uist and Eriskay*, ed. J. L. Campbell, (Dublin, 1958).

41. M. Martin, *A Description of the Western Island of Scotland* (1703), 28–9.

42. Alexander Carmichael, *Carmina Gadelica* (Edinburgh, 1900), i. 163.

CHAPTER 36

1. BL Add. MS 38174. fo. 34ᵛ.

2. The parish sources are given in Ronald Hutton, *The Rise and Fall of Merry England* (Oxford, 1994), 305, n. 121 and appendix. Additional material is from *The Earl of Northumberland's Household Book*, ed. Thomas Percy (1905), 320, 324; and Robert Ricart, *The Maire of Bristowe is Kalendar*, ed. Lucy Toulmin Smith (Camden Society, 1872), 79.

3. Thomas Cranmer, *Miscellaneous Writings*, ed. J. E. Cox (Parker Society, 1844), 415; John Foxe, *Acts and Monuments*, ed. Stephen Reed Cattley (1938), v. 561–2.

4. HMC Dean and Chapter of Wells MSS, ii. 264–5.

5. Sources in Hutton, *Merry England*, 315, n. 76, and appendix.

6. Sources ibid. 317, n. 136, and appendix.

7. Ibid. 160–7, and sources given there.

8. J. Weld, *A History of Leagram* (Chetham Society, 1913), 132–3.

9. W. Holden, 'Tindles', *Derbyshire Archaeological and Natural History Society Journal*, 65 (1944), 86–8; *Sanas Chormaic: Cormac's Glossary*, trans. John O'Donovan, ed. Whitley Stokes (Calcutta, 1868), 157.

10. Charles Hardwick, *Traditions, Superstitions and Folk-Lore* (Manchester, 1872), 31–4.
11. A. R. Wright, *British Calendar Customs*, ed. T. E. Lones, (Folk-Lore Society, 1936), iii. 108, 144.
12. Quoted in Brand, *Observations*, i. 391.
13. Holden, 'Tindles', 86–7.
14. Doris Jones-Baker, *The Folklore of Hertfordshire* (1977), 165–6.
15. Cited in Brand, *Observations*, i. 391.
16. Cited ibid. i. 392.
17. Cited ibid. i. 392.
18. John Aubrey, *Remaines of Gentilisme and Judaisme*, ed. James Britten, (1881), 23.
19. Charlotte S. Burne, 'Souling, Clementing and Catterning', *Folk-Lore*, 25 (1914), 285–99; Bob Bushaway, *By Rite* (1982), 184; Brand, *Observations*, i. 391–3; J. Bridge, 'Souling Songs', *Journal of the Architectural, Archaeological and Historic Society of Chester and North Wales*, 6 (1897); R. L. Tongue, *Somerset Folklore*, ed. K. M. Briggs (Folklore Society County Folklore 8; 1965), 170; Hardwick, *Traditions*, 31; E. Beck, 'Children's Hallowe'en Customs in Sheffield', *Lore and Language*, 3: 9 (1983), 70–88; Frederick William Hackwood, *Staffordshire Customs, Superstitions and Folklore* (Lichfield, 1924), 45–6; T. F. Thiselton Dyer, *British Popular Customs* (1876), 406–7; Ella Mary Leather, *The Folk-Lore of Herefordshire* (Hereford, 1912), 107; Trefor M. Owen, *Welsh Folk Customs* (St Fagans, 1974), 136–40; John Harland and T. T. Wilkinson, *Lancashire Folk-Lore* (1867), 251; Charlotte Sophia Burne, *Shropshire Folk-Lore* (1883), 382–8; Wright, *British Calendar Customs*, iii. 121–43; Robert Holland, *A Glossary of Words Used in the County of Chester* (English Dialect Society, 1886), 506–13; Jones-Baker, *Folklore of Hertfordshire*, 166; Jacqueline Simpson, *The Folklore of the Welsh Border* (1976), 168–70.
20. Owen, *Welsh Folk Customs*, 136; T. Gwynn Jones, *Welsh Folklore and Folk-Custom* (Cambridge, 1979), 152.
21. Hardwick, *Traditions*, 31.
22. Dyer, *British Popular Customs*, 407.
23. Hackwood, *Staffordshire*, 45–6.
24. Bridge, 'Souling Songs', 74–6.
25. Mary Macleod Banks (ed.), *British Calendar Customs: Scotland* (Folk-Lore Society, 1939), iii. 175.
26. Burne, 'Souling, Clementing and Catterning'.
27. Burne, *Shropshire Folk-Lore*, 387–8. For similar versions, see Hackwood, *Staffordshire Customs*, 45–6; Owen, *Welsh Folk Customs*, 134.
28. Jones-Baker, *Hertfordshire*, 166.
29. Iona and Peter Opie, *The Lore and Language of Schoolchildren* (Oxford, 1959), 275.
30. Tongue, *Somerset Folklore*, 170.
31. Cf. Burne, *Shropshire Folk-Lore*, 388.
32. Opie and Opie, *Lore and Language*, 275.
33. Beck, 'Children's Hallowe'en Customs', 70–88.
34. Holland, *Glossary of Words*, 507–8. For other versions see Simpson, *Welsh Border*, 168–70.
35. Sources at n. 34. plus Peter Wright and P. F. M McDonald, 'The Cheshire Soul-Cakers' Play', *Lore and Language*, 1: 3 (1970), 9–11: and Alex Helm, 'The Cheshire Soul-Caking Play' *JEFDS* 6: 2 (1950), 450–50.
36. Susan Pattison, 'The Antrobus Soulcaking Play: An Alternative Approach to the Mummers' Play', *Folklife* 15 (1977), 5–11; A. E. Green, 'Popular Drama and the Mummers' Play', in David Bradby, Louis James, and Bernard Sharratt (eds.), *Performance and Politics in Popular Drama* (Cambridge, 1980), 139–66.

37. Sidney Oldall Addy, *Household Talles with Other Traditional Remains* (1895), 125.

38. Lawrence Whistler, *The English Festivals* (1947), 201.

39. Bob Bushaway, 'Name upon Name: The Great War and Remembrance', in Roy Porter (ed.), *Myths of the English* (Cambridge, 1992), 136–56.

CHAPTER 37

1. William Hone, *The Every-Day Book and table Book* (1852), i. 1415; Kevin Danaher, *The Year in Ireland* (Cork, 1972), 204–6; Lady Jane Francesca Wilde, *Ancient Cures, Charms and Usage of Ireland* (1890), 115–16.

2. William Grant Stewart, *The Popular Superstitions and Festive Amusements of the Highlanders of Scotland* (Edinburgh, 1823), 227.

3. I. F. Grant, *Highland Folkways* (1961), 359; James R. Nicolson, *Shetland Folklore* (1981), 144.

4. T. Gwynne Jones, *Welsh Folklore and Folk Customs* (Cambridge, 1979), 146–50; D. E. Owen, 'Pre-Reformation Survivals in Radnorshire', *Transactions of the Honourable Society of Cymmrodorion* (1910–11), 107; Elias Owen, 'Folk-Lore, Superstitions, or What-Not, in Montgomeryshire', *Montgomeryshire Collections*, 15 (1882), 131–2; William Howells, *Cambrian Superstitions* (1831), 174; Trefor M. Owen, *Welsh Folk Customs* (St Fagans, 1974), 125.

5. *The Autobiography of Samuel Bamford*, ed. W. H. Chaloner (1967), 160–1.

6. Enid Porter, *Cambridgeshire Customs and Folklore* (1969), 125. For comparable West Country measures, see Ruth Tongue, *Somerset Folklore* (1965), 171.

7. Nicholson, *Shetland Folklore*, 142–4; Jones, *Welsh Folklore*, 150–1; Grant, *Highland Folkways*, 65, 297; Stewart, *Popular Superstitions*, 227; Hugh Miller, *Scenes and Legends of the North of Scotland* (1850), 63; Edward W. B. Nicholson, *Golspie* (1897), 95–9; Wilde, *Ancient Cures*, 115–16; Allan Mcdonald, *Gaelic Words and Expressions from South Uist and Eriskay*, ed. J. L. Campbell (Dublin, 1958), 103; Maria J. MacCulloch, 'Folk-Lore of the Isle of Skye', *Folk-Lore*, 34 (1923), 86–7; Danaher, *Year in Ireland*, 202.

8. Jones, *Welsh Folklore*, 150; R. T. Hampson, *Medii Aevi Kalendarium* (1841), i. 363–4; F. Sawyer, 'Sussex Folklore and Customs Connected with the Seasons', *Sussex Archaeological Collections*, 33 (1883), 250–1; John Brand, *Observations on the Popular Antiquities of Great Britain*, ed. Sir Henry Ellis (1908), i. 378–89; Howells, *Cambrian Superstitions*, 174; *British Calendar Customs: Scotland*, ed. Mary Macleod Banks, iii (Folk-Lore Society, 1941), 174; William Hutchinson, *A View of Northumberland* (Newcastle, 1778), ii, appendix, 18.

9. Alan Gailey, *Irish Folk Drama* (Cork, 1969), 89.

10. Nicholson, *Shetland Folklore*, 141–2; Joseph Train, *An Historical and Statistical Account of the Isle of Man* (Douglas, 1845), ii. 123; C. I. Paton, 'Manx Calendar Customs', *Folk-Lore*, 52 (1941), 54.

11. Ruth Glass, 'Seven Decades of Hallowe'en', *Folklore Society News*, 17 (June 1993), 3; Maria J. McCulloch, 'Folk-Lore of the Isle of Skye', *Folk-Lore*, 34 (1923).

12. Iona and Peter Opie, *The Lore and Language of Schoolchildren* (Oxford, 1959), 270; Glass, 'Seven Decades', 3.

13. Jones, *Welsh Folklore*, 149–50; Owen, *Welsh Folk Customs*, 133–5; Jane C. Beck, 'The White Lady of Great Britain and Ireland', *Folklore*, 81 (1970), 292–306.

14. Danaher, *Year in Ireland*, 210–11.

15. Banks, *British Calendar Customs: Scotland*, iii. 159–63.

16. Miller, *Scenes and Legends*, 63.

17. Nicholson, *Golspie*, 91–4. For other north Scottish examples see *British Calendar Customs: Scotland*, iii. 159–63, 173–4.

18. *British Calendar Customs: Scotland*, iii. 159–63, 173–4; MacCulloch, 'Isle of Skye', 88.

19. Danaher, *Year in Ireland*, 214–17.

20. Nicholson, *Golspie*, 91.

21. Kingsley Palmer, *The Folklore of Somerset* (1976), 105–6; R. L. Tongue, *Somerset Folklore*, ed. K. M. Briggs (Folklore Society County Folklore, 8; 1965), 169–70; K. Palmer, 'Punkies', *Folklore*, 83 (1972), 240–4. I visited Hinton St George on Punky Night 1982.

22. Peter Robson, 'Calendar Customs in Nineteenth and Twentieth Century Dorset' (Sheffield University M.Phil. thesis, 1988), 116–17; Doris Jones-Baker, *The Folklore of Hertfordshire* (1977), 165–6.

23. William Brenchley Rye (ed.), *England as Seen by Foreigners in the Days of Elizabeth and James the First* (1865), 112.

24. Lesley Pratt Bannatyne, *Halloween: An American Holiday* (New York, 1990), *passim*.

25. Opie and Opie, *Lore and Language*, 268–75; David Clark, *Between Pulpit and Pew* (Cambridge, 1982), 106–7; E. Beck, 'Children's Hallowe'en Customs in Sheffield', *Lore and Language*, 3: 9 (1983), 70–88.

26. *British Calendar Customs: Scotland*, iii. 159–63, 173–4; Glass, 'Seven Decades', 3–4; Opie and Opie, *Lore and Language*, 268–75.

27. Quoted in the *Observer*, 31 Oct. 1993.

28. At the time of writing, important research into modern British celebrations of Hallowe'en, and Pagan observation in particular, is being conducted at the University of Sheffield by Leila Dudley-Edwards.

CHAPTER 38

1. William Warner, *Albions England* (1589), bk. 5, p. 121.

2. C. A. Burland, *Echoes of Magic: A Study of Seasonal Festivals Throughout the Ages* (1972), 207.

3. Kevin Danaher, *The Year in Ireland* (Cork, 1972), 230–2; 'Irish Folk-Lore', *Folk-Lore Journal*, 6 (1888), 56; Leland L. Duncan, 'Fairy Beliefs and Other Folklore Notes from County Leitrim', *Folk-Lore*, 7 (1896), 178–9.

4. J. E. Neale, *Essays in Elizabethan History* (1958), 10–12; Roy C. Strong, 'The Popular Celebration of the Accession Day of Queen Elizabeth I', *Journals of the Warburg and Courtauld Institutes*, 21 (1958), 86–103.

5. Frances A. Yates, *Astraea* (1975), 88–108; David Cressy, *Bonfires and Bells* (1989), 50–7.

6. Ronald Hutton, *The Rise and Fall of Merry England* (Oxford, 1994), 149–51.

7. Ibid. 153–4.

8. Ibid. 186–7.

9. Ibid. 222.

10. Ibid. 253: Sheila Williams, 'The Pope-Burning Processions of 1679, 1680 and 1681', *Journals of the Warburg and Courtauld Institutes*, 21 (1958), 104–18: O. W. Furley. 'The Pope-Burning Processions of the Late Seventeenth Century', *History*, 44 (1959), 16–23: Tim Harris, *London Crowds in the Reign of Charles II* (Cambridge, 1987), 26, 31, 93, 104–6, 120–1, 123–4, 157, 169, 180, 219: Cressy, *Bonfires and Bells*, 173–84.

11. Hutton, *Merry England*, 253, 255.

12. Tim Harris, *Politics under the Later Stuarts* (1993), 185.

CHAPTER 39

1. C. C. Bell *et al.*, 'Fifth of November Customs', *Folk-Lore*, 14 (1903), 185–8.

2. Esp. *Balder the Beautiful* (1914).

3. Such as those of Christina Hole, *English Custom and Usage* (1941), 86–7, and 'Winter Bonfires', *Folklore*, 71 (1960), 217–23; Lord Raglan, analysed (and pulverized) in Joseph Fontenrose, *The Ritual Theory of Myth* (Berkeley, 1966), 19–20; Charlotte S. Burne, 'Guy Fawkes's Day', *Folk-Lore*, 23 (1912), 409–26.

4. In *By Rite* (1982), 66–7.

5. *Bonfires and Bells* (1989), 57–8.

6. Thomas Birch, *The Court and Times of James I* (1848), i. 46–51; *Journals of the House of Commons*, i. 258–60; *Journals of the House of Lords*, ii. 363, 365; *Statutes of the Realm* (1819), v. ii. 1067–8.

7. Cressy, *Bonfires and Bells*, ch. 9; Ronald Hutton, *The Rise and Fall of Merry England* (Oxford, 1994), 183–5.

8. Hutton, *Merry England*, 185–7.

9. Ibid. 221–2; Cressy, *Bonfires and Bells*, 164–5; John Morrill, 'The Church in England, 1642–9', in Morrill (ed.), *Reactions to the English Civil War* (1982), 114.

10. Hutton, *Merry England*, 252–3; Cressy, *Bonfires and Bells*, 171–4; *The Journal of William Shellinks' Travels in England*, trans. and ed. Maurice Exwood and H. L. Lehrmann (Camden Society, 5th ser. 1; 1993), 172.

11. Hutton, *Merry England*, 255–6; Cressy, *Bonfires and Bells*, 185–6.

12. Hutton, *Merry England*, 256–7.

13. Robert D. Storch, 'Please to Remember the Fifth of November', in Storch (ed.), *Popular Culture and Custom in Nineteenth-Century England* (1982), 71–2; Robert W. Malcolmson, *Popular Recreations in English Society 1700–1850* (Cambridge, 1973), 26.

14. Storch, 'Please to Remember', 71; R. P. Chope, 'Devonshire Calendar Customs, Part II. Fixed Festivals', *Transactions of the Devonshire Association*, 70 (1938), 402–3.

15. Malcolmson, *Popular Recreations*, 25.

16. David Cressy, 'The Fifth of November Remembered', in Roy Porter (ed.), *Myths of the English* (Cambridge, 1992), 76–7.

17. Malcolmson, *Popular Recreations*, 26.

18. Chope, 'Devonshire Calendar Customs', 402–3.

19. *The Autobiography of Samuel Bamford*, ed. W. H. Chaloner (1967), i. 159–60.

20. William Hone, *The Every-Day Book and Table Book* (1832), i. 1431–3.

21. Cressy, 'The Fifth of November', 77–8, 83.

22. Ibid. 78.

23. Bushaway, *By Rite*, 67–8, 71–2.

24. Cressy, 'The Fifth of November', 78.

25. Storch, 'Please to Remember', 74–85.

26. Robert Gifford, 'Guy Fawkes: Who Celebrated What?', in Theresa Buckland and Juliette Wood (eds.), *Aspects of British Calendar Customs* (Folklore Society Mistletoe Series, 22; Sheffield, 1993), 147–54.

27. Storch, 'Please to Remember', 79; Malcolmson, *Popular Recreations*, 79–80.

28. Storch, 'Please to Remember', 79.

29. Hone, *Every-Day Book*, i. 1433.

30. Bushaway, *By Rite*, 69–70.

31. J. B. Partridge, 'Cotswold Place-Lore and Customs', *Folk-Lore*, 23 (1912), 455.

32. Craig Fees, 'Christmas Mumming in a North Cotswold Town' (Leeds Ph.D. thesis, 1988), II. ii. 49.

33. John Symonds Udal, *Dorsetshire Folk-Lore* (Hertford, 1922), 48; Charlotte Sophia Burne, *Shropshire Folk-Lore* (1833), 389–90.

34. Jacqueline Simpson, *The Folk-Lore of the Welsh Border* (1976), 173.

35. Peter Robson, 'Calendar Customs in Nineteenth and Twentieth Century Dorset' (Sheffield University M.Phil. thesis, 1988), 122–4.

36. Storch, 'Please to Remember', 86–8.

37. Bushaway, *By Rite*, 252–3.

38. Storch, 'Please to Remember', 89–92; Burne, 'Guy Fawkes's Day', 418–19.

39. Owen Chadwick, *The Victorian Church* (1966), i. 491.

40. Storch, 'Please to Remember', 81–2; Cressy, 'The Fifth of November', 81; D. G. Paz, 'Bonfire Night in Mid-Victorian Northants: The Politics of a Popular Revel', *Bulletin of the Institute of Historical Research*, 63 (1990), 316–28.

41. *Parliamentary Debates* (1858), 151, 475–502, 1392–4, 1660–2; *Statutes at Large*, xxiv. 329–30.

42. Storch, 'Please to Remember', 88–95; Cressy, 'The Fifth of November', 85–6; Burne, 'Guy Fawkes's Day', 409–26; Robson, 'Calendar Customs', 124–6; Keith Leech, 'The Oldest Guy in the World', *English Dance and Song* 49.2 (1987), 2–4; Laurence Whistler, *The English Festivals* (1947), 207.

43. *Oxfordshire Archaeological Society Reports* (1903), 31.

44. John Nicholson, *Folk-Lore of East Yorkshire* (1890), 15–16; Enid Porter, *The Folklore of East Anglia* (1974), 71; John Harland and T. T. Wilkinson, *Lancashire Folk-Lore* (1867), 251–2; Percy Manning, 'Stray Notes on Oxfordshire Folklore', *Folk-Lore*, 14 (1903), 175–6; Ethel H. Rudkin, 'Lincolnshire Folklore', *Folk-Lore*, 44 (1933), 287; A. R. Wright, *British Calendar Customs*, ed. T. E. Lones (Folk-Lore Society, 1936), iii. 146–9; G. F. Northall, *English Folk-Rhymes* (1892), 245–50; M. A. Courtney, *Cornish Feasts and Folklore* (1890), 4–5; Doris Jones-Baker, *The Folklore of Hertfordshire* (1977), 167; Roy Palmer, *The Folklore of Warwickshire* (1976), 168; Jacqueline Simpson, *The Folklore of Sussex* (1973), 136–7; T. F. Thiselton Dyer, *British Popular Customs* (1876), 412–15.

45. Virtually all are from the early nineteenth century and not before, a selection from the period 1820–50 being provided in Manning, 'Stray Notes', 176, and Dyer, *British Popular Customs*, 412–15. The exception is a specimen sung or chanted by 'Boys' in 1742: 'Don't you Remember, | The Fifth of November, | 'Twas Gunpowder Treason Day, | I let off my gun, | And made'em all run. | And stole all their Bonfire away' | (Iona and Peter Opie, *The Lore and Language of Schoolchildren* (Oxford, 1959), 282).

46. Northall, *English Folk-Rhymes*, 246.

47. Sources at n. 44, plus 'Scraps of English Folklore', *Folk-Lore*, 37 (1926), 77; 'Scraps of English Folklore', *Folk-Lore*, 40 (1929), 77; Ella Mary Leather, *The Folk-Lore of Herefordshire* (Hereford, 1912), 107–8; Mabel Peacock, 'Fifth of November Customs', *Folk-Lore*, 14 (1903), 89–90; John Symonds Udal, *Dorsetshire Folk-Lore* (Hertford, 1922), 48; Burne, *Shropshire*, 389–90; Richard Blakeborough, *Wit, Character, Folklore and Customs of the North Riding of Yorkshire* (1898); John Noake, *Notes and Queries for Worcestershire* (1856), 209; C. C. Bell *et al.*, 'Fifth of November Customs', 185–8; Partridge, 'Cotswold Place-Lore', 455; 'Scraps of English Folklore', *Folk-Lore*, 24 (1913), 236–7; J. B. Partridge, 'Folklore from Yorkshire (North Riding)', *Folk-Lore*, 25 (1914), 376; *Oxfordshire Village Life*, ed. Pamela Horn (Abingdon, 1983), 36, 62, 67, 94.

48. R. B. Sayce, 'A Survey of Montgomeryshire Folklore', *Montgomeryshire Collections*, 47 (1942), 21, and 'The Seasonal Bonfires', ibid. 50 (1948), 87.

49. Blakeborough, *Character, Folklore and Customs*, 86–7.

50. Ralph Whitlock, *The Folklore of Wiltshire* (1976), 64.

51. 'Botley Bonfire Night', *Folk-Lore*, 42 (1931), 465.

52. Ralph Whitlock, *The Folklore of Devon* (1977), 153.
53. Enid Porter, *Cambridgeshire Customs and Folklore* (1969), 125; Simon Hoggart, 'The Tax Man', *Observer Magazine* (28 Nov. 1993).
54. Opie and Opie, *Lore and Language*, 276–80.
55. Cressy, 'The Fifth of November', 86.
56. Opie and Opie, *Lore and Language*, 280–3.
57. Nicholas Timmins, 'What It Costs to Remember', *The Times* (31 Oct. 1980).
58. R. P. Chope, '36th Report on Devonshire Folk-Lore', *Transactions of the Devonshire Association*, 68 (1936), 95–6.

CHAPTER 40

1. Charles Hardwick, *Traditions, Superstitions, and Folk-Lore* (Manchester, 1872), 30–40.
2. e.g. T. G. E. Powell, *The Celts* (1958); Nora K. Chadwick, *Celtic Britain* (1963); Stuart Piggott, *The Druids* (1968).
3. *Pagan Celtic Britain* (1967), 57.
4. *The Celtic Realms* (1967), 108.
5. *The Celts* (1970), 180–1.
6. *Everyday Life of the Pagan Celts* (1970), 151–4.
7. e.g. Charles Thomas, *Celtic Britain* (1980); and Lloyd and Jennifer Laing, *Celtic Britain and Ireland, AD 200–800* (Dublin, 1990).
8. *Celtic Britain* (1979), 40–1.
9. *The Gods of the Celts* (1986), 15 and 74.
10. *The British Celts and their Gods under Rome* (1986), 31–5. Perhaps I should also include here the paragraph in Hilda Ellis Davidson, *Myths and Symbols in Pagan Europe* (Manchester, 1988), 38–9, the hesitation being that to ignore it might seem a discourtesy but to discuss it could equally seem an unnecessary finding of fault in another fine book by an eminent scholar expert in, and interested in, other matters. She talks briefly of the usual four festivals in the usual way, her principal citations being not to medievial sources but to the folklorists Máire MacNeill and Kevin Danaher, behind whom stand (again) Rhŷs and Frazer.
11. Outlined in a paper at the Institute of Historical Research, and also in a recent volume of *Eriu* which I was not able to obtain at the time of writing.
12. Before writing this, I telephoned five colleagues in British universities celebrated for their knowledge of early Irish or Welsh literature, to check this point with them. I would never have dared to assert it so roundly if they had not all endorsed it.
13. I am aware that these suggestions may come to take their place in a diffuse, fitful, and yet still immensely important debate which has been developing since the mid-1980s, over the existence and identity of a Celtic cultural province. At times it has been concentrated briefly and fiercely, such as in a discussion group at the British Museum in November 1992, but these moments have so far been little reflected in print. The only observation which I would make upon the wider issue at this stage is how much the belief in such a province is sustained by linguists rather than by historians or archaeologists. A striking example of this is D. E. Evans, 'Celts and Germans', *Bulletin of the Board of Celtic Studies*, 29 (1982), 230–55, and esp. 239, 253, 255. He asserts that 'there was a fundamental difference; there was antagonism' between Celtic-speaking and Teutonic-speaking peoples in ancient Europe, and that 'Celts and Germans were in turn expanding, marauding, and conquering peoples, markedly different from each other and for ever, it seems, consciously or unconsciously rejecting each other because of a deep-seated and pernicious incompatibility'. The only evidence offered

for these dramatic statements is taken neither from history, nor archaeology, nor literature, but consists of the relative absence of transference from Celtic to Germanic of loan-words for legal, administrative, or political matters! The obvious rejoinder, that cultures frequently use loan-words for objects or concepts unfamiliar or alien to them, not those for which they have domestic parallels, is nowhere confronted. At the same time he notes that 'there may have been a shared Celto-Germanic heritage in material culture, in cult and mythology, in social structure, in language', just to dismiss all this as irrelevant. I would not bother to pick on an essay written some years ago, were it not so characteristic of the genre and by such a distinguished philologist, and were it not still cited as an important prop of the argument that Celts and Germans represented two distinct cultures as opposed to a spectrum or a patchwork; cf. Hilda Ellis Davidson, *The Lost Beliefs of Northern Europe* (1993), 4.

14. Ronald Hutton, *The Rise and Fall of Merry England* (Oxford, 1994), ch. 2.

15. 'Round the Maypole', *Times Literary Supplement* (14 Oct. 1994), 6.

16. Eamon Duffy, *The Stripping of the Altars* (New Haven, 1992); Clive Burgess, 'By Quick and by Dead: Wills and Pious Provision in Late Medieval Bristol', *English Historical Review*, 102 (1987), 837–58; 'A Fond Thing Vainly Invented', in S. J. Wright (ed.), *Parish, Church and People* (Leicester, 1988), 56–85; 'For the Increase of Divine Service: Chantries in the Parish in Late Medieval Bristol', *Journal of Ecclesiastical History*, 36 (1985), 48–65, and 'A Service for the Dead: The Form and Function of the Anniversary in Late Medieval Bristol', *Transactions of the Bristol and Gloucestershire Archaeological Society*, 105 (1987), 183–211.

17. *Adolescence and Youth in Early Modern England* (New Haven, 1994). The section on culture is on pp. 183–207, the quotation from p. 205.

18. The discussion in this section is much extended, and attached directly to the evidence extrapolated from the book, in an essay, 'The English Reformation and the Evidence of Folklore', *Past and Present*, 148 (1995), 89–116.

19. Christopher Haigh, 'Puritan Evangelism in the reign of Elizabeth I', *English Historical Review*, 92 (1977), 30–58, and 'The Church of England, Catholics and the People', in Christopher Haigh (ed.), *The Reign of Elizabeth I* (1984), 195–220; J. J. Scarisbrick, *The Reformation and the English People* (Oxford, 1984); Christopher Haigh (ed.), *The English Reformation Revised* (Cambridge, 1987); Duffy, *Stripping of the Altars;* Christopher Haigh, *English Reformations* (Oxford, 1992). Into this category rather than the other I would put Robert Whiting, *The Blind Devotion of the People* (Cambridge, 1989), because although it postulates a far more rapid impact of the reforms upon popular belief than the works listed above, it portrays this impact as essentially a negative one.

20. G. R. Dickens, 'The Early Expansion of Protestantism in England, 1520–58', *Archiv fur Reformationsgeschichte* 78 (1987), 187–221; Patrick Collinson, *The Birthpangs of Protestant England* (1988); Diarmaid MacCulloch, *The Later Reformation in England, 1547–1603* (1990), and *Building a Godly Realm* (1992); Peter Lake, 'Deeds against Nature: Cheap Print, Protestantism and Murder in Early Seventeenth-Century England', in Kevin Sharpe and Peter Lake (eds.), *Culture and Politics in Early Stuart England* (1994), 257–84.

21. *Cheap Print and Popular Piety* (Cambridge, 1991).

22. These seem to be the conclusions and emphases made by Dr Watt herself, although there have been attempts to conscript her work into the debate outlined above, esp. in Lake, 'Deeds against Nature', 362 n. 1. Professor Lake himself employs very similar source material for that piece but treats it in an altogether different manner.

23. In (of course) large sections of *Religion and the Decline of Magic*.

24. Theo Brown, *The Fate of the Dead* (Folklore Society, 1979). I am very grateful to Dr P. R. Newman for presenting me with a copy long ago and so first alerting me to its existence.

25. Ibid. 83.

26. Diego Duran, *Book of the Gods and Rites*, trans. and ed. F. Horcasitas and D. Heyden (Norman, Okla., 1971), 169–77, 251–97.

27. R. A. Markus, *The End of Ancient Christianity* (Cambridge, 1990), 1–38.

28. Henry Bourne, *Antiquitates Vulgares* (Newcastle upon Tyne, 1725), pp. ix–xi.

29. Exposed and excoriated in David Harker, 'Cecil Sharp in Somerset', *Folk Music Journal*, 2 (1972), 220–40; Vic Gammon, 'Folk Song Collecting in Sussex and Surrey 1843–1914', *History Workshop*, 10 (1980), 72–85; Gillian Bennett, 'Folklore Studies and the English Rural Myth', *Rural History*, 4 (1993), 77–91; Georgina Boyes, *The Imagined Village* (Manchester, 1993).

30. Georgina Smith, 'Social Bases of Tradition: The Limitations and Implications of "The Search for Origins"', in A. E. Green and J. D. A. Widdowson (eds.), *Language, Culture and Tradition* (Centre for English Cultural Tradition and Language, Sheffield, 1981); Theresa Buckland, 'English Folk Dance Scholarship: An Overview', in Buckland (ed.), *Traditional Dance* (Crewe, 1982), i. 3–18; Georgina Boyes, 'Cultural Survivals Theory and Traditional Customs', *Folk Life*, 26 (1987–8), 5–9; Theresa Buckland and Juliette Wood (eds.), *Aspects of British Calendar Customs* (Folklore Society, 1993).

31. *Carmina Gadelica* (Edinburgh, 1900).

32. *Folk-Lore and Folk-Stories of Wales* (1909).

33. The controversy over *Carmina Gadelica* is summarized in the preface by John MacInnes to the Floris Books edition in 1992. It is now generally accepted that Carmichael conflated and rewrote the Gaelic hymns, chants, and charms which he collected in such a way as to give them that haunting beauty which is the chief attraction of the work; the degree of 'improvement' varied greatly between the individual pieces. The suspicion must remain that he standarized and embellished the accounts of folk customs which he collected in just the same way, but the apparent loss of his field notes makes this difficult to prove. As for Trevelyan, even the earliest and most enthusiastic reviewers of her book, such as Charlotte Burne in *Folk-Lore*, noticed that she sometimes seemed to pass off accounts copied word for word from earlier printed sources as original material collected from oral tradition. One of the publisher's readers of my related essay in *Past and Present* objected to my use of her work at all, calling it 'very unreliable'.

34. E. P. Thompson, 'Patrician Society, Plebeian Culture', *Journal of Social History*, 7 (1974), 390–410, *Whigs and Hunters* (1975), and *Customs in Common* (1991), which reprints several earlier pieces; Robert W. Malcolmson, *Popular Recreations in English Society 1700–1850* (Cambridge, 1973); Robert D. Storch (ed.), *Popular Culture and Custom in Nineteenth-Century England* (1982); Bob Bushaway, *By Rite* (1982).

35. *Folklore*, 105 (1994), 89–96.

36. Ibid.; and see also Hilda Ellis Davidson, 'Changes in the Folklore Society, 1949–1986', *Folklore*, 98 (1987), 123–4.

37. Other examples of which are in the sources at nn. 29 and 30.

38. Ronald Hutton, *The Pagan Religions of the Ancient British Isles* (Oxford, 1991), 300–6.

39. In *The God of the Witches* (1933), and *The Divine King in England* (1954).

40. Listed by Keith Thomas, in *Religion and the Decline of Magic* (1971), 514–19, to which I would add the work of the very influential scholar of pagan Celtic Britain, Anne Ross.

41. All this can be found in *Folk-Lore*, 28 (1917), 228–58, 453; 31 (1920), 204–9; 33 (1922), 224–30; 43 (1932), 114–15; 45 (1934), 95–6; 57 (1946), 12–33; 58 (1947), 285–7; 60 (1952), 244–5; 66 (1955), 307–8.
42. 'Female Fertility Figures', *Journal of the Royal Anthropological Institute*, 64 (1934), 93–100.
43. Hutton, *Pagan Religions*, 308–16.
44. *Folk-Lore*, 28 (1917), 453.
45. *Pan the Goat-God: His Myth in Modern Times* (Cambridge, Mass., 1969).

✠ INDEX ✠